THE UNIVERSITY OF VIRGINIA EDITION OF
THE WORKS OF STEPHEN CRANE

VOLUME III

THE THIRD VIOLET
and
ACTIVE SERVICE

Crane in Corwin Knapp Linson's studio (George Arents Research
Library, Syracuse University)

STEPHEN CRANE

THE THIRD VIOLET
and
ACTIVE SERVICE

EDITED BY
FREDSON BOWERS
LINDEN KENT PROFESSOR OF ENGLISH AT
THE UNIVERSITY OF VIRGINIA

WITH AN INTRODUCTION BY
J. C. LEVENSON
EDGAR ALLAN POE PROFESSOR OF ENGLISH AT
THE UNIVERSITY OF VIRGINIA

THE UNIVERSITY PRESS OF VIRGINIA

CHARLOTTESVILLE

CENTER FOR EDITIONS OF
AMERICAN AUTHORS

AN APPROVED TEXT

MODERN LANGUAGE
ASSOCIATION OF AMERICA

®

Editorial expenses for this volume have been
met in part by grants from the National
Endowment for the Humanities administered
through the Center for Editions of American
Authors of the Modern Language Association.

ISBN: 0–8139–0666–0
Library of Congress Catalog Card Number: 68–8536
Printed in the United States of America

To
Clifton Waller Barrett

FOREWORD

THIS volume presents two of Crane's novels edited with the assistance of textual documents not previously utilized. In *The Third Violet* the newspaper syndicated versions may preserve more faithfully than the somewhat heavily styled book certain details of Crane's general "accidental" texture and thus enable an editor to attempt a critical text that in considerable part reconstructs the lost typescript behind both versions. For *Active Service* the use of the Heinemann printer's-copy typescript as copy-text leads to a purified text superior in its authority to either the English or the American book versions.

The introduction by Professor Levenson analyzes the sources and the growth of these novels against the background of Crane's literary development. The editor's "The Text: History and Analysis" details the physical forms of these texts, their authority and transmission (tortuous for *Active Service*), and examines specific problems concerned with the establishment of the texts in their present critical form. The general principles on which the editing has been based are stated in "The Text of the Virginia Edition" prefixed to Volume I, BOWERY TALES (1969).

The expenses of the preparation of this volume with its introductions and apparatus have been subsidized by a grant from the National Endowment for the Humanities administered through the Modern Language Association of America and its Center for Editions of American Authors, but with generous support, as well, from the University of Virginia.

The editor is much in debt for assistance and various courtesies to a number of friends and colleagues. Mr. Kenneth A. Lohf, Librarian of Rare Books and Manuscripts of the Columbia University Libraries, has been of unfailing and particular help and made available the typescript of *Active Service* and other documents for study and use. Miss Joan Crane kindly checked the bibliographical descriptions and furnished the color designations. The editor is grateful to Miss Judith Nelson, Mrs. Malcolm Craig, Miss Susan Hitchcock, Miss Rosalie Hardin, and Mr. Richard Rainville, all of whom assisted at various stages in the collation of texts, the checking of the apparatus, and the reading of proofs. The editor's deepest obligation is reserved for Miss Gillian G. M. Kyles, who has been in complete charge of the organization of textual research and proofreading. In these days of relatively rapid editorial publication no single scholar can hope to assume the burden of the repeated checking for accuracy of collation, transcription, and notation enforced by the standards set for CEAA editions, all of which Miss Kyles has organized and personally supervised as well as taking an important part herself in the actual operations behind any CEAA text. Mr. William Matheson, Curator of Rare Books, the Library of Congress, was of especial assistance in searching the copyright records. Professor Kean Butterworth of the University of South Carolina, who examined this volume for the seal of the Center for Editions of American Authors, made various useful suggestions. The frontispiece appears by permission of the Stephen Crane Collection, the George Arents Research Library for Special Collections at Syracuse University, Syracuse, New York.

A considerable amount of the editor's textual analysis and of the final editing of the text was performed during a period of leisure afforded by a Visiting Fellowship at All Souls College, Oxford, during Trinity Term 1974, for which grateful acknowledgment is made.

The editor's personal debt to Mr. Clifton Waller Barrett and his magnificent collection at the University of Virginia remains constant and can be expressed only by the dedication of this edition to him.

F. B.

Charlottesville, Virginia
May 19, 1975

CONTENTS

INTRODUCTION

THE THIRD VIOLET

STEPHEN CRANE started writing *The Third Violet* in the flush of youthful confidence, contracted doubts as he went along, and ended with mixed feelings. In the fall of 1894, when the work can be said to have germinated, he had already written two novels that men of judgment told him were masterpieces, and he was finishing a third that he liked even better. The author of *Maggie* and *The Red Badge of Courage* and *George's Mother* was just turning twenty-three. He was readying a book of poetry for the press, and he was placing his freelance newspaper pieces with some frequency at last. Endowed with seemingly limitless energies, he came easily to the notion of turning his hand to a new kind of novel and he would be taken aback to find that there were some things he could not do. Even as he thus defined his limitations as a novelist, he was of course exploring what he could do. Therefore the work he produced has an interest and integrity which cannot be denied. There are no grounds for suggesting that he crassly undertook this novel as a potboiler. Like any professional writer he hoped to make money by the practice of his craft, but like any good writer he undertook the work with serious intentions. Fair critical questioning arises, however, from the fact that a new kind of novel for him was not a new kind for the reading public. Crane, who all his life thought of himself as a realist in pretty much the sense that Howells defined the term, came closest in this novel to practicing realism in the Howells mode. The results were paradoxical. Howells, supposed to be the high priest of the genteel tradition, welcomed *Maggie* for its going so courageously beyond the limits of middle-class fiction, but he seems never to have had a word to say about *The Third Violet*. Crane, turning in good faith to the novel of manners and sentiment, quickly saw that his simple love story lacked the intensity of his earlier work. The two writers, sharing basic principles as they did, never could account for their differences. Yet the differences, which are to be discriminated in *The Third Violet* more finely than elsewhere, help us to see how two writers with shared principles express a wider range of values than either alone could realize.

On October 28, 1894, the New York *Times* printed an interview with Howells by Stephen Crane. The relaxed and admiring tone of the interviewer bespoke a literary and personal relation of some years' standing. Crane's first ideas on writing stemmed from a Hamlin Garland lecture on Howells that he covered as a reporter in the summer of 1891; at the secular Chautauqua of a New Jersey Coast resort, he first heard expounded the "truthful treatment of material" and the dependence of such truth on relation, perspective, and the widening of sympathy.[1] Almost two years later, in the spring of 1893, he met Howells in New York through the good offices of Garland. Howells read *Maggie*, and it had a powerful effect on him—without in any way changing his basic premises about novel-writing. Though he admired Crane for his insights into "New York Low Life," he continued to find the challenge of fiction for himself in honestly rendering the familiar experience of the middle class. Such difference of subject seemed less important than the common purpose of honest rendering. Howells of course was very widely read and his literary purpose had complex literary origins, but even more than Crane he had grown up in a newspaper world—setting type as a boy in his father's shop, becoming a city editor by twenty-one. He never entirely lost the newspaperman's conception of the reading public as consumers of print and of serious literature as competing for attention, not with monuments of unaging intellect, but with the inane amusement or heavy-handed moralizing which the mass market preferred. Now the young reporter could nod in agreement as the older novelist-critic denounced the writer as "trained bear" or as cudgeling preacher. Crane would have continued his assent as Howells went on to declare: "It is the business of the novel to picture the daily life in the most exact terms possible with an absolute and clear sense of proportion." It hardly mattered that the lesson in perspective and honest rendering was not about low life, as Howells went on:

[1] TALES, SKETCHES, AND REPORTS, *Works*, VIII (1973), 507–508.

"I suppose that when a man tries to write 'what the people want'
—when he tries to reflect the popular desire, it is a bad quarter of an
hour for the laws of proportion."

"Do you recall any of the hosts of stories that began in love and
end a little further on. Those stories used to represent life to the people and I believe they do now to a large class. Life began when the
hero saw a certain girl, and it ended abruptly when he married her.
Love and courtship was not an incident, a part of life—it was the
whole of it. All else was of no value. Men of that religion must have
felt very stupid when they were engaged at anything but courtship.
Do you see the false proportion?" [2]

Now *The Third Violet* was to begin when a young man sees a
certain girl and end abruptly when marriage seems certain, and
Crane surely saw the challenge in handling so overworked a subject and trying to restore it to proportion. More than a year after
the Howells interview, when he was two-thirds of the way
through writing the novel, he told of his own experience with
the nonliterary public: "I gave the first eighteen chapters to my
brother Teddie to read. He finished them up without a halt. He
is an awful stuff in literature. I am a little dubious about his performance. Seems to me it throws rather a grimly humorous light
on the situation. Understand, he thinks my style wouldn't be
used by the devil to patch his trousers with. I think he—Teddie—
discovered the fellow and the girl in the story and read on to find
out if they married. He hung around for a time asking for more
chapters but I sent him away." [3] Whatever his brother Edmund
might think, Crane did not agree that his novel treated courtship
as if it were the whole of life. Nevertheless, he did not say what
else besides style made the difference between his story and his
reader's oversimplification. To find what he was not saying it is
necessary to go back to the Howells interview and the earliest
germ-time of the novel.

Howells at the time was willing to muse upon "a little scheme"
for a novel he had. He remembered fondly a girl from a little
Ohio village, whose mother eked out a living by making rag-
carpets for the villagers—"And this girl had the most wonderful

[2] *Works*, VIII, 636, 637.
[3] To Willis Brooks Hawkins, Hartwood, [N.Y.], Nov. 19, [1895], *Stephen Crane:
Letters*, ed. R. W. Stallman and Lillian Gilkes (New York University Press,
1960), p. 76.

instinct in manner and dress. Her people were of the lowest of the low in a way and yet this girl was a lady." [4] He thought too of another such girl in Boston with a natural taste that belied her modest background and, by so doing, undermined common assumptions about class and rank. These American success stories, even so barely sketched, set themselves apart from the popular type at the same time that they took up the popular subject. No Horatio Alger fantasy ever dealt with cultural rise, and no businessman's autobiography measured the handicaps to social mobility by Howells' standards of education. Taking one of the most hackneyed themes of mass-market writing and seeing what seriously could be done with it, Howells proposed a method that was characteristic of Crane's best work all his life, and so naturally the younger man could be expected to respond. He could leave to Howells the girl who started literally from rags and became "as chic as chic could be" and yet work out a variation of his own. So in *The Third Violet* he would not focus on, though he would assume, the rise of the gifted and successful young artist from humble origins, and he would indeed stress the humble background by bringing his hero back to the upstate farm which his hardworking father and family worked by themselves. Initially he even used the Howells technique of giving the family speech in marked vernacular dialect, but as he had in the case of *The Red Badge*, he cut most of the dialect in revision. The hero encounters, when he first alights from the train that brings him home, the rich young woman who will be staying at a nearby resort hotel. So Crane, for the first half of his story, was able to modulate his scenes from the simple family home, much like his brother Edmund's house in Hartwood where he himself liked to stay the summer—and other seasons too—to the resort hotel such as he knew less well but could put together from his knowledge of the Hartwood Club and the chaperoned guest camp for young men and women like the one he had stayed at in Pike's County, Pennsylvania, the previous summer. He could work up the Howells subject matter of summer visitors and native folks out of his own experience. The possibility that Howells gave him the first suggestion is enhanced by the fact that even when his scheme was at a most preliminary stage, Howells had a name

[4] *Works*, VIII, 635.

for the novel, which he wanted to call after the wildflower known as ragged lady, and that Crane too finally settled for a floral title; also, the novel includes a successful young writer who has given up being a prophet in order to become, instead, a "trained bear of the magazines." [5] In any case, it was to be five years before Howells published *Ragged Lady* while Crane worked out his treatment of the topic in 1895, a year after the interview and not long after a second summer holiday in Pike County. So whatever he owed to the spoken suggestion for the origin of his story, he would have felt, in the course of writing, little sense of literary dependence on Howells and a strong sense of relying on his own powers of observation.

The rising novelist-poet-journalist, who spoke to Howells so confidently as one realist to another, had two other newspaper pieces come out on the same day as his interview. They were both sketches for the many-sectioned Sunday edition of the New York *Press* of October 28, 1894, and each in its own way relates to the novel whose prehistory may be said to begin on that date. The first of these, "Stories Told by an Artist" (*Works*, VIII, 68–75), catches the life of impecunious young artists like those with whom Crane had moved in that fall. A friend was later to reminisce:

I wish you could have known that old shack of a studio building. It had been the home of the Art Students' League. There were three street entrances, and it had been remodeled and twisted about so much at various times, to suit the growing needs of the League, that it took an expert pilot to guide a stranger through its mysteries. The upper floors were filled with artists, musicians and writers, young men and women, decent people all, who were glad of the low rents and really congenial atmosphere. The landlord was an artist, and as considerate of our financial difficulties as he could be in reason. Our life there was free, gay, hard working—and *decent*.

Such is the ambience of the sketch and, later, of the novel when it moves from the country to the city. In the newspaper piece Crane wrote vignettes of making two eggs into a dinner for three and of having the rent fall due when no one in the studio

[5] P. 16. Crane liked the phrase so well he used it twice. Marston LaFrance first noticed Crane's adoption of the Howells formula in *A Reading of Stephen Crane* (Oxford: Clarendon Press, 1971), p. 175.

has money, much of which he would use with but little change in Chapters XIX and XX of the novel. The supporting cast—Wrinkles, Great Grief (Warwickson), Penny (Pennoyer), and Purple Sanderson (who doubled in his old trade of gas fitter when he wanted money)—are present, but not the leading character Billie Hawker or the model Florinda O'Connor (called Splutter) who loves him and stands as foil to the heiress he chooses to court. In the sketch there is a successful young artist called Corinson, whose name suggests that he is modeled on Corwin K. Linson, the friend of studio days who painted the best portrait of Crane and left the fullest memoir.[6] When Corinson comes in, the talk turns to banter about art. In the novel the background scene is the same, but it is Splutter O'Connor who comes in, and the conversation mainly gives the young artists a chance to note how she reacts to the mention of Hawker's name. Given the plot of the rising young painter who courts the wealthy and highborn young woman, Crane had already sketched the social setting for the second half of his story in which the summer romance is tested for its viability in a workaday world.[7]

Crane's other newspaper piece of October 28, "In a Park Row Restaurant" (*Works*, VIII, 328–332), also bears a relation to *The Third Violet*. For one thing, it was to contribute half a dozen colorful lines of description to the restaurant scene (Chapter XXVII) in which against a background of uproar Hawker and his friend Hollanden still manage, not too directly, to talk about love. More important, I believe, though less immediately pertinent, this little

[6] Frederick C. Gordon to Thomas Beer, Westfield, N.J., May 25, 1923, *Letters*, p. 330. Linson, *My Stephen Crane*, ed. Edwin H. Cady (Syracuse University Press, 1958), mentions (p. 66) a painting of Linson's that Crane may have used in the novel. Linson also claimed, in a note he slipped into his copy of *The Third Violet*, "Crane jocularly informed me that I was 'Hawker' in the book" (Joseph Katz, "Corwin Knapp Linson and *The Third Violet*," *Stephen Crane Newsletter*, III [Fall, 1968], 5).

[7] In "Stories Told by an Artist" there is a third vignette, "How Pennoyer Disposed of His Sunday Dinner," in which the artist gives his meager bit of food to an old model who is more desperately hungry than he. Fragments from this sketch concerning coffee cakes from the baker's, and delays at the cash-windows of magazine offices, supply details for the beginnings of Chapters XXI and XXV. Yet another sketch with the studio characters, probably dating from this same period, is "The Silver Pageant" (*Works*, VIII, 76–77), unpublished in Crane's lifetime. In short, his fund of sketched material was greater than what he re-used in the novel, just as the studio material he used in the novel went well beyond what he had already sketched. New York artists' life thus gave him ample material for a realistic social environment in which to set his novel.

sketch indicates the way in which the Howells theory of picturing daily life in the most exact terms possible could be true
but insufficient. The insufficiency did not have a drastic effect
on Howells' practice, for he knew and was to some degree in
dialogue with all the great realistic novelists of the nineteenth
century. Thus, when he came to write *Ragged Lady*, he offered
something more than the exact record of unpredictable gifts and
social mobility. Consciously or unconsciously, Howells wrote a
novel which stands in parodic relation to Henry James's *Portrait
of a Lady*, with the action lowered by several social notches.
Clementina Claxon (the phonetic Down East spelling of her
name and the ineradicable accent that goes with it suggest her
native strength of character) is, far more literally than Isabel
Archer, plucked from poverty by a wealthy older woman who
sees her possibilities and carries her onto the international scene.
Her head unturned by an English lord, she chooses between two
Americans, a thin-blooded expatriate and a representative of rising industry—the former is a zealous would-be missionary of
the sort that must have outnumbered aesthetes and collectors
like Gilbert Osmond on the order of ten to one, and the latter is
a pleasant and right smart young man from rural Ohio with an
invention to sell rather than an emergent tycoon like Caspar
Goodwood. The question of how Clementina chooses can become
for the reader a kind of game of probabilities, Howells versus
James, and thus give an otherwise slight novel precisely the kind
of interest Howells wanted, namely, reflective curiosity on what
are the "more American" qualities of life. Even the most committed realism derives value not only from the direct treatment
of subject matter but also from the relation it establishes with
what has already been written. And even Crane's little sketch,
"In a Park Row Restaurant," shows how truthful rendering exists
in relation to literature as well as to fact. For in his notebook
draft Crane literally transcribed a random series of customers'
shouts at harried waiters and thus directly rendered the uproar
in the background. These lines are cut from the revised version
that was printed, and instead, Crane developed the character of
the observer, a retired Nevada sheriff who comes to the restaurant when he wants to recapture the "fever and exhilaration" of
old times. The Wild West convention and battle imagery that

seemed to come naturally to him provided the occasion for a descriptive passage such as had not appeared in the draft:

Meanwhile the waiters dashed about the room as if a monster pursued them and they sought escape wildly through the walls. It was like the scattering and scampering of a lot of water bugs, when one splashes the surface of the brook with a pebble. Withal, they carried incredible masses of dishes and threaded their swift ways with rare skill. Perspiration stood upon their foreheads, and their breaths came strainedly. They served customers with such speed and violence that it often resembled a personal assault. The crumbs from the previous diner were swept off with one fierce motion of a napkin. A waiter struck two blows at the table and left there a knife and a fork. And then came the viands in a volley, thumped down in haste, causing men to look sharp to see if their trousers were safe.

There was in the air an endless clatter of dishes, loud and bewilderingly rapid, like the gallop of a thousand horses. From afar back, at the places of communication to the kitchen, there came the sound of a continuing roaring altercation, hoarse and vehement, like the cries of the officers of a regiment under attack.[8]

In the novel Crane cut and toned down the passage a bit, substituted a band of guitars and mandolins for some of the clatter, and made the figurative altercation into an actual brawl going on at the edge of perception. He dropped the Wild West altogether in order to fit the background to the advancement of his main plot through the dialogue of protagonist and confidant. Yet it was first by adding such fiction to his account and dropping the merely literal that he got to a satisfactory rendering of the material, and when he dropped the Wild West in its turn he kept some of the fever and exhilaration of his own responses in the style.

Yet there is less fever, exhilaration, or intensity of style in *The Third Violet* than in any other of Crane's early works. He himself recognized almost as soon as he started writing that he had committed himself to a kind of plainness that was uncharacteristic. In the year since the seedtime of the novel he had made his momentous trip to the West and Mexico where vivid impressions, often played off against vivid preconceptions, livened his reports with colorful and rapidly shifting images. Moreover, the stories

[8] *Works*, VIII, 329.

which were to come out of that experience—he wrote the first, "One Dash Horses," in September, 1895, just a month before he began work on the novel—required focal characters whose inward response to ultimate dangers was itself part of the ordeal. Writing a novel of manners, Crane made his action turn on the interpretation of outward signs, gestures, verbal formalities. Because his hero had to master an outer world rather than an inner one, the presented drama tended to take place in only half the imaginative theater that Crane usually used. So in the first letter in which he talked about his new novel, he reported on October 29, 1895, to Ripley Hitchcock at Appleton's: "The story is working out fine. I have made seven chapters in the rough and they have given me the proper enormous interest in the theme. I have adopted such a quick style for the story that I don't believe it can work out much beyond twenty-five thousand words—perhaps thirty—possibly thirty-five. Can you endure that length?—I mean, should you like the story otherwise, can you use a story that length?" [9]

The quick style went so quickly that it was only about a week later that Crane wrote his friend Willis Hawkins of surprising progress and unexpected doubts: "The novel is one-third completed. I am not sure that it is any good. It is easy work. I can finish a chapter each day. I want you to see it before it goes to Appletons." Perhaps ten days after that, he sent the same kind of report: "The novel is exactly half finished. It seems clever sometimes and sometimes it seems nonsensical. I hope to show it you in less than two months." [10] Crane knew Hawkins so well that he could unblushingly adapt his name for his fictional hero William Hawker—well enough so that he could express doubts privately that he would not mention elsewhere. At the same time that he was expressing unsureness about his work in progress, he was telling his doubts also about the forthcoming literary dinner in his honor being arranged by Elbert Hubbard, the arty editor of *The Philistine* who enthusiastically published Crane's poems and backed *The Red Badge*. Crane at twenty-four was entering new territory about which he knew little.

[9] *Letters*, p. 65.
[10] [Hartwood, Nov. 6 or 7, 1895], date corrected; Hartwood, [about Nov. 15, 1895], *Letters*, pp. 70, 74.

Writing about a successful young artist as lover, he was himself but an incipient success and an incipient suitor. Reviews and sales reports of *The Red Badge*, published at the end of September, were coming in, but not money—not even enough to outfit him, without friends' assistance, for the *Philistine* dinner. As for honors, the staff of the Philadelphia *Press* had given him a rousing informal welcome in their editorial offices the previous December when the serialized version of the war novel came out. A year went by before Hubbard's formal dinner took place on December 19, 1895, by which time *The Third Violet* was complete and in the hands of a typist. Besides, the dinner turned more or less into a shambles and Crane was to have as many doubts after the affair as before. In contrast to the world of outlaws and violence that he had entered with such relish, the world of dress suits and too many jovial toasts hardly provided the high-keyed inner life that tallied so well with Crane's lively eye for the outer scene.

Crane's experience as a lover was also, from a literary point of view, negligible. His gift for easy decorous social life is attested by the idyllic summer holidays he enjoyed at Camp Interlaken in Pike County. On the other hand, his major episodes of sentiment did not suggest that his social instincts were being trained into worldliness. Far from it. He began unshrewdly by not accommodating to convention, falling in love first with a girl who was already engaged and then with one, somewhat older, who was already married. From the epistolary record we learn that he could stand on the pavement all night and gaze pathetically at his truelove's window and that he could declare without a hint of irony, "It is better to have known you and suffered, than never to have known you." [11] He had already in the early winter of 1894–95, before his January departure for the West and Mexico, met Nellie Crouse, who more than any other affected his writing of *The Third Violet*. He cannot be said to have fallen in love with her until he began his spirited epistolary campaign for her heart, and that was not until he had finished the novel. What he had to go on till then amounted to one formal call which was a fiasco. When he later reminded her of the oc-

[11] To Helen Trent, [Lake View, N.J., Sept. 19, 1891]; to Lily Brandon Munroe, New York, [winter 1893–1894], *Letters*, pp. 10, 22.

casion, he could not make much of a compliment of his tale: "Your admission that many people find you charming, leads me to be honest. So prepare. I called once in 34th St., when you were there, didn't I? Well, I was rather bored. I thought you very attractive but then I was bored, because I had always believed that when I made calls I was bored. However to some sentence of mine you said: 'Yes, I know,' before I had quite finished. I don't remember what I had said but I always remembered your saying: 'Yes, I know.' I knew then that you had lived a long time. And so in some semi-conscious manner, you stood forth very distinctly in my memory." [12] Some months after that meeting his memory was jolted when he saw, as he wandered without purpose through the Mexican provinces, an American girl who resembled Miss Crouse. He felt startled out of his "mountaineer senses," he later said, and ran at once to the railroad station to buy his ticket back to New York. But when he paid another call at 34th Street and found no one at home, he left it at that for another seven months. Obviously the matter was not so urgent at the time as it seemed in retrospect. When he completed the novel, indeed, he had some idea of the art which he might want life to imitate, but the contrary cannot be said. He did not bring to the writing any very rich experience, introspective or observational, from which to work out plausible complications of so interesting but hackneyed a subject as love.[13]

[12] Hartwood, Jan. 12, [1896], *Letters*, pp. 100–101.

[13] Crane's sexual experience at this time also fits the canons of genteel decorum at least to the extent of leaving no flagrant evidence. Among the testimonies gathered by Thomas Beer and others and conveniently reprinted in the Appendix of *Letters*, those from friends with whom he was on the closest terms declare him to be gentlemanly, proper, even chivalric. John Northern Hilliard claimed in 1922 an intimacy in no way borne out by the internal evidence of his remarks or by the formal letters he exchanged with Crane beginning in mid-December 1895. He attributed to Crane a promiscuity ("He took up with many a drab. . . . Time and again he would bring a lady of the streets to his room" [p. 324]) and a coarse braggadocio ("Many a time I have heard him say that he would have to go out and get a nigger wench 'to change his luck.'") which do not fit Crane's character. Disbelief in Hilliard does not, of course, require belief in young Crane's innocence. Whatever his initiatory experiences in New York, they did not disturb physically or verbally the living at close quarters with other hardworking and decent young people who had good times together. Only in 1896 did his more flamboyant adventures occur—with Amy Leslie, a somewhat superannuated actress still active as a theater critic, with Dora Clark, the chorus girl and sometime prostitute for whom he gallantly testified when she was wrongly accused of soliciting, and with Cora Taylor, proprietress of the Hotel de Dream in Jacksonville. The affair with Cora Howorth Stewart Taylor

Given that Crane worked from limited personal knowledge and truly minimal literary knowledge, he could not offer the dense specification which so often provides interest to the novel of manners. His opening scene on the station platform presents a monster locomotive and passengers who swarm from the train like escaping prisoners, but the self-conscious rhetoric seems thin beside the similar train arrival that opens Howells' *The Quality of Mercy* (1891). Even before that train pulls in, Howells individualizes the people on the platform and classifies them socially both by graphic detail and by the language they speak. The older novelist was not only an astute social historian but also a representational artist with a very wide technical range. Crane, neither a historian nor a knowing and avid listener to American speech, had technical skills of his own. He had an eye that did not see things conventionally, and he enjoyed noting fresh details like a very small boy's cautiously "disembarking backward" down the steps of the railroad car.[14] He could render inner drama with remarkable immediacy, so that when Billie Hawker is asked how to find the hotel stage and turns to see Grace Fanhall for the first time, "a wave of astonishment whirled into his hair and he turned his eyes quickly for fear that she would think that he had looked at her." Hawker's intense feeling and naive shyness justified only very brief direct treatment, however, for though they underlie the presented action, they are not the center of interest. What Crane focused on was the young artist's effort to enter a world where he must express his feelings by formal and indirect means. Hawker as a social being called for a narrative of formal conduct rather than inner feelings, but Hawker at work not only justified vivid glimpses of the things he painted but also set the narrator to seeing country and, later, city scenes in painterly ways. When Hawker approaches his family home, he sees light coming from the kitchen and then his sisters "shading their eyes

---

would hardly be called courtship in any usual sense, and she became Cora Crane without benefit of formalities and Crane became a husband without having mastered the art of being a suitor.

[14] For touches like that, he often used his newspaper pieces as a painter would use his sketchbook drawings. So he had noted a very small boy going downstairs backward in one of the Tommie stories he wrote about New York tenement life, "A Dark-Brown Dog" (*Works*, VIII, 58). Freshness, needless to say, depends on context and convention and not on the fortuitous circumstance in this case that the sketch had gone unpublished.

and peering down the yellow stream"; and when, back in the city, he escorts Splutter O'Connor home, the grim and lonely side street where she lives is contrasted with the great avenue from which they enter, now "no more than a level stream of yellow light." [15] Such bold visual effects do not in themselves account for Crane's most characteristic style, often called Impressionist as if he were approximating the painter's art in prose. The signature of Crane's genius, almost, consists of rapid staccato shifts of imagery and point of view and a readiness on the part of the narrator to project himself animistically into the scene, sometimes in fear as in *The Red Badge*, sometimes in play. John Berryman singles out two such sentences in *The Third Violet* as the rewarding moments of an uncertain book, one describing a country scene, the other a studio interior:

A little brook, a brawling, ruffianly little brook, swaggered from side to side down the glade, swirling in white leaps over the great dark rocks and shouting challenge to the hillsides.

A long stove-pipe wandered off in the wrong direction and then turned impulsively toward a hole in the wall.[16]

Sentences like these, with their unpredictable imaginative energy, are rare in the book, for narrators in Crane do not usually project themselves into the scene except in a kind of reciprocal relation when the action is deeply internalized in one of the characters. Hawker's drama is mostly externalized, and without much occasion to render inner consciousness, Crane also had little occasion to use the complex, nervous style which seems to have an effect like broken color. He did, however, use a kind of broken syntax which, just as much as his more colorful prose, could be likened to the Impressionist assault on conventionalized perception. On Hawker's arrival home, for example, a question does not signal for an answer as it usually does. "What made you so late?" functions, rather, as affectionate family greeting. Simi-

15 Milne Holton puts Crane's divided intention thus: "Crane never seems to decide whether his book is to be a Howells-like story of New York or a record of an artist's vision," and while he is severe with the way Crane handled the former, he shows how much of the latter actually got into the novel (*Cylinder of Vision: The Fiction and Journalistic Writing of Stephen Crane* [Baton Rouge: Louisiana State University Press, 1972], pp. 132–135).

16 John Berryman, *Stephen Crane* (New York: Sloan, 1950), p. 123. The sentences occur on pp. 41, 72 below.

larly, later in the novel, "Here she comes now" ends a scene instead of functioning as it usually does to introduce one. Other rhetorical devices serve the same end, quirky repetitions in particular. "What made you so late?" thrice repeated is among the first of many iterated phrases which break the pattern of common usage and emphasize the pattern of rhetoric that stands between the reader and the action of the novel. Whereas Howells had a broad range of representational technique, Crane had what one might call a vertical range from simple realistic representation, in which language is conceived as a transparent medium through which one looks directly upon the object, to such stylized, almost affected, discourse as calls attention to the fact that language mediates between subject and object, that there is no such thing as beholding an object without benefit of the verbal, conceptual, conventional means we bring to the looking. At its best the self-conscious rhetoric that seems thin as realism turns into an artistic detachment from literary and social convention that gives the whole novel a somewhat different slant.

Just as Hawker's arrival home involves visual and rhetorical effects beyond simple realism, so with many of the seemingly plain notations of fact. For example, readers have from the beginning liked Crane's treatment in this novel of the family dog, a creature modeled from life. The daughter of Edmund Crane, to whose house Stephen came home to write *The Third Violet*, later reminisced about *their* family dog: "When Chester was a pup, father was teaching him to lie down at the command, 'Charge!' One of his brothers began to quote:

> 'Charge, Chester, charge!
> On, Stanley, on!'

Thereupon the dog was named Chester, and when he appears in 'The Third Violet,' he is called Stanley." [17] The dog barks fiercely on the homecoming night till Hawker's voice identifies him as the approaching stranger, and then "the ardour for battle was instantly smitten from the dog, and his barking swallowed in a gurgle of delight." What there is besides literal representation in

[17] Edna Crane Sidbury, "My Uncle, Stephen Crane, As I Knew Him," *Literary Digest*, IV (1926), 248–250. The reviewer in the *Spectator* (LXXVIII [May 29, 1897], 771) seems to have been the first in print to single out "the humblest, but not the least engaging, of the dramatis personae" for praise.

that sentence becomes much clearer in what follows: "He was a large orange and white setter, and he partly expressed his emotion by twisting his body into a fantastic curve and then dancing over the ground with his head and his tail very near to each other. He gave vent to little sobs in a wild attempt to vocally describe his gladness." Crane, who hewed so close to neutral objectivity in much of the novel, personified unabashedly in saying that the dog "partly expressed his emotion" and made a "wild attempt to vocally describe his gladness." The irony is not an inconsistency. The dog becomes a touchstone of direct vocal and bodily expression, precisely what one might wish for but cannot have in the world of social convention and language. The point is made rather more invidiously by John Berryman, who very much approves the rendering of Stanley but goes on to say that the book "produces in many of its human passages an odd, slight sense of *instead*, as if we were not hearing whatever it is that matters." [18]

The value Crane put on naturalness is made equally clear by the way he portrayed those "middle-aged ladies of the most aggressive respectability" who make up more than a third of the summer hotel guests. Crane detested the small-town moral censors, often with prurient minds, like the "feminine mule" in Port Jervis who greeted him with outrageous innuendo when he had given a thirteen-year-old girl a Sunday buggy ride and who was so much like, he said, "those hunks of women who squat on porches of hotels in summer and wherever their eye lights there blood rises." [19] In the novel, Grace Fanhall meets Billie Hawker's father with his ox team and after some friendly conversation accepts a ride back to the hotel on the ox wagon, "right to the door." The next day a female censor at the hotel lets her know disapprovingly that only her family's wealth and position enable her to do so unconventional a thing. The young woman, angered by the meddling, nevertheless recognizes that Hawker himself seems to harbor some of the same stuffy feelings. He had been reluctant to introduce the girl to his father when the sounds of ox-driving announced him to the couple on a country

---

[18] *Crane*, p. 123.
[19] To an unknown recipient, [Port Jervis, N.Y., after Dec. 15, 1894], *Letters*, pp. 42–43.

walk; he had held back from the conversation that followed; he had winced at the idea of a ride to the hotel. By contrast, the girl could with equal ease ask sensible questions about the oxen or playful ones—"Do you think they are happy?"—and the old farmer can answer both kinds with equal ease also. Their mutual courtesy should have taught Billie Hawker that naturalness and manners can go together, but he knows only enough of convention to feel its constraints. He cannot rightly explain his embarrassment, and he doesn't realize, until he is told, how close he has come to apologizing for his father's owning an ox wagon. The middle-class righteousness of the hotel women is relevant to the protagonist himself, whose conformist reactions might otherwise seem natural just because they are immediate. His later profession that he regards the poverty of his earlier struggling-artist years as a matter for shame, though he possibly half-meant it as a witticism, underscores how far he has to go in learning to be natural.

Did Crane mean the incident of the ox wagon to signify so much? There is reason to think so in a letter he wrote at just the time he was composing these chapters.[20] As usual he reported his progress on the novel without any specific discussion of substantive problems in the writing, but just before mentioning his progress he got at its themes in quite other terms. Commenting on the death of Eugene Field, the professional-Westerner columnist of the Chicago *Daily News*, he said: "I never thought him a western barbarian. I have always believed the western people to be much truer than the eastern people. We in the east are overcome a good deal by a detestable superficial culture which I think is the real barbarism. Culture in its true sense, I take it, is a comprehension of the man at one's shoulder." After going on and on about straight-out honest Westerners in contrast to effete Easterners, he paused to note that these convenient, conventional tokens of American discourse might be

---

[20] Chapters xiv and xv. On October 29 (to Ripley Hitchcock, *Letters*, p. 65) he had written seven chapters, and on November 6 or 7 (to Willis Brooks Hawkins, date corrected, *Letters*, pp. 69–70) he was writing a chapter a day. With Sunday off and possibly Election Day (the 5th) also, since his brother William's running for Probate was his great interest, the letter in which he reported disastrous election results would date from the time he was getting at Chapter xiv.

somewhat too simple: "Garland will wring every westerner by the hand and hail him as a frank honest man. I wont. No, sir. But what I contend for is the atmosphere of the west which is really frank and honest and is bound to make eleven honest men for one pessimistic thief. More glory be with them." [21] From this play with Western stereotypes, such as he would never use without qualification and irony when writing of the West, he went on without a pause to announce that his novel was one-third completed and that he hoped to have Hawkins' criticism before turning it in to the publisher. For a social novel, once he turned to classes above those which appear in *Maggie* and *George's Mother*, he had no recourse to popular conventions closer than the West-East contrast. His hero, a talented artist but in social matters a decent but confused young man, must, without the help of mediating convention, learn to tell the true, frank, and honest from the superficial and effete.

The episode with the ox wagon and its sequel are crucial, also, in that they make the heroine of the novel come alive as the more stilted courtship scenes do not. Her unaffected warmth, her capacity for play, her freedom from and sensitivity to the prejudices of class give assurance that Grace Fanhall is something more than a mechanical stimulus to love at first sight. If she were not thus made to appear worth the seeking, the model Splutter O'Connor would alone be attractive and, as so often with genteel romance, the protagonist would seem silly in his choice. The very fact that Florinda O'Connor, like the young artists in the studio, is known by nickname betokens camaraderie, informality, frankness. She is more natural in her readiness to stake the hungry to a meal than are the young artists who refuse her offer on grounds of genteel decorum. She does not tell her emotions with unbecoming candor, but when her knowing friends tease her, she does not coyly dodge the issue either. Class and sex may have something to do with help refused and teasing indulged, and so may caste, as Crane seems casually to disclose the ethnocentric premises of his American comedy of manners. When Hawker returns from a formal call on Grace Fanhall at her city home, he is easily made to feel self-conscious about the gray gloves he is wearing. His retort to Florinda

---

[21] *Letters*, pp. 69–70.

O'Connor—"I suppose your distinguished ancestors in Ireland did not educate their families in the matter of gloves"—is as dubious in him as his embarrassment at ox-driving. Caste-consciousness has perhaps been stronger than class-consciousness in genteel America, and the author of *Maggie* well knew what this anti-Irish remark implied. But Crane once more left Hawker's confusions undeveloped. Hawker is shown to be capable of vulgar errors, for otherwise his movement into the world of high manners would not have the interest of an initiatory ordeal. But he does not reject Splutter O'Connor's love because he is a snob; the book depends on his being better than that, and to that purpose the convincing characterization of Grace Fanhall is essential.

A closer look at Hawker's defects is necessary if his decency is to be believed in. Decency, and not some nobler quality, is in question. At a later time when Crane was eloquently courting Nellie Crouse by letter, he would "swear by the real aristocrat" who can stand any strain, be reliable in any crisis.[22] But what he had behind him as he wrote this novel was *The Red Badge*, in which a man's faults, by romantic standards unforgivable, do not keep him from acting well in a next episode. And what he had immediately ahead was the ordeal of the *Philistine* dinner, where he behaved with dignity but other guests did not. He would write his uncertainty to Willis Hawkins: "I am very anxious to hear wether you are satisfied with the dinner. I did not drink much but the excitement soon turned everything into a grey haze for me and I am not sure that I came off decently." [23] Hawker's problems stem from a social imperceptiveness that is ironic but not 'implausible' in one who is visually so acute. In affairs of the heart, he has a knack for being the last to know. He only learns of Splutter O'Connor's feeling for him on the night when he escorts her home from the studio. The dark loneliness of the side street where she lives seems to prompt the model's question, "Billie . . . what makes you so mean to me?" When he suddenly sees her face and understands what she means, he gasps with surprise. Then they part in silence, both chastened by the pathetic truth that has come out. Both prob-

22 Hartwood, Feb. 11, [1896], *Letters*, p. 115.
23 Hartwood, N.Y., Dec. 31, [1895], *Letters*, p. 84.

ability and pathos are enhanced by the fact that the same problem underlies the main plot as the subordinate one. Hawker's inability to tell whether his love for Grace Fanhall is returned is important enough to give the novel its title. The first violet that he takes as a memento has accidentally been dropped by the girl. The second one she gives him, but with so simple a gesture and such formal words that he cannot tell whether it conveys any special affection or not. When back in the city where even greater formality prevails, he decides that she does not love him and calls to take his leave. When she offers him a third violet, his "Please don't pity me" tone makes her angry enough almost to fling it at him, angry enough finally so that his plea for dismissal is answered by her tearful "Oh, do go! Go! Please! I want you to go!" Once again Hawker is amazed by sudden recognition, only this time the outcome is delight rather than pathos. In the moment when formalities break down, there is "anger, defiance, unhappiness," but with the message of love that is thus conveyed, decorum is soon restored. The sequence—and the novel—ends: "Later, she told him that he was perfectly ridiculous."

Hawker has hardly mastered the arts of courtliness and courtship, but he gets by. In this respect he stands in relation to the comedy of manners as Crane's Henry Fleming to the narrative of heroic exploit. He is no great shakes compared to what literary tradition may make us wish for, but in his way he affirms the human possibility of fallible men. The theme of the novel, stated thus, is thoroughly Howellsian, but something more is added in Hawker's need to submit himself to formality in manners and language and yet have confidence that natural emotion can still be expressed. As a problem of perception, his situation affects the novel as a whole, of which H. G. Wells observed: "The characters act, and on reflection one admits that they act, *true*, but the play of their emotions goes on behind the curtain of the style." [24] What Wells describes as a defect is, it happens, a clue to the way Crane was going beyond Howellsian realism, beyond the belief that an artist can present unmediated reality, to a recognition that life always goes on behind the curtain of style.

[24] H. G. Wells, "Stephen Crane from an English Standpoint," *North American Review*, CLXXI (August, 1900), 240.

The protagonist's name Billie, the curious fillips of thrice-repeated phrases, an occasional archness like swearing by "the nine mad blacksmiths of Donawhiroo" remind us that Crane was preparing in this slight novel those elements of style which would stand in "The Open Boat" for what the human will can keep between itself and reduction to mere thing. In the novel life is curtained not only by language but also by manners, and the protagonist has to learn—to use the phrase which Crane used for a while as the title of the book—"The Eternal Patience." [25] That phrase defines the discipline which must constantly be undergone for the sake of organized social life. Regarded as tragic necessity, it suggests the theme of Freud's *Civilization and Its Discontents*. Regarded as a learnable skill that leads at last both to civilized life and to enhanced fulfillment of natural desire, it is and has been the theme of comedy of manners ever since courtship became a literary subject.

On finishing the novel, Crane had before him a demonstration that something less than mastery, something more like muddling through, might be qualification enough for courtship. The day after he sent off the manuscript he wrote his first letter to Nellie Crouse. Writing could not convey any better than speech all that he wished to say, but he was no longer inclined to apologize for the inadequacy: "I go through the world unexplained, I suppose. Perhaps this letter may look like an incomparable insolence. Who knows. Script is an infernally bad vehicle for thoughts. I know that, at least." [26] There followed a series of letters in which he expressed his thoughts on character, art, and the world as clearly and directly as on any occasion of his life. But the letters

[25] Ames W. Williams and Vincent Starrett, *Stephen Crane: A Bibliography* (Glendale, Calif., 1948), p. 127. Williams and Starrett simply say that "prior to publication" the novel "was tentatively entitled 'The Eternal Patience.'" At first one might think that this was a working title during composition and that like *Maggie*, *The Red Badge*, and *George's Mother* the novel got its final title very late. However, *The Third Violet*, signifying that real emotion lies behind the conventional token, is conceptually built into the narrative from early on. Another hypothesis is that Crane temporarily relinquished his title because, in December, 1895, *Ladies' Home Journal* began to serialize Julia Magruder's *The Violet*. This simpy society romance, complete with illustrations by Charles Dana Gibson, was on the bookstands and being reviewed by the time Crane's novel was serialized in the fall of 1896. Someone had to have made the conscious decision that the similarity of titles did not matter because the two works were so different in kind.

[26] Hartwood, N.Y., Dec. 31, [1895], *Letters*, p. 86.

which served so well as the vehicle of thought were not so effective as the instrument of persuasion. After two months or so, Crane received his dismissal.[27] In real life the successful artist turned suitor did not win the heiress.

As a successful artist Crane had another field to master and another kind of prize to seek. With *The Third Violet* he became more enterprising than he had yet been in the management of his own affairs. But the business history of the novel began quietly in the details of winding up the writing and getting over an awful pang of diffidence that followed. Crane probably finished the writing by December 15, 1895, the day he moved from his brother Edmund's house in Hartwood for a few days' visit with his brother William in Port Jervis. He left for Buffalo on the eighteenth and, after the *Philistine* dinner there, stayed over for a few days in East Aurora as Elbert Hubbard's guest, returning to Hartwood no earlier than Christmas Eve. While he was gone a local typist had been transcribing the manuscript, but on December 27 he sent word to Ripley Hitchcock, his editor at Appleton's, that he was forwarding the manuscript itself, "for the typewriting was so bad I am obliged to consider the original better." In the note enclosed with the manuscript, he repeated that "typewriting is too new an art for the woods" and asked that Hitchcock have it typed for him in New York. Evidently he waited from Friday till Monday before posting it, for in a letter to Hawkins on December 31 he reported, "I sent my new novel down to Appleton's yesterday." On that day after shipping off the novel, he was taking time to look before and after. All on the same day he summoned the boldness to open his corre-

[27] Crane left unfinished a letter to Nellie Crouse from New York, March 1, [1896], but sent the fragment from Washington on March 18 with the postscript: "Really, by this time I should have recovered enough to be able to write you a sane letter but I cannot—my pen is dead. I am simply a man struggling with a life that is no more than a mouthful of dust to him" (*Letters*, pp. 119–120). On March 15 from Washington he wrote Hawkins, whom he had evidently stood up: "How sorry I am that I treated you so badly and yet how full how absolute is the explanation—a woman" (*Letters*, p. 118). He wrote a letter of apology to Ripley Hitchcock also, and his less personal terms with the publisher suggest that his vanishing act in New York was connected, not with a scarlet episode as the editors of *Letters* suggest (p. 119 n.), but with his having had enough of formal society such as Nellie Crouse represented for him. He mentions no woman in the letter to Hitchcock, but concludes with an indirection that he consistently used to symbolize gentility: "I have had enough tea" (Washington, [about March 15, 1896], *Letters*, p. 119).

spondence with Nellie Crouse, expressed some uncertainty to Hawkins about how the *Philistine* affair had come out, and in a third letter—to Curtis Brown—got to the far end of the emotional spectrum and sounded completely down about the book he had just sent off: "I have finished my new novel—'The Third Violet' —and sent it to Appleton and Co., as per request, but I've an idea it won't be accepted. It's pretty rotten work. I used myself up in the accursed 'Red Badge.' " [28]

Transferring some of his faintheartedness as a suitor to a matter of business was an imprudence Crane did not permit himself for long. He had worried about the great difference in style between *The Red Badge* and this new work even as he wrote, and although he was anything but well off—most of his outfit for the *Philistine* dinner, from overcoat to patent-leather shoes, was borrowed—he saw the problem at least in part as learning to live with prosperity. Commenting on his own career and on writing in general, he described the earlier book as "an effort born of pain—despair, almost" and compared it invidiously to the work of "prosperous and contented" writers, work which "lacks the sting it would have if written under the spur of pain." [29] That was in November. At his low point at the end of December, he saw the matter as the draining of psychic energy. In January, when his editor Hitchcock had read the new novel and proposed the same comparison to *The Red Badge*—tactfully, no doubt—Crane had recovered from his diffidence and arrived at a more reasonable and prudent literary view: "I think it is as well to go ahead with The Third Violet. People may just as well discover now that the high dramatic key of The Red Badge cannot be sustained. You know what I mean. I dont think The Red Badge to be any great shakes but then the very theme of it gives

[28] To Hitchcock, Hartwood, N.Y., Dec. 27, 1895, and undated; to Hawkins, Dec. 31; to Brown, Dec. 31, *Letters*, pp. 83, 85, 87. Unfortunately, Brown was not only a friend but also an editor, and having been prejudiced by the author himself, he would one day turn down *The Third Violet* for the New York *Press* (Curtis Brown, *Contacts* [New York: Harper & Brothers, 1935], pp. 261–262).

[29] To the Editor of *Leslie's Weekly*, [Hartwood, Nov. 1895], *Letters*, pp. 78–79. Although Crane did not identify himself overtly with the prosperous writers whose work lacked sting, he ended with a word of nostalgia for "the uncertain, happy-go-lucky newspaper writing days": "I used to dream continually of success then. Now that I have achieved it in some measure it seems like mere flimsy paper."

it an intensity that a writer cant reach every day. The Third Violet is a quiet little story but then it is serious work and I should say let it go. If my health and my balance remains to me, I think I will be capable of doing work that will dwarf both books." The conceptual process of absorbing *The Third Violet* into the canon of his work, begun thus, was completed when he inscribed a copy of the published novel, "This book is even worse than any of the others." Such assured self-deprecation was obviously equivalent to saying that he thought it as good in its way as any of the rest.[30]

Whatever questions Hitchcock may have raised about the manuscript and the possibilities of some rewriting, there seems never to have been a doubt about publication by Appleton's. Shortly after Crane made his first progress report, with the warning that his quick style would lead to a short novel, he was saying confidently that the firm wanted "to put my new story in their Zeit-Geist series." The only uncertainty he felt had to do with German pronunciation, not with the fate of his story. When the novel was turned in and read, he went to New York to confer with Hitchcock in full confidence; and he came back with his tone virtually unchanged, depending somewhat on how sincere his modesty was when he told Nellie Crouse: "I have about four new books coming out. Sometimes I feel like sitting still and watching them appear. However, they are not good enough to delight me at all."[31] In his first letter saying in so many words that Appleton would publish the novel, Crane made it clear that he had a rather different problem—not rejection but too many acceptances at once. Out of consideration of timing, *The Third Violet* would have to wait until the revised *Maggie* came out, since that was already under contract for simultaneous London publication by Heinemann. He also mentioned "The Little Regiment," which he was writing for McClure; a literary business-man could have told him that with McClure guaranteeing prompt magazine or syndicate publication of his war stories, the volume built around that novelette might garner its journalistic

---

[30] To Hitchcock, Hartwood, Jan. 27, [1896]; to Mr. Harris, inscribed in a copy of *The Third Violet*, London, June 1897, *Letters*, pp. 106–107, 143.

[31] To Willis Brooks Hawkins, Hartwood, Nov. 1, 1895; to Nellie Crouse, Hartwood, Jan. 12, [1896], and Feb. 5, [1896], *Letters*, pp. 66, 100, 111–112.

income before serialization of *The Third Violet* even began.[32] What he did not mention was the fourth of the four books he had coming out. When Appleton's learned that the firm of Edward Arnold was going to bring out *George's Mother* at almost exactly the time planned for *Maggie*, there may have been a small explosion; but Hitchcock, waiting for final copy for *Maggie* and thereafter for *The Little Regiment*, could hardly say all he may have thought. Not even Crane could miss the fact that his bargaining position was the best it would ever be. Crane's apology for violating his understanding with Appleton was a masterly act of aggression:

I have not told you that I am beset—quite—with publishers of various degrees who wish—or seem to wish—to get my books and who make me various offers. Some of them are little firms but I think nearly every representative American house has made overtures of some kind to me as well as five or six London firms. I have not thought it worth while to talk much about it and in fact this letter contains the first mention of it, I believe. I have not considered at all the plan of playing one house against another but have held that the house of Appleton would allow me all the benefits I deserved. Without vanity I may say that I dont care a snap for money until I put my hand in my pocket and find none there. If I make ill terms now there may come a period of reflection and so I expect you to deal with me precisely as if I was going to write a GREAT book ten years from now and might wreak a terrible vengeance upon you by giving it to the other fellow. And so we understand each other.[33]

Whether or not the idea of playing one house against another originated with Hitchcock, as Crane's tone of assumed innocence suggested, the young novelist used it well. He had, when he was really innocent in such matters, agreed to a most ungenerous Appleton contract for *The Red Badge*, with among other stipulations a royalty of only 10 percent. A few years later, when he was to become a jaded compounder of debts, he would contrive an extra advance from another publisher on the basis of "a little temporary mortgage upon the royalties of my four Appleton books viz: The Red Badge of Courage, The Little Regiment, Maggie, and The Third Violet, the royalties being at fifteen per

---

[32] To the Editor of *The Critic*, Hartwood, Feb. 15, 1896, *Letters*, p. 117.
[33] To Hitchcock, Washington, March 26, [1896], *Letters*, p. 121.

cent and free of all claims." [34] Evidently the change from 10 to
15 percent was made about this time, for Crane's next letters
to Hitchcock were tranquil businesslike communications. But
when Arnold, having lost out on *Maggie*, tried to get the English
rights to later works and thus undo Appleton's arrangement with
Heinemann, the old problem came to a head. The matter was
cleared up when Crane wrote, not to Hitchcock, but to Mr.
Appleton himself: "I have written to Arnold that your arrangement with Heinemann concerning The Little Regiment and The
Third Violet must stand—that it was a prior and just contract
and that I intend to see that Heinemann's rights in the books
shall be guarded." This letter, written on Appleton stationery and
bearing a date filled in by someone other than Crane, bears the
marks of having been done in the Appleton office with Hitchcock
standing over Crane's shoulder and breathing some strong words
on the meaning of legal obligation. [35]

Although there was a moment of acute doubt among his
friends and a time of serious if not really open reconsideration
with his publisher, Crane almost always kept a good face before
the wider world on *The Third Violet*. That wider world, commer-
cially speaking, consisted of magazine and newspaper editors,
syndicate managers, and literary agents. As his reputation
spread, he got letters like the inquiry from *Youth's Companion*
which came in the fall of 1895. In excusing himself from providing them with a story at once, he explained that his time was
"now possessed by a small novel" and by his serious tone made
it clear that "small" was not at all a pejorative word for him. [36]
At the turn of the year, in writing an autobiographical sketch for
the Rochester *Union and Advertiser*, he was pleased to announce: "Last week I finished my new novel: 'The Third Violet.'

[34] To James B. Pinker, [Oxted, Surrey], Feb. 4, 1899, *Letters*, p. 208. Whether
or not Crane actually was getting a 15 percent royalty, it was to his advantage
to say so both for negotiating new contracts and for assuring this creditor of
early repayment from ample income; however, 15 percent was by no means a
large royalty, and with four Crane books to be on sale at once, one of them a
proven best seller, Appleton can be expected to have adjusted its original hard
terms up to the customary norm.

[35] To Appleton, New York, July [16, 1896], ALS in Lilly Library, Indiana University, printed in *Stephen Crane Newsletter*, I, no. 1 (Fall, 1966), 1–2.

[36] Corresponding Editor of *Youth's Companion* to Crane, Boston, Oct. 31,
[1895], *Letters*, pp. 67–68; Crane to Corresponding Editor, Hartwood, Nov. 5,
[1895], *Stephen Crane Newsletter*, II, no. 2 (Winter, 1967), 5.

It is a story of life among the younger and poorer artists of New York." [37] When salesmanship entered, the language became somewhat more emphatic. So, in September, 1896, Crane arranged an interview with the city editor of the New York *Journal* to propose a series of city sketches, and on the note confirming time and place, he jotted down the blurb: "The Third Violet is really the history of the love of one of the younger and brilliant American artists for an heiress of the ancient New York family kind. The girl spends her summer near the home [. . .]." [38] But Crane's intensified language was nothing compared to what a true huckster could do, and the "really" in his first sentence sounds as if it is intended as a correction to the circular McClure put out when marketing the novel as one dealing with "the seamy side of glorious love." [39] But the history of Crane's relation with McClure involves more than hucksterism, and their deal on *The Third Violet* presages the fate of the author as entrepreneur.

Need was stronger than pride or prudence in bringing Crane back to McClure more than once. Despite his early experience of standing around in McClure's waiting room and never being called in, Crane was glad enough to go armed with a letter from Hamlin Garland and try again. He gave McClure the first chance to read *The Red Badge* and was kept dangling for almost six months, during which vague promises were made and nothing at all happened. The poor young artist learned a good deal about hardship and, worse than that, depression at having his work reach no one, until finally he was angry enough to take his manuscript back and try elsewhere. He should not have forgotten such treatment, but a year later, in the fall of 1895, he proved that he held no grudges. While writing *The Third Violet*, he necessarily withdrew himself from the day-to-day opportunities of freelance journalism, and before long he felt the lack of income. When McClure approached him for a war story, he agreed to do one. The promise was easier than the execution, he

---

[37] To John Northern Hilliard, Hartwood, Jan. 2, [1896], *Letters*, p. 95.

[38] H. R. Huxton to Crane, New York, Sept. 13, 1896, TLS in Crane Collection, Columbia University Libraries. Huxton's letter setting up the appointment for Crane served well. On September 20, the *Journal* printed the first article, with prefatory reference to the arrangement that came from the meeting (see *Works*, VIII, 937–938).

[39] Peter Lyon, *Success Story: The Life and Times of S. S. McClure* (New York: Scribner, 1963), p. 140.

quickly found. He wrote of "The Little Regiment," "I have invented the sum of my invention in regard to war and this story keeps me in internal despair." What he had hoped to do with his left hand while keeping up progress on his novel, he in fact could do only when he had finished the very different work on which he was engaged. McClure, shrewdly judging how *The Red Badge* typed Crane for the market, not only got several war stories out of him but also projected a series of articles on battles of the Civil War. McClure was economically on a crest at the moment, and as often at such times, he was full of projects. Of his various projects for Crane, which included sending him into Virginia to study battles and to Washington to report on the political scene, his most ingenious was to put the impecunious young man on a kind of retainer. Crane sensed in a generous and naive way that the agreement might be too good, for at the rates McClure would pay, his writing, sometimes slow and sometimes sporadic, might not keep up with obligations. Naiveté was one day to wither in the discovery that he was in virtual peonage. For the moment, however, he had ample energies (even if he had proved that he could not intensively imagine a war tale while writing a comedy of manners) and many ways of satisfying his side of the contract. In a tally of his economic situation, he made a list on a sheet of McClure's stationery of seven newspaper pieces that he turned in for syndication between May and August, 1896, and which earned him credit for the sum of $155; to the list he added his story "The Veteran," which came out in *McClure's Magazine* in August and was worth an additional $75 for the author's account; then finally he added *The Third Violet* with the notation "30,000 words." What the list makes clear, with its various prices for newspaper pieces separately written in, perhaps by someone in McClure's office, is that the syndicate was an agent for newspaper publication and not the outright purchaser of serial rights. Also, the last addition on the list dates it in the late summer of 1896 when the other work was not only turned in but distributed and printed and subject to accounting. By August he was in deep.[40]

---

[40] To Hawkins, Hartwood, [Nov. 12, 1895], and *re* agreement, to McClure, Hartwood, Jan. 27, [1896], *Letters*, pp. 72, 108; manuscript list in Crane Collection, Columbia University Libraries.

Crane turned to McClure for serializing the novel when it appeared that Hitchcock at Appleton's would perform no such service: he had sent Hitchcock an inquiry from the *Atlantic Monthly* with the suggestion that *The Third Violet* might interest them, but nothing came of it. Once he found out from his McClure accounting what American and British serial rights might be worth, he recognized that he would be better off with access to the whole market rather than dependent on a single syndicate, and so in September he engaged Paul Revere Reynolds as his agent and, leaving his first story with Reynolds, advised him, "Don't go to Bacheller or McClure," that is, advised him that he didn't care to pay a fee for placing work with syndicates to which he had direct access.[41] Quite apart from questions of simplicity or deviousness, hopefulness or despair—and all these terms apply to Crane's business dealings at this point—the poor but brilliant young writer had entered a world of success that was very much more complicated than he knew. Although he was hoping through Reynolds to crack the great international magazines that published simultaneously in New York and London, he retained him as an agent for any purchasers. Also, the *Sun,* the usual New York outlet for McClure's syndicate, did not take everything of Crane's that was offered. So Reynolds got the chance to sell *The Third Violet* to the New York *World* for $150. As to the settlement, he got his commission of $25 before remitting the money to McClure, who presumably then got another healthy cut before sending any money to the author or, more likely, crediting it to his account. Economic disaster was still a fairly long way off, but Crane was well started on the way to convert success into failure.[42]

[41] To Hitchcock, Washington, March 23, [1896]; to Reynolds, [New York], Sept. 9, 1896, *Letters*, pp. 121, 130–131. Crane had also tried to sell the newspaper rights himself; see note 28 above.

[42] Ernest O. Chamberlin, New York Evening *World*, to Reynolds, New York, Oct. 20, 1896:

"The first installments of the Crane story are received and being put into type.

"I had supposed from the circular you presented on your first visit that we were dealing with the McClure Syndicate.

"It seems from your note accompanying the copy that the affair is with you personally.

"Under the circumstances you will pardon me for asking for assurance of your authority to sell the story.

"We wish to advertise it extensively before publication and want to be sure of our ground first" (ALS in Barrett Collection, University of Virginia Library).

Robert Finley, S. S. McClure Co., wrote to Reynolds, New York, Oct. 30, 1896:

The timing of Crane's several projects gave him one more chance to revise *The Third Violet*, for while the novel was running as a newspaper serial, *The Little Regiment* was coming from the printer (copyright deposit October 30, 1896) in the nick of time for the winter trade. There would be a pause before the new novel would be brought out for the spring market. Hitchcock evidently asked Crane to use the interval to lengthen and perhaps to thicken the spare prose of the book, and as noted earlier, Crane did cut down the use of dialect and make other minor revisions. But just as he had found it impossible to oblige McClure and think war while writing about love, he now declined to oblige Hitchcock. It would have been hard to renew his imaginative immersion in the novel now that he no longer lived the same life "among the younger and poorer artists in New York." The Dora Clark affair had put him in conflict with the New York police and brought on harassment that made the city almost impossible for him to live in at all. As he looked for out-of-town newspaper assignments that would take him farther and farther away, what most caught his imagination was Bacheller's proposal that he become a war correspondent and cover the Cuban revolution. The day before the serial finished running in the *World*, Crane departed for Jacksonville with Bacheller's advance for expenses in his money belt. There, with war on his mind, he found love at the Hotel de Dream. With life providing lurid ironies like that, it is perhaps a little lame to recall the literary reasons why Crane thought his one comedy of manners could be neither elaborated nor bespangled. With so many reasons not to revise his novel in any basic way, he took his stand on the highest. According to Thomas Beer, Crane was willing to concede some of Hitchcock's points about compression "but the story had appeared as a serial and it was 'dishonest' to change the thing now that it had been offered to readers." According to

"Would you please remind Mr. Chamberland of the Eve. Post that the last instalment of the Crane story is not to appear before the afternoon of Saturday Nov. 14. earlier publication of this instalment by the World would bring our whole syndicate down on our heads" (TLS in Barrett Collection, University of Virginia Library).

Finley wrote again to Reynolds, New York, Nov. 13, 1896:

"Your letter to the effect that you have received $150 for us from the Evening World, in payment for the New York rights to the Stephen Crane serial received.

"According to our arrangement with you, you are to take $25 out of this sum as your commission for placing this serial" (TLS in Barrett Collection, University of Virginia Library).

Linson, Beer's probable source, Crane's "scrupulous sincerity" was "carried to the limit when he refused to elaborate parts of *The Third Violet* for their betterment because the story had already appeared in print. One would suppose that an artist had the privilege of improving his work for the benefit of his next audience, if not for his own sake." [43] The serious trouble with the chronology of such accounts is, of course, that Crane had left New York before one could say that the serial had already appeared. If Hitchcock really did raise the question of basic revision after the serial was in print, and the incident was within Linson's knowledge of day-to-day conversation with Crane, then the request was put during that brief period in March, 1897, when Crane stopped in New York en route from Jacksonville to Europe, where he would cover the Greek-Turkish War. With less than a week in the city and more pressing matters to occupy him, Crane did what he could. The revised copy must have gone to the printer even before he boarded ship on March 20, for after copyright was applied for on April 15 the printed book was ready for deposit on April 30. By that time Crane was in Greece, and Cora was with him. A very different story had begun.

ACTIVE SERVICE

SOMETIME in October, 1897, Stephen Crane conceived the book which was to become *Active Service*. Having played his part as a star reporter in the Greek-Turkish War, he had come back to England in the late summer and settled down to serious work as a writer of fiction. When he surveyed his economic situation, he found it tight but not hopeless, and he tried to plan his work so that he could properly support the household he and Cora Howorth Stewart were now establishing as Mr. and Mrs. Crane. He had reason to believe that a war novel making use of his Greek experience might be a commercial success. The project was strongly urged by his newspaper friend Harold Frederic, who had helped to sponsor Crane's fame by his New York *Times* article on English response to *The Red Badge of Courage*, and

---

[43] Thomas Beer, *Stephen Crane: A Study in American Letters* (New York: Knopf, 1923), p. 228; Linson, *My Stephen Crane*, p. 34.

who would willingly have helped sponsor Crane's success in new ways. The matter was worth the serious thought Crane evidently gave it, and toward the end of October he wrote to his brother back home: "I am working now on a big novel. It will be much longer than The Red Badge." For the time being, however, he left the project a mere intention. Other forces intervened, principally the momentum of imaginative energy at the flood— he had just written "The Monster" and "The Bride Comes to Yellow Sky" and he knew how good they were—and partly the making of a new literary friend in Joseph Conrad, whose profound responsiveness to Crane's art helped elicit more work of a high order. To a later generation it must seem that instead of seizing the main chance Crane was distracted by greatness. A few weeks after his first mention of the big novel, it still existed only in thought. Instead, he sent his agent the short story of the Greek war "Death and the Child." By this time he was broke and feeling the first painful tightening of the web of debt, but he continued to plan on the novel as a sure thing. He reported to the agent Paul Reynolds, "I have made a proposition to McClure that he advance £200 on the 1st of January for the book rights of my new Greek novel—not yet begun." The split between intention and performance, so far as he was aware of it, was explainable entirely in economic terms: short stories brought in money fairly promptly, though in pitifully small amounts, while novels took a long time to write and bring to publication but could sell well enough to provide a comfortable income. The principle is illustrated by his finally beginning his Greek novel now that he had finished his Greek story. By December 20 he claimed to have some 12,000 words of it on hand. Without other income, however, he simply could not survive the five or six months it would take to complete the work. He chose instead to work up a backlog of "short stuff" so that he could be free thereafter to devote himself to his "big book." Accordingly he forsook the novel to write "The Blue Hotel," and he did not return to it for some months.[1]

---

[1] Thomas Beer, *Stephen Crane: A Study in American Letters* (New York: Knopf, 1923), p. 162. Beer's statement that Crane "was ordered by Harold Frederic to write a novel about his trip to Greece" has been tempered but not substantively revised by subsequent biographers. Crane to William Howe Crane, London, Oct. 29, [1897]; to Paul Revere Reynolds, [Oxted, Surrey, Dec. 1897],

As this account of its earliest stage indicates, conscious economic motivation hardly applied more to *Active Service* than to any other of Crane's work. Yet artistic motivation somehow applied less, as can be seen in comparing his Greek war story and his eventual Greek war novel. The central figure of "Death and the Child" happens to be a correspondent, but even more he is a young man who gets initiated into a reality, both inward and objective, that is constructed according to Crane's characteristic vision. Emotionally caught up by the war in unexpected ways, young Peza feels as if he has "resolved willy-nilly to swing to the bottom of the abyss." He becomes the special witness of soldiers in battle and civilians in flight. Then caught by panic, he encounters death and the child, ultimate negation and natural renewal. In the collapse of his own personality as well as of the commonsense world around him, he touches bottom, though since he has not died, there is the chance of his reviving as a new man. There the story ends, a glimpse of reality and possibility that is powerful in its conciseness and resistant to elaboration. The novel, on the other hand, has a plot that could be extended in either direction. In the main action, Coleman, the college-bred Sunday editor turned war correspondent, seeks out and rescues the archaeological party that includes his beloved Marjory Wainwright, and this adventure beyond the battle lines into Turkish territory serves also to overcome her parents' resistance to his marrying her. At the end of 12,000 words, that is, after Crane's first writing stint, we have not yet done with the prehistory of this action. Coleman is presented on a visit to his old college and at work in the editorial rooms of the New York *Eclipse*, but he is only on the point of becoming a war corre-

---

Stephen Crane: Letters (New York University Press, 1960), pp. 146, 156–157. To Reynolds, Oxted, Dec. 20, [1897], typed copy in Syracuse University Library: "Now comes the question of the big book. I am writing now a novel which is to be at least 75000 words. It is only started now (12000 words) but it will be finished in April or May and as soon as The Open Boat volume comes out and makes its little hit as I am sure it will, I want you to drop some news of the novel here and there. Perhaps by that time I will be able to send you a third of it and at any rate I will send you a synopsis. We should make a big serial amout and a round sum in advance." To Reynolds, Oxted, Jan. 31, [1898], typed copy in Syracuse University Library, announcing that manuscript of "The Blue Hotel" will follow shortly: "I am going to write about a thousand or twelve hundred more dollars in short stuff and work only on my big book."

spondent. These preliminaries, though they are different from the main narrative and more interesting, are nonetheless merely preliminary. Even the refusal of Marjory Wainwright's parents to accept Coleman as a possible suitor for their daughter's hand serves mainly to establish the situation of her being taken to Greece for the conventionally prescribed change of scene. After the outbreak of war, the story of rescue and courtship properly begins. The complications of romance and adventure delay the happy ending, but they are spun out without much suspense. The book falls short of being sensational. Nor does it make a clear appeal to interest in other ways. The fundamental insight of Crane's best fiction, especially his best stories about war, is the precariousness of personality and institutions, but it is scarcely detectable in this novel. There is no swinging to the bottom of the abyss and very little exuberance at missing such a fate. When so much is missing, one must be puzzled at what Crane put in.

Unlike Crane's short story of the Greek war, his novel centers on the idea of the war correspondent more than the character of the man who becomes one. When Crane, working on the main part of the narrative, saw the gist of things, he settled on the appropriate title, *Active Service*. That military term asserts a maximum claim for journalists in the war zone by likening them to soldiers in their dangers, their duties, and their possible heroism. The implicit claim is all the stronger in a war novel that gives so little attention to the duties, dangers, and heroism of soldiers. A correspondent in this sense is an adventurous figure whose doings are themselves the raw materials of publicity. Coleman understands this yellow-press conception of reality. When in Greece he gets a cable from his home office, "Find Wainwright party all hazards much talk here success means red fire by ton," he immediately sees in his mind's eye all the newspaper readers from every walk of life who will follow his story "as a sort of sensational novel." He is not averse to the spurious glamour that will come his way and not deceived by it even when he most relishes the game. But once he is cast in that role, the role seems more important than any private purposes or individual sensibility in determining his consciousness and behavior. So long as he sticks to what is prescribed for the part, abysses will not exist for him and adventures will provide both fun and fame. Besides, this fictitious war correspondent should be all the more interesting to the reading public in that the author of the novel was himself an actual attested war correspondent, thought by some to be the best of them all. Like the fictitious correspondent, the actual one was consciously performing for an audience rather than discovering inner and outer reality.

Above all else the experience that lies behind *Active Service* is Crane's becoming a war correspondent. It involves a transaction between the artist and his society far more complex than figuring out how to make a living by what one writes. Through a sequence of coercive economic events and minor social adjustments, Crane gradually changed his conception of himself. The change was complicated, drawn out over a long period, and—fortunately—never quite complete. Because it profoundly affected his practice as a novelist, it is worth sketching briefly here. In part it is the depressing story of a young man with inadequate resources, intellectual and cultural even more than economic, giving way before the institutional pressures of his time. It is also the story, abruptly broken off by early death, of his first tentative efforts to find how his vision of things, a vision of the world in general and of the private inner life, connected with day-to-day social existence. Ironically, his first artistic triumph, based on his insights into the world and the psyche, led to his involvement with the new corporate powers of journalism. When Hamlin Garland read *The Red Badge* in manuscript and suggested that he take it to S. S. McClure, Crane's transformation from a newspaper free lance into a correspondent began. Although Crane never entirely lost the old-fashioned notion of the newspaperman as an individual editor, he dealt from then on with new institutions of journalism bigger than he had ever known and more complex than he ever quite understood.

McClure's economic and literary influence on Crane defined itself in the first dealings they had and was to be repeated with variations thereafter. The young novelist hopefully brought his manuscript and letter of introduction to a man who could arrange lucrative serial publication in papers across the country.

McClure, founder of one of the recently organized syndicates that were nationalizing the press, was a rising tycoon who knew a promising young man when he saw one. He generated ideas as he talked, and enterprising as he was, he almost immediately proposed sending Crane on assignment to write an article on life in the Pennsylvania coal mines and having Crane's friend Corwin Linson go along on commission to do the illustrations. Obviously he wasted no time with an idea that would pay off. As for the novel, however, he held the manuscript almost six months without either accepting or rejecting it. It did not fit his current schemes, but he did not want to give up a good thing. His entrepreneurial heartiness toward Crane did not extend to personal consideration: the enthusiastic commissioner of the coal-mining article was in the matter of the book downright cruel. Crane, after being put off time and again until he could stand it no longer, finally took the novel away. He could not afford, of course, to hold a grudge even for such outrageous treatment. McClure, rising to the top of the syndicate business, would get him back whenever money pressure provided the occasion. In the meantime, even when Crane dealt with a man who was as generous as McClure was hard, he would be dealing with the same economic institutions and reshaping his journalistic career in the same way.

Crane on his second try brought *The Red Badge* to Irving Bacheller, the originator of the syndicate scheme and McClure's great rival. Temperamentally Bacheller was more an ingenious small-town newsman than a high-powered operator. He read the manuscript in a night, and without having to calculate the market first, he jumped at the chance to buy it. When the novel was serialized soon after, he acted not only as promoter but also as friend in taking Crane to Philadelphia to meet the staff of the *Press* who liked the book so much. He listened to Crane's ideas of what he wanted to write and sponsored his 1895 trip to the West and Mexico, thus first making him a regular correspondent with a national audience. When Crane returned to New York, the well-meaning older friend welcomed him back by enlisting him as a charter member of the Lantern Club. Sharing Crane's literary ambitions himself, he had founded the club in much the same spirit as he had founded his college fraternity, out of natural congeniality and a sense that voluntary associations could serve humane purposes. He and his fellow club members offered Crane sociability, encouragement, criticism, and on occasion the chance to lunch informally with established writers as distinguished as Mark Twain and William Dean Howells. The comfortable dining room with its big fireplace was in a quaint rooftop structure on an old downtown building, reached by an outdoor stairway that was lighted by a ship's lantern. There a serious young journalist had an ideal alternative to the din of Park Row restaurants or the rougher geniality of newspapermen's saloons. Crane liked that choice and became a regular attendant there, so much so that he began using the club as his mailing address. More important, the amiable Bacheller provided Crane with ideal working conditions editorially as well as socially. As an editor he took things as they came. Unlike the more aggressive McClure, whose tempting advances soon had Crane back in his pool of talent, he never urged Crane to capitalize on his early success with *The Red Badge*. Notoriously McClure pressed Crane to do articles on great battles of the Civil War and to turn out more war stories when he was sick of writing war stories, as Bacheller did not. Yet it was Bacheller who first made Crane a war correspondent, sending him in November, 1896, to cover the Cuban Revolution. No longer a loner as he had been on his trip West, Crane began to live his part. In Florida he chummed with other newsmen who waited for the chance to ship out, and during that time of delay, he began his grand romantic liaison with Cora Stewart. Then, with the sinking of the *Commodore* on its way to the rebels with guns, he figured in an adventure which made him famous for what he did, not just for what he wrote. For Bacheller, the loss of the money with which he staked his correspondent helped him go broke as a syndicate operator. For Crane, the headline adventure confirmed his status as someone who made news as well as reporting it, a correspondent with a public image to purvey.

As support from Bacheller petered out, Crane made a new arrangement that involved him with still larger enterprises and more powerful entrepreneurs. He signed on with the New York *Journal* to become one of William Randolph Hearst's staff covering the Greek-Turkish War. When he had worked for the *Journal* before, he had achieved a New York notoriety in the Dora Clark case. Defending an accused prostitute whom the police were out to get, he made headlines as well as sending in copy. He also brought on himself the police harassment that ultimately forced him to leave New York. So Hearst, from his own knowledge as publisher of the *Journal*, could well guess that the star of the *Commodore* affair would be a good correspondent. Evidently he signed him on somewhat casually, for Crane's delayed response seems to keep up a tone already set. Halfway across Europe en route to Greece, it occurred to Crane that he lacked the languages that a reporter would need, and he jauntily concluded: "Willie Hearst has made a bad bargain." Whatever contact he may have made with the great captain of yellow journalism, there was also a more homely personal aspect to his getting the new job. His friend Edward Marshall, who had once published his work in the New York *Press*, had shifted to the *Journal*. Marshall responded both as friend and as wide-awake editor to the news of Crane's shipwreck and ordeal at sea, and he telegraphed the survivor: "Congratulations on plucky and successful fight for life. Dont wire. But write fully from Jax. Will wire money to-day." [2] A couple of months later, when his hope of getting to Cuba for Bacheller had faded, Crane found that there was Hearst money ready to outfit him and send him to Greece, and presumably Marshall had something to do with it. Marshall's own switch from Sunday editor to war correspondent in the Spanish-American War gave Crane a model for the fictive career of Rufus Coleman in *Active Service*. In the novel the publisher's spontaneous and lavish response to the proposed assignment could be Crane's version of what happened to Marshall or possibly of what happened to himself. Either way, contact with Hearst gave Crane the notion of a new scale of doing things.

In no sense did Hearst get a bad bargain, but perhaps Crane did. The young correspondent wrote headline dispatches and had headline dispatches written about him. He was a big enough name to come into the friendly ambience of the American minister to Greece, Eben Alexander, to whom he was to dedicate *Active Service*. He did not become a particular expert on the

---

[2] Beer, *Crane*, p. 154; Marshall's telegram relayed by Morton to Stephen Crane, [Jacksonville, Jan., 1897], *Letters*, p. 138.

war or show a lucky talent for scoops, but he wrote with fresh sensitivity of both soldiers and civilians, battles and aftermath. He worked hard to earn the public image of star reporter, but he also kept up his jaunty side. When Cora Stewart, who had come with him to England and Europe, joined him in Greece, he saw that a place was made for her—in name at least—on the *Journal* staff. With his behind-the-scenes assistance, she became "Imogene Carter," the *Journal's* own "Woman Correspondent at the Front." Later when they returned to England and thought of putting their peacetime domesticity on a sound financial basis, they hoped that by syndicating a weekly London Letter by Imogene Carter, they could assure some regular income. That Crane thought the product was shoddy—"rotten bad" was his phrase—did not seem to matter; exploiting the name did not seem to affect any real person, and for a syndicate payment he would see that the writing was better. Besides such commercialization of his standards, Crane paid other costs for his new role. When he went over his affairs with his agent Reynolds, he simply could not explain his situation with Hearst: "As for the *Journal* I have quite a big misunderstanding with them and can't get it pulled out straight. They say I am over-drawn. I say I am not. I have sent them an installment of my Irish Notes that I am doing here for the Westminster *Gazette* and would send them more if it were possible to hear from them. . . . My idea was that they would go in with that stuff on the editorial page. Twenty-five dollars per installment would be enough. If the *Journal* will explain why they say I am overdrawn I am the last man in the world to kick and will pay the a/c in work." [3]

In the autumn of 1897 Crane was in debt to both McClure and Hearst. The former characteristically held a work in manuscript —"The Monster"—that he did not want to publish; instead of letting Crane sell it elsewhere, he kept it as security till his debt was paid off. The latter turned out not to be so lavish with expense money as Crane thought; out of the initial stake and later payments, a large part was debited against the correspondent's day-to-day earnings. [4] With such debts plus his household expenses in

[3] For "Imogene Carter," see REPORTS OF WAR, *Works*, IX (1971), 267–273, 523–526, and TALES, SKETCHES, AND REPORTS, *Works*, VIII (1973), 693–726, 943–960. Crane to Reynolds, [Oxted, Oct., 1897], *Letters*, p. 145.

[4] To Reynolds, [Oxted, Oct., 1897], *Letters*, pp. 144–145. McClure held "The

Surrey, where he and Cora established themselves with liberal use of local credit, Crane had no choice but to keep economic considerations in mind even while he pursued the uneconomical course of writing remarkable stories with great expenditure of time and pains. Under the circumstances, getting a novel written was impossible even though it might prove a bonanza. But thinking of newspaper work as a source of regular income was reasonable enough, and the possibility could only become more attractive as Crane's finances went from bad to worse that winter and spring. With the approach of the Spanish-American War, the thought also occurred to him, "This war will be fought in English." Even before McKinley's war message to Congress, he decided that he must start "for the war" at once. He explained his haste, in Conrad's account, as prompted by concern "lest peace should be declared and the opportunity of seeing a war missed." On his prospects as a war correspondent he was able to raise £60 as a loan-advance from *Blackwood's Magazine* to be paid off with articles "from the seat of war in the event of war breaking out." [5] When he got to New York his intention swerved, momentarily at least, and he tried to get into the navy. But he failed to pass the navy physical—an unsettling sign that economic stress and imaginative strain were taking a toll. On the other hand, though he had no job lined up when he left England, Pulitzer's *World* was waiting to sign him on as a correspondent, and he came to terms at once.

Crane's 1898 performance as a war correspondent, though it was prelude to his writing *Active Service*, differed radically from the role he was to describe in the novel. For one thing, the zest was gone. Conrad thought, from his London perspective and his acute sympathetic insight, that Crane disappeared into the war "like a wilful man walking away into the depths of an ominous

---

Monster," which was a novelette in length, till he got Crane to agree to give him his next collection of short stories, centered on "The Open Boat": "It turned out that I only owed McClure $71.09 and of course he copped that out of the $200 [i.e., the advance on *The Open Boat and Other Stories*]. And at the same time, he has already 53000 words for a book—at least he has as soon as he gets a copy of Death and the Child" (Crane to Reynolds, Oxted, Jan. 31, [1898], typed copy in Syracuse University Library).

[5] Beer, *Crane*, p. 177; Conrad, introd. to Beer, *Crane*, p. 32; receipt for £60 from *Blackwood's* (author's copy, unsigned), dated April 7, 1898, MS in Columbia University Libraries.

twilight." Whatever personal twilight he may have been in, Crane worked hard at his job. He became an expert reporter who managed with good frequency to be on the spot for important events even though he was not always prompt to file his story. Richard Harding Davis, the star correspondent of them all, testified to his expertness, relieved perhaps that Crane played the role of rival star much less than in Greece. Crane for his part became a kind of spokesman for the regular soldiers who got so much less glory than the well-publicized gentlemen volunteers. He found that they did their duty without question, without show, and without self-consciousness, and he admired bravery that did not lend itself to sensational reporting.[6] He showed himself to be brave too, doing his duty like a regular perhaps, but also something more. In exposing himself to risk he showed a curiously mechanical bravado that evidently came from the depressed state he was in. After the intense work and desperate pressures of his first English winter, after his flight and then his rejection from the navy on physical grounds, he had sufficient cause to be depressed. Insofar as depression exceeds its manifest causes, his slovenly appearance and, for once, his unpopularity among his fellow journalists on the dispatch boats confirmed that something was wrong. Then tropical fever (probably malaria, possibly a flaring of the tuberculosis which was to kill him within two years) set in, and with it, acute fatigue. Sick and exhausted though he was, Crane could still rise to an occasion. At the battle of Las Guasimas, when a random bullet wounded Ed Marshall, Crane took his story from him, ran with it to the *Journal* outpost some five miles away, and brought back help. When he was sent back to the United States in July to recuperate, he found that the *World* did not think well of such gallant but economically absurd behavior. So he said good-bye to Pulitzer's paper and signed on again with Hearst's. The ease of the switch proved that he was still a big-name correspondent, but he was also to find that the big-name publishers were equally sharp about getting their

[6] Conrad, introd. to Beer, *Crane*, p. 31; Davis, "Our War Correspondents in Cuba and Puerto Rico," *Harper's*, xcviii (May, 1899), 942. Crane produced his American equivalent of *Barrack-Room Ballads*, only a bit thicker than anything of Kipling's, in "Regulars Get No Glory," *Works*, ix, 170–173; the emphasis on "fatalism" and "unquestioning obedience" is closer to Kipling than to Hemingway, but the filiation of an American pattern is evident.

money's worth. When the military campaigns were over and despite official discouragements he got into Havana, Crane set himself up as he thought a Hearst correspondent should. He seems to have expected that the *Journal* would cover his expenses at the elegant Hotel Pasaje and forward his pay, through its London office, to Cora. When he learned at last that he was mistaken, he moved to a cheap boarding house—with an enormous hotel bill, an overdraft with Hearst that he must work off at twenty dollars a column, and word coming through that Cora was getting no *Journal* payments and was being served with bailiffs' writs. Under such circumstances he began writing hard—columns for Hearst, war stories for the young publisher Frederick Stokes with whom he had reached an understanding on his short home leave, and various other work that probably included some of his novel about a dashing, carefree, sure-of-himself war correspondent.[7]

How much Crane got done before his return to England remains obscure. The widely accepted belief that he did a lot is mainly traceable to the imperfectly reliable biography by Thomas Beer. According to him, Crane's active concern for the novel began in the long hours on board the dispatch boat during the military campaign, when he "lounged and wondered, with crescent boredom, how to make an end of 'Active Service' and out of that contemplation, rose a remark on a postcard: 'A reporter is no hero for a novel.'" The note of frustration, cited so circumstantially, sounds authentic but hardly demonstrates accomplishment. As for the autumn months he spent in Havana, there is little reason to believe Beer's assertion that "he finished 'Active Service' before starting North, then threw the last chapters aside and wrote them afresh." The strongest evidence that Crane worked on the novel at all, much less finished it, is indirect and uncertain. Cora wrote in January, 1899, when Stephen was on his way home: "He has been hard at work upon a war story but what it is like I do not know." Since she had just been declaring her hopes for his next book, her sentence could be construed as

---

[7] Marshall, *The Story of the Rough Riders* (New York, 1899), pp. 76, 85, 143; Ames W. Williams, "Stephen Crane: War Correspondent," *New Colophon*, 1 (April, 1948), 113–124; J. C. Levenson, "Introduction," TALES OF ADVENTURE, *Works*, v (1970), cviii–cxii; Crane to Reynolds, Havana, Nov. 1, [1898], typed copy in Syracuse University Library.

referring to a novel; the inference is not strengthened, however, by the circumstance that she was notoriously out of touch with Crane. The writer's own surviving letters to his agent do not, during the spring, summer, or autumn of 1898, mention a novel. During the period of his virtual disappearance in Havana, when he seemed to be in documentable contact with no one but the agent Reynolds, he wrote war stories which he sent on to New York, and he wrote Havana sketches for Hearst even after he became aware that Hearst had cut off the flow of payments to Cora. He had time for other work as well. His fellow reporter Otto Carmichael, who testifies to Crane's physical debilitation in that Havana interval, to his slack appearance, irregular habits, and seemingly callous unresponsiveness to cables from England, bears witness differently when he speaks of Crane and work: "When I saw him he was doing 600 words a day. This was the only thing he did with regularity. He was very particular about his work." [8] But if 600 words a day was a reasonable minimum output for him when he was writing steadily, he had time enough to complete the first half of *Active Service* later, between his getting back to England in January, 1899, and his first mention of the novel since he had laid it aside to write "short stuff" and then to go to war. He had presumably given it some thought in the interval and perhaps had realized some of his thought on paper, but he did not mention it again as work in progress until February 13, 1899, when he wrote to Reynolds: "I'm going to have two big novels this year. I have got half of one of the big novels very nearly finished to my satisfaction and I will send the half to you in about three weeks if you think there is any possibility of getting any goodly sum (advance) upon the exhibition of half of a novel for serialization. The book-rights belong to Stokes." [9]

[8] Beer, *Crane*, pp. 183–184, 199. Cora Crane to Edward Garnett, [Oxted, first week of Jan., 1899], *Letters*, p. 203. Between January 31, 1898, and February 13, 1899, a sequence of sixteen letters from Crane to Reynolds omit mention of the Greek war novel (typed copies in Syracuse University Library). Carmichael's article in the Omaha *Daily Bee*, discovered by Virginia Knoll and reprinted in *Prairie Schooner*, XLIII (Summer, 1969), 200–204.

[9] Crane evidently made his first contact with Stokes during his recuperation trip to the United States in July, 1898, and very likely he did so through Reynolds since his November 1 letter to the agent from Havana asked that he "convey to Stokes the pleasing information that I have completed about 15000 words of Cuban stories and that he shall have the book for spring" (typed copy in Syracuse University Library). Although Beer observed that Stokes "was

By the time he did the main work on the novel, then, Crane's two-part career as a war correspondent was over. After the Greek episode, he learned for the first time what it was to be in debt to Hearst. In Cuba he learned the lesson again, much more painfully. At these two early stages of composing the novel, and thereafter, he had no reason to think of war as a lark, a reporter as a hero, or a mass-circulation newspaper publisher as an easygoing benefactor of young journalists. It was a sign of extraordinary magnanimity, or forgetfulness, or responsiveness to the conventions of popular fiction, that he should have Rufus Coleman of the New York *Eclipse* come into his boss's office to announce his need of a change and to have the publisher Sturgeon reach at once for his checkbook, saying: "Where do you want to go? How long do you want to be gone? How much money do you want?" As soon as Greece is proposed, Sturgeon agrees

---

anxious for a novel" (*Crane*, p. 200), neither Reynolds nor Crane thought one was forthcoming enough to be worth a preliminary negotiation. But after Crane returned to England and the financial troubles that awaited him there, matters came to a head. Before he could leave his Oxted house and move to Brede, he had to make some settlement with his creditors; and on February 4, 1899, he reported to his British agent James B. Pinker that he had spent a long day with Dominick, the head of Stokes's London office, and arranged a loan for which he gave as security a "mortgage" on his future Appleton royalties (*Letters*, pp. 207–208). Between February 4 and February 13, the date Crane reported that "the book-rights belong to Stokes," the informal mortgage had evidently been negotiated into an advance on *Active Service*. Although Crane said that half of the novel was "very nearly finished to my satisfaction" on February 13, Cora Crane wrote Pinker three weeks later on Monday, March 6: "Half of the novel should reach you by Thursday" (*Letters*, p. 217). Not all that time was necessary for the preparation of typescript.

Crane's bypassing his agent in selling the book rights was matched by his pressure to have Reynolds sell the serial rights despite the wishes (and perhaps the expectations) of the publisher. On March 2 Crane wrote Reynolds from Brede: "My big novel of 80000-words should be finished by the end of March. It is full of love and war. Stokes and Co. dont wish me to sell the American serial rights but I think if you tackled all those news-papers for a big summer serial we could make fifteen hundred dollars out of it. Would a good half of the novel be of any service to you to begin preliminary work with? If so I can send it to you upon reciept of your reply to this letter. On this side of the water Pinker is going to take half of the novel immediately out among the Englishmen." On March 16 he returned to the subject: "I dont suppose that the Stokes Co. will be pleased to have the story run as a serial in America but the more I look at it the more I feel that we might get even two or three thousand dollars out of newspapers like the Sun or the Herald in New York, the Press in Philla. and others" (typed copies in Syracuse University Library). Reynolds did not set up an ad hoc syndicate for the novel as Crane suggested, but he may have put enough effort into the attempt so as to become permanently disaffected from Crane (see note 14 below).

and writes a check: "Here's a thousand dollars. Will that do you to start with?" The only way Crane could indicate the anti-realism of his main plot was by exuberant storytelling that would remind his readers that it was make-believe. But he could not sustain such exuberance. For the most part his narrative follows popular convention without a hint that the world may be constructed in accordance with other principles. That Crane lost his critical awareness is suggested also by a remark he made to Reynolds when he was about two-thirds through the writing, as if he saw for the first time how his sentimental plot was going to end. On March 25, after reporting his progress, he went on: "For your own edification and also for business reasons I think it should be announced that Coleman simply drowns all opposition and marries Marjory." [10]

It was not only economic pressure and money-making calculation that kept Crane closely bound to popular conventionality. He was hard up for imaginative resources too: no one has yet suggested a specific literary source for the novel even though it is the nature of literature that it stand in some kind of dialectical relation to what has been said before. By the time he had worked himself up to writing, as he put it, "at a clipping gait of some ten thousand words per week," there was hardly a chance for literary reflection or even critical control.[11] Under such conditions one might expect more personal history and unconscious projection to enter the narrative, so that readers have often seen hints and disclosures in Crane's perfectly conventional doubling of romantic objects. But it adds little to the book to identify Marjory Wainwright with Nellie Crouse or Lily Brandon Munroe, to whom Crane had been romantically attracted; like so many sentimental heroines she is thoroughly simpy and not much else. On the other hand, the temptress rival Nora Black has attributes that link her both with Crane's inconvenient friend Amy Leslie and

[10] To Reynolds, Brede, March 25, 1899, typed copy in Syracuse University Library.

[11] In his letter to Reynolds from Brede, March 16, 1899, Crane gave the optimistic report on his prospect for early completion as prelude to his optimistic estimate of two or three thousand dollars that the agent might get for serializing the novel in newspapers across the country: "The new novel 'Active Service' now stands at 47000 words and I am going at a clipping gait of some ten thousand words per week. The end of the first week in April should see it finished" (typed copy in Syracuse University Library).

with Cora herself. Like the former she is an actress who seems to have set her cap for the unwilling protagonist, and she travels "with her saddle bags packed with inflammable substances," i.e., she drinks. But she gives up her London musical comedy run and, like Cora, comes to Greece as a war correspondent. Like Cora, too, she mixes her styles: she travels genteelly with a duenna, yet she also affects camaraderie and even puts on a hearty Irish accent when she speaks as one journalist to another. In the great temptation scene, instead of playing the tippler herself, she almost conquers Coleman's resistance by means of brandy and champagne as much as by her physical charms. Given the unresolved mixture of characteristics—weak, strong, pal, temptress—she can best be classified simply as the "other woman" of romantic fiction. More revealing than conjectural identifications are the details that meet the eye—Coleman the rejected lover drinking to drown his sorrows, Coleman the tempted hero barely overcoming the effects of drink, Coleman the worldly correspondent slipping whiskey to the college boys in the Wainwright party when the professor and his ultra-proper wife are out of sight. Such moderate sinning as would not basically compromise his leading character may have been analogous, in Crane's view, to sexual freedom or the prostitution of literary talent, but the realistic details stand only for themselves and they are banal. Before he had turned eight years old, little Stevie Crane had shed his temperance background more interestingly than that, plunking down his dime for his first beer and insisting that the mug be properly filled all the way up. "Beer ain't nothing at all," he told his awed playmate. "How was I going to know what it tasted like less'n I tasted it? How you going to know about things at all less'n you do 'em?" [12] The child's act, which stunned barman and

[12] Post Wheeler, in Post Wheeler and Hallie Erminie Rives, *Dome of Many-Coloured Glass* (New York: Doubleday, 1955), pp. 21–22. The boys had accompanied their mothers to a WCTU convention only a couple of days earlier, and little Wheeler had joined the "blue-ribbon army" of pledge-signers some time before. The emancipated Stephen undid all that with his beer-drinking. Partly he sowed doubt about the absolute and irrevocable nature of the sin. "Anyway I didn't want to be so much better than Stevie. When he was looking the other way, I pulled off the blue ribbon and put it in my pocket." The incident took place just after the centenary pageant commemorating the 1788 Indian massacre at Wyoming, Pa., not far from where the Wheelers lived. Mrs. Crane and Stephen went on to visit the Wheelers after the convention. R. W. Stallman (*Stephen Crane, A Biography* [New York: Braziller, 1968], pp. 11–12),

playmate alike, had a comic vitality that did not survive in the man's fable of twenty years later. The correspondent novelist, and therefore the correspondent protagonist, could not sustain the performance which was promised in the beginning.

Crane had committed himself to a kind of fiction which throve on sin, suspense, and sensation, but even though his taste might not forbid, he lacked the narrative skills required for a truly vulgar success. Sometimes comically, sometimes banally, sometimes merely unobtrusively, he undercut the great moments of romance and adventure. Coleman with some intelligence heads himself in the right direction to find the Wainwright party and then has the luck to stumble across them and effect the purposed rescue. The moment of recognition he understands to be "the most theatric moment of his life," and even though he knows that return within the Greek lines will be easy, he is confident that "anyhow his heroism should be preserved." But he does not know how to press his advantage except by making his candor seem put on: "Of course I worked rather hard to reach you but the final meeting was purely accidental and does not redound to my credit in the least." As he becomes less the performing hero, he becomes more the correspondent according to another definition than the one which prevails in the novel. This other conception, making claims for newspapermen which are modest and tentative, more like the "active service" of regulars than of glamorous volunteers, becomes explicit in the novel for a moment only. At one point the narrative jumps ahead of the fictive action, and we learn that "in later years" Coleman would develop a theory of war correspondents that tallied with the one Crane himself developed in his own later years, that is, not during the Greek war but in Cuba:

In the minds of governments, war-offices and generals they have no function save one of disturbance but Coleman deemed it proven that the common men, and many uncommon men, when they go away to the fighting ground, out of the sight, out of the hearing of the world known to them and are eager to perform feats of war in this new place they feel an absolute longing for a spectator. . . .

though he cites no source but Wheeler, places the incident in Ocean Grove, N.J., but the hawker of beer would not have stood a chance in that 100 percent Methodist, Prohibitionist town.

There is not too much vanity of the street in this desire of men to have some disinterested fellows perceive their deeds. It is merely that a man doing his best in the middle of a sea of war longs to have people see him doing his best. This feeling is often notably serious if, in peace, a man has done his worst or part of his worst. Coleman believed that, above everybody, young, proud and brave subalterns had this itch but it existed, truly enough, from lieutenants to colonels. None wanted to conceal from his left hand that his right hand was performing a manly and valiant thing although there might be times when an application of the principle would be immensely inconvenient. The war-correspondent arises, then, to become a sort of cheap telescope for the people at home; further still, there have been fights where the eyes of a solitary man were the eyes of the world; one spectator whose business it was to transfer, according to his ability, his visual impressions to other minds.

Popular convention established the correspondent as an adventurous figure compelling attention to himself, and the pressure of convention was stronger on the would-be popular novelist than it had been on Crane the reporter. Yet he could not banish from his book that other, functional definition of a correspondent as having a responsibility not simply to capture the literary market but rather to present his honest impressions of an objective world. His task was to do justice to his materials as he found them, minimizing the distortion between the objective image and the ultimate viewer. But the optical figure of a "cheap telescope for the people at home" goes too far in depersonalizing the process. The transfer of visual impressions is not enough to explain the interest of the little sketches which, had they existed more profusely, might have made up for the thinness of the narrative. Washurst College, where Coleman goes to pay court to the professor's daughter, provides a more than visual image of the higher learning in America. The first scene opens on the professor, "interrupted in the writing of one of his sentences, ponderous, solemn and endless, in which wandered multitudes of homeless and friendless prepositions, adjectives looking for a parent, and quarreling nouns, sentences which no longer symbolized the language form of thought but which had about them a quaint aroma from the dens of long-dead scholars." And the second scene opens with the mass scrimmage of freshmen and sophomores, who, as the professor notes, "display an energy in the halls which I do not detect in the classroom." Thus are introduced the obdurate father of the sentimental comedy and the youthful chorus of the adventure drama. Their nonexistent intellectual relation is a joke serious enough to suggest why the novelist, who had sampled American college education for a year, could make a good initial sketch and yet lack resources for filling in his plot. So too with the introduction of Coleman at work on the New York *Eclipse*. Out of all the items which he can feature in his next Sunday edition, young Coleman instinctively fastens on the grotesque story of a child born without arms in one of the remote hill counties of western Massachusetts, complete with photograph. The flurry of work which begins with that brilliant judgment of what the public wants ends with his contemptuous dismissal of an eccentric German who claims to have invented a long-range gun: " 'That's a comic old boy,' he said to himself." In both vignettes—of the college and of the newspaper —Crane sketched materials which were new to the apprehension of serious novel readers, and he handled the materials with intelligence and liveliness. But it took a lot of experience, direct or acquired by strenuous learning, to go but a little way with such circumstantial narration. In late 1897, when Crane seems to have written these scenes, he was being imaginatively prodigal and reaping great artistic success. Quite apart from economic pressure, one literary reason for his first breaking off his narrative before the main action had begun was his demonstration, so to speak, in "Death and the Child" that what he knew of the Greek war did not lend itself to a comic narrative set in a realistic if ironically simplified background. After the Cuban war, he had no more experience to draw on of the sort that could contribute to the adventure-romance to which he was committed.

Yet another possible novel which Crane chose not to write cropped up in the narrative, and it too is suggested by the passage on other conceptions of the correspondent. Talking of the world which the correspondent reports, the narrator speaks of men "in the middle of a sea of war." The "Open Boat" figure of speech, when referred to its original context, conveys a situation in which man is beset by engulfing chaos. Laboring so intently to survive that one is unconscious even of the color of the sky, a man loses his commonsense perspective on things and finds that outer and inner experience become deeply intermixed in the world of consciousness. The correspondent, in that ultimate encounter with reality, is totally identified with the action of which he may later be an interpreter. So, almost, is the case of Coleman, who begins his rescue mission full of fantasies of war and love and tilting "with one lance at both gods" and is startled to rather different reveries by his first experience in the war zone.[13] At the end of Chapter IX Coleman and his party come at last within the sound of artillery and the sight of black masses of troops:

They finally came up with one of these black bodies of men and found it to be composed of a considerable number of soldiers who were idly watching some hospital people bury a dead Turk. The dragoman at once rushed forward to peer through the throng and see the face of the corpse. Then he came and supplicated Coleman as if he were hawking him to look at a relic and Coleman, moved by a strong mysterious impulse, went forward to look at the poor little clay-colored body. At that moment a snake ran out from a tuft of grass at his feet and wriggled wildly over the sod. The dragoman shrieked, of course, but one of the soldiers put his heel upon the head of the reptile and it flung itself into the agonized knot of death. Then the whole crowd pow-wowed, turning from the dead man to the dead snake. Coleman signaled his contingent and proceeded along the road.

This incident, this paragraph, had seemed a strange introduction to war. The snake, the dead man, the entire sketch, made him shudder of itself but, more than anything he felt an uncanny symbolism. It was no doubt a mere occurrence; but inasmuch as all the detail of this daily life associated itself with Marjory, he felt a different horror. . . .

And now he interwove his memory of Marjory with a dead man and with a snake in the throes of the end of life. They crossed, intersected, tangled, these two thoughts. He perceived it clearly, the incongruity of it. He academically reflected upon the mysteries of the human mind, this homeless machine which lives here and there and often lives in two or three opposing places at the same instant. He

---

[13] The theme of the novel did not merely slip in unconsciously. In Crane's letter to Reynolds of March 2 (cited in note 9 above), written about halfway along in the composition of his "big novel," he made clear what he had in mind: "It is full of love and war."

decided that the incident of the snake and the dead man had no more meaning than the greater number of things which happen to us in our daily lives. Nevertheless it bore upon him.

Had Crane chosen to penetrate the inner life which he here dismissed as meaningless, he might have written a psychological novel more original than *The Red Badge*, but such a novel would have been correspondingly more demanding than the book to which he had given the most sustained effort of study and re-flection, writing and rewriting, of his whole career. As with the filling in of the social background which his opening vignettes suggested, he simply did not have the resources or the time to acquire them. So he worked as rapidly as he could on his ro-mance-melodrama. Like all his writing it took longer than he expected. The work went on through March and April.[14] It was mid-May when he finished. He then wrote Mrs. Moreton Frewen, the American woman through whose kindness the Cranes had Brede Place at moderate rent, to tell her how he was adding his bit to the history of the house. In announcing completion of the

[14] His March 16 letter to Reynolds, cited in note 11, reported the novel at 47,-000 words. The next day in a letter to Pinker, he reported it at 48,000. On March 25, when he sent the first batch of eighteen chapters in typescript to Reynolds, he reported that he had reached 53,000 words. On March 30, he sent Reynolds Chapters XIX–XXII. It was not until April 25 (Tuesday) that he sent Pinker the first twenty-two chapters; he then promised the rest at week's end, although he had three weeks' work left, as it turned out, not three days' (to Reynolds, typed copies in Syracuse University Library; to Pinker, *Letters*, pp. 218, 219). The delays affected the campaign for serial publication. In an un-dated letter to Pinker (about March 10, *Letters*, p. 218), Crane made it clear that he was committed to have serial publication end by November 1 and that beyond that he foresaw no difficulty in coordinating British and American seri-als. Pinker's deflationary view of the project led to Crane's giving the British agent low priority in getting copy (letter of March 17). When he sent copy to Reynolds on March 25, he warned: "I would not like it left long in the hands of any one man." He still hoped for money for serial rights by May 1. The same kind of pressure would be applied, he hoped, to British publishers. When copy was sent Pinker on April 25 with a covering letter from Cora, she instructed the agent: "Please do your very best to sell serially and give editors to understand that two weeks is the limit to keep Mr. Crane's copy." With all this pressure on his agents, neither sold the serial, it seems. In an undated letter to Reynolds, Crane apologized that Stokes should "have, without my knowledge or permission, been attempting to sell it serially" (*Letters*, p. 219). As the textual evidence indicates (see Fredson Bowers, Textual Introduction, pp. 351–358 below), Stokes seems indeed to have made the sale, and the buyer was the most notorious of manuscript holders and delayers McClure, who took copyright on the serial on July 1. At about that time Reynolds gave up Crane as a client, and Pinker be-came his sole agent.

novel, Crane adopted a tone of self-deprecating candor which she could, being generous, take as charming affectation:

May 15
(Monday)

Dear Mrs. Frewen: I am an honest man above all and—according to promise—I must confess to you that on Saturday morning at 11.15 —after dismal sorrow and travail—there was born into an unsuspecting world a certain novel called "Active Service", full and complete in all its shame—79000 words.—which same is now being sent forth to the world to undermine whatever reputation for excellence I may have achieved up to this time and may heaven forgive it for being so bad.

Yours faithfully
Stephen Crane[15]

There are two odd postscripts to the writing of *Active Service* which indicate that Crane did not think so ill of his novel as he said. One is the fragment of a Spanish-American war play (POETRY AND LITERARY REMAINS, *Works*, x, 139–158), a romantic melodrama of wartime rescue which is set on an English-owned sugar plantation in Cuba. One of the planter's daughters is named Marjorie (Crane was ever parsimonious in inventing names), and one of the characters is a reporter for the New York *Eclipse* (named Sylvester Thorpe, somewhat after Sylvester Scovel, Crane's fellow correspondent on the *World*, and thus balancing Crane's use of Marshall of the *Journal* as his model in the novel). With its comic-opera extravagance, the play might with lively enough music have had some appeal, but Crane never finished it. It seems to date from late 1899 when Crane was exploring possibilities of what would sell. The other postscript was *The Ghost*, a musical farce by Crane with help from numerous guests and fellow writers, with the great collaborative production presented to the villagers of Brede on December 28, 1899. James, Conrad, Gissing, Wells, and Rider Haggard were among the participants in the lark, though for the most part their contribution to the writing seems to have been the inscription of a word or two. The play features the Ghost of Brede Place, and one

[15] ALS from Brede, University of Virginia Library. An earlier letter of March 17 was a kind of progress report, stating like the letter to Pinker of the same date that the novel was at 48,000 words and that he wished it were better.

of the characters is Rufus Coleman, Crane thus complimenting his own work as he did that of Gilbert and Sullivan when he composed a little number called "Three Little Maids from Rye." The house party that centered on producing *The Ghost* barely came to its end when Crane collapsed with tuberculosis.

The most serious postscripts to *Active Service* were in Crane's most serious later writings. By the time the novel came out—copyright deposit was made on October 7 in the United States, on November 2 in England—Crane had given up the idea for what was to have been his second big war novel of the year. Instead of doing the American Revolution as he had done Greece and started to do Cuba, he undertook his Irish Romance, as he called it, *The O'Ruddy*. By this time he knew something of the picaresque tradition, and he cultivated narrative exuberance more purposefully than before. That was the hopeful direction perhaps, but it was not the whole story. Crane the typecast war correspondent and storyteller received a proposal from *Lippincott's* that he do a series on *Great Battles of the World*, and though he resisted for a while, he yielded to economic pressure and began work almost at the same time as he got his Irish Romance under way. What mattered for that project was first of all his name. In the beginning he delegated much of the research, but as his tuberculosis got worse and worse he delegated even the preparation of draft. His research assistant Kate Lyon became his ghostwriter, as he played his role to the end. The split between these two possibilities of what his talent might become was not to be resolved. He died leaving both works unfinished.

THE THIRD VIOLET

CHAPTER I

THE engine bellowed its way up the slanting, winding valley. Grey crags, and trees with roots fastened cleverly to the steeps, looked down at the struggles of the black monster.

When the train finally released its passengers, they burst forth with the enthusiasm of escaping convicts. A great bustle ensued on the platform of the little mountain station. The idlers and philosophers from the village were present to examine the consignment of people from the city. These latter, loaded with bundles and children, thronged at the stage drivers. The stage drivers thronged at the people from the city.

Hawker, with his clothes case, his paint box, his easel, climbed awkwardly down the steps of the car. The easel swung uncontrolled and knocked against the head of a little boy who was disembarking backward with fine caution. "Hello, little man," said Hawker, "did it hurt?" The child regarded him in silence and with sudden interest as if Hawker had called his attention to a phenomenon. The young painter was politely waiting until the little boy should conclude his examination, but a voice behind him cried: "Roger, go on down." A nurse maid was conducting a little girl where she would probably be struck by the other end of the easel. The boy resumed his cautious descent.

The stage drivers made such great noise as a collection that as individuals their identities were lost. With a highly important air, as a man proud of being so busy, the baggageman of the train was thundering trunks at other employees on the platform. Hawker, prowling through the crowd, heard a voice near his shoulder say: "Do you know where is the stage for Hemlock Inn?" Hawker turned and found a young woman regarding him. A wave of astonishment whirled into his hair and he turned his eyes quickly for fear that she would think that he had looked at her. He said: "Yes—certainly—I think I can find it." At the same time he was crying to himself: "Wouldn't I like to paint her, though. What a glance—oh, murder. The—the—the distance in her eyes."

He went fiercely from one driver to another. That obdurate stage for Hemlock Inn must appear at once. Finally he perceived a man who grinned expectantly at him. "Oh," said Hawker, "you drive the stage for Hemlock Inn." The man admitted it. Hawker said: "Here is the stage." The young woman smiled.

The driver inserted Hawker and his luggage far into the end of the vehicle. He sat there, crooked forward so that his eyes should see the first coming of the girl into the frame of light at the other end of the stage. Presently she appeared there. She was bringing the little boy, the little girl, the nurse maid, and another young woman who was at once to be known as the mother of the two children. The girl indicated the stage with a small gesture of triumph. When they were all seated uncomfortably in the huge covered vehicle, the little boy gave Hawker a glance of recognition. "It hurted then, but it's all right now," he informed him cheerfully.

"Did it?" replied Hawker. "I'm sorry."

"Oh, I didn't mind it much," continued the little boy, swinging his long red-leather leggins bravely to and fro. "I don't cry when I'm hurt, anyhow." He cast a meaning look at his tiny sister, whose soft lips set defensively.

The driver climbed into his seat and after a scrutiny of the group in the gloom of the stage, he chirped to his horses. They began a slow and thoughtful trotting. Dust streamed out behind the vehicle. In front, the green hills were still and serene in the evening air. A beam of gold struck them a-slant and on the sky was lemon and pink information of the sun's sinking. The driver knew many people along the road and from time to time he conversed with them in yells.

The two children were opposite Hawker. They sat very correctly mucilaged to their seats, but their large eyes were always upon Hawker, calmly valuing him.

"Do you think it nice to be in the country? I do," said the boy.

"I like it very well," answered Hawker.

"I shall go fishing and hunting and everything. Maybe I shall shot a bears."

"I hope you may."

"Did you ever shot a bears?"

"No."

"Well, I didn't, too, but maybe I will. Mister Hollanden, he said he'd look around for one. Where I live——"

"Roger," interrupted the mother from her seat at Hawker's side, "perhaps every one is not interested in your conversation." The boy seemed embarrassed at this interruption, for he leaned back in silence with an apologetic look at Hawker. Presently the stage began to climb the hills and the two children were obliged to take grip upon the cushions for fear of being precipitated upon the nurse maid.

Fate had arranged it so that Hawker could not observe the girl with the—the—the distance in her eyes without leaning forward and discovering to her his interest. Secretly and impiously he wriggled in his seat and as the bumping stage swung its passengers this way and that way, he obtained fleeting glances of a cheek, an arm or a shoulder.

The driver's conversation tone to his passengers was also a yell. "Train was an hour late t'night," he said, addressing the interior. "It'll be nine o'clock before we git t' th' inn an' it'll be perty dark travellin'."

Hawker waited decently, but at last he said: "Will it?"

"Yes. No moon." He turned to face Hawker and roared: "You're ol' Jim Hawker's son, hain't yeh?"

"Yes."

"I thort I'd seen yeh b'fore. Live in the city, now, don't yeh?"

"Yes."

"Want t' git off at th' cross-road?"

"Yes."

"Come up fer a little stay doorin' th' summer?"

"Yes."

"On'y charge yeh a quarter if yeh git off at cross-road. Useter charge 'em fifty cents, but I ses t' th' ol' man: ' 'Tain't no use. Goldern 'em, they'll walk ruther'n put up fifty cents.' Yep. On'y a quarter."

In the shadows, Hawker's expression seemed assassin-like. He glanced furtively down the stage. She was apparently deep in talk with the mother of the children.

CHAPTER II

WHEN Hawker pushed at the old gate, it hesitated because of a broken hinge. A dog barked with loud ferocity and came headlong over the grass.

"Hello, Stanley, old man," cried Hawker. The ardor for battle was instantly smitten from the dog and his barking swallowed in a gurgle of delight. He was a large orange and white setter and he partly expressed his emotion by twisting his body into a fantastic curve and then dancing over the ground with his head and his tail very near to each other. He gave vent to little sobs in a wild attempt to vocally describe his gladness. "Well, 'e was a dreat dod," said Hawker, and the setter, overwhelmed, contorted himself wonderfully.

There were lights in the kitchen and at the first barking of the dog the door had been thrown open. Hawker saw his two sisters shading their eyes and peering down the yellow stream. Presently they shouted: "Here he is." They flung themselves out and upon him. "Why, Will—why, Will—" they panted. "We're awful glad to see you." In a whirlwind of ejaculation and unanswerable interrogation, they grappled the clothes case, the paint box, the easel, and dragged him toward the house.

He saw his old mother seated in a rocking chair by the table. She had laid aside her paper and was adjusting her glasses as she scanned the darkness. "Hello, mother," cried Hawker, as he entered. His eyes were bright. The old mother reached her arms to his neck. She murmured soft and half-articulate words. Meanwhile, the dog writhed from one to another. He raised his muzzle high to express his delight. He was always fully convinced that he was taking a principal part in this ceremony of welcome and that everybody was heeding him.

"Have you had your supper?" asked the old mother as soon as she recovered herself. The girls clamored sentences at him. "Pa's out in the barn, Will. What made you so late? He said maybe he'd go up to the cross-roads to see if he could see the stage. Maybe he's gone. What made you so late? And, oh, we got a new buggy."

The old mother repeated anxiously, "Have you had your supper?"

"No," said Hawker, "but——"

The three women sprang to their feet. "Well! We'll git you something right away." They bustled about the kitchen and dove from time to time into the cellar. They called to each other in happy voices.

Steps sounded on the line of stones that led from the door toward the barn and a shout came from the darkness. "Well, William, home again, hey?" Hawker's grey father came stamping genially into the room. "I thought maybe you got lost. I was comin' to hunt you," he said, grinning, as they stood with gripped hands. "What made you so late?"

While Hawker confronted the supper, the family sat about and contemplated him with shining eyes. His sisters noted his tie and propounded some questions concerning it. His mother watched to make sure that he should consume a notable quantity of the preserved cherries. "He used to be so fond of 'em when he was little," she said.

"Oh, Will," cried the younger sister, "do you remember Lil' Johnson? Yeh. She's married. Married las' June."

"Is the boy's room all ready, mother?" asked the father.

"We fixed it this mornin'," she said.

"And do you remember Jeff Decker?" shouted the elder sister. "Well, he's dead. Yep. Drowned pickerel fishin'—poor feller."

"Well, how are you getting along, William?" asked the father. "Sell many pictures?"

"An occasional one."

"Saw your illustrations in the May number of *Perkinson's*." The old man paused for a moment and then added quite weakly: "Pretty good."

"How's everything about the place?"

"Oh, just about the same—'bout the same. The colt run away with me last week, but didn't break nothin', though. I was scared because I had out the new buggy—we got a new buggy—but it didn't break nothin'. I'm goin' to sell the oxen in the fall. I don't want to winter 'em. And then in the spring I'll get a good hoss team. I rented th' back five-acre to John Westfall. I had more'n I could handle with only one hired hand. Times is pickin' up a little, but not much—not much."

"And we got a new school teacher," said one of the girls.

"Will, you never noticed my new rocker," said the old mother, pointing. "I set it right where I thought you'd see it and you never took no notice. Ain't it nice? Father bought it at Monticello for my birthday. I thought you'd notice it first thing."

When Hawker had retired for the night, he raised a sash and sat by the window smoking. The odor of the woods and the fields came sweetly to his nostrils. The crickets chanted their hymn of the night. On the black brow of the mountain he could see two long rows of twinkling dots which marked the position of Hemlock Inn.

CHAPTER III

HAWKER had a writing friend named Hollanden. In New York, Hollanden had announced his resolution to spend the summer at Hemlock Inn. "I don't like to see the world progressing," he had said. "I shall go to Sullivan county for a time."

In the morning Hawker took his painting equipment and after maneuvering in the fields until he had proved to himself that he had no desire to go toward the inn, he went toward it. The time was only nine o'clock and he knew that he could not hope to see Hollanden before eleven, as it was only through rumor that Hollanden was aware that there was a sunrise and an early morning.

Hawker encamped in front of some fields of vivid yellow stubble on which trees made olive shadows and which was overhung by a china-blue sky and sundry little white clouds. He fiddled away perfunctorily at it. A spectator would have believed probably that he was sketching the pines on the hill where shone the red porches of Hemlock Inn.

Finally a white-flannel young man walked into the landscape. Hawker waved a brush. "Hi, Hollie, get out of the color-scheme." At this cry the white-flannel young man looked down at his feet apprehensively. Finally he came forward grinning. "Why, hello, Hawker, old boy. Glad to find you here." He perched on a boulder and began to study Hawker's canvas, and the vivid yellow stubble with the olive shadows. He wheeled his eyes from one to the other. "Say, Hawker," he said suddenly, "why don't you marry Miss Fanhall?"

Hawker had a brush in his mouth, but he took it quickly out and said: "Marry Miss Fanhall? Who the devil is Miss Fanhall?"

Hollanden clasped both hands about his knee and looked thoughtfully away. "Oh, she's a girl."

"She is?" said Hawker.

"Yes. She came to the inn last night with her sister-in-law and a small tribe of young Fanhalls. There's six of them, I think."

"Two," said Hawker. "A boy and a girl."

"How do you—oh, you must have come up with them. Of course. Why, then you saw her."

"Was that her?" asked Hawker, listlessly.

"Was that her?" cried Hollanden, with indignation. "Was that her?"

"Oh," said Hawker.

Hollanden mused again. "She's got lots of money," he said. "Loads of it. And I think she would be fool enough to have sympathy for you in your work. They are a tremendously wealthy crowd, although they treat it simply. It would be a good thing for you. I believe—yes, I am sure she could be fool enough to have sympathy for you in your work. And now if you weren't such a hopeless chump——"

"Oh, shut up, Hollie," said the painter.

For a time Hollanden did as he was bid, but at last he talked again. "Can't think why they came up here. Must be her sister-in-law's health. Something like that. She——"

"Great heavens," said Hawker, "you speak of nothing else."

"Well, you saw her, didn't you?" demanded Hollanden. "What can you expect, then, from a man of my sense? You—you old stick—you——"

"It was quite dark," protested the painter.

" 'Quite dark,' " repeated Hollanden in a wrathful voice. "What if it was?"

"Well, that is bound to make a difference in a man's opinion, you know."

"No, it isn't. It was light down at the railroad station, anyhow. If you had any sand—thunder, but I did get up early this morning. Say, do you play tennis?"

"After a fashion," said Hawker. "Why?"

"Oh, nothing," replied Hollanden, sadly. "Only they are wearing me out at the game. I had to get up and play before breakfast this morning with the Worcester girls, and there is a lot more mad players who will be down on me before long. It's a terrible thing to be a tennis player."

"Why, you used to put yourself out so little for people," remarked Hawker.

"Yes, but up there"—Hollanden jerked his thumb in the direction of the inn—"they think I'm so amiable."

"Well, I'll come up and help you out."

"Do," Hollanden laughed. "You and Miss Fanhall can team it against the littlest Worcester girl and me." He regarded the landscape and meditated. Hawker struggled for a grip on the thought of the stubble.

"That color of hair and eyes always knocks me ke-plunk," observed Hollanden, softly.

Hawker looked up irascibly. "What color hair and eyes?" he demanded. "I believe you're crazy."

" 'What color hair and eyes?' " repeated Hollanden, with a savage gesture. "You've got no more appreciation than a post."

"They are good enough for me," muttered Hawker, turning again to his work. He scowled first at the canvas and then at the stubble. "Seems to me you had best take care of yourself instead of planning for me," he said.

"Me!" cried Hollanden. "Me! Take care of myself! My boy, I've got a past of sorrow and gloom. I——"

"You're nothing but a kid," said Hawker, glaring at the other man.

"Oh, of course," said Hollanden, wagging his head with midnight wisdom. "Oh, of course."

"Well, Hollie," said Hawker, with sudden affability, "I didn't mean to be unpleasant, but then you are rather ridiculous, you know, sitting up there and howling about the color of hair and eyes."

"I'm not ridiculous."

"Yes, you are, you know, Hollie."

The writer waved his hand despairingly. "And you rode in the train with her and in the stage."

"I didn't see her in the train," said Hawker.

"Oh, then you saw her in the stage. Ha-ha, you old thief. I sat up here and you sat down there and lied." He jumped from his perch and belabored Hawker's shoulders.

"Stop that," said the painter.

"Oh, you old thief, you lied to me. You lied—— Hold on— bless my life, here she comes now."

CHAPTER IV

ONE day Hollanden said: "There are forty-two people at Hemlock Inn, I think. Fifteen are middle-aged ladies of the most aggressive respectability. They have come here for no discernible purpose save to get where they can see people and be displeased at them. They sit in a large group on that porch and take measurements of character as importantly as if they constituted the jury of heaven. When I arrived at Hemlock Inn I at once cast my eye searchingly about me. Perceiving this assemblage, I cried: 'There they are.' Barely waiting to change my clothes, I made for this formidable body and endeavored to conciliate it. Almost every day I sit down among them and lie like a machine. Privately I believe they should be hanged, but publicly I glisten with admiration. Do you know, there is one of 'em who I know has not moved from the inn in eight days, and this morning I said to her: 'These long walks in the clear mountain air are doing you a world of good.' And I keep continually saying: 'Your frankness is so charming.' Because of the great law of universal balance, I know that this illustrious corps will believe good of themselves with exactly the same readiness that they will believe ill of others. So I ply them with it. In consequence, the worst they ever say of me is: 'Isn't that Mr. Hollanden a peculiar man?' And you know, my boy, that's not so bad for a literary person." After some thought he added: "Good people, too. Good wives—good mothers—and everything of that kind, you know. But conservative, very conservative. Hate anything radical. Cannot endure it. Were that way themselves once, you know. They hit the mark, too, sometimes. Such general volleyings can't fail to hit everything. May the devil fly away with them."

Hawker regarded the group nervously, and at last propounded a great question. "Say, I wonder where they all are recruited.

When you come to think that almost every summer hotel——"

"Certainly," said Hollanden. "Almost every summer hotel. I've studied the question and have nearly established the fact that almost every summer hotel is furnished with a full corps of——"

"To be sure," said Hawker. "And if you search for them in the winter, you can find barely a sign of them until you examine the boarding-houses and then you observe——"

"Certainly," said Hollanden. "Of course. By the way," he added, "you haven't got any obviously loose screws in your character, have you?"

"No," said Hawker, after consideration. "Only general poverty —that's all."

"Of course, of course," said Hollanden. "But that's bad. They'll get on to you—sure. Particularly since you come up here to see Miss Fanhall so much."

Hawker glinted his eyes at his friend. "You've got a deuced open way of speaking," he observed.

"Deuced open, is it?" cried Hollanden. "It isn't near so open as your devotion to Miss Fanhall, which is as plain as a red petticoat hung on a hedge."

Hawker's face gloomed and he said: "Well, it might be plain to you, you infernal cat, but that doesn't prove that all those old hens can see it."

"I tell you that if they look twice at you they can't fail to see it. And it's bad, too. Very bad. What's the matter with you? Haven't you ever been in love before?"

"None of your business," replied Hawker.

Hollanden thought upon this point for a time. "Well," he admitted finally, "that's true in a general way, but I hate to see you managing your affairs so stupidly."

Rage flamed into Hawker's face and he cried passionately: "I tell you it is none of your business." He suddenly confronted the other man.

Hollanden surveyed this outburst with a critical eye and then slapped his knee with emphasis. "You certainly have got it. A million times worse than I thought. Why, you—you—you're heels over head."

"What if I am?" said Hawker, with a gesture of defiance and despair.

Hollanden saw a dramatic situation in the distance and with a bright smile he studied it. "Say," he exclaimed, "suppose she should not go to the picnic to-morrow. She said this morning she did not know if she could go. Somebody was expected from New York, I think. Wouldn't it break you up, though! Eh?"

"You're so dev'lish clever," said Hawker with sullen irony.

Hollanden was still regarding the distant dramatic situation. "And rivals, too. The woods must be crowded with them. A girl like that, you know. And then, all that money. Say, your rivals must number enough to make a brigade of militia. Imagine them, swarming around. But then it doesn't matter so much," he went on cheerfully. "You've got a good play there. You must appreciate them to her—you understand—appreciate them kindly like a man in a watch-tower. You must laugh at them only about once a week and then very tolerantly, you understand—and kindly and —and appreciatively."

"You're a colossal ass, Hollie," said Hawker. "You——"

"Yes—yes—I know," replied the other peacefully. "A colossal ass. Of course." After looking into the distance again he murmured: "I'm worried about that picnic. I wish I knew she was going. By heavens, as a matter of fact, she must be made to go."

"What have you got to do with it?" cried the painter in another sudden outburst.

"There—there," said Hollanden, waving his hand. "You fool. Only a spectator, I assure you."

Hawker seemed overcome then with a deep dislike of himself. "Oh, well, you know, Hollie, this sort of thing——" He broke off and gazed at the trees. "This sort of thing—— It——"

"How?" asked Hollanden.

"Confound you for a meddling, gabbling idiot," cried Hawker suddenly.

Hollanden replied: "What did you do with that violet she dropped at the side of the tennis court yesterday?"

CHAPTER V

MRS. FANHALL, with the two children, the Worcester girls, and Hollanden, clambered down the rocky path. Miss Fanhall and Hawker had remained on top of the ledge. Hollanden showed much zeal in conducting his contingent to the foot of the falls. Through the trees they could see the cataract, a great shimmering white thing, booming and thundering until all the leaves gently shuddered.

"I wonder where Miss Fanhall and Mr. Hawker have gone," said the younger Miss Worcester. "I wonder where they've gone."

"Millicent," said Hollanden, looking at her fondly, "you always had such great thought for others."

"Well, I wonder where they've gone."

At the foot of the falls where the mist arose in silver clouds and the green water swept into the pool, Miss Worcester, the elder, seated on the moss, exclaimed: "Oh, Mr. Hollanden, what makes all literary men so peculiar?"

"And all that just because I said that I could have made better digestive organs than Providence if it is true that he made mine," replied Hollanden with reproach. "Here, Roger," he cried, as he dragged the child away from the brink. "Don't fall in there, or you won't be the full-back at Yale in 1907, as you have planned. I'm sure I don't know how to answer you, Miss Worcester. I've inquired of innumerable literary men and none of 'em know. I may say I have chased that problem for years. I might give you my personal history and see if that would throw any light on the subject." He looked about him with chin high until his glance had noted the two vague figures at the top of the cliff. "I might give you my personal history——"

Mrs. Fanhall looked at him curiously, and the elder Worcester girl cried: "Oh, do!"

After another scanning of the figures at the top of the cliff,

Hollanden established himself in an oratorical pose on a great weather-beaten stone. "Well—you must understand—I started my career—my career, you understand—with a determination to be a prophet and, although I have ended in being an acrobat, a trained bear of the magazines, and a juggler of comic paragraphs, there was once carven upon my lips a smile which made many people detest me, for it hung before them like a banshee whenever they tried to be satisfied with themselves. I was informed from time to time that I was making no great holes in the universal plan, and I came to know that one person in every two thousand of the people I saw had heard of me, and that four out of five of these had forgotten it. And then one in every two of those who remembered that they had heard of me regarded the fact that I wrote as a great impertinence. I admitted these things and in defense merely builded a maxim that stated that each wise man in this world is concealed amid some twenty thousand fools. If you have eyes for mathematics this conclusion should interest you. Meanwhile I created a gigantic dignity, and when men saw this dignity and heard that I was a literary man they respected me. I concluded that the simple campaign of existence for me was to delude the populace or as much of it as would look at me. I did. I do. And now I can make myself quite happy concocting sneers about it. Others may do as they please, but as for me," he concluded ferociously, "I shall never disclose to anybody that an acrobat, a trained bear of the magazines, a juggler of comic paragraphs is not a priceless pearl of art and philosophy."

"I don't believe a word of it is true," said Miss Worcester.

"What do you expect of autobiography?" demanded Hollanden with asperity.

"Well, anyhow, Hollie," exclaimed the younger sister. "You didn't explain a thing about how literary men came to be so peculiar, and that's what you started out to do, you know."

"Well," said Hollanden, crossly, "you must never expect a man to do what he starts to do, Millicent. And besides," he went on, with the gleam of a sudden idea in his eyes, "literary men are not peculiar, anyhow."

The elder Worcester girl looked angrily at him. "Indeed? Not you, of course, but the others?"

"They are all asses," said Hollanden, genially.

The elder Worcester girl reflected. "I believe you try to make us think and then just tangle us up purposely."

The younger Worcester girl reflected. "You are an absurd old thing, you know, Hollie."

Hollanden climbed offendedly from the great weather-beaten stone. "Well, I shall go and see that the men have not spilled the luncheon while breaking their necks over these rocks. Would you like to have it spread here, Mrs. Fanhall? Never mind consulting the girls. I assure you I shall spend a great deal of energy and temper in bullying them into doing just as they please. Why, when I was in Brussels——"

"Oh, come now, Hollie. You never were in Brussels, you know," said the younger Worcester girl.

"What of that, Millicent?" demanded Hollanden. "This is autobiography."

"Well, I don't care, Hollie. You tell such whoppers."

With a gesture of despair he again started away. Whereupon the Worcester girls shouted in chorus: "Oh, I say, Hollie, come back. Don't be angry. We didn't mean to tease you, Hollie—really, we didn't."

"Well, if you didn't," said Hollanden, "why did you——"

The elder Worcester girl was gazing fixedly at the top of the cliff. "Oh, there they are. I wonder why they don't come down?"

CHAPTER VI

STANLEY, the setter, walked to the edge of the precipice and looking over at the falls, wagged his tail in friendly greeting. He was braced warily so that if this howling white animal should reach up a hand for him he could flee in time.

The girl stared dreamily at the red-stained crags that projected from the pines of the hill across the stream. Hawker lazily aimed bits of moss at the oblivious dog and missed him.

"It must be fine to have something to think of beyond just living," said the girl to the crags.

"I suppose you mean art?" said Hawker.

"Yes. Of course. It must be finer at any rate than the ordinary thing."

He mused for a time. "Yes. It is—it must be," he said. "But then—I'd rather just lie here."

The girl seemed aggrieved. "Oh, no, you wouldn't. You couldn't stop. It's dreadful to talk like that, isn't it. I always thought that painters were——"

"Of course. They should be. Maybe they are. I don't know. Sometimes I am. But not to-day."

"Well, I should think you ought to be so much more contented than just ordinary people. Now, I——"

"You," he cried—"you are not 'just ordinary people.'"

"Well, but when I try to recall what I have thought about in my life I can't remember, you know. That's what I mean."

"You shouldn't talk that way," he told her.

"But why do you insist that life should be so highly absorbing for me?"

"You have everything you wish for," he answered in a voice of deep gloom.

"Certainly not. I am a woman."

"But——"

"A woman to have everything she wishes for would have to be Providence. There are some things that are not in the world."

"Well, what are they?" he asked of her.

"That's just it," she said, nodding her head. "No one knows. That's what makes the trouble."

"Well, you are very unreasonable."

"What?"

"You are very unreasonable. If I were you—an heiress——"

The girl flushed and turned upon him angrily.

"Well!" He glowered back at her. "You are, you know. You can't deny it."

She looked at the red-stained crags. At last she said: "You seemed really contemptuous."

"Well, I assure you that I do not feel contemptuous. On the contrary, I am filled with admiration. Thank heaven, I am a man of the world. Whenever I meet heiresses, I always have the deepest admiration." As he said this, he wore a brave hang-dog expression. The girl surveyed him coldly from his chin to his eyebrows. "You have a handsome audacity, too."

He lay back in the long grass and contemplated the clouds.

"You should have been a Chinese soldier of fortune," she said.

He threw another little clod at Stanley and struck him on the head.

"You are the most scientifically unbearable person in the world," she said.

Stanley came back to see his master and to assure himself that the clump on the head was not intended as a sign of serious displeasure. Hawker took the dog's long ears and tried to tie them into a knot.

"And I don't see why you so delight in making people detest you," she continued.

Having failed to make a knot of the dog's ears, Hawker leaned back and surveyed his failure admiringly. "Well—I don't," he said.

"You do."

"No, I don't."

"Yes, you do. You just say the most terrible things as if you positively enjoyed saying them."

"Well, what did I say, now? What did I say?"

"Why, you said that you always had the most extraordinary admiration for heiresses whenever you met them."

"Well, what's wrong with that sentiment?" he said. "You can't find fault with that."

"It is utterly detestable."

"Not at all," he answered sullenly. "I consider it a tribute—a graceful tribute."

Miss Fanhall arose and went forward to the edge of the cliff. She became absorbed in the falls. Far below her, a bough of a hemlock drooped to the water and each swirling mad wave caught it and made it nod—nod—nod. Her back was half turned toward Hawker.

After a time Stanley, the dog, discovered some ants scurrying in the moss and he at once began to watch them and wag his tail.

"Isn't it curious," observed Hawker, "how an animal as large as a dog will sometimes be so entertained by the very smallest things?"

Stanley pawed gently at the moss and then thrust his head forward to see what the ants did under the circumstances.

"In the hunting season," continued Hawker, having waited a moment, "this dog knows nothing on earth but his master and the partridges. He is lost to all other sound and movement. He moves through the woods like a steel machine. And when he scents the bird—ah, it is beautiful. Shouldn't you like to see him then?"

Some of the ants had perhaps made war-like motions and Stanley was pretending that this was a reason for excitement. He reared a-back and made grumbling noises in his throat.

After another pause Hawker went on: "And now see the precious old fool. He is deeply interested in the movements of little ants and as childish and ridiculous over them as if they were highly important. There, you old blockhead, let them alone."

Stanley could not be induced to end his investigations and he told his master that the ants were the most thrilling and dramatic animals of his experience.

"Oh, by the way," said Hawker, at last, as his glance caught upon the crags across the river, "did you ever hear the legend of those rocks yonder? Over there where I am pointing. Where I'm pointing. Did you ever hear it? What? Yes? No? Well, I shall tell it you." He settled comfortably in the long grass.

CHAPTER VII

ONCE upon a time, there was a beautiful Indian maiden, of course. And she was, of course, beloved by a youth from another tribe who was very handsome and stalwart and a mighty hunter, of course. But the maiden's father was, of course, a stern old chief, and when the question of his daughter's marriage came up, he, of course, declared that the maiden should be wedded only to a warrior of her tribe. And, of course, when the young man heard this he said that in such case he would, of course, fling himself headlong from that crag. The old chief was, of course, obdurate, and, of course, the youth did, of course, as he had said. And, of course, the maiden wept." After Hawker had waited for some time, he said with severity: "You seem to have no great appreciation of folk-lore."

The girl suddenly bended her head. "Listen," she said. "They're calling. Don't you hear Hollie's voice?"

They went to another place, and looking down over the shimmering tree-tops they saw Hollanden waving his arms. "It's luncheon," said Hawker. "Look how frantic he is."

The path required that Hawker should assist the girl very often. His eyes shone at her whenever he held forth his hand to help her down a blessed steep place. She seemed rather pensive. The route to luncheon was very long. Suddenly he took seat on an old tree and said: "Oh, I don't know why it is. Whenever I'm with you, I—I have no wits—nor good nature—nor anything. It's the worst luck."

He had left her standing on a boulder, where she was provisionally helpless. "Hurry," she said. "They're waiting for us."

Stanley, the setter, had been sliding down cautiously behind them. He now stood wagging his tail and waiting for the way to be cleared.

Hawker leaned his head on his hand and pondered dejectedly. "It's the worst luck."

"Hurry," she said. "They're waiting for us."

At luncheon the girl was for the most part silent. Hawker was superhumanly amiable. Somehow he gained the impression that they all quite fancied him, and it followed that being clever was very easy. Hollanden listened and approved him with a benign countenance.

There was a little boat fastened to the willows at the edge of the black pool. After the spread, Hollanden navigated various parties around to where they could hear the great hollow roar of the falls beating against the sheer rocks. Stanley swam after sticks at the request of little Roger.

Once Hollanden succeeded in making the others so engrossed in being amused that Hawker and Miss Fanhall were left alone staring at the white bubbles that floated solemnly on the black water. After Hawker had stared at them a sufficient time, he said: "Well, you are an heiress, you know."

In return she chose to smile radiantly. Turning toward him, she said: "If you will be good, now—always—perhaps I'll forgive you."

They drove home in the sombre shadows of the hills with Stanley padding along under the wagon. The Worcester girls tried to induce Hollanden to sing and in consequence there was quarreling until the blinking lights of the inn appeared above them as if a great lantern hung there.

Hollanden conveyed his friend some distance on the way home from the inn to the farm. "Good time at the picnic?" said the writer.

"Yes."

"Picnics are mainly places where the jam gets on the dead leaves and from thence to your trousers. But this was a good little picnic." He glanced at Hawker. "But you don't look as if you had such a swell time."

Hawker waved his hand tragically. "Yes—no. I don't know."

"What's wrong with you?" asked Hollanden.

"I tell you what it is, Hollie," said the painter, darkly, "whenever I'm with that girl I'm such a blockhead. I'm not so stupid, Hollie. You know I'm not. But when I'm with her I can't be clever to save my life."

Hollanden pulled contentedly at his pipe. "Maybe she don't notice it."

"Notice it!" muttered Hawker, scornfully. "Of course she notices it. In conversation with her I tell you I am as interesting as an iron dog." His voice changed as he cried: "I don't know why it is. I don't know why it is."

Blowing a huge cloud of smoke into the air, Hollanden studied it thoughtfully. "Hits some fellows that way," he said. "And of course it must be deuced annoying. Strange thing, but now under those circumstances I'm very glib. Very glib, I assure you."

"I don't care what you are," answered Hawker. "All those con-founded affairs of yours—they were not——"

"No," said Hollanden, stolidly puffing. "Of course not. I under-stand that. But, look here, Billie," he added, with sudden bright-ness, "maybe you are not a blockhead, after all. You are on the inside, you know, and you can't see from there. Besides, you can't tell what a woman will think. You can't tell what a woman will think."

"No," said Hawker, grimly. "And you suppose that is my only chance."

"Oh, don't be such a chump," said Hollanden in a tone of vast exasperation.

They strode for some time in silence. The mystic pines swaying over the narrow road made talk sibilantly to the wind. Stanley the setter took it upon himself to discover some menacing pres-ence in the woods. He walked on his toes and with his eyes glint-ing sideways. He swore half under his breath.

"And work, too," burst out Hawker at last. "I came up here this season to work and I haven't done a thing that ought not to be shot at."

"Don't you find that your love sets fire to your genius?" asked Hollanden gravely.

"No. I'm hanged if I do."

Hollanden sighed then with an air of relief. "I was afraid that a popular impression was true," he said. "But it's all right. You would rather sit still and moon, wouldn't you?"

"Moon—blast you. I couldn't moon to save my life."

"Oh, well, I didn't mean moon, exactly."

CHAPTER VIII

THE blue night of the lake was embroidered with black tree forms. Silver drops sprinkled from the lifted oars. Somewhere in the gloom of the shore there was a dog who from time to time raised his sad voice to the stars.

"But, still, the life of the studios——" began the girl.

Hawker scoffed. "There were six of us. Mainly we smoked. Sometimes we played hearts and at other times poker—on credit, you know—credit. And when we had the materials and got something to do, we worked. Did you ever see these beautiful red and green designs that surround the common tomato can?"

"Yes."

"Well," he said proudly, "I have made them. Whenever you come upon tomatoes remember that they might once have been encompassed in my design. When first I came back from Paris I began to paint, but nobody wanted me to paint. Later, I got into green corn and asparagus——"

"Truly?"

"Yes, indeed. It is true."

"But, still, the life of the studios——"

"There were six of us. Fate ordained that only one in the crowd could have money at one time. The other five lived off him and despised themselves. We despised ourselves five times as long as we had admiration."

"And was this just because you had no money?"

"It was because we had no money in New York," said Hawker.

"Well, after a while, something happened——"

"Oh, no, it didn't. Something impended always, but it never happened."

"In a case like that one's own people must be such a blessing. The sympathy——"

" 'One's own people,' " said Hawker.

"Yes," she said. "One's own people and more intimate friends. The appreciation——"

" 'The appreciation,' " said Hawker. "Yes, indeed."

He seemed so ill-tempered that she became silent. The boat floated through the shadows of the trees and out to where the water was like a blue crystal. The dog on the shore threshed about in the reeds and waded in the shallows, mourning his unhappy state in an occasional cry. Hawker stood up and sternly shouted. Thereafter silence was among the reeds. The moon slipped sharply through the little clouds.

The girl said: "I liked that last picture of yours."

"What?"

"At the last exhibition, you know, you had that one with the cows—and things—in the snow—and—and a haystack."

"Yes," he said. "Of course. Did you like it really? I thought it about my best. And you really remembered it? Oh," he cried, "Hollanden, perhaps, recalled it to you."

"Why, no," she said. "I remembered it. Of course."

"Well, what made you remember it?" he demanded, as if he had cause to be indignant.

"Why—I just remembered it because—I liked it and because— well, the people with me said—said it was about the best thing in the exhibit and they talked about it a good deal. And then I remembered that Hollie had spoken of you and then I—I——"

"Never mind," he said. After a moment he added: "The confounded picture was no good anyhow."

The girl started. "What makes you speak so of it? It was good. Of course, I don't know—I can't talk about pictures, but," she said in distress, "everybody said it was fine."

"It wasn't any good," he persisted with dogged shakes of the head.

From off in the darkness they heard the sound of Hollanden's oars splashing in the water. Sometimes there was squealing by the Worcester girls and at other times loud arguments on points of navigation.

"Oh," said the girl, suddenly. "Mr. Oglethorpe is coming tomorrow."

"Mr. Oglethorpe?" said Hawker. "Is he?"

"Yes." She gazed off at the water. "He's an old friend of ours.

He is always so good and Roger and little Helen simply adore him. He was my brother's chum in college and they were quite inseparable until Herbert's death. He always brings me violets. But I know you will like him."

"I shall expect to," said Hawker.

"I'm so glad he is coming. What time does that morning stage get here?"

"About eleven," said Hawker.

"He wrote that he would come then. I hope he won't disappoint us."

"Undoubtedly he will be here," said Hawker.

The wind swept from the ridge top where some great bare pines stood in the moonlight. A loon called in its strange unearthly note from the lake shore. As Hawker turned the boat toward the dock, the flashing rays from the moon fell upon the head of the girl in the rear seat and he rowed very slowly.

The girl was looking away somewhere with a mystic, shining glance. She leaned her chin in her hand. Hawker facing her, merely paddled sub-consciously. He seemed greatly impressed and expectant.

At last she spoke very slowly. "I wish I knew Mr. Oglethorpe was not going to disappoint us."

Hawker said: "Why, no, I imagine not."

"Well, he is a trifle uncertain in matters of time. The children —and all of us—will be anxious. I know you will like him."

CHAPTER IX

"EH?" said Hollanden. "Oglethorpe? Oglethorpe? Why, he's that friend of the Fanhalls. Yes, of course, I know him. Deuced good fellow, too. What about him?"

"Oh, nothing, only he's coming here to-morrow," answered Hawker. "What kind of a fellow did you say he was?"

"Deuced good fellow. What are you so—— Say, by the nine mad blacksmiths of Donawhiroo, he's your rival. Why, of course. Glory, but I must be thick-headed to-night."

Hawker said: "Where's your tobacco?"

"Yonder in that jar. Got a pipe?"

"Yes. How do you know he's my rival?"

"Know it? Why, hasn't he been—— Say, this is getting thrilling." Hollanden sprang to his feet and, filling a pipe, flung himself into the chair and began to rock himself madly to and fro. He puffed clouds of smoke.

Hawker stood with his face in shadow. At last he said in tones of deep weariness: "Well, I think I'd better be going home and turning in."

"Hold on," Hollanden exclaimed, turning his eyes from a prolonged stare at the ceiling. "Don't go yet. Why, man, this is just the time when—— Say, who would ever think of Jem Oglethorpe's turning up to harry you. Just at this time, too."

"Oh," cried Hawker, suddenly filled with rage, "you remind me of an accursed duffer. Why can't you tell me something about the man instead of sitting there and gibbering those crazy things at the ceiling."

"By the piper——"

"Oh, shut up. Tell me something about Oglethorpe, can't you? I want to hear about him. Quit all that other business."

"Why, Jem Oglethorpe—he—why, say, he's one of the best

fellows going. If he were only an ass! If he were only an ass, now, you could feel easy in your mind. But he isn't. No, indeed. Why, blast him, there isn't a man that knows him who doesn't like Jem Oglethorpe. Excepting the chumps."

The window of the little room was open and the voices of the pines could be heard as they sang of their long sorrow. Hawker pulled a chair close and stared out into the darkness. The people on the porch of the inn were frequently calling: "Good night! Good night!"

Hawker said: "And of course he's got train loads of money."

"You bet he has. He can pave streets with it. Lordie, but this is a situation."

A heavy scowl settled upon Hawker's brow and he kicked at the dressing case. "Say, Hollie, look here, sometimes I think you regard me as a bug and like to see me wriggle. But——"

"Oh, don't be a fool," said Hollanden, glaring through the smoke. "Under the circumstances you are privileged to rave and ramp around like a wounded lunatic, but for heaven's sake don't swoop down on me like that. Especially when I'm—when I'm doing all I can for you."

"Doing all you can for me! Nobody asked you to. You talk as if I was an infant."

"There! That's right. Blaze up like a fire balloon just because I said that, will you? A man in your condition—why, confound you, you are an infant."

Hawker seemed again overwhelmed in a great dislike of himself. "Oh, well, of course, Hollie, it——" He waved his hand. "A man feels like—like——"

"Certainly he does," said Hollanden. "That's all right, old man."

"And, look now, Hollie, here's this Oglethorpe——"

"May the devil fly away with him."

"Well, here he is, coming along when I thought maybe—after awhile, you know—I might stand some show. And you are acquainted with him, so give me a line on him."

"Well, I would advise you to——"

"Blow your advice. I want to hear about Oglethorpe."

"Well, in the first place, he is a rattling good fellow, as I told you before, and this is what makes it so——"

"Oh, hang what it makes it. Go on."

"He is a rattling good fellow, and he has stacks of money. Of course in this case, his having money doesn't affect the situation much. Miss Fanhall——"

"Say, can you keep to the thread of the story, you infernal literary man?"

"Well, he's popular. He don't talk money—ever. And if he's wicked, he's not sufficiently proud of it to be perpetually describing his sins. And then he is not so hideously brilliant, either. That's great credit to a man in these days. And then he—well, take it altogether, I should say Jem Oglethorpe was a smashing good fellow."

"I wonder how long he is going to stay?" murmured Hawker.

During this conversation his pipe had often died out. It was out at this time. He lit another match. Hollanden had watched the fingers of his friend as the match was scratched. "You're nervous, Billie," he said.

Hawker straightened in his chair. "No, I'm not."

"I saw your fingers tremble when you lit that match."

"Oh, you lie."

Hollanden mused again. "He's popular with women, too," he said ultimately. "And often a woman will like a man and hunt his scalp just because she knows other women like him and want his scalp."

"Yes, but not——"

"Hold on. You were going to say that she was not like other women, weren't you?"

"Not exactly that, but——"

"Well, we will have all that understood."

After a period of silence, Hawker said: "I must be going."

As the painter walked toward the door, Hollanden cried to him: "Heavens! Of all pictures of a weary pilgrim." His voice was very compassionate.

Hawker wheeled and an oath spun through the smoke clouds.

CHAPTER X

"WHERE'S Mr. Hawker this morning?" asked the younger Miss Worcester. "I thought he was coming up to play tennis."

"I don't know. Confound him, I don't see why he didn't come," said Hollanden, looking across the shining valley. He frowned questioningly at the landscape. "I wonder where in the mischief he is?"

The Worcester girls began also to stare at the great gleaming stretch of green and gold. "Didn't he tell you he was coming?" they demanded.

"He didn't say a word about it," answered Hollanden. "I supposed of course he was coming. We will have to postpone the melee."

Later he met Miss Fanhall. "You look as if you were going for a walk."

"I am," she said, swinging her parasol. "To meet the stage. Have you seen Mr. Hawker to-day?"

"No," he said. "He is not coming up this morning. He is in a great fret about that field of stubble and I suppose he is down there sketching the life out of it. These artists—they take such a fiendish interest in their work. I dare say we won't see much of him until he has finished it. Where did you say you were going to walk?"

"To meet the stage."

"Oh, well, I won't have to play tennis for an hour, and if you insist——"

"Of course."

As they strolled slowly in the shade of the trees, Hollanden began: "Isn't that Hawker an ill-bred old thing?"

"No. He is not." Then after a time she said: "Why?"

"Oh, he gets so absorbed in a beastly smudge of paint that I really suppose he cares nothing for anything else in the world. Men who are really artists—I don't believe they are capable of deep human affections. So much of them is occupied by art. There's not much left over, you see."

"I don't believe it at all," she exclaimed.

"You don't, eh?" cried Hollanden, scornfully. "Well, let me tell you, young woman, there is a great deal of truth in it. Now, there's Hawker, as good a fellow as ever lived, too, in a way, and yet he's an artist. Why, look how he treats—look how he treats that poor setter dog."

"Why, he's as kind to him as he can be," she declared.

"And I tell you he is not," cried Hollanden.

"He is, Hollie. You—you are unspeakable when you get in these moods."

"There—that's just you in an argument. I'm not in a mood at all. Now, look—the dog loves him with simple unquestioning devotion that fairly brings tears to one's eyes——"

"Yes," she said.

"And he—why, he's as cold and stern——"

"He isn't. He isn't, Hollie. You are awf'ly unfair."

"No, I'm not. I am simply a liberal observer. And Hawker with his people, too," he went on darkly. "You can't tell—you don't know anything about it—but I tell you that what I have seen proves my assertion that the artistic mind has no space left for the human affections. And as for the dog——"

"I thought you were his friend, Hollie?"

"Whose?"

"No. Not the dog's. And yet you—really, Hollie, there is something unnatural in you. You are so stupidly keen in looking at people that you do not possess common loyalty to your friends. It is because you are a writer, I suppose. That has to explain so many things. Some of your traits are very disagreeable."

"There—there," plaintively cried Hollanden. "This is only about the treatment of a dog, mind you. Goodness, what an oration."

"It wasn't about the treatment of a dog. It was about your treatment of your friends."

"Well," he said, sagely, "it only goes to show that there is nothing impersonal in the mind of a woman. I undertook to discuss broadly——"

"Oh, Hollie!"

"At any rate it was rather below you to do such scoffing at me."

"Well, I didn't mean—not all of it, Hollie."

"Well, I didn't mean what I said about the dog and all that, either."

"You didn't?" She turned toward him, large-eyed.

"No. Not a single word of it."

"Well, what did you say it for, then?" she demanded indignantly.

"I said it," answered Hollanden placidly, "just to tease you." He looked abstractedly up to the trees.

Presently she said slowly: "Just to tease me?"

At this time Hollanden wore an unmistakable air of having a desire to turn up his coat collar. "Oh, come now——" he began nervously.

"George Hollanden," said the voice at his shoulder. "You are not only disagreeable, but you are hopelessly ridiculous. I—I wish you would never speak to me again."

"Oh, come now, Grace, don't—don't—— Look! There's the stage coming, isn't it?"

"No, the stage is not coming. I wish—I wish you were at the bottom of the sea, George Hollanden. And—and Mr. Hawker, too. There!"

"Oh, bless my soul! And all about an infernal dog," wailed Hollanden. "Look! Honest, now, there's the stage. See it! See it!"

"It isn't there at all," she said.

Gradually he seemed to recover his courage. "What made you so tremendously angry? I don't see why."

After consideration, she said decisively: "Well, because."

"That's why I teased you," he rejoined.

"Well, because—because——"

"Go on," he told her finally. "You are doing very well." He waited patiently.

"Well," she said, "it is dreadful to defend somebody so—so excitedly and then have it turn out just a tease. I don't know what he would think."

"Who would think?"

"Why—he."

"What could he think? Now, what could he think? Why," said

Hollanden, waxing eloquent, "he couldn't under any circumstances think—think anything at all. Now, could he?"

She made no reply.

"Could he?"

She was apparently reflecting.

"Under any circumstances," persisted Hollanden, "he couldn't think anything at all. Now, could he?"

"No," she said.

"Well, why are you angry at me, then?"

CHAPTER XI

J OHN," said the old mother from the profound mufflings of the pillow and quilts.

"What?" said the old man. He was tugging at his right boot and his tone was very irascible.

"I think William's changed a good deal."

"Well, what if he has?" replied the father in another burst of ill-temper. He was then tugging at his left boot.

"Yes, I'm afraid he's changed a good deal," said the muffled voice from the bed. "He's got a good many fine friends, now, John. Folks what put on a good many airs, and he don't care for his home like he did."

"Oh, well, I don't guess he's changed very much," said the old man, cheerfully. He was now free of both boots.

She raised herself on an elbow and looked out with a troubled face. "John, I think he likes that girl."

"What girl?" said he.

" 'What girl!' Why that awful handsome girl you see around— of course."

"Do you think he likes 'er?"

"I'm afraid so—I'm afraid so," murmured the mother, mournfully.

"Oh, well," said the old man without alarm, nor grief, nor pleasure in his tone.

He turned the lamp's wick very low and carried the lamp to the head of the stairs where he perched it on the step. When he returned he said: "She's mighty good-lookin'."

"Well, that ain't everything," she snapped. "How do we know she ain't proud and selfish, and—everything?"

"How do you know she is?" returned the old man.

"And she may just be leading him on."

"Do him good, then," said he with impregnable serenity. "Next time he'll know better."

"Well, I'm worried about it," she said, as she sank back on the pillow again. "I think William's changed a good deal. He don't seem to care about—us—like he did."

"Oh, go to sleep," said the father, drowsily.

She was silent for a time and then she said: "John!"

"What?"

"Do you think I better speak to him about that girl?"

"No."

She grew silent again, but at last she demanded: "Why not?"

" 'Cause it's none of your business. Go to sleep, will you." And presently he did, but the old mother lay blinking wide-eyed into the darkness.

In the morning Hawker did not appear at the early breakfast eaten when the blue glow of dawn shed its ghostly lights upon the valley. The old mother placed various dishes on the back part of the stove. At ten o'clock he came downstairs. His mother was sweeping busily in the parlor at the time, but she saw him and ran to the back part of the stove. She slid the various dishes onto the table. "Did you oversleep?" she asked.

"Yes. I don't feel very well this morning," he said. He pulled his chair close to the table and sat there staring.

She renewed her sweeping in the parlor. When she returned, he sat still staring undeviatingly at nothing.

"Why don't you eat your breakfast?" she said, anxiously.

"I tell you, mother, I don't feel very well this morning," he answered quite sharply.

"Well," she said meekly, "drink some coffee and you'll feel better."

Afterward he took his painting machinery and left the house. His younger sister was at the well. She looked at him with a little smile and a little sneer. "Going up to the inn this morning?" she said.

"I don't see how that concerns you, Mary?" he rejoined with dignity.

"Oh, my," she said airily.

"But since you are so interested I don't mind telling you that I'm not going up to the inn this morning."

His sister fixed him with her eye. "She ain't mad at you, is she, Will?"

"I don't know what you mean, Mary." He glared hatefully at her and strode away.

Stanley saw him going through the fields and leaped a fence jubilantly in pursuit. In a wood, the light sifted through the foliage and burned with a peculiar reddish lustre on the masses of dead leaves. He frowned at it for a while from different points. Presently he erected his easel and began to paint. After a time he threw down his brush and swore. Stanley, who had been solemnly staring at the scene as if he too was sketching it, looked up in surprise.

In wandering aimlessly through the fields and the forest, Hawker once found himself near the road to Hemlock Inn. He shied away from it quickly as if it were a great snake.

While most of the family were at supper, Mary, the younger sister, came charging breathlessly into the kitchen. "Ma—sister—" she cried. "I know why—why Will didn't go to the inn to-day. There's another fellow come. Another fellow."

"Who? Where? What do you mean?" exclaimed her mother and her sister.

"Why, another fellow up at the inn," she shouted, triumphant in her information. "Another fellow come up on the stage this morning. And she went out driving with him this afternoon."

"Well!" exclaimed her mother and her sister.

"Yep! And he's an awful good-looking fellow, too. And she—oh, my—she looked as if she thought the world and all of him."

"Well!" exclaimed her mother and her sister again.

"Sho!" said the old man. "You wimen leave William alone and quit your gabbling."

The three women made a combined assault upon him. "Well, we ain't a-hurting him, are we, Pa? You needn't be so snifty. I guess we ain't a-hurting him much."

"Well," said the old man. And to this argument he added: "Sho!"

They kept him out of the subsequent consultations.

CHAPTER XII

THE next day, as little Roger was going toward the tennis court, a large orange and white setter ran effusively from around the corner of the inn and greeted him. Miss Fanhall, the Worcester girls, Hollanden and Oglethorpe faced to the front like soldiers. Hollanden cried: "Why, Billie Hawker must be coming." Hawker at that moment appeared, coming toward them with a smile which was not overconfident.

Little Roger went off to perform some festivities of his own on the brown carpet under a clump of pines. The dog to join him felt obliged to circle widely about the tennis court. He was much afraid of this tennis court with its tiny round things that sometimes hit him. When near it he usually slunk along at a little sheep-trot and with an eye of wariness upon it.

At her first opportunity the younger Worcester girl said: "You didn't come up yesterday, Mr. Hawker?"

Hollanden seemed to think that Miss Fanhall turned her head as if she wished to hear the explanation of the painter's absence, so he engaged her in swift and fierce conversation.

"No," said Hawker. "I was resolved to finish a sketch of a stubble field which I began a good many days ago. You see, I was going to do such a great lot of work this summer and I've done hardly a thing. I really ought to compel myself to do some, you know."

"There," said Hollanden, with a victorious nod. "Just what I told you."

"You didn't tell us anything of the kind," retorted the Worcester girls with one voice.

A middle-aged woman came upon the porch of the inn and after scanning for a moment the group at the tennis court, she hurriedly withdrew. Presently she appeared again accompanied by five more middle-aged women. "You see," she said to the others. "It is as I said. He has come back."

The five surveyed the group at the tennis court and then said: "So he has. I knew he would. Well, I declare. Did you ever." Their voices were pitched at low keys and they moved with care, but their smiles were broad and full of a strange glee.

"I wonder how he feels," said one in subtle ecstasy.

Another laughed. "You know how you would feel, my dear, if you were him and saw yourself suddenly cut out by a man who was so hopelessly superior to you. Why, Oglethorpe's a thousand times better looking. And then think of his wealth and social position."

One whispered dramatically: "They say he never came up here at all yesterday."

Another replied: "No more he did. That's what we've been talking about. Stayed down at the farm all day, poor fellow."

"Do you really think she cares for Oglethorpe?"

"Care for him? Why, of course she does. Why, when they came up the path yesterday morning I never saw a girl's face so bright. I asked my husband how much of the Chambers Street Bank stock Oglethorpe owned and he said that if Oglethorpe took his money out there wouldn't be enough left to buy a pie."

The youngest woman in the corps said: "Well, I don't care. I think it is too bad. I don't see anything so much in that Mr. Oglethorpe."

The others at once patronized her. "Oh, you don't, my dear. Well, let me tell you that bank stock waves in the air like a banner. You would see it if you were her."

"Well, she don't have to care for his money."

"Oh, no, of course she don't have to. But they are just the ones that do, my dear. They are just the ones that do."

"Well, it's a shame."

"Oh, of course. It's a shame."

The woman who had assembled the corps said to one at her side: "Oh, the commonest kind of people, my dear, the commonest kind. The father is a regular farmer, you know. He drives oxen. Such language! You can really hear him miles away bellowing at those oxen. And the girls are shy, half-wild things— oh, you have no idea. I saw one of them yesterday when we were out driving. She dodged as we came along, for I suppose she was ashamed of her frock, poor child. And the mother—well, I wish

you could see her. A little old dried-up thing. We saw her carrying a pail of water from the well, and, oh, she bent and staggered dreadfully, poor thing."

"And the gate to their front yard, it has a broken hinge, you
know. Of course, that's an awful bad sign. When people let their
front gate hang on one hinge, you know what that means."

After gazing again at the group at the court, the youngest
member of the corps said: "Well, he's a good tennis player, anyhow."

The others smiled indulgently. "Oh, yes, my dear, he's a good
tennis player."

CHAPTER XIII

ONE day Hollanden said in greeting to Hawker: "Well, he's gone."

"Who?" asked Hawker.

"Why, Oglethorpe, of course. Who did you think I meant?"

"How did I know?" said Hawker, angrily.

"Well," retorted Hollanden, "your chief interest was in his movements, I thought."

"Why, of course not, hang you. Why should I be interested in his movements?"

"Well, you weren't then. Does that suit you?"

After a period of silence Hawker asked: "What did he—what made him go?"

"Who?"

"Why—Oglethorpe."

"How was I to know you meant him? Well, he went because some important business affairs in New York demanded it, he said, but he is coming back again in a week. They had rather a late interview on the porch last evening."

"Indeed," said Hawker, stiffly.

"Yes, and he went away this morning looking particularly elated. Aren't you glad?"

"I don't see how it concerns me," said Hawker, with still greater stiffness.

In a walk to the lake that afternoon Hawker and Miss Fanhall found themselves side by side and silent. The girl contemplated the distant purple hills as if Hawker were not at her side and silent. Hawker frowned at the roadway. Stanley the setter scouted the fields in a genial gallop.

At last the girl turned to him. "Seems to me—" she said. "Seems to me you are dreadfully quiet this afternoon."

"I am thinking about my wretched field of stubble," he answered, still frowning.

Her parasol swung about until the girl was looking up at his inscrutable profile. "Is it then so important that you haven't time to talk to me?" she asked with an air of what might have been timidity.

A smile swept the scowl from his face. "No, indeed," he said, instantly. "Nothing is so important as that."

She seemed aggrieved then. "Hum—you didn't look so," she told him.

"Well, I didn't mean to look any other way," he said contritely. "You know what a bear I am sometimes. Hollanden says it is a fixed scowl from trying to see uproarious pinks, yellows and blues."

A little brook, a brawling, ruffianly little brook, swaggered from side to side down the glade, swirling in white leaps over the great dark rocks and shouting challenge to the hillsides. Hollanden and the Worcester girls had halted in a place of ferns and wet moss. Their voices could be heard quarreling above the clamor of the stream. Stanley the setter had soused himself in a pool and then gone and rolled in the dust of the road. He blissfully lolled there with his coat now resembling an old door mat.

"Don't you think Jem is a wonderfully good fellow," said the girl to the painter.

"Why, yes, of course," said Hawker.

"Well, he is," she retorted, suddenly defensive.

"Of course," he repeated loudly.

She said: "Well, I don't think you like him as well as I like him."

"Certainly not," said Hawker.

"You don't?" She looked at him in a kind of astonishment.

"Certainly not," said Hawker again and very irritably. "How in the wide world do you expect me to like him as well as you like him?"

"I don't mean as well——" she explained.

"Oh," said Hawker.

"But I mean you don't like him the way I do at all—the way I expected you to like him. I thought men of a certain pattern always fancied their kind of men wherever they met them, don't you know. And I was so sure you and Jem would be friends."

"Oh," cried Hawker. Presently he added: "But he isn't my kind of a man at all."

"He is. Jem is one of the best fellows in the world."

Again Hawker cried: "Oh!"

They paused and looked down at the brook. Stanley sprawled panting in the dust and watched them. Hawker leaned against a hemlock. He sighed and frowned and then finally coughed with great resolution. "I suppose, of course, that I am unjust to him. I care for you myself, you understand, and so it becomes——"

He paused for a moment because he heard a rustling of her skirts as if she had moved suddenly. Then he continued: "And so it becomes difficult for me to be fair to him. I am not able to see him with a true eye." He bitterly addressed the trees on the opposite side of the glen. "Oh, I care for you, of course. You might have expected it." He turned from the trees and strode toward the roadway. The uninformed and disreputable Stanley arose and wagged his tail.

As if the girl had cried out at a calamity, Hawker said again: "Well, you might have expected it."

CHAPTER XIV

AT THE lake Hollanden went pickerel fishing, lost his hook in a gaunt, grey stump, and earned much distinction by his skill in discovering words to express his emotion without resorting to the list ordinarily used in such cases. The younger Miss Worcester ruined a new pair of boots, and Stanley sat on the bank and howled the song of the forsaken. At the conclusion of the festivities, Hollanden said: "Billie, you ought to take the boat back."

"Why had I? You borrowed it."

"Well, I borrowed it, and it was a lot of trouble and now you ought to take it back."

Ultimately Hawker said: "Oh, let's both go."

On this journey Hawker made a long speech to his friend, and at the end of it he exclaimed: "And now do you think she cares so much for Oglethorpe? Why, she as good as told me that he was only a very great friend."

Hollanden wagged his head dubiously. "What a woman says doesn't amount to shucks. It's the way she says it—that's what counts. Besides," he cried in a brilliant afterthought, "she wouldn't tell you, anyhow, you fool."

"You're an encouraging brute," said Hawker with a rueful grin.

Later the Worcester girls seized upon Hollanden and piled him high with ferns and mosses. They dragged the long grey lichens from the chins of venerable pines and ran with them to Hollanden and dashed them into his arms. "Oh, hurry up, Hollie," they cried, because with his great load he frequently fell behind them in the march. He once positively refused to carry these things another step. Some distance further on the road he positively refused to carry this old truck another step. When almost to the inn he positively refused to carry this senseless rubbish another step. The Worcester girls had such vivid contempt for his expressed unwillingness that they neglected to tell him of any appreciation they might have had for his noble struggle.

As Hawker and Miss Fanhall proceeded slowly, they heard a voice ringing through the foliage. "Whoa! Haw! Git-ap! Blast you! Haw! Haw, drat your hides! Will you haw? Git-ap! Gee! Whoa!"

Hawker said: "The others are a good ways ahead. Hadn't we better hurry a little."

The girl obediently mended her pace.

"Whoa! Haw! Git-ap!" shouted the voice in the distance. "Git over there, Red. Git over! Gee! Git-ap!" And these cries pursued the man and the maid.

At last Hawker said: "That's my father."

"Where?" she asked, looking bewildered.

"Back there. Driving those oxen."

The voice shouted: "Whoa! Git-ap! Gee! Red, git over there now, will you? I'll trim the skin off'n you in a minute. Whoa! Haw! Haw! Whoa! Git-ap!"

Hawker repeated: "Yes, that's my father."

"Oh, is it?" she said. "Let's wait for him."

"All right," said Hawker, sullenly.

Presently a team of oxen waddled into view around the curve of the road. They swung their heads slowly from side to side, bended under the yoke and looking out at the world with their great eyes in which was a mystic note of their humble, submissive, toilsome lives. An old wagon creaked after them and erect upon it was the tall and tattered figure of the farmer swinging his whip and yelling: "Whoa! Haw there! Git-ap!" The lash flicked and flew over the broad backs of the animals.

"Hello, father," said Hawker.

"Whoa—back—whoa! Why, hello, William, what you doing here?"

"Oh, just taking a walk. Miss Fanhall, this is my father. Father——"

"How d' you do!" The old man balanced himself with care and then raised his straw hat from his head with a quick gesture and with what was perhaps a slightly apologetic air, as if he feared that he was rather overdoing the ceremonial part.

The girl, later, became very intent upon the oxen. "Aren't they nice old things," she said as she stood looking into the faces of the team. "But what makes their eyes so very sad?"

"I dunno," said the old man.

She was apparently unable to resist a desire to pat the nose of the nearest ox and for that purpose she stretched forth a cautious hand. But the ox moved restlessly at the moment and the girl put her hand apprehensively behind herself and backed away. The old man on the wagon grinned. "They won't hurt you," he told her.

"They won't bite, will they?" she asked, casting a glance of inquiry at the old man, and then turning her eyes again upon the fascinating animals.

"No," said the old man, still grinning. "Just as gentle as kittens."

She approached them circuitously. "Sure?" she said.

"Sure," replied the old man. He climbed from the wagon and came to the heads of the oxen. With him as an ally, she finally succeeded in patting the nose of the nearest ox. "Aren't they solemn, kind old fellows. Don't you get to think a great deal of them?"

"Well, they're kind of aggravating beasts sometimes," he said. "But they're a good yoke—a good yoke. They can haul with anything in this region."

"It doesn't make them so terribly tired, does it?" she said, hopefully. "They are such strong animals."

"No-o-o," he said. "I dunno. I never thought much about it."

With their heads close together they became so absorbed in their conversation that they seemed to forget the painter. He sat on a log and watched them.

Ultimately the girl said: "Won't you give us a ride?"

"Sure," said the old man. "Come on and I'll help you up." He assisted her very painstakingly to the old board that usually served him as a seat and he clambered to a place beside her. "Come on, William," he called. The painter climbed into the wagon and stood behind his father, putting his hand on the old man's shoulder to preserve his balance.

"Which is the near ox?" asked the girl with a serious frown.

"Git-ap! Haw! That one there," said the old man.

"And this one is the off ox?"

"Yep."

"Well, suppose you sat here where I do? Would this one be the near ox and that one the off ox, then?"

"Nope. Be just same."

"Then the near ox isn't always the nearest one to a person, at all. That ox there is always the near ox?"

"Yep. Always. 'Cause when you drive 'em a-foot, you always walk on the left side."

"Well! I never knew that before."

After studying them in silence for a while, she said: "Do you think they are happy?"

"I dunno," said the old man. "I never thought." As the wagon creaked on they gravely discussed this problem, contemplating profoundly the backs of the animals. Hawker gazed in silence at the meditating two before him. Under the wagon Stanley the setter walked slowly, wagging his tail in placid contentment and ruminating upon his experiences.

At last the old man said cheerfully: "Shall I take you around by the inn?"

Hawker started and seemed to wince at the question. Perhaps he was about to interrupt, but the girl cried: "Oh, will you? Take us right to the door? Oh, that will be awf'ly good of you."

"Why—" began Hawker. "You don't want—you don't want to ride to the inn on an—on an ox wagon, do you?"

"Why, of course I do," she retorted, directing a withering glance at him.

"Well——" he protested.

"Let 'er be, William," interrupted the old man. "Let 'er do what she wants to. I guess everybody in th' world ain't even got an ox wagon to ride in. Have they?"

"No, indeed," she returned, while withering Hawker again.

"Gee! Gee! Whoa! Haw! Git-ap! Haw! Whoa! Back!"

After these two attacks, Hawker became silent.

"Gee! Gee! Gee there, blast—s'cuse me! Gee! Whoa! Git-ap!"

All the boarders of the inn were upon its porches waiting for the dinner gong. There was a surge toward the railing as a middle-aged woman passed the word along her middle-aged friends that Miss Fanhall, accompanied by Mr. Hawker, had arrived on the ox cart of Mr. Hawker's father.

"Whoa! Haw! Git-ap!" said the old man in more subdued tones. "Whoa there, Red! Whoa, now! Wh-o-a!"

Hawker helped the girl to alight and she paused for a moment conversing with the old man about the oxen. Then she ran smiling up the steps to meet the Worcester girls.

"Oh, such a lovely time. Those dear old oxen—you should have been with us."

CHAPTER XV

O H, Miss Fanhall."

"What is it, Mrs. Truscot?"

"That was a great prank of yours last night, my dear. We all enjoyed the joke so much."

" 'Prank'?"

"Yes, your riding on the ox cart with that old farmer and that young Mr. What's-his-name, you know. We all thought it delicious. Ah, my dear, after all—don't be offended—if we had your people's wealth and position we might do that sort of unconventional thing, too, but, ah, my dear, we can't, we can't. Isn't the young painter a charming man?"

Out on the porch Hollanden was haranguing his friends. He heard a step and glanced over his shoulder to see who was about to interrupt him. He suddenly ceased his oration and said: "Hello! What's the matter with Grace?" The heads turned promptly.

As the girl came toward them, it could be seen that her cheeks were very pink and her eyes were flashing general wrath and defiance.

The Worcester girls burst into eager interrogations. "Oh, nothing," she replied at first, but later she added in an undertone: "That wretched Mrs. Truscot——"

"What did she say?" whispered the younger Worcester girl.

"Why, she said—oh, nothing."

Both Hollanden and Hawker were industriously reflecting.

Later in the morning, Hawker said privately to the girl: "I know what Mrs. Truscot talked to you about."

She turned upon him belligerently. "You do?"

"Yes," he answered with meekness. "It was undoubtedly some reference to your ride upon the ox wagon."

She hesitated a moment and then said: "Well?"

With still greater meekness he said: "I am very sorry."

"Are you—indeed?" she inquired loftily. "Sorry for what? Sorry that I rode upon your father's ox wagon, or sorry that Mrs. Truscot was rude to me about it?"

"Well—in some ways it was my fault."

"Was it? I suppose you intend to apologize for your father's owning an ox wagon, don't you?"

"No, but——"

"Well, I am going to ride in the ox wagon whenever I choose. Your father, I know, will always be glad to have me. And if it so shocks you there is not the slightest necessity of your coming with us."

They glowered at each other and he said: "You have twisted the question with the usual ability of your sex."

She pondered as if seeking some particularly destructive retort. She ended by saying bluntly: "Did you know that we were going home next week?"

A flush came suddenly to his face. "No! Going home? Who? You?"

"Why, of course." And then with an indolent air she continued: "I meant to have told you before this, but somehow it quite escaped me."

He stammered: "Are—are you, honestly?"

She nodded. "Why, of course. Can't stay here forever, you know."

They were then silent for a long time.

At last Hawker said: "Do you remember what I told you yesterday?"

"No. What was it?"

He cried indignantly: "You know very well what I told you."

"I do not."

"No," he sneered. "Of course not. You never take the trouble to remember such things. Of course not. Of course not."

"You are a very ridiculous person," she vouchsafed after eyeing him coldly.

He arose abruptly. "I believe I am. By heavens, I believe I am," he cried in a fury.

She laughed. "You are more ridiculous now than I have yet seen you."

After a pause he said magnificently: "Well, Miss Fanhall, you will doubtless find Mr. Hollanden's conversation to have a much greater interest than that of such a ridiculous person."

Hollanden approached them with the blithesome step of an untroubled man. "Hello, you two people, why don't you—oh—ahem. Hold on, Billie, where you going?"

"I——" began Hawker.

"Oh, Hollie," cried the girl impetuously, "do tell me how to do that slam-thing, you know. I've tried it so often, but I don't believe I hold my racquet right. And you do it so beautifully."

"Oh, that," said Hollanden. "It's not so very difficult. I'll show it you. You don't want to know this minute, do you?"

"Yes," she answered.

"Well, come over to the court, then. Come ahead, Billie."

"No," said Hawker, without looking at his friend. "I can't this morning, Hollie. I've got to go to work. Good-by." He comprehended them both in a swift bow and stalked away.

Hollanden turned quickly to the girl. "What was the matter with Billie? What was he grinding his teeth for? What was the matter with him?"

"Why, nothing—was there?" she asked in surprise.

"Why, he was grinding his teeth until he sounded like a stone crusher," said Hollanden in a severe tone. "What was the matter with him?"

"How should I know?" she retorted.

"You've been saying something to him."

"I! I didn't say a thing."

"Yes, you did."

"Hollie, don't be absurd."

Hollanden debated with himself for a time and then observed: "Oh, well, I always said he was an ugly-tempered fellow——"

The girl flashed him a little glance.

"And now I am sure of it. As ugly-tempered a fellow as ever lived."

"I believe you," said the girl. Then she added: "All men are. I declare I think you to be the most incomprehensible creatures. One never knows what to expect of you. And you explode and go into rages and make yourselves utterly detestable over the most trivial matters and at the most unexpected times. You are all mad, I think."

"I!" cried Hollanden wildly. "What in the mischief have I done?"

CHAPTER XVI

L OOK here," said Hollanden at length, "I thought you were so wonderfully anxious to learn that stroke?"

"Well, I am," she said.

"Come on, then." As they walked toward the tennis court he seemed to be plunged in mournful thought. In his eyes was a singular expression which perhaps denoted the woe of the optimist pushed suddenly from his height. He sighed. "Oh, well, I suppose all women, even the best of them, are that way."

"What way?" she said.

"My dear child," he answered in a benevolent manner, "you have disappointed me because I have discovered that you resemble the rest of your sex."

"Ah?" she remarked, maintaining a non-committal attitude.

"Yes," continued Hollanden with a sad but kindly smile, "even you, Grace, were not above fooling with the affections of a poor country swain until he don't know his ear from the tooth he had pulled two years ago."

She laughed. "He would be furious if he heard you call him a country swain."

"Who would?" said Hollanden.

"Why the country swain, of course," she rejoined.

Hollanden seemed plunged in mournful reflection again. "Well, it's a shame, Grace, anyhow," he observed, wagging his head dolefully. "It's a howling, wicked shame."

"Hollie, you have no brains at all," she said, "despite your opinion."

"No," he replied, ironically. "Not a bit."

"Well, you haven't, you know, Hollie."

"At any rate," he said in an angry voice, "I have some comprehension and sympathy for the feelings of others."

"Have you?" she asked. "How do you mean, Hollie? Do you

mean you have feeling for them in their various sorrows? Or do you mean that you understand their minds?"

Hollanden ponderously began: "There have been people who have not questioned my ability to——"

"Oh, then, you mean that you both feel for them in their sorrows and comprehend the machinery of their minds. Well, let me tell you that in regard to the last thing, you are wrong. You know nothing of any one's mind. You know less about human nature than anybody I have met."

Hollanden looked at her in artless astonishment. He said: "Now, I wonder what made you say that?" This interrogation did not seem to be addressed to her, but was evidently a statement to himself of a problem. He meditated for some moments. Eventually he said: "I suppose you mean that I do not understand you?"

"Why do you suppose I mean that?"

"That's what a person usually means when he—or she—charges another with not understanding the entire world."

"Well, at any rate, it is not what I mean at all," she said. "I mean that you habitually blunder about other people's affairs in the belief, I imagine, that you are a great philanthropist, when you are only making an extraordinary exhibition of yourself."

"The dev——" began Hollanden. Afterward he said: "Now, I wonder what in blue thunder you mean this time?"

" 'Mean this time?' My meaning is very plain, Hollie. I supposed the words were clear enough."

"Yes," he said, thoughtfully, "your words were clear enough, but then you were of course referring back to some event or series of events in which I had the singular ill-fortune to displease you. Maybe you don't know yourself and spoke only from the emotion generated by the event or series of events in which, as I have said, I had the singular ill-fortune to displease you."

"How awf'ly clever," she said.

"But I can't recall the event or series of events at all," he continued, musing with a scholarly air and disregarding her mockery. "I can't remember a thing about it. To be sure, it might have been that time when——"

"I think it very stupid of you to hunt for a meaning when I believe I made everything so perfectly clear," she said, wrathfully.

"Well, you yourself might not be aware of what you really meant," he answered, sagely. "Women often do that sort of thing, you know. Women often speak from motives which, if brought face to face with them, they wouldn't be able to distinguish from any other thing which they had never before seen."

"Hollie, if there is a disgusting person in the world it is he who pretends to know so much concerning a woman's mind."

"Well, that's because they who know or pretend to know so much about a woman's mind are invariably satirical, you understand," said Hollanden, cheerfully.

A dog ran frantically across the lawn, his nose high in the air and his countenance expressing vast perturbation and alarm. "Why, Billie forgot to whistle for his dog when he started for home," said Hollanden. "Come here, old man. Well, 'e was a nice dog." The girl also gave invitation, but the setter would not heed them. He spun wildly about the lawn until he seemed to strike his master's trail and then with his nose near to the ground went down the road at an eager gallop. They stood and watched him.

"Stanley's a nice dog," said Hollanden.

"Indeed, he is," replied the girl fervently.

Presently Hollanden remarked: "Well, don't let's fight any more, particularly since we can't decide what we're fighting about. I can't discover the reason and you don't know it, so——"

"I do know it. I told you very plainly."

"Well, all right. Now, this is the way to work that slam. You give the ball a sort of a lift—see—underhanded and with your arm crooked and stiff. Here, you smash this other ball into the net. Hi! Look out! If you hit it that way you'll knock it over the hotel. Let the ball drop nearer to the ground. Oh, heavens, not on the ground. Well, it's hard to do it from the serve, anyhow. I'll go over to the other court and bat you some easy ones."

Afterward when they were going toward the inn, the girl suddenly began to laugh.

"What you giggling at?" said Hollanden.

"I was thinking how furious he would be if he heard you call him a country swain," she rejoined.

"Who?" asked Hollanden.

CHAPTER XVII

OGLETHORPE contended that the men who made the most money from books were the best authors. Hollanden contended that they were the worst. Oglethorpe said that such a question should be left to the people. Hollanden said that the people habitually made wrong decisions on questions that were left to them. "That is the most odiously aristocratic belief," said Oglethorpe.

"No," said Hollanden. "I like the people. But, considered generally, they are a collection of ingenuous blockheads."

"But they read your books," said Oglethorpe, grinning.

"That is through a mistake," replied Hollanden.

As the discussion grew in size it incited the close attention of the Worcester girls, but Miss Fanhall did not seem to hear it. Hawker, too, was staring into the darkness with a gloomy and preoccupied air.

"Are you sorry that this is your last evening at Hemlock Inn?" said the painter at last in a low tone.

"Why, yes—certainly," said the girl.

Under the sloping porch of the inn the vague orange light from the parlors drifted to the black wall of the night.

"I shall miss you," said the painter.

"Oh, I dare say," said the girl.

Hollanden was lecturing at length and wonderfully. In the mystic spaces of the night the pines could be heard in their weird monotone as they softly smote branch and branch as if moving in some solemn and sorrowful dance.

"This has been quite the most delightful summer of my experience," said the painter.

"I have found it very pleasant," said the girl.

From time to time Hawker glanced furtively at Oglethorpe,

Hollanden and the Worcester girls. This glance expressed no desire for their well being.

"I shall miss you," he said to the girl again. His manner was rather desperate. She made no reply, and, after leaning toward her, he subsided with an air of defeat.

Eventually he remarked: "It will be very lonely here again. I dare say I shall return to New York myself in a few weeks."

"I hope you will call," she said.

"I shall be delighted," he answered, stiffly and with a dissatis-fied look at her.

"Oh, Mr. Hawker," cried the younger Worcester girl, suddenly emerging from the cloud of argument which Hollanden and Oglethorpe kept in the air, "won't it be sad to lose Grace? Indeed, I don't know what we shall do. Sha'n't we miss her dreadfully?"

"Yes," said Hawker, "we shall, of course, miss her dreadfully."

"Yes, won't it be frightful?" said the elder Worcester girl. "I can't imagine what we will do without her. And Hollie is only going to spend ten more days. Oh, dear—mamma, I believe, will insist on staying the entire summer. It was papa's orders, you know, and I really think she is going to obey them. He said he wanted her to have one period of rest at any rate. She is such a busy woman in town, you know."

"Here," said Hollanden, wheeling to them suddenly, "you all look as if you were badgering Hawker, and he looks badgered. What are you saying to him?"

"Why," answered the younger Worcester girl, "we were only saying to him how lonely it would be without Grace."

"Oh!" said Hollanden.

As the evening grew old, the mother of the Worcester girls joined the group. This was a sign that the girls were not to long delay the vanishing time. She sat almost upon the edge of her chair, as if she expected to be called upon at any moment to arise and bow "good-night," and she repaid Hollanden's eloquent attentions with the placid and absent-minded smiles of the chaperone who waits.

Once the younger Worcester girl shrugged her shoulders and turned to say: "Mamma, you make me nervous." Her mother merely smiled in a still more placid and absent-minded manner.

Oglethorpe arose to drag his chair nearer to the railing, and when he stood the Worcester mother moved and looked around expectantly, but Oglethorpe took seat again. Hawker kept an anxious eye upon her.

Presently Miss Fanhall arose.

"Why, you are not going in already, are you?" said Hawker and Hollanden and Oglethorpe. The Worcester mother moved toward the door, followed by her daughters, who were protesting in muffled tones. Hollanden pitched violently upon Oglethorpe. "Well, at any rate——" he said. He picked the thread of a past argument with great agility.

Hawker said to the girl: "I—I—I shall miss you dreadfully."

She turned to look at him and smiled. "Shall you?" she said in a low voice.

"Yes," he said. Thereafter he stood before her awkwardly and in silence. She scrutinized the boards of the floor. Suddenly she drew a violet from a cluster of them upon her gown and thrust it out to him as she turned toward the approaching Oglethorpe.

"Good-night, Mr. Hawker," said the latter. "I am very glad to have met you, I'm sure. Hope to see you in town. Good-night."

He stood near when the girl said to Hawker: "Good-by. You have given us such a charming summer. We shall be delighted to see you in town. You must come some time when the children can see you, too. Good-by."

"Good-by," replied Hawker, eagerly and feverishly trying to interpret the inscrutable feminine face before him. "I shall come at my first opportunity."

"Good-by."

"Good-by."

Down at the farmhouse, in the black quiet of the night, a dog lay curled on the door mat. Of a sudden the tail of this dog began to thump-thump on the boards. It began as a lazy movement, but it passed into a state of gentle enthusiasm and then into one of curiously loud and joyful celebration. At last the gate clicked. The dog uncurled and went to the edge of the steps to greet his master. He gave adoring, tremulous welcome with his clear eyes shining in the darkness. "Well, Stan, old boy," said Hawker, stooping to stroke the dog's head. After his master had entered the house the dog went forward and sniffed at something that lay on the top step. Apparently it did not interest him greatly, for he returned in a moment to the door mat.

But he was again obliged to uncurl himself, for his master

came out of the house with a lighted lamp and made search of the door mat, the steps and the walk, swearing meanwhile in an undertone. The dog wagged his tail and sleepily watched this ceremony. When his master had again entered the house, the dog went forward and sniffed at the top step, but the thing that had lain there was gone.

CHAPTER XVIII

IT was evident at breakfast that Hawker's sisters had achieved information. "What's the matter with you this morning?" asked one. "You look as if you hadn't slep' well."

"There is nothing the matter with me," he rejoined, looking glumly at his plate.

"Well, you look kind of broke up."

"How I look is of no consequence. I tell you there is nothing the matter with me."

"Oh," said his sister. She exchanged meaning glances with the other feminine members of the family. Presently the other sister observed: "I heard she was going home to-day."

"Who?" said Hawker, with a challenge in his tone.

"Why, that New York girl. Miss What's-her-name," replied the sister, with an undaunted smile.

"Did you, indeed? Well, perhaps she is."

"Oh, you don't know for sure, I s'pose."

Hawker arose from the table and taking his hat went away.

"Mary!" said the mother in the sepulchral tone of belated but conscientious reproof.

"Well, I don't care. He needn't be so grand. I didn't go to tease him. I don't care."

"Well, you ought to care," said the old man suddenly. "There's no sense in you wimen folks pestering the boy all the time. Let him alone with his own business, can't you?"

"Well, ain't we leaving him alone?"

"No, you ain't. 'Cept when he ain't here. I don't wonder the boy grabs his hat and skips out when you git to going."

"Well, what did we say to him, now? Tell us what we said to him that was so dreadful."

"Aw, thunder an' lightnin'," cried the old man, with a sudden great snarl. They seemed to know by this ejaculation that he had emerged in an instant from that place where man endures, and they ended the discussion. The old man continued his breakfast.

During his walk that morning Hawker visited a certain cascade, a certain lake, and some roads, paths, groves, nooks. Later in the day he made a sketch, choosing an hour when the atmosphere was of a dark blue, like powder smoke in the shade of trees, and the western sky was burning in strips of red. He painted with a wild face like a man who is killing.

After supper he and his father strolled under the apple boughs in the orchard and smoked. Once he gestured wearily. "Oh, I guess I'll go back to New York in a few days."

"Um," replied his father calmly. "All right, William."

Several days later Hawker accosted his father in the barnyard. "I suppose you think sometimes I don't care so much about you and the folks and the old place any more. But I do."

"Um," said the old man. "When you goin'?"

"Where?" asked Hawker, flushing.

"Back to New York."

"Why—I hadn't thought much about—— Oh, next week, I guess."

"Well, do as you like, William. You know how glad me an' mother and the girls are to have you home with us whenever you can come. You know that. But you must do as you think best and if you ought to go back to New York, now, William, why— do as you think best."

"Well, my work——" said Hawker.

From time to time the mother made wondering speech to the sisters. "How much nicer William is now. He's just as good as he can be. There for a while he was so cross and out of sorts. I don't see what could have come over him. But now he's just as good as he can be."

Hollanden told him: "Come up to the inn more, you fool."

"I was up there yesterday."

"Yesterday! What of that? I've seen the time when the farm couldn't hold you for two hours during the day."

"Go to blazes."

"Millicent got a letter from Grace Fanhall the other day."

"That so?"

"Yes, she did. Grace wrote—— Say, does that shadow look pure purple to you?"

"Certainly it does or I wouldn't paint it so, duffer. What did she write?"

"Well, if that shadow is pure purple my eyes are liars. It looks a kind of a slate color to me. Lord, if what you fellows say in your pictures is true, the whole earth must be blazing and burning and glowing and——"

Hawker went into a rage. "Oh, you don't know anything about color, Hollie. For heaven's sake, shut up or I'll smash you with the easel."

"Well, I was going to tell you what Grace wrote in her letter. She said——"

"Go on."

"Gimme time, can't you? She said that town was stupid and that she wished she was back at Hemlock Inn."

"Oh! Is that all?"

" 'Is that all!' I wonder what you expected? Well, and she asked to be recalled to you."

"Yes? Thanks."

"And that's all. 'Gad, for such a devoted man as you were, your enthusiasm and interest is stupendous."

The father said to the mother: "Well, William's going back to New York next week."

"Is he? Why, he ain't said nothing to me about it."

"Well, he is, anyhow."

"I declare. What do you s'pose he's going back before September for, John?"

"How do I know?"

"Well, it's funny. John, I bet—I bet he's going back so's he can see that girl."

"He says it's his work."

CHAPTER XIX

WRINKLES had been peering into the little dry goods box that acted as a cupboard. "There are only two eggs and half a loaf of bread left," he announced brutally.

"Heavens," said Warwickson from where he lay smoking on the bed. He spoke in a dismal voice. This tone, it is said, had earned him his popular name of Great Grief.

From different points of the compass Wrinkles looked at the little cupboard with a tremendous scowl, as if he intended thus to frighten the eggs into becoming more than two and the bread into becoming a loaf. "Plague take it," he exclaimed.

"Oh, shut up, Wrinkles," said Grief from the bed.

Wrinkles sat down with an air austere and virtuous. "Well, what are we going to do?" he demanded of the others.

Grief, after swearing, said: "There! That's right. Now, you're happy. The holy office of the inquisition. Blast your buttons, Wrinkles, you always try to keep us from starving peacefully. It is two hours before dinner, anyhow, and——"

"Well, but what are we going to do?" persisted Wrinkles.

Pennoyer with his head bended afar down had been busily scratching at a pen-and-ink drawing. He looked up from his board to utter a plaintive optimism. "The *Monthly Amazement* may pay me to-morrow. They ought to. I've waited over three months now. I'm going down there to-morrow and perhaps I'll get it."

His friends listened with airs of tolerance. "Oh, no doubt, Penny, old man." But at last Wrinkles giggled pityingly. Over on the bed Grief croaked deep down in his throat. Nothing was said for a long time thereafter.

The crash of the New York streets came faintly to this room. Occasionally one could hear the tramp of feet in the intricate corridors of the begrimed building which squatted, slumbering and old, between two exalted commercial structures that would have had to bend afar down to perceive it. The northward march of the city's progress had happened not to overturn this aged structure and it huddled there, lost and forgotten, while the cloud-veering towers strode on.

Meanwhile the first shadows of dusk came in at the blurred windows of the room. Pennoyer threw down his pen and tossed his drawing over on the wonderful heap of stuff that hid the table. "It's too dark to work." He lit a pipe and walked about stretching his shoulders like a man whose labor was valuable.

When the dusk came fully, the youths grew apparently sad. The solemnity of the gloom seemed to make them ponder. "Light the gas, Wrinkles," said Grief fretfully.

The flood of orange light showed clearly the dull walls lined with sketches, the tousled bed in one corner, the masses of boxes and trunks in another, a little dead stove and the wonderful table. Moreover, there were wine-colored draperies flung in some places and on a shelf, high up, there were plaster casts with dust in the creases. A long stove-pipe wandered off in the wrong direction and then turned impulsively toward a hole in the wall. There were some elaborate cobwebs on the ceiling.

"Well, let's eat," said Grief.

"Eat!" said Wrinkles with a jeer. "I told you there was only two eggs and a little bread left. How are we going to eat?"

Again brought face to face with this problem and at the hour for dinner, Pennoyer and Grief thought profoundly. "Thunder and turf," Grief finally announced as the result of his deliberations.

"Well, if Billie Hawker was only home——" began Pennoyer.

"But he isn't," objected Wrinkles. "And that settles that."

Grief and Pennoyer thought more. Ultimately Grief said: "Oh, well, let's eat what we've got." The others at once agreed to this suggestion, as if it had been in their minds.

Later there came a quick step in the passage and a confident little thunder upon the door. Wrinkles arranging the tin pail on the gas stove, Pennoyer engaged in slicing the bread and Great Grief affixing the rubber tube to the gas stove, yelled: "Come in."

The door opened and Miss Florinda O'Connor, the model, dashed into the room like a gale of obstreperous autumn leaves.

"Why, hello, Splutter," they cried.

"Oh, boys, I've come to dine with you."

It was like a squall striking a fleet of yachts.

Grief spoke first. "Yes, you have?" he said incredulously.

"Why, certainly I have. What's the matter?"

They grinned. "Well, old lady," responded Grief, "you've hit us at the wrong time. We are, in fact, all out of everything. No dinner—to mention—and, what's more, we haven't got a sou."

"What? Again?" cried Florinda.

"Yes, again. You'd better dine home to-night."

"But I'll—I'll stake you," said the girl eagerly. "Oh, you poor old idiots. It's a shame. Say, I'll stake you."

"Certainly not," said Pennoyer sternly.

"What are you talking about, Splutter?" demanded Wrinkles in an angry voice.

"No, that won't go down," said Grief in a resolute yet wistful tone.

Florinda divested herself of her hat, jacket and gloves and put them where she pleased. "Got coffee, haven't you? Well, I'm not going to stir a step. You're a fine lot of birds," she added bitterly. "You've all pulled me out of a whole lot of scrapes—oh, any number of times—and now you're broke, you go acting like a set of dudes."

Great Grief had fixed the coffee to boil on the gas stove, but he had to watch it closely, for the rubber tube was short and a chair was balanced on a trunk and two bundles of kindling were balanced on the chair and the gas stove was balanced on the kindling. Coffee-making was here accounted a feat.

Pennoyer dropped a piece of bread to the floor. "There! I'll have to go shy one."

Wrinkles sat playing serenades on his guitar and staring with a frown at the table as if he was applying some strange method of clearing it of its litter.

Florinda assaulted Great Grief. "Here! That's not the way to make coffee."

"What ain't?"

"Why, the way you're making it. You want to take——" She explained some way to him which he couldn't understand.

"For heaven's sake, Wrinkles, tackle that table. Don't sit there like a music box," said Pennoyer, grappling the eggs and starting for the gas stove.

Later as they sat around the board, Wrinkles said with satisfaction: "Well, the coffee's good, anyhow."

" 'Tis good," said Florinda. "But it isn't made right. I'll show you how, Penny. You first——"

"Oh, dry up, Splutter," said Grief. "Here, take an egg."

"I don't like eggs," said Florinda.

"Take an egg," said the three hosts menacingly.

"I tell you I don't like eggs."

"Take—an—egg," they said again.

"Oh, well," said Florinda, "I'll take one, then. But you needn't act like such a set of dudes. And, oh, maybe you didn't have much lunch. I had such a daisy lunch. Up at Pontiac's studio. He's got a lovely studio."

The three looked to be oppressed. Grief said sullenly: "I saw some of his things over in Stencil's gallery and they're rotten."

"Yes, rotten," said Pennoyer.

"Rotten," said Grief.

"Oh, well," retorted Florinda, "if a man has a swell studio and dresses—oh, sort of like a Willie, you know, you fellows sit here like owls in a cave and say rotten—rotten—rotten. You're away off. Pontiac's landscapes——"

"Landscapes be blowed. Put any of his work alongside of Billie Hawker's and see how it looks."

"Oh, well, Billie Hawker's," said Florinda. "Oh, well."

At the mention of Hawker's name, they had all turned to scan her face.

CHAPTER XX

H E wrote that he was coming home this week," said Pen-noyer.

"Did he?" asked Florinda, indifferently.

"Yes. Aren't you glad?"

They were still watching her face.

"Yes, of course, I'm glad. Why shouldn't I be glad?" cried the girl with defiance.

They grinned.

"Oh, certainly. Billie Hawker is a good fellow, Splutter. You have a particular right to be glad."

"You people make me tired," Florinda retorted. "Billie Hawker doesn't give a rap about me and he never tried to make out that he did."

"No," said Grief. "But that isn't saying that you don't care a rap about Billie Hawker. Ah, Florinda."

It seemed that the girl's throat suffered a slight contraction. "Well, and what if I do?" she demanded finally.

"Have a cigarette?" answered Grief.

Florinda took a cigarette, lit it, and perching herself on a divan which was secretly a coal box, she smoked fiercely.

"What if I do?" she again demanded. "It's better than liking one of you dubs, anyhow."

"Oh, Splutter, you poor little outspoken kid," said Wrinkles in a sad voice.

Grief searched among the pipes until he found the best one. "Yes, Splutter, don't you know that when you are so frank you defy every law of your sex, and wild eyes will take your trail?"

"Oh, you talk through your hat," replied Florinda. "Billie don't care whether I like him or whether I don't. And if he should hear me now he wouldn't be glad or give a hang either way. I know that." The girl paused and looked at the row of plaster casts. "Still, you needn't be throwing it at me all the time."

"We didn't," said Wrinkles, indignantly. "You threw it at yourself."

"Well," continued Florinda. "It's better than liking one of you dubs, anyhow. He makes money and——"

"There," said Grief. "Now you've hit it. Bedad, you've reached a point in eulogy where if you move again you will have to go backwards."

"Of course I don't care anything about a fellow's having money——"

"No, indeed, you don't, Splutter," said Pennoyer.

"But then you know what I mean. A fellow isn't a man and doesn't stand up straight unless he has some money. And Billie Hawker makes enough so that you feel that nobody could walk over him, don't you know. And there isn't anything jay about him, either. He's a thoroughbred, don't you know?"

After reflection Pennoyer said: "It's pretty hard on the rest of us, Splutter."

"Well, of course, I like him, but—but——"

"What?" said Pennoyer.

"I don't know," said Florinda.

Purple Sanderson lived in this room, but he usually dined out. At a certain time in his life, before he came to be a great artist, he had learned the gas-fitter's trade and when his opinions were not identical with the opinions of the art managers of the greater number of New York publications he went to see a friend who was a plumber, and the opinions of this man he was thereafter said to respect. He frequented a very neat restaurant on Twenty-third street. It was known that on Saturday nights Wrinkles, Grief and Pennoyer frequently quarreled with him.

As Florinda ceased speaking Purple entered. "Hello, there, Splutter." As he was neatly hanging up his coat he said to the others: "Well, the rent will be due in four days."

"Will it?" asked Pennoyer, astounded.

"Certainly it will," responded Purple, with the air of a superior financial man.

"My soul," said Wrinkles.

"Oh, shut up, Purple," said Grief. "You make me weary, coming around here with your chin about rent. I was just getting happy."

"Well, how are we going to pay it? That's the point," said Sanderson.

Wrinkles sank deeper in his chair and played despondently on his guitar. Grief cast a look of rage at Sanderson and then stared at the wall. Pennoyer said: "Well, we might borrow it from Billie Hawker."

Florinda laughed then.

"Or," continued Pennoyer, hastily, "if those *Amazement* people pay me when they said they would, I'll have money."

"So you will," said Grief. "You will have money to burn. Did the *Amazement* people ever pay you when they said they would? You are wonderfully important all of a sudden, it seems to me. You talk like an artist."

Wrinkles, too, smiled at Pennoyer. "The *Eminent Magazine* people wanted Penny to hire models and make a try for them, too. It would only cost him a stack of blues. By the time he has invested all his money he hasn't got and the rent is three weeks overdue he will be able to tell the landlord to wait seven months until the Monday morning after the day of publication. Go ahead, Penny."

After a period of silence Sanderson, in an obstinate manner, said: "Well, what's to be done? The rent has got to be paid."

Wrinkles played more sad music. Grief frowned deeper. Pennoyer was evidently searching his mind for a plan.

Florinda took the cigarette from between her lips that she might grin with greater freedom.

"We might throw Purple out," said Grief with an inspired air. "That would stop all this discussion."

"You," said Sanderson, furiously. "You can't keep serious a minute. If you didn't have us to take care of you, you wouldn't even know when they threw you out in the street."

"Wouldn't I?" said Grief.

"Well, look here," interposed Florinda. "I'm going home unless you can be more interesting. I am dead sorry about the rent, but I can't help it and——"

"Here! Sit down! Hold on, Splutter," they shouted. Grief turned to Sanderson. "Purple, you shut up."

Florinda curled again on the divan and lit another cigarette. The talk waged about the names of other and more successful painters whose work they usually pronounced "Rotten."

CHAPTER XXI

PENNOYER coming home one morning with two gigantic cakes to accompany the coffee at the breakfast in the den, saw a young man bounce from a horse-car. He gave a shout. "Hello there, Billie! Hello!"

"Hello, Penny," said Hawker. "What you doing out so early?" It was somewhat after nine o'clock.

"Out to get breakfast," said Pennoyer, waving the cakes. "Have a good time, old man?"

"Great."

"Do much work?"

"No. Not so much. How are all the people?"

"Oh, pretty good. Come in and see us eat breakfast," said Pennoyer, throwing open the door of the den. Wrinkles, in his shirt, was making coffee. Grief sat in a chair trying to loosen the grasp of sleep. "Why, Billie Hawker, b'ginger," they cried.

"How's the wolf, boys? At the door yet?"

" 'At the door yet?' He's half way up the back stairs and coming fast. He and the landlord will be here to-morrow. 'Mr. Landlord, allow me to present Mr. F. Wolf of Hunger, N.J. Mr. Wolf —Mr. Landlord.' "

"Bad as that?" said Hawker.

"You bet it is. Easy street is somewhere in heaven for all we know. Have some breakfast—coffee and cake, I mean."

"No, thanks, boys. Had breakfast."

Wrinkles added to the shirt, Grief aroused himself and Pennoyer brought the coffee. Cheerfully throwing some drawings from the table to the floor, they thus made room for the breakfast and grouped themselves with beaming smiles at the board.

"Well, Billie, come back to the old gang again, eh? How did the country seem? Do much work?"

"Not very much. A few things. How's everybody?"

"Splutter was in last night. Looking out of sight. Seemed glad to hear that you were coming back soon."

"Did she? Penny, did anybody call wanting me to do a ten-thousand-dollar portrait for them?"

"No. That frame-maker, though, was here with a bill. I told him——"

Afterward Hawker crossed the corridor and threw open the door of his own large studio. The great skylight, far above his head, shed its clear rays upon a scene which appeared to indicate that some one had very recently ceased work here and started for the country. A distant closet door was open and the interior showed the effects of a sudden pillage.

There was an unfinished "Girl in Apple Orchard" upon the tall Dutch easel and sketches and studies were thick upon the floor. Hawker took a pipe and filled it from his friend, the tan and gold jar. He cast himself into a chair and taking an envelope from his pocket, emptied two violets from it to the palm of his hand and stared long at them. Upon the walls of the studio, various labors of his life in heavy gilt frames contemplated him and the violets.

At last Pennoyer burst impetuously in upon him. "Hi, Billie, come over and—— What's the matter?"

Hawker had hastily placed the violets in the envelope and hurried it to his pocket. "Nothing," he answered.

"Why, I thought——" said Pennoyer. "I thought you looked rather rattled. Didn't you have—I thought I saw something in your hand."

"Nothing, I tell you," cried Hawker.

"Er—oh, I beg your pardon," said Pennoyer. "Why, I was going to tell you that Splutter is over in our place and she wants to see you."

"Wants to see me? What for?" demanded Hawker. "Why don't she come over here, then?"

"I'm sure I don't know," replied Pennoyer. "She sent me to call you."

"Well, do you think I'm going to—— Oh, well, I suppose she wants to be unpleasant and knows she loses a certain mental position if she comes over here, but if she meets me in your place she can be as infernally disagreeable as she—— That's it, I'll bet."

When they entered the den, Florinda was gazing from the window. Her back was toward the door.

At last she turned to them, holding herself very straight. "Well, Billie Hawker," she said grimly. "You don't seem very glad to see a fellow."

"Why, heavens, did you think I was going to turn somersaults in the air?"

"Well, you didn't come out when you heard me pass your door," said Florinda with gloomy resentment.

Hawker appeared to be ruffled and vexed. "Oh, Great Scott," he said, making a gesture of despair.

Florinda returned to the window. In the ensuing conversation she took no part save when there was opportunity to harry some speech of Hawker's, which she did in short contemptuous sentences. Hawker made no reply save to glare in her direction. At last he said: "Well, I must go over and do some work." Florinda did not turn from the window. "Well, so long, boys," said Hawker. "I'll see you later."

As the door slammed Pennoyer apologetically said: "Billie is a trifle off his feed this morning."

"What about?" asked Grief.

"I don't know. But when I went to call him, he was sitting deep in his chair staring at some——" He looked at Florinda and became silent.

"Staring at what?" asked Florinda, turning then from the window.

Pennoyer seemed embarrassed. "Why, I don't know—nothing, I guess—I couldn't see very well—I was only fooling."

Florinda scanned his face suspiciously. "Staring at what?" she demanded imperatively.

"Nothing, I tell you," shouted Pennoyer.

Florinda looked at him and wavered and debated. Presently she said softly: "Ah, go on, Penny. Tell me."

"It wasn't anything at all, I say," cried Pennoyer stoutly. "I was only giving you a jolly. Sit down, Splutter, and hit a cigarette."

She obeyed, but she continued to cast the dubious eye at Pennoyer. Once she said to him privately: "Go on, Penny, tell me. I know it was something from the way you are acting."

"Oh, let up, Splutter, for heaven's sake."

"Tell me," beseeched Florinda.

"No."

"Tell me."

"No."

"Pl-e-a-se, tell me."

"No."

"Oh, go on."

"No."

"Ah, what makes you so mean, Penny. You know I'd tell you if it was the other way about."

"But it's none of my business, Splutter. I can't tell you something which is Billie Hawker's private affair. If I did I would be a chump."

"But I'll never say you told me. Go on."

"No."

"Pl-e-a-se, tell me."

"No."

CHAPTER XXII

WHEN Florinda had gone, Grief said: "Well, what was it?" Wrinkles looked curiously from his drawing board. Pennoyer lit his pipe and held it at the side of his mouth in the manner of a deliberate man. At last he said: "It was two violets."

"You don't say," ejaculated Wrinkles.

"Well, I'm hanged," cried Grief. "Holding them in his hand and moping over them, eh?"

"Yes," responded Pennoyer. "Rather that way."

"Well, I'm hanged," said both Grief and Wrinkles. They grinned in a pleased, urchin-like manner. "Say, who do you suppose she is? Somebody he met this summer, no doubt. Would you ever think old Billie would get into that sort of a thing. Well, I'll be gol-durned."

Ultimately Wrinkles said: "Well, it's his own business." This was spoken in a tone of duty.

"Of course, it's his own business," retorted Grief. "But who would ever think——" Again they grinned.

When Hawker entered the den some minutes later, he might have noticed something unusual in the general demeanor. "Say, Grief, will you loan me your—— What's up?" he asked.

For answer they grinned at each other and then grinned at him.

"You look like a lot of Chessy cats," he told them.

They grinned on.

Apparently feeling unable to deal with these phenomena, he went at last to the door. "Well, this is a fine exhibition," he said, standing with his hand on the knob and regarding them. "Won election bets? Some good old auntie just died? Found something new to pawn? No? Well, I can't stand this. You resemble those fish they discover at deep sea. Good-by."

As he opened the door, they cried out: "Hold on, Billie. Billie, look here. Say, who is she?"

"What?"

"Who is she?"

"Who is who?"

They laughed and nodded. "Why, you know. She. Don't you understand? She."

"You talk like a lot of crazy men," said Hawker. "I don't know what you mean."

"Oh, you don't, eh? You don't? Oh, no. How about those violets you were moping over this morning? Eh, old man? Oh, no, you don't know what we mean. Oh, no. How about those violets, eh? How about 'em?"

Hawker with flushed and wrathful face looked at Pennoyer. "Penny——" But Grief and Wrinkles roared an interruption. "Oh, ho, Mr. Hawker, so it's true, is it? It's true? You are a nice bird, you are. Well, you old rascal. Durn your picture."

Hawker, menacing them once with his eyes, went away. They sat cackling.

At noon when he met Wrinkles in the corridor he said: "Hey, Wrinkles, come here for a minute, will you? Say, old man, I—— I——"

"What?" said Wrinkles.

"Well, you know, I—I—of course, every man is likely to make an accursed idiot of himself once in a while, and I——"

"And you what?" asked Wrinkles.

"Well, we are a kind of a band of hoodlums, you know, and I'm just enough idiot to feel that I don't care to hear—don't care to hear—well, her name used, you know."

"Bless your heart," replied Wrinkles. "We haven't used her name. We don't know her name. How could we use it?"

"Well, I know," said Hawker. "But you understand what I mean, Wrinkles."

"Yes, I understand what you mean," said Wrinkles with dignity. "I don't suppose you are any worse of a stuff than common. Still, I didn't know that we were such outlaws."

"Of course, I have overdone the thing," responded Hawker hastily. "But—you ought to understand how I mean it, Wrinkles."

After Wrinkles had thought for a time he said: "Well, I guess I do. All right. That goes."

Upon entering the den, Wrinkles said: "You fellows have got to quit guying Billic, do you hear?"

"We?" cried Grief. "We've got to quit? What do you do?"

"Well, I quit, too."

Pennoyer said: "Ah, ha, Billie has been jumping on you."

"No, he didn't," maintained Wrinkles. "But he let me know it was—well, rather a—rather a—sacred subject." Wrinkles blushed when the others snickered.

In the afternoon, as Hawker was going slowly down the stairs, he was almost impaled upon the feather of a hat which, upon the head of a lithe and rather slight girl, charged up at him through the gloom.

"Hello, Splutter," he cried. "You are in a hurry."

"That you, Billie?" said the girl peering, for the hallways of this old building remained always in a dungeon-like darkness.

"Yes, it is. Where are you going at such a headlong gait?"

"Up to see the boys. I've got a bottle of wine and some—some pickles, you know. I'm going to make them let me dine with them to-night. Coming back, Billie?"

"Why, no, I don't expect to."

He moved then accidentally in front of the light that sifted through the dull grey panes of a little window.

"Oh, cracky," cried the girl. "How fine you are, Billie. Going to a coronation?"

"No," said Hawker, looking seriously over his collar and down at his clothes. "Fact is—er—well, I've got to make a call."

"A call—bless us. And are you really going to wear those grey gloves you're holding there, Billie? Say, wait until you get around the corner. They won't stand 'em on this street."

"Oh, well," said Hawker, deprecating the gloves. "Oh, well."

The girl looked up at him. "Who you going to call on?"

"Oh," said Hawker. "A friend."

"Must be somebody most extraordinary. You look so dreadfully correct. Come back, Billie, won't you? Come back and dine with us?"

"Why I—I don't believe I can."

"Oh, come on. It's fun when we all dine together. Won't you, Billie?"

"Well, I——"

"Oh, don't be so stupid." The girl stamped her foot and flashed her eyes at him angrily.

"Well, I'll see—I will if I can—I can't tell——" He left her rather precipitately.

Hawker eventually appeared at a certain austere house where he rang the bell with quite nervous fingers.

But she was not at home. As he went down the steps, his eyes were as those of a man whose fortunes have tumbled upon him. As he walked down the street he wore in some subtle way, the air of a man who has been grievously wronged. When he rounded the corner, his lips were set strangely as if he were a man seeking revenge.

CHAPTER XXIII

I T'S just right," said Grief.

"It isn't quite cool enough," said Wrinkles.

"Well, I guess I know the proper temperature for claret."

"Well, I guess you don't. If it was buttermilk, now, you would know, but you can't tell anything about claret."

Florinda ultimately decided the question. "It isn't quite cool enough," she said, laying her hand on the bottle. "Put it on the window ledge, Grief."

"Hum! Splutter, I thought you knew more than——"

"Oh, shut up," interposed the busy Pennoyer from a remote corner. "Who is going after the potato salad? That's what I want to know. Who is going?"

"Wrinkles," said Grief.

"Grief," said Wrinkles.

"There," said Pennoyer, coming forward and scanning a late work with an eye of satisfaction. "There's the three glasses and the little tumbler and then, Grief, you will have to drink out of a mug."

"I'll be double-dyed black if I will!" cried Grief. "I wouldn't drink claret out of a mug to save my soul from being pinched."

"You duffer. You talk like a bloomin' British chump, on whom the sun never sets. What do you want?"

"Well, there's enough without that—what's the matter with you? Three glasses and the little tumbler."

"Yes, but if Billie Hawker comes——"

"Well, let him drink out of the mug, then. He——"

"No, he won't," said Florinda, suddenly. "I'll take the mug myself."

"All right, Splutter," rejoined Grief, meekly. "I'll keep the mug. But still, I don't see why Billie Hawker——"

"I shall take the mug," reiterated Florinda, firmly.

"But I don't see why——"

"Let her alone, Grief," said Wrinkles. "She has decided that it is heroic. You can't move her now."

"Well, who is going for the potato salad?" cried Pennoyer again. "That's what I want to know."

"Wrinkles," said Grief.

"Grief," said Wrinkles.

"Do you know," remarked Florinda, raising her head from where she had been toiling over the spaghetti, "I don't care so much for Billie Hawker as I did once." Her sleeves were rolled above the elbows of her wonderful arms and she turned from the stove and poised a fork as if she had been smitten at her task with this inspiration.

There was a short silence, and then Wrinkles said politely: "No?"

"No," continued Florinda. "I really don't believe I do." She suddenly started. "Listen! Isn't that him coming now?"

The dull trample of a step could be heard in some distant corridor, but it died slowly to silence.

"I thought that might be him," she said, turning to the spaghetti again.

"I hope the old Indian comes," said Pennoyer. "But I don't believe he will. Seems to me he must be going to see——"

"Who?" asked Florinda.

"Well, you know, Hollanden and he usually dine together when they are both in town."

Florinda looked at Pennoyer. "I know, Penny. You must have thought I was remarkably clever not to understand all your blundering. But I don't care so much. Really I don't."

"Of course not," assented Pennoyer.

"Really I don't."

"Of course not."

"Listen," exclaimed Grief, who was near the door. "There he comes now." Somebody approached, whistling an air from "Traviata," which rang loud and clear and low and muffled as the whistler wound among the intricate hallways. This air was as much a part of Hawker as his coat. The spaghetti had arrived at a critical stage. Florinda gave it her complete attention.

When Hawker opened the door he ceased whistling and said gruffly: "Hello!"

"Just the man," said Grief. "Go after the potato salad, will you, Billie? There's a good boy. Wrinkles has refused."

"He can't carry the salad with those gloves," interrupted Florinda, raising her eyes from her work and contemplating them with displeasure.

"Hang the gloves," cried Hawker, dragging them from his hands and hurling them at the divan. "What's the matter with you, Splutter?"

Pennoyer said: "My, what a temper you are in, Billie."

"I am," replied Hawker. "I feel like an Apache. Where do you get this accursed potato salad?"

"On Second avenue. You know where. At the old place."

"No, I don't," snapped Hawker.

"Why——"

"Here," said Florinda. "I'll go." She had already rolled down her sleeves and was arraying herself in her hat and jacket.

"No, you won't," said Hawker, filled with wrath. "I'll go myself."

"We can both go, Billie, if you are so bent," replied the girl in a conciliatory voice.

"Well, come on, then. What are you standing there for?"

When these two had departed, Wrinkles said: "Lordie! What's wrong with Billie?"

"He's been discussing art with some pot-boiler," said Grief, speaking as if this was the final condition of human misery.

"No, sir," said Pennoyer. "It's something connected with the now celebrated violets."

Out in the corridor Florinda said: "What—what makes you so ugly, Billie?"

"Why, I am not ugly, am I?"

"Yes, you are. Ugly as anything."

Probably he saw a grievance in her eyes, for he said: "Well, I don't want to be ugly." His tone seemed tender. The halls were intensely dark and the girl placed her hand on his arm. As they rounded a turn in the stairs a straying lock of her hair brushed against his temple. "Oh," said Florinda in a low voice.

"We'll get some more claret," observed Hawker, musingly.

"And some cognac for the coffee. And some cigarettes. Do you think of anything more, Splutter?"

As they came from the shop of the illustrious purveyors of potato salad on Second avenue, Florinda cried anxiously: "Here, Billie, you let me carry that."

"What infernal nonsense," said Hawker, flushing. "Certainly not."

"Well," protested Florinda. "It might soil your gloves somehow."

"In heaven's name, what if it does? Say, young woman, do you think I am one of these cholly boys?"

"No, Billie, but then you know——"

"Well, if you don't take me for some kind of a Willie, give us peace on this blasted glove business!"

"I didn't mean——"

"Well, you've been intimating that I've got the only pair of grey gloves in the universe, but you are wrong. There are several pairs, and these need not be preserved as unique in history."

"They're not grey. They're——"

"They are grey. I suppose your distinguished ancestors in Ireland did not educate their families in the matter of gloves, and so you are not expected to——"

"Billie!"

"You are not expected to believe that people wear gloves excepting in cold weather, and then you expect to see mittens."

On the stairs in the darkness he suddenly exclaimed: "Here! Look out, or you'll fall." He reached for her arm, but she evaded him. Later he said again: "Look out, girl. What makes you stumble around so? Here! Give me the bottle of wine. I can carry it all right. There! Now, can you manage?"

CHAPTER XXIV

PENNY," said Grief, looking across the table at his friend, "if a man thinks a heap of two violets, how much would he think of a thousand violets?"

"Two into a thousand goes five hundred times, you fool," said Pennoyer. "I would answer your question if it were not upon a forbidden subject."

In the distance Wrinkles and Florinda were making Welsh rabbits.

"Hold your tongues," said Hawker. "Barbarians!"

"Grief," said Pennoyer, "if a man loves a woman better than the whole universe, how much does he love the whole universe?"

"Gawd knows," said Grief, piously. "Although it ill befits me to answer your question."

Wrinkles and Florinda came with the Welsh rabbits very triumphant. "There," said Florinda. "Soon as these are finished I must go home. It is after eleven o'clock. Pour the ale, Grief."

At a later time Purple Sanderson entered from the world. He hung up his hat and cast a look of proper financial dissatisfaction at the remnants of the feast. "Who has been——"

"Before you breathe, Purple, you graceless scum, let me tell you that we will stand no reference to the two violets here," said Pennoyer.

"What the——"

"Oh, that's all right, Purple," said Grief, "but you were going to say something about the two violets right then. Weren't you now, you old bat?"

Sanderson grinned expectantly. "What's the row?" said he.

"No row at all," they told him. "Just an agreement to keep you from chattering obstinately about the two violets."

"What two violets?"

"Have a rabbit, Purple," advised Wrinkles, "and never mind those maniacs."

"Well, what is this business about two violets?"

"Oh, it's just some dream. They gibber at anything."

"I think I know," said Florinda, nodding. "It is something that concerns Billie Hawker."

Grief and Pennoyer scoffed, and Wrinkles said: "You know nothing about it, Splutter. It doesn't concern Billie Hawker at all."

"Well, then, what is he looking sideways for?" cried Florinda.

Wrinkles reached for his guitar and played a serenade. "The silver moon is shining——"

"Dry up," said Pennoyer.

Then Florinda cried again: "What does he look sideways for?"

Pennoyer and Grief giggled at the imperturbable Hawker, who destroyed rabbit in silence.

"It's you, is it, Billie?" said Sanderson. "You are in this two-violet business."

"I don't know what they're talking about," replied Hawker.

"Don't you, honestly?" asked Florinda.

"Well, only a little."

"There!" said Florinda, nodding again. "I knew he was in it."

"He isn't in it at all," said Pennoyer and Grief.

Later, when the cigarettes had become exhausted, Hawker volunteered to go after a further supply, and as he arose a question seemed to come to the edge of Florinda's lips and pend there. The moment that the door was closed upon him she demanded: "What is that about the two violets?"

"Nothing at all," answered Pennoyer, apparently much aggrieved. He sat back with an air of being a fortress of reticence.

"Oh, go on, tell me. Penny, I think you are very mean. Grief, you tell me."

> "The silver moon is shining.
> Oh, come my love to me.
> My heart——"

"Be still, Wrinkles, will you. What was it, Grief? Oh, go ahead and tell me."

"What do you want to know for?" cried Grief, vastly exasperated. "You've got more blamed curiosity. It isn't anything at all, I keep saying to you."

"Well, I know it is," said Florinda, sullenly, "or you would tell me."

When Hawker brought the cigarettes, Florinda smoked one and then announced: "Well, I must go now."

"Who is going to take you home, Splutter?"

"Oh, any one," replied Florinda.

"I tell you what," said Grief. "We'll throw some poker hands, and the one who wins will have the distinguished honor of conveying Miss Splutter to her home and mother."

Pennoyer and Wrinkles speedily routed the dishes to one end of the table. Grief's fingers spun the halves of a pack of cards together with the pleased eagerness of a good player. The faces grew solemn with the gambling solemnity. "Now, you Indians," said Grief, dealing. "A draw, you understand, and then a show-down."

Florinda leaned forward in her chair until it was poised on two legs. The cards of Purple Sanderson and of Hawker were faced toward her. Sanderson was gravely regarding two pair— aces and queens. Hawker scanned a little pair of sevens. "They draw, don't they?" she said to Grief.

"Certainly," said Grief. "How many, Wrink?"

"Four," replied Wrinkles, plaintively.

"Gimme three," said Pennoyer.

"Gimme one," said Sanderson.

"Gimme three," said Hawker. When he picked up his hand again Florinda's chair was tilted perilously. She saw another seven added to the little pair. Sanderson's draw had not assisted him.

"Same to the dealer," said Grief. "What you got, Wrink?"

"Nothing," said Wrinkles, exhibiting it face upward on the table. "Good-by, Florinda."

"Well, I've got two small pair," ventured Pennoyer, hopefully. "Beat 'em?"

"No good," said Sanderson. "Two pair—aces up."

"No good," said Hawker. "Three sevens."

"Beats me," said Grief. "Billie, you are the fortunate man. Heaven guide you on Third avenue."

Florinda had gone to the window. "Who won?" she asked, wheeling about carelessly.

"Billie Hawker."

"What? Did he?" she said in surprise.

"Never mind, Splutter. I'll win sometime," said Pennoyer. "Me, too," cried Grief. "Good-night, old girl," said Wrinkles. They crowded in the doorway. "Hold onto Billie. Remember the two steps going up." Pennoyer called intelligently into the stygian blackness: "Can you see all right?"

Florinda lived in a flat with fire escapes written all over the face of it. The street in front was being repaired. It had been said by imbecile residents of the vicinity that the paving was never allowed to remain down for a sufficient time to be invalided by the tramping millions, but that it was kept perpetually stacked in little mountains through the unceasing vigilance of a virtuous and heroic city government which insisted that everything should be repaired. The alderman for the district had sometimes asked indignantly of his fellow-members why this street had not been repaired, and they, aroused, had at once ordered it to be repaired. Moreover, shopkeepers whose stables were adjacent placed trucks and other vehicles strategically in the darkness. Into this tangled midnight Hawker conducted Florinda. The great avenue behind them was no more than a level stream of yellow light, and the distant merry bells might have been on boats floating down it. Grim loneliness hung over the uncouth shapes in the street which was being repaired.

"Billie," said the girl suddenly, "what makes you so mean to me?"

A peaceful citizen emerged from behind a pile of debris, but he might not have been a peaceful citizen, so the girl clung to Hawker.

"Why, I'm not mean to you, am I?"

"Yes," she answered. As they stood on the steps of the flat of innumerable fire escapes, she slowly turned and looked up at him. Her face was of a strange pallor in this darkness and her eyes were as when the moon shines in a lake of the hills.

He returned her glance. "Florinda," he cried, as if enlightened, and gulping suddenly at something in his throat. The girl studied the steps and moved from side to side, as do the guilty ones in country schoolhouses. Then she went slowly into the flat.

There was a little red lamp hanging on a pile of stones to warn people that the street was being repaired.

CHAPTER XXV

I'LL get my check from the *Gamin* on Saturday," said Grief. "They bought that string of comics."

"Well, then, we'll arrange the present funds to last until Saturday noon," said Wrinkles. "That gives us quite a lot. We can have a table d'hote on Friday night."

However, the cashier of the *Gamin* office looked under his respectable brass wiring and said: "Very sorry, Mr.—er—Warwickson, but our payday is Monday. Come around any time after ten."

"Oh, it doesn't matter," said Grief.

When he plunged into the den his visage flamed with rage. "Don't get my check until Monday morning, any time after ten," he yelled, and flung a portfolio of mottled green into the danger zone of the casts.

"Thunder," said Pennoyer, sinking at once to a profound despair.

"Monday morning, any time after ten," murmured Wrinkles in astonishment and sorrow.

While Grief marched to and fro threatening the furniture, Pennoyer and Wrinkles allowed their under jaws to fall and remained as men smitten between the eyes by the god of calamity.

"Singular thing," muttered Pennoyer at last. "You get so frightfully hungry as soon as you learn that there are no more meals coming."

"Oh, well——" said Wrinkles. He took up his guitar.

> Oh, some folks say dat a niggah won' steal,
> 'Way down yondeh in d' cohn'fiel',
> But Ah caught two in my cohn'fiel',
> 'Way down yondeh in d' cohn'fiel'.

"Oh, let up," said Grief, as if unwilling to be moved from his despair.

"Oh, let up," said Pennoyer, as if he disliked the voice and the ballad.

In his studio Hawker sat braced nervously forward on a little stool before his tall Dutch easel. Three sketches lay on the floor near him and he glared at them constantly while painting at the large canvas on the easel.

He seemed engaged in some kind of a duel. His hair dishevelled, his eyes gleaming, he was in a deadly scuffle. In the sketches was the landscape of heavy blue, as if seen through powder smoke, and all the skies burned red. There was in these notes a sinister quality of hopelessness, eloquent of a defeat, as if the scene represented the last hour on a field of disastrous battle. Hawker seemed attacking with this picture something fair and beautiful of his own life, a possession of his mind, and he did it fiercely, mercilessly, formidably. His arm moved with the energy of a strange wrath. He might have been thrusting with a sword.

There was a knock at the door. "Come in." Pennoyer entered sheepishly. "Well?" cried Hawker, with an echo of savagery in his voice. He turned from the canvas precisely as one might emerge from a fight. "Oh," he said, perceiving Pennoyer. The glow in his eyes slowly changed. "What is it, Penny?"

"Billie," said Pennoyer, "Grief was to get his check to-day, but they put him off until Monday, and so, you know—er—well——"

"Oh," said Hawker again.

When Pennoyer had gone, Hawker sat motionless before his work. He stared at the canvas in a meditation so profound that it was probably unconscious of itself.

The light from above his head slanted more and more toward the east.

Once he arose and lighted a pipe. He returned to the easel and stood staring with his hands in his pockets. He moved like one in a sleep. Suddenly the gleam shot into his eyes again. He dropped to the stool and grabbed a brush. At the end of a certain long tumultuous period he clinched his pipe more firmly in his teeth and puffed strongly. The thought might have occurred to him that it was not a-light, for he looked at it with a vague, questioning glance. There came another knock at the door. "Go to the devil," he shouted without turning his head.

Hollanden crossed the corridor then to the den.

"Hi, there, Hollie! Hello, boy! Just the fellow we want to see! Come in—sit down—hit a pipe. Say, who was the girl Billie Hawker went mad over this summer?"

"Blazes!" said Hollanden, recovering slowly from this onslaught. "Who—what—how did you Indians find it out?"

"Oh, we tumbled," they cried in delight. "We tumbled."

"There!" said Hollanden, reproaching himself. "And I thought you were such a lot of blockheads."

"Oh, we tumbled," they cried again, in their ecstasy. "But who is she? That's the point."

"Well, she was a girl."

"Yes. Go on."

"A New York girl."

"Yes."

"A perfectly stunning New York girl."

"Yes. Go ahead."

"A perfectly stunning New York girl of a very wealthy and rather old-fashioned family."

"Well, I'll be shot! You don't mean it? She is practically seated on top of the Matterhorn. Poor old Billie!"

"Not at all," said Hollanden, composedly.

It was a common habit of Purple Sanderson to call attention at night to the resemblance of the den to some little ward in a hospital. Upon this night, when Sanderson and Grief were buried in slumber, Pennoyer moved restlessly. "Wrink," he called softly into the darkness in the direction of the divan which was secretly a coal box.

"What?" said Wrinkles in a surly voice. His mind had evidently been caught at the threshold of sleep.

"Do you think Florinda cares much for Billie Hawker?"

Wrinkles fretted through some oaths. "How in thunder do I know?" The divan creaked as he turned his face to the wall.

"Well——" muttered Pennoyer.

CHAPTER XXVI

THE harmony of summer sunlight on leaf and blade of green was not known to the two windows which looked forth at an obviously endless building of brown stone about which there was the poetry of a prison. Inside, great folds of lace swept down in orderly cascades, as water trained to fall mathematically. The colossal chandelier, gleaming like a Siamese head-dress, caught the subtle flashes from unknown places.

Hawker heard a step and the soft swishing of a woman's dress. He turned toward the door swiftly with a certain dramatic impulsiveness. But when she entered the room he said: "How delighted I am to see you again."

She had said: "Why, Mr. Hawker, it was so charming in you to come."

It did not appear that Hawker's tongue could wag to his purpose. The girl seemed in her mind to be frantically shuffling her pack of social receipts and finding none of them made to meet this situation. Finally Hawker said that he thought "Hearts at War" was a very good play.

"Did you?" she said in surprise. "I thought it much like the others."

"Well, so did I," he cried hastily. "The same figures moving around in the mud of modern confusion. I really didn't intend to say that I liked it. Fact is—meeting you rather moved me out of my mental track."

"Mental track?" she said. "I didn't know clever people had mental tracks. I thought it was a privilege of the theologians."

"Who told you I was clever?" he demanded.

"Why—" she said, opening her eyes wider. "Nobody."

Hawker smiled and looked upon her with gratitude. "Of course! 'Nobody!' There couldn't be such an idiot. I am sure you should be astonished to learn that I believed such an imbecile existed. But——"

"Oh," she said.

"But I think you might have spoken less bluntly."

"Well," she said, after wavering for a time, "you are clever, aren't you?"

"Certainly," he answered reassuringly.

"Well, then?" she retorted with triumph in her tone. And this interrogation was apparently to her the final victorious argument.

At his discomfiture, Hawker grinned.

"You haven't asked news of Stanley," he said. "Why don't you ask news of Stanley?"

"Oh, and how was he?"

"The last I saw of him he stood down at the end of the pasture —the pasture, you know—wagging his tail in blissful anticipation of an invitation to come with me and when it finally dawned upon him that he was not to receive it, he turned and went back toward the house 'like a man suddenly stricken with age,' as the story-tellers eloquently say. Poor old dog."

"And you left him?" she said reproachfully. Then she asked: "Do you remember how he amused you playing with the ants at the falls?"

"No."

"Why, he did. He pawed at the moss and you sat there laughing. I remember distinctly."

"You remember distinctly? Why, I thought—well, your back was turned, you know. Your gaze was fixed upon something before you and you were utterly lost to the rest of the world. You could not have known if Stanley pawed the moss and I laughed. So, you see, you are mistaken. As a matter of fact, I utterly deny that Stanley pawed the moss or that I laughed or that any ants appeared at the falls at all."

"I have always said that you should have been a Chinese soldier of fortune," she observed, musingly. "Your daring and ingenuity would be prized by the Chinese."

"There are innumerable tobacco jars in China," he said, measuring the advantages. "Moreover, there is no perspective. You don't have to walk two miles to see a friend. No. He is always there near you, so that you can't move a chair without hitting your distant friend. You——"

"Did Hollie remain as attentive as ever to the Worcester girls?"

"Yes, of course. As attentive as ever. He dragged me into all manner of tennis games——"

"Why, I thought you loved to play tennis?"

"Oh, well——" said Hawker. "I did until you left."

"My sister has gone to the park with the children. I know she will be vexed when she finds that you have called."

Ultimately Hawker said: "Do you remember our ride behind my father's oxen?"

"No," she answered. "I had forgotten it completely. Did we ride behind your father's oxen?"

After a moment he said: "That remark would be prized by the Chinese. We did. And you most graciously professed to enjoy it, which earned my deep gratitude and admiration. For no one knows better than I," he added meekly, "that it is no great comfort or pleasure to ride behind my father's oxen."

She smiled retrospectively. "Do you remember how the people on the porch hurried to the railing?"

CHAPTER XXVII

NEAR the door, the stout proprietress sat entrenched behind the cash desk in a Parisian manner. She looked with practiced amiability at her guests, who dined noisily and with great fire, discussing momentous problems furiously, making wide maniacal gestures through the cigarette smoke. Meanwhile the little handful of waiters ran to and fro wildly. Imperious and importunate cries rang at them from all directions. "Gustave! Adolphe!" Their faces expressed a settled despair. They answered calls, commands, oaths, in a semi-distraction, fleeting among the tables as if pursued by some dodging animal. Their breaths came in gasps. If they had been convict laborers they could not have surveyed their positions with countenances of more unspeakable injury. Withal they carried incredible masses of dishes and threaded their ways with skill. They served people with such speed and violence that it often resembled a personal assault. They struck two blows at a table and left there a knife and a fork. Then came the viands in a volley. The clatter of this business was loud and bewilderingly rapid like the gallop of a thousand horses.

In a remote corner a band of mandolins and guitars played the long, sweeping, mad melody of a Spanish waltz. It seemed to go tingling to the hearts of many of the diners. Their eyes glittered with enthusiasm, with abandon, with deviltry. They swung their heads from side to side in rhythmic movement. High in air curled the smoke from the innumerable cigarettes. The long black claret bottles were in clusters upon the tables. At an end of the hall, two men with maudlin grins sang the waltz uproariously, but always a trifle belated.

An unsteady person leaning back in his chair to murmur swift compliments to a woman at another table, suddenly sprawled out upon the floor. He scrambled to his feet, and turning to the escort of the woman, heatedly blamed him for the accident. They exchanged a series of tense bitter insults, which spatted back and forth between them like pellets. People arose from their chairs and stretched their necks. The musicians stood in a body, their faces turned with expressions of keen excitement toward this quarrel, but their fingers still twinkling over their instruments, sending into the middle of this turmoil the passionate mad Spanish music. The proprietor of the place came in agitation and plunged headlong into the argument, where he thereafter appeared as a frantic creature, harried to the point of insanity, for they buried him at once in long vociferous threats, explanations, charges, every form of declamation known to their race. The music, the noise of the galloping horses, the voices of the brawlers gave the whole thing the quality of war.

There were two men in the cafe who seemed to be tranquil. Hollanden carefully stacked one lump of sugar upon another in the middle of his saucer and poured cognac over them. He touched a match to the cognac and the blue and yellow flames eddied in the saucer. "I wonder what those two fools are bellowing at?" he said, turning about irritably.

"Hanged if I know," muttered Hawker in reply. "This place makes me weary anyhow. Hear the blooming din."

"What's the matter?" said Hollanden. "You used to say this was the one natural, the one truly Bohemian resort in the city. You swore by it."

"Well, I don't like it so much any more."

"Ho," cried Hollanden. "You're getting correct—that's it exactly. You will become one of these intensely—— Look, Billie, the little one is going to punch him."

"No, he isn't. They never do," said Hawker, morosely. "Why did you bring me here to-night, Hollie?"

"I? I bring you? Good heavens, I came as a concession to you. What are you talking about? Hi, the little one is going to punch him—sure!"

He gave the scene his undivided attention for a moment. Then he turned again. "You will become correct. I know you will. I have been watching. You are about to achieve a respectability that will make a stone saint blush for himself. What's the matter with you? You act as if you thought falling in love with a girl was a most extraordinary circumstance. I wish they would put those people out. Of course, I know that you—— There! The little one has swiped at him at last."

After a time he resumed his oration. "Of course, I know that you are not reformed in the matter of this uproar and this remarkable consumption of bad wine. It is not that. It is a fact that there are indications that some other citizen was fortunate enough to possess your napkin before you, and moreover you are sure that you would hate to be caught by your correct friends with any such consomme in front of you as we had to-night. You have got an eye suddenly for all kinds of gilt. You are in the way of becoming a most unbearable person. Oh, look—the little one and the proprietor are having it now. You are in the way of becoming a most unbearable person. Presently many of your friends will not be fine enough. In heaven's name, why don't they throw him out? Are they going to howl and gesticulate there all night?"

"Well," said Hawker, "a man would be a fool if he did like this dinner."

"Certainly. But what an immaterial part in the glory of this joint is the dinner. Who cares about the dinner? No one comes here to eat—that's what you always claimed. Well, there, at last they are throwing him out. I hope he lands on his head. Really, you know, Billie, it is such a fine thing being in love that one is sure to be detestable to the rest of the world, and that is the reason they created a proverb to the other effect. You want to look out."

"You talk like a blasted old granny," said Hawker. "Haven't changed at all. This place is all right. Only——"

"You are gone," interrupted Hollanden in a sad voice. "It is very plain. You are gone."

CHAPTER XXVIII

THE proprietor of the place, having pushed to the street the little man who may have been the most vehement, came again and resumed the discussion with the remainder of the men of war. Many of these had volunteered, and they were very enduring.

"Yes, you are gone," said Hollanden, with the sobriety of graves in his voice. "You are gone! Hi," he cried, "there is Lucian Pontiac! Hi, Pontiac! Sit down here!"

A man with a tangle of hair and with that about his mouth which showed that he had spent many years in manufacturing a proper modesty with which to bear his greatness, came toward them smiling.

"Hello, Pontiac," said Hollanden. "Here's another great painter. Do you know Mr. Hawker? Mr. William Hawker—Mr. Pontiac."

"Mr. Hawker—delighted," said Pontiac. "Although I have not known you personally, I can assure you that I have long been a great admirer of your abilities."

The proprietor of the place and the men of war had at length agreed to come to an amicable understanding. They drank liquors, while each firmly but now silently upheld his dignity.

"Charming place," said Pontiac. "So thoroughly Parisian in spirit. And from time to time, Mr. Hawker, I use one of your models. Must say she has the best arm and wrist in the universe. Stunning figure—stunning."

"You mean Florinda?" said Hawker.

"Yes. That's the name. Very fine girl. Lunches with me from time to time and chatters so volubly. That's how I learned you posed her occasionally. If the models didn't gossip, we would never know what painters were addicted to profanity. Now that old Thorndike—he told me you swore like a drill-sergeant if the model winked a finger at the critical time. Very fine girl, Florinda. And honest, too. Honest as the devil. Very curious thing. Of course, honesty among the girl models is very common, very common—quite universal thing, you know—but then it always strikes me as being very curious, very curious. I've been much attracted by your girl, Florinda."

"My girl?" said Hawker.

"Well, she always speaks of you in a proprietory way, you know. And then she considers that she owes you some kind of obedience and allegiance and devotion. I remember last week I said to her: 'You can go now. Come again Friday.' But she said: 'I don't think I can come on Friday. Billie Hawker is home now, and he may want me then.' Said I: 'The devil take Billie Hawker. He hasn't engaged you for Friday, has he? Well, then, I engage you now.' But she shook her head. No, she couldn't come on Friday. Billie Hawker was home, and he might want her any day. 'Well, then,' said I, 'you have my permission to do as you please, since you are resolved upon it anyway. Go to your Billie Hawker.' Did you need her on Friday?"

"No," said Hawker.

"Well, then, the minx, I shall scold her. Stunning figure—stunning. It was only last week that old Charley Master said to me mournfully: 'There are no more good models. Great Scott, not a one.' 'You're 'way off, my boy,' I said. 'There is one good model.' And then I named your girl. I mean the girl who claims to be yours."

"Poor little beggar," said Hollanden.

"Who?" said Pontiac.

"Florinda," answered Hollanden. "I suppose——"

Pontiac interrupted. "Oh, of course, it is too bad. Everything is too bad. My dear sir, nothing is so much to be regretted as the universe. But this Florinda is such a sturdy young soul. The world is against her, but, bless your heart, she is equal to the battle. She is strong in the manner of a little child. Why, you don't know her. She——"

"I know her very well."

"Well, perhaps you do, but for my part I think you don't appreciate her formidable character. And stunning figure—stunning."

"Damn it," said Hawker to his coffee cup, which he had accidentally overturned.

"Well," resumed Pontiac, "she is a stunning model and I think, Mr. Hawker, you are to be envied."

"Eh?" said Hawker.

"I wish I could inspire my models with such obedience and devotion. Then I would not be obliged to rail at them for being late and have to badger them for not showing up at all. She has a beautiful figure—beautiful."

CHAPTER XXIX

WHEN Hawker went again to the house of the great windows, he looked first at the colossal chandelier, and perceiving that it had not moved, he smiled in a certain friendly and familiar way.

"It must be a fine thing," said the girl, dreamily. "I always feel envious of that sort of life."

"What sort of life?"

"Why—I don't know exactly—but there must be a great deal of freedom about it. I went to a studio tea once, and——"

"A studio tea! Merciful heavens! Go on."

"Yes. A studio tea. Don't you like them? To be sure, we didn't know whether the man could paint very well, and I suppose you think it is an imposition for any one who is not a great painter to give a tea."

"Go on."

"Well, he had the dearest little Japanese servants, and some of the cups came from Algiers and some from Turkey and some from—— What's the matter?"

"Go on. I'm not interrupting you."

"Well, that's all. Excepting that everything was charming in color and I thought what a lazy, beautiful life the man must lead, lounging in such a studio, smoking monogrammed cigarettes and remarking how badly all the other men painted."

"Very fascinating. But——"

"Oh, you are going to ask if he could draw. I'm sure I don't know, but the tea that he gave was charming."

"I was on the verge of telling you something about artist life, but if you have seen a lot of draperies and drank from a cup of Algiers, you know all about it."

"You, then, were going to make it something very terrible and tell how young painters struggled and all that."

"No, not exactly. But listen. I suppose there is an aristocracy who, whether they paint well or paint ill, certainly do give charming teas, as you say, and all other kinds of charming affairs, too, but when I hear people talk as if that was the whole life it makes my hair rise, you know, because I am sure that as they get to know me better and better they will see how I fall short of that kind of an existence, and I shall probably take a great tumble in their estimation. They might even conclude that I cannot paint, which would be very unfair, because I can paint, you know."

"Well, proceed to arrange my point of view so that you sha'n't tumble in my estimation when I discover that you don't lounge in a studio, smoke monogrammed cigarettes and remark how badly the other men paint."

"That's it. That's precisely what I wish to do."

"Begin."

"Well, in the first place——"

"In the first place—what?"

"Well, I started to study when I was very poor, you understand. Look here, I'm telling you these things because I want you to know, somehow. It isn't that I'm not ashamed of it. Well, I began very poor, and I—as a matter of fact—I—well, I earned myself over half the money for my studying and the other half I bullied and badgered and beat out of my poor old dad. I worked pretty hard in Paris and I returned here expecting to become a great painter at once. I didn't, though. In fact, I had my worst moments then. It lasted for some years. Of course, the faith and endurance of my father was by this time worn to a shadow. This time when I needed him the most. However, things got a little better and a little better, until I found that by working quite hard I could make what was to me a fair income. That's where I am now, too."

"Why are you so ashamed of this story?"

"The poverty."

"Poverty isn't anything to be ashamed of."

"Great heavens, have you the temerity to get off that old nonsensical remark. Poverty is everything to be ashamed of. Did you ever see a person not ashamed of his poverty? Certainly not. Of course when a man gets very rich he will brag so loudly of the poverty of his youth that one would never suppose that he was once ashamed of it. But he was."

"Well, anyhow, you shouldn't be ashamed of the story you have just told me."

"Why not? Do you refuse to allow me the great right of being like other men?"

"I think it was—brave, you know."

"Brave—nonsense. Those things are not brave. Impression to that effect created by the men who have been through the mill for the greater glory of the men who have been through the mill."

"I don't like to hear you talk that way. It sounds wicked, you know."

"Well, it certainly wasn't heroic. I can remember distinctly that there was not one heroic moment."

"No, but it was—it was——"

"It was what?"

"Well, somehow I like it, you know."

CHAPTER XXX

T HERE'S three of them," said Grief, in a hoarse whisper.
"Four, I tell you!" said Wrinkles, in a low, excited
tone.

"Four!" breathed Pennoyer, with decision.

They held fierce pantomimic argument. From the corridor
came sounds of rustling dresses and rapid feminine conversation.

Grief had kept his ear to the panel of the door. His hand was
stretched back warning the others to silence. Presently he turned
his head and whispered: "Three!"

"Four!" whispered Pennoyer and Wrinkles.

"Hollie is there, too," whispered Grief. "Billie is unlocking the
door. Now, they're going in. Hear them cry out, 'Oh, isn't it
lovely!' Jinks!" He began a noiseless dance about the room. "Jinks,
don't I wish I had a big studio and a little reputation. Wouldn't
I have my swell friends come to see me and wouldn't I entertain
'em." He adopted a descriptive manner and with his forefinger
indicated various spaces of the wall. "Here is a little thing I did
in Brittany. Peasant woman in sabots. This brown spot here is
the peasant woman and those two white things are the sabots.
Peasant woman in sabots, don't you see? Women in Brittany,
of course, all wear sabots, you understand. Convenience of the
painters. I see you are looking at that little thing I did in Morocco. Ah, you admire it? Well, not so bad—not so bad. Arab
smoking pipe squatting in doorway. This long streak here is the
pipe. Clever, you say? Oh, thanks. You are too kind. Well, all
Arabs do that, you know. Sole occupation. Convenience of the
painters. Now, this little thing here I did in Venice. Grand canal,
you know. Gondolier leaning on his oar. Convenience of the
painters. Oh, yes, American subjects are well enough, but hard

to find, you know, hard to find. Morocco, Venice, Brittany, Holland—all ablaze with color, you know—quaint form—all that. We are so hideously modern over here. And besides nobody has painted us much. How the devil can I paint America when nobody has done it before me? My dear sir, are you aware that that would be originality? Good heavens! We are not aesthetic, you understand. Oh, yes, some good mind comes along and understands a thing and does it, and after that it is aesthetic—yes, of course, but then—well—— Now, here is a little Holland thing of mine—it——"

The others had evidently not been heeding him. "Shut up," said Wrinkles, suddenly. "Listen." Grief paused his harangue and they sat in silence, their lips apart, their eyes from time to time exchanging eloquent messages. A dulled melodious babble came from Hawker's studio.

At length Pennoyer murmured wistfully: "I would like to see her."

Wrinkles started noiselessly to his feet. "Well, I tell you she's a peach. I was going up the steps, you know, with a loaf of bread under my arm when I chanced to look up the street and saw Billie and Hollanden coming with four of them."

"Three," said Grief.

"Four! And I tell you I scattered. One of the two with Billie was a peach—a peach."

"Oh, lord," groaned the others, enviously. "Billie's in luck."

"How do you know," said Wrinkles. "Billie is a blamed good fellow, but that doesn't say she will care for him—more likely that she won't."

They sat again in silence, grinning and listening to the murmur of voices.

There came the sound of a step in the hallway. It ceased at a point opposite the door of Hawker's studio. Presently it was heard again. Florinda entered the den. "Hello," she cried. "Who is over in Billie's place. I was just going to knock——"

They motioned at her violently. "Sh," they whispered. Their countenances were very impressive.

"What's the matter with you fellows," asked Florinda, in her ordinary tone. Whereupon they made gestures of still greater wildness. "S-s-sh."

Florinda lowered her voice properly. "Who is over there?"

"Some swells," they whispered.

Florinda bended her head. Presently she gave a little start. "Who is over there?" Her voice became a tone of deep awe. "She?"

Wrinkles and Grief exchanged a swift glance. Pennoyer said gruffly: "Who do you mean?"

"Why," said Florinda, "you know. She. The—the girl that Billie likes."

Pennoyer hesitated for a moment, and then said wrathfully: "Of course she is! Who do you suppose?"

"Oh," said Florinda. She took a seat upon the divan, which was privately a coal box, and unbuttoned her jacket at the throat. "Is she—is she—very handsome, Wrink?"

Wrinkles replied stoutly: "No."

Grief said: "Let's make a sneak down the hall to the little unoccupied room at the front of the building and look from the window there. When they go out we can pipe 'em off."

"Come on," they exclaimed, accepting this plan with glee.

Wrinkles opened the door and seemed about to glide away, when he suddenly turned and shook his head. "It's dead wrong," he said, ashamed.

"Oh, go on," eagerly whispered the others. Presently they stole pattering down the corridor, grinning, exclaiming and cautioning each other.

At the window Pennoyer said: "Now, for heaven's sake, don't let them see you. Be careful, Grief, you'll tumble. Don't lean on me that way, Wrink. Think I'm a barn door? Here they come. Keep back. Don't let them see you."

"O-o-oh," said Grief. "Talk about a peach. Well, I should say so."

Florinda's fingers tore at Wrinkles' coat sleeve. "Wrink, Wrink, is that her? Is that her? On the left of Billie? Is that her, Wrink?"

"What? Yes. Stop pinching me. Yes, I tell you. That's her. Are you deaf?"

IN the evening Pennoyer conducted Florinda to the flat of many fire escapes. After a period of silent tramping through the great golden avenue and the street that was being repaired, she said: "Penny, you are very good to me."

"Why?" said Pennoyer.

"Oh, because you are. You—you are very good to me, Penny."

"Well, I guess I'm not killing myself."

"There isn't many fellows like you."

"No?"

"No. There isn't many fellows like you, Penny. I tell you most everything and you just listen and don't argue with me and tell me I'm a fool because you know that it—because you know that it can't be helped anyhow."

"Oh, nonsense, you kid. Almost anybody would be glad to——"

"Penny, do you think she is very beautiful?" Florinda's voice had a singular quality of awe in it.

"Well," replied Pennoyer, "I don't know."

"Yes, you do, Penny. Go ahead and tell me."

"Well——"

"Go ahead."

"Well, she is rather handsome, you know."

"Yes," said Florinda, dejectedly. "I suppose she is." After a time she cleared her throat and remarked indifferently: "I suppose Billie cares a lot for her?"

"Oh, I imagine that he does. In a way."

"Why, of course he does," insisted Florinda. "What do you mean by 'in a way'? You know very well that Billie thinks his eyes of her."

"No, I don't."

"Yes you do. You know you do. You are talking in that way just to brace me up. You know you are."

"No, I'm not."

"Penny," said Florinda, thankfully, "what makes you so good to me?"

"Oh, I guess I'm not so astonishingly good to you. Don't be silly."

"But you are good to me, Penny. You don't make fun of me the way—the way the other boys would. You are just as good as you can be. But you do think she is beautiful, don't you?"

"They wouldn't make fun of you," said Pennoyer.

"But do you think she is beautiful?"

"Look here, Splutter, let up on that, will you? You keep harping on one string all the time. Don't bother me."

"But, honest now, Penny, you do think she is beautiful?"

"Well, then, confound it—no. No. No."

"Oh, yes, you do, Penny. Go ahead now. Don't deny it just because you are talking to me. Own up now, Penny. You do think she is beautiful?"

"Well," said Pennoyer, in a dull roar of irritation, "do you?"

Florinda walked in silence, her eyes upon the yellow flashes which lights sent to the pavement. In the end she said: "Yes."

"Yes, what?" asked Pennoyer sharply.

"Yes, she—yes, she is—beautiful."

"Well, then?" cried Pennoyer, abruptly closing the discussion.

Florinda announced something as a fact. "Billie thinks his eyes of her."

"How do you know he does?"

"Don't scold at me, Penny. You—you——"

"I'm not scolding at you. There! What a goose you are, Splutter. Don't for heaven's sake go to whimpering on the street. I didn't say anything to make you feel that way. Come, pull yourself together."

"I'm not whimpering."

"No, of course not; but then you look as if you were on the edge of it. What a little idiot!"

CHAPTER XXXII

WHEN the snow fell upon the clashing life of the city, the exiled stones, beaten by myriad strange feet, were told of the dark silent forests where the flakes swept through the hemlocks and swished softly against the boulders.

In his studio Hawker smoked a pipe, clasping his knee with thoughtful interlocked fingers. He was gazing sourly at his finished picture. Once he started to his feet with a cry of vexation. Looking back over his shoulder, he swore an insult into the face of the picture. He paced to and fro smoking belligerently and from time to time eyeing it. The helpless thing remained upon the easel facing him.

Hollanden entered and stopped abruptly at sight of the great scowl. "What's wrong, now?" he said.

Hawker gestured at the picture. "That dunce of a thing. It makes me tired. It isn't worth a hang. Blame it!"

"What?" Hollanden strode forward and stood before the painting with legs apart in a properly critical manner. "What? Why, you said it was your best thing."

"Aw," said Hawker, waving his arms, "it's no good. I abominate it. I didn't get what I wanted, I tell you. I didn't get what I wanted. That?" he shouted, pointing thrust-way at it. "That? It's vile. Aw, it makes me weary."

"You're in a nice state," said Hollanden, turning to take a critical view of the painter. "What has got into you now. I swear —you are more kinds of a chump!"

Hawker crooned dismally. "I can't paint. I can't paint for a damn. I'm no good. What in thunder was I invented for, anyhow, Hollie?"

"You're a fool," said Hollanden. "I hope to die if I ever saw such a complete idiot. You give me a pain. Just because she don't——"

"It isn't that. She has nothing to do with it, although I know well enough—I know well enough——"

"What?"

"I know well enough she doesn't care a hang for me. It isn't that. It is because—it is because I can't paint. Look at that thing over there. Remember the thought and energy I—— Damn the thing."

"Why, did you have a row with her?" asked Hollanden, perplexed. "I didn't know——"

"No, of course, you didn't know," cried Hawker, sneering. "Because I had no row. It isn't that, I tell you. But I know well enough"—he shook his fist, vaguely—"that she don't care an old tomato can for me. Why should she?" he demanded, with a curious defiance. "In the name of heaven, why should she?"

"I don't know," said Hollanden. "I don't know, I'm sure. But then, women have no social logic. This is the great blessing of the world. There is only one thing which is superior to the multiplicity of social forms, and that is a woman's mind—a young woman's mind. Oh, of course, sometimes they are logical, but let a woman be so once and she will repent of it to the end of her days. The safety of the world's balance lies in woman's illogical mind. I think— "

"Go to blazes," said Hawker. "I don't care what you think. I am sure of one thing, and that is that she doesn't care a hang for me."

"I think," Hollanden continued, "that society is doing very well in its work of bravely lawing away at Nature, but there is one immovable thing—a woman's illogical mind. That is our safety. Thank heaven, it——"

"Go to blazes," said Hawker again.

CHAPTER XXXIII

AS Hawker again entered the room of the great windows he glanced in sidelong bitterness at the chandelier. When he was seated, he looked at it in open defiance and hatred.

Men in the street were shovelling at the snow. The noise of their instruments scraping on the stones came plainly to Hawker's ears in a harsh chorus, and this sound at this time was perhaps to him a miserere.

"I came to tell you," he began. "I came to tell you that perhaps I am going away."

"Going away?" she cried. "Where?"

"Well, I don't know—quite. You see I am rather indefinite as yet. I thought of going for the winter somewhere in the Southern States. I am decided merely this much, you know—I am going somewhere. But I don't know where. 'Way off, anyhow."

"We shall be very sorry to lose you," she remarked. "We——"

"And I thought," he continued, "that I would come and say 'adios' now for fear that I might leave very suddenly. I do that sometimes. I'm afraid you will forget me very soon, but I want to tell you that——"

"Why," said the girl in some surprise, "you speak as if you were going away for all time. You surely do not mean to utterly desert New York?"

"I think you misunderstand me," he said. "I give this important air to my farewell to you because to me it is a very important event. Perhaps you recollect that once I told you that I cared for you. Well, I still care for you and so I can only go away somewhere—some place 'way off—where—where—— See?"

"New York is a very large place," she observed.

"Yes, New York is a very large—— How good of you to remind me. But then you don't understand. You can't understand. I know I can find no place where I will cease to remember you, but then I can find some place where I can cease to remember in a way that I am myself. I shall never try to forget you. Those two violets, you know—one I found near the tennis court and the other you gave me, you remember—I shall take them with me."

"Here," said the girl, tugging at her gown for a moment. "Here. Here's a third one." She thrust a violet toward him.

"If you were not so serenely insolent," said Hawker, "I would think that you felt sorry for me. I don't wish you to feel sorry for me. And I don't wish to be melodramatic. I know it is all commonplace enough, and I didn't mean to act like a tenor. Please don't pity me."

"I don't," she replied. She gave the violet a little fling.

Hawker lifted his head suddenly and glowered at her. "No, you don't," he at last said slowly, "you don't. Moreover there is no reason why you should take the trouble. But——"

He paused when the girl leaned and peered over the arm of her chair precisely in the manner of a child at the brink of a fountain. "There's my violet on the floor," she said. "You treated it quite contemptuously, didn't you?"

"Yes."

Together they stared at the violet. Finally he stooped and took it in his fingers. "I feel as if this third one was pelted at me, but I shall keep it. You are rather a cruel person, but, heaven guard us, that only fastens a man's love the more upon a woman."

She laughed. "That is not a very good thing to tell a woman."

"No," he said gravely, "it is not, but then I fancy that somebody may have told you previously."

She stared at him and then said: "I think you are revenged for my serene insolence."

"Great heavens, what an armor," he cried. "I suppose after all, I did feel a trifle like a tenor when I first came here, but you have chilled it all out of me. Let's talk upon indifferent topics." But he started abruptly to his feet. "No," he said, "let us not talk upon indifferent topics. I am not brave, I assure you, and it—it might be too much for me." He held out his hand. "Good-by."

"You are going?"

"Yes, I am going. Really I didn't think how it would bore you for me to come around here and croak in this fashion."

"And you are not coming back for a long, long time?"

"Not for a long, long time." He mimicked her tone. "I have the three violets, now, you know, and you must remember that I took the third one even when you flung it at my head. That will remind you how submissive I was in my devotion. When you recall the two others, it will remind you of what a fool I was. Dare say you won't miss three violets."

"No," she said.

"Particularly the one you flung at my head. That violet was certainly freely-given."

"I didn't fling it at your head." She pondered for a time with her eyes upon the floor. Then she murmured: "No more freely-given than the one I gave you that night—that night at the inn."

"So very good of you to tell me so."

Her eyes were still upon the floor.

"Do you know," said Hawker, "it is very hard to go away and leave an impression in your mind that I am a fool. That is very hard. Now, you do think I am a fool, don't you?"

She remained silent. Once she lifted her eyes and gave him a swift look with much indignation in it.

"Now you are enraged. Well, what have I done?"

It seemed that some tumult was in her mind, for she cried out to him at last in sudden tearfulness: "Oh, do go. Go. Please. I want you to go."

Under this swift change, Hawker appeared as a man struck from the sky. He sprang to his feet, took two steps forward and spoke a word which was an explosion of delight and amazement. He said: "What?"

With heroic effort, she slowly raised her eyes until, a-light with anger, defiance, unhappiness, they met his eyes.

Later, she told him that he was perfectly ridiculous.

ACTIVE SERVICE

CHAPTER I

MARJORY walked pensively along the hall. In the cold shadows made by the palms on the window ledge, her face wore the expression of thoughtful melancholy expected on the faces of the devotees who pace in cloistered gloom. She halted before a door at the end of the hall and laid her hand upon the knob. She stood hesitating, her head bowed. It was evident that this mission was to require great fortitude.

At last, she opened the door. "Father," she began at once. There was disclosed an elderly narrow-faced man seated at a large table and surrounded by manuscripts and books. The sunlight flowing through curtains of Turkey red fell sanguinely upon the bust of dead-eyed Pericles on the mantle. A little clock was ticking, hidden somewhere among the countless leaves of writing, the maps and broad heavy tomes that swarmed upon the table.

Her father looked up quickly with an ogrish scowl. "Go away!" he cried in a rage. "Go away! Go away! Get out!" He seemed on the point of arising to eject the visitor. It was plain to her that he had been interrupted in the writing of one of his sentences, ponderous, solemn and endless, in which wandered multitudes of homeless and friendless prepositions, adjectives looking for a parent, and quarreling nouns, sentences which no longer symbolized the language form of thought but which had about them a quaint aroma from the dens of long-dead scholars. "Get out," snarled the professor.

"Father," faltered the girl. Either because his formulated thought was now completely knocked out of his mind by his own emphasis in defending it or because he detected something of portent in her expression, his manner suddenly changed and with a petulant glance at his writing he laid down his pen and sank back in his chair to listen. "Well, what is it, my child?"

The girl took a chair near the window and gazed out upon the snow-stricken campus, where at that moment a group of students returning from a class-room were festively hurling snowballs. "I've got something important to tell you, father," said she, "but I don't quite know how to say it."

"Something important?" repeated the professor. He was not habitually interested in the affairs of his family but this proclamation that something important could be connected with them, filled his mind with a capricious interest. "Well, what is it, Marjory?"

She replied calmly: "Rufus Coleman wants to marry me."

"What?" demanded the professor loudly. "Rufus Coleman. What do you mean?"

The girl glanced furtively at him. She did not seem to be able to frame a suitable sentence.

As for the professor, he had, like all men both thoughtful and thoughtless, told himself that one day his daughter would come to him with a tale of this kind. He had never forgotten that the little girl was to be a woman and he had never forgotten that this tall lithe creature, the present Marjory, was a woman. He had been entranced and confident or entranced and apprehensive, according to the time. A man focussed upon astronomy, the pig-market or social progression, may nevertheless have a secondary mind which hovers like a spirit over his dahlia tubers and dreams upon the mystery of their slow and tender revelations. The professor's secondary mind had dwelt always with his daughter and watched with faith and delight the changing to a woman of a certain fat and mumbling babe. However he now saw this machine, this self-sustaining, self-operative love, which had run with the ease of a clock, suddenly crumble to ashes and leave the mind of a great scholar staring at a calamity. "Rufus Coleman," he repeated stunned. Here was his daughter very obviously desirous of marrying Rufus Coleman. "Marjory," he cried in amazement and fear, "what possesses you? Marry Rufus Coleman!"

The girl seemed to feel a strong sense of relief at this prompt recognition of a fact. Being freed from the necessity of making a flat declaration, she simply hung her head and blushed impressively. A hush fell upon them. The professor stared long at his daughter. The shadow of unhappiness deepened upon his face. "Marjory! Marjory!" he murmured at last. He had trampled heroically upon his panic and devoted his strength to bringing thought into some kind of attitude toward this terrible fact. "I am—I am surprised," he began. Fixing her then with a stern eye he asked: "Why do you wish to marry this man? You with your opportunities of meeting persons of intelligence. And you want to marry——" His voice grew tragic. "You want to marry the Sunday Editor of the *New York Eclipse*."

"It is not so very terrible, is it?" said Marjory sullenly.

"Wait a moment; don't talk," cried the professor. He arose and walked nervously to and fro, his hands flying in the air. He was very red behind the ears as when in the class-room some student offended him. "A gambler, a sporter of fine clothes, an expert on champagne, a polite loafer, a witless knave who edits the Sunday edition of a great outrage upon our sensibilities! You want to marry him, this man? Marjory, you are insane! This fraud who asserts that his work is intelligent, this fool comes here to my house and——"

He became aware that his daughter was regarding him coldly. "I thought we had best have all this part of it over at once," she remarked.

He confronted her in a new kind of surprise. The little keen-eyed professor was at this time imperial, on the verge of a majestic outburst. "Be still," he said. "Don't be clever with your father. Don't be a dodger. Or, if you are, don't speak of it to me. I suppose this fine young man expects to see me personally?"

"He was coming tomorrow," replied Marjory. She began to weep. "He was coming tomorrow."

"Um," said the professor. He continued his pacing while Marjory wept with her head bowed to the arm of the chair. His brow made the three dark vertical crevices well-known to his students. Sometimes he glowered murderously at the photographs of ancient temples which adorned the walls. "My poor child," he said once as he paused near her, "to think I never knew you were a fool. I have been deluding myself. It has been my fault quite as much as it has been yours. I will not readily forgive myself."

The girl raised her face and looked at him. Finally resolved to disregard the dishevelment wrought by tears she presented a desperate front with her wet eyes and flushed cheeks. Her hair was disarrayed. "I don't see why you can call me a fool," she said. The pause before this sentence had been so portentous of a wild and rebellious speech that the professor almost laughed now. But still the father for the first time knew that he was being undauntedly faced by his child in his own library, in the presence of three hundred and seventy-two pages of the book that was to be his masterpiece. At the back of his mind he felt a great awe as if his own youthful spirit had come from the past and challenged him with a glance. For a moment he was almost a defeated man. He dropped into a chair. "Does your mother know of this?" he asked mournfully.

"Yes," replied the girl. "She knows. She has been trying to make me give up Rufus."

" 'Rufus'!" cried the professor rejuvenated by anger.

"Well, his name *is* Rufus," said the girl.

"But please do not call him so before me," said the father with icy dignity. "I do not recognize him as being named Rufus. That is a contention of yours which does not arouse my interest. I know him very well as a gambler and a drunkard and if incidentally he is named Rufus, I fail to see any importance to it."

"He is not a gambler and he is not a drunkard," she said.

"Um. He drinks heavily—that is well-known. He gambles. He plays cards for money—more than he possesses—at least he did when he was in college."

"You often said you liked him when he was in college."

"So I did! So I did!" answered the professor sharply. "I often find myself liking that kind of a boy in college. Don't I know them—those lads with their beer and their poker games in the dead of night with a towel hung over the key-hole. Their habits are often vicious enough but something remains in them through it all and they may go away and do great things. This happens. We know it. It happens with confusing insistence. It destroys theories. There—there is not much to say about it. And sometimes we like this kind of a boy better than we do the—the others. For my part I know of many a pure, pious and fine-minded student that I have positively loathed from a personal point-of-view. But," he added, "this Rufus Coleman, his life in college and his life since, go to prove how often we get off the track. There is no gauge of collegiate conduct whatever, until we can get evidence of the man's work in the world. Your precious scoundrel's evidence is now all in and he is a failure, or worse."

"You are not habitually so fierce in judging people," said the girl.

"I would be if they all wanted to marry my daughter," rejoined the professor. "Rather than let that man make love to you, or even be within a short railway journey of you, I'll cart you off to Europe this winter and keep you there until you forget. If you persist in this silly fancy, I shall at once become medieval."

Marjory had evidently recovered much of her composure. "Yes, father, new climates are always supposed to cure one," she remarked with a kind of lightness.

"It is not so much the old expedient," said the professor musingly, "as it is that I would be afraid to leave you here with no protection against that drinking gambler and gambling drunkard."

"Father, I have to ask you not to use such terms in speaking of the man that I shall marry."

There was a silence. To all intents, the professor remained unmoved. He smote the tips of his fingers thoughtfully together. "Ye—es," he observed. "That sounds reasonable from your standpoint." His eyes studied her face in a long and steady glance. He arose and went into the hall. When he returned he wore his hat and great-coat. He took a book and some papers from the table and went away.

Marjory walked slowly through the halls and up to her room. From a window she could see her father making his way across the campus laboriously against the wind and whirling snow. She watched it, this little black figure, bent forward, patient, steadfast. It was an inferior fact that her father was one of the famous scholars of the generation. To her, he was now a little old man facing the wintry wind. Recollecting herself and Rufus Coleman she began to weep again, wailing amid the ruins of her tumbled hopes. Her skies had turned to paper and her trees were mere bits of green sponge. But amid all this woe appeared the little black image of her father making its way against the storm.

CHAPTER II

IN a high-walled corridor of one of the college buildings, a crowd of students waited amid jostlings and a loud buzz of talk. Suddenly a huge pair of doors flew open and a wedge of young men inserted itself boisterously and deeply into the throng. There was a great scuffle attended by a general banging of books upon heads. The two lower classes engaged in herculean play while members of the two higher classes, standing aloof, devoted themselves strictly to the encouragement of whichever party for a moment lost ground or heart. This was in order to prolong the conflict.

The combat, waged in the desperation of proudest youth, waxed hot and hotter. The wedge had been instantly smitten into a kind of a block of men. It had crumpled into an irregular square and on three sides it was now assailed with remarkable ferocity.

It was a matter of wall meeting wall in terrific rushes during which lads could feel their very hearts leaving them in the compress of friends and foes. They on the outskirts upheld the honor of their classes by squeezing into paper thickness the lungs of those of their fellows who formed the centre of the melee. In some way it resembled a panic at a theater.

The first lance-like attack of the Sophomores had been formidable, but the Freshmen outnumbering their enemies and smarting from continual Sophomoric oppression, had swarmed to the front like drilled collegians and given the arrogant foe the first serious check of the year. Therefore the tall Gothic windows which lined one side of the corridor looked down upon as incomprehensible and enjoyable a tumult as could mark the steps of advanced education. The Seniors and Juniors cheered themselves ill. Long freed from the joy of such meetings, their only means for this kind of recreation was to involve the lower classes and they had never seen the victims fall to with such vigor and courage.

Bits of printed leaves, torn note-books, dismantled collars and cravats, all floated to the floor beneath the feet of the warring hordes. There were no blows; it was a battle by pressure. It was a deadly pushing where the leaders on either side often suffered the most cruel and sickening agony caught thus between phalanxes of shoulders with friend as well as foe contributing to the pain.

Charge after charge of Freshmen beat upon the now compact and organized Sophomores. Then finally the rock began to give slow way. A roar came from the Freshmen and they hurled themselves in a frenzy upon their betters.

To be under the gaze of the Juniors and Seniors is to be in sight of all men and so the Sophomores at this important moment labored with the desperation of the half-doomed to stem the terrible Freshmen.

In the kind of game, it was the time when bad tempers came strongly to the front and in many Sophomore minds a thought arose of the incomparable insolence of the Freshmen. A blow was struck; an infuriated Sophomore had swung an arm high and smote a Freshman.

Although it had seemed that no greater noise could be made by the given numbers, the din that succeeded this manifestation surpassed everything. The Juniors and Seniors immediately set up an angry howl. These veteran classes projected themselves into the middle of the fight, buffeting everybody with small thought as to merit. This method of bringing peace was as militant as a landslide but they had much trouble before they could separate the central clump of antagonists into its parts. A score of Freshmen had cried out: "It was Coke! Coke punched him! Coke!" A dozen of them were tempestuously endeavoring to register their protest against fisticuffs by means of an introduction of more fisticuffs.

The upper classmen were swift, harsh and hard. "Come now Freshies, quit it! Get back! Get back, d'y' hear?" With a wrench of muscles they forced themselves in front of Coke who was being blindly defended by his class-mates from intensely earnest attacks by outraged Freshmen.

These meetings between the lower classes at the door of a recitation room were accounted quite comfortable and idle affairs and a blow delivered openly and in hatred fractured a sharply defined rule of conduct. The corridor was in a hub-bub. Many Seniors and Juniors bursting from old and iron discipline wildly clamored that some Freshman should be given the privilege of a single encounter with Coke. The Freshmen themselves were frantic. They besieged the tight and dauntless circle of men that encompassed Coke. None dared confront the Seniors openly but by headlong rushes at auspicious moments they tried to come to quarters with the rings of dark-browed Sophomores. It was no longer a festival, a game; it was a riot. Coke, wild-eyed, pallid with fury, a ribbon of blood on his chin, swayed in the middle of the mob of his class-mates, comrades who waived the ethics of the blow under the circumstance of being obliged as a corps to stand against the scorn of the whole college as well as against the tremendous assaults of the Freshmen. Shamed by their own man but knowing full well the right time and the wrong time for a palaver of regret and disavowal, this battalion struggled in the desperation of despair. Once they were upon the verge of making unholy campaign against the interfering Seniors. This fiery impertinence was the measure of their state.

It was a critical moment in the play of the college. Four or five defeats from the Sophomores during the fall had taught the Freshmen much. They had learned the comparative measurements and they knew now that their prowess was ripe to enable them to amply revenge what was according to their standards an execrable deed by a man who had not the virtue to play the rough game but was obliged to resort to uncommon methods. In short the Freshmen were almost out of control and the Sophomores, debased but defiant, were quite out of control. The Senior and Junior classes which in most American colleges dictate in these affrays found their dignity toppling and in consequence there was a sudden on-come of the entire force of upper classmen, foot-ball players naturally in advance. All distinctions were dissolved at once in a general fracas. The stiff and still Gothic windows surveyed a scene of dire carnage.

Suddenly a voice rang brazenly through the tumult. It was not loud but it was different. "Gentlemen! Gentlemen!" Instantly there was a remarkable number of haltings, abrupt replacements, quick changes. Professor Wainwright stood at the door of his recitation room looking into the eyes of each member of the mob of three hundred. "Ssh!" said the mob. "Ssh! Quit! Stop! It's the Embassador! Stop!" He had once been minister to Austro-Hungary and forever now to the students of the college his name was Embassador. He stepped into the corridor and they cleared for him a little respectful zone of floor. He looked about him coldly. "It seems a quite general dishevelment. The Sophomores display an energy in the halls which I do not detect in the class-room." A feeble murmur of appreciation arose from the outskirts of the throng. While he had been speaking several remote groups of battling men had been violently signaled and suppressed by other students. The professor gazed into terraces of faces that were still inflamed. "I need not say that I am surprised," he remarked in the accepted rhetoric of his kind. He added musingly: "There seems to be a great deal of torn linen. Who is the young gentleman with blood on his chin?"

The throng moved restlessly. A manful silence such as might be in the tombs of stern and honorable knights, fell upon the shadowed corridor. The subdued rustling had fainted to nothing. Then out of the crowd Coke, pale and desperate, delivered himself.

"Oh, Mr. Coke," said the professor, "I would be glad if you would tell the gentlemen they may retire to their dormitories." He waited while the students passed out to the campus.

The professor returned to his room for some books and then began his march across the snowy campus. The wind twisted his coat-tails fantastically and he was obliged to keep one hand firmly on the top of his hat. When he arrived home he met his wife in the hall. "Look here, Mary," he cried. She followed him into the library. "Look here," he said. "What is this all about? Marjory tells me that she wants to marry Rufus Coleman!"

Mrs. Wainwright was a fat woman who was said to pride herself upon being very wise and if necessary sly. In addition she laughed continually in an inexplicably personal way which made everybody who heard her feel offended. Mrs. Wainwright laughed.

"Well," said the professor bristling, "what do you mean by that?"

"Oh, Harris!" she replied. "Oh, Harris!"

The professor straightened in his chair. "I do not see any illumination in those remarks, Mary. I understand from Marjory's manner that she is bent upon marrying Rufus Coleman. She said you knew of it."

"Why of course I knew! It was as plain!"

" 'Plain'!" scoffed the professor. " 'Plain'!"

"Why, of course," she cried. "I knew it all along." There was nothing in her tone which proved that she admired the event itself. She was evidently carried away by the triumph of her penetration. "I knew it all along," she added nodding.

The professor looked at her affectionately. "You knew it all along then, Mary? Why didn't you tell me, dear?"

"Because you ought to have known," she answered blatantly.

The professor was glaring. Finally he spoke in tones of grim reproach. "Mary, whenever you happen to know anything, dear, it seems only a matter of partial recompense that you should tell me."

The wife had been taught in a terrible school that she should never invent any inexpensive retorts concerning bookworms, and so she yawed at once. "Really, Harris. Really I didn't suppose the affair was serious. You could have knocked me down with a feather. Of course he has been here very often but then Marjory gets a great deal of attention. A great deal of attention."

The professor had been thinking. "Rather than let my girl marry that scallywag I'll take you and her to Greece this winter with the class. Separation! It is a cure that has the sanction of antiquity."

"Well," said Mrs. Wainwright, "you know best, Harris. You know best." It was a common remark with her and it probably meant either approbation or disapprobation if it did not mean simple discretion.

CHAPTER III

THERE had been a babe with no arms born in one of the western counties of Massachusetts. In place of upper limbs the child had growing from its chest a pair of fin-like hands, mere bits of skin covered bones. Furthermore it had only one eye. This phenomenon lived four days but the news of the birth had travelled up this country-road and through that village until it had reached the ears of the editor of the *Michaelstown Tribune*. He was also a correspondent of the *New York Eclipse*. On the third day he appeared at the home of the parents accompanied by a photographer. While the latter arranged his instrument, the correspondent talked to the father and mother, two cow-eyed and yellow-faced people who seemed to suffer a primitive fright of the strangers. Afterward as the correspondent and the photographer were climbing into their buggy, the mother crept furtively down to the gate and asked, in a foreigner's dialect, if they would send her a copy of the photograph. The correspondent, carelessly indulgent, promised it. As the buggy swung away, the father came from behind an apple tree and the two semi-humans watched it with its burden of glorious strangers until it rumbled across the bridge and disappeared. The correspondent was elate; he told the photographer that the *Eclipse* would probably pay fifty dollars for the article and the photograph.

The office of the *New York Eclipse* was at the top of an immense building on Broadway. It was a sheer mountain to the heights of which the interminable thunder of the streets arose faintly. The Hudson was a broad path of silver in the distance. Its edge was marked by the tracery of sailing ships' rigging and by the huge and many-colored stacks of ocean liners. At the foot of the cliff lay City Hall Park. It seemed no larger than a quilt. The grey walks patterned the snow-covering into triangles and ovals and upon them many tiny people scurried here and there, without sound, like fish at the bottom of a pool. It was only the vehicles that sent high, unmistakably, the deep bass of their movement. And yet after listening one seemed to hear a singular murmurous note, a pulsation, as if the crowd made noise by its mere living, a mellow hum of the eternal strife. Then suddenly out of the deeps might ring a human voice, a newsboy shout perhaps, the cry of a faraway jackal at night.

From the level of the ordinary roofs, combined in many plateaus, dotted with short iron chimneys from which curled wisps of steam, arose other mountains like the *Eclipse* Building. They were great peaks, ornate, glittering with paint or polish. Northward they subsided to sun-crowned ranges.

From some of the windows of the *Eclipse* office dropped the walls of a terrible chasm in the darkness of which could be seen vague and struggling figures. Looking down into this appalling crevice one discovered only tops of hats and knees which in spasmodic jerks seemed to touch the rims of the hats. The scene represented some weird fight or dance or carouse. It was not an exhibition of men hurrying along a narrow street.

It was good to turn one's eyes from that place to the vista of the city's splendid reaches, with spire and spar shining in the clear atmosphere and the marvel of the Jersey shore, pearl-misted or brilliant with detail. From this height the sweep of a snow-storm was defined and majestic. Even a slight summer shower, with swords of lurid yellow sunlight piercing its edges as if warriors were contesting every foot of its advance, was, from the *Eclipse* office, something so inspiring that the chance pilgrim felt a sense of exultation as if from this peak he was surveying the world-wide war of the elements and life. The staff of the *Eclipse* usually worked without coats and amid the smoke from pipes.

To one of the editorial chambers came a photograph and an article from Michaelstown, Massachusetts. A boy placed the packet and many others upon the desk of a young man who was standing before a window and thoughtfully drumming upon the pane. He turned at the thudding of the packets upon his desk. "Blast you," he remarked amiably. "Oh, I guess it won't hurt you to work," answered the boy grinning with a comrade's insolence.

Baker, an assistant editor for the Sunday paper, took seat at his desk and began the task of examining the packets. His face could not display any particular interest because he had been at the same work for nearly a fortnight.

The first long envelope he opened was from a woman. There was a neat little manuscript accompanied by a letter which explained that the writer was a widow who was trying to make her living by her pen and who, further, hoped that the generosity of the editor of the *Eclipse* would lead him to give her article the opportunity which she was sure it deserved. She hoped that the editor would pay her as well as possible for it as she needed the money greatly. She added that her brother was a reporter on the *Little Rock Sentinel* and he had declared that her literary style was excellent.

Baker really did not read this note. His vast experience of a fortnight had enabled him to detect its kind in two glances. He unfolded the manuscript, looked at it woodenly and then tossed it with the letter to the top of his desk where it lay with other corpses. None could think of widows in Arkansas, ambitious from the praise of the reporter on the *Little Rock Sentinel,* waiting for a crown of literary glory and money. In the next envelope a man using the note-paper of a Boston journal begged to know if the accompanying article would be acceptable; if not it was to be kindly returned in the enclosed envelope. It was a humorous essay on trolley cars. Adventuring through the odd scraps that were come to the great mill, Baker paused occasionally to re-light his pipe.

As he went through envelope after envelope, the desks about him gradually were occupied by young men who entered from the hall with their faces still red from the cold of the streets. For the most part they bore the unmistakable stamp of the American college. They had that confident poise which is easily brought from the athletic field. Moreover their clothes were quite in the way of being of the newest fashion. There was an air of precision about their cravats and linen. But on the other hand there might be with them some indifferent Westerner who was obliged to resort to irregular means and harangue startled shop-keepers in order to provide himself with collars of a strange kind. He was usually very quick and brave of eye and noted for his inability to perceive a distinction between his own habit and the habit of others, his Western character preserving itself inviolate amid a confusion of manners.

The men, coming one and one, or two and two, flung badinage to all corners of the room. Afterward, as they wheeled from time to time in their chairs, they bitterly insulted each other with the utmost good nature, taking unerring aim at faults and riddling personalities with the quaint and cynical humor of a newspaper office. Throughout the banter, it was strange to note how infrequently the men smiled, particularly when directly engaged in an encounter.

A wide door opened into another apartment where there were many little slanted tables each under an electric globe with a green shade. Here a curly-headed scoundrel with a corn-cob pipe was hurling paper balls of the size of apples at the head of an industrious man who, under these difficulties, was trying to draw a picture of an awful wreck with ghastly-faced sailors frozen in the rigging. Near this pair a lad was challenging a German artist who resembled Napoleon III with having been publicly drunk at a music-hall on the previous night. Next to the great gloomy corridor of this sixteenth floor was a little office presided over by an austere boy and here waited in enforced patience a little dismal band of people who wanted to see the Sunday Editor.

Baker took a manuscript and after glancing about the room walked over to a man at another desk. "Here is something that I think might do," he said. The man at the desk read the first two pages. "But where is the photograph?" he asked then. "There should be a photograph with this thing."

"Oh, I forgot," said Baker. He brought from his desk a photograph of the babe that had been born lacking arms and one eye. Baker's superior braced a knee against his desk and settled back to a judicial attitude. He took the photograph and looked at it impassively. "Yes," he said after a time, "that's a pretty good thing. You better show that to Coleman when he comes in."

In the little office where the dismal band waited there had been a sharp hopeful stir when Rufus Coleman, the Sunday Editor, passed rapidly from door to door and vanished within the holy precincts. It had evidently been in the minds of some to accost him then but his eyes did not turn once in their direction. It was as if he had not seen them. Many experiences had taught him that the proper manner of passing through this office was at a blind gallop.

The dismal band turned then upon the austere office-boy. Some demanded with terrible dignity that he should take in their cards at once. Others sought to ingratiate themselves by smiles of tender friendliness. He for his part employed what he would have called his knowledge of men and women upon the group and in consequence blundered and bungled vividly, freezing with a glance an annoyed and importunate Arctic explorer who was come to talk of illustrations for an article that had been lavishly paid for in advance. The hero might have thought he was again in the northern seas. At the next moment the boy was treating almost courteously a German from the East-side who wanted the *Eclipse* to print a grand full-page advertising description of his invention, a gun which was supposed to have a range of forty miles and to be able to penetrate anything with equanimity and joy. The gun, as a matter of fact, had once been induced to go off when it had hurled itself passionately upon its back, incidentally breaking its inventor's leg. The projectile had wandered some four hundred yards seaward where it had dug a hole in the water which was really a menace to navigation. Since then there had been nothing tangible save the inventor, in splints or out of splints as the fortunes of science decreed. In short, this office-boy mixed his business in the perfect manner of an underdone lad dealing with matters too large for him and, throughout, he displayed the pride and assurance of a god.

As Coleman crossed the large office his face still wore the stern expression which he invariably used to carry him unmolested through the ranks of the dismal band. As he was removing his London over-coat he addressed the imperturbable back of one of his staff who had a desk against the opposite wall. "Has Hasskins sent in that drawing of the mine accident yet?" The man did not lift his head from his work but he answered at once. "No; not yet." Coleman was laying his hat on a chair. "Well, why hasn't he?" he demanded. He glanced toward the door of the room in which the curly-headed scoundrel with the corn-cob pipe was still hurling paper balls at the man who was trying to invent the postures of dead mariners frozen in the rigging. The office-boy came timidly from his post and informed Coleman of the waiting people. "All right," said the editor. He dropped into his chair and began to finger his letters which had been neatly opened and placed in a little stack by a boy. Baker came with the photograph of the miserable babe.

It was publicly believed that the Sunday staff of the *Eclipse* must have a kind of æsthetic delight in pictures of this kind but Coleman's face betrayed no emotion as he looked at this speci-men. He lit a fresh cigar, tilted his chair and surveyed it with a cold and stony stare. "Yes, that's all right," he said slowly. There seemed to be no affectionate relation between him and this pic-ture. Evidently he was weighing its value as a morsel to be flung to a ravenous public whose wolf-like appetite could only satisfy itself upon mental entrails, abominations. As for himself, he seemed to be remote, exterior. It was a matter of the *Eclipse* business.

Suddenly Coleman became executive. "Better give it to—Schooner and tell him to make a half-page—or, no, send him in here and I'll tell him my idea. How's the article? Any good? Well, give it to Smith to rewrite."

An artist came from the other room and presented for inspec-tion his drawing of the seamen dead in the rigging of the wreck, a company of grisly and horrible figures, bony-fingered, shrunken and with awful eyes. "Hum," said Coleman after a prolonged study, "that's all right. That's good, Jimmie. But you'd better work 'em up around the eyes a little more." The office-boy was de-ploying in the distance waiting for the correct moment to present some cards and names.

The artist was cheerfully taking away his corpses when Cole-man hailed him. "Oh, Jim, let me see that thing again, will you? Now how about this spar? This don't look right to me."

"It looks right to me," replied the artist sulkily.

"But see! It's going to take up half a page. Can't you change it somehow?"

"How am I going to change it?" said the other glowering at Coleman. "That's the way it ought to be. How am I going to change it? That's the way it ought to be."

"No, it isn't at all," said Coleman. "You've got a spar sticking out of the main body of the drawing in a way that will spoil the look of the whole page."

The artist was a man of remarkable popular reputation and he was very stubborn and conceited of it, constantly making himself unbearable with covert threats that if he was not delicately placated at all points, he would freight his genius over to the office of the great opposition journal.

"That's the way it ought to be," he repeated in a tone at once sullen and superior. "The spar is all right. I can't rig spars on ships just to suit you."

"And I can't give up the whole paper to your accursed spars either," said Coleman with animation. "Don't you see you use about a third of a page with this spar sticking off into space? Now you were always so clever, Jimmie, in adapting yourself to the page. Can't you shorten it or cut it off or something? Or, break it—that's the thing. Make it a broken spar dangling down. See?"

"Yes, I s'pose I could do that," said the artist mollified by a thought of the ease with which he could make the change and mollified, too, by the brazen tribute to a part of his cleverness.

"Well, do it, then," said the Sunday Editor, turning abruptly away. The artist, with his head high, walked majestically back to the other room. Whereat the curly-headed one immediately resumed the rain of paper balls upon him. The office-boy came timidly to Coleman and suggested the presence of the people in the outer office. "Let them wait until I read my mail," said Coleman. He shuffled the pack of letters indifferently through his hands. Suddenly he came upon a little grey envelope. He opened it at once and scanned its contents with the speed of his craft. Afterward he laid it down before him on the desk and surveyed it with a cool and musing smile. "So?" he remarked. "That's the case, is it?"

He presently swung around in his chair and for a time held the entire attention of the men at the various desks. He outlined to them again their various parts in the composition of the next great Sunday edition. In a few brisk sentences he set a complex machine in proper motion. His men no longer thrilled with admiration at the precision with which he grasped each obligation of the campaign toward a successful edition. They had grown to accept it as they accepted his hat or his London clothes. At this time his face was lit with something of the self-contained enthusiasm of a general. Immediately afterward he arose and reached for his coat and hat.

The office-boy coming circuitously forward, presented him with some cards and also with a scrap of paper upon which was scrawled a long and semi-coherent word. "What are these?" grumbled Coleman.

"They are waiting outside," answered the boy with trepidation. It was part of the law that the lion of the ante-room should cringe like a cold monkey more or less, as soon as he was out of his private jungle. "Oh, Tallerman," called the Sunday Editor, "here's this Arctic man come to arrange about his illustrations. I wish you'd go and talk it over with him." By chance he picked up the scrap of paper with its cryptic word. "Oh," he said, scowling at the office-boy. "Pity you can't remember that fellow. If you can't remember faces any better than that you should be a detective. Get out now and tell him to go to the devil." The wilted slave turned at once but Coleman hailed him. "Hold on. Come to think of it, I will see this idiot. Send him in," he commanded grimly.

Coleman lapsed into a dream over the sheet of grey note-paper. Presently, a middle-aged man, a palpable German, came hesitatingly into the room and bunted among the desks as unmanageably as a tempest-tossed scow. Finally he was impatiently towed in the right direction. He came and stood at Coleman's elbow and waited nervously for the engrossed man to raise his eyes. It was plain that this interview meant important things to him. Somewhere in his common-place countenance was to be found the expression of a dreamer, a fashioner of great and absurd projects, a fine tender fool. He cast hopeful and reverent glances at the man who was deeply contemplative of the grey note. He evidently believed himself on the threshold of a triumph of some kind and he awaited its fruition with a joy that was only made sharper by the usual human suspicion of coming events.

Coleman glanced up at last and saw his visitor. "Oh, it's you, is it?" he remarked icily, bending upon the German the stare of a tyrant. "So you've come again, have you?" He wheeled in his chair until he could fully display a contemptuous merciless smile. "Now, Mr. What's-your-name, you've called here to see me about twenty times already and at last I am going to say something definite about your invention." His listener's face which had worn for a moment a look of fright and bewilderment gladdened swiftly to a gratitude that seemed the edge of an outburst of tears. "Yes," continued Coleman, "I am going to say something definite. I am going to say that it is the most imbecile bit of nonsense that has come within the range of my large newspaper experience. It is simply the aberration of a rather remarkable lunatic. It is no good; it is not worth the price of a cheese-sandwich. I understand that its one feat has been to break your leg; if it ever goes off again, persuade it to break your neck. And now I want you to take this nursery rhyme of yours and get out. And don't ever come here again. Do you understand? You understand, do you?" He arose and bowed in courteous dismissal.

The German was regarding him with the surprise and horror of a youth shot mortally. He could not find his tongue for a moment. Ultimately he gasped: "But, Mister Edidor——" Coleman interrupted him tigerishly. "You heard what I said? Get out!" The man bowed his head and went slowly toward the door.

Coleman placed the little grey note in his breast pocket. He took his hat and top-coat and evading the dismal band by a shameless manœuvre, passed through the halls to the entrance to the elevator shaft. He heard a movement behind him and saw that the German was also waiting for the elevator.

Standing in the gloom of the corridor, Coleman felt the mournful owlish eyes of the German resting upon him. He took a case from his pocket and elaborately lit a cigarette. Suddenly there was a flash of light and a cage of bronze, gilt and steel dropped magically from above. Coleman yelled: "Down." A door flew open. Coleman, followed by the German, stepped upon the elevator. "Well, Johnnie," he said cheerfully to the lad who operated this machine, "is business good?" "Yes, sir, pretty good," answered the boy grinning. The little cage sank swiftly; floor after floor seemed to be rising with marvelous speed; the whole building was winging straight into the sky. There were soaring lights, figures and the opalescent glow of ground-glass doors marked with black inscriptions. Other lifts were springing heavenwards. All the lofty corridors rang with cries. "Up!" "Down!" "Down!" "Up!" The boy's hand grasped a lever and his machine obeyed his slightest movement with sometimes an unbalancing swiftness.

Coleman discoursed briskly to the youthful attendant. Once he turned and regarded with a quick stare of insolent annoyance the despairing countenance of the German whose eyes had never left him. When the elevator arrived at the ground-floor, Coleman departed with the outraged air of a man who for a time has been compelled to occupy a cell in company with a harmless spectre.

He walked quickly away. Opposite a corner of the City Hall he was impelled to look behind him. Through the hordes of people with cable cars marching like panoplied elephants, he was able to distinguish the German, motionless and gazing after him. Coleman laughed. "That's a comic old boy," he said to himself.

In the grill-room of a Broadway hotel he was obliged to wait some minutes for the fulfillment of his orders and he spent the time in reading and studying the little grey note. When his luncheon was served he ate with an expression of morose dignity.

CHAPTER IV

MARJORY paused again at her father's door. After hesitating in the original way she entered the library. Her father almost represented an emblematic figure seated upon a column of books. "Well?" he cried. Then seeing it was Marjory he changed his tone. "Ah, under the circumstances, my dear, I admit your privilege of interrupting me at any hour of the day. You have important business with me." His manner was satanically indulgent.

The girl fingered a book. She turned the leaves in absolute semblance of a person reading. "Rufus Coleman has called."

"Indeed," said the professor.

"And I've come to you, father, before seeing him."

The professor was silent for a time. "Well, Marjory," he said at last, "what do you want me to say?" He spoke very deliberately. "I am sure this is a singular situation. Here appears the man that I formally forbid you to marry. I am sure I do not know what I am to say."

"I wish to see him," said the girl.

"You wish to see him?" enquired the professor. "You wish to see him? Marjory, I may as well tell you now that with all the books and plays I have read, I really do not know how the obdurate father should conduct himself. He is always pictured as an exceedingly dense gentleman with white whiskers who does all the unintelligent things in the plot. You and I are going to play no drama, are we, Marjory? I admit that I have white whiskers and I am an obdurate father. I am, as you well may say, a very obdurate father. You are not to marry Rufus Coleman. I settle that point. You are not to marry Rufus Coleman. You understand the rest of the matter. He is here; you want to see him. What will you say to him when you see him?"

"I will say that you refuse to let me marry him, father,

and——" She hesitated a moment before she lifted her eyes fully and formidably to her father's face. "And that I shall marry him anyhow."

The professor did not cavort when this statement came from his daughter. He nodded and then passed into a period of reflection. Finally he asked: "But when? That is the point. When?"

The girl made a sad gesture. "I don't know. I don't know. Perhaps when you come to know Rufus better——"

"Know him better! Know that rapscallion better! Why I know him much better than he knows himself. I know him too well. Do you think I am talking off-hand about this affair? Do you think I am talking without proper information?"

Marjory made no reply.

"Well," said the professor, "you may see Coleman on condition that you inform him at once that I forbid your marriage to him. I do not understand at all how to manage these situations. I do not know what to do. I suppose I should go myself and—— No, you can not see him, Marjory."

Still the girl made no reply. Her head sank forward and she breathed a trifle heavily.

"Marjory!" cried the professor. "It is impossible that you should think so much of this man!" He arose and went to his daughter. "Marjory, many wise children have been guided by foolish fathers but we both suspect that no foolish child has ever been guided by a wise father. Let us change it. I present myself to you as a wise father. Follow my wishes in this affair and you will be at least happier than if you marry this wretched Coleman."

She answered: "He is waiting for me."

The professor turned abruptly from her and dropped into his chair at the table. He resumed a grip on his pen. "Go!" he said wearily. "Go! But if you have a remnant of sense remember what I have said to you. Go!" He waved his hand in a dismissal that was slightly scornful. "I hoped you would have a minor conception of what you were doing. It seems a pity." Drooping and in tears the girl slowly left the room.

Coleman had an idea that he had occupied the chair for several months. He gazed about at the pictures and the odds and ends of a drawing-room in an attempt to make an interest in them. The great garlanded paper shade over the piano-lamp consoled his impatience in a mild degree because he knew that Marjory had made it. He noted the clusters of cloth violets which she had pinned upon the yellow paper and he dreamed over the fact. He was able to endow this shade with certain qualities of sentiment that caused his stare to become almost a part of an intimacy, a communion. He looked as if he could have unburdened his soul to this shade over the piano-lamp.

Upon the appearance of Marjory he sprang up and came forward rapidly. "Dearest," he murmured, stretching out both hands. She gave him one set of fingers with chilling convention. She said something which he understood to be, "Good afternoon." He started as if the woman before him had suddenly drawn a knife. "Marjory," he cried, "what is the matter." They walked together toward a window. The girl looked at him in polite enquiry. "Why?" she said. "Do I seem strange?"

There was a moment's silence while he gazed into her eyes, eyes full of innocence and tranquillity. At last she tapped her foot upon the floor in expression of mild impatience. "People do not like to be asked what is the matter when there is nothing the matter. What do you mean?"

Coleman's face had gradually hardened. "Well, what is wrong?" he demanded abruptly. "What has happened? What is it, Marjory?"

She raised her glance in a perfect reality of wonder. " 'What is wrong? What has happened?' How absurd. Why, nothing, of course." She gazed out of the window. "Look," she added brightly, "the students are rolling somebody in the drift. Oh, the poor man!"

Coleman, now wearing a bewildered air, made some pretence of being occupied with the scene. "Yes," he said ironically. "Very interesting, indeed."

"Oh," said Marjory suddenly, "I forgot to tell you! Father is going to take mother and me to Greece this winter with him and the class."

Coleman replied at once. "Ah, indeed? That will be jolly."

"Yes! Won't it be charming?"

"I don't doubt it," he replied. His composure may have displeased her for she glanced at him furtively and in a way that denoted surprise perhaps.

"Oh, of course," she said in a glad voice. "It will be more fun!

We expect to have a fine time. There is such a nice lot of boys going. Sometimes father chooses these dreadfully studious ones. But this time he acts as if he knew precisely how to make up a party."

He reached for her hand and grasped it vise-like. "Marjory," he breathed passionately, "don't treat me so! Don't treat me——"

She wrenched her hand from him in regal indignation. "One or two rings make it uncomfortable for the hand that is grasped by an angry gentleman." She held her fingers and gazed as if she expected to find them mere debris. "I am sorry that you are not interested in the students rolling that man in the snow. It is the greatest scene our quiet life can afford."

He was regarding her as a judge faces a lying culprit. "I know," he said after a pause. "Somebody has been telling you some stories. You have been hearing something about me."

"Some stories?" she enquired. "Some stories about you? What do you mean? Do you mean that I remember stories I may happen to hear about people?"

There was another pause and then Coleman's face flared red. He beat his hand violently upon a table. "Good God, Marjory! Don't make a fool of me! Don't make this kind of a fool of me, at any rate. Tell me what you mean! Explain——"

She laughed at him. " 'Explain'? Really, your vocabulary is getting extensive, but it is dreadfully awkward to ask people to explain when there is nothing to explain."

He glared at her. "I know as well as you do that your father is taking you to Greece in order to get rid of me."

"And do people have to go to Greece in order to get rid of you?" she asked civilly. "I think you are getting excited."

"Marjory——" he began stormily.

She raised her hand. "Hush," she said, "there is somebody coming." A bell had rung. A maid entered the room. "Mr. Coke," she said. Marjory nodded. In the interval of waiting, Coleman gave the girl a glance that mingled despair with rage and pride. Then Coke burst with half-tamed rapture into the room. "Oh, Miss Wainwright," he almost shouted, "I can't tell you how glad I am! I just heard today you were going! Imagine it! It will be more—oh, how are you, Coleman, how are you?"

Marjory welcomed the new-comer with a cordiality that might

not have thrilled Coleman with pleasure. They took chairs that formed a triangle and one side of it vibrated with talk. Coke and Marjory engaged in a tumultuous conversation concerning the prospective trip to Greece. The Sunday Editor, as remote as if the apex of his angle was the top of a hill, could only study the girl's clear profile. The youthful voices of the two others rang like bells. He did not scowl at Coke; he merely looked at him as if he gently disdained his mental calibre. In fact all the talk seemed to tire him; it was idle and childish; as for him, he apparently found this babble almost insupportable.

"And just think of the camel rides we'll have!" cried Coke.

" 'Camel rides'," repeated Coleman dejectedly. "My dear Coke!"

Finally he arose like an old man climbing from a sick-bed. "Well, I am afraid I must go, Miss Wainwright." Then he said affectionately to Coke: "Good-bye, old boy. I hope you have a good time."

Marjory walked with him to the door. He shook her hand in friendly fashion. "Good-bye, Marjory," he said. "Perhaps it may happen that I shan't see you again before you start for Greece and so I had best bid you God-speed—or whatever the term is—now. You will have a charming time; Greece must be a delightful place. Really, I envy you, Marjory! And now my dear child—" His voice grew brotherly, filled with the patronage of generous fraternal love. "—although I may never see you again, let me wish you fifty as happy years as this last one has been for me." He smiled frankly into her eyes; then dropping her hand, he went away.

Coke renewed his tempest of talk even as Marjory turned toward him. But after a series of splendid eruptions whose red fire illumined all of ancient and modern Greece, he too went away.

The professor was in his library apparently absorbed in a book when a tottering pale-faced woman appeared to him and, in her course toward a couch in a corner of the room, described almost a semi-circle. She flung herself face downward. A thick strand of hair swept over her shoulder. "Oh, my heart is broken! My heart is broken!"

The professor arose, grizzled and thrice-old with pain. He went to the couch but he found himself a handless, feckless man. "My poor child," he said. "My poor child." He remained listening stupidly to her convulsive sobbing. A ghastly kind of solemnity came upon the room.

Suddenly the girl lifted herself and swept the strand of hair away from her face. She looked at the professor with the wide-open dilated eyes of one who still sleeps. "Father," she said in a hollow voice, "he don't love me! He don't love me! He don't love me at all. You were right, father." She began to laugh.

"Marjory," said the professor, trembling. "Be quiet, child. Be quiet."

"But," she said, "I thought he loved me.——— I was sure of it.——— But it don't—don't matter. I—I can get over it. Women—women, they——— But it don't matter."

"Marjory!" said the professor. "Marjory, my poor daughter!"

She did not heed this appeal but continued in a dull whisper. "He was playing with me. He was—was—was—flirting with me. He didn't care when I told him—I told him—I was going—going away." She turned her face wildly to the cushions again. Her young shoulders shook as if they might break. "Women—women, they always———"

CHAPTER V

BY a strange mishap of management, the train which bore Coleman back toward New York was fetched into an obscure side-track of some lonely region and there compelled to bide a change of fate. The engine wheezed and sneezed like a paused fat man. The lamps in the cars pervaded a stuffy odor of smoke and oil. Coleman examined his case and found only one cigar. Important brakemen proceeded rapidly along the aisles and when they swung open the doors, a polar wind circled the legs of the passengers. "Well, now, what is all this for?" demanded Coleman furiously. "I want to get back to New York."

The conductor replied with sarcasm: "Maybe you think I'm stuck on it? I ain't running the road. I'm running this train and I run it according to orders." Amid the dismal comforts of the waiting cars Coleman felt all the profound misery of the rebuffed true lover. He had been sentenced, he thought, to a penal servitude of the heart as he watched the dusky vague ribbons of smoke come from the lamps and felt to his knees the cold winds from the brakeman's busy flights. When the train started with a whistle and a jolt, he was elate as if in his abjection his beloved's hand had reached to him from the clouds.

When he had arrived at New York, a cab rattled him to an uptown hotel with speed. In the restaurant he first ordered a large bottle of champagne. The last of the wine he finished in sombre mood like an unbroken and defiant man who chews the straw that litters his prison house. During his dinner he was continually sending out messenger boys. He was arranging a poker party. Through a window he watched the beautiful moving life of upper Broadway at night with its crowds and clanging cable cars and its electric signs, mammoth and glittering like the jewels of a giantess.

Word was brought to him that the poker players were arriving.

He arose joyfully, leaving his cheese. In the broad hall occupied mainly by miscellaneous people and actors, all deep in leather chairs, he found some of his friends waiting. They trooped upstairs to Coleman's rooms where as a preliminary Coleman began to hurl books and papers from the table to the floor. A boy came with drinks. Most of the men in order to prepare for the game removed their coats and cuffs and drew up the sleeves of their shirts. The electric globes shed a blinding light upon the table. The sound of clinking chips arose; the elected banker spun the cards, careless and dexterous.

Later, during a pause of dealing, Coleman said: "Billie, what kind of a lad is that young Coke up at Washurst?" He addressed an old college friend.

"Oh, you mean the Sophomore Coke?" asked the friend. "Seems a decent sort of fellow. I don't know. Why?"

"Well, who is he? Where does he come from? What do you know about him?"

"He's one of those Ohio Cokes—regular thing—father millionaire—used to be a barber—good old boy—why?"

"Nothin'," said Coleman, looking at his cards. "I know the lad. I thought he was a good deal of an ass. I wondered who his people were."

"Oh, his people are all right—in one way. Father owns rolling mills. Do you raise it, Henry? Well, in order to make vice abhorrent to the young, I'm obliged to raise back."

"I'll see it," observed Coleman, slowly pushing forward two blue chips. Afterward he reached behind him and took another glass of wine.

To the others Coleman seemed to have something bitter upon his mind. He played poker quietly, steadfastly, and without change of eye, following the mathematical religion of the game. Outside of the play he was savage, almost insupportable.

"What's the matter with you, Rufus?" said his old college friend. "Lost your job? Girl gone back on you? You're a hell of a host. We don't get anything but insults and drinks."

Late at night Coleman began to lose steadily. In the meantime he drank glass after glass of wine. Finally he made reckless bets on a mediocre hand and an opponent followed him thoughtfully bet by bet, undaunted, calm, absolutely without emotion. Coleman lost; he hurled down his cards. "Nobody but a damned fool would have seen that last raise on anything less than a full hand."

"Steady! Come off! What's wrong with you, Rufus?" cried his guests.

"You're not drunk, are you?" said his old college friend, puritanically.

" 'Drunk'?" repeated Coleman.

"Oh, say," cried a man, "let's play cards. What's all this gabbling?"

It was when a grey dirty light of dawn evaded the thick curtains and fought on the floor with the feebled electric glow that Coleman, in the midst of play, lurched his chest heavily upon the table. Some chips rattled to the floor. "I'll call you," he murmured sleepily.

"Well," replied a man sternly, "three kings."

The other players with difficulty extracted five cards from beneath Coleman's pillowed head. "Not a pair! Come, come, this won't do. Oh, let's stop playing. This is the rottenest game I ever sat in. Let's go home. Why don't you put him to bed, Billie?"

When Coleman awoke next morning, he looked back upon the poker game as something that had transpired in previous years. He dressed and went down to the grill-room. For his breakfast he ordered some eggs on toast and a pint of champagne. A privilege of liberty belonged to a certain Irish waiter, and this waiter looked at him, grinning. "Maybe you had a pretty lively time last night, Mr. Coleman?"

"Yes, Pat," answered Coleman, "I did. It was all because of an unrequited affection, Patrick." The man stood near, a napkin over his arm. Coleman went on impressively. "The ways of the modern lover are strange. Now I, Patrick, am a modern lover, and when yesterday, the dagger of disappointment was driven deep into my heart, I immediately played poker as hard as I could and incidentally got loaded. This is the modern point-of-view. I understand on good authority that in old times lovers used to languish. That is probably a lie, but at any rate we do not in these times languish to any great extent. We get drunk. Do you understand, Patrick?"

The waiter was used to a harangue at Coleman's breakfast

time. He placed his hand over his mouth and giggled. "Yessir."

"Of course," continued Coleman thoughtfully. "It might be pointed out by uneducated persons that it is difficult to maintain a high standard of drunkenness for the adequate length of time, but in the series of experiments which I am about to make, I am sure I can easily prove them to be in the wrong."

"I am sure, sir," said the waiter, "the young ladies would not like to be hearing you talk this way."

"Yes; no doubt, no doubt. The young ladies have still quite medieval ideas. They don't understand. They still prefer lovers to languish."

"At any rate, sir, I don't see that your heart is sure enough broken. You seem to take it very easy."

"Broken!" cried Coleman. "Easy? Man, my heart is in fragments. Bring me another small bottle."

CHAPTER VI

SIX weeks later, Coleman went to the office of the proprietor of the *Eclipse*. Coleman was one of those smooth-shaven old-young men who wear upon some occasions a singular air of temperance and purity. At these times, his features lost their quality of worldly shrewdness and endless suspicion and bloomed as the face of some innocent boy. It then would be hard to tell that he had ever encountered even such a crime as a lie or a cigarette. As he walked into the proprietor's office he was a perfect semblance of fine inexperienced youth. People usually concluded this change was due to a Turkish bath or some other expedient of recuperation but it was due probably to the power of a singular physical characteristic.

"Boss in?" said Coleman.

"Yeh," said the secretary, jerking his thumb toward an inner door. In his private office, Sturgeon sat on the edge of the table dangling one leg and dreamily surveying the wall. As Coleman entered he looked up quickly. "Rufus," he said, "you're just the man I wanted to see. I've got a scheme. A great scheme." He slid from the table and began to pace briskly to and fro, his hands deep in his trousers pockets, his chin sunk in his collar, his light blue eyes afire with interest. "Now listen. This is immense. The *Eclipse* enlists a battalion of men to go to Cuba and fight the Spaniards under its own flag—the *Eclipse* flag. Collect trained officers from here and there—enlist every young devil we see—drill 'em—best rifles—loads of ammunition—provisions—staff of doctors and nurses—a couple of dynamite guns—everything complete—best in the world. Now, isn't that great? What's the matter with that now? Eh? Eh? Isn't that great? It's great, isn't it? Eh? Why, my boy, we'll free——"

Coleman did not seem to ignite. "I have been arrested four or five times already on fool-matters connected with the newspaper business," he observed gloomily, "but I've never yet been hung. I think your scheme a beauty."

Sturgeon paused in astonishment. "Why what happens to be the matter with you? What are you kicking about?"

Coleman made a slow gesture. "I'm tired," he answered. "I need a vacation."

"Vacation!" cried Sturgeon. "Why don't you take one then?"

"That's what I've come to see you about. I've had a pretty heavy strain on me for three years now and I want to get a little rest."

"Well, who in thunder has been keeping you from it? It hasn't been me."

"I know it hasn't been you but of course I wanted the paper to go and I wanted to have my share in its success but now that everything is all right I think I might go away for a time if you don't mind."

"Mind!" exclaimed Sturgeon falling into his chair and reaching for his cheque-book. "Where do you want to go? How long do you want to be gone? How much money do you want?"

"I don't want very much. And as for where I want to go, I thought I might like to go to Greece for awhile."

Sturgeon had been writing a cheque. He poised his pen in the air and began to laugh. "That's a queer place to go for a rest. Why the biggest war of modern times—a war that may involve all Europe—is likely to start there at any moment. You are not likely to get any rest in Greece."

"I know that," answered Coleman. "I know there is likely to be a war there. But I think that is exactly what would rest me. I would like to report the war."

"You are a queer bird," murmured Sturgeon, deeply fascinated with this new idea. He had apparently forgotten his vision of a Cuban volunteer battalion. "War-correspondence is about the most original medium for a rest I ever heard of."

"Oh, it may seem funny but, really, any change will be good for me now. I've been whacking at this old Sunday edition until I'm sick of it and sometimes I wish the *Eclipse* was in hell."

"That's all right," laughed the proprietor of the *Eclipse*. "But still I don't see how you are going to get any vacation out of a war that will upset the whole of Europe. But that's your affair. If you want to become the chief correspondent in the field, in case of any such war, why, of course I would be glad to have you. I couldn't get anybody better. But I don't see where your vacation comes in."

"I'll take care of that," answered Coleman. "When I take a vacation I want to take it my own way and I think this will be a vacation because it will be different—don't you see—different?"

"No, I don't see any sense in it but if you think that is the way that suits you, why, go ahead. How much money do you want?"

"I don't want much. Just enough to see me through nicely."

Sturgeon scribbled on his cheque-book and then ripped a cheque from it. "Here's a thousand dollars. Will that do you to start with?"

"That's plenty."

"When do you want to start?"

"Tomorrow."

"Oho," said Sturgeon. "You're in a hurry." This impetuous manner of exit from business seemed to appeal to him. " 'Tomorrow'," he repeated smiling. In reality he was some kind of a poet using his millions romantically, spending wildly on a sentiment that might be with beauty or without beauty, according to the momentary vacillation. The vaguely-defined desperation in Coleman's last announcement appeared to delight him. He grinned and placed the points of his fingers together, stretching out his legs in a careful attitude of indifference which might even mean disapproval. " 'Tomorrow'," he murmured teasingly.

"By jiminy," exclaimed Coleman, ignoring the other man's mood. "I'm sick of the whole business. I've got out a Sunday paper once a week for three years and I feel absolutely incapable of getting out another edition. It would be all right if we were running on ordinary lines but when each issue is more or less of an attempt to beat the previous issue, it becomes rather wearing, you know. If I can't get a vacation now I take one later in a lunatic asylum."

"Why, I'm not objecting to your having a vacation. I'm simply marveling at the kind of vacation you want to take. And 'tomorrow', too, eh?"

"Well, it suits me," muttered Coleman sulkily.

"Well, if it suits you, that's enough. Here's your cheque. Clear out now and don't let me see you again until you are thoroughly rested even if it takes a year." He arose and stood smiling. He was mightily pleased with himself. He liked to perform in this way. He was almost seraphic as he thrust the cheque for a thousand dollars toward Coleman.

Then his manner changed abruptly. "Hold on a minute. I must think a little about this thing if you are going to manage the correspondence. Of course it will be a long and bloody war."

"You bet."

"The big chance is that all Europe will be dragged into it. Of course then you would have to come out of Greece and take up a better position—say Vienna."

"No, I wouldn't care to do that," said Coleman positively. "I just want to take care of the Greek end of it."

"It will be an idiotic way to take a vacation," observed Sturgeon.

"Well, it suits me," muttered Coleman again. "I tell you what it is—" he added suddenly. "I've got some private reasons—see?"

Sturgeon was radiant with joy. "Private reasons." He was charmed by the sombre pain in Coleman's eyes and his own ability to eject it. "Good. Go now and be blowed. I will cable final instructions to meet you in London. As soon as you get to Greece cable me an account of the situation there and we will arrange our plans." He began to laugh. "Private reasons! Come out to dinner with me."

"I can't very well," said Coleman. "If I go tomorrow, I've got to pack——"

But here the real tyrant appeared, emerging suddenly from behind the curtain of sentiment, appearing like a red devil in a pantomime. "You can't?" snapped Sturgeon. "Nonsense——"

CHAPTER VII

SWEEPING out from between two remote half-submerged dunes on which stood slender sentry light-houses, the steamer began to roll with a gentle insinuating motion. Passengers in their staterooms saw at rhythmical intervals, the spray race fleetly past the port-holes. The waves grappled hurriedly at the sides of the great flying steamer and boiled discomfited astern in a turmoil of green and white. From the tops of the enormous funnels streamed level masses of smoke which were immediately torn to nothing by the headlong wind. Meanwhile as the steamer rushed into the north-east, men in caps and ulsters comfortably paraded the deck and stewards arranged deck-chairs for the reception of various women who were coming from their cabins with rugs.

In the smoking-room, old voyagers were settling down comfortably while new voyagers were regarding them with diffident respect. Among the passengers Coleman found a number of people whom he knew, including a whole-sale wine-merchant, a Chicago railway magnate and a New York millionaire. They lived practically in the smoking-room. Necessity drove them from time to time to the salon, or to their berths. Once indeed the millionaire was absent from the group while penning a short note to his wife.

When the Irish coast was sighted Coleman came on deck to look at it. A tall young woman immediately halted in her walk until he had stepped up to her. "Well, of all ungallant men, Rufus Coleman, you are the star!" she cried laughing and held out her hand.

"Awfully sorry, I'm sure," he murmured. "Been playing poker in the smoking-room all voyage. Didn't have a look at the passenger list until just now. Why didn't you send me word?" These lies were told so modestly and sincerely that when the girl flashed her brilliant eyes full upon their author there was a mixture of admiration in the indignation.

"Send you a card? I don't believe you can read, Rufus. Else you would have known that I was to sail on this steamer. If I hadn't been ill until today you would have seen me in the salon. I open at the Folly Theater next week. Dear ol' Lunnon, y'know."

"Of course, I knew you were going," said Coleman. "But I thought you were to go later. What do you open in?"

"*Fly by Night.* Come walk along with me. See those two old ladies? They've been watching for me like hawks ever since we left New York. They expected to see me flirt with every man on board. But I've fooled them. I've been just as g-o-o-d. I had to be."

As the pair moved toward the stern, enormous and radiant green waves were crashing futilely after the steamer. Ireland showed a dreary coast-line to the north. A wretched man who had crossed the Atlantic eighty-four times was declaiming to a group of novices. A venerable banker, bundled in rugs, was asleep in his deck-chair.

"Well, Nora," said Coleman, "I hope you make a hit in London. You deserve it if anybody does. You've worked hard."

" 'Worked hard'!" cried the girl. "I should think so. Eight years ago I was in the rear row. Now I have the centre of the stage whenever I want it. I made Chalmers cut out that great scene in the second act between the queen and Rodolfo. The idea. Did he think I would stand that! And just because he was in love with Clara Trotwood, too."

Coleman was dreamy. "Remember when I was dramatic man for the *Gazette* and wrote that first notice?"

"Indeed, I do," answered the girl affectionately. "Indeed I do, Rufus. Ah, that was a great lift. I believe that was the first thing that had any effect on old Oliver. Before that, he never would believe that I was any good. Give me your arm, Rufus. Let's parade before the two old women." Coleman glanced at her keenly. Her voice had trembled slightly. Her eyes were lustrous as if she were about to weep.

"Good heavens," he said. "You are the same old Nora Black. I thought you would be proud and 'aughty by this time."

"Not to my friends," she murmured. "Not to my friends. I'm always the same and I never forget, Rufus."

"Never forget what?" asked Coleman.

"If anybody does me a favor I never forget it as long as I live," she answered fervently.

"Oh, you mustn't be so sentimental, Nora. You remember that play you bought from little Ben Whipple just because he had once sent you some flowers in the old days when you were poor and happened to be sick? A sense of gratitude cost you over eight thousand dollars that time, didn't it?" Coleman laughed heartily.

"Oh, it wasn't the flowers at all," she interrupted seriously. "Of course Ben was always a nice boy but then his play was worth a thousand dollars. That's all I gave him. I lost some more in trying to make it go. But it was too good. That was what was the matter. It was altogether too good for the public. I felt awfully sorry for poor little Ben."

"Too good?" sneered Coleman. "Too good? Too differently bad, you mean. My dear girl, you mustn't imagine that you know a good play. You don't, at all."

She paused abruptly and faced him. This regal creature was looking at him so sternly that Coleman felt awed for a moment as if he were in the presence of a great mind. "Do you mean to say I'm not an artist?" she asked.

Coleman remained cool. "I've never been decorated for informing people of their own affairs," he observed. "But I should say that you were about as much of an artist as I am."

Frowning slightly, she reflected upon this reply. Then, of a sudden, she laughed. "There is no use in being angry with you, Rufus. You were always a hopeless scamp. But," she added, childishly wistful, "have you ever seen *Fly by Night*? Don't you think my dance in the second act is artistic?"

"No," said Coleman, "I haven't seen *Fly by Night* yet but of course I know that you are the most beautiful dancer on the stage. Everybody knows that."

It seemed that her hand tightened on his arm. Her face was radiant. "There!" she exclaimed. "Now you are forgiven. You are a nice boy, Rufus—sometimes."

When Miss Black went to her cabin, Coleman strolled into the smoking-room. Every man there covertly or openly surveyed him. He dropped lazily into a chair at a table where the wine-

merchant, the Chicago railway king and the New York millionaire were playing cards. They made a noble pretense of not being aware of him. On the oil-cloth top of the table the cards
were snapped down, turn by turn.

Finally the wine-merchant without lifting his head to address
a particular person said: "New conquest?"

Hailing a steward Coleman asked for a brandy and soda.

The millionaire said: "He's a sly cuss anyhow." The railway
man grinned. After an elaborate silence the wine-merchant
asked: "Known Miss Black long, Rufus?" Coleman looked scornfully at his friends. "What's wrong with you fellows, anyhow?"
The Chicago man answered airily. "Oh, nothin', whatever."

At dinner in the crowded salon, Coleman was aware that
more than one passenger glanced first at Nora Black and then
at him, as if connecting them in some train of thought, moved
to it by the narrowed horizon of ship-board and by a sense of
the mystery that surrounds the lives of the beauties of the stage.
Near the captain's right hand sat the glowing and splendid Nora,
exhibiting under the gaze of the persistent eyes of many meanings, a practised and profound composure that to the populace
was terrifying dignity.

Strolling toward the smoking-room after dinner, Coleman met
the New York millionaire who seemed much agitated. He took
Coleman fraternally by the arm. "Say, old man, introduce me,
won't you? I'm crazy to know her."

"Do you mean Miss Black?" asked Coleman. "Why, I don't
know that I have a right. Of course, you know, she hasn't been
meeting anybody aboard. I'll ask her, though—certainly."

"Thanks, old man, thanks. I'd be tickled to death. Come along
and have a drink. When will you ask her?"

"Why, I don't know when I'll see her. Tomorrow, I suppose——"

They had not been long in the smoking-room, however, when
the deck-steward came with a card to Coleman. Upon it was
written: "Come for a stroll?" Everybody saw Coleman read this
card and then look and whisper to the deck-steward. The deck-
steward bent his head and whispered discreetly in reply. There
was an abrupt pause in the hum of conversation. The interest
was acute.

Coleman leaned carelessly back in his chair, puffing at his cigar. He mingled calmly in a discussion of the comparative merits of certain trans-Atlantic lines. After a time, he threw away his cigar and arose. Men nodded. "Didn't I tell you?" His studiously languid exit was made dramatic by the eagle-eyed attention of the smoking-room.

On deck, he found Nora pacing to and fro. "You didn't hurry yourself," she said, as he joined her. The lights of Queenstown were twinkling. A warm wind, wet with the moisture of rain-stricken sod, was coming from the land.

"Why," said Coleman, "we've got all these duffers very much excited."

"Well, what do you care?" asked the girl. "You don't care, do you?"

"No, I don't care. Only it's rather absurd to be watched all the time." He said this precisely as if he abhorred being watched in this case. "Oh, by the way——" he added. Then he paused for a moment. "Aw—a friend of mine—not bad fellow—he asked me for an introduction. Of course, I told him I'd ask you."

She made a contemptuous gesture. "Oh, another Willie. Tell him no. Tell him to go home to his family. Tell him to run away."

"He isn't a bad fellow. He—" said Coleman diffidently, "he would probably be at the theater every night in a box."

"Yes and get drunk and throw a bottle of wine on the stage instead of a bouquet. No," she declared positively, "I won't see him."

Coleman did not seem oppressed by this ultimatum. "Oh, all right. I promised him—that was all."

"Besides, are you in such a hurry to get rid of me?"

"Rid of you? Nonsense." They walked in the shadows.

"How long are you going to be in London, Rufus?" asked Nora softly.

"Who? I? Oh, I'm going right off to Greece. First train. There's going to be a war, you know."

"A war? Why, who is going to fight? The Greeks and the—the —the what?"

"The Turks. I'm going right over there."

"Why that's dreadful, Rufus," said the girl, mournful and shocked. "You might get hurt or something." Presently, she asked: "And aren't you going to be in London any time at all?"

"Oh," he answered, puffing out his lips, "I may stop in London for three or four days on my way home. I'm not sure of it."

"And when will that be?"

"Oh, I can't tell. It may be in three or four months or it may be a year from now. When the war stops."

There was a long silence as they walked up and down the swaying deck.

"Do you know," said Nora at last, "I like you, Rufus Coleman. I don't know any good reason for it either unless it is because you are such a brute. Now when I was asking you if you were to be in London, you were perfectly detestable. You knew I was anxious."

"I—detestable?" cried Coleman, feigning amazement. "Why, what did I say?"

"It isn't so much what you said——" began Nora slowly. Then she suddenly changed her manner. "Oh, well, don't let's talk about it any more. It's too foolish. Only—you are a disagreeable person sometimes."

In the morning, as the vessel steamed up the Irish channel, Coleman was on deck, keeping furtive watch on the cabin-stairs. After two hours of waiting, he scribbled a message on a card and sent it below. He received an answer that Miss Black had a headache and felt too ill to come on deck. He went to the smoking-room. The three card-players glanced up grinning. "What's the matter?" asked the wine-merchant. "You look angry." As a matter of fact, Coleman had purposely wreathed his features in a pleasant and satisfied expression so he was for a moment furious at the wine-merchant.

"Confound the girl," he thought to himself. "She has succeeded in making all these beggars laugh at me." He mused that if he had another chance he would show her how disagreeable or detestable or scampish he was under some circumstances. He reflected ruefully that the complacence with which he had accepted the comradeship of the belle of the voyage might have been somewhat over-done. Perhaps he had got a little out of proportion. He was annoyed at the stares of the other men in the smoking-room who seemed now to be reading his discomfiture. As for Nora Black he thought of her wistfully and angrily as a superb woman whose company was honor and joy, a payment for any sacrifices.

"What's the matter?" persisted the wine-merchant. "You look grumpy."

Coleman laughed. "Do I?"

At Liverpool, as the steamer was being slowly warped to the landing-stage by some tugs, the passengers crowded the deck with their hand-bags. Adieus were falling as dead leaves fall from a great tree. The stewards were handling small hills of luggage marked with flaming red labels. The ship was firmly against the dock before Miss Black came from her cabin. Coleman was at the time gazing shoreward but his three particular friends instantly nudged him. "What?" "There she is." "Oh, Miss Black?" He composedly walked toward her. It was impossible to tell whether she saw him coming or whether it was accident but at any rate she suddenly turned and moved toward the stern of the ship. Ten watchful gossips had noted Coleman's travel in her direction and more than half the passengers noted his defeat. He wheeled casually and returned to his three friends. They were colic-stricken with a coarse and yet silent merriment. Coleman was glad that the voyage was over.

After the polite business of an English custom-house, the travellers passed out to the waiting train. A nimble little theatrical agent of some kind, sent from London, dashed forward to receive Miss Black. He had a first-class compartment engaged for her and he bundled her and her maid into it in an exuberance of enthusiasm and admiration. Coleman passing moodily along the line of coaches heard Nora's voice hailing him.

"Rufus."

There she was framed in a carriage window, beautiful and smiling brightly. Every near-by person turned to contemplate this vision.

"Oh," said Coleman advancing, "I thought I was not going to get a chance to say good-bye to you." He held out his hand. "Good-bye."

She pouted. "Why, there's plenty of room in this compartment." Seeing that some forty people were transfixed in observation of her, she moved a short way back. "Come on in this compartment, Rufus," she said.

"Thanks. I prefer to smoke," said Coleman. He went off abruptly. On the way to London, he brooded in his corner on the two divergent emotions he had experienced when refusing her invitation. At Euston Station in London, he was directing a porter who had his luggage when he heard Nora speak at his shoulder. "Well, Rufus, you sulky boy," she said, "I shall be at the Cecil. If you have time, come and see me."

"Thanks, I'm sure, my dear Nora," answered Coleman effusively. "But, honestly, I'm off for Greece."

A brougham was drawn up near them and the nimble little agent was waiting. The maid was directing the establishment of a mass of luggage on and in a four-wheeler cab. "Well, put me into my carriage anyhow," said Nora. "You will have time for that."

Afterward she addressed him from the dark interior. "Now, Rufus, you must come to see me the minute you strike London again—" She hesitated a moment and then smiling gorgeously upon him, she said: "Brute!"

CHAPTER VIII

AS soon as Coleman had planted his belongings in a hotel he was bowled in a hansom briskly along the smoky Strand, through a dark city whose walls dripped like the walls of a cave and whose passages were only illuminated by flaring yellow and red signs.

Walkley, the London correspondent of the *Eclipse*, whirled from his chair with a shout of joy and relief at sight of Coleman. "Cables," he cried, "nothin' but cables. All the people in New York are writing cables to you. The wires groan with them. And we groan with them too. They come in here in bales. However there is no reason why you should read them all. Many are similar in words and many more are similar in spirit. The sense of the whole thing is that you get to Greece quickly taking with you *immense* sums of money and *enormous* powers over nations."

"Well, when does the row begin?"

"The most astute journalists in Europe have been predicting a general European smash-up every year since 1878," said Walkley, "and the prophets weep. The English are the only people who can pull off wars on schedule time and they have to do it in odd corners of the globe. I fear me the war business is getting tuckered. There is sorrow in the lodges of the lone wolves, the war-correspondents. However, my boy, don't bury your face in your blanket. This Greek business looks very promising, very promising." He then began to proclaim trains and connections. "Dover—Calais—Paris—Brindisi—Corfu—Patras—Athens. That is your game. You are supposed to sky-rocket yourself over that route in the shortest possible time but you would gain no time by starting before tomorrow so you can cool your heels here in London until then. I wish I was going along."

Coleman returned to his hotel, a knight impatient and savage at being kept for a time out of the saddle. He went for a late supper to the grill-room and as he was seated there alone, a party of four or five people came to occupy the table directly behind him. They talked a great deal even before they arrayed themselves at the table and he at once recognized the voice of Nora Black. She was queening it, apparently, over a little band of awed masculine worshippers.

Either by accident or for some curious reason, she took a chair back to back with Coleman's chair. Her sleeve of fragrant stuff almost touched his shoulder and he felt appealing to him seductively a perfume of orris-root and violet. He was drinking bottled stout with his chop; he sat with a face of wood.

"Oh, the little lord?" Nora was crying to some slave. "Now, do you know, he won't do at all. He is too awfully charming. He sits and ruminates for fifteen minutes and then he pays me a lovely compliment. Then he ruminates for another fifteen minutes and cooks up another fine thing. It is too tiresome. Do you know what kind of a man I like?" she asked softly and confidentially. And here she sank back in her chair until Coleman knew from the tingle that her head was but a few inches from his head. Her sleeve touched him. He turned more wooden under the spell of the orris-root and violet. Her courtiers thought it all a graceful pose but Coleman believed otherwise. Her voice sank to the liquid siren note of a succubus. "Do you know what kind of a man I like? Really like? I like a man that a woman can't bend in a thousand different ways in five minutes. He must have some steel in him. He obliges me to admire him the most when he remains stolid; stolid to my lures. Ah, that is the only kind of a man who can ever break a heart among us women of the world. His stolidity is not real; no; it is mere art but it is a highly finished art and often enough we can't cut through it. Really we can't. And then we may actually come to—er—care for the man. Really we may. Isn't it funny?"

At the end Coleman arose and strolled out of the room, smoking a cigarette. He did not betray a sign. Before the door clashed softly behind him, Nora laughed a little defiantly, perhaps a little loudly. It made every man in the grill-room perk up his ears. As for her courtiers, they were entranced. In her description of the conquering man, she had easily contrived that each one of them wondered if she might not mean him. Each man was perfectly sure that he had plenty of steel in his composition and that seemed to be a main point.

Coleman delayed for a time in the smoking-room and then went to his own quarters. In reality he was somewhat puzzled in his mind by a projection of the beauties of Nora Black upon his desire for Greece and Marjory. His thoughts formed a duality. Once he was on the point of sending his card to Nora Black's parlor inasmuch as Greece was very distant and he could not start until the morrow. But he suspected that he was holding the interest of the actress because of his recent appearance of impregnable serenity in the presence of her fascinations. If he now sent his card, it was a form of surrender and he knew her to be one to take a merciless advantage. He would not make this tactical mistake. On the contrary, he would go to bed and think of war.

In reality he found it easy to fasten his mind upon the prospective war. He regarded himself cynically in most affairs but he could not be cynical of war. Because he had seen none of it. His rejuvenated imagination began to thrill to the roll of battle, through his thought passing all the lightning in the pictures of Detaille, de Neuville and Morot; lashed battery horses roaring over bridges; grand cuirassiers dashing headlong against stolid invincible red-faced lines of German infantry; furious and bloody grapplings in the streets of little villages of north-eastern France. There was one thing at least of which he could still feel the spirit of a debutante. In this matter of war he was not too unlike a young girl embarking upon her first season of opera. Walkley, the next morning, saw this mood sitting quaintly upon Coleman and cackled with astonishment and glee. Coleman's usual manner did not return until he detected Walkley's appreciation of his state and then he snubbed him according to the ritual of the Sunday Editor of the *New York Eclipse*. Parenthetically, it might be said that if Coleman now recalled Nora Black to his mind at all, it was only to think of her for a moment with a sort of an ironical complacence. He had beaten her.

When the train drew out of the station, Coleman felt himself thrill. Was ever fate less perverse? War and love—war and Marjory—were in conjunction—both in Greece—and he could tilt with one lance at both gods. It was a great fine game to play and no man was ever so blessed in vacations. He was smiling continually to himself and sometimes actually on the point of talking aloud. This was despite the presence in the compartment of two fellow passengers who preserved in their uncomfortably rigid, icy and uncompromising manners many of the more or less ridiculous traditions of the English first-class carriage. Coleman's fine humor betrayed him once into addressing one of these passengers and the man responded simply with a wide look of incredulity, as if he discovered that he was travelling in the same compartment with a zebu. It turned Coleman suddenly to evil temper and he wanted to ask the man questions concerning his education and his present mental condition; and so until the train arrived at Dover, his ballooning soul was in danger of collapsing. On the packet crossing the channel, too, he almost returned to the usual Rufus Coleman since all the world was seasick and he could not get a cabin in which to hide himself from it. However he reaped much consolation by ordering a bottle of champagne and drinking it in sight of the people which made them still more seasick. From Calais to Brindisi really nothing met his disapproval save the speed of the train, the conduct of some of the passengers, the quality of the food served, the manners of the guards, the temperature of the carriages, the prices charged, and the length of the journey.

In time he passed as in a vision from wretched Brindisi to charming Corfu, from Corfu to the little war-bitten city of Patras and from Patras by rail at the speed of an ox cart to Athens.

With a smile of grim content and surrounded in his carriage with all his beautiful brown luggage, he swept through the dusty streets of the Greek capital. Even as the vehicle arrived in a great terraced square in front of the yellow palace, Greek recruits in garments representing many trades and many characters were marching up cheering for Greece and the king. Officers stood up on the little iron chairs in front of the cafes; all the urchins came running and shouting; ladies waved their handkerchiefs from the balconies; the whole city was vivified with a leaping and joyous enthusiasm. The Athenians—as dragomen or otherwise—had preserved an ardor for their glorious traditions and it was as if that in the white dust which lifted from the plaza and floated across the old-ivory face of the palace, there were the souls of the capable soldiers of the past. Coleman was almost intoxicated with it. It seemed to celebrate his own reasons, his reasons of love and ambition to conquer in love.

When the carriage arrived in front of the hotel D'Angleterre, Coleman found the servants of the place with more than one eye upon the scene in the plaza but they soon paid heed to the arrival of a gentleman with such an amount of beautiful brown leather luggage, all marked boldly with the initials "R. C." Coleman let them lead him and follow him and conduct him and use bad English upon him without noting either their words, their salaams or their work. His mind had quickly fixed upon the fact that here was the probable head-quarters of the Wainwright party and, with the rush of his western race fleeting through his veins, he felt that he would choke and die if he did not learn of the Wainwrights in the first two minutes. It was a tragic venture to attempt to make the Levantine mind understand something off the course, that the new arrival's first thought was to establish a knowledge of the whereabouts of some friends rather than to swarm helter-skelter into that part of the hotel for which he was willing to pay rent. In fact he failed to thus impress them; failed in dark wrath, but, nevertheless, failed. At last he was simply forced to concede the travel of files of men up the broad, red-carpeted staircase, each man being loaded with Coleman luggage. The men in the hotel-bureau were then able to comprehend that the foreign gentleman might have something else on his mind. They raised their eye-brows languidly when he spoke of the Wainwright party in gentle surprise that he had not yet learned that they were gone some time. They were departed on some excursion. Where? Oh, really—it was almost laughable, indeed—they didn't know. Were they sure? Why, yes—it was almost laughable, indeed—they were quite sure. Where could the gentleman find out about them? Well, they—as they had explained—did not know but—it was possible—the American minister might know. Where was he to be found? Oh, that was very simple. It was well-known that the American minister had apartments in the hotel. Was he in? Ah, that they could not say.

So Coleman, rejoicing at his final emancipation and with the grime of travel still upon him, burst in somewhat violently upon the secretary of the Hon. Thomas M. Gordner of Nebraska, the

United States minister to Greece. From his desk the secretary arose from behind an accidental bulwark of books and governmental pamphlets. "Yes, certainly. Mr. Gordner is in. If you would give me your card——"

Directly, Coleman was introduced into another room where a quiet man who was rolling a cigarette looked him frankly but carefully in the eye. "The Wainwrights?" said the minister immediately after the question. "Why, I myself am immensely concerned about them at present. I'm afraid they've gotten themselves into trouble."

"Really?" said Coleman.

"Yes. That little professor is rather—er—stubborn, isn't he? He wanted to make an expedition to Nikopolis and I explained to him all the possibilities of war and begged him to at least not take his wife and daughter with him."

" 'Daughter'," murmured Coleman as if in his sleep.

"But that little old man had a head like a stone and only laughed at me. Of course those villainous young students were only too delighted at a prospect of war but it was a stupid and absurd thing for the man to take his wife and daughter there. They are up there now. I can't get a word from them or get a word to them."

Coleman had been choking. "Where is Nikopolis?" he asked.

The minister gazed suddenly in comprehension of the man before him. "Nikopolis is in Turkey," he answered gently.

Turkey at that time was believed to be a country of delay, corruption, turbulence and massacre. It meant everything. More than a half of the Christians of the world shuddered at the name of Turkey. Coleman's lips tightened and perhaps blanched and his chin moved out strangely, once, twice, thrice. "How can I get to Nikopolis?" he said.

The minister smiled. "It would take you the better part of four days if you *could* get there but as a matter of fact you *can't* get there at the present time. A Greek army and a Turkish army are looking at each other from the sides of the river at Arta—the river is there the frontier—and Nikopolis happens to be on the wrong side. You can't reach them. The forces at Arta will fight within three days. I know it. Of course I've notified our legation at Constantinople but, with Turkish methods of communication, Nikopolis is about as far from Constantinople as New York is from Pekin."

Coleman arose. "They've run themselves into a nice mess," he said crossly. "Well, I'm a thousand times obliged to you, I'm sure."

The minister opened his eyes a trifle. "You're not going to try to reach them, are you?"

"Yes," answered Coleman, abstractedly, "I'm going to have a try at it. Friends of mine, you know——"

At the bureau of the hotel, the correspondent found several cables awaiting him from the alert office of the *New York Eclipse*. One of them read: "State department gives out bad plight Wainwright party lost somewhere find them *Eclipse*." When Coleman perused the message he began to smile with seraphic bliss. Could fate have ever been less perverse.

Whereupon he whirled himself in Athens. And it was to the considerable astonishment of some Athenians. He discovered and instantly subsidized a young Englishman who during his absence at the front, would act as correspondent for the *Eclipse* at the capital.

He took unto himself a dragoman and then bought three horses and hired a groom at a speed that caused a little crowd at the horse dealer's place to come out upon the pavement and watch this surprising man ride back to his hotel. He had already driven his dragoman into a curious state of oriental bewilderment and panic in which he could only lumber hastily and helplessly here and there, with his face in the meantime marked with agony. Coleman's own field equipment had been ordered by cable from New York to London but it was necessary to buy much tinned meats, chocolate, coffee, candles, patent food, brandy, tobaccos, medicines and other things.

He went to bed that night feeling more placid. The train back to Patras was to start in the early morning and he felt the satisfaction of a man who is at last about to start on his own great quest. Before he dropped off to slumber, he heard crowds cheering exultantly in the streets and the cheering moved him as it had done in the morning. He felt that the celebration of the people was really an accompaniment to his primal reason—a reason of love and ambition to conquer in love—even as in the theater, the music accompanies the hero in his progress. He arose once during the night to study a map of the Balkan peninsula and get nailed into his mind the exact position of Nikopolis. It was important.

CHAPTER IX

COLEMAN'S dragoman aroused him in the blue before dawn. The correspondent arrayed himself in one of his new khaki suits—riding breeches and a tunic well marked with buttoned pockets—and accompanied by some of his beautiful brown luggage, they departed for the station.

The ride to Patras is a terror under ordinary circumstances. It begins in the early morning and ends in the twilight. To Coleman having just come from Patras to Athens, this journey from Athens to Patras had all the exasperating elements of a forced recantation. Moreover, he had not come prepared to view with awe the ancient city of Corinth nor to view with admiration the limpid beauties of the gulf of that name with its olive grove shore. He was not stirred by Parnassus, a faraway snow-field high on the black shoulders of the mountains across the gulf. No; he wished to go to Nikopolis. He passed over the graves of an ancient race, the gleam of whose mighty minds shot, hardly dimmed, through the clouding ages. No; he wished to go to Nikopolis. The train went at a snail's pace and if Coleman had an interest it was in the people who lined the route and cheered the soldiers on the train. In Coleman's compartment there was a greasy person who spoke a little English. He explained that he was a poet, a poet who now wrote of nothing but war. When a man is in pursuit of his love and success is known to be at least remote, it often relieves his strain if he is deeply bored from time to time.

The train was really obliged to arrive finally at Patras, even if it was a tortoise, and when this happened, a hotel runner appeared who lied for the benefit of the hotel in saying that there was no boat over to Mesalonghi that night. When, all too late, Coleman discovered the truth of the matter, his wretched dragoman came in for a period of infamy and suffering. However, while strolling in the plaza at Patras, amid newsboys howling out the names of war extras, amid people who were attacked from every side by rumor and truth, Coleman learned things to his advantage. A Greek fleet was bombarding Prevasa. Prevasa was near Nikopolis. The opposing armies at Arta were engaged, principally in an artillery duel. Arta was on the road from Nikopolis into Greece. Hearing this news in the sun-lit square made him betray no weakness but in the darkness of his room at the hotel, he seemed to behold Marjory encircled by insurmountable walls of flame. He could look out of his window into the black night of the north and feel every ounce of a hideous circumstance. It appalled him; here was no power of calling up a score of reporters and sending them scampering to accomplish everything. He even might as well have been without a tongue as far as it could serve him in goodly speech. He was alone, confronting the black ominous Turkish north behind which were the deadly flames; behind the flames was Marjory. It worked upon him until he felt obliged to call in his dragoman and then seated upon the edge of his bed and waving his pipe eloquently, he described the plight of some of his very dear friends who were cut off at Nikopolis in Epirus. Some of his talk was almost wistful in its wish for sympathy from his servant but at the end he bade the dragoman understand that he, Coleman, was going to their rescue and he defiantly asked the hireling if he was prepared to go with him. But he did not know the Greek nature. In two minutes the dragoman was weeping tears of enthusiasm and, for these tears, Coleman was over-grateful because he had not been told that any of the more crude forms of sentiment arouse the common Greek to the highest pitch but sometimes when it comes to what the Americans call a "show-down," when he gets backed toward his last corner with a solitary privilege of dying for these sentiments, perhaps he does not always exhibit those talents which are supposed to be possessed by the bull-dog. He often, then, goes into the cafes and takes it all out in oration like any common Parisian.

In the morning, a steamer carried them across the strait and landed them near Mesalonghi at the foot of the railroad that leads to Agrinion. At Agrinion Coleman at last began to feel that he was nearing his goal. There were plenty of soldiers in the town who received with delight and applause this gentleman in the distinguished-looking khaki clothes with his revolver and his field-glasses, and his canteen and his dragoman. The dragoman lied of course and vociferated that the gentleman in the distinguished-looking khaki clothes was an English soldier of reputation who had, naturally, come to help the cross in its fight against the crescent. He also said that his master had three superb horses coming from Athens in charge of a groom and was undoubtedly going to join the cavalry. Whereupon the soldiers wished to embrace and kiss the gentleman in the distinguished-looking khaki clothes.

There was more or less of a scuffle. Coleman would have taken to kicking and punching but he found that by a series of elusive movements he could dodge the demonstrations of affection without losing his popularity. Escorted by soldiers, citizens, children and dogs, he went to the diligence which was to take him and others the next stage of the journey.

As the diligence proceeded, Coleman's mind suffered another little inroad of ill-faith as to the success of his expedition. In the first place it seemed foolish to expect that this diligence would ever arrive anywhere. Moreover, the accommodations were about equal to what one would endure if one undertook to sleep for a night in a tree. Then there was a devil-dog, a little black-and-tan terrier in a blanket gorgeous and belled, whose duty it was to stand on the top of the coach and bark incessantly to keep the driver fully aroused to the enormity of his occupation. To have this cur silenced either by strangulation or ordinary clubbing, Coleman struggled with his dragoman as Jacob struggled with the angel but, in the first place, the dragoman was a Greek whose tongue could go quite drunk, a Greek who had become a slave to the heralding and establishment of one certain fact, or lie, and now he was engaged in describing to every village and to all the countryside the prowess of the gentleman in the distinguished-looking khaki clothes. It was the general absurdity of this advance to the frontier and the fighting, to the crucial place where he was resolved to make an attempt to rescue his sweetheart; it was this ridiculous aspect that caused to come to Coleman a

premonition of failure. No knight ever went out to recover a lost
love in such a diligence and with such a devil-dog, tinkling his
little bells and yelping insanely to keep the driver awake.

After night-fall, they arrived at a town on the southern coast
of the Gulf of Arta and the goaded dragoman was thrust forth
from the little inn into the street to find the first possible means
of getting on to Arta. He returned at last to tremulously say that
there was no single chance of starting for Arta that night.
Whereupon he was again thrust into the street with orders, strict
orders. In due time, Coleman spread his rugs upon the floor of
his little room and thought himself almost asleep when the dragoman entered with a really intelligent man who for some reason
had agreed to consort with him in the business of getting the
stranger off to Arta. They announced that there was a brigantine
about to sail with a load of soldiers for a little port near Arta and
if Coleman hurried he could catch it, permission from an officer
having already been obtained. He was up at once and the dragoman and the unaccountably intelligent person hastily gathered
his chattels. Stepping out into a black street **and** moving to the
edge of black water and embarking in a black boat filled with
soldiers whose rifles dimly shone, was as impressive to Coleman
as if, really, it was the first start. He had endured many starts, it
is true, but the last one always touched him as being final.

There were no lights on the brigantine and the men swung
precariously up her sides to the deck which was already occupied by a babbling multitude. The dragoman judiciously found a
place for his master where during the night the latter had to
move quickly every time the tiller was shifted to starboard. The
craft raised her shadowy sails and swung slowly off into the deep
gloom. Forward, some of the soldiers began to sing weird minor
melodies. Coleman, enveloped in his rugs, smoked three or four
cigars. He was content and miserable, lying there, hearing these
melodies which defined to him his own affairs.

At dawn they were at the little port. First, in the carmine and
grey tints from a sleepy sun, they could see little mobs of soldiers
working amid boxes of stores. And then from back in some dun
and green hills sounded a deep-throated thunder of artillery. An
officer gave Coleman and his dragoman positions in one of the
first boats but of course it could not be done without an almost

endless amount of palaver. Eventually they landed with their traps. Coleman felt through the sole of his boot his foot upon the shore. He was within striking distance.

But here it was smitten into the head of Coleman's servant to turn into the most inefficient dragoman, probably, in the entire East. Coleman discerned it, immediately, before any blunder could tell him. He at first thought that it was the voices of the guns which had made a chilly inside for the man but when he reflected upon the incompetency, or childish courier falsity, at Patras and his discernible lack of sense from Agrinion onward he felt that the fault was elemental in his nature. It was a mere basic inability to front novel situations which was somehow in the dragoman; he retreated from everything difficult in a smoke of gibberish and gesticulation. Coleman glared at him with the hatred that sometimes ensues when breed meets breed but he saw that this man was indeed a golden link in his possible success. This man connected him with Greece and its language. If he destroyed him he delayed what was now his main desire in life. However this truth did not prevent him from addressing the man in inelegant speech.

The two little men who were induced to carry Coleman's luggage as far as the Greek camp were really procured by the correspondent himself who pantomimed vigorously and with unmistakable vividness. Followed by his dragoman and the two little men, he strode off along a road which led straight as a stick to where the guns were at intervals booming. Meanwhile the dragoman and the two little men talked, talked, talked. Coleman was silent, puffing his cigar and reflecting upon the odd things that happen to chivalry in the modern age.

He knew of many men who would have been astonished if they could have seen into his mind at that time and he knew of many more men who would have laughed if they had the same privilege of sight. He made no attempt to conceal from himself that the whole thing was romantic, romantic despite the little tinkling dog, the decrepit diligence, the palavering natives, the super-idiotic dragoman. It was fine. It was from another age and even the actors could not deface the purity of the picture. However it was true that upon the brigantine the previous night he had unaccountably wetted all his available matches. This was momentous, important, cruel truth but Coleman, after all, was taking—as well as he could forget—a solemn and knightly joy of this adventure and there were as many portraits of his lady envisioning before him as ever held the heart of an armor-encased young gentleman of medieval poetry. If he had been travelling in this region as an ordinary tourist, he would have been apparent mainly for his lofty impatience over trifles but now there was in him a positive assertion of direction which was undoubtedly one of the reasons for the despair of the accomplished dragoman.

Before them the country slowly opened and opened, the straight white road always piercing it like a lance shaft. Soon they could see black masses of men marking the green knolls—the artillery thundered loudly and now vibrated augustly through the air. Coleman quickened his pace, to the despair of the little men carrying the traps.

They finally came up with one of these black bodies of men and found it to be composed of a considerable number of soldiers who were idly watching some hospital people bury a dead Turk. The dragoman at once dashed forward to peer through the throng and see the face of the corpse. Then he came and supplicated Coleman as if he were hawking him to look at a relic and Coleman, moved by a strong mysterious impulse, went forward to look at the poor little clay-colored body. At that moment a snake ran out from a tuft of grass at his feet and wriggled wildly over the sod. The dragoman shrieked, of course, but one of the soldiers put his heel upon the head of the reptile and it flung itself into the agonized knot of death. Then the whole crowd pow-wowed, turning from the dead man to the dead snake. Coleman signaled his contingent and proceeded along the road.

This incident, this paragraph, had seemed a strange introduction to war. The snake, the dead man, the entire sketch, made him shudder of itself but, more than anything he felt an uncanny symbolism. It was no doubt a mere occurrence; nothing but an occurrence; but inasmuch as all the detail of this daily life associated itself with Marjory, he felt a different horror. He had thought of the little devil-dog and Marjory in an interwoven way. Supposing Marjory had been riding in the diligence with the little devil-dog a-top? What would she have said? Of her fund of expressions, a fund uncountable, which would she have innocently projected against the background of the green Greek hills? Would it have smitten her nerves badly or would she have laughed? And supposing Marjory could have seen him in his new khaki clothes cursing his dragoman as he listened to the devil-dog?

And now he interwove his memory of Marjory with a dead man and with a snake in the throes of the end of life. They crossed, intersected, tangled, these two thoughts. He perceived it clearly, the incongruity of it. He academically reflected upon the mysteries of the human mind, this homeless machine which lives here and then there and often lives in two or three opposing places at the same instant. He decided that the incident of the snake and the dead man had no more meaning than the greater number of the things which happen to us in our daily lives. Nevertheless it bore upon him.

CHAPTER X

ON a spread of plain they saw a force drawn up in long line. It was a flagrant inky streak on the verdant prairie. From somewhere near it sounded the timed reverberations of guns. The brisk walk of the next ten minutes was acutely exciting to Coleman. He could not but reflect that those guns were being fired with serious purpose at certain human bodies much like his own.

As they drew nearer they saw that the inky streak was composed of cavalry, the troopers standing at their bridles. The sunlight flickered upon their bright weapons. Now the dragoman developed in one of his extraordinary directions. He announced forsooth that an intimate friend was a captain of cavalry in this command. Coleman at first thought that this was some kind of mysterious lie but when they arrived where they could hear the stamping of hoofs, the clank of weapons, and the murmur of men, behold, a most dashing young officer gave a shout of joy and he and the dragoman hurled themselves into a mad embrace. After his first ecstasy was over, the dragoman bethought him of his employer and looking toward Coleman hastily explained him to the officer. The latter, it appeared, was very affable indeed. Much had happened. The Greeks and Turks had been fighting over a shallow part of the river nearly opposite this point and the Greeks had driven back the Turks and succeeded in throwing a bridge of casks and planking across the stream. It was now the duty and the delight of this force of cavalry to cross the bridge and, passing the little force of covering Greek infantry, to proceed into Turkey until they came in touch with the enemy.

Coleman's eyes dilated. Was ever fate less perverse. Partly in wretched French to the officer and partly in idiomatic English to the dragoman, he proclaimed his fiery desire to accompany the expedition. The officer immediately beamed upon him. In fact, he was delighted. The dragoman had naturally told him many falsehoods concerning Coleman, incidentally referring to himself more as a philanthropic guardian and valuable friend of the correspondent than as a plain unvarnished dragoman with an exceedingly good eye for the financial possibilities of his position.

Coleman wanted to ask his servant if there was any chance of the scout taking them near Nikopolis but he delayed being informed upon this point until such a time as he could find out, secretly, for himself. To ask the dragoman would be mere stupid questioning which would surely make the animal shy. He tried to be content that fate had given him this early opportunity of dealing with a medieval situation with some show of proper form; that is to say, armed, a-horseback and in danger. Then he could feel that to the gods of the game, he was not laughable, as when he rode to rescue his love in a diligence with a devil-dog yelping a-top.

With some flourish, the young captain presented him to the major who commanded the cavalry. This officer stood with his legs wide apart eating the rind of a fresh lemon and talking betimes to some of his officers. The major also beamed upon Coleman when the captain explained that the gentleman in the distinguished-looking khaki clothes wished to accompany the expedition. He at once said that he would provide two troop horses for Coleman and the dragoman. Coleman thanked fate for this behavior and his satisfaction was not without a vestige of surprise. At that time he judged it to be a remarkable amiability of individuals but in later years he came to believe in certain laws which he deemed existent solely for the benefit of war-correspondents. In the minds of governments, war-offices and generals they have no function save one of disturbance but Coleman deemed it proven that the common men, and many uncommon men, when they go away to the fighting-ground, out of the sight, out of the hearing of the world known to them and are eager to perform feats of war in this new place they feel an absolute longing for a spectator. It is indeed the veritable coronation of this world. There is not too much vanity of the street in this desire of men to have some disinterested fellows perceive their deeds. It is merely that a man doing his best in the middle of a sea of war longs to have people see him doing his best. This feeling is often notably serious if, in peace, a man has done his worst or part of his worst. Coleman believed that, above everybody, young, proud and brave subalterns had this itch but it existed, truly enough, from lieutenants to colonels. None wanted to conceal from his left hand that his right hand was performing a manly and valiant thing although there might be times when an application of the principle would be immensely convenient. The war-correspondent arises, then, to become a sort of cheap telescope for the people at home; further still, there have been fights where the eyes of a solitary man were the eyes of the world; one spectator whose business it was to transfer, according to his ability, his visual impressions to other minds.

Coleman and his servant were conducted to two saddled troop horses and beside them, waited decently in the rear of the ranks. The uniforms of the troopers were of plain dark green cloth and they were well and sensibly equipped. The mounts however had in no way been picked; there were little horses and big horses, fat horses and thin horses. They looked the result of a wild conscription. Coleman noted the faces of the troopers and they were calm enough, save when a man betrayed himself by perhaps a disproportionate angry jerk at the bridle of his restive horse.

The major, artistically drooping his cloak from his left shoulder and tenderly and musingly fingering his long yellow moustache, rode slowly to the middle of the line and wheeled his horse to face his men. A bugle called attention and then he addressed them in a loud and rapid speech which did not seem to have an end. Coleman imagined that the major was paying tribute to the Greek tradition of the power of oratory.

Again the trumpet rang out and this parade front swung off into column formation. Then Coleman and the dragoman trotted at the tails of the squadrons, restraining with difficulty their horses who could not understand their new places in the procession and worked feverishly to regain what they considered their positions in life.

The column jangled musically over the sod, passing between two hills on one of which a Greek light battery was posted. Its men climbed to the tops of their intrenchments to witness the going of the cavalry. Then the column curved along over ditch and through hedge to the shallows of the river. Across this narrow stream was Turkey. Turkey, however, presented nothing to the eye but a muddy bank with fringes of trees back of it. It seemed to be a great plain with sparse collections of foliage marking it, whereas the Greek side presented in the main a vista of high gaunt rocks. Perhaps one of the first effects of war upon the mind is a new recognition and fear of the circumscribed ability of the eye, making all landscape seem inscrutable. The cavalry drew up in platoon formation on their own bank of the stream, and waited. If Coleman had known anything of war he would have known, from appearances, that there was nothing in the immediate vicinity to cause heart-jumping, but as a matter of truth he was deeply moved and wondered what was hidden, what was veiled by those trees. Moreover, the squadrons resembled an old picture of a body of horse awaiting Napoleon's order to charge. In the meantime his mount fumed at the bit, plunging to get back to the ranks. The sky was without a cloud and the sunrays swept down upon them. Sometimes Coleman was on the verge of addressing the dragoman according to his anxiety but in the end he simply told him to go to the river and fill the canteens.

At last an order came and the first troop moved with muffled tumult across the bridge. Coleman and his dragoman followed the last troop. The horses scrambled up the muddy bank much as if they were merely breaking out of a pasture but probably all the men felt a sudden tightening of their muscles. Coleman in his excitement felt, more than he saw, glossy heaving horse flanks, green-clothed men chumping in their saddles, banging sabres and canteens, and carbines slanted in line.

There were some Greek infantry in a trench. They were heavily over-coated despite the heat and some were engaged in eating loaves of round thick bread. They called out lustily as the cavalry passed them. The troopers smiled slowly, somewhat proudly in response.

Presently there was another halt and Coleman saw the major trotting busily here and there while troop-commanders rode out to meet him. Spreading groups of scouts and flankers moved off and disappeared. Their dashing young officer friend cantered past them with his troop at his heels. He waved a joyful good-bye. It was the doings of cavalry in actual service, horsemen fanning out in all forward directions. There were two troops held in reserve and as they jangled ahead at a foot-pace, Coleman and his dragoman followed them.

The dragoman was now moved to erect many reasons for an immediate return. It was plain that he had no stomach at all for this business and that he wished himself safely back on the other side of the river. Coleman looked at him askance. When these men talked together Coleman might as well have been a Polar bear for all he understood of it. When he saw the trepidation of his dragoman he did not know what it fore-boded. In this situation it was not for him to say that the dragoman's fears were founded on nothing. And ever the dragoman raised his reasons for a retreat. Coleman spoke to himself. "I am just a trifle rattled," he said to his heart and after he had communed for a time upon the duty of steadiness he addressed the dragoman in cool language. "Now, my persuasive friend, just quit all that because business is business and it may be rather annoying business but you will have to go through with it." Long afterward when ruminating over the feelings of that morning he saw with some astonishment that there was not a single thing within sound or sight to cause a rational being any quaking. He was simply riding with some soldiers over a vast tree-dotted prairie.

Presently the commanding officer turned in his saddle and told the dragoman that he was going to ride forward with his orderly to where he could see the flanking parties and the scouts and courteously, with the manner of a gentleman entertaining two guests, he asked if the civilians cared to accompany him. The dragoman would not have passed this question correctly to Coleman if he had thought he could have avoided it but, with both men regarding him, he considered that a lie probably meant instant detection. He spoke almost the truth, contenting himself with merely communicating to Coleman in a subtle way his sense that a ride forward with the commanding officer and his orderly would be a depressing and dangerous occupation. But Coleman immediately accepted the invitation mainly because it was the invitation of the major and in war it is a brave man who can refuse the invitation of a commanding officer. The little party of four trotted away from the reserves, curving in single file about the water-holes. In time they arrived at where the plain lacked trees and was one great green lake of grass; grass and scrub. On this expanse they could see the Greek horsemen riding, mainly appearing as little black dots. Far to the left there was a squad said to be composed of only twenty troopers but in the distance their black mass seemed to be a regiment.

As the officer and his guests advanced they came in view of what one may call the shore of the plain. The rise of ground was heavily clad with trees and over the tops of them appeared the cupola and part of the walls of a large white house and there were glimpses of huts near it as if a village was marked. The black specks seemed to be almost to it. The major galloped forward and the others followed at his pace. The white house grew larger and larger and they came nearly to the advance scouts who they could now see were not quite close to the village. There had been a deception of the eye precisely as occurs at sea. Herds of unguarded sheep drifted over the plain and little ownerless horses, still cruelly hobbled, leaped painfully away, frightened, as if they understood that an anarchy had come upon them. The party rode until they were very nearly up with the scouts and then from low down at the very edge of the plain there came a long rattling noise which endured as if some kind of grinding machine had been put in motion. Smoke arose, faintly marking the position of an intrenchment. Sometimes a swift spitting could be heard from the air over the party.

It was Coleman's fortune to think at first that the Turks were not firing in his direction but as soon as he heard the weird voices in the air he knew that war was upon him. But it was plain that the range was almost excessive, plain even to his ignorance. The major looked and laughed; he found no difficulty in smiling in response. If this was war, it could be withstood somehow. He could not at this time understand what a mere trifle was the present incident. He felt upon his cheek a little breeze which was moving the grass-blades. He had tied his canteen in a wrong place on the saddle and every time the horse moved quickly the canteen banged the correspondent, to his annoyance and distress, forcibly on the knee.

He had forgotten about his dragoman but happening to look upon that faithful servitor, he saw him gone white with horror.

A bullet at that moment twanged near his head and the slave to fear ducked in a spasm. Coleman called the little orderly's attention and they both laughed discreetly. They made no pretension of being heroes but they saw plainly that they were better than this man.

Coleman said to him: "How far is it now to Nikopolis?" The dragoman replied only with a look of agonized impatience.

But of course there was no going to Nikopolis that day. The officer had advanced his men as far as he was intended by his superiors and presently they were all recalled and trotted back to the bridge. They crossed it to their old camp.

An important part of Coleman's traps was back with his Athenian horses and their groom but with his present equipment he could at least lie, smoking, on his blankets and watch the dragoman prepare food. But he reflected that for that day he had only attained the simple discovery that the approach to Nikopolis was surrounded with difficulties.

CHAPTER XI

THE same afternoon, Coleman and the dragoman rode up to Arta on their borrowed troop horses. The correspondent first went to the telegraph office and found there the usual number of despairing clerks. They were outraged when they found he was going to send messages and thought it preposterous that he insisted upon learning if there were any in the office for him. They had trouble enough with endless official communications without being hounded about private affairs by a confident young man in khaki. But Coleman at last unearthed six cablegrams which collectively said that the *Eclipse* wondered why they did not hear from him, that Walkley had been relieved from duty in London and sent to join the army of the Crown Prince, that young Point, the artist, had been shipped to Greece, that if he, Coleman, succeeded in finding the Wainwright party the paper was prepared to make a tremendous uproar of a celebration over it and, finally, the paper wondered twice more why they had not heard from him.

When Coleman went forth to enquire if anybody knew of the whereabouts of the Wainwright party he thought first of his fellow correspondents. He found most of them in a cafe where was to be had about the only food in the soldier-laden town. It was a slothful den where even an ordinary boiled egg could be made unpalatable. Such a common matter as the salt, men watched with greed and suspicion as if they were always about to grab it from each other. The proprietor, in a dirty shirt, could always be heard whining, evidently telling the world that he was being abused but he had spirit enough remaining to charge three prices for everything with an almost Jewish fluency.

The correspondents consoled themselves largely upon black bread and the native wines. Also there were certain little oiled fishes, and some green odds and ends for salads. The correspondents were practically all Englishmen. Some of them were veterans of journalism in the Sudan, in India, in South Africa; and there were others who knew as much of war as they could learn by sitting at a desk and editing the London stock reports. Some were on large salaries; some were on their own hook; some had horses and dragomen and some had neither the one nor the other; many knew how to write and a few had it yet to learn. The thing in common was a spirit of adventure which found pleasure in the extraordinary business of seeing how men kill each other.

They were talking of an artillery duel which had been fought the previous day between the Greek batteries above the town and the Turkish batteries across the river. Coleman took seat at one of the long tables and the astute dragoman got somebody in the street to hold the horses in order that he might be present at any feasting.

One of the experienced correspondents was remarking that the fire of the Greek batteries in the engagement had been the finest artillery practise of the century. He spoke a little loudly perhaps in the wistful hope that some of the Greek officers would understand enough English to follow his meaning for it is always good for a correspondent to admire the prowess on his own side of the battlefield. After a time Coleman spoke in a lull and describing the supposed misfortunes of the Wainwright party, asked if any one had news of them. The correspondents were surprised; they had none of them heard even of the existence of a Wainwright party. Also none of them seemed to care exceedingly. The conversation soon changed to a discussion of the probable result of the general Greek advance, announced for the morrow.

Coleman silently commented that this remarkable appearance of indifference to the mishap of the Wainwrights, a little party, a single group, was a better definition of a real condition of war than that bit of long-range futile musketry of the morning. He took a certain despatch out of his pocket and again read it. "Find Wainwright party all hazards much talk here success means red fire by ton *Eclipse*." It was an important matter. He could imagine how the American people, vibrating for years to stories of the cruelty of the Turk, would tremble—indeed, was now trembling—while the newspaper howled out the dire possibilities. He saw all the kinds of people, from those who would read the Wainwright chapters from day to day as a sort of sensational novel, to those who would work up a gentle sympathy for the woe of others around the table in the evenings. He saw bar-keepers and policemen taking a high gallery thrill out of this kind of romance. He saw even the emotion among the American colleges over the tragedy of a professor and some students. It certainly was a big affair. Marjory of course was everything in one way but that to the world was not a big affair. It was the romance of the Wainwright party in its simplicity that to the American world was arousing great sensation; one that in the old days would have made his heart leap like a colt.

Still, when batteries had fought each other savagely and horse, foot and guns were now about to make a general advance, it was difficult, he could see, to stir men to think and feel out of the present zone of action; to adopt for a time in fact the thoughts and feelings of the other side of the world. It made Coleman dejected as he saw clearly that the task was wholly on his own shoulders.

Of course they were men who when at home manifested the most gentle and wide reaching feelings; most of them could not by any possibility have slapped a kitten merely for the prank and yet all of them who had seen an unknown man shot through the head in battle had little more to think of it than if the man had been a rag-baby. Tender they might be; poets they might be; but they were all horned with a provisional, temporary, but absolutely essential callous which was formed by their existence amid war with its quality of making them always think of the sights and sounds concealed in their own direct future.

They had been simply polite. "Yes?" said one to Coleman. "How many people in the party? Are they all Americans? Oh, I suppose it will be quite right. Your minister in Constantinople will arrange all that easily. Where did you say? At Nikopolis? Well, we conclude that the Turks will make no stand between here and Pentepigadia. In that case, your Nikopolis will be uncovered unless the garrison at Prevasa intervenes. That garrison at Prevasa, by the way, may make a deal of trouble. Remember Plevna."

"Exactly how far is it to Nikopolis?" asked Coleman.

"Oh, I think it is about thirty kilometers," replied the other. "There is a good military road as soon as you cross the Louros river. I've got the map of the Austrian General Staff. Would you like to look at it?"

Coleman studied the map speeding with his eye rapidly to and fro between Arta and Nikopolis. To him it was merely a brown lithograph of mystery but he could study the distances.

He had received a cordial invitation from the commander of the cavalry to go with him for another ride into Turkey and he inclined to believe that his project would be furthered if he stuck close to the cavalry. So he rode back to the cavalry camp and went peacefully to sleep on the sod. He awoke in the morning with chattering teeth to find his dragoman saying that the major had unaccountably withdrawn his loan of the two troop horses. Coleman of course immediately said to himself that the dragoman was lying again in order to prevent another expedition into ominous Turkey but after all if the commander of the cavalry had suddenly turned the light of his favor from the correspondent it was only a proceeding consistent with the nature which Coleman now thought he was beginning to discern, a nature which can never think twice in the same place, a gaseous mind which drifts, dissolves, combines, vanishes with the ability of an aerial thing until the man of the north feels that when he clutches it with full knowledge of his senses he is only the victim of his ardent imagination. It is the difference in standards, in creeds, which is the more luminous when men call out that they are all alike.

Coleman and his dragoman loaded their traps and moved out to again invade Turkey. It was not yet clear day-light but they felt that they might well start early since they were no longer mounted men.

On the way to the bridge, the dragoman although he was curiously in love with his forty francs a day and his opportunities, ventured a stout protest based apparently on the fact that after all this foreigner, four days out from Athens, was somewhat at his mercy. "Meester Coleman," he said, stopping suddenly, "I think we make no good if we go there. Much better we wait Arta for our horse. *Much* better. I think this no good. There is coming one big fight and I think much better we go stay Arta. *Much* better."

"Oh, come off," said Coleman. And in clear language he began to labor with the man. "Look here, now, if you think you are engaged in steering a bunch of wooden-headed guys about the Acropolis, my dear partner of my joys and sorrows, you are extremely mistaken. As a matter of fact you are now the dragoman of a war-correspondent and you were engaged and are paid to be one. It becomes necessary that you make good. Make good, do you understand? I'm not out here to be buncoed by this sort of a game." . . . He continued indefinitely in this strain and at intervals he asked sharply: "Do you understand?"

Perhaps the dragoman was dumbfounded that the laconic Coleman could on occasion talk so much or perhaps he understood everything and was impressed by the argumentative power. At any rate he suddenly wilted. He made a gesture which was a protestation of martyrdom and picking up his burden proceeded on his way.

When they reached the bridge, they saw strong columns of Greek infantry, dead black in the dim light, crossing the stream and slowly deploying on the other shore. It was a bracing sight to the dragoman who then went into one of his absurd babbling moods in which he would have talked the head off any man who was not born in a country laved by the childish Mediterranean. Coleman could not understand what he said to the soldiers as they passed but it was evidently all grandiose nonsense.

Two light batteries had precariously crossed the rickety bridge during the night and now this force of several thousand infantry with the two batteries was moving out over the territory which the cavalry had reconnoitred on the previous day. The ground being familiar to Coleman he no longer knew a tremor and, regarding his dragoman, he saw that that invaluable servitor was also in better form. They marched until they found one of the light batteries unlimbered and aligned on the lake of grass about a mile from where parts of the white house appeared above the tree-tops. Here the dragoman talked with the captain of artillery, a tiny man on an immense horse, who for some unknown reason told him that this force was going to raid into Turkey and try to swing around the opposing army's right flank. He announced, as he showed his teeth in a smile, that it would be very dangerous work. The dragoman precipitated himself upon Coleman.

"This is much danger. The copten he tell me the trups go now in back of the Turks. It will be much danger. I think much better we go Arta wait for horse. *Much* better." Coleman although he believed he despised the dragoman could not help but be influenced by his fears. They were, so to speak, in a room with one window and only the dragoman looked forth from the window, so if he said that what he saw outside frightened him, Coleman was perforce frightened also in a measure. But when the correspondent raised his eyes he saw the captain of the battery looking at him, his teeth still showing in a smile, as if his information whether true or false had been given to convince the foreigner that the Greeks were a very superior and brave people, notably one little officer of artillery. He had apparently assumed that Coleman would baulk from venturing with such a force upon an excursion to trifle with the rear of a hard-fighting Ottoman army. He exceedingly disliked that man sitting up there on his tall horse and grinning like a cruel little ape with a secret. In truth, Coleman was taken back at the outlook but he could no more refrain from instantly accepting this half-concealed challenge than he could have refrained from resenting an ordinary form of insult. His mind was not at peace but the small vanities are very large. He was perfectly aware that he was being misled into the thing by some odd pride but anyhow it easily might turn out to be a stroke upon the doors of Nikopolis. He nodded and smiled at the officer in grateful acknowledgment of his service.

The infantry was moving steadily a-field. Black blocks of men were trailing in column slowly over the plain. They were not unlike the backs of dominoes on a green baize table; they were so vivid, so startling. The correspondent and his servant followed them. Eventually they over-took two companies in command of a captain who seemed immensely glad to have the strangers with him. As they marched, the captain spoke through the dragoman upon the virtues of his men announcing with other news the fact that his first serjeant was the bravest man in the world.

A number of columns were moving across the plain parallel to their line of march and the whole force seemed to have orders to halt when they reached a long ditch about four-hundred yards from where the shore of the plain arose to the luxuriant groves with the cupola of the big white house sticking above them. The soldiers lay along the ditch and the bravest man in the world spread his blanket on the ground for the captain, Coleman and himself. During a long pause, Coleman tried to elucidate the question of why the Greek soldiers wore heavy over-coats even in the bitter heat of mid-day but he could only learn that the dews when they came were very destructive to the lungs. Further, he convinced himself anew that talking through an interpreter to the minds of other men was as satisfactory as looking at landscape through a stained-glass window.

After a time there was, in front, a stir near where a curious hedge of dry brambles seemed to outline some sort of a garden-patch.

Many of the soldiers exclaimed and raised their guns. But there seemed to come a general understanding to the line that it was wrong to fire. Then presently into the open came a dirty brown figure and Coleman could see through his glasses that its head was crowned with a dirty fez which had once been white. This indicated that the figure was that of one of the Christian peasants of Epirus. Obedient to the captain the serjeant arose and waved invitation. The peasant wavered, changed his mind, was obviously terror stricken, regained confidence and then began to advance circuitously toward the Greek lines. When he arrived within hailing distance, the captain, the serjeant, Coleman's dragoman and many of the soldiers yelled human messages and a moment later he was seen to be a poor yellow-faced stripling with a body which seemed to have been first twisted by an ill-birth and afterward maimed by either labor or oppression, these being often identical in their effects.

His reception of the Greek soldiery was no less fervid than their welcome of him to their protection. He threw his grimy fez in the air and croaked out cheers while tears wet his cheeks. When he had come upon the right side of the ditch he ran capering among them and the captain, the serjeant, the dragoman and a number of soldiers received wild embraces and kisses. He made a dash at Coleman but Coleman was now wary in the game and retired dexterously behind different groups with a finished appearance of not noting that the young man wished to greet him.

Behind the hedge of dry brambles there were more indications of life and the peasant stood up and made beseeching gestures. Soon a whole flock of miserable people in crude and comic smocks, pranced here and there uproariously embracing and kissing their deliverers. An old tearful, toothless hag flung herself rapturously into the arms of the captain and Coleman's brick-and-iron soul was moved to admiration at the way in which the officer administered a chaste salute upon that furrowed cheek. The dragoman told the correspondent that the Turks had run away from this village on up a valley toward Jannina. Everybody was proud and happy.

A major of infantry came from the rear at this time and asked the captain in sharp tones who were the two strangers in civilian attire. When the captain had answered correctly, the major was immediately mollified and had it announced to the correspondent that his battalion was going to move immediately into the village and that he would be delighted to have his company.

The major strode at the head of his men with the group of villagers singing and dancing about him and looking upon him as if he were a god. Coleman and the dragoman, at the officer's request, marched one on either side of him and in this manner they entered the village. From all sorts of hedges and thickets, people came creeping out to pass into a delirium of joy. The major borrowed three little pack-horses with rope bridles and thus mounted and followed by the clanking column they rode on in triumph.

It was probably more of a true festival than most men experience in the longest life-time. The major with his Greek instinct of drama was a splendid personification of poetic quality; in fact he was himself almost a lyric. From time to time he glanced back at Coleman with eyes half dimmed with appreciation. The people gathered flowers, great blossoms of purple and corn-color. They sprinkled them over the three horsemen and flung them deliriously under the feet of the little nags. Being now mounted Coleman had no difficulty in avoiding the embraces of the peasants but he felt to the tips of his toes an abandonment to a kind of pleasure with which he was not at all familiar. Riding thus amid cries of thanksgiving addressed at him equally with the others he felt a burning virtue and quite lost his old self in an illusion of noble benignity. And there continued the fragrant hail of blossoms.

Miserable little huts straggled along the sides of the village street as if they were following at the heels of the great white house of the bey. The column proceeded north-ward announcing laughingly to the glad villagers that they would never see another Turk. Before them on the road was here and there a fez from the head of a fled Turkish soldier and they lay like drops of blood from some wounded leviathan. Ultimately it grew cloudy. It even rained slightly. In the misty downfall the column of soldiers in blue was dim as if it were merely a long trail of low-hung smoke.

They came to the ruins of a church and there the major halted his battalion. Coleman worried at his dragoman to learn if the halt was only temporary. It was a long time before there was answer from the major for he had drawn up his men in platoons and was addressing them in a speech as interminable as any that Coleman had heard in Greece. The officer waved his arms and roared out, evidently, the glories of patriotism and soldierly honor, the glories of their ancient people, and he may have included any subject in this wonderful speech for the reason that he had plenty of time in which to do it. It was impossible to tell whether the oration was a good one or a bad one because the men stood in their loose platoons without discernible feeling as if to them this appeared merely as one of the inevitable consequences of a campaign, an established rule of warfare. Coleman ate black bread and chocolate tablets while the dragoman hovered near the major with the intention of pouncing upon him for information as soon as his lungs yielded to the strain upon them.

The dragoman at last returned with a very long verbal treatise from the major who apparently had not been as exhausted after his speech to the men as one would think. The major had said that he had been ordered to halt here to form a junction with some of the troops coming direct from Arta and that he expected that in the morning the army would be divided and one wing would chase the retreating Turks on toward Jannina while the other wing would advance upon Prevasa because the enemy had a garrison there which had not retreated an inch and although it was cut off, it was necessary to send either a force to hold it in its place or a larger force to go through with the business of capturing it, else there would be left in the rear of the left flank of a Greek advance upon Jannina a body of the enemy which at any moment might become active. The major said that his battalion would probably form part of the force to advance upon Prevasa. Nikopolis was on the road to Prevasa and only three miles from it.

CHAPTER XII

COLEMAN spent a long afternoon in the drizzle. Enveloped in his macintosh he sat on a boulder in the lee of one of the old walls and moodily smoked cigars and listened to the ceaseless clatter of tongues. A ray of light penetrated the mind of the dragoman and he labored assiduously with wet fuel until he had accomplished a tin of coffee. Bits of cinder floated in it but Coleman rejoiced and was kind to the dragoman.

The night was of cruel monotony. Afflicted by the wind and the darkness, the correspondent sat with nerves keyed high waiting to hear the pickets open fire on the night attack. He was so unaccountably sure that there would be a tumult and panic of this kind at some time of the night that he prevented himself from getting a reasonable amount of rest. He could hear the soldiers breathing in sleep all about him; he wished to arouse them from this slumber which, to his ignorance, seemed stupid. Often he bent near to the embers of the fire and looked at his watch. The quality of mysterious menace in the great gloom and the silence would have caused him to pray if prayer would have transported him magically to New York and made him a young man with no coat playing billiards at his club.

The chill dawn came at last and with it a fine elation which ever follows a dismal night in war; an elation which bounds in the bosom as soon as day has knocked the shackles from a trembling mind. Although Coleman had slept but a short time he was now as a total abstainer coming from the bath. He heard the creak of battery wheels; he saw crawling bodies of infantry moving in the dim light like ghostly processions. He felt a tremendous virility come with this new hope in the day-light. He again took satisfaction in his sentimental journey. It was a shining affair. He was on active service, an active service of the heart, and he felt that he was a strong man ready to conquer difficulty even as the olden heroes conquered difficulty. He imagined himself in a way like them. He, too, had come out to fight for love with giants, dragons and witches. He had never known that he could be so pleased with that kind of a parallel.

The dragoman announced that the major had suddenly lent their horses to some other people and after cursing this versatility of interest, he summoned his henchman and they moved out on foot, following the sound of the creaking wheels. They came in time to a bridge and on the other side of this bridge was a hard military road which sprang away in two directions, north and west. Some troops were creeping out the west-ward way and the dragoman pointing at them said: "They going Prevasa. That is road to Nikopolis."

Coleman grinned from ear to ear and slapped his dragoman violently on the shoulder. For a moment he intended to hand the man a louis of reward but he changed his mind.

Their traps were in the way of being heavy but they minded little since the dragoman was now a victim of the influence of Coleman's enthusiasm. The road wound along the base of a mountain range, sheering around the abutments in wide and white curves and then circling into glens where immense trees spread their shade over it. Some of the great trunks were oppressed with vines green as garlands and these vines even ran like verdant foam over the rocks. Streams of translucent water showered down from the hills and made pools in which every pebble, every leaf of a water plant shone with magic lustre and if the bottom of a pool was only of clay, the clay glowed with sapphire light. The day was fair. The country was part of that land which turned the minds of its ancient poets toward a more tender dreaming so that indeed their nymphs would die, one is sure, in the cold mythology of the north with its storms amid the gloom of pine forests. It was all wine to Coleman's spirit. It enlivened him to think of success with absolute surety. To be sure one of his boots began soon to rasp his toes but he gave it no share of his attention. They passed at a much faster pace than the troops and everywhere they met laughter and confidence and the cry: "On to Prevasa."

At mid-day they were at the heels of the advance battalion,

among its stragglers, taking its white dust into their throats and eyes. The dragoman was waning and he made a number of attempts to stay Coleman but no one could have had influence upon Coleman's steady rush, with his eyes always straight to the front as if thus to symbolize his steadiness of purpose.

Rivulets of sweat marked the dust on his face and two of his toes were now paining as if they were being burned off. He was obliged to concede himself a privilege of limping but he would not stop.

At night-fall they halted with the outpost battalion of the infantry. All the cavalry had in the meantime come up and they saw their old friends. There was a village from which the Christian peasants came and cheered like a trained chorus. Soldiers were driving a great flock of fat sheep into a corral. They had belonged to a Turkish bey and they bleated as if they knew that they were now mere spoils of war. Coleman lay on the steps of the bey's house smoking with his head on his blanket-roll. Camp-fires glowed off in the fields. He was now about four miles from Nikopolis.

Within the house, the commander of the cavalry was writing despatches. Officers clanked up and down the stairs. The dashing young captain came and said that there would be a general assault on Prevasa at the dawn of the next day. Afterward, the dragoman descended upon the village and in some way wrenched a little grey horse from an inhabitant. Its pack-saddle was on its back and it would very handily carry the traps. In this matter the dragoman did not consider his master; he considered his own sore back.

Coleman ate more bread and chocolate tablets and also some tinned sardines. He was content with the day's work. He did not see how he could have improved it. There was only one route by which the Wainwright party could avoid him and that was by going to Prevasa and thence taking ship. But since Prevasa was blockaded by a Greek fleet, he conceived that event to be impossible. Hence, he had them hedged on this peninsula and they must be either at Nikopolis or Prevasa. He would probably know all early in the morning. He reflected that he was too tired to care if there might be a night attack and then wrapped in his blankets he went peacefully to sleep in the grass under a big tree with the crooning of some soldiers around their fire blending into his slumber.

And now although the dragoman had performed a number of feats of incapacity he achieved during the one hour of Coleman's sleeping a blunder which for real finish was simply a perfection of art. When Coleman, much later, extracted the full story, it appeared that ringing events happened during that single hour of sleep. Ten minutes after he had lain down for a night of oblivion, the battalion of infantry which had advanced a little beyond the village was recalled and began a hurried night march back on the way that it had so festively come. It was significant enough to appeal to almost any mind but the dragoman was able not to understand it. He remained jabbering to some acquaintances among the troopers. Coleman had been asleep his hour when the dashing young captain perceived the dragoman and completely horrified by his presence at that place, ran to him and whispered to him swiftly that the game was to flee, flee, flee. The wing of the army which had advanced north-ward upon Jannina had already been tumbled back by the Turks and all the other wing had been recalled to the Louros river and there was now nothing practically between him and his sleeping master and the enemy but a cavalry picket. The cavalry was immediately going to make a forced march to the rear. The stricken dragoman could even then see troopers getting into their saddles. He rushed to the tree and in a panic simply bundled Coleman upon his feet before he was awake. He stuttered out his tale and the dazed correspondent heard it punctuated by the steady trample of the retiring cavalry. The dragoman saw a man's face then turn in a flash from an expression of luxurious drowsiness to an expression of utter malignancy. However he was in too much of a hurry to be afraid of it; he ran off to the little grey horse and frenziedly but skilfully began to bind the traps upon the pack-saddle. "Come. Come. Come. Queek! Queek!" They slid hurriedly down a bank to the road and started to do again that which they had accomplished with considerable expenditure of physical power during the day. The hoof-beats of the cavalry had already died away and the mountains shadowed them in lonely silence. They were the rear-guard after the rear-guard.

The dragoman muttered hastily his last dire rumors. Five hundred Circassian cavalry were coming. The mountains were now infested with the dread Albanian irregulars. Coleman had thought in his day-light tramp that he had appreciated the noble distances but he found that he knew nothing of their nobility until he tried this night stumbling. And the hoofs of the little horse made on the hard road more noise than could be made by men beating with hammers upon brazen cylinders. The correspondent glanced continually up at the crags. From the other side he could sometimes hear the metallic clink of water deep down in a glen. For the first time in his life he seriously opened the flap of his holster and let his fingers remain on the handle of his revolver. From just in front of him he could hear the chattering of the dragoman's teeth which no attempt at more coolness could seem to prevent. In the meantime the casual manner of the little grey horse struck Coleman with maddening vividness. If the black darkness was simply filled with ferocious Albanians, the horse did not care a button; he leisurely put his feet down with a resounding ring. Coleman whispered hastily to the dragoman: "If they rush us, jump down the bank, no matter how deep it is. That's our only chance. And try to keep together."

All they saw of the universe was, in front of them, a plane faintly luminous near their feet but fading in six yards to the darkness of a dungeon. This represented the bright white road of the daytime. It had no end. Coleman had thought that he could tell from the very feel of the air some of the landmarks of his daytime journey but he had now no sense of location at all. He would not have denied that he was squirming on his belly like a worm through black mud.

They went on and on. Visions of his past were sweeping through Coleman's mind precisely as they are said to sweep through the mind of a drowning person. But he had no regret for any bad deeds; he regretted merely distant hours of peace and protection. He was no longer a hero going to rescue his love. He was a slave making a gasping attempt to escape from the most incredible tyranny of circumstance. He half vowed to himself that if the God whom he had in no wise heeded, would permit him to crawl out of this slavery he would never again venture a yard toward a danger any greater than may be incurred from the police of a most proper metropolis. If his juvenile and up-lifting thoughts of other days had reproached him he would simply have repeated and repeated: "Adventure be damned."

It became known to them that the horse had to be led. The debased creature was asserting its right to do as it had been trained, to follow its customs; it was asserting this right during a situation which required conduct superior to all training and custom. It was so grossly conventional that Coleman would have understood that demoniac form of anger which sometimes leads men to jab knives into warm bodies. Coleman from cowardice tried to induce the dragoman to go ahead leading the horse and the dragoman from cowardice tried to induce Coleman to go ahead leading the horse. Coleman of course had to succumb. The dragoman was only good to walk behind and tearfully whis-per maledictions as he prodded the flanks of their tranquil beast.

In the absolute black of the frequent forests, Coleman could not see his feet and he often felt like a man walking forward to fall at any moment down a thousand yards of chasm. He heard whispers; he saw skulking figures and these frights turned out to be the voice of a little trickle of water or the effect of wind among the leaves but they were replaced by the same terrors in slightly different forms.

Then the poignant thing interpolated. A volley crashed ahead of them some half of a mile away and another volley answered from a still nearer point. Swishing noises which the correspond-ent had heard in the air he now knew to have been from the passing of bullets. He and the dragoman came stock still. They heard three other volleys sounding with the abrupt clamor of a hail of little stones upon a hollow surface. Coleman and the dragoman came close together and looked into the whites of each other's eyes. The ghastly horse at that moment stretched down his neck and began placidly to pluck the grass at the road-side. The two men were equally blank with fear and each seemed to seek in the other some newly rampant manhood upon which he could lean at this time. Behind them were the Turks. In front of them was a fight in the darkness. In front it was mathematic to suppose in fact were also the Turks. They were barred; en-closed; cut off. The end was come.

Even at that moment they heard behind them the sound of slow stealthy footsteps. They both wheeled instantly, choking with this additional terror. Coleman saw the dragoman move swiftly to the side of the road, ready to jump into whatever abyss happened to be there. Coleman still gripped the halter as if it were in truth a straw. The stealthy footsteps were much nearer. Then it was that an insanity came upon him as if fear had flamed up within him until it gave him all the magnificent desperation of a mad-man. He jerked the grey horse broadside to the approaching mystery and grabbing out his revolver aimed it from the top of his improvised bulwark. He hailed the darkness.

"Halt. Who's there?" He had expected his voice to sound like a groan but instead it happened to sound clear, stern, commanding like the voice of a young sentry at an encampment of volunteers. He did not seem to have any privilege of selection as to the words. They were born of themselves.

He waited then, blanched and hopeless, for death to wing out of the darkness and strike him down. He heard a voice. The voice said—"Do you speak English?" For one or two seconds he could not even understand English and then the great fact swelled up and up within him. This voice with all its new quavers was still undoubtedly the voice of Professor Harrison B. Wainwright of Washurst College.

CHAPTER XIII

A CHANGE flashed over Coleman as if it had come from an electric storage. He had known the professor long but he had never before heard a quaver in his voice and it was this little quaver that seemed to impel him to a supreme disregard of the dangers which he had looked upon as being the final dangers. His own voice had not quavered.

When he spoke, he spoke in a low tone but it was the voice of the master of the situation. He could hear his dupes fluttering there in the darkness. "Yes," he said, "I speak English. There is some danger. Stay where you are and make no noise." He was as cool as an iced drink. To be sure the circumstances had in no wise changed as to his personal danger but beyond the important fact that there were now others to endure it with him, he seemed able to forget it in a strange unauthorized sense of victory. It came from the professor's quavers.

Meanwhile he had forgotten the dragoman but he recalled him in time to bid him wait. Then, as well concealed as a monk hiding in his cowl, he tip-toed back into the group of people who knew him intimately. He discerned two women mounted on little horses and about them were dim men. He could hear them breathing hard. "It is all right," he began smoothly. "You only need to be very careful——"

Suddenly out of the blackness projected a half-phosphorescent face. It was the face of the little professor. He stammered. "We —we—do you really speak English?" Coleman in his feeling of superb triumph could almost have laughed. His nerves were steady as hemp but he was in haste and his haste allowed him to administer rebuke to his old professor. "Didn't you hear me?" he hissed through his tightening lips. "They are fighting just ahead of us on the road and if you want to save yourselves don't waste time."

Another face loomed faintly like a mask painted in dark grey. It belonged to Coke and it was a mask figured in profound stupefaction. The lips opened and tensely breathed out the name: "Coleman." Instantly the correspondent felt about him that kind of a tumult which tries to suppress itself. He knew that it was the most theatric moment of his life. He glanced quickly toward the two figures on horse-back. He believed that one was making foolish gesticulation while the other sat rigid and silent. This latter one he knew to be Marjory. He was content that she did not move. Only a woman who was glad he had come but did not care for him would have moved. This applied directly to what he thought he knew of Marjory's nature.

There was confusion among the students but Coleman suppressed it as in such a situation might a centurion. "S-s-steady." He seized the arm of the professor and drew him forcibly close. "The condition is this," he whispered rapidly. "We are in a fix with this fight on up the road. I was sent after you but I can't get you into the Greek lines tonight. Mrs. Wainwright and Marjory must dismount and I and my man will take the horses on and hide them. All the rest of you must go about a hundred feet into the woods and hide. When I come back, I'll hail you and you answer low." The professor was like pulp in his grasp. He choked out the word "Coleman" in agony and wonder but he obeyed with a palpable gratitude. Coleman sprang to the side of the shadowy figure of Marjory. "Come," he said authoritatively. She laid in his palm a little icy cold hand and dropped from her horse. He had an impulse to cling to the small fingers but he loosened them immediately, imparting to his manner as well as the darkness permitted him, a kind of casual politeness as if he were too intent upon the business in hand. He bunched the crowd and pushed them into the woods. Then he and the dragoman took the horses a hundred yards onward and tethered them. No one would care if they were stolen; the great point was to get them where their noise would have no power of revealing the whole party. There had been no further firing.

After he had tied the little grey horse to a tree he unroped his luggage and carried the most of it back to the point where the others had left the road. He called out cautiously and received a sibilant answer. He and the dragoman bunted among the trees until they came to where a forlorn company was seated awaiting them, lifting their faces like frogs out of a pond. His first question did not give them any assurance. He said at once: "Are any of you armed?" Unanimously they breathed: "No." He searched them out one by one and finally sank down by the professor. He kept a sort of hypnotic handcuff upon the dragoman because he foresaw that this man was really going to be the key to the best means of escape. To a large neutral party wandering between hostile lines there was technically no danger but actually there was a great deal. Both armies had too many irregulars, lawless hillsmen come out to fight in their own way, and if they were encountered in the dead of the night on such hazardous ground the Greek hillsmen with their white cross on a blue field would be precisely as dangerous as the blood-hungry Albanians. Coleman knew that the rational way was to reach the Greek lines and he had no intention of reaching the Greek lines without a tongue and the only tongue was in the mouth of the dragoman. He was correct in thinking that the professor's deep knowledge of the ancient language would give him small clue to the speech of the modern Greek.

As he settled himself by the professor the band of students, eight in number, pushed their faces close.

He did not see any reason for speaking. There were thirty seconds of deep silence in which he felt that all were bending to hearken to his words of counsel. He said nothing because it increased his strange prestige and because in the second place he had to bestow only a most minute amount of counsel. The professor huskily broke the stillness. "Well——what are we to do now?"

Coleman was decisive, indeed absolute. "We'll stay here until day-light unless you care to get shot."

"All right," answered the professor. He turned and made a useless remark to his flock: "Stay here."

Coleman asked civilly: "Have you had anything to eat? Have you got anything to wrap around you?"

"We have absolutely nothing," answered the professor. "Our servants ran away and . . . we left everything behind us and . . . I've never been in such a position in my life."

Coleman moved softly in the darkness and unbuckled some of

his traps. On his knee he broke the hard cakes of bread and with his fingers he broke the little tablets of chocolate. These he distributed to his people. And at this time he felt fully an appreciation of the conduct of the eight American college students. They had not yet said a word—with the exception of the bewildered exclamation from Coke. They all knew him well. In any circumstance of life which as far as he truly believed, they had yet encountered, they would have been privileged to accost him in every form of their remarkable vocabulary. They were as new to this game as would have been eight newly caught Apache Indians if such were set to run the elevators in the Tract Society Building. He could see their eyes gazing at him anxiously and he could hear their deep-drawn breaths. But they said no word. He knew that they were looking upon him as their leader, almost as their saviour, and he knew also that they were going to follow him without a murmur in the conviction that he knew ten-fold more than they knew. It occurred to him that his position was ludicrously false but, anyhow, he was glad. Surely it would be a very easy thing to lead them to safety in the morning and he foresaw the credit which would come to him. He concluded that it was beneath his dignity as preserver to vouchsafe them many words. His business was to be the cold, masterful, enigmatic man. It might be said that these reflections were only half-thoughts in his mind. Meanwhile a section of his intellect was flying hither and thither, speculating upon the Circassian cavalry and the Albanian guerillas and even the Greek outposts.

He unbuckled his blanket-roll and taking one blanket placed it about the shoulders of the shadow which was Mrs. Wainwright. The shadow protested incoherently but he muttered: "Oh, that's all right." Then he took his other blanket and went to the shadow which was Marjory. It was something like putting a wrap about the shoulders of a statue. He was base enough to linger in the hopes that he could detect some slight trembling but as far as he knew, she was of stone. His macintosh he folded around the body of the professor amid quite senile protests, so senile that the professor seemed suddenly proven to him as an old old man, a fact which had never occurred to Washurst or her children. Then he went to the dragoman and pre-empted half of his blankets. The dragoman grunted but Coleman was panther

fashion with him. It would not do to have this dragoman develope a luxurious temperament when eight American college
students were, without speech, shivering in the cold night.

Coleman really began to ruminate upon his glory but he
found that he could not do this well without smoking so he crept
away some distance from the fireless encampment and bending
his face to the ground at the foot of a tree he struck a match
and lit a cigar. His return to the others would have been somewhat in the manner of coolness as displayed on the stage if he
had not been prevented by the necessity of making no noise. He
saw regarding him as before the dimly visible eyes of the eight
students and Marjory and her father and mother. Then he whispered the conventional words: "Go to sleep if you can. You'll
need your strength in the morning. I and this man here will keep
watch." Three of the college students of course crawled up to
him and each said: "I'll keep watch, old man."

"No. We'll keep watch. You people try to sleep."

He deemed that it might be better to yield the dragoman his
blanket and so he got up and leaned against a tree smoking,
holding his hand to the brilliant point of his cigar. He knew
perfectly well that none of them could sleep but he stood there
somewhat like a sentry without the attitude but with all the effect of responsibility.

He had no doubt but what escape to civilization would be easy
but anyhow his heroism should be preserved. He was the rescuer.
His thoughts of Marjory were somewhat in a puzzle. The meeting had placed him in such a position that he had expected a lot
of condescension on his own part. Instead, she had exhibited
about as much recognition of him as would a stone fountain on
his grandfather's place in Connecticut. This in his opinion was
not the way to greet the knight who had come to the rescue of
his lady. He had not expected it so to happen. In fact from
Athens to this place he had engaged himself with imagery of possible meetings. He was vexed, certainly, but far beyond that he
knew a deeper admiration for this girl. To him she represented
the sex and the sex as embodied in her seemed a mystery to be
feared. He wondered if safety came on the morrow he would not
surrender to this feminine invulnerability. She had not done anything that he had expected of her and so inasmuch as he loved

her he loved her more. It was bewitching. He half considered himself a fool. But at any rate he thought resentfully she should be thankful to him for having rendered her a great service. However when he came to consider this proposition he knew that on a basis of absolute manly endeavor he had rendered her little or no service. The night was long.

CHAPTER XIV

COLEMAN suddenly found himself looking upon his pallid dragoman. He saw that he had been asleep crouched at the foot of the tree. Without any exchange of speech at all he knew there had been alarming noises. Then shots sounded from near by. Some were from rifles aimed in that direction and some were from rifles opposed to them. This was distinguishable to the experienced man but all that Coleman knew was that the conditions of danger were now triplicated. Unconsciously he stretched his hands in supplication over his charges. "Don't move! Don't move! And keep close to the ground!" All heeded him but Marjory. She still sat straight. He himself was on his feet but he now knew the sound of bullets and he knew that no bullets had spun through the trees. He could not see her distinctly but it was known to him in some way that she was mutinous. He leaned toward her and spoke as harshly as was possible. "Marjory! Get down!" She wavered for a moment as if resolved to defy him. As he turned again to peer in the direction of the firing it went through his mind that she must love him very much indeed. He was assured of it.

It must have been some small out-pour between nervous pickets and eager hillsmen for it ended in a moment. The party waited in abasement for what seemed to them a long time and the blue dawn began to laggardly shift the night as they waited. The dawn itself seemed prodigiously long in arriving at anything like discernible landscape. When this was consummated, Coleman in somewhat the manner of the father of a church, dealt bits of chocolate out to the others. He had already taken the precaution to confer with the dragoman so he said: "Well, come ahead. We'll make a try for it." They arose at his bidding and followed him to the road. It was the same broad white road only that the white was in the dawning something like the grey of a veil. It took some courage to venture upon this thoroughfare but Coleman stepped out after looking quickly in both directions. The party tramped to where the horses had been left and there they were found without change of a rope. Coleman rejoiced to see that his dragoman now followed him in the way of a good lieutenant. They both dashed in among the trees and had the horses out into the road in a twinkle. When Coleman turned to direct that utterly subservient group he knew that his face was drawn from hardship and anxiety but he saw everywhere the same style of face with the exception of the face of Marjory who looked simply of lovely marble. He noted with a curious satisfaction, as if the thing were a tribute to himself, that his macintosh was over the professor's shoulders, that Marjory and her mother were each carrying a blanket and that the corps of students had dutifully brought all the traps which his dragoman had forgotten. It was grand.

He addressed them to say: "Now, approaching outposts is very dangerous business at this time in the morning. So my man who can talk both Greek and Turkish will go ahead forty yards and I will follow somewhere between him and you. Try not to crowd forward."

He directed the ladies upon their horses and placed the professor upon the little grey nag. Then they took up their line of march. The dragoman had looked somewhat dubiously upon this plan of having him go forty yards in advance but he had the utmost confidence in this new Coleman whom yesterday he had not known. Besides he himself was a very gallant man indeed and it befitted him to take the post of danger before the eyes of all these foreigners. In his new position he was as proud and unreasonable as a rooster. He was continually turning his head to scowl back at them when only the clank of hoofs was sounding. An impenetrable mist lay on the valley and the hill-tops were shrouded. As for the people they were like mice. Coleman paid no attention to the Wainwright party but walked steadily along near the dragoman.

Perhaps the whole thing was a trifle absurd but to a great percentage of the party it was terrible. For instance those eight boys fresh from a school could in no wise gauge the dimensions. And if this was true of the students it was more distinctly true of

Marjory and her mother. As for the professor he seemed weighted to the earth by his love and his responsibility.

Suddenly the dragoman wheeled and made demoniac signs. Coleman half turned to survey the main body and then paid his attention swiftly to the front. The white road sped to the top of a hill where it seemed to make a rotund swing into oblivion. The top of the curve was framed in foliage and therein was a horseman. He had his carbine slanted on his thigh and his bridle-rein taut. Upon sight of them he immediately wheeled and galloped down the other slope and vanished.

The dragoman was throwing wild gestures into the air. As Coleman looked back at the Wainwright party he saw plainly that to an ordinary eye they might easily appear as a strong advance of troops. The peculiar light would emphasize such theory. The dragoman ran to him jubilantly but he contained now a form of intelligence which caused him to whisper. "That was one Greek. That was one Greek—what do you call—sentree."

Coleman addressed the others. He said: "It's all right. Come ahead. That was a Greek picket. There is only one trouble now and that is to approach them easy—do you see—easy."

His obedient charges came forward at his word. When they arrived at the top of this rise they saw nothing. Coleman was very uncertain. He was not sure that this picket had not carried with him a general alarm and in that case there would soon occur a certain amount of shooting. However as far as he understood the business, there was no way but forward. Inasmuch as he did not indicate to the Wainwright party that he wished them to do differently, they followed on doggedly after him and the dragoman. He knew now that the dragoman's heart had for the tenth time turned to dog-biscuit so he kept a-breast of him. And soon together they walked into a cavalry outpost commanded by no less a person than the dashing young captain who came laughing out to meet them.

Suddenly losing all color of war, the condition was now such as might occur in a drawing-room. Coleman felt the importance of establishing highly conventional relations between the captain and the Wainwright party. To compass this he first seized his dragoman and the dragoman enlightened immediately spun a series of lies which must have led the captain to believe that the entire heart of the American Republic had been taken out of the western continent and transported to Greece. Coleman was proud of the captain. The latter immediately went and bowed in the manner of the French school and asked everybody to have a cup of coffee although acceptation would have proved his ruin and disgrace. Coleman refused in the name of courtesy. He called his party forward and now they proceeded merely as one crowd. Marjory had dismounted in the meantime.

The moment was come. Coleman felt it. The first rush was from the students. Immediately he was buried in a thrashing mob of them. "Good boy! Good boy! Great man! Oh, isn't he a peach? How did he do it? He came in at the strong finish! Good boy Coleman." Through this mist of glowing youthful congratulation he saw the professor standing at the outskirts with direct formal thanks already moving on his lips while near him his wife wept joyfully. Marjory was evidently enduring some inscrutable emotion.

After all it did penetrate his mind that it was indecent to accept all this gratitude but there was built within him no intention of positively declaring himself lacking in all credit or at least lacking in all credit in the way their praises defined it. In truth he had assisted them but he had been at the time largely engaged in assisting himself and their coming had been more of a boon to his loneliness than an addition to his care. However he soon had no difficulty in making his conscience appropriate every line in these hymns sung in his honor. The students, curiously wise of men, thought his conduct quite perfect. "Oh, say come off," he protested. "Why, I didn't do anything. You fellows are crazy. You would have gotten in all right by yourselves. Don't act like asses——"

As soon as the professor had opportunity he came to Coleman. He was a changed little man and his extraordinary bewilderment showed in his face. It was the disillusion and amazement of a stubborn mind that had gone implacably in its one direction and found in the end that the direction was all wrong and that really a certain mental machine had not been infallible. Coleman remembered what the American minister in Athens had described of his protests against the starting of the professor's party on this journey and of the complete refusal of the little professor to recognize any value in the advice. And here now was the consequent defeat. It was mirrored in the professor's astonished eyes. Coleman went directly to his dazed old teacher. "Well, you're out of it now, professor," he said warmly. "I congratulate you on your escape, sir." The professor looked at him, helpless to express himself, but the correspondent was at that time suddenly enveloped in the hysterical gratitude of Mrs. Wainwright who hurled herself upon him with extravagant manifestations. Coleman played his part with skill. To both the professor and Mrs. Wainwright his manner was a combination of modestly filial affection and a pretentious disavowal of his having done anything at all. It seemed to charm everybody but Marjory. It irritated him to see that she was apparently incapable of acknowledging that he was a grand man.

He was actually compelled to go to her and offer congratulations upon her escape as he had congratulated the professor.

If his manner to her parents had been filial, his manner to her was parental. "Well, Marjory," he said kindly, "you have been in considerable danger. I suppose you're glad to be through with it." She at that time made no reply but by her casual turn he knew that he was expected to walk along by her side. The others knew it too and the rest of the party left them free to walk side by side in the rear.

"This is a beautiful country hereabouts if one gets a good chance to see it," he remarked. Then he added: "But I suppose you had a view of it when you were going up to Nikopolis?"

She answered in muffled tones. "Yes. We thought it very beautiful."

"Did you note those streams from the mountains? That seemed to me the purest water I'd ever seen. But I bet it would make one ill to drink it. There is, you know, a prominent German chemist who has almost proven that really pure water is practical poison to the human stomach."

"Yes?" she said.

There was a period of silence during which he was perfectly comfortable because he knew that she was ill at ease. If the silence was awkward, she was suffering from it. As for himself he had no inclination to break it. His position was, as far as the entire Wainwright party was concerned, a place where he could afford to wait. She turned to him at last. "Of course I know how much you have done for us and I want you to feel that we all appreciate it deeply—deeply." There was discernible to the ear a certain note of desperation.

"Oh, not at all," he said generously. "Not at all. I didn't do anything. It was quite an accident. Don't let that trouble you for a moment."

"Well, of course you would say that," she said more steadily. "But I—we—we know how good and how—brave it was in you to come for us and I—we must never forget it."

"As a matter of fact," replied Coleman with an appearance of ingenuous candor, "I was sent out here by the *Eclipse* to find you people and of course I worked rather hard to reach you but the final meeting was purely accidental and does not redound to my credit in the least."

As he had anticipated, Marjory shot him a little glance of disbelief. "Of course you would say that," she repeated with gloomy but flattering conviction.

"Oh, if I had been a great hero," he said smiling, "no doubt I would have kept up this same manner which now sets so well upon me but I am telling you the truth when I say that I had no part in your rescue at all."

She became slightly indignant. "Oh, if you care to tell us constantly that you were of no service to us, I don't see what we can do but continue to declare that you were."

Suddenly he felt vulgar. He spoke to her this time with real meaning. "I beg of you never to mention it again. That will be the best way."

But to this she would not accede. "No; we will often want to speak of it."

He replied: "How do you like Greece? Don't you think some of these ruins are rather out of shape in the popular mind? Now, for my part I would rather look at a good strong finish at a horse-race than to see ten-thousand Parthenons in a bunch."

She was immediately in the position of defending him from himself. "You would rather see no such thing. You shouldn't talk in that utterly trivial way. I like the Parthenon of course but I can't think of it now because my head is too full of my escape from where I was so—so frightened."

Coleman grinned. "Were you really frightened?"

"Naturally," she answered. "I suppose I was more frightened for mother and father but I was frightened enough for myself. It was not—not a nice thing."

"No it wasn't," said Coleman. "I could hardly believe my senses when the minister at Athens told me that you all had ventured into such a trap and there is no doubt but what you can be glad that you are well out of it."

She seemed to have some struggle with herself and then she deliberately said: "Thanks to you."

Coleman embarked on what he intended to make a series of high-minded protests. "Not at all——" but at that moment the dragoman whirled back from the van-guard with a great collection of the difficulties which had been gathering upon him. Coleman was obliged to resign Marjory and again take up the active leadership. He disposed of the dragoman's difficulties mainly by declaring that they were not difficulties at all. He had learned that this was the way to deal with dragomen.

The fog had already lifted from the valley and as they passed along the wooded mountain-side the fragrance of leaves and earth came to them. Ahead, along the hooded road, they could see the blue-clad figures of Greek infantry-men. Finally they passed an encampment of a battalion whose line was at a right angle to the highway. A hundred yards in advance was the bridge across the Louros river. And there a battery of artillery was encamped. The dragoman became involved in all sorts of discussions with other Greeks but Coleman stuck to his elbow and stifled all aimless oration. The Wainwright party waited for them to the rear in an observant but patient group.

Across a plain the hills directly behind Arta loomed up showing the straight yellow scar of a modern intrenchment. To the north of Arta were some grey mountains with a dimly marked road winding to the summit. On one side of this road were two shadows. It took a moment for the eye to find these shadows but when this was accomplished it was plain that they were men. The captain of the battery explained to the dragoman that he did not know that they were not also Turks. In which case the road to Arta was a dangerous path. It was no good news to Coleman. He waited a moment in order to gain composure and then walked back to the Wainwright party. They must have known at once from his peculiar gravity that all was not well. Five of the students and the professor immediately asked: "What is it?"

He had at first some old fashioned idea of concealing the ill tidings from the ladies but he perceived what flagrant nonsense this would be in circumstances in which all were fairly likely to incur equal dangers and at any rate he did not see his way clear to allow their imaginations to run riot over a situation which might not turn out to be too bad. He said slowly: "You see those mountains over there? Well, troops have been seen there and the captain of this battery thinks they are Turks. If they are Turks the road to Arta is distinctly—er—unsafe."

This new blow first affected the Wainwright party as being too much to endure. They thought they had gone through enough. This was a general sentiment. Afterward the emotion took color according to the individual character. One student laughed and said: "Well, I see our finish."

Another student piped out: "How do they know they are Turks? What makes them think they are Turks?"

Another student expressed himself with a sigh. "This is a long way from the Bowery."

The professor said nothing but looked annihilated; Mrs. Wainwright wept profoundly; Marjory looked expectantly toward Coleman.

As for the correspondent he was adamantine and reliable and stern for he had not the slightest idea that those men on the distant hill were Turks at all.

"OH," said a student, "this game ought to quit. I feel like thirty cents. We didn't come out here to be pursued about the country by these Turks. Why don't they stop it?"

Coleman was remarking: "Really the only sensible thing to do now is to have breakfast. There is no use in worrying ourselves silly over this thing until we've got to."

They spread the blankets on the ground and sat about a feast of bread, water-cress and tinned beef. Coleman was the real host but he contrived to make the professor appear as that honorable person. They ate, casting their eyes from time to time at the distant mountain with its two shadows. People began to fly down the road from Jannina, peasants hurriedly driving little flocks, women and children on donkeys and little horses which they clubbed unceasingly. One man rode at a gallop, shrieking and flailing his arms in the air. They were all Christian peasants of Turkey but they were in flight now because they did not wish to be at home if the Turk was going to return and reap revenge for his mortification. The Wainwright party looked at Coleman in abrupt questioning. "Oh, it's all right," he said easily. "They are always taking on that way."

Suddenly, the dragoman gave a shout and dashed up the road to the scene of a melee where a little rat-faced groom was vociferously defending three horses from some Greek officers who as vociferously were stating their right to requisition them. Coleman ran after his dragoman. There was a sickening pow-wow but in the end, Coleman straight and easy in the saddle came cantering back on a superb open-mouthed snorting bay horse. He did not mind if the half-wild animal plunged crazily. It was part of his role. "They were trying to steal my horse," he explained. He leaped to the ground and holding the horse by the bridle, he addressed his admiring companions. "The groom—the man who has charge of the horses—says that he thinks that the people on the mountain-side are Turks but I don't see how that is possible. You see—" he pointed wisely—"that road leads directly south to Arta and it is hardly possible that the Greek army would come over here and leave that approach to Arta utterly unguarded. It would be too foolish. They must have left some men to cover it and that is certainly what those troops are. If you are all ready and willing, I don't see anything to do but make a stout-hearted dash for Arta. It would be no more dangerous than to sit here."

The professor was at last able to make his formal speech. "Mr. Coleman," he said distinctly, "we place ourselves entirely in your hands." It was somehow pitiful. This man who for years and years had reigned in a little college town almost as a monarch, passing judgement with the air of one who words the law, dealing criticism upon the universe as one to whom all things are plain, publicly disdaining defeat as one to whom all things are easy—this man was now veritably appealing to Coleman to save his wife, his daughter and himself and really declared himself dependent for safety upon the ingenuity and courage of the correspondent.

The attitude of the students was utterly different. They did not consider themselves helpless at all. They were evidently quite ready to withstand anything but they looked frankly up to Coleman as their intelligent leader. If they suffered any, their only expression of it was in the simple grim slang of their period.

"I wish I was at Coney Island."

"This is not so bad as trigonometry but it's worse than playing billiards for the beers."

And Coke said privately to Coleman: "Say what in hell are these two peoples fighting for anyhow?"

When he saw that all opinions were in favor of following him loyally Coleman was impelled to feel a responsibility. He was now no errant rescuer but a properly elected leader of fellow beings in distress. While one of the students held his horse, he took the dragoman for another consultation with the captain of the battery. The officer was sitting on a large stone with his eyes fixed into his field-glasses. When again questioned he could give no satisfaction as to the identity of the troops on the distant mountain. He merely shrugged his shoulders and said that if they were Greeks it was very good but if they were Turks it was very bad. He seemed more occupied in trying to impress the correspondent that it was a matter of soldierly indifference to himself. Coleman after loathing him sufficiently in silence returned to the others and said: "Well, we'll chance it."

They looked to him to arrange the caravan. Speaking to the men of the party he said: "Of course any one of you is welcome to my horse if you can ride but—if you're not too tired—I think I had myself better ride so that I can go ahead at times."

His manner was so fine as he said this that the students seemed fairly to worship him. Of course it had been most improbable that any of them could have ridden that volcanic animal even if one of them had tried it.

He saw Mrs. Wainwright and Marjory upon the backs of their two little native horses and hoisted the professor into the saddle of the groom's horse leaving instructions with the servant to lead the animal always and carefully. He and the dragoman then mounted at the head of the procession and amid curious questionings from the soldiery they crossed the bridge and started on the trail to Arta. The rear was brought up by the little grey horse with the luggage led by one student and flogged by another.

Coleman checking with difficulty the battling disposition of his horse was very uneasy in his mind because the last words of the captain of the battery had made him feel that perhaps on this ride he would be placed in a position where only the best courage would count and he did not see his way clear to feeling very confident about his conduct in such a case. Looking back upon the caravan, he saw it as a most unwieldy thing, not capable of even running away. He hurried it, with sudden sharp contemptuous phrases.

On the march there incidentally flashed upon him a new truth. More than half of that student band were deeply in love with Marjory. Of course when he had been distant from her he had had an eternal jealous reflection to that effect. It was natural that he should have thought of the intimate camping relations between Marjory and these young students with a great deal of bitterness, grinding his teeth when picturing their opportunities to make Marjory fall in love with some one of them. He had raged particularly about Coke whose father had millions of dollars. But he had forgotten all these jealousies in the general splendor of his exploits. Now when he saw the truth it seemed to bring him back to his common life and he saw himself suddenly as not being frantically superior in any way to those other young men. The more closely he looked at this last fact the more convinced he was of its truth. He seemed to see that he had been improperly elated over his services to the Wainwrights and that in the end the girl might fancy a man because the man had done her no service at all. He saw his proud position lower itself to be a pawn in the game. Looking back over the students he wondered which one Marjory might love. This hideous Nikopolis had given eight men a chance to win her. His scorn and his malice quite centred upon Coke for he could never forget that the man's father had millions of dollars. The unfortunate Coke chose that moment to address him querulously. "Look here, Coleman, can't you tell us how far it is to Arta?"

"Coke," said Coleman, "I don't suppose you take me for a tourist agency but if you can only try to distinguish between me and a map with the scale of miles printed in the lower left-hand corner, you will not contribute so much to the sufferings of the party which you now adorn."

The students within hearing guffawed and Coke retired in confusion.

The march was not rapid. Coleman almost wore out his arms holding in check his impetuous horse. Often the caravan floundered through mud, while at the same time a hot yellow dust came from the north.

They were perhaps half way to Arta when Coleman decided that a rest and luncheon were the things to be considered. He halted his troop then in the shade of some great trees and privately he bade his dragoman prepare the best feast which could come out of those saddle-bags fresh from Athens. The result was rather gorgeous in the eyes of the poor wanderers. First of all there were three knives, three forks, three spoons, three tin-cups, and three tin-plates, which the entire party of twelve used on a most amiable socialistic principle. There were crisp salty biscuits and olives for which they speared in the bottle. There was potted turkey and potted ham and potted tongue, all tasting precisely alike. There were sardines and the ordinary tinned beef disguised sometimes with onions, carrots and potatoes. Out of the saddle-bags came pepper and salt and even mustard. The dragoman made coffee over a little fire of sticks that blazed with a white light. The whole thing was prodigal but any philanthropist would have approved of it if he could have seen the way in which the eight students laid into the spread. When there came polite remonstrance—notably from Mrs. Wainwright—Coleman merely pointed to a large bundle strapped back of the groom's saddle. During the coffee he was considering how best to get the students one by one out of the sight of the Wainwrights where he could give them good drinks of whiskey.

There was an agitation on the road toward Arta. Some people were coming on horses. He paid small heed until he heard a thump of pausing hoofs near him and a musical voice say: "Rufus."

He looked up quickly and then all present saw his eyes really bulge. There on a fat and glossy horse sat Nora Black dressed in probably one of the most correct riding habits which had ever been seen in the East. She was smiling a radiant smile which held the eight students simply spell-bound. They all would have recognized her if it had not been for this apparitional coming in the wilds of south-eastern Europe. Behind her were her people— some servants and an old lady on a very little pony. "Well, Rufus," she said.

Coleman had made the mistake of hesitating. For a fraction of a moment he had acted as if he were embarrassed and was only going to nod and say: "How d' do."

He arose and came forward too late. She was looking at him with a menacing glance which meant difficulties for him if he was not skilful. Keen as an eagle, she swept her glance over the face and figure of Marjory. Without further introduction the girls seemed to understand that they were enemies.

Despite his feeling of awkwardness Coleman's mind was mainly occupied by pure astonishment. "Nora Black?" he said as if even then he could not believe his senses. "How in the world did you get down here?"

She was not too amiable evidently over his reception and she seemed to know perfectly that it was in her power to make him feel extremely unpleasant. "Oh, it's not so far," she answered. "I don't see where you come in to ask me what I'm doing here. What are you doing here?" She lifted her eyes and shot the half of a glance at Marjory. Into her last question she had interjected a spirit of ownership in which he saw some future woe. It turned him cowardly. "Why, you know I was sent up here by the paper to rescue the Wainwright party and I've got them. Here they are. I'm taking them to Arta. But why are you here?"

"I am here," she said giving him the most defiant of glances, "principally to look for you."

Even the horse she rode betrayed an intention of abiding upon that spot forever. She had made her communication with Coleman appear to the Wainwright party as a sort of tender reunion.

Coleman looked at her with a steely eye. "Nora, you can certainly be a devil when you choose."

"Why don't you present me to your friends? Miss Nora Black, special correspondent of the *New York Daylight*, if you please. I belong to your opposition. I am your rival, Rufus, and I draw a bigger salary—see? Funny looking gang, that. Who is the old Johnnie in the white wig?"

"Er—where you goin'—you can't——" blundered Coleman miserably. "Aw—the army is in retreat and you must go back to—don't you see?"

"Is it?" she asked. After a pause she added coolly: "Then I shall go back to Arta with you and your precious Wainwrights."

CHAPTER XVI

GIVING Coleman another glance of subtle menace Nora repeated: "Why don't you present me to your friends?" Coleman had been swiftly searching the whole world for a way clear of this unhappiness but he knew at last that he could only die at his guns. "Why certainly," he said quickly, "if you wish it." He sauntered easily back to the luncheon blanket. "This is Miss Black of the *New York Daylight* and she says that those people on the mountain are Greeks." The students were gaping at him and Marjory and her father sat in the same silence. But to the relief of Coleman and to the high edification of the students Mrs. Wainwright cried out: "Why, is she an American woman?" and seeing Coleman's nod of assent she rustled to her feet and advanced hastily upon the complacent horse-woman. "I'm delighted to see you. Who would think of seeing an American woman 'way over here. Have you been here long? Are you going on further? Oh, we've had *such* a dreadful time." Coleman remained long enough to hear Nora say: "Thank you very much but I shan't dismount. I am going to ride back to Arta presently."

Then he heard Mrs. Wainwright cry: "Oh, are you indeed? Why we, too, are going at once to Arta. We can all go together." Coleman fled then to the bosom of the students who all looked at him with eyes of cynical penetration. He cast a glance at Marjory more than fearing a glare which denoted an implacable resolution never to forgive this thing. On the contrary he had never seen her so content and serene. "You have allowed your coffee to get chilled," she said considerately. "Won't you have the man warm you some more?"

"Thanks no," he answered with gratitude.

Nora, changing her mind, had dismounted and was coming with Mrs. Wainwright. That worthy lady had long had a fund of information and anecdote the sound of which neither her husband nor her daughter would endure for a moment. Of course the rascally students were out of the question. Here then was really the first ear amiably and cheerfully open and she was talking at what the students called her "thirty knot gait."

"Lost everything. Absolutely everything. Neither of us have even a brush and comb, or a cake of soap, or enough hair-pins to hold up our hair. I'm going to take Marjory's away from her and let her braid her hair down her back. You can imagine how dreadful it is——"

From time to time the cool voice of Nora sounded without effort through this clamor. "Oh, it will be no trouble at all. I have more than enough of everything. We can divide very nicely."

Coleman broke somewhat imperiously into this feminine chat. "Well, we must be moving you know," and his voice started the men into activity. When the traps were all packed again on the horses Coleman looked back surprised to see the three women engaged in the most friendly discussion. The combined parties now made a very respectable squadron. Coleman rode off at its head without glancing behind at all. He knew that they were following from the soft pounding of the horses' hoofs on the sod and from the mellow hum of human voices.

For a long time he did not think to look upon himself as anything but a man much injured by circumstance. Among his friends he could count numbers who had lived long lives without having this peculiar class of misfortune come to them. In fact it was so unusual a misfortune that men of the world had not found it necessary to pass from mind to mind a perfect formula for dealing with it. But he soon began to consider himself an extraordinary lucky person inasmuch as Nora Black had come upon him with her saddle-bags packed with inflammable substance, so to speak, and there had been as yet only fire to boil coffee for luncheon. He laughed tenderly when he thought of the innocence of Mrs. Wainwright but his face and back flushed with heat when he thought of the canniness of the eight American college students.

He heard a horse cantering up on his left side and looking he saw Nora. She was beaming with satisfaction and good nature. "Well, Rufus," she cried flippantly, "how goes it with the gallant rescuer? You've made a hit, my boy. You are the success of the season."

Coleman reflected upon the probable result of a direct appeal to Nora. He knew of course that such appeals were usually idle but he did not consider Nora an ordinary person. His decision was to venture it. He drew his horse close to hers. "Nora," he said, "do you know that you are raising the very devil?"

She raised her finely-pencilled eye-brows and looked at him with the baby-stare. "How?" she enquired.

"You know well enough," he gritted out wrathfully.

"Raising the very devil?" she asked. "How do you mean?" She was palpably interested for his answer. She waited for his reply for an interval and then she asked him outright: "Rufus Coleman do you mean that I am not a respectable woman?"

In reality he had meant nothing of the kind but this direct throttling of a great question stupefied him utterly for he saw now that she would probably never understand him in the least and that she would at any rate always pretend not to understand him and that the more he said the more harm he manufactured. She studied him over carefully and then wheeled her horse toward the rear with some parting remarks. "I suppose you should attend more strictly to your own affairs, Rufus. Instead of raising the devil I am lending hair-pins. I have seen you insult people but I have never seen you insult anyone quite for the whim of the thing. Go soak your head."

Not considering it advisable to then indulge in such immersion Coleman rode moodily onward. The hot dust continued to sting the cheeks of the travellers and in some places great clouds of dead leaves roared in circles about them. All of the Wainwright party were utterly fagged. Coleman felt his skin crackle and his throat seemed to be coated with the white dust. He worried his dragoman as to the distance to Arta until the dragoman lied to the point where he always declared that Arta was only off some hundreds of yards.

At their place in the procession, Mrs. Wainwright and Marjory were animatedly talking to Nora and the old lady on the little pony. They had at first suffered great amazement at the voluntary presence of the old lady but she was there really because she knew no better. Her colossal ignorance took the form, mainly, of a most obstreperous patriotism and indeed she always acted in a foreign country as if she were the special commissioner of the President or perhaps as a special commissioner could not act at all. She was very aggressive and when any of the travelling arrangements in Europe did not suit her ideas she was wont to shrilly exclaim: "Well! New York is good enough for me." Nora, morbidly afraid that her expense bill to the *Daylight* would not be large enough, had dragged her bodily off to Greece as her companion, friend and protection. At Arta they had heard of the grand success of the Greek army. The Turks had not stood for a moment before that gallant and terrible advance; no; they had scampered howling with fear into the north. Jannina would fall—well, Jannina would fall as soon as the Greeks arrived. There was no doubt of it. The correspondent and her friend, deluded and hurried by the light-hearted confidence of the Greeks in Arta, had hastened out then on a regular tourist's excursion to see Jannina after its capture. Nora concealed from her friend the fact that the editor of the *Daylight* particularly wished her to see a battle so that she might write an article on actual warfare from a woman's point-of-view. With her name as a queen of comic opera, such an article from her pen would be a burning sensation.

Coleman had been the first to point out to Nora that instead of going on a picnic to Jannina, she had better run back to Arta. When the old lady heard that they had not been entirely safe, she was furious with Nora. "The idea!" she exclaimed to Mrs. Wainwright. "They might have caught us. They might have caught us!"

"Well," said Mrs. Wainwright, "I verily believe they would have caught *us* if it had not been for Mr. Coleman."

"Is he the gentleman on the fine horse?"

"Yes; that's him. Oh, he has been sim-plee splendid. I confess I was a little bit—er—surprised. He was in college under my husband. I don't know that we thought very great things of him but if ever a man won golden opinions he has done so from us."

"Oh, that must be the Coleman who is such a great friend of Nora's."

"Yes?" said Mrs. Wainwright insidiously. "Is he? I didn't know. Of course he knows so many people." Her mind had been suddenly illumined by the old lady and she thought extravagantly of the arrival of Nora on the scene. She remained all sweetness to the old lady. "Did you know he was here? Did you expect to meet him? It seems such a delightful coincidence." In truth she was subterraneously clever.

"Oh, no; I don't think so. I didn't hear Nora mention it. Of course she would have told me. You know, our coming to Greece was such a surprise. Nora had an engagement in London at the Folly Theater in *Fly by Night* but the manager was insufferable, oh, insufferable. So of course Nora wouldn't stand it a minute and then these newspaper people came along and asked her to go to Greece for them and she accepted. I am sure I never expected to find us—aw—fleeing from the Turks or I shouldn't have come."

Mrs. Wainwright was gasping. "You don't mean that she is— she is Nora Black, the actress."

"Of course, she is," said the old lady jubilantly.

"Why, how strange," choked Mrs. Wainwright. Nothing she knew of Nora could account for her stupefaction and grief. What appeared glaringly to her was the duplicity of man. Coleman was a ribald deceiver. He must have known and yet he had pretended throughout that the meeting was a pure accident. She turned with a nervous impulse to sympathize with her daughter but despite the lovely tranquillity of the girl's face there was something about her which forbade the mother to meddle. Anyhow Mrs. Wainwright was sorry that she had told nice things of Coleman's behavior so she said to the old lady: "Young men of these times get a false age so quickly. We have always thought it a great pity about Mr. Coleman."

"Why, how so?" asked the old lady.

"Oh, really, nothing. Only, to us he seems rather—er—prematurely experienced or something of that kind."

The old lady did not catch the meaning of the phrase. She seemed surprised. "Why, I've never seen any full-grown person in this world who got experience any too quick for his own good."

At the tail of the procession there was talk between the two students who had in charge the little grey horse—one to lead and one to flog. "Billie," said one, "it now becomes necessary to lose this hobby into the hands of some of the other fellows. Whereby, we will gain opportunity to pay homage to the great Nora. Why, you egregious thick-head, this is the chance of a life-time. I'm damned if I'm going to tow this beast of burden much further."

"You wouldn't stand a show," said Billie pessimistically. "Look at Coleman."

"That's all right. Do you mean to say that you prefer to continue towing pack-horses in the presence of this queen of song and the dance just because you think Coleman can throw out his chest a little more than you. Not so. Think of your bright and sparkling youth. There's Coke and Pete Tounley near Marjory. We'll call 'em." Whereupon he set up a cry. "Say, you people, we're not getting a salary for this. Supposin' you try it for a time. It'll do you good." When the two addressed had halted to await the arrival of the little grey horse, they took on glum expressions. "You look like poisoned pups," said the student who led the horse. "Too strong for light work? Grab onto the halter, now, Peter, and tow. We are going ahead to talk to Nora Black."

"Good time you'll have," answered Peter Tounley. "Coleman is cuttin' up scandalous. You won't stand a show."

"What do you think of him?" said Coke. "Seems curious, all 'round. Do you suppose he knew she would show up? It was nervy to——"

"Nervy to what?" asked Billie.

"Well," said Coke, "seems to me he is playing both ends against the middle. I don't know anything about Nora Black but——"

The three other students expressed themselves with conviction and in chorus: "Coleman's all right."

"Well, anyhow," continued Coke, "I don't see my way free to admiring him introducing Nora Black to the Wainwrights."

"He didn't," said the others, still in chorus.

"Queer game," said Peter Tounley. "He seems to know her pretty well."

"Pretty damned well," said Billie.

"Anyhow, he's a brick," said Peter Tounley. "We mustn't forget that. Lo, I begin to feel that our Rufus is a fly guy of many different kinds. Any play that he is in commands my respect. He won't be hit by a chimney in the daytime for unto him has come much wisdom. I don't think I'll worry."

"Is he stuck on Nora Black, do you know?" asked Billie.

"One thing is plain," replied Coke. "She has got him somehow by the short hair and she intends him to holler murder. Anybody can see that."

"Well, he won't holler murder," said one of them with conviction. "I'll bet you he won't. He'll hammer the war-post and beat the tom-tom until he drops but he won't holler murder."

"Old Mother Wainwright will be in his wool presently," quoth Peter Tounley musingly. "I could see it coming in her eye. Somebody has given his snap away, or something."

"Aw, he had no snap," said Billie. "Couldn't you see how rattled he was? He would have given a lac if dear Nora hadn't turned up."

"Of course," the others assented. "He was rattled."

"Looks queer! And nasty," said Coke.

"Nora herself had an axe ready for him."

They began to laugh. "If she had had an umbrella she would have basted him over the head with it. Oh, my! He was *green*."

"Nevertheless," said Peter Tounley, "I refuse to worry over our Rufus. When he can't take care of himself the rest of us want to hunt cover. He is a fly guy."

Coleman in the meantime had become aware that the light of Mrs. Wainwright's countenance was turned from him. The party stopped at a well and when he offered her a drink from his cup he thought she accepted it with scant thanks. Marjory was still gracious, always gracious, but this did not re-assure him because he felt there was much unfathomable deception in it. When he turned to seek consolation in the manner of the professor he found him as before, stunned with surprise, and the only idea he had was to be as tractable as a child.

When he returned to the head of the column, Nora again cantered forward to join him. "Well, me gay Lochinvar," she cried. "And has your disposition improved?"

"You are very fresh," he said.

She laughed loudly enough to be heard the full length of the caravan. It was a beautiful laugh but full of insolence and confidence. He flashed his eyes malignantly upon her but then she only laughed more. She could see that he wished to strangle her. "What a disposition!" she said. "What a disposition! You are not nearly so nice as your friends. Now, they are charming but you

—Rufus, I wish you would get that temper mended. Dear Rufus, do it to please me. You know you like to please me. Don't you now, dear?"

He finally laughed. "Confound you, Nora. I would like to kill you."

But at his laugh, she was all sunshine. It was as if she had been trying to taunt him into good humor with her. "Aw, now, Rufus, don't be angry. I'll be good, Rufus. Really I will. Listen. I want to tell you something. Do you know what I did? Well, you know, I never was cut out for this business and, back there, when you told me about the Turks being near and all that sort of thing, I was frightened almost to death. Really I was. So then when nobody was looking I sneaked two or three little drinks out of my flask. Two or three little drinks——"

CHAPTER XVII

"GOOD God," said Coleman, "you don't mean——"

Nora smiled rosily at him. "Oh, I'm all right," she answered. "Don't worry about your Aunt Nora, my precious boy. Not for a minute."

Coleman was horrified. "But you are not going to—— You are not going to——"

"Not at all, me son. Not at all," she answered. "I'm not going to prance. I'm going to be as nice as pie and just ride quietly along here with dear little Rufus. Only . . . you know what I can do when I get started so you had better be a very good boy. I might take it into my head to say some things, you know."

Bound hand and foot to his stake he could not even chant his defiant torture song. It might precipitate—in fact he was sure it would precipitate the grand smash. But to the very core of his soul, he for the time hated Nora Black. He did not dare to remind her that he would revenge himself; he dared only to dream of this revenge but it fairly made his thoughts flame and deep in his throat he was swearing an inflexible persecution of Nora Black. The old expression of his sex came to him. "Oh, if she were only a man!" If she had been a man he would have fallen upon her tooth and nail. Her motives for all this impressed him not at all; she was simply a witch who bound him helpless with the power of her femininity and made him eat cinders. He was so sure that his face betrayed him that he did not dare let her see it. "Well, what are you going to do about it?" he asked, over his shoulder.

"O-o-oh," she drawled impudently. "Nothing." He could see that she was determined not to be confessed. "I may do this or I may do that. It all depends upon your behavior, my dear Rufus."

As they rode on, he deliberated as to the best means of dealing with this condition. Suddenly he resolved to go with the whole tale direct to Marjory and to this end he half-wheeled his horse. He would reiterate that he loved her and then explain—— Explain! He groaned when he came to the word and ceased formulation.

The cavalcade reached at last the bank of the Aracthus river with its lemon groves and lush grass. A battery wheeled before them over the ancient bridge—a flight of short broad cobbled steps up as far as the centre of the stream and a similar flight down to the other bank. The returning aplomb of the travellers was well illustrated by the professor who upon sighting this bridge murmured: "Byzantine." This was the first indication that he had still within him a power to resume the normal.

The steep and narrow street was crowded with soldiers; the smoky little coffee-shops were a-babble with people discussing the bad news from the front. None seemed to heed the remarkable procession that wended its way to the cable office. Here Coleman resolutely took precedence. He knew that there was no good in expecting intelligence out of the chaotic clerks but he managed to get upon the wires this message: "*Eclipse,* New York: Got Wainwright party all well Coleman." The students had struggled to send messages to their people in America but they had only succeeded in deepening the tragic boredom of the clerks.

When Coleman returned to the street he thought that he had seldom looked upon a more moving spectacle than the Wainwright party presented at that moment. Most of the students were seated in a row, dejectedly, upon the kerb. The professor and Mrs. Wainwright looked like two old pictures which after an existence in a considerate gloom had been brought out in their tawdriness to the clear light. Hot white dust covered everybody and from out the grimy faces the eyes blinked red-fringed with sleeplessness. Desolation sat upon all, all save Marjory. She possessed some marvelous power of looking always fresh. This quality had indeed impressed the old lady on the little pony until she had said to Nora Black: "That girl would look well anywhere." Nora Black had not been amiable in her reply.

Coleman called the professor and the dragoman for a durbar. The dragoman said: "Well, I can get one carriage and we can go immediate-lee."

"Carriage be blowed," said Coleman. "What these people need is rest, sleep. You must find a place at once. These people can't remain in the street." He spoke in anger as if he had previously told the dragoman and the latter had been inattentive. The man immediately departed.

Coleman remarked that there was no course but to remain in the street until his dragoman had found them a habitation. It was a mournful waiting. The students sat on the kerb. Once they whispered to Coleman suggesting a drink but he told them that he knew only one cafe, the entrance of which would be in plain sight of the rest of the party. The ladies talked together in a group of four. Nora Black was bursting with the fact that her servant had hired rooms in Arta on their out-coming journey and she wished Mrs. Wainwright and Marjory to come to them at least for a time but she dared not risk a refusal and she felt something in Mrs. Wainwright's manner which led her to be certain that such would be the answer to her invitation. Coleman and the professor strolled slowly up and down the walk.

"Well, my work is over, sir," said Coleman. "My paper told me to find you and, through no virtue of my own, I found you. I am very glad of it. I don't know of anything in my life that has given me greater pleasure."

The professor was himself again in so far as he had lost all manner of dependence. But still he could not yet be bumptious. "Mr. Coleman," he said, "I am placed under life-long obligation to you. . . . I am not thinking of myself so much. . . . My wife and daughter——" His gratitude was so genuine that he could not finish its expression.

"Oh, don't speak of it," said Coleman. "I really didn't do anything at all."

The dragoman finally returned and led them all to a house which he had rented for gold. In the great bare upper chamber, the students dropped wearily to the floor while the woman of the house took the Wainwrights to a more secluded apartment. As the door closed on them, Coleman turned like a flash. "Have a drink," he said. The students arose around him like the wave of a flood. "You bet." In the absence of changes of clothing, ordinary food, the possibility of a bath and in the presence of great weariness and dust, Coleman's whiskey seemed to them a glistening luxury. Afterward they laid down as if to sleep but in reality they were too dirty and too fagged to sleep. They simply lay murmuring. Peter Tounley even developed a small fever.

It was at this time that Coleman suddenly discovered that his acute interest in the progressive troubles of his affair of the heart had placed the business of his newspaper in the rear of his mind. The greater part of the next hours he spent in a new wrangle with the clerks in the cable office and finally succeeded in getting off to New York that despatch which created so much excitement for him later. Afterward he was free to reflect moodily upon the ability of Nora Black to distress him. She with her retinue had disappeared toward her own rooms. At dusk he went into the street and was edified to see Nora's dragoman dodging along in his wake. He thought that this was simply another manifestation of Nora's interest in his movements and so he turned a corner and there pausing waited until the dragoman spun around directly into his arms. But it seemed that the man had a note to deliver and this was only his oriental way of doing it.

The note read: "Come and dine with me tonight." It was not a request. It was peremptory. "All right," he said scowling at the man.

He did not go at once for he wished to reflect for a time and find if he could not evolve some weapons of his own. It seemed to him that all the others were liberally supplied with weapons.

A clear cold night had come upon the earth when he signified to the lurking dragoman that he was in readiness to depart with him to Nora's abode. They passed finally into a dark court-yard up a winding staircase across an embowered balcony and Coleman entered alone a room where there were lights.

His feet were scarcely over the threshold before he had concluded that the tigress was now going to try some velvet purring. He noted that the arts of the stage had not been thought too cheaply obvious for use. Nora sat facing the door. A bit of yellow silk had been twisted about the crude shade of the lamp and it made the play of light, amber-like, shadowy and yet perfectly clear, the light which women love. She was arrayed in a puzzling gown of that kind of Grecian silk which is so docile that one can pull yards of it through a ring. It was of the color of new straw.

Her chin was leaned pensively upon her palm and the light fell on a pearly rounded fore-arm. She was looking at him with a pair of famous eyes, azure perhaps—certainly purple at times—and it may be black at odd moments—a pair of eyes that had made many an honest man's heart jump if he thought they were looking at him. It was a vision, yes, but Coleman's cynical knowledge of drama overpowered his sense of its beauty. He broke out brutally in the phrases of the American street: "Your dragoman is a rubber-neck. If he keeps darking me I will simply have to kick the stuffing out of him."

She was alone in the room. Her old lady had been instructed to have a headache and send apologies. She was not disturbed by Coleman's words. "Sit down, Rufus, and have a cigarette and don't be cross because I won't stand it."

He obeyed her glumly. She had placed his chair where not a charm of her could be lost upon an observant man. Evidently she did not purpose to allow him to irritate her away from her original plan. Purring was now her method and none of his insolence could achieve a growl from the tigress. She arose saying softly: "You look tired, almost ill, poor boy. I will give you some brandy. I have almost everything that I could think to make those *Daylight* people buy." With a sweep of her hand she indicated the astonishing opulence of her possessions in different parts of the room.

As she stood over him with the brandy there came through the smoke of his cigarette the perfume of orris-root and violet.

A servant began to arrange the little cold dinner on a camp-table and Coleman saw with an enthusiasm which he could not fully master four quart bottles of a notable brand of champagne placed in a rack on the floor.

At dinner Nora was sisterly. She watched him, waited upon him, treated him to an affectionate intimacy for which he knew a thousand men who would have hated him. The champagne was cold.

Slowly he melted. By the time that the boy came with little cups of Turkish coffee he was at least amiable. Nora talked dreamily. "The dragoman says this room used to be part of the harem long ago." She shot him a watchful glance as if she had expected the fact to affect him. "Seems curious doesn't it? A harem. Fancy that." He smoked one cigar and then discarded tobacco for the perfume of orris-root and violet was making him meditate. Nora talked on in a low voice. She knew that through half-closed lids he was looking at her in steady speculation. She knew that she was conquering but no movement of hers betrayed an elation. With the most exquisite art she aided his contemplation, baring for instance, the glories of a statuesque neck, doing it all with the manner of a splendid and fabulous virgin who knew not that there was such a thing as shame. Her stockings were of black silk.

Coleman presently answered her only in monosyllable, making small distinction between yes and no. He simply sat watching her with eyes in which there were two little covetous steel colored flames.

He was thinking. To go to the devil—to go to the devil—to go to the devil with this girl was not a bad fate—not a bad fate— not a bad fate.

CHAPTER XVIII

COME out on the balcony," cooed Nora. "There are some funny old storks on top of some chimneys near here and they clatter like mad all day and all night."

They moved together out to the balcony but Nora retreated with a little cry when she felt the coldness of the night. She said that she would get a cloak. Coleman was not unlike a man in a dream. He walked to the rail of the balcony where a great vine climbed toward the roof. He noted that it was dotted with blossoms which in the deep purple of the oriental night were colored in strange shades of maroon. This truth penetrated his abstraction until when Nora came she found him staring at them as if their color was a revelation which affected him vitally. She moved to his side without sound and he first knew of her presence from the damning fragrance. She spoke just above her breath. "It's a beautiful evening."

"Yes," he answered. She was at his shoulder. If he moved two inches he must come in contact. They remained in silence leaning upon the rail. Finally he began to mutter some commonplaces which meant nothing particularly but into his tone as he mouthed them was the note of a forlorn and passionate lover. Then as if by accident he traversed the two inches and his shoulder was against the soft and yet firm shoulder of Nora Black. There was something in his throat at this time which changed his voice into a mere choking noise. She did not move. He could see her eyes glowing innocently out of the pallor which the darkness gave to her face. If he was touching her, she did not seem to know it.

"I am awfully tired," said Coleman thickly. "I think I will go home and turn in."

"You must be, poor boy," said Nora tenderly. "Wouldn't you like a little more of that champagne?"

"Well, I don't mind another glass."

She left him again and his galloping thought pounded to the old refrain. To go to the devil—to go to the devil—to go to the devil with this girl was not a bad fate—not a bad fate—not a bad fate. When she returned he drank his glass of champagne. Then he mumbled: "You must be cold. Let me put your cape around you better. It won't do to catch cold here, you know."

She made a sweet pretense of rendering herself to his care. "Oh, thanks . . . I am not really cold . . . there, that's better."

Of course all his manipulation of the cloak had been a fervid caress and although her acting up to this point had remained in the role of the splendid and fabulous virgin she now turned her liquid eyes to his with a look that expressed knowledge, triumph and delight. She was sure of her victory. And she said: "Sweetheart . . . don't you think I am as nice as Marjory?" The impulse had been airily confident.

It was as if the silken cords had been parted by the sweep of a sword. Coleman's face had instantly stiffened and he looked like a man suddenly recalled to the ways of light. It may easily have been that in a moment he would have relapsed again to his luxurious dreaming. But in his face the girl had read a fatal character to her blunder and her resentment against him took precedence of any other emotion. She wheeled abruptly from him and said with great contempt: "Rufus, you had better go home. You're tired and sleepy and more or less drunk."

He knew that the grand tumble of all their little embowered incident could be neither stayed nor mended. "Yes," he answered sulkily, "I think so too." They shook hands huffily and he went away.

When he arrived among the students he found that they had appropriated everything of his which would conduce to their comfort. He was furious over it. But to his bitter speeches they replied in jibes.

"Rufus is himself again. Admire his angelic disposition. See him smile. Gentle soul."

A sleepy voice said from a corner: "I know what pinches him."

"What?" asked several.

"He's been to see Nora and she flung him out bodily."

"Yes?" sneered Coleman. "At times I seem to see in you, Coke, the fermentation of some primeval form of sensation as if it were possible for you to develope a mind in two or three thousand years and then at other times you appear . . . much as you are now."

As soon as they had well measured Coleman's temper all of the students save Coke kept their mouth tightly closed. Coke either did not understand or his mood was too vindictive for silence. "Well, I know you got a throw-down all right," he muttered.

"And how would you know when I got a throw-down? You pimply milk-fed Sophomore."

The others perked up their ears in mirthful appreciation of this language.

"Of course," continued Coleman, "no one would protest against your continued existence, Coke, unless you insist on recalling yourself violently to people's attention in this way. The mere fact of your living would not usually be offensive to people if you weren't eternally turning a sort of calcium light on your prehensile attributes."

Coke was suddenly angry, angry much like a peasant and his anger first evinced itself in a mere sputtering and spluttering. Finally he got out a rather long speech, full of grumbling noises, but he was understood by all to declare that his prehensile attributes had not led him to cart a notorious woman about the world with him. When they quickly looked at Coleman they saw that he was livid. "You ——"

But of course there immediately arose all sorts of protesting cries from the seven non-combatants. Coleman as he took two strides toward Coke's corner looked fully able to break him across his knee, but for this Coke did not seem to care at all. He was on his feet with a challenge in his eye. Upon each cheek burned a sudden hectic spot. The others were clamoring. "Oh, say, this won't do! Quit it! Oh, we mustn't have a fight! He didn't mean it, Coleman." Peter Tounley pressed Coke to the wall saying: "You damned young jackass, be quiet."

They were in the midst of these festivities when a door opened and disclosed the professor. He might have been coming into the middle of a row in one of the corridors of the college at home only this time he carried a candle. His speech, however, was a

Washurst speech: "Gentlemen, gentlemen, what does this mean?" All seemed to expect Coleman to make the answer. He was suddenly very cool. "Nothing, professor," he said, "only that this—only that Coke has insulted me. I suppose that it was only the irresponsibility of a boy, and I beg that you will not trouble over it."

"Mr. Coke," said the professor indignantly, "what have you to say to this?" Evidently he could not clearly see Coke and he peered around his candle at where the virtuous Peter Tounley was expostulating with the young man. The figures of all the excited group moving in the candle light caused vast and uncouth shadows to have Titanic conflicts in the end of the room.

Peter Tounley's task was not light, and beyond that he had the conviction that his struggle with Coke was making him also to appear as a rowdy. This conviction was proven to be true by a sudden thunder from the old professor. "Mr. Tounley, desist!"

In wrath he desisted and Coke flung himself forward. He paid less attention to the professor than if the latter had been a jack-rabbit. "You say I insulted you?" he shouted crazily in Coleman's face. "Well . . . I meant to, do you see?"

Coleman was glacial and lofty beyond everything. "I am glad to have you admit the truth of what I have said."

Coke was still suffocating with this peasant rage which would not allow him to meet the clear, calm expressions of Coleman. "Yes . . . I insulted you . . . I insulted you because what I said was correct . . . my prehensile attributes . . . yes . . . but I have never——"

He was interrupted by a chorus from the other students. "Oh, no, that won't do. Don't say that. Don't repeat that, Coke."

Coleman remembered the weak bewilderment of the little professor in hours that had not long passed and it was with something of an impersonal satisfaction that he said to himself: "The old boy's got his war paint on again." The professor had stepped sharply up to Coke and looked at him with eyes that seemed to throw out flame and heat. There was a moment's pause and then the old scholar spoke, biting out his words as if they were each a short section of steel wire. "Mr. Coke, your behavior will end your college career abruptly and in gloom, I promise you. You have been drinking."

Coke, his head simply floating in a sea of universal defiance, at once blurted out: "Yes sir."

"You have been drinking?" cried the professor ferociously. "Retire to your . . . retire to your . . . retire . . ." and then in a voice of thunder he shouted: "Retire!" Whereupon seven hoodlum students waited a decent moment, then shrieked with laughter. But the old professor would have none of their nonsense. He quelled them all with force and finish.

Coleman now spoke a few words. "Professor, I can't tell you how sorry I am that I should be concerned in any such riot as this and since we are doomed to be bound so closely into each other's society I offer myself without reservation as being willing to repair the damage as well as may be done. I don't see how I can forget at once that Coke's conduct was insolently unwarranted but . . . if he has anything to say . . . of a nature that might heal the breach . . . I would be willing to . . . to meet him in the openest manner." As he made these remarks Coleman's dignity was something grand and moreover there was now upon his face that curious look of temperance and purity which had been noted in New York as a singular physical characteristic. If he was guilty of anything in this affair at all— in fact if he had ever at any time been guilty of anything—no mark had come to stain that bloom of innocence. The professor nodded in the fullest appreciation and sympathy. "Of course . . . really there is no other sleeping place . . . I suppose it would be better——" Then he again attacked Coke. "Young man you have chosen an unfortunate moment to fill us with suspicion that you may not be a gentleman. For the time there is nothing to be done with you." He addressed the other students. "There is nothing for me to do young gentlemen but to leave Mr. Coke in your care. Good-night sirs. Good-night Coleman." He left the room with his candle.

When Coke was bade to "retire" he had of course simply retreated fuming to a corner of the room where he remained looking with yellow eyes like an animal from a cave. When the others were able to see through the haze of mental confusion they found that Coleman was with deliberation taking off his boots. Afterward when he removed his waistcoat he took great care to wind his large gold watch.

The students, much subdued, lay again in their places and when there was any talking it was of an extremely local nature referring principally to the floor as being unsuitable for beds and also referring from time to time to a real or an alleged selfishness on the part of some one of the recumbent men. Soon there was only the sound of heavy breathing.

When the professor had returned to what may be called the Wainwright part of the house he was greeted instantly with the question: "What was it?" His wife and daughter were up in alarm. "What was it?" they repeated wildly.

He was peevish. "Oh, nothing, nothing. But that young Coke is a regular ruffian. He had gotten himself into some tremendous uproar with Coleman. When I arrived he seemed actually trying to assault him. Revolting! He had been drinking. Coleman's behavior, I must say, was splendid. Recognized at once the delicacy of my position—he not being a student. If I had found him in the wrong it would have been simpler than finding him in the right. Confound that rascal of a Coke." Then as he began a partial disrobing, he treated them to grunted scraps of information. "Coke was quite insane . . . I feared that I could not control him . . . Coleman was like ice . . . and as much as I have seen to admire in him during the last few days, this quite beat it . . . all . . . if he had not recognized my helplessness as far as he was concerned the whole thing might have been a most miserable business . . . he is a very fine young man." The dissenting voice to this last tribute was the voice of Mrs. Wainwright. She said: "Well, Coleman drinks too—everybody knows that."

"I know," repeated the professor rather bashfully, "but . . . I am confident that he had not touched a drop."

Marjory said nothing.

The earlier artillery battles had frightened most of the furniture out of the houses of Arta and there was left in this room only a few old red cushions and the Wainwrights were camping upon the floor. Marjory was enwrapped in Coleman's macintosh and while the professor and his wife maintained some low talk of the recent incident she in silence had turned her cheek into the yellow velvet collar of the coat. She felt something against her bosom and putting her hand carefully into the top pocket of

the coat she found three cigars. These she took in the darkness
and laid aside telling herself to remember their position in the
morning. She had no doubt that Coleman would rejoice over
them before he could get back to Athens when there were other
good cigars.

CHAPTER XIX

THE ladies of the Wainwright party had not complained at all when deprived of even such civilized advantages as a shelter and a knife and fork and soap and water but Mrs. Wainwright complained bitterly amid the half-civilization of Arta. She could here see no excuse for the absence of several hundred things which she had always regarded as essential to life. She began at 8.30 a.m. to make both the professor and Marjory woeful with an endless dissertation upon the beds in the hotel at Athens. Of course she had not regarded them at the time as being exceptional beds . . . that was quite true . . . but then one really never knew what one was really missing until one really missed it. . . . She would never have thought that she would come to consider those Athenian beds as excellent . . . but experience is a great teacher . . . makes one reflect upon the people who year in and year out have no beds at all, poor things. . . . Well, it made one glad if one *did* have a good bed even if it was at the time on the other side of the world. . . . If she ever reached it she did not know what could ever induce her to leave it again. . . . She would never be induced——

" 'Induced'," snarled the professor. The word represented to him a practised feminine misusage of truth and at such his white warlock always arose. " 'Induced'. Out of four American women I have seen lately, you seem to be the only one who would say that you had endured this thing because you had been 'induced' by others to come over here. How absurd."

Mrs. Wainwright fixed her husband with a steely eye. She saw opportunity for a shattering retort. "You don't mean, Harrison, to include Marjory and I in the same breath with those two women?"

The professor saw no danger ahead for himself. He merely answered: "I had no thought either way. It did not seem important."

"Well, it *is* important," snapped Mrs. Wainwright. "Do you know that you are speaking in the same breath of Marjory and Nora Black the actress?"

"No," said the professor. "Is that so?" He was astonished but he was not aghast at all. "Do you mean to say that is Nora Black the comic opera star?"

"That's exactly who she is," said Mrs. Wainwright dramatically. "And I consider that . . . I consider that Rufus Coleman has done no less than . . . mislead us."

This last declaration seemed to have no effect upon the professor's pure astonishment but Marjory looked at her mother suddenly. However she said no word, exhibiting again that strange and inscrutable countenance which masked even the tiniest of her maidenly emotions.

Mrs. Wainwright was triumphant and she immediately set about celebrating her victory. "Men never see those things," she said to her husband. "Men never see those things. You would have gone on forever without finding out that your . . . your . . . hospitality was being abused by that Rufus Coleman."

The professor woke up. "Hospitality?" he said indignantly. " 'Hospitality'? I have not had any hospitality to be abused. Why don't you talk sense? It is not that, but . . . it might——" he hesitated and then spoke slowly. "It might be very awkward. Of course one never knows anything definite about such people but I suppose. . . . Anyhow it was strange in Coleman to allow her to meet us."

"It was all a prearranged plan," announced the triumphant Mrs. Wainwright. "She came here on purpose to meet Rufus Coleman and he knew it and I should not wonder if they had not the exact spot picked out where they were going to meet."

"I can hardly believe that," said the professor in distress. "I can hardly believe that. It does not seem to me that Coleman——"

"Oh, yes. Your dear Rufus Coleman," cried Mrs. Wainwright. "You think he is very fine now. But I can remember when you didn't think——"

And the parents turned together and abashed looked at their daughter. The professor actually flushed with shame. It seemed to him that he had just committed an atrocity upon the heart of his child. The instinct of each of them was to go to her and console her in their arms. She noted it immediately and seemed to fear it. She spoke in a clear and even voice. "I don't think, father, that you should humiliate me by supposing that I am concerned at all if Mr. Coleman cares to meet Nora Black over here."

"Not at all," stuttered the professor. "I——"

Mrs. Wainwright's consternation turned suddenly to anger. "He is a scapegrace. A rascal. A—a——"

"Oh," said Marjory coolly, "I don't see why it isn't his own affair. He didn't really present her to you, mother, you remember? She seemed quite to force her way at first and then you—you did the rest. It should be very easy to avoid her now that we are out of the wilderness. And then it becomes a private matter of Mr. Coleman's. For my part, I rather liked her. I don't see such a dreadful calamity."

"Marjory!" screamed her mother. "How dreadful. Liked her. Don't let me hear you say such shocking things."

"I fail to see anything shocking," answered Marjory stolidly.

The professor was looking helplessly from his daughter to his wife and from his wife to his daughter like a man who was convinced that his troubles would never end. This new catastrophe created a different kind of difficulty but he considered that the difficulties were as robust as had been the preceding ones. He put on his hat and went out of the room. He felt an impossibility of saying anything to Coleman but he felt that he must look upon him. He must look upon this man and try to know from his manner the measure of guilt. And incidentally he longed for the machinery of a finished society which prevents its parts from clashing, prevents it with its great series of law upon law, easily operative but relentless. Here he felt as a man flung into the jungle with his wife and daughter where they could become the victims of any sort of savagery. His thought referred once more to what he considered the invaluable services of Coleman and as he observed them in conjunction with the present accusation, he was simply dazed. It was then possible that one man could play two such divergent parts. He had not learned this at Washurst. But no; the world was not such a bed of putrefaction. He would not believe it; he would not believe it.

After adventures which require great nervous endurance, it is only upon the second or third night that the common man sleeps hard. The students had expected to slumber like dogs on the first night after their trials but none slept long and few slept soundly.

Coleman was the first man to arise. When he left the room the students were just beginning to blink. He took his dragoman among the shops and he bought there all the little odds and ends which might go to make up the best breakfast in Arta. If he had had news of certain talk he probably would not have been playing dragoman for eleven people. Instead, he would have been buying breakfast for one. During his absence, the students arose and performed their frugal toilets. Considerable attention was paid to Coke by the others. "He made a monkey of you," said Peter Tounley with unction. "He twisted you until you looked like a wet grey rag. You had better leave this wise guy alone."

It was not the night nor was it meditation that had taught Coke anything but he seemed to have learned something from the mere lapse of time. In appearance he was subdued but he managed to make a temporary jauntiness as he said: "Oh, I don't know."

"Well you ought to know," said he who was called Billie. "You ought to know. You made an egregious snark of yourself. Indeed you sometimes resembled a boojum. Anyhow you were a plain chump. You exploded your face about something of which you knew nothing and I'm damned if I believe you'd make even a good retriever."

"You're a half-bred water-spaniel," blurted Peter Tounley. "And," he added musingly, "that is a pretty low animal."

Coke was argumentative. "Why am I?" he asked, turning his head from side to side. "I don't see where I was so wrong."

"Oh, dances, balloons, picnics, parades and ascensions!" they retorted profanely. "You swam voluntarily into water that was too deep for you. Swim out. Get dry. Here's a towel."

Coke smitten in the face with a wet cloth rolled into a ball grabbed it and flung it futilely at a well-dodging companion. "No," he cried. "I don't see it. Now look here. I don't see why we shouldn't all resent this Nora Black business."

One student said: "Well, what's the matter with Nora Black anyhow?"

Another student said: "I don't see how you've been issued any license to say things about Nora Black."

Another student said: "All anybody can say will not make me believe that he had a thing to do with it."

Another student said dubiously: "Well, he knows her well."

And then three or four spoke at once. "He was very badly rattled when she appeared upon the scene."

Peter Tounley asked: "Well, which of you people know anything wrong about Nora Black?"

There was a pause and then Coke said: "Oh, of course . . . I don't know . . . but——"

He who was called Billie then addressed his companions. "It wouldn't be right to repeat any old lie about Nora Black and by the same token it wouldn't be right to see Old Mother Wainwright chummin' it with her. There is no wisdom in going further than that. Old Mother Wainwright don't know that her fair companion of yesterday is the famous comic opera star. For my part I believe that Coleman is simply afraid to tell her. I don't think he wished to see Nora Black yesterday any more than he wished to see the devil. The discussion as I understand it . . . concerned itself only with what Coleman had to do with the thing and yesterday anybody could see that he was in a panic."

They heard a step on the stair and directly Coleman entered followed by his dragoman. They were laden with the raw material for breakfast. The correspondent looked keenly among the students for it was plain that they had been talking of him. It filled him with rage and for a stifling moment he could not think why he failed to immediately decamp in chagrin and leave eleven orphans to whatever fate their general incompetence might lead them. It struck him as a deep shame that even then he and his paid man were carrying in the breakfast. He wanted to fling it all on the floor and walk out. Then he remembered Marjory. She was the reason. She was the reason for everything.

But he could not repress certain of his thoughts. "Say, you people," he said icily, "you had better soon learn to hustle for yourselves. I may be a dragoman, and a butler, and a cook, and a housemaid but I'm blowed if I'm a wet nurse." In reality he had taken the most generous pleasure in working for the others before their eyes had even opened from sleep but it was now all turned to worm-wood. It is certain that even this could not have deviated this executive man from labor and management because these were his life. But he felt that he was about to walk out of the room, consigning them all to hades. His glance of angry reproach fastened itself mainly upon Peter Tounley because he knew that of all Peter was the most innocent.

Peter Tounley was abased by this glance. "So you've brought us something to eat, old man. . . . That is tremendously nice of you . . . we . . . appreciate it like . . . everything."

Coleman was mollified by Peter's tone. Peter had had that emotion which is equivalent to a sense of guilt although in reality he was speckless. Two or three of the other students bobbed up to a sense of the situation. They ran to Coleman and with polite cries took his provisions from him. One dropped a bunch of lettuce on the floor, and others reproached him with scholastic curses. Coke was seated near the window, half militant, half conciliatory. It was impossible for him to keep up a manner of deadly enmity while Coleman was bringing in his breakfast. He would have much preferred that Coleman had not brought in his breakfast. He would have much preferred to have forgone breakfast altogether. He would have much preferred anything. There seemed to be a conspiracy of circumstance to put him in the wrong and make him appear as a ridiculous young peasant. He was the victim of a benefaction and he hated Coleman harder now than at any previous time. He saw that if he stalked out and took his breakfast alone in a cafe, the others would consider him still more of an outsider. Coleman had expressed himself like a man of the world and a gentleman and Coke was convinced that he was a superior man of the world and a superior gentleman but that he simply had not had words to express his position at the proper time. Coleman was glib. Therefore Coke had been the victim of an attitude as well as of a benefaction. And so he deeply hated Coleman.

The others were talking cheerfully. "What the deuce are these, Coleman? Sausages? Oh, my. And look at these burlesque fishes. Say, these Greeks don't care *what* they eat. Them thar things am sardines in the crude state. No? Great God, look at those things. Look. What? Yes, they are. Radishes. Greek synonym for radishes."

The professor entered. "Oh," he said apologetically as if he were intruding in a boudoir. He looked, too, as if he thought it Coleman's boudoir. All his serious desire to probe Coleman to the bottom ended in embarrassment. Mayhap it was not a law of feeling but it happened at any rate. He had come in a puzzled frame of mind, even an accusative frame of mind, and almost immediately he found himself suffering like a culprit before his judge. It is a phenomenon of what we call guilt and innocence.

Coleman welcomed him cordially. "Well, professor, good morning. . . . I've rounded up some things that at least *may* be eaten."

"You are very good; very considerate, Mr. Coleman," answered the professor hastily. "I am sure we are much indebted to you." He had scanned the correspondent's face and it had been so devoid of guile that he was fearful that his suspicion, a base suspicion, of this noble soul would be detected. "No, no; we can never thank you enough."

Some of the students began to caper with a sort of decorous hilarity before their teacher. "Look at the sausage, professor. Did you ever see such sausage? Isn't it salubrious? And see these other things, sir. Aren't they curious? I shouldn't wonder if they were alive. Turnips, sir? No, sir. I think they are Pharisees. I have seen a Pharisee look like a pelican but I have never seen a Pharisee look like a turnip, so I think these turnips must be Pharisees, sir. Yes, they may be walrus. We're not sure. Anyhow, their angles are geometrically all wrong. Peter, look out." Some green stuff was flung across the room. The professor laughed; Coleman laughed. Despite Coke, dark-browed, sulking and yet desirous of reinstating himself, the room had waxed warm with the old college feeling, the feeling of lads who seemed never to treat anything respectfully and yet at the same time managed to treat the real things with respect. The professor himself contributed to their wild carouse over the strange Greek viands. It was a vivacious moment common to this class in times of relaxation and it was understood perfectly.

Coke arose. "I don't see that I have any friends here," he said hoarsely, "and in consequence I don't see why I should remain here."

All looked at him. At the same moment Mrs. Wainwright and Marjory entered the room.

CHAPTER XX

G OOD MORNING," said Mrs. Wainwright jovially to the students and then she stared at Coleman as if he were a sweep at a wedding.

"Good morning," said Marjory.

Coleman and the students made reply. "Good morning. Good morning. Good morning. Good morning——"

It was curious to see this greeting, this common phrase, this bit of old ware, this antique, come upon a dramatic scene and pulverize it. Nothing remained but a ridiculous dust. Coke, glowering, with his lips still trembling from heroic speech, was an angry clown, a pantaloon in rage. Nothing was to be done to keep him from looking like an ass. He strode toward the door mumbling something about a walk before breakfast.

Mrs. Wainwright beamed upon him. "Why, Mr. Coke, not before breakfast? You surely won't have time." It was grim punishment. He appeared to go blind and he fairly staggered out of the door mumbling again, mumbling thanks or apologies or explanations. About the mouth of Coleman played a sinister smile. The professor cast upon his wife a glance expressing weariness. It was as if he had said: "There you go again. You *can't* keep your foot out of it." She understood the glance and so she asked blankly: "Why. What's the matter? Oh." Her belated mind grasped that it was an aftermath of the quarrel of Coleman and Coke. Marjory looked as if she was distressed in the belief that her mother had been stupid. Coleman was outwardly serene. It was Peter Tounley who finally laughed a cheery healthy laugh and they all looked at him with gratitude as if his sudden mirth had been a real statement of reconciliation and consequent peace.

The dragoman and others disported themselves until a breakfast was laid upon the floor. The adventurers squatted upon the floor. They made a large company. The professor and Coleman discussed the means of getting to Athens. Peter Tounley sat next to Marjory. "Peter," she said privately, "what was all this trouble between Coleman and Coke?"

Peter answered blandly: "Oh, nothing at all. Nothing at all."

"Well, but—" she persisted, "what was the cause of it?"

He looked at her quaintly. He was not one of those in love with her but he was interested in the affair. "Don't you know?" he asked.

She understood from his manner that she had been some kind of an issue in the quarrel. "No," she answered hastily. "I don't."

"Oh, I don't mean that," said Peter. "I only meant—I only meant—oh, well, it was about nothing—really."

"It must have been about something," continued Marjory. She continued because Peter had denied that she was concerned in it. "Whose fault?"

"I really don't know. It was all rather confusing," lied Peter tranquilly.

Coleman and the professor decided to accept a plan of the correspondent's dragoman to start soon on the first stage of the journey to Athens. The dragoman had said that he had found two large carriages rentable.

Coke, the out-cast, walked alone in the narrow streets. The flight of the Crown Prince's army from Larissa had just been announced in Arta but Coke was probably the most woebegone object on the Greek peninsula.

He encountered a strange sight on the streets. A woman garbed in the style for walking of an afternoon on upper Broadway was approaching him through a mass of kilted mountaineers and soldiers in soiled over-coats. Of course he recognized Nora Black.

In his conviction that everybody in the world was at this time considering him a mere worm, he was sure that she would not heed him. Beyond that he had been presented to her notice in but a transient and cursory fashion. But contrary to his conviction, she turned a radiant smile upon him. "Oh," she said brusquely, "you are one of the students. Good morning." In her manner was all the confidence of an old warrior, a veteran, who addresses the universe with assurance because of his past battles.

Coke grinned at this strange greeting. "Yes, Miss Black," he answered, "I am one of the students."

She did not seem to quite know how to formulate her next speech. "Er—I suppose you're going to Athens at once? You must be glad after your horrid experiences."

"I believe *they* are going to start for Athens today," said Coke.

Nora was all attention. "'They'?" she repeated. "Aren't you going with them?"

"Well," he said. ". . . Well——"

She saw of course that there had been some kind of trouble. She laughed. "You look as if somebody had kicked you down stairs," she said candidly. She at once assumed an intimate manner toward him which was like a temporary motherhood. "Come, walk with me and tell me all about it." There was in her tone a most artistic suggestion that whatever had happened, she was on his side. He was not loath. The street was full of soldiers whose tongues clattered so loudly that the two foreigners might have been wandering in a great cave of the winds. "Well what was the row about?" asked Nora. "And who was in it?"

It would have been no solace to Coke to pour out his tale even if it had been a story that he could have told Nora. He was not stopped by the fact that he had gotten himself in the quarrel because he had insulted the name of the girl at his side. He did not think of it at that time. The whole thing was now extremely vague in outline to him and he only had a dull feeling of misery and loneliness. He wanted her to cheer him.

Nora laughed again. "Why you're a regular little kid. Do you mean to say you've come out here sulking alone because of some nursery quarrel?" He was ruffled by her manner. It did not contain the cheering he required. "Oh, I don't know that I'm such a regular little kid," he said sullenly. "The quarrel was not a nursery quarrel."

"Why don't you challenge him to a duel?" asked Nora suddenly. She was watching him closely.

"Who?" said Coke.

"Coleman you stupid," answered Nora.

They stared at each other, Coke paying her first the tribute of astonishment and then the tribute of admiration. "Why how did you guess that?" he demanded.

"Oh," said Nora, "I've known Rufus Coleman for years and he is always rowing with people."

"That is just it," cried Coke eagerly. "That is just it. I fairly hate the man. Almost all of the other fellows will stand his abuse but it riles me I tell you. I think he is a beast. And of course if you seriously meant what you said about challenging him to a duel—I mean if there is any sense in that sort of thing —I would challenge Coleman. I swear I would. I think he's a great bluffer anyhow. Shouldn't wonder if he would back out. Really I shouldn't."

Nora smiled humorously at a house on her side of the narrow way. "I wouldn't wonder if he did either," she answered. After a time she said: "Well do you mean to say that you have definitely shaken them? Aren't you going back to Athens with them or anything?"

"I—I don't see how I can," he said morosely.

"Oh," she said. She reflected for a time. At last she turned to him archly and asked: "Some words over a lady?"

Coke looked at her blankly. He suddenly remembered the horrible facts. "No . . . no . . . not over a lady."

"My dear boy, you are a liar," said Nora freely. "You are a little unskilful liar. It *was* some words over a lady and the lady's name is Marjory Wainwright."

Coke felt as if he had suddenly been let out of a cell but he continued a mechanical denial. "No, no . . . It wasn't truly . . . upon my word. . . ."

"Nonsense," said Nora. "I know better. Don't you think you can fool me you little cub. I know you're in love with Marjory Wainwright and you think Coleman is your rival. What a blockhead you are. Can't you understand that people see these things?"

"Well——" stammered Coke.

"Nonsense," said Nora again. "Don't try to fool me, you may as well understand that it's useless. I am too wise."

"Well——" stammered Coke.

"Go ahead," urged Nora. "Tell me about it. Have it out."

He began with great importance and solemnity. "Now, to tell you the truth . . . that *is* why I hate him . . . I hate him like anything. . . . I can't see why everybody admires him so. I don't see anything to him myself. I don't believe he's got any more principle than a wolf. I wouldn't trust him with two dollars. Why, I know stories about him that would make your hair curl. When I think of a girl like Marjory——"

His speech had become a torrent. But here Nora raised her hand. "Oh! Oh! Oh! That will do. That will do. Don't lose your senses. I don't see why this girl Marjory is any too good. She is no chicken, I'll bet. Don't let yourself get fooled with that sort of thing."

Coke was unaware of his incautious expressions. He floundered on while Nora looked at him as if she wanted to wring his neck. "No . . . she's too fine and too good . . . for him or anybody like him . . . she's too fine and too good——"

"Aw, rats," interrupted Nora furiously. "You make me tired."

Coke had a wooden-headed conviction that he must make Nora understand Marjory's infinite superiority to all others of her sex and so he passed into a panegyric each word of which was a hot coal to the girl addressed. Nothing would stop him apparently. He even made the most stupid repetitions. Nora finally stamped her foot formidably. "*Will* you stop? *Will* you stop?" she said through her clenched teeth. "Do you think I want to listen to your everlasting twaddle about her? Why, she's—she's no better than other people, you ignorant little mamma's boy. She's no better than other people. You swab."

Coke looked at her with the eyes of a fish. He did not understand. "But she *is* better than other people," he persisted.

Nora seemed to decide suddenly that there would be no accomplishment in flying persistently against this rock-walled conviction. "Oh, well," she said with marvelous good nature, "perhaps you are right, numbskull. But, look here, do you think she cares for him?"

In his heart, his jealous heart, he believed that Marjory loved Coleman but he reiterated eternally to himself that it was not true. As for speaking it to another; that was out of the question. "No," he said, stoutly, "she doesn't care a snap for him." If he had admitted it, it would have seemed to him that he was somehow advancing Coleman's chances.

"Oh, she doesn't, eh?" said Nora enigmatically. "She doesn't?" He studied her face with an abrupt miserable suspicion but he repeated doggedly: "No she doesn't."

"Ahem," replied Nora. "Why, she's set her cap for him all right. She's after him for certain. It's as plain as day. Can't you see that, stupidity?"

"No," he said hoarsely.

"You are a fool," said Nora. "It isn't Coleman that's after her. It is she that is after Coleman."

Coke was mulish. "No such thing. Coleman's crazy about her. Everybody has known it ever since he was in college. You ask any of the other fellows."

Nora was now very serious, almost doleful. She remained still for a time, casting at Coke little glances of hatred. "I don't see my way clear to ask any of the other fellows," she said at last with considerable bitterness. "I'm not in the habit of conducting such inquiries."

Coke felt now that he disliked her and he read plainly her dislike of him. If they were the two villains of the play they were not having fun together at all. Each had some kind of a deep knowledge that their aspirations, far from colliding, were of such character that the success of one would mean at least assistance to the other but neither could see how to confess it. Perhaps it was from shame; perhaps it was because Nora thought Coke to have little wit; perhaps it was because Coke thought Nora to have little conscience. Their talk was mainly rudderless. From time to time Nora had an inspiration to come boldly at the point but this inspiration was commonly defeated by some extraordinary manifestation of Coke's incapacity. To her mind then it seemed like a proposition to ally herself to a butcher-boy in a matter purely sentimental. She wondered indignantly how she was going to conspire with this lad who puffed out his infantile cheeks in order to conceitedly demonstrate that he did not understand the game at all. She hated Marjory for it. Evidently it was only the weaklings who fell in love with that girl. Coleman was an exception but then Coleman was misled by extraordinary artifices. She meditated for a moment if she should tell Coke to go home and not bother her. What at last decided the question was his unhappiness. She clung to this unhappiness for its value as it stood alone and because its reason for existence was related to her own unhappiness. "You say you are not going back to Athens with your party. I don't suppose you're going to stay here. I'm going back to Athens today. I came up here to see a battle but it doesn't seem that there are to be any more battles. The fighting will now all be on the other side of the mountains." Apparently she had learned in some haphazard way that the Greek peninsula was divided by a spine of almost inaccessible mountains and the war was thus split into two simultaneous campaigns. The Arta campaign was known to be ended. "If you want to go back to Athens without consorting with your friends you had better go back with me. I can take you in my carriage as far as the beginning of the railroad. Don't you worry. You've got money haven't you? The professor isn't keeping your money?"

"Yes," he said slowly, "I've got money enough." He was apparently dubious over the proposal.

In their abstracted walk they had arrived in front of the house occupied by Coleman and the Wainwright party. Two carriages forlorn in dusty age, stood before the door. Men were carrying out new leather luggage and flinging it into the traps amid a great deal of talk which seemed to refer to nothing. Nora and Coke stood looking at the scene without either thinking of the importance of running away, when out tumbled seven students followed immediately but in more decorous fashion by the Wainwrights and Coleman.

Some student set up a whoop. "Oh, there he is. There's Coke. Hey, Coke, where you been? Here he is, professor."

For a moment after the hoodlum had subsided, the two camps stared at each other in silence.

CHAPTER XXI

NORA and Coke were an odd-looking pair at the time. They stood indeed as if rooted to the spot, staring vacuously, like two villagers, at the surprising travellers. It was not an eternity before the practised girl of the stage recovered her poise but to the end of the incident the green youth looked like a culprit and a fool. Mrs. Wainwright's glower of offensive incredulity was a masterpiece. Marjory nodded pleasantly; the professor nodded. The seven students clambered boisterously into the forward carriage making it clang with noise like a rook's nest. They shouted to Coke: "Come on; all aboard; come on, Coke; we're off. Hey, there, Cokey, hurry up." The professor as soon as he had seated himself on the forward seat of the second carriage, turned in Coke's general direction and asked formally: "Mr. Coke, are you or are you not coming with us?" He felt seemingly much in doubt as to the propriety of abandoning the headstrong young man and this doubt was not at all decreased by Coke's appearance with Nora Black. As far as he could tell, any assertion of authority on his part would end only in a scene in which Coke would probably insult him with some gross violation of collegiate conduct. As at first the young man made no reply the professor after waiting spoke again. "You understand Mr. Coke that if you separate yourself from the party you encounter my strongest disapproval and if I did not feel responsible to the college and your father for your safe journey to New York I—I don't know but what I would have you expelled by cable if that were possible."

Although Coke had been silent and Nora Black had had the appearance of being silent in reality she had lowered her chin and whispered sideways and swiftly. She had said: "Now here's your time. Decide quickly and don't look like such a wooden Indian."

Coke pulled himself together with a visible effort and spoke to the professor from an inspiration in which he had no faith. "I understand my duties to you, sir, perfectly. I also understand my duty to the college. But I fail to see where either of these obligations require me to accept the introduction of objectionable people into the party. If I owe a duty to the college and to you, I don't owe any to Coleman and as I understand it Coleman was not in the original plan of this expedition. If such had been the case, I would not have been here. I can't tell what the college may see fit to do but as for my father I have no doubt of how he will view it."

The first one to be electrified by the speech was Coke himself. He saw with a kind of sub-conscious amazement this volley of bird-shot take effect upon the face of the old professor. The face of Marjory flushed crimson as if her mind had sprung to a fear that if Coke could develope ability in this singular fashion he might succeed in humiliating her father in the street in the presence of the seven students, her mother, Coleman and—herself. She had felt the bird-shot sting her father.

When Coke had launched forth, Coleman with his legs stretched far apart had just struck a match on the wall of the house and was about to light a cigar. His groom was leading up his horse. He saw the value of Coke's argument more appreciatively and sooner perhaps than did Coke. The match dropped from his fingers and in the white sunshine and still air it burnt on the pavement orange colored and with langour. Coleman held his cigar with all five fingers—in a manner out of all the laws of smoking. He turned toward Coke. There was danger in the moment but then in a flash it came upon him that his role was not one of squabbling with Coke, far less of punching him. On the contrary he was to act the part of a cool and instructed man who refused to be waylaid into foolishness by the outcries of this pouting youngster and who placed himself in complete deference to the wishes of the professor. Before the professor had time to embark upon any reply to Coke, Coleman was at the side of the carriage and, with a fine assumption of distress, was saying: "Professor, I could very easily ride back to Agrinion alone. It would be all right. I don't want to——"

To his surprise the professor waved at him to be silent as if he were a mere child. The old man's face was set with the resolution of exactly what he was going to say to Coke. He began in measured tone, speaking with feeling but with no trace of anger. "Mr. Coke, it has probably escaped your attention that Mr. Coleman, at what I consider a great deal of peril to himself, came out to rescue this party—you and others—and although he studiously disclaims all merit in his finding us and bringing us in, I do not regard it in that way and I am surprised that any member of this party should conduct himself in this manner toward a man who has been most devotedly and generously at our service." It was at this time that the professor raised himself and shook his finger at Coke, his voice now ringing with scorn. In such moments words came to him and formed themselves into sentences almost too rapidly for him to speak them. "You are one of the most remarkable products of our civilization which I have yet come upon. What do you mean sir? Where are your senses? Do you think that all this puling and puking is manhood? I will tell you what I will do with you. I thought I brought out eight students to Greece but when I find that I brought out seven students and—er an—ourang-outang—don't get angry, sir—I don't care for your anger—I say when I discover this I am naturally puzzled for a moment. I will leave you to the judgement of your peers. Young gentlemen!"

Of the seven heads of the forward carriage none had to be turned. All had been turned since the beginning of the talk. If the professor's speech had been delivered in one of the classrooms of Washurst they would have glowed with delight over the butchery of Coke but here they felt its portentous aspect. Butchery here in Greece thousands of miles from home presented to them more of the emphasis of down-right death and destruction. The professor called out: "Young gentlemen, I have done all that I can do without using force which, much to my regret, is impracticable. If you will persuade your fellow student to accompany you I think our consciences will be the better for not having left a weak minded brother alone among the by-paths."

The valuable aggregation of intelligence and refinement which decorated the interior of the first carriage did not hesitate over answering this appeal. In fact his fellow students had worried among themselves over Coke and their desire to see him come out of his troubles in fair condition was intensified by the fact that they had lately concentrated much thought upon him. There was a somewhat comic pretense of speaking so that only Coke could hear. Their chorus was low sung. "Oh, cheese it, Coke. Let up on yourself you blind ass. Wait till you get to Athens and then go and act like a monkey. All this is no good——"

The advice which came from the carriage was all in one direction and there was so much of it that the hum of voices sounded like a wind blowing through a forest.

Coke spun suddenly and said something to Nora Black. Nora laughed rather loudly and then the two turned squarely and the Wainwright party contemplated what were surely at that time the two most insolent backs in the world.

The professor looked as if he might be going to have a fit. Mrs. Wainwright lifted her eyes toward high heaven and flinging out her trembling hands cried: "Oh, what an outrage! *What an outrage!* That minx——" The consensus of opinion in the first carriage was perfectly expressed by Peter Tounley who with a deep-drawn breath said: "Well, I'm damned." Marjory had moaned and lowered her head as from a sense of completely personal shame. Coleman lit his cigar and mounted his horse. "Well, I suppose there is nothing for it but to be off, professor?" His tone was full of regret, with a sort of poetic regret. For a moment the professor looked at him blankly and then gradually recovered part of his usual manner. "Yes," he said sadly, "there is nothing for it but to go on." At a word from the dragoman the two impatient drivers spoke gutturally to their horses and the carriages whirled out of Arta. Coleman, his dragoman and the groom trotted in the dust from the wheels of the Wainwright carriage. The correspondent always found his reflective faculties improved by the constant pounding of a horse on the trot and he was not sorry to have now a period for reflection as well as this artificial stimulant. As he viewed the game he had in his hand about all the cards that were valuable. In fact he considered that the only ace against him was Mrs. Wainwright. He had always regarded her as a stupid person concealing herself behind a mass of trivialities which were all conventional but he thought now that the more stupid she was and the more conventional in her triviality, the more she approached to being the very ace of trumps itself. She was just the sort of a card that would come upon the table mid the neat play of experts and by some inexplicable arrangement of circumstance lose a whole game for the wrong man.

After Mrs. Wainwright he worried over the students. He believed them to be reasonable enough; in fact he honored them distinctly in regard to their powers of reason but he knew that people generally hated a row. It put them off their balance, made them sweat over a lot of pros and cons and prevented them from thinking for a time at least only of themselves. Then they came to resent the principals in a row. Of course the principal who was thought to be in the wrong was the most resented but Coleman believed that after all people always came to resent the other principal or at least be impatient and suspicious of him. If he was a correct person why was he in a row at all? The principal who had been in the right often brought this impatience and suspicion upon himself no doubt by never letting the matter end, continuing to yawp about their virtuous suffering and not allowing people to return to the steady contemplation of their own affairs. As a precautionary measure he decided to say nothing at all about the late trouble unless someone addressed him upon it. Even then he would be serenely laconic. He felt that he must be popular with the seven students. In the first place it was nice that in the presence of Marjory they should like him and in the second place he feared to displease them as a body because he believed that he had some dignity. Hoodlums are seldom dangerous to other hoodlums but if they catch pomposity alone in the field, pomposity is their prey. They tear him to mere bloody ribbons amid heartless shrieks. When Coleman put himself on the same basis with the students he could cope with them easily but he did not want the wild pack after him when Marjory could see the chase. And so he reasoned that his best attitude was to be one of rather taciturn serenity.

On the hard military road the hoofs of the horses made such clatter that it was practically impossible to hold talk between the carriages and the horsemen without all parties bellowing. The professor, however, strove to overcome the difficulties. He was apparently undergoing a great amiability toward Coleman. Frequently he turned with a bright face and pointing to some object in the landscape obviously tried to convey something entertaining to Coleman's mind. Coleman could see his lips mouth the words. He always nodded cheerily in answer and yelled.

The road ultimately became that straight lance-handle which Coleman—it seemed as if many years had passed—had traversed with his dragoman and the funny little carriers. He was fixing in his mind a possible story to the Wainwrights about the snake and his first dead Turk. But suddenly the carriages left this road and began a circuit of the Gulf of Arta, winding about an endless series of promontories. The journey developed into an excess of dust whirling from a road which half circled the waist of cape after cape. All dramatics were lost in the rumble of wheels and in the click of hoofs. They passed a little soldier leading a prisoner by a string. They passed more frightened peasants who seemed resolved to flee down into the very boots of Greece. And people looked at them with scowls envying them their speed. At the little town from which Coleman had embarked at one stage of the upward journey, they found crowds in the streets. There was no longer any laughter, any confidence, any vim. All the spirit of the visible Greek nation seemed to have been knocked out of it in two blows. But still they talked and never ceased talking. Coleman noted that the most curious changes had come upon them since his journey to the frontier. They no longer approved of foreigners. They seemed to blame the travellers for something which had transpired in the past few days. It was not that they really blamed the travellers for the nation's calamity; it was simply that their minds were half stunned by the news of defeats and, not thinking for a moment to blame themselves or even not thinking to attribute the defeats to mere numbers and skill, they were savagely eager to fasten it upon something near enough at hand for the operation of vengeance.

Coleman perceived that the dragoman, all his former plumage gone, was whining and snivelling as he argued to a dark-browed crowd that was running beside the cavalcade. The groom, who always had been a miraculously laconic man, was suddenly launched forth garrulously. The drivers from their high seats palavered like mad-men, driving with one hand and gesturing with the other, explaining evidently their own great innocence.

Coleman saw that there was trouble but he only sat more stiffly in his saddle. The eternal gabble moved him to despise the situation. At any rate, the travellers would soon be out of this town and on to a more sensible region.

However, he saw the driver of the first carriage suddenly pull up before a little blackened coffee-shop and inn. The dragoman spurred forward and began wild expostulation. The second carriage pulled up close behind the other. The crowd, murmuring like a Roman mob in Nero's time, closed around them.

CHAPTER XXII

OLEMAN pushed his horse coolly through the throng to the dragoman's side. "What is it?" he demanded. The dragoman was broken-voiced. "These peoples, they say you are Germans, all Germans, and they are ongry," he wailed. "I can do nossing—nossing."

"Well, tell these men to drive on," said Coleman, "tell them they *must* drive on."

"They will note drive on," wailed the dragoman still more loudly. "I can do nossing. They say here is place for feed the horse. It is the custom and they will note drive on."

"*Make* them drive on."

"They will *note*," shrieked the agonized servitor.

Coleman looked from the men waving their arms and chattering on the box-seats to the men of the crowd who also waved their arms and chattered. In this throng far to the rear of the fighting armies there did not seem to be a single man who was not able-bodied, who had not been free to enlist as a soldier. They were of that scurvy behind-the-rear-guard which every nation has in degree proportionate to its worth. The man-hood of Greece had gone to the frontier leaving at home this rabble of talkers most of whom were armed with rifles for mere pretention. Coleman loathed them to the end of his soul. He thought them a lot of infants who would like to prove their courage upon eleven innocent travellers, all but unarmed, and in this fact he was quick to see a great danger to the Wainwright party. One could deal with soldiers; soldiers would have been ashamed to bait helpless people; but this rabble——

The fighting blood of the correspondent began to boil and he really longed for the privilege to run amok through the multitude. But a look at the Wainwrights kept him in his senses. The

professor had turned pale as a dead man. He sat very stiff and
still while his wife clung to him, hysterically beseeching him to
do something, do something, although what he was to do she
could not have even imagined.

Coleman took the dilemma by its beard. He dismounted from
his horse into the depths of the crowd and addressed the Wainwrights. "I suppose we had better go into this place and have
some coffee while the men feed their horses. There is no use in
trying to make them go on." His manner was fairly casual but
they looked at him in glazed horror. "It is the only thing to do.
This crowd is not nearly so bad as they think they are. But we've
got to look as if we felt confident." He himself had no confidence
with this angry buzz in his ears but he felt certain that the only
correct move was to get everybody as quickly as possible within
the shelter of the inn. It might not be much of a shelter for them
but it was better than the carriages in the street.

The professor and Mrs. Wainwright seemed to be considering
their carriage as a castle and they looked as if their terror had
made them physically incapable of leaving it. Coleman stood
waiting. Behind him the clapper-tongued crowd was moving
ominously. Marjory arose and stepped calmly down to him.

He thrilled to the end of every nerve. It was as if she had
said: "I don't think there is great danger but if there *is* great
danger why . . . here I am . . . ready . . . with you." It
conceded everything, admitted everything. It was a surrender
without a blush and it was only possible in the shadow of the
crisis when they did not know what the next moments might
contain for them. As he took her hand and she stepped past him
he whispered swiftly and fiercely in her ear: "I love you." She
did not look up but he felt that in this quick incident they had
claimed each other, accepted each other with a far deeper meaning and understanding than could be possible in a mere drawing-
room. She laid her hand on his arm and with the strength of
four men he twisted his horse into the making of furious prancing side-steps toward the door of the inn, clanking side-steps
which mowed a wide lane through the crowd for Marjory, his
Marjory. He was as haughty as a new German lieutenant and
although he held the fuming horse with only his left hand, he

seemed perfectly capable of hurling the animal over a house without calling into service the arm which was devoted to Marjory.

It was not an exhibition of coolness such as wins applause on the stage when the hero placidly lights a cigarette before the mob which is clamoring for his death. It was, on the contrary, an exhibition of down-right classic disdain, a disdain which with the highest arrogance declared itself in every glance of his eye into the faces about him. "Very good . . . attack me if you like . . . there is nothing to prevent it . . . you mongrels." Every step of his progress was made a renewed insult to them. The very air was charged with what this lone man was thinking of this threatening crowd.

His audacity was invincible. They actually made way for it as quickly as children would flee from a ghost. The horse, dancing with ringing steps, with his glistening neck arched toward the iron hand at his bit, this powerful quivering animal was a regular engine of destruction and they gave room until Coleman halted him at an exclamation from Marjory. "My mother and father." But they were coming close behind and Coleman resumed this contemptuous journey to the door of the inn. The groom, with his new-born tongue, was clattering there to the populace. Coleman gave him the horse and passed after the Wainwrights into the public room of the inn. He was smiling. What simpletons.

A new actor suddenly appeared in the person of the keeper of the inn. He too had a rifle and a prodigious belt of cartridges but it was plain at once that he had elected to be a friend of the worried travellers. A large part of the crowd were thinking it necessary to enter the inn and pow-wow more. But the innkeeper stayed at the door with the dragoman and together they vociferously held back the tide. The spirit of the mob had subsided to a more reasonable feeling. They no longer wished to tear the strangers limb from limb on the suspicion that they were Germans. They now were frantic to talk as if some inexorable law had kept them silent for ten years and this was the very moment of their release. Whereas, their simultaneous and interpolating orations had, throughout, made noise much like a coal-breaker.

Coleman led the Wainwrights to a table in a far part of the room. They took chairs as if he had commanded them. "What an outrage," he said jubilantly. "The apes." He was keeping more than half an eye upon the door because he knew that the quick coming of the students was important.

Then suddenly the storm broke in wrath. Something had happened in the street. The jabbering crowd at the door had turned and were hurrying upon some central tumult. The dragoman screamed to Coleman. Coleman jumped and grabbed the dragoman. "Tell this man to take them somewheres—upstairs," he cried, indicating the Wainwrights with a sweep of his arm. The inn-keeper seemed to understand sooner than the dragoman and he nodded eagerly. The professor was crying: "What is it, Mr. Coleman? What is it?" An instant later, the correspondent was out in the street, buffeting toward a scuffle. Of course it was the students. It appeared, afterward, that those seven young men, with their feelings much ruffled, had been making the best of their way toward the door of the inn when a large man in the crowd, during a speech which was surely most offensive, had laid an arresting hand on the shoulder of Peter Tounley. Whereupon the excellent Peter Tounley had hit the large man on the jaw in such a swift and skilful manner that the large man had gone spinning through a group of his countrymen to the hard earth where he lay holding his face together, and howling. Instantly of course there had been a riot. It might well be said that even then the affair could have ended in a lot of talking but in the first place the students did not talk modern Greek and in the second place they were now past all thought of talking. They regarded this affair seriously as a fight and now that they at last were in it, they were in it for every pint of blood in their bodies. Such a pack of famished wolves had never before been let loose upon men armed with Gras rifles.

They all had been expecting the row and when Peter Tounley had found it expedient to knock over the man, they had counted it a signal; their arms had immediately begun to swing out as if they had been wound up. It was at this time that Coleman swam brutally through the Greeks and joined his countrymen. He was more frightened than any of those novices. When he saw Peter Tounley over-throw a dreadful-looking brigand whose wide belt was full of knives and who crashed to the ground amid a clang of cartridges, he was appalled by the utter simplicity with which the lads were treating the crisis. It was to them no common scrimmage at Washurst, of course, but it flashed through Coleman's mind that they had not the slightest sense of the size of the thing. He expected every instant to see the flash of knives or to hear the deafening intonation of a rifle fired against his ear. It seemed to him miraculous that the tragedy was so long delayed.

In the meantime he was in the affray. He jolted one man under the chin with his elbow in a way that reeled him off from Peter Tounley's back; a little person in checked clothes he smote between the eyes; he received a gun-butt emphatically on the side of the neck; he felt hands tearing at him; he kicked the pins out from under three men in rapid succession. He was always yelling. "Try to get to the inn, boys, try to get to the inn. Look out, Peter. Take care for his knife, Peter——" Suddenly he whipped a rifle out of the hands of a man and swung it, whistling. He had gone stark mad with the others.

The boy Billie, drunk from some blows and bleeding, was already staggering toward the inn over the clearage which the wild Coleman made with the clubbed rifle. The others followed as well as they might while beating off a discouraged enemy. The remarkable inn-keeper had barred his windows with strong wood shutters. He held the door on the crack for them and they stumbled one by one through the portal. Coleman did not know why they were not all dead nor did he understand the intrepid and generous behavior of the inn-keeper but at any rate he felt that the fighting was suspended and he wanted to see Marjory. The inn-keeper was doing a great pantomime in the middle of the darkened room, pointing to the outer door and then aiming his rifle at it to explain his intention of defending them at all costs. Some of the students moved to a billiard table and spread themselves wearily upon it. Others sank down where they stood. Outside the crowd was beginning to roar. Coleman's groom crept out from under the little coffee-bar and comically saluted his master. The dragoman was not present. Coleman felt that he must see Marjory and he made signs to the inn-keeper. The latter understood quickly and motioned that Coleman should follow him. They passed together through a dark hall and up a darker stairway whereafter Coleman stepped out into a sun-lit room saying loudly: "Oh, it's all right. It's all over. Don't worry."

Three wild people were instantly upon him. "Oh, what was it? What *did* happen? Isn't anybody hurt? Oh, tell us, quick." It seemed at the time that it was an avalanche of three of them and it was not until later that he recognized that Mrs. Wainwright had tumbled the largest number of questions upon him. As for Marjory she had said nothing until the time when she cried: "Oh . . . he is bleeding . . . he is bleeding. Oh, come, quick." She fairly dragged him out of one room into another room where there was a jug of water. She wet her handkerchief and softly smote his wounds. "Bruises," she said piteously tearful. "Bruises. Oh, dear. How they must hurt you." The handkerchief was soon stained crimson.

When Coleman spoke his voice quavered. "It isn't anything. Really, it isn't anything." He had not known of these wonderful wounds but he almost choked in the joy of Marjory's ministry and her half-coherent exclamations. This proud and beautiful girl, this superlative creature, was reddening her handkerchief with his blood and no word of his could have prevented her from thus attending him. He could hear the professor and Mrs. Wainwright fussing near him, trying to be of use. He would have liked to have been able to order them out of the room. Marjory's cool fingers on his face and neck had conjured within him a vision of an intimacy that was even sweeter than anything which he had imagined and he longed to pour out to her the bubbling impassioned speech which came to his lips. But, always doddering behind him, were the two old people, strenuous to be of help to him.

Suddenly a door opened and a youth appeared simply red with blood. It was Peter Tounley. His first remark was cheerful. "Well, I don't suppose *those* people will be any too quick to look for more trouble."

Coleman felt a swift pang because he had forgotten to announce the dilapidated state of all the students. He had been so submerged by Marjory's tenderness that all else had been drowned from his mind. His heart beat quickly as he waited for Marjory to leave him and rush to Peter Tounley.

But she did nothing of the sort. "Oh, Peter," she cried in distress and then she turned back to Coleman. It was the professor and Mrs. Wainwright who, at last finding a field for their kindly ambitions, flung themselves upon Tounley and carried him off to another place. Peter was removed crying: "Oh, now, look here, professor, I'm not dying or anything of that sort——"

Coleman and Marjory were left alone. He suddenly and forcibly took one of her hands and the blood-stained handkerchief dropped to the floor.

CHAPTER XXIII

FROM below, they could hear the thunder of weapons and fists upon the door of the inn amid a great clamor of tongues. Sometimes there arose the argumentative howl of the inn-keeper. Above this roar Coleman's quick words sounded in Marjory's ear. "I've got to go. I've got to go back to the boys but—I love you."

"Yes, go, go," she whispered hastily. "You should be there but —come back."

He held her close to him. "But you are mine, remember," he said fearfully and sternly. "You are mine—forever—as I am yours—remember."

Her eyes half closed. She made intensely solemn answer. "Yes." He released her and was gone.

In the glooming coffee-room of the inn he found the students, the dragoman, the groom and the inn-keeper armed with a motley collection of weapons which ranged from the rifle of the inn-keeper to the table leg in the hands of Peter Tounley. The last named young student of archaeology was in a position of temporary leadership and holding a great pow-wow with the inn-keeper through the medium of piercing outcries by the dragoman. Coleman had not yet understood why none of them had been neither stabbed nor shot in the fight in the street but it seemed to him now that affairs were leading toward a crisis of tragedy. He thought of the possibilities of having the dragoman go to an upper window and harangue the people but he saw no chance of success in such a plan. He saw that the crowd would merely howl at the dragoman while the dragoman howled at the crowd. He then asked if there was any other exit from the inn by which they could secretly escape. He learned that the door into the coffee-room was the only door which pierced the four great walls. All he could then do was to find out from the inn-keeper how much of a siege the place could stand and to this the inn-keeper answered volubly and with smiles that this hostelry would easily endure until the mercurial temper of the crowd had darted off in a new direction. It may be curious to note here that all of Peter Tounley's impassioned communication with the inn-keeper had been devoted to an endeavor to learn what in the devil was the matter with these people as a man about to be bitten by poisonous snakes should, first of all, furiously insist upon learning their exact species before deciding upon either his route if he intended to run away or his weapon if he intended to fight them.

The inn-keeper was evidently convinced that his house would withstand the rage of the populace and he was such an unaccountably gallant little chap that Coleman trusted entirely to his word. His only fear or suspicion was an occasional one as to the purity of the dragoman's translation.

Suddenly there was half a silence on the mob without the door. It is inconceivable that it could become altogether silent but it went as near to a rational stillness of tongues as it was able. Then there was a loud knocking by a single fist and a new voice began to spin Greek, a voice that was somewhat like the rattle of pebbles in a tin box. Then a startling feminine voice called out in English. "Are you in there, Rufus?"

Answers came from every English speaking person in the room in one great outburst. "Yes."

"Well, let us in," called Nora Black. "It is all right. We've got an officer with us."

"Open the door," said Coleman with speed. The little inn-keeper laboriously unfastened the great bars and when the door was finally opened there appeared on the threshold Nora Black with Coke and an officer of infantry, Nora's little old companion and Nora's dragoman. "We saw your carriages in the street," cried the queen of comic opera as she swept into the room. She was beaming with delight. "What is all the row anyway. O-o-oh, look at that student's nose. Who hit him? And look at Rufus. What *have* you boys been doing?"

Her little Greek officer of infantry had stopped the mob from flowing into the room. Coleman looked toward the door at times with some anxiety. Nora, noting it, waved her hand in careless re-assurance. "Oh, it's all right. Don't worry about them any more. He is perfectly devoted to me. He would die there on the threshold if I told him it would please me. Speaks splendid French. I found him limping along the road and gave him a lift. And now *do* hurry up and tell me exactly what happened."

They all told what had happened, while Nora and Coke listened agape. Coke, by the way, had quite floated back to his old position with the students. It had been easy in the stress of excitement and wonder. Nobody had time to think of the excessively remote incidents of the early morning. All minor interests were lost in their marvel of the present situation.

"Who landed you in the eye, Billie?" asked the awed Coke. "That was a bad one."

"Oh, I don't know," said Billie. "You really couldn't tell who hit you, you know. It was like a foot-ball rush. They had guns and knives but they didn't use 'em. I don't know why. Jinks. I'm getting pretty stiff. My face feels as if it were made of tin. Did they give you people a row, too?"

"No; only talk. That little officer managed them. Out-talked them, I suppose. Hear him buzz, now."

The Wainwrights came down stairs. Nora Black went confidently forward to meet them. "You've added one more to your list of rescuers," she cried with her glowing triumphant smile. "Miss Black of the *New York Daylight*—at your service. How in the world do you manage to get yourselves into such dreadful scrapes? You are the most remarkable people. You *need* a guardian. Why, you might have all been killed. How exciting it must seem to be regularly of your party." She had shaken cordially one of Mrs. Wainwright's hands without that lady in any way indicating assent to the proceeding but Mrs. Wainwright had not felt repulsion. In fact she had had no emotion springing directly from it. Here again the marvel of the situation came to deny Mrs. Wainwright the right to resume a state of mind which had been so painfully interesting to her a few hours earlier.

The professor, Coleman and all the students were talking together. Coke had addressed Coleman civilly and Coleman had made a civil reply. Peace was upon them.

Nora slipped her arm lovingly through Marjory's arm. "That Rufus. Oh, that Rufus," she cried joyously. "I'll give him a good scolding as soon as I see him alone. I might have foreseen that he would get you all into trouble. The old stupid."

Marjory did not appear to resent anything. "Oh, I don't think it was Mr. Coleman's fault at all," she answered calmly. "I think it was more the fault of Peter Tounley, poor boy."

"Well, I'd be glad to believe it, I'd be glad to believe it," said Nora. "I want Rufus to keep out of that sort of thing but he is *so* hot-headed and foolish." If she had pointed out her proprietary stamp on Coleman's cheek she could not have conveyed what she wanted to convey with more clearness.

"Oh," said the impassive Marjory, "I don't think you need have any doubt as to whose fault it was, if there were any of our boys at fault. Mr. Coleman was inside when the fighting commenced and only ran out to help the boys. He had just brought us safely through the mob and, far from being hot-headed and foolish, he was utterly cool in manner, impressively cool, I thought. I am glad to be able to re-assure you on these points for I see that they worry you."

"Yes, they *do* worry me," said Nora densely. "They worry me night and day when he is away from me."

"Oh," responded Marjory, "I have never thought of Mr. Coleman as a man that one would worry about much. We consider him very self-reliant, able to take care of himself under almost any conditions but then of course we do not know him at all in the way that you know him. I should think that you would find that he came off rather better than you expected from most of his difficulties. But then of course as I said you know him so much better than we do." Her easy indifference was a tacit dismissal of Coleman as a topic.

Nora, now thoroughly alert, glanced keenly into the other girl's face but it was inscrutable. The actress had intended to go careering through a whole circle of daring allusions to an intimacy with Coleman but here, before she had really developed her attack, Marjory, with a few conventional and indifferent sentences, almost expressive of boredom, had made the subject of Coleman impossible. An effect was left upon Nora's mind that Marjory had been extremely polite in listening to much nervous talk about a person in whom she had no interest.

The actress was dazed. She did not know how it had all been done. Where was the head of this thing? And where was the tail?

A fog had mysteriously come upon all her brilliant prospects of seeing Marjory Wainwright suffer and this fog was the product of a kind of magic with which she was not familiar. She could not think how to fight it. After being simply dubious throughout a long pause, she in the end went into a great rage. She glared furiously at Marjory, dropped her arm as if it had burned her and moved down upon Coleman. She must have reflected that at any rate she could make him wriggle. When she was come near to him, she called out: "Rufus." In her tone was all the old insolent statement of ownership. Coleman might have been a poodle. She knew how to call his name in a way that was nothing less than a public scandal. On this occasion everybody looked at him and then went silent as people awaiting the startling denouement of a drama. "Rufus." She was baring his shoulder to show the fleur de lys of the criminal. The students gaped.

Coleman's temper was, if one may be allowed to speak in that way, broken loose inside of him. He could hardly breathe; he felt that his body was about to explode into a thousand fragments. He simply snarled out:—"What?" Almost at once he saw that she had at last goaded him into making a serious tactical mistake. It must be admitted that it is only when the relations between a man and a woman are the relations of wed-lock or at least of an intimate resemblance to it that the man snarls out—"What?"— to the woman. Mere lovers say: "I beg your pardon?" It is only Cupid's finished product that spits like a cat. Nora Black had called him like a wife and he had answered like a husband. For his cause, his manner could not possibly have been worse. He saw the professor stare at him in surprise and alarm and felt the excitement of the eight students. These latter were diabolic in the celerity with which they picked out meanings. It was as plain to them as if Nora Black had said: "He is my property."

Coleman would have given his nose to have been able to recall that single reverberating word. But he saw that the scene was spelling downfall for him and he went still more blind and desperate of it. His despair made him burn to make matters worse. He did not want to improve anything at all. "What?" he demanded. "What do ye' want?"

Nora was sweetly reproachful. "I left my jacket in the carriage and I want you to get it for me."

"Well, get it for yourself, do ye' see? Get it for yourself."

Now it is plainly to be seen that no one of the people listening there had ever heard a man speak thus to a woman who was not his wife. Whenever they had heard that form of spirited repartee it had come from the lips of a husband. Coleman's rude speech was to their ears a flat announcement of an extraordinary intimacy between Nora Black and the correspondent. Any other interpretation would not have occurred to them. It was so palpable that it greatly distressed them with its arrogance and boldness. The professor had blushed. The very milkiest word in his mind at the time was the word vulgarity.

Nora Black had won a great battle. It was her Agincourt. She had beaten the clever Coleman in a way that had left little of him but rags. However, she could have lost it all again if she had shown her feeling of elation. At Coleman's rudeness her manner indicated a mixture of sadness and embarrassment. Her suffering was so plain to the eye that Peter Tounley was instantly moved. "Can't I get your jacket for you, Miss Black?" he asked hastily and at her grateful nod he was off at once.

Coleman was resolved to improve nothing. His over-throw seemed to him to be so complete that he could not in any way mend it without a sacrifice of his dearest prides. He turned away from them all and walked to an isolated corner of the room. He would abide no longer with them. He had been made an out-cast by Nora Black and he intended to be an out-cast. There was no sense in attempting to stem this extraordinary deluge. It was better to acquiesce.

Then suddenly he was angry at Marjory. He did not exactly see why he was angry at Marjory but he was angry at her nevertheless. He thought of how he could revenge himself upon her. He decided to take horse with his groom and dragoman and proceed forthwith on the road, leaving the jumble as it stood. This would pain Marjory anyhow, he hoped. She would feel it deeply, he hoped.

Acting upon this plan, he went to the professor. "Well, of course you are all right now, professor, and if you don't mind, I would like to leave you—go on ahead. I've got a considerable pressure of business on my mind and I think I should hurry on to Athens, if you don't mind."

The professor did not seem to know what to say. "Of course,

if you wish it—sorry, I'm sure—of course it is as you please—but you have been such a power in our favor—it seems too bad to lose you—but—if you wish it—if you insist——"

"Oh, yes, I quite insist," said Coleman calmly. "I quite insist. Make your mind easy on that score, professor. I insist."

"Well, Mr. Coleman," stammered the old man. "Well, it seems a great pity to lose you—you have been such a power in our favor——"

"Oh, you are now only eight hours from the railway. It is very easy. You would not need my assistance even if it were a benefit."

"But——" said the professor.

Coleman's dragoman came to him then and said: "There is one man here who says you made to take one rifle in the fight and was break his head. He was say he want sumthing for you was break his head. He says hurt."

"How much does he want?" asked Coleman impatiently.

The dragoman wrestled then evidently with a desire to protect this mine from outside fingers. "I—I think two gold piece plenty."

"Take them," said Coleman. It seemed to him preposterous that this idiot with a broken head should interpolate upon his tragedy. "Afterward, you and the groom get the three horses and we will start for Athens at once."

"For Athens? At once?" said Marjory's voice in his ear.

CHAPTER XXIV

O H," said Coleman, "I was thinking of starting."

"Why?" asked Marjory unconcernedly.

Coleman shot her a quick glance. "I believe my period of usefulness is quite ended," he said with just a small betrayal of bitter feeling.

"It is certainly true that you have had a remarkable period of usefulness to us," said Marjory with a slow smile, "but if it is ended, you should not run away from us."

Coleman looked at her to see what she could mean. From many women, these words would have been equal, under the circumstances, to a command to stay but he felt that none might know what impulses moved the mind behind that beautiful mask. In his misery, he thought to hurt her into an expression of feeling by a rough speech. "I'm so in love with Nora Black, you know, that I have to be very careful of myself."

"Oh," said Marjory, "I never thought of that. I should think you would have to be careful of yourself." She did not seem moved in any way. Coleman despaired of finding her weak spot. She was adamantine, this girl. He searched his mind for something to say which would be still more gross than his last outbreak but when he felt that he was about to hit upon it, the professor interrupted with an agitated speech to Marjory: "You had better go to your mother, my child, and see that you are all ready to leave here as soon as the carriages come up."

"We have absolutely nothing to make ready," said Marjory, laughing. "But I'll go and see if mother needs anything before we start that I can get for her." She went away without bidding good-bye to Coleman. The sole maddening impression to him was that the matter of his going had not been of sufficient importance to remain longer than a moment upon her mind. At the same time he decided that he would go, irretrievably go.

Even then the dragoman entered the room. "We will pack everything upon the horse?"

"Everything—yes."

Peter Tounley came afterward. "You are not going to bolt?"

"Yes, I'm off," answered Coleman recovering himself for Peter's benefit. "See you in Athens, probably."

Presently the dragoman announced the readiness of the horses. Coleman shook hands with the students and the professor amid cries of surprise and polite regret. "What? Going, old man? Really? What for? Oh, wait for us. We're off in a few minutes. Sorry as the devil, old boy, to see you go." He accepted their protestations with a somewhat sour face. He knew perfectly well that they were thinking of his departure as something that related to Nora Black. At the last, he bowed to the ladies as a collection. Marjory's answering bow was affable; the bow of Mrs. Wainwright spoke a resentment for something; and Nora's bow was triumphant mockery. As he swung into the saddle an idea struck him with overwhelming force. The idea was that he was a fool. He was a colossal imbecile. He touched the spur to his horse and the animal leaped superbly, making the Greeks hasten for safety in all directions. He was off; he could no more turn to retract his devious idiocy than he could make his horse fly to Athens. What was done was done. He could not mend it. And he felt like a man that had broken his own heart; perversely, childishly, stupidly broken his own heart.

He was sure that Marjory was lost to him. No man could be degraded so publicly and resent it so crudely and still retain a Marjory. In his abasement from his defeat at the hands of Nora Black he had performed every imaginable block-headish act and had finally climaxed all by a departure which left the tongue of Nora to speak unmolested into the ear of Marjory. Nora's victory had been a serious blow to his fortunes but it had not been so serious as his own subsequent folly. He had generously muddled his own affairs until he could read nothing out of them but despair.

He was in the mood for hatred. He hated many people. Nora Black was the principal item but he did not hesitate to detest the professor, Mrs. Wainwright, Coke and all the students. As for Marjory, he would revenge himself upon her. She had done nothing that he defined clearly but, at any rate, he would take revenge for it. As much as was possible, he would make her suffer. He would convince her that he was a tremendous and inexorable person. But it came upon his mind that he was powerless in all ways. If he hated many people they probably would not be even interested in his emotion and, as for his revenge upon Marjory, it was beyond his strength. He was nothing but the complaining victim of Nora Black and of himself.

He felt that he would never again see Marjory and while feeling it, he began to plan his attitude when next they met. He would be very cold and reserved.

At Agrinion, he found that there would be no train until the next daybreak. The dragoman was excessively annoyed over it but Coleman did not scold at all. As a matter of fact his heart had given a great joyous bound. He could not now prevent his being over-taken. They were only a few leagues away and while he was waiting for the train, they would easily cover the distance. If anybody expressed surprise at seeing him, he could exhibit the logical reasons.

If there had been a train starting at once, he would have taken it. His pride would have put up with no subterfuge. If the Wainwrights over-took him, it was because he could not help it. But he was delighted that he could not help it. There had been an interposition by some specially beneficent fate. He felt like whistling. He spent the early half of the night in blissful smoke, striding the room which the dragoman had found for him. His head was full of plans and detached impressive scenes in which he figured before Marjory. The simple fact that there was no train away from Agrinion until the next daybreak had wrought a stupendous change in his outlook. He unhesitatingly considered it an omen of a good future.

He was up before the darkness even contained presage of coming light but near the railway station was a little hut where coffee was being served to several prospective travellers who had come even earlier to the rendezvous. There was no evidence of the Wainwrights.

Coleman sat in the hut and listened for the rumble of wheels. He was suddenly appalled that the Wainwrights were going to miss the train. Perhaps they had decided against travelling during the night. Perhaps this thing and perhaps that thing. The morning was very cold. Closely muffled in his cloak, he went to the door and stared at where the road was whitening out of night. At the station stood a little spectral train and the engine at intervals emitted a long piercing scream which informed the echoing land that, in all probability, it was going to start after a time for the south. The Greeks in the coffee-room were, of course, talking.

At last Coleman did hear the sound of hoofs and wheels. The three carriages swept up in grand procession. The first was laden with students; in the second was the professor, the Greek officer, Nora Black's old lady and other persons, all looking marvelously unimportant and shelved. It was the third carriage at which Coleman stared. At first he thought the dim light deceived his vision but in a moment he knew that his first leaping conception of the arrangement of the people in this vehicle had been perfectly correct. Nora Black and Mrs. Wainwright sat side by side on the back seat while facing them were Coke and Marjory. They looked cold but intimate.

The oddity of the grouping stupefied Coleman. It was anarchy naked and unashamed. He could not imagine how such changes could have been consummated in the short time he had been away from them but he laid it all to some startling necromancy on the part of Nora Black, some wondrous play which had captured them all because of its surpassing skill and because they were, in the main, rather gullible people. He was wrong. The magic had been wrought by the unaided foolishness of Mrs. Wainwright. As soon as Nora Black had succeeded in creating an effect of an affectionate intimacy and dependence between herself and Coleman, the professor had flatly stated to his wife that the presence of Nora Black in the party, in the inn, in the world, was a thing that did not meet his approval in any way. She should be abolished. As for Coleman he would not defend him. He preferred not to talk of him. It made him sad. Coleman at least had been very indiscreet, very indiscreet. It was a great pity. But as for this blatant woman, the sooner they rid themselves of her, the sooner he would feel that all the world was not evil.

Whereupon Mrs. Wainwright had changed front with the speed of light and attacked with horse, foot and guns. She failed to see, she had declared, where this poor lone girl was in great fault. Of course it was probable that she had listened to this snaky-tongued Rufus Coleman but that was ever the mistake that women made. Oh, certainly; the professor would like to let Rufus Coleman off scot-free. That was the way with men. They defended each other in all cases. If wrong were done it was the woman who suffered. Now since this poor girl was alone far off here in Greece, Mrs. Wainwright announced that she had such full sense of her duty to her sex that her conscience would not allow her to scorn and desert a sister even if that sister was, approximately, the victim of a creature like Rufus Coleman. Perhaps the poor thing loved this wretched man although it was hard to imagine any woman giving her heart to such a monster.

The professor had then asked with considerable spirit for the proofs upon which Mrs. Wainwright named Coleman a monster and had made a wry face over her completely conventional reply. He had told her categorically his opinion of her erudition in such matters.

But Mrs. Wainwright was not to be deterred from an exciting espousal of the cause of her sex. Upon the instant that the professor strenuously opposed her she became an apostle, an enlightened uplifted apostle to the world on the wrongs of her sex. She had come down with this thing as if it were a disease. Nothing could stop her. Her husband, her daughter, all influences in other directions, had been over-turned with a roar and the first thing fully clear to the professor's mind had been that his wife was riding affably in the carriage with Nora Black.

Coleman aroused when he heard one of the students cry out: "Why, there is Rufus Coleman's dragoman. He must be *here*." A moment later they thronged upon him. "Hi, old man, caught you again. Where did you break to? Glad to catch you, old boy. How are you making it? Where's your horse?"

"Sent the horses on to Athens," said Coleman. He had not yet recovered his composure and he was glad to find available this common-place return to their exuberant greetings and questions. "Sent 'em on to Athens with the groom."

In the meantime the engine of the little train was screaming to heaven that its intention of starting was serious. The carriages careered to the station platform and unburdened. Coleman had his dragoman place his luggage in a little first-class carriage and he defiantly entered it and closed the door. He had a sudden return to the old sense of downfall and with it came the original rebellious desires. However he hoped that somebody would intrude upon him.

It was Peter Tounley. The student flung open the door and then yelled to the distance: "Here's an empty one." He clattered into the compartment. "Hello, Coleman. Didn't know you were in here." At his heels came Nora Black, Coke and Marjory.

"Oh," they said when they saw the occupant of the carriage. "Oh." Coleman was furious. He could have distributed some of his traps in a way to create more room but he did not move.

CHAPTER XXV

THERE was a demonstration of the unequaled facilities of a European railway carriage for rendering unpleasant things almost intolerable. These people could find no way to alleviate the poignancy of their position. Coleman did not know where to look. Every personal mannerism becomes accentuated in a European railway carriage. If you glance at a man, your glance defines itself as a stare. If you carefully look at nothing, you create for yourself a resemblance to all wooden-headed things. A newspaper is then in the nature of a preservative and Coleman longed for a newspaper.

It was this abominable railway carriage which exacted the first display of agitation from Marjory. She flushed rosily and her eyes wavered over the compartment. Nora Black laughed in a way that was a shock to the nerves. Coke seemed very angry indeed and Peter Tounley was in pitiful distress. Everything was acutely, painfully vivid, bald, painted as glaringly as a grocer's new wagon. It fulfilled those conditions which the artists deplore when they use their pet phrase on a picture. "It hurts." The damnable power of accentuation of the European railway carriage seemed, to Coleman's amazed mind, to be redoubled and redoubled.

It was Peter Tounley who seemed to be in the greatest agony. He looked at the correspondent beseechingly and said: "It's a very cold morning, Coleman." This was an actual appeal in the name of humanity.

Coleman came squarely to the front and even grinned a little at poor Peter Tounley's misery. "Yes it is a cold morning, Peter. I should say it is one of the coldest mornings in my recollection."

Peter Tounley had not intended a typical American emphasis on the polar conditions which obtained in the compartment at this time but Coleman had given the word this meaning. Spontaneously everybody smiled and at once the tension was relieved. But of course the satanic powers of the railway carriage could not be altogether set at naught. Of course it fell to the lot of Coke to get the seat directly in front of Coleman and thus face to face they were doomed to stare at each other.

Peter Tounley was inspired to begin a conventional babble in which he took great care to make an appearance of talking to all the carriage. "Funny thing. I never knew these mornings in Greece were so cold. I thought the climate here was quite tropical. It must have been inconvenient in the ancient times when, I am told, people didn't wear near so many—er—clothes. Really I don't see how they stood it. For my part I would like nothing so much as a buffalo robe. I suppose when those great sculptors were doing their masterpieces, they had to wear gloves. Ever think of that? Funny isn't it? Aren't you cold Marjory? I am. Jingo! Imagine the Spartans in ulsters going out to meet an enemy in cape over-coats and being desired by their mothers to return with their ulsters or wrapped in them."

It was rather hard work for Peter Tounley. Both Marjory and Coleman tried to display an interest in his labors and they laughed not at what he said but because they believed it assisted him. The little train, meanwhile, wandered up a great green slope and the day rapidly colored the land.

At first Nora Black did not display a militant mood but as time passed Coleman saw clearly that she was considering the advisability of a new attack. She had Coleman and Marjory in conjunction and where they were unable to escape from her. The opportunities were great. To Coleman, she seemed to be gloating over the possibilities of making more mischief. She was looking at him speculatively as if considering the best place to hit him first. Presently she drawled: "Rufus, I wish you would fix my rug about me a little better." Coleman saw that this was a beginning.

Peter Tounley sprang to his feet with speed and enthusiasm. "Oh, let me do it for you." He had her well muffled in the rug before she could protest even if a protest had been rational. The young man had had no plan of defending Coleman. He had no knowledge of the necessity for it. It had been merely the exercise of his habit of amiability, his chronic desire to see everybody comfortable. His passion in this direction was well-known in

Washurst where the students had borrowed a phrase from the photographers in order to describe him fully in a nickname. They called him "Look-Pleasant Tounley." This did not in any way antagonize his perfect willingness to fight on occasions with a singular desperation which usually has a small stool in every mind where good nature has a throne.

"Oh thank you very much, Mr. Tounley," said Nora Black, without gratitude. "Rufus is always so lax in these matters."

"I don't know how you know it," said Coleman boldly and he looked her fearlessly in the eye. The battle had begun.

"Oh," responded Nora airily, "I have had opportunity enough to know it, I should think, by this time."

"No," said Coleman, "since I have never paid you particular and direct attention, you cannot possibly know what I am lax in and what I am not lax in. I would be delighted to be of service at any time, Nora, but surely you do not consider that you have a right to my services superior to any other right."

Nora Black simply went mad but fortunately part of her madness was in the form of speechlessness. Otherwise there might have been heard something approaching to billings-gate.

Marjory and Peter Tounley turned first hot and then cold and looked as if they wanted to fly away and even Coke, penned helplessly in with this unpleasant incident, seemed to have a sudden attack of distress. The only frigid person was Coleman. He had made his declaration of independence and he saw with glee that the victory was complete. Nora Black might storm and rage but he had announced his position in an unconventionally blunt way which nobody in the carriage could fail to understand. He felt somewhat like smiling with confidence and defiance in Nora's face but he still had the fear for Marjory.

Unexpectedly, the fight was all out of Nora Black. She had the fury of a woman scorned but evidently she had perceived that all was over and lost. The remainder of her wrath dispensed itself in glares which Coleman withstood with great composure.

A strained silence fell upon the group which lasted until they arrived at the little port of Mesalonghi whence they were to take ship for Patras. Coleman found himself wondering why he had not gone flatly at the great question at a much earlier period, indeed at the first moment when the great question began to make life exciting for him. He thought that if he had charged Nora's guns in the beginning they would have turned out to be the same incapable artillery. Instead of that he had run away and continued to run away until he was actually cornered and made to fight and his easy victory had defined him as a person who had, earlier, indulged in much stupidity and cowardice.

Everything had worked out so simply, his terrors had been dispelled so easily, that he probably was led to over-estimate his success. And it occurred suddenly to him. He foresaw a fine occasion to talk privately to Marjory when all had boarded the steamer for Patras and he resolved to make use of it. This he believed would end the strife and conclusively laurel him.

The train finally drew up on a little stone pier and some boatmen began to scream like gulls. The steamer lay at anchor in the placid blue cove. The embarkation was chaotic in the oriental fashion and there was the customary misery which was only relieved when the travellers had set foot on the deck of the steamer. Coleman did not devote any premature attention to finding Marjory, but when the steamer was fairly out on the calm waters of the Gulf of Corinth, he saw her pacing to and fro with Peter Tounley. At first he lurked in the distance waiting for an opportunity, but ultimately he decided to make his own opportunity. He approached them. "Marjory, would you let me speak to you alone for a few moments? You won't mind, will you, Peter?"

"Oh no, certainly not," said Peter Tounley.

"Of course. It is not some dreadful revelation, is it?" said Marjory, bantering him coolly.

"No," answered Coleman abstractedly. He was thinking of what he was going to say. Peter Tounley vanished around the corner of a deck-house and Marjory and Coleman began to pace to and fro even as Marjory and Peter Tounley had done. Coleman had thought to speak his mind frankly and once for all, and on the train he had invented many clear expressions of his feeling. It did not appear that he had forgotten them. It seemed, more, that they had become entangled in his mind in such a way that he could not unravel the end of his discourse.

In the pause, Marjory began to speak in admiration of the scenery. "I never imagined that Greece was so full of mountains.

One reads so much of the Attic plains, but aren't these mountains royal? They look so rugged and cold, whereas the bay is absolutely as blue as the old descriptions of a summer sea."

"I wanted to speak to you about Nora Black," said Coleman.

"Nora Black? Why?" said Marjory, lifting her eye-brows.

"You know well enough," said Coleman in a headlong fashion. "You must know, you must have seen it. She knows I care for you and she wants to stop it. And she has no right to—to interfere. She is a fiend, a perfect fiend. She is trying to make you feel that I care for her."

"And don't you care for her?" asked Marjory.

"No," said Coleman vehemently. "I don't care for her at all."

"Very well," answered Marjory simply. "I believe you." She managed to give the words the effect of a mere announcement that she believed him and it was in no way plain that she was glad or that she esteemed the matter as being of consequence.

He scowled at her in dark resentment. "You mean by that, I suppose, that you don't believe me?"

"Oh," answered Marjory wearily, "I believe you. I said so. Don't talk about it any more."

"Then," said Coleman slowly, "you mean that you do not care whether I'm telling the truth or not?"

"Why, of course I care," she said. "Lying is not nice."

He did not know, apparently, exactly how to deal with her manner, which was actually so pliable that it was marble, if one may speak in that way. He looked ruefully at the sea. He had expected a far easier time. "Well——" he began.

"Really," interrupted Marjory, "this is something which I do not care to discuss. I would rather you not speak to me at all about it. It seems too—too—bad. I can readily give you my word that I believe you, but I would prefer you would not try to talk to me about it or—anything of that sort. Mother!"

Mrs. Wainwright was hovering anxiously in the vicinity, and she now bore down rapidly upon the pair. "You are very nearly to Patras," she said reproachfully to her daughter, as if the fact had some fault of Marjory's concealed in it. She in no way acknowledged the presence of Coleman.

"Oh, are we?" cried Marjory.

"Yes," said Mrs. Wainwright. "We are."

She stood waiting as if she expected Marjory to instantly quit Coleman. The girl wavered a moment and then followed her mother. "Good-bye," she said to Coleman. "I hope we may see you again in Athens." It was a command to him to travel alone with his servant on the long railway journey from Patras to Athens. It was a dismissal of a casual acquaintance given so graciously that it stung him to the depths of his pride. He bowed his adieu and his thanks. When the yelling boatmen came again, he and his man proceeded to the shore in an early boat without looking in any way after the welfarc of the others.

At the train the party split into three sections. Coleman and his man had one compartment, Nora Black and her squad had another, and the Wainwrights and students occupied two more.

The little officer was still in tow of Nora Black. He was very enthusiastic. In French she directed him to remain silent, but he did not appear to understand. "You tell him," she then said to her dragoman, "to sit in a corner and not to speak until I tell him to, or I won't have him in here." She seemed to be anxious to unburden herself to the old lady companion. "Do you know," she said, "that girl has a nerve like steel. I tried to break it therc in that inn but I couldn't *budge* her. If I am going to have her beaten I must prove myself to be a very, very artful person."

"Why did you try to break her nerve?" asked the old lady, yawning. "Why do you want to have her beaten?"

"Because I do, old stupid," answered Nora. "You should have heard the things I said to her."

"About what?"

"About Coleman. Can't you understand anything at all?"

"And why would you say anything about Coleman to her?" queried the old lady, still hopelessly befogged.

"Because," cried Nora, darting a look of wrath at her companion, "I want to prevent that marriage." She had been betrayed into this avowal by the singular opaque mind of the old lady. The latter at once sat erect. "Oh, ho!" she said, as if a ray of light had been let into her head. "Oh, ho! So that's it, is it?"

"Yes, that's it," rejoined Nora shortly.

The old lady was amazed into a long period of silent meditation. At last she spoke depressingly. "Well, how are you going to prevent it? Those things can't be done in these days at all. If they care for each other——"

Nora burst out furiously. "Don't venture opinions until you know what you are talking about, please. They don't care for each other, do you see? *She* cares for *him*, but *he* don't give a snap of his fingers for *her*."

"But," cried the bewildered old lady, "if *he* don't care for *her*, there will be nothing to prevent. If he don't care for her, he won't ask her to marry him, and so there won't be anything to prevent."

Nora made a broad gesture of impatience. "Oh, can't you get anything through your head? Haven't you seen that the girl has been the only young woman in that whole party lost up there in the mountains, and that naturally more than half the men still think they are in love with her? That's what it is. Can't you see? It always happens that way. Then Coleman comes along and makes a fool of himself with the others."

The old lady spoke up brightly as if at last feeling able to contribute something intelligent to the talk. "Oh, then, he *does* care for her."

Nora's eyes looked as if their glance might shrivel the old lady's hair. "Don't I keep telling you that it is no such thing? Can't you understand? It is all glamour! Fascination! 'Way up there in the wilderness! Only one even passable woman in sight."

"I don't say that I am so very keen," said the old lady, somewhat offended, "but I fail to see where I could improve when first you tell me he don't care for her, and then you tell me that he does care for her."

"'Glamour', 'Fascination'," quoted Nora. "Don't you understand the meaning of the words?"

"Well," asked the other, "didn't he know her, then, before he came over here?"

Nora was silent for a time, while the gloom upon her face deepened. It had struck her that the theories for which she protested so energetically might be not of such value. Spoken aloud, they had a sudden new flimsiness. It is even doubtful if she had ever really believed in them. Perhaps she had reiterated to herself that Coleman was the victim of glamour only because she wished it to be true. One theory, however, remained unshaken. Marjory was an artful minx, with no truth in her.

She presently felt the necessity of replying to the question of her companion. "Oh," she said carelessly, "I suppose they were acquainted—in a way."

The old lady was giving the best of her mind to the subject. "If that's the case—" she observed musingly, "if that's the case, you can't tell what is between 'em."

The talk had so slackened that Nora's unfortunate Greek admirer felt that here was a good opportunity to present himself again to the notice of the actress. The means was a smile and a French sentence, but his reception would have frightened a man in armor. His face blanched with horror at the storm he had invoked, and he dropped limply back as if someone had shot him. "You tell this little snipe to let me alone!" cried Nora to the dragoman. "If he dares to come around me with any more of those Parisian dude speeches, I—I don't know what I'll do! I won't have it, I say!" The impression upon the dragoman was hardly less in effect. He looked with bulging eyes at Nora, and then began to stammer at the officer. The latter's voice could sometimes be heard in awed whispers for the more elaborate explanation of some detail of the tragedy. Afterward, he remained meek and silent in his corner, barely more than a shadow, like the proverbial husband of imperious beauty.

"Well," said the old lady after a long and thoughtful pause, "I don't know, I'm sure, but it seems to me that if Rufus Coleman really cares for that girl, there isn't much use in trying to stop him from getting her. He isn't that kind of a man."

"For heaven's sake, will you stop assuming that he *does* care for her?" demanded Nora breathlessly.

"And I don't see," continued the old lady, "what you want to prevent him for anyhow."

CHAPTER XXVI

I FEEL in this radiant atmosphere that there could be no such thing as war—men striving together in black and passionate hatred." The professor's words were for the benefit of his wife and daughter. He was viewing the sky-blue waters of the Gulf of Corinth with its background of mountains that in the sunshine were touched here and there with a copperish glare. The train was slowly sweeping along the southern shore. "It is strange to think of those men fighting up there in the north. And it is strange to think that we ourselves are but just returning from it."

"I cannot begin to realize it yet," said Mrs. Wainwright in a high voice.

"Quite so," responded the professor, reflectively. "I do not suppose any of us will realize it fully for some time. It is altogether too odd, too very odd."

"To think of it!" cried Mrs. Wainwright. "To think of it! Supposing those dreadful Albanians or those awful men from the Greek mountains had caught us! Why, years from now I'll wake up in the night and think of it!"

The professor mused. "Strange that we cannot feel it strongly now. My logic tells me to be aghast that we ever got into such a place but my nerves at present refuse to thrill. I am very much afraid that this singular apathy of ours has led us to be unjust to poor Coleman."

Here Mrs. Wainwright objected. " 'Poor Coleman'! I don't see why you call him 'poor Coleman'."

"Well," answered the professor slowly, "I am in doubt about our behavior. It——"

"Oh," cried the wife gleefully, "in doubt about *our* behavior! I am in doubt about *his* behavior."

"So, then, you do have a doubt of his behavior?"

"Oh, no," responded Mrs. Wainwright hastily. "Not about its badness. What I meant to say was that in the face of his outrageous conduct with that—that woman, it is curious that you should worry about *our* behavior. It surprises me, Harrison."

The professor was wagging his head sadly. "I don't know . . . I don't know . . . It seems hard to judge . . . I hesitate to——"

Mrs. Wainwright treated this attitude with disdain. "It is not hard to judge," she scoffed, "and I fail to see why you have any reason for hesitation at all. Here he brings this woman——"

The professor got angry. "Nonsense! Nonsense! I do not believe that he brought her. If I ever saw a spectacle of a woman bringing herself, it was then. You keep chanting that thing like an outright parrot."

"Well," retorted Mrs. Wainwright, bridling, "I suppose you imagine that you understand such things. Men usually think that, but I want to tell you that you seem to me utterly blind."

"Blind or not, do stop the everlasting reiteration of that sentence."

Mrs. Wainwright passed into an offended silence, and the professor, also silent, looked with a gradually dwindling indignation at the scenery.

Night was suggested in the sky before the train was near to Athens. "My trunks," sighed Mrs. Wainwright. "How glad I will be to get back to my trunks! Oh, the dust! Oh, the misery! Do find out when we will get there, Harrison. Maybe the train is late."

But, at last, they arrived in Athens amid a darkness which was confusing and, after no more than the common amount of trouble, they procured carriages and were taken to the hotel. Mrs. Wainwright's impulses now dominated the others in the family. She had one passion after another. The majority of the servants in the hotel pretended that they spoke English, but, in three minutes, she drove them distracted with the abundance and violence of her requests. It came to pass that in the excitement the old couple quite forgot Marjory. It was not until Mrs. Wainwright, then feeling splendidly, was dressed for dinner that she thought to open Marjory's door and go to render a usual motherly supervision of the girl's toilet.

There was no light; there did not seem to be anybody in the room. "Marjory!" called the mother in alarm. She listened for a moment and then ran hastily out again. "Harrison!" she cried. "I can't find Marjory!" The professor had been tying his cravat. He let the loose ends fly. "What?" he ejaculated, opening his mouth wide. Then they both rushed into Marjory's room. "Marjory!" beseeched the old man in a voice which would have invoked from the grave.

The answer was from the bed. "Yes?" It was low, weary, tearful. It was not like Marjory. It was dangerously like the voice of a heart-broken woman. They hurried forward with outcries. "Why, Marjory! Are you ill, child? How long have you been lying here in the dark? Why didn't you call us? Are you ill?"

"No," answered this changed voice, "I am not ill. I only thought I'd rest for a time. Don't bother."

The professor hastily lit the gas and then father and mother turned hurriedly to the bed. In the first of the illumination they saw that tears were flowing unchecked down Marjory's face.

The effect of this grief upon the professor was, in part, an effect of fear. He seemed afraid to touch it, to go near it. He could, evidently, only remain in the outskirts, a horrified spectator. The mother, however, flung her arms about her daughter. "Oh, Marjory!" She, too, was weeping.

The girl turned her face to the pillow and held out a hand of protest. "Don't, mother! Don't!"

"Oh, Marjory! Oh, Marjory!"

"Don't, mother. Please go away. Please go away. Don't speak at all, I beg of you."

"Oh, Marjory! Oh, Marjory!"

"Don't." The girl lifted a face which appalled them. It had something entirely new in it. "Please go away, mother. I will speak to father, but I won't—I can't—I can't be pitied."

Mrs. Wainwright looked at her husband. "Yes," said the old man, trembling. "Go!" She threw up her hands in a sorrowing gesture that was not without its suggestion that her exclusion would be a mistake. She left the room.

The professor dropped on his knees at the bedside and took one of Marjory's hands. His voice dropped to its tenderest note. "Well, my Marjory?"

She had turned her face again to the pillow. At last she answered in muffled tones. "You know."

Thereafter, came a long silence full of sharpened pain. It was Marjory who spoke first. "I have saved my pride, daddy, but—I have—lost—everything—else." Even her sudden resumption of the old epithet of her childhood was an additional misery to the old man. He still said no word. He knelt gripping her fingers and staring at the wall.

"Yes, I have lost . . . everything . . . else."

The father gave a low groan. He was thinking deeply, bitterly. Since one was only a human being how was one going to protect beloved hearts assailed with sinister fury by the inexplicable zenith? In this tragedy he felt as helpless as an old grey ape. He did not see a possible weapon with which he could defend his child from the calamity which was upon her. There was no wall, no shield which could turn this sorrow from the heart of his child. If one of his hands' loss could have spared her, there would have been a sacrifice of his hand, but he was potent for nothing. He could only groan and stare at the wall.

He reviewed the past half in fear that he would there suddenly come upon his error which was now the cause of Marjory's tears. He dwelt long upon the fact that in Washurst he had refused his consent to Marjory's marriage with Coleman, but even now he could not say that his judgement was not correct. It was simply that the doom of woman's woe was upon Marjory, this ancient woe of the silent tongue and the governed will, and he could only kneel at the bedside and stare at the wall.

Marjory raised her voice in a laugh. "Did I betray myself? Did I become the maiden all forlorn? Did I giggle to show people that I did not care? No—I did not—I did not. And it was a long time, daddy! Oh, such a long time! I thought we would never get here. I thought I would never get where I could be alone like this, where I could—cry—if I wanted to. I am not much of a crier, am I, daddy? But this time—this time——"

She suddenly drew herself over near to her father and looked at him. "Oh, daddy, I want to tell you one thing. Just one simple little thing." She waited then, and while she waited her father's head went lower and lower. "Of course, you know—I told you once. I love him! I love him! Yes, probably he is a rascal, but, do you know, I don't think I would mind if he was a—an assassin. This morning I sent him away, but, daddy, he didn't want to go at all. I know he didn't. This Nora Black is nothing to him. I know she is not. I am sure of it. Yes—I am sure of it. . . . I never expected to talk this way to any living creature, but—you are so good, daddy. . . . Dear old daddy——"

She ceased, for she saw that her father was praying. The sight brought to her a new outburst of sobbing, for her sorrow now had dignity and solemnity from the bowed white head of her old father, and she felt that her heart was dying amid the pomp of the church. It was the last rites being performed at the death-bed. Into her ears came some imagining of the low melancholy chant of monks in a gloom.

Finally her father arose. He kissed her on the brow. "Try to sleep, dear," he said. He turned out the gas and left the room. His thought was full of chastened emotion.

But if his thought was full of chastened emotion, it received some degree of shock when he arrived in the presence of Mrs. Wainwright. "Well, what is all this about?" she demanded irascibly. "Do you mean to say that Marjory is breaking her heart over that man Coleman? It is all your fault——" She was apparently still ruffled over her exclusion.

When the professor interrupted her he did not speak with his accustomed spirit, but from something novel in his manner she recognized a danger signal.

"Please do not burst out at it in that way."

"Then, it is true?" she asked. Her voice was a mere awed whisper.

"It is true," answered the professor.

"Well," she said after reflection, "I knew it. I always knew it. If you hadn't been so blind! You turned like a weather-cock in your opinions of Coleman. You never *could* keep your opinion about him for more than an hour. Nobody could imagine what you might think next. And now you see the result of it! I warned you! I told you what this Coleman was, and if Marjory is suffering now you have only yourself to blame for it. I warned you."

"If it is my fault," said the professor drearily, "I hope God may forgive me, for here is a great wrong to my daughter."

"Well, if you had done as I told you——" she began.

Here the professor revolted. "Oh, now, do not begin on that," he snarled peevishly. "Do not begin on that."

"Anyhow," said Mrs. Wainwright, "it is time that we should be going down to dinner. Is Marjory coming?"

"No, she is not," answered the professor, "and I do not know as I shall go myself."

"But you must go. Think how it would look! All the students down there dining without us and cutting up capers! You must come."

"Yes," he said dubiously, "but who will look after Marjory?"

"She wants to be left alone," announced Mrs. Wainwright as if she was the particular herald of this news. "She wants to be left alone."

"Well, I suppose we may as well go down."

Before they went the professor tip-toed into his daughter's room. In the darkness he could see her waxen face on the pillow and her two eyes gazing fixedly at the ceiling. He did not speak, but immediately withdrew, closing the door noiselessly behind him.

I F the professor and Mrs. Wainwright had descended sooner to a lower floor of the hotel, they would have found reigning there a form of anarchy. The students were in a smoking-room which was also an entrance hall to the diningroom, and because there was in the middle of the apartment a fountain containing gold fish, they had been moved to license and sin. They had all been tubbed and polished and brushed and dressed until they were exuberantly beyond themselves. The proprietor of the hotel brought in his dignity and showed it to them, but they minded it no more than if he had been only a common man. He drew himself to his height and looked gravely at them and they jovially said: "Hello, Whiskers." American college students are notorious in their country for the inclination to scoff at robed and crowned authority, and, far from being awed by the dignity of the hotel-keeper, they were delighted with it. It was something with which to sport. With immeasurable impudence, they copied his attitude, and, standing before him, made long comic speeches, always alluding with blinding vividness to his beard. His exit disappointed them. He had not remained long under fire. They felt that they could have interested themselves with him an entire evening. "Come back, Whiskers! Oh, come back!" Out in the main hall he made a gesture of despair to some of his gaping minions and then fled to seclusion.

A formidable majority then decided that Coke was a gold fish, and that therefore his proper place was in the fountain. They carried him to it while he struggled madly. This quiet room with its crimson rugs and gilded mirrors seemed suddenly to have become an important apartment in hell. There being as yet no traffic in the dining-room, the waiters were all at liberty to come to the open doors, where they stood as men turned to stone. To them, it was no less than incendiarism.

Coke, standing with one foot on the floor and the other on the bottom of the shallow fountain, blasphemed his comrades in a low tone, but with intention. He was certainly desirous of lifting his foot out of the water, but it seemed that all movement to that end would have to wait until he had successfully expressed his opinions. In the meantime, there was heard slow footsteps and the rustle of skirts and then some people entered the smoking-room on their way to dine. Coke took his foot hastily out of the fountain.

The faces of the men of the arriving party went blank, and they turned their cold and pebbly eyes straight to the front, while the ladies, after little expressions of alarm, looked as if they wanted to run. In fact, the whole crowd rather bolted from this extraordinary scene.

"There, now," said Coke bitterly to his companions. "You see? We looked like little schoolboys——"

"Oh, never mind, old man," said Peter Tounley. "We'll forgive you, although you did embarrass us. But, above everything, don't drip. Whatever you do, don't drip."

The students took this question of dripping and played upon it until they would have made quite insane anybody but another student. They worked it into all manner of forms, and hacked and naggled at Coke until he was driven to his room to seek other apparel. "Be sure and change both legs," they told him. "Remember, you can't change one leg without changing both legs."

After Coke's departure, the United States minister entered the room, and instantly they were subdued. It was not his lofty station that affected them. There are probably few stations that would have at all affected them. They became subdued because they unfeignedly liked the United States minister. They were suddenly a group of well-bred, correctly attired young men who had not put Coke's foot in the fountain. Nor had they desecrated the majesty of the hotel-keeper.

"Well, I am delighted," said the minister, laughing as he shook hands with them all. "I was not sure I would ever see you again. You are not to be trusted, good boys as you are; I'll be glad to see you once and forever over the boundary of my jurisdiction. Leave Greece, you vagabonds. However, I am truly delighted to see you all safe."

"Thank you, sir," they said.

"How in the world did you get out of it? You must be remarkable chaps. I thought you were in a hopeless position. I wired and cabled everywhere I could, but I could find out nothing."

"A correspondent," said Peter Tounley. "I don't know if you have met him. His name is Coleman. He found us."

"Coleman?" asked the minister quickly.

"Yes, sir. He found us and brought us out safely."

"Well, glory be to Coleman," exclaimed the minister after a long sigh of surprise. "Glory be to Coleman! I never thought he could do it."

The students were alert immediately. "Why, did you know about it, sir? Did he tell you he was coming after us?"

"Of course. He came to me here at Athens and asked where you were. I told you were in a peck of trouble. He acted quietly and somewhat queerly, and said that he would try to look you up. He said you were friends of his. I warned him against trying it. Yes, I said it was impossible. I had no idea that he would really carry the thing out. But didn't he tell you anything about this himself?"

"No, sir," answered Peter Tounley. "He never said much about it. I think he usually contended that it was mainly an accident."

"It was no accident," said the minister sharply. "When a man starts out to do a thing and does it, you can't say it is an accident."

"I didn't say so, sir," said Peter Tounley diffidently.

"Quite true, quite true! You didn't, but—this Coleman must be a *man*!"

"We think so, sir," said he who was called Billie. "He certainly brought us through in style."

"But how did he manage it?" cried the minister, keenly interested. "How did he do it?"

"It is hard to say, sir. But he did it. He met us in the dead of night out near Nikopolis——"

"Near Nikopolis?"

"Yes, sir. And he hid us in a forest while a fight was going on, and then in the morning he brought us inside the Greek lines. Oh, there is a lot to tell——"

Whereupon they told it, or as much as they could of it. In the end, the minister said: "Well, where is the professor and Mrs. Wainwright? I want you all to dine with me tonight. I am dining in the public room, but you won't mind that after Epirus."

"They should be down now, sir," answered a student.

People were now coming rapidly to dinner and presently the professor and Mrs. Wainwright appeared. The old man looked haggard and white. He accepted the minister's warm greeting with a strained pathetic smile. "Thank you. We are glad to return safely."

Once at dinner the minister launched immediately into the subject of Coleman. "He must be altogether a most remarkable man. When he told me, very quietly, that he was going to try to rescue you, I frankly warned him against any such attempt. I thought he would merely add one more to a party of suffering people. But the boys tell me that he did actually rescue you."

"Yes, he did," said the professor. "It was a very gallant performance and we are very grateful."

"Of course," spoke Mrs. Wainwright, "we *might* have rescued ourselves. We were on the right road and all we had to do was to keep going on."

"Yes, but I understand—" said the minister. "I understand he took you into a wood to protect you from that fight and generally protected you from all kinds of trouble. It seems wonderful to me not so much because it was done as because it was done by the man who, some time ago, calmly announced to me that he was going to do it. Extraordinary."

"Oh, of course," said Mrs. Wainwright. "Oh, of course."

"And where is he now?" asked the minister suddenly. "Has he now left you to the mercies of civilization?"

There was a moment's curious stillness and then Mrs. Wainwright used that high voice which—the students believed—could only come to her when she was about to say something peculiarly destructive to the sensibilities. "Oh, of course, Mr. Coleman rendered us a great service but in his private character he is not a man whom we exactly care to associate with."

"Indeed!" said the minister staring. Then he hastily addressed the students. "Well, isn't this a comic war? Did you ever imagine war could be like this?" The professor remained looking at his wife with an air of stupefaction as if she had opened up to him visions of imbecility of which he had not even dreamed. The students loyally began to chatter at the minister. "Yes, sir, it is a queer war. After all their bragging, it is funny to hear that they are running away with such agility. We thought of course of the old Greek wars."

Later, the minister asked them all to his rooms for coffee and cigarettes but the professor and Mrs. Wainwright apologetically retired to their own quarters. The minister and the students made clouds of smoke through which sang their eloquent descriptions of late adventures.

The minister had spent days of listening to questions from the State Department at Washington as to the whereabouts of the Wainwright party. "I suppose you know that you are very prominent people in the United States just now? Your pictures must have been in all the papers and there must have been columns printed about you. My life here was made almost insupportable by your friends who consist, I should think, of about half the population of the country. Of course they laid regular siege to the Department. I am angry at Coleman for only one thing. When he cabled the news of your rescue to his newspaper from Arta, he should have also wired me, if only to relieve my failing mind. My first news of your escape was from Washington—think of that."

"Coleman had us all on his hands at Arta," said Peter Tounley. "He was a fairly busy man."

"I suppose so," said the minister. "By the way," he asked bluntly, "what is wrong with him? What did Mrs. Wainwright mean?"

They were silent for a time but it seemed plain to him that it was not evidence that his question had demoralized them. They seemed to be deliberating upon the form of answer. Ultimately, Peter Tounley coughed behind his hand. "You see, sir," he began, "there is—well, there is a woman in the case. Not that anybody would care to speak of it excepting to you. But that is what is the cause of things and then, you see, Mrs. Wainwright is—well——" He hesitated a moment and then completed his sentence in the ingenuous profanity of his age and condition.—"She is rather an extraordinary old bird."

"But who is the woman?"

"Why, it is Nora Black, the actress."

"Oh," cried the minister enlightened. "Her? Why, I saw her here. She was very beautiful but she seemed harmless enough. She was somewhat—er— confident perhaps but she did not alarm me. She called upon me and I confess I—why, she seemed charming."

"She's sweet on little Rufus. That's the point," said an oracular voice.

"Oh," cried the host suddenly, "I remember. She asked me where he was. She said she had heard he was in Greece and I told her he had gone knight-erranting off after you people. I remember now. I suppose she posted after him up to Arta, eh?"

"That's it. And so she asked you where he was?"

"Yes."

"Why, that old flamingo——Mrs. Wainwright insists that it was a rendezvous."

Everyone exchanged glances and laughed a little.

"And did you see any actual fighting?" asked the minister.

"No. We only heard it——"

Afterward as they were trooping up to their rooms, Peter Tounley spoke musingly. "Well, it looks to me now as if Old Mother Wainwright was just a bad-minded old hen."

"Oh, I don't know. How is one going to tell what the truth is?"

"At any rate, we are sure now that Coleman had nothing to do with Nora's *debut* in Epirus."

They had talked much of Coleman but in their tones there always had been a note of indifference or carelessness. This matter which to some people was as vital and fundamental as existence remained to others who knew of it only a harmless detail of life with no terrible powers and its significance had faded greatly when had ended the close associations of the late adventure.

After dinner, the professor had gone directly to his daughter's room. Apparently she had not moved. He knelt by the bedside again and took one of her hands. She was not weeping. She looked at him and smiled through the darkness. "Daddy, I would like to die," she said. "I think—yes—I would like to die."

For a long time the old man was silent but he arose at last with a definite abruptness and said hoarsely: "Wait!"

Mrs. Wainwright was standing before her mirror with her elbows thrust out at angles above her head while her fingers moved in a disarrangement of her hair. In the glass, she saw a reflection of her husband coming from Marjory's room and his face was set with some kind of alarming purpose. She turned to watch him actually but he walked toward the door into the corridor and did not in any wise heed her. "Harrison!" she called. "Where are you going?"

He turned a troubled face upon her and, as if she had hailed him in his sleep, he vacantly said: "What?"

"Where *are* you going?" she demanded with increasing trepidation.

He dropped heavily into a chair. " 'Going?' " he repeated.

She was angry. "Yes! Going! Where are you going?"

"I am going——" he answered. "I am going to see Rufus Coleman."

Mrs. Wainwright gave voice to a muffled scream. "Not about Marjory?"

"Yes," he said. "About Marjory."

It was now Mrs. Wainwright's turn to look at her husband with an air of stupefaction as if he had opened up to her visions of imbecility of which she had not even dreamed. "About Marjory!" she gurgled. Then suddenly her wrath flamed out. "Well, upon my word, Harrison Wainwright, you are of all men in the world the most silly and stupid. You are absolutely beyond belief. Of all projects! And what do you think Marjory would have to say of it if she knew it? I suppose you think she would like it? Why, I tell you she would keep her right hand in the fire until it was burned off before she would allow you to do such a thing."

"She must never know it," responded the professor in dull misery.

"Then think of yourself! Think of the shame of it! The shame of it!"

The professor raised his eyes for an ironical glance at his wife. "Oh . . . I have thought of the shame of it!"

"And you'll accomplish nothing," cried Mrs. Wainwright. "You'll accomplish nothing. He'll only laugh at you!"

"If he laughs at me, he will laugh at nothing but a poor weak unworldly old man. It is my duty to go."

Mrs. Wainwright opened her mouth as if she was about to shriek. After a choking moment she said: "Your duty? Your duty to go and bend the knee to that man? Your duty?"

" 'It is my duty to go'," he repeated humbly, "if I can find even one chance for my daughter's happiness in a personal sacrifice. He can do no more than—he can do no more than make me a little sadder."

His wife evidently understood his humility as a tribute to her arguments and as a clear indication that she had fatally undermined his original intention. "Oh, he would have made you sadder," she quoth grimly. "No fear! Why, it was the most insane idea I ever heard of."

The professor arose wearily. "Well, I must be going to this work. It is a thing to have ended quickly." There was something almost biblical in his manner.

"Harrison!" burst out his wife in amazed lamentation. "You are not really going to do it? Not really!"

"I am going to do it," he answered.

"Well, there!" ejaculated Mrs. Wainwright to the heavens. She was, so to speak, prostrate. "Well, there!"

As the professor passed out of the door she cried beseechingly but futilely after him. "Harrison!" In a mechanical way she turned then back to the mirror and resumed the disarrangement of her hair. She addressed her image. "Well, of all stupid creatures under the sun, men are the very *worst!*" And her image said this to her even as she informed it and afterward they stared at each other in a profound and tragic reception and acceptance of this great truth.

Presently she began to consider the advisability of going to Marjory with the whole story. Really, Harrison must not be allowed to go on blundering until the whole world heard that Marjory was trying to break her heart over that common scamp of a Coleman. It seemed to be about time for her, Mrs. Wainwright, to come into the situation and mend matters.

CHAPTER XXVIII

WHEN the professor arrived before Coleman's door, he paused a moment and looked at it. Previously, he could not have imagined that a simple door would ever so affect him. Every line of it seemed to express cold superiority and disdain. It was only the door of a former student's, one of his old boys, whom, as the need arrived, he had whipped with his satire in the class-rooms at Washurst until the mental blood had come and all without a conception of his ultimately arriving before the door of this boy in the attitude of a—supplicant. He would not say it; Coleman probably would not say it; but—they would both know it. A single thought of it, made him feel like running away. He would never dare to knock on that door. It would be too monstrous. And even as he decided that he was afraid to knock, he knocked.

Coleman's voice said: "Come in." The professor opened the door. The correspondent, without a coat, was seated at a paper-littered table. Near his elbow, upon another table, was a tray from which he had evidently dined and also a brandy bottle with several recumbent bottles of soda. Although he had so lately arrived at the hotel he had contrived to diffuse his traps over the room in an organized disarray which represented a long and careless occupation if it did not represent the scene of a scuffle. His pipe was in his mouth.

After a first murmur of surprise, he arose and reached in some haste for his coat. "Come in, professor, come in," he cried, wriggling deeper into his jacket as he held out his hand. He had laid aside his pipe and had also been very successful in flinging a newspaper so that it hid the brandy and soda. This act was a feat of deference to the professor's well-known principles.

"Won't you sit down, sir?" said Coleman cordially. His quick glance of surprise had been immediately suppressed and his manner was now as if the professor's call was a common matter.

"Thank you, Mr. Coleman, I—yes, I will sit down," replied the old man. His hand shook as he laid it on the back of the chair and steadied himself down into it. "Thank you!"

Coleman looked at him with a great deal of expectation.

"Mr. Coleman!"

"Yes, sir?"

"I——"

He halted and passed his hand over his face. His eyes did not seem to rest upon Coleman but they occupied themselves in furtive and frightened glances over the room. Coleman could make neither head nor tail of the affair. He would not have believed any man's statement that the professor could act in such an extraordinary fashion. "Yes, sir?" he said again suggestively. The simple strategy resulted in a silence that was acutely awkward. Coleman, despite his bewilderment, hastened into a preserving gossip. "I've had a great many cables waiting for me for heaven knows how long and others have been arriving in flocks tonight. You have no idea of the row in America, professor. Why everybody must have gone wild over the lost sheep. My paper has cabled some things that are evidently for you. For instance here is one that says a new puzzle-game called 'Find the Wainwright Party' has had a big success. Think of that, would you." Coleman grinned at the professor. "'Find the Wainwright Party,' a new puzzle-game."

The professor had seemed grateful for Coleman's tangent off into matters of a light vein. "Yes?" he said, almost eagerly. "Are they selling a game really called that?"

"Yes, really," replied Coleman. "And of course you know that —er—well, all the Sunday papers would of course have big illustrated articles—full pages—with your photographs and general private histories pertaining mostly to things which are none of their business?"

"Yes, I suppose they would do that," admitted the professor. "But I dare say it may not be as bad as you suggest."

"Very likely not," said Coleman. "I put it to you forcibly so that in the future the blow will not be too cruel. They are often a weird lot."

"Perhaps they can't find anything very bad about us."

"Oh, no. And besides the whole episode will probably be forgotten by the time you return to the United States."

They talked on in this way, slowly, strainedly, until they each found that the situation would soon become insupportable. The professor had come for a distinct purpose and Coleman knew it; they could not sit there lying at each other forever. Yet when he saw the pain deepening in the professor's eyes, the correspondent again ordered up his trivialities. "Funny thing. My paper has been congratulating me, you know, sir, in a whole-sale fashion and I think—I feel sure—that they have been exploiting my name all over the country as the Heroic Rescuer. There is no sense in trying to stop them because they don't *care* whether it is true or not true. All they want is the privilege of howling out that their correspondent rescued you and they would take that privilege without in any ways worrying if I refused my consent. You see, sir? I wouldn't like you to feel that I was such a strident idiot as I doubtless am appearing now before the public."

"No," said the professor absently. It was plain that he had been a very slack listener. "I—Mr. Coleman——" he began.

"Yes, sir?" answered Coleman promptly and gently.

It was obviously only a recognition of the futility of further dallying that was driving the old man onward. He knew of course that, if he was resolved to take this step, a longer delay would simply make it harder for him. The correspondent, leaning forward, was watching him almost breathlessly.

"Mr. Coleman, I understand—or, at least, I am led to believe —that you—at one time, proposed marriage to my daughter?"

The faltering words did not sound as if either man had aught to do with them. They were an expression by the tragic muse herself. Coleman's jaw fell and he looked glassily at the professor. He said: "Yes!" But already his blood was leaping as his mind flashed everywhere in speculation.

"I refused my consent to that marriage," said the old man more easily. "I do not know if the matter has remained important to you but at any rate I—I retract my refusal."

Suddenly the blank expression left Coleman's face and he smiled with sudden intelligence as if information of what the professor had been saying had just reached him. In this smile there was a sudden betrayal, too, of something keen and bitter which had lain hidden in the man's mind. He arose and made a step toward the professor and held out his hand. "Sir, I thank you from the bottom of my heart!" And they both seemed to note with surprise that Coleman's voice had broken.

The professor had arisen to receive Coleman's hand. His nerve was now of iron and he was very formal. "I judge from your tone that I have not made a mistake—something which I feared."

Coleman did not seem to mind the professor's formality. "Don't fear anything, sir, don't fear anything. Won't you sit down again? Will you have a cigar. . . . No, I couldn't tell you how glad I am. How glad I am. I feel like a fool. . . . It——"

But the professor fixed him with an Arctic eye and bluntly said: "You love her?"

The question steadied Coleman at once. He looked undauntedly straight into the professor's face. He simply said: "I love her!"

"You love her?" repeated the professor.

"I love her," repeated Coleman.

After some seconds of pregnant silence, the professor arose. "Well, if she cares to give her life to you, I will allow it but I must say that I do not consider you nearly good enough. Good-night." He smiled faintly as he held out his hand.

"Good-night, sir," said Coleman. "And I can't tell you how——"

Mrs. Wainwright, in her room, was languishing in a chair and applying to her brow a handkerchief wet with cologne water. She kept her feverish glance upon the door. Remembering well the manner of her husband when he went out she could hardly identify him when he came in. Serenity, composure, even self-satisfaction, was written upon him. He paid no attention to her but going to a chair sat down with a groan of contentment.

"Well?" cried Mrs. Wainwright, starting up. "Well?"

"Well—what?" he asked.

She waved her hand impatiently. "Harrison, don't be absurd. You know perfectly well what I mean. It is a pity you couldn't think of the anxiety I have been in." She was going to weep.

"Oh, I'll tell you after a while," he said stretching out his legs with the complacency of a rich merchant after a successful day.

"No! Tell me now," she implored him. "Can't you see I've worried myself nearly to death?" She was not going to weep; she was going to wax angry.

"Well, to tell the truth," said the professor with considerable pomposity, "I've arranged it. Didn't think I could do it at first but it turned out——"

" 'Arranged it'," wailed Mrs. Wainwright. "Arranged what?"

It seemed to strike the professor suddenly that he was not such a flaming example for diplomatists as he might have imagined. "Arranged," he stammered. "Arranged——"

"Arranged what?"

"Why, I fixed—I fixed it up."

"Fixed what up?"

"It—it——" began the professor. Then he swelled with indignation. "Why, can't you understand anything at all? I—I fixed it."

"Fixed what?"

"Fixed it. Fixed it with Coleman."

"Fixed what with Coleman?"

The professor's wrath now took control of him. "Thunder and lightnin'! You seem to jump at the conclusion that I've made some horrible mistake. For goodness' sake, give me credit for a particle of sense."

"What did you do?" she asked in a sepulchral voice.

"Well," said the professor in a flaming defiance, "I'll tell you what I did. I went to Coleman and told him that once—as he of course knew—I had refused his marriage with my daughter but that now——"

"Grrr," said Mrs. Wainwright.

"But that now—" continued the professor, "I retracted that refusal."

"Mercy on us!" cried Mrs. Wainwright throwing herself back in the chair. "Mercy on us! What fools men are!"

"Now, wait a minute——"

But Mrs. Wainwright began to croon: "Oh, if Marjory should hear of this! Oh, if she should hear of it! Just let her hear——"

"But she must not," cried the professor tigerishly. "Just you *dare!*" And the woman saw before her a man whose eyes were lit with a flame which almost expressed a temporary hatred.

*　　　*　　　*　　　*　　　*

The professor had left Coleman so abruptly that the correspondent found himself murmuring half-coherent gratitude to the closed door of his room. Amazement soon began to be mastered by exultation. He flung himself upon the brandy and soda and negotiated a strong glass. Pacing the room with nervous steps, he caught a vision of himself in a tall mirror. He halted before it. "Well, well," he said. "Rufus, you're a grand man. There is not your equal anywhere. You are a great bold strong player fit to sit down to a game with the best."

A moment later it struck him that he had appropriated too much. If the professor had paid him a visit and made a wonderful announcement, he, Coleman, had not been the engine of it. And then he enunciated clearly something in his mind which even in a vague form had been responsible for much of his early elation. Marjory herself had compassed this thing. With shame he rejected a first wild and preposterous idea that she had sent her father to him. He reflected that any man who for an instant could conceive such a thing was a natural-born idiot. With an equal feeling, he rejected also an idea that she could have known anything of her father's visit. If she had known of his purpose, there would have been no visit.

What then was the cause? Coleman soon decided that the professor had witnessed some demonstration of Marjory's emotion which had been sufficiently severe in its character to force him to the extraordinary visit. But then this also was wild and preposterous. That coldly beautiful goddess would not have given a demonstration of emotion over Rufus Coleman sufficiently alarming to have forced her father on such an errand. That was impossible. No, he was wrong; Marjory even indirectly could not be connected with the visit. As he arrived at this decision, the enthusiasm passed out of him and he wore a doleful monkish face.

Well, what, then, was the main cause? After eliminating Marjory from the discussion waging in his mind, he found it hard to hit upon anything rational. The only remaining theory was to the effect that the professor, having a very high sense of the correspondent's help in the escape of the Wainwright party, had decided that the only way to express his gratitude was to revoke a certain decision which he now could see had been unfair. The retort to this theory seemed to be that if the professor had had such a fine conception of the services rendered by Coleman, he had had ample time to display his appreciation on the road to Arta and on the road down from Arta. There was no necessity for his waiting until their arrival in Athens. It was impossible to concede that the professor's emotion could be a new one; if he had it now, he must have had it in far stronger measure directly after he had been hauled out of danger.

So, it may be seen that after Coleman had eliminated Marjory from the discussion that was waging in his mind, he had practically succeeded in eliminating the professor as well. This, he thought dolefully, was eliminating with a vengeance. If he dissolved all the factors he could hardly proceed.

The mind of a lover moves in a circle or at least on a more circular course than other minds some of which at times seem to move almost in a straight line. Presently, Coleman was at the point where he had started and he did not pause until he reached that theory which asserted that the professor had been inspired to his visit by some sight or knowledge of Marjory in distress. Of course Coleman was wistfully desirous of proving to himself the truth of this theory.

The palpable agitation of the professor during the interview seemed to support it. If he had come on a mere journey of conscience, he would have hardly appeared as a white and trembling old man. But then, said Coleman, he himself probably exaggerated this idea of the professor's appearance. It might have been that he was only sour and distressed over the performance of a very disagreeable duty.

The correspondent paced his room and smoked. Sometimes he halted at the little table where was the brandy and soda. He thought so hard that sometimes it seemed that Marjory had been to him to propose marriage and at other times it seemed that there had been no visit from any one at all.

A desire to talk to somebody was upon him. He strolled down stairs and into the smoking and reading rooms, hoping to see somebody he knew even if it were Coke. But the only occupants were two strangers furiously debating the war. Passing the minister's room, Coleman saw that there was a light within and he could not forbear knocking. He was bidden to enter and opened the door upon the minister carefully reading his *Spectator* fresh from London.

He looked up and seemed very glad. "How are you!" he cried. "I was tremendously anxious to see you, do you know! I looked for you to dine with me tonight but you were not down?"

"No; I had a great deal of work."

"Over the Wainwright affair? By the way, I want you to accept my personal thanks for that work. In a week more I would have gone demented and spent the rest of my life in some kind of a cage, shaking the bars and howling out State Department messages about the Wainwrights. You see, in my territory there are no missionaries to get into trouble and I was living a life of undisturbed and innocent calm, ridiculing the sentiments of men from Smyrna and other interesting towns who maintained that the diplomatic service was exciting. However when the Wainwright party got lost, my life at once became active. I was all but helpless, too, which was the worst of it. I suppose Terry at Constantinople must have got grandly stirred up, also. Pity he can't see you to thank you for saving him from probably going mad. By the way," he added while looking keenly at Coleman, "the Wainwrights don't seem to be smothering you with gratitude?"

"Oh, as much as I deserve—sometimes more," answered Coleman. "My exploit was more or less of a fake, you know. I was between the lines by accident or through the efforts of that blockhead of a dragoman. I didn't intend it. And then in the night when we were waiting in the road because of a fight they almost bunked into us. That's all."

"They tell it better," said the minister severely. "Especially the youngsters."

"Those kids got into a high old fight at a town up there beyond Agrinion. Tell you about that, did they? I thought not. Clever kids. You have noted that there are signs of a few bruises and scratches?"

"Yes but I didn't ask——"

"Well, they are from the fight. It seems the people took us for Germans and there was an awful palaver which ended in a proper and handsome shin-dig. It raised the town, I tell you."

The minister sighed in mock despair. "Take these people home, will you? Or at any rate conduct them out of the field of my responsibility. Now, they would like Italy immensely, I am sure."

Coleman laughed and they smoked for a time. "That's a charming girl—Miss Wainwright," said the minister musingly. "And what a beauty! It does my exiled eyes good to see her. I suppose all those youngsters are madly in love with her? I don't see how they could help it."

"Yes," said Coleman glumly. "More than half of 'em."

The minister seemed struck with a sudden thought. "You ought to try to win that splendid prize yourself. The rescuer! Perseus! What more fitting?"

Coleman answered calmly: "Well . . . I think I'll take your advice."

CHAPTER XXIX

THE next morning, Coleman awoke with a sign of a resolute decision on his face as if it had been a developement of his sleep. He would see Marjory as soon as possible, see her despite any barbed-wire entanglements which might be placed in his way by her mother whom he regarded as his strenuous enemy. And he would ask Marjory's hand in the presence of all Athens if it became necessary.

He sat a long time at his breakfast in order to see the Wainwrights enter the dining-room and as he was about to surrender to the will of time, they came in, the professor placid and self-satisfied, Mrs. Wainwright worried and injured and Marjory cool, beautiful, serene. If there had been any kind of a storm there was no trace of it on the white brow of the girl. Coleman studied her closely but furtively while his mind spun around his circle of speculation.

Finally he noted the waiter who was observing him with a pained air as if it was on the tip of his tongue to ask this guest if he was going to remain at breakfast forever. Coleman passed out to the reading-room where upon the table a multitude of great red guide books were crushing the fragile magazines of London and Paris. On the walls were various depressing maps with the name of a tourist agency luridly upon them and there were also some pictures of hotels with their rates—in francs—printed beneath. The room was cold, dark, empty, with the trail of the tourist upon it.

Coleman went to the picture of a hotel in Corfu and stared at it precisely as if he was interested. He was standing before it when he heard Marjory's voice just without the door. "All right! I'll wait." He did not move for the reason that the hunter moves not when the unsuspecting deer approaches his hiding place. She entered rather quickly and was well toward the centre of the room before she perceived Coleman. "Oh!" she said and stopped. Then she spoke the immortal sentence, a sentence which, curiously enough, is common to the drama, to the novel, and to life. "I thought no one was here." She looked as if she was going to retreat but it would have been hard to make such retreat graceful and probably for this reason she stood her ground.

Coleman immediately moved to a point between her and the door. "You are not going to run away from me, Marjory Wainwright," he cried angrily. "You at least owe it to me to tell me definitely that you don't love me—that you can't love me——"

She did not face him with all of her old spirit but she faced him and in her answer there was the old Marjory. "A most common question. Do you ask all your feminine acquaintances that?"

"I mean——" he said. "I mean that I love you and——"

"Yesterday—no. Today—yes. Tomorrow—who knows. Really, you ought to take some steps to know your own mind."

"Know *my* own mind," he retorted in a burst of indignation. "You mean *you* ought to take steps to know *your* own mind."

"*My* own mind! *You*——" Then she halted in acute confusion and all her face went pink. She had been far quicker than the man to define the scene. She lowered her head. "Let me pass, please——"

But Coleman sturdily blocked the way and even took one of her struggling hands. "Marjory——" And then his brain must have roared with a thousand quick sentences for they came tumbling out, one over the other. . . . Her resistance to the grip of his fingers grew somewhat feeble. Once she raised her eyes in a quick glance at him. . . . Then suddenly she wilted. She surrendered, she confessed without words. "Oh, Marjory, thank God, thank God——"

Peter Tounley made a dramatic entrance on the gallop. He stopped, petrified. "Whoo!" he cried. "My stars!" He turned and fled. But Coleman called after him in a low voice, intense with agitation. "Come back here, you young scoundrel! Come back here!"

Peter returned looking very sheepish. "I hadn't the slightest idea you——"

"Never mind that now. But look here, if you tell a single soul

—particularly those other young scoundrels—I'll break——"

"I won't, Coleman. Honest, I won't." He was far more embarrassed than Coleman and almost equally so with Marjory. He was like a horse tugging at a tether. "I won't, Coleman! Honest!"

"Well, all right, then." Peter escaped.

*   *   *   *   *

The professor and his wife were in their sitting-room writing letters. The cablegrams had all been answered but as the professor intended to prolong the journey homeward into a month of Paris and London, there remained the arduous duty of telling their friends at length exactly what had happened. There was considerable of the lore of olden Greece in the professor's descriptions of their escape and in those of Mrs. Wainwright there was much about the lack of hair-pins and soap.

Their heads were lowered over their writing when the door into the corridor opened and shut quickly and upon looking up they saw in the room a radiant girl, a new Marjory. She dropped to her knees by her father's chair and reached her arms to his neck. "Oh, daddy! I'm happy! I'm so happy!"

"Why—what——" began the professor stupidly.

"Oh, I am so happy, daddy!"

Of course he could not be long in making his conclusion. The one who could give such joy to Marjory was the one who, last night, gave her such grief. The professor was only a moment in understanding. He laid his hand tenderly upon her head. "Bless my soul," he murmured. "And so—and so—he——"

At the personal pronoun, Mrs. Wainwright lumbered frantically to her feet. "What?" she shouted. "Coleman?"

"Yes," answered Marjory. "Coleman." As she spoke the name her eyes were shot with soft yet tropic flashes of light.

Mrs. Wainwright dropped suddenly back into her chair. "Well —of—all—things!"

The professor was stroking his daughter's hair and although for a time after Mrs. Wainwright's outbreak there was little said, the old man and the girl seemed in gentle communion, she making him feel her happiness, he making her feel his appreciation. Providentially Mrs. Wainwright had been so stunned by the first blow that she was evidently rendered incapable of speech.

"And are you sure you will be happy with him?" asked her father gently.

"All my life long," she answered.

"I am glad! I am glad!" said the father but even as he spoke a great sadness came to blend with his joy. The hour when he was to give this beautiful and beloved life into the keeping of another had been heralded by the god of the sexes, the ruthless god that devotes itself to the tearing of children from the parental arms and casting them amid the mysteries of an irretrievable wed-lock. The thought filled him with solemnity.

But in the dewy eyes of the girl, there was no question. The world to her was a land of glowing promise.

"I am glad," repeated the professor.

The girl arose from her knees. "I must go away and—think all about it," she said smiling. When the door of her room closed upon her, the mother arose in majesty.

"Harrison Wainwright," she declaimed. "You are not going to allow this monstrous thing!"

The professor was aroused from a reverie by these words. "What monstrous thing?" he growled.

"Why, this between Coleman and Marjory."

"Yes," he answered boldly.

"Harrison! That man who——"

The professor crashed his hand down on the table. "Mary! I will not hear another word of it!"

"Well," said Mrs. Wainwright sullen and ominous, "time will tell! Time will tell!"

*   *   *   *   *

When Coleman had turned from the fleeing Peter Tounley again to Marjory, he found her making the preliminary movements of a flight. "What's the matter?" he demanded anxiously.

"Oh, it's too dreadful!"

"Nonsense," he retorted stoutly. "Only Peter Tounley! He don't count. What of that?"

"Oh, dear!" She pressed her palm to a burning cheek. She gave him a star-like beseeching glance. "Let me go now—please."

"Well," he answered, somewhat affronted. "If you like——"

At the door she turned to look at him and this glance expressed in its elusive way a score of things which she was not yet able to speak. It explained that she was loth to leave him, that she asked forgiveness for leaving him, that even for a short absence she wished to take his image in her eyes, that he must please not bully her, that there was something now in her heart which frightened her, that she loved him, that she was happy——

When she had gone, Coleman went to the rooms of the American minister. A Greek was there who talked wildly as he waved his cigarette. Coleman waited in well-concealed impatience for the evaporation of this man. Once the minister regarding the correspondent hurriedly interpolated a comment. "You look very cheerful?"

"Yes," answered Coleman, "I've been taking your advice."

"Oh, ho!" said the minister.

The Greek with the cigarette jawed endlessly. Coleman began to marvel at the enduring good-manners of the minister who continued to nod and nod in polite appreciation of the Greek's harangue which, Coleman firmly believed, had no point or interest whatever. But at last the man after an effusive farewell, went his way.

"Now," said the minister, wheeling in his chair. "Tell me all about it."

Coleman arose and thrusting his hands deep in his trousers pockets began to pace the room with long strides. He said nothing but kept his eyes on the floor.

"Can I have a drink?" he asked abruptly pausing.

"What would you like?" asked the minister benevolently as he touched the bell.

"A brandy and soda. I'd like it very much. You see," he said, as he resumed his walk, "I have no kind of right to burden you with my affairs but, to tell the truth, if I don't get this news off my mind and into somebody's ear, I'll die. It's this—I asked Marjory Wainwright to marry me,—and—she accepted, and—that's all."

"Well, I am very glad," cried the minister arising and giving his hand. "And as for burdening me with your affairs, no one has a better right, you know, since you released me from the persecution of Washington and the friends of the Wainwrights. May good luck follow you both forever. You, in my opinion, are a very very fortunate man. And, for her part—she has not done too badly."

Seeing that it was important that Coleman should have his spirits pacified in part, the minister continued: "Now, I have got to write an official letter so you just walk up and down here and use up this surplus steam. Else you'll explode."

But Coleman was not to be detained. Now that he had informed the minister, he must rush off somewhere, anywhere, and do—he knew not what.

"All right," said the minister laughing. "You have a wilder head than I thought. But look here," he called, as Coleman was making for the door. "Am I to keep this news a secret?"

Coleman with his hand on the knob turned impressively. He spoke with deliberation. "As far as I am concerned, I would be glad to see a man paint it in red letters, eight feet high, on the front of the king's palace."

The minister, left alone, wrote steadily and did not even look up when Peter Tounley and two others entered in response to his cry of permission. However, he presently found time to speak over his shoulder to them. "Hear the news?"

"No, sir," they answered.

"Well, be good boys, now, and read the papers and look at pictures until I finish this letter. Then I'll tell you."

They surveyed him keenly. They evidently judged that the news was worth hearing but, obediently, they said nothing. Ultimately the minister affixed a rapid signature to the letter and turning looked at the students with a smile.

"Haven't heard the news, eh?"

"No, sir."

"Well, Marjory Wainwright is engaged to marry Coleman."

The minister was amazed to see the effect of this announcement upon the three students. He had expected the crows and cackles of rather absurd merriment with which unbearded youth often greets such news. But there was no crow nor cackle. One young man blushed scarlet and looked guiltily at the floor. With a great effort he muttered: "She's too good for him." Another student had turned ghastly pale and was staring. It was Peter Tounley who relieved the minister's mind for upon that young man's face was a broad jack-o'-lantern grin and the minister saw, that, at any rate, he had not made a complete massacre.

Peter Tounley said triumphantly: "I knew it!"

The minister was anxious over the havoc he had wrought with the two other students but slowly the color abated in one face and grew in the other. To give them opportunity the minister talked busily to Peter Tounley. "And how did you know it, you young scamp?"

Peter was jubilant. "Oh, I knew it! I knew it! I am very clever."

The student who had blushed now addressed the minister in a slightly strained voice. "Are you positive that it is true, Mr. Gordner?"

"I had it on the best authority," replied the minister gravely.

The student who had turned pale said: "Oh, it's true, of course."

"Well," said crudely the one who had blushed, "she's a great sight too good for Coleman or anybody like him. That's all I've got to say."

"Oh, Coleman is a good fellow," said Peter Tounley reproachfully. "You've no right to say that—exactly. You don't know where you'd be now if it were not for Coleman."

The response was, first, an angry gesture. "Oh, don't keep everlastingly rubbing that in. For heaven's sake, let up. Supposing I don't know where I'd be now if it were not for Rufus Coleman? What of it? For the rest of my life, have I got to——"

The minister saw that this was the embittered speech of a really defeated youth so, to save scenes, he gently ejected the trio. "There, there, now! Run along home like good boys. I'll be busy until luncheon. And I dare say you won't find Coleman such a bad chap."

In the corridor, one of the students said offensively to Peter Tounley: "Say, how in hell did *you* find out all this so early?"

Peter's reply was amiable in tone. "You are a damned bleating little kid and you made a holy show of yourself before Mr. Gordner. There's where *you* stand. Didn't you see that he turned us out because he didn't know but what you were going to blubber or something. You are a sucking pig and if you want to know how I find out things go ask the Delphic Oracle, you blind ass."

"You better look out or you may get a punch in the eye!"

"You take one punch in the general direction of my eye, me son," said Peter cheerfully, "and I'll distribute your remains over this hotel in a way that will cause your friends years of trouble to collect you. Instead of anticipating an attack upon my eye, you had much better be engaged in improving your mind which is not at present a fit machine to cope with exciting situations. There's Coke! Hello, Coke, hear the news? Well, Marjory Wainwright and Rufus Coleman are engaged. Straight? Certainly! Go ask the minister."

Coke did not take Peter's word. "Is that so?" he asked the others.

"So the minister told us," they answered and then these two, who seemed so unhappy, watched Coke's face to see if they could not find surprised misery there. But Coke coolly said: "Well, then, I suppose it's true."

It soon became evident that the students did not care for each other's society. Peter Tounley was probably an exception but the others seemed to long for quiet corners. They were distrusting each other and, in a boyish way, they were even capable of malignant things. Their excuses for separation were badly made.

"I—I think I'll go for a walk."

"I'm going upstairs to read."

"Well, so long, old man." "So long." There was no heart to it.

Peter Tounley went to Coleman's door where he knocked with noisy hilarity. "Come in!" The correspondent apparently had just come from the street for his hat was on his head and a light topcoat was on his back. He was searching hurriedly through some papers. "Hello, you young devil. What are you doing here?"

Peter's entrance was a somewhat elaborate comedy which Coleman watched in icy silence. Peter, after a long and impudent pantomime, halted abruptly and fixing Coleman with his eye demanded: "Well?"

"Well—what?" said Coleman bristling a trifle.

"Is it true?"

"Is what true?"

"*Is it true?*" Peter was extremely solemn.

"Say, me bucko," said Coleman suddenly, "if you've come up here to twist the beard of the patriarch, don't you think you are running a chance?"

"All right. I'll be good," said Peter and he sat on the bed. "But —is it true?"

"Is what true?"

"What the whole hotel is saying."

"I haven't heard the hotel making any remarks lately. Been talking to the other buildings, I suppose."

"Well I want to tell you that everybody knows that you and Marjory have done gone and got yourselves engaged," said Peter bluntly.

"And well?" asked Coleman imperturbably.

"Oh, nothing," replied Peter waving his hand. "Only—I thought it might interest you."

Coleman was silent for some time. He fingered his papers. At last he burst out joyously. "And so they know it already, do they? Well—damn them—*let* them know it. But you didn't tell them yourself?"

"I!" quoth Peter wrathfully. "No! The minister told us."

Then Coleman was again silent for a time and Peter Tounley sat on the bed reflectively nursing his knee. "Funny thing," said the latter looking at the ceiling. "Funny thing, Marjory 'way over here in Greece and then you happening over here the way you did."

"It isn't funny at all."

"Why isn't it?"

"Because," said Coleman impressively, "that is why I came to Greece. It was all planned. See?"

"Whirroo," exclaimed Peter. "This here is magic."

"No magic at all." Coleman displayed some complacence. "No magic at all. Just pure plain—whatever you choose to call it."

"Holy smoke," said Peter, admiring the situation. "Why, this is plumb romance, Coleman. I'm blowed if it isn't."

Coleman was grinning with delight. He took a fresh cigar and his bright eyes looked at Peter through the smoke. "Seems like it, don't it? Yes. Regular romance. Have a drink, my boy, just to celebrate my good luck. And be patient if I talk a great deal of my—my—future. My head spins with it." He arose to pace the room flinging out his arms in a great gesture. "God! When I think yesterday was not like today I wonder how I stood it." There was a knock at the door and a waiter left a note in Coleman's hand.

"Dear Rufus:

We are going for a drive this afternoon at three and mother wishes you to come, if you care to. I too, wish it, if you care to.

Yours,

Marjory."

With a radiant face, Coleman gave the note a little crackling flourish in the air. "Oh, you don't know what life is, kid."

"S-steady the Blues," said Peter Tounley seriously. "You'll lose your head if you don't watch out."

"Not I," cried Coleman with irritation. "But a man must turn loose *some*times, mustn't he?"

*   *   *   *   *

When the four students had separated in the corridor, Coke had posted at once to Nora Black's sitting-room. His entrance was somewhat precipitate but he cooled down almost at once for he reflected that he was not bearing good news. He ended by perching in awkward fashion on the brink of his chair and fumbling his hat uneasily. Nora floated in to him in a cloud of a white dressing-gown. She gave him a plump hand. "Well, young man?" she said with a glowing smile. She took a chair and the stuff of her gown fell in curves over the arms of it.

Coke looked hot and bothered, as if he could have more than half wanted to retract his visit. "I—aw—we haven't seen much of you lately," he began, sparring. He had expected to tell his news at once.

"No," said Nora, languidly, "I have been resting after that horrible journey—that *horrible* journey. Dear, dear! Nothing will ever induce me to leave London, New York and Paris. I am at home there. But, here! Why, it is worse than living in Brooklyn. And that journey into the wilds! No, no; not for me!"

"I suppose we'll all be glad to get home," said Coke aimlessly.

At the moment a waiter entered the room and began to lay the table for luncheon. He kept open the door to the corridor and he had the luncheon at a point just outside the door. His excursions to the trays were flying ones so that, as far as Coke's purpose was concerned, the waiter was always in the room. Moreover Coke was obliged, naturally, to depart at once. He had bungled everything.

As he arose, he whispered hastily. "Does this waiter understand English?"

"Yes," answered Nora. "Why?"

"Because I have something to tell you—important."

"What is it?" whispered Nora eagerly.

He leaned toward her and replied: "Marjory Wainwright and
Coleman are engaged."

To his unfeigned astonishment, Nora Black burst into peals of
silvery laughter. "Oh, indeed? And so this is your tragic story,
poor innocent lambkin? And what did you expect? That I would
faint?"

"I thought—I don't know——" murmured Coke in confusion.

Nora became suddenly business-like. "But how do you know?
Are you sure? Who told you? Anyhow, stay to luncheon. Do—
like a good boy. Oh, you must."

Coke dropped again into his chair. He studied her in some
wonder. "I thought you'd be more surprised," he said ingenu-
ously.

"Oh, you did, did you? Well, you see I'm not. And now tell me
all about it."

"There's really nothing to tell but the plain fact. Some of the
boys dropped in at the minister's rooms a little while ago and he
told them of it. That's all."

"Well, how did _he_ know?"

"I am sure I can't tell you. Got it first hand, I suppose. He likes
Coleman and Coleman is always hanging up there."

"Oh, perhaps Coleman was lying," said Nora easily. Then suddenly her face brightened and she spoke with animation. "Oh,
I haven't told you how my little Greek officer has turned out.
Have I? No. Well, it is simply lovely. Do you know, he belongs
to one of the best families in Athens? He does. And they're _rich_
—rich as can be. My courier tells me that the marble palace
where they live is enough to blind you and that if titles hadn't
gone out of style—or something—here in Greece, my little officer
would be a _prince_! Think of that! The courier didn't know it until we got to Athens and the little officer—the _prince_—gave me
his card, of course. One of the oldest, noblest and richest families
in Greece. Think of that! There I thought he was only a bother-
some little officer who came in handy at times and there he turns

out to be a *prince*. I could hardly keep myself from rushing right off to find him and apologize to him for the way I treated him. It was *awful!* And—" added the fair Nora pensively, "if he *does* meet me in Paris, I'll make him wear that title down to a shred, you can bet. What's the good of having a title unless you make it work."

CHAPTER XXX

COKE did not stay to luncheon with Nora Black. He went away saying to himself: "Either that girl don't care a straw for Coleman or she has got a heart absolutely of flint or she is the greatest actress on earth or—there is some other reason."

At his departure, Nora turned and called into an adjoining room. "Maude!" The voice of her companion and friend answered her peevishly. "What? Don't bother me. I'm reading."

"Well, anyhow, luncheon is ready so you will have to stir your precious self," responded Nora. "You're lazy."

"I don't want any luncheon. Don't bother me. I've got a headache."

"Well, if you don't come out, you'll miss the news. That's all I've got to say."

There was a rustle in the adjoining room and immediately the companion appeared, seeming much annoyed but curious. "Well, what is it?"

"Rufus Coleman is engaged to be married to that Wainwright girl, after all."

"Well, I declare," ejaculated the little old lady. "Well, I declare." She meditated for a moment and then continued in a tone of satisfaction. "I told you that you couldn't stop that man Coleman if he had really made up his mind to——"

"You're a fool," said Nora pleasantly.

"Why?" said the old lady.

"Because you are. Don't talk to me about it. I want to think of Marco."

" 'Marco'," quoted the old lady startled.

"The prince. The prince. Can't you understand? I mean the prince."

" 'Marco'!" again quoted the old lady under her breath.

"Yes, 'Marco'," cried Nora belligerently. " 'Marco'. Do you object to the name? What's the matter with you anyhow?"

"Well," rejoined the other nodding her head wisely, "he may be a prince but I've always heard that these continental titles are no good in comparison to the English titles."

"Yes but who told you so, eh?" demanded Nora noisily. She herself answered the question. "The English!"

"Anyhow that little marquis who tagged after you in London is a much bigger man in every way, I'll bet, than this little prince of yours."

"But—good heavens—he didn't mean it. Why, he was only one of the regular rounders. But, Marco, he is *serious*! He *means* it. He'd go through fire and water for me and be glad of the chance."

"Well," proclaimed the old lady, "if you are not the strangest woman in the world, I'd like to know. Here I thought——"

"What did you think?" demanded Nora suspiciously.

"I thought that Coleman——"

"Bosh!" interrupted the graceful Nora. "I tell you what, Maude; you'd better try to think as little as possible. It will suit your style of beauty better. And above all, don't think of my affairs. I myself am taking pains not to think of them. It's easier."

*   *   *   *   *

Mrs. Wainwright, with no spirit of intention whatever, had set about re-adjusting her opinions. It is certain that she was unconscious of any evolution. If some one had said to her that she was surrendering to the inevitable, she would have been immediately on her guard and would have opposed forever all suggestions of a match between Marjory and Coleman. On the other hand if some one had said to her that her daughter was going to marry a human serpent and that there were people in Athens who would be glad to explain his treacherous character, she would have haughtily scorned the tale-bearing and would have gone with more haste into the professor's way of thinking. In fact she was in process of undermining herself and the work could have been retarded or advanced by any irresponsible gossipy tongue.

The professor, from the depths of his experience of her, arranged a course of conduct. "If I just leave her to herself she will come around all right but if I go 'striking while the iron is hot' or any of those things, I'll bungle it surely."

As they were making ready to go down to luncheon, Mrs. Wainwright made her speech which first indicated a changing mind. "Well, what will be, will be," she murmured with a prolonged sigh of resignation. "What will be, will be. Girls are very headstrong in these days and there is nothing much to be done with them. They go their own roads. It wasn't so in my girlhood. *We* were obliged to pay attention to our mothers' wishes."

"I did not notice that you paid much attention to your mother's wishes when you married me," remarked the professor. "In fact I thought——"

"That was another thing," retorted Mrs. Wainwright with severity. "You were a steady young man who had taken the highest honors all through your college course and my mother's sole objection was that we were too hasty. She thought we ought to wait until you had a penny to bless yourself with and I can see now where she was quite right."

"Well, you married me anyhow," said the professor victoriously.

Mrs. Wainwright allowed her husband's retort to pass over her thoughtful mood. "They say . . . they say Rufus Coleman makes as much as fifteen thousand dollars a year. That's more than three times your income. . . . I don't know. . . . It all depends on whether they try to save or not. His manner of life is no doubt very luxurious. I don't suppose he knows how to economize at all. That kind of a man usually doesn't. And then in the newspaper world, positions are so very precarious. Men may have valuable positions one minute and be penniless in the street the next minute. It isn't as if they had any real *income* and of course he has no real *ability*. If he was suddenly thrown out of his position, goodness knows what would become of him. Still . . . still . . . fifteen thousand dollars a year is a big income . . . while it lasts. I suppose he is very extravagant. That kind of a man usually is. And I wouldn't be surprised if he was heavily in debt; very heavily in debt. Still . . . if Marjory has set her heart there is nothing to be done, I suppose. It wouldn't have happened if you had been as wise as you thought you were. . . . I suppose he thinks I have been very rude to him. Well sometimes I wasn't nearly so rude as I felt like being. Feeling as I did, I could hardly be very amiable. . . . Of course this drive this afternoon was all your affair and Marjory's. But, of course, I shall be nice to him."

"And what of all this Nora Black business?" asked the professor with a display of valor but really with much trepidation.

"She is a hussy," responded Mrs. Wainwright with energy. "Her conversation in the carriage on the way down to Agrinion, sickened *me*."

"I really believe that her plan was simply to break everything off between Marjory and Coleman," said the professor, "and I don't believe she had any grounds for all that appearance of owning Coleman and the rest of it."

"Of course, she didn't," assented Mrs. Wainwright. "The vicious thing!"

"On the other hand," said the professor, "there might be *some* truth in it."

"I don't think so," said Mrs. Wainwright seriously. "I don't believe a word of it."

"You do not mean to say that you think Coleman a model man?" demanded the professor.

"Not at all! Not at all!" she hastily answered. "But . . . one doesn't look for model men these days."

"Who told you he made fifteen thousand a year?" asked the professor.

"It was Peter Tounley this morning. We were walking upstairs after breakfast and he remarked that if he could make fifteen thousand a year like Coleman, he'd—I've forgotten what—some fanciful thing."

"I doubt if it is true," muttered the old man wagging his head.

"Of course, it's true," said his wife emphatically. "Peter Tounley says everybody knows it."

"Well . . . anyhow . . . money is not everything."

"But it's a great deal, you know well enough. You know you are always speaking of poverty as an evil, as a grand resultant, a collaboration of many lesser evils. Well, then?"

"But," began the professor meekly, "when I say that I mean——"

"Well, money is money and poverty is poverty," interrupted his wife. "You don't have to be very learned to know that."

"I do not say that Coleman has not a very nice thing of it but

I must say it is hard to think of his getting any such sum as you mention."

"Isn't he known as a most brilliant journalist in New York?" she demanded harshly.

"Y-yes, as long as it lasts but then one never knows when he will be out in the street penniless. Of course he has no particular ability which would be marketable if he suddenly lost his present employment. Of course, it is not as if he was a really talented young man. He might not be able to make his way at all in any new direction."

"I don't know about that," said Mrs. Wainwright in reflective protestation. "I don't know about that. I think he would."

"I thought you said a moment ago——" The professor spoke with an air of puzzled hesitancy. "I thought you said a moment ago that he *wouldn't* succeed in anything but journalism."

Mrs. Wainwright swam over the situation with a fine tranquillity. "Well-l-l," she answered musingly, "if I *did* say that, I didn't mean it *exactly*."

"No, I suppose not," spoke the professor and despite the necessity for caution he could not keep out of his voice a faint note of annoyance.

"Of course," continued the wife, "Rufus Coleman is known everywhere as a brilliant man, a very brilliant man, and he even might do well in—in politics or something of that sort."

"I have a very poor opinion of that kind of a mind which does well in American politics," said the professor, speaking as a collegian, "but I suppose there may be something in it."

"Well, at any rate," decided Mrs. Wainwright. "At any rate——"

At that moment, Marjory attired for luncheon and the drive entered from her room and Mrs. Wainwright checked the expression of her important conclusion. Neither father nor mother had ever seen her so glowing with triumphant beauty, a beauty which would carry the mind of a spectator far above physical appreciation into that realm of poetry where creatures of light move and are beautiful because they cannot know pain or a burden. It carried tears to the old father's eyes. He took her hands. "Don't be *too* happy, my child, don't be *too* happy," he admonished her tremulously. "It makes me afraid—it makes me afraid."

CHAPTER XXXI

IT seems strange that the one who was the most hilarious over the engagement of Marjory and Coleman should be Coleman's dragoman who was indeed in a state bordering on transport. It is not known how he learned the glad tidings but it is certain that he learned them before luncheon. He told all the visible employees of the hotel and allowed them to know that the betrothal really had been his handiwork. He had arranged it. He did not make quite clear how he had performed this feat but at least he was perfectly frank in acknowledging it.

When some of the students came down to luncheon, they saw him but could not decide what ailed him. He was in the main corridor of the hotel, grinning from ear to ear, and when he perceived the students he made signs to intimate that they possessed in common a joyous secret. "What's the matter with that idiot?" asked Coke morosely. "Looks as if his wheels were going around too fast."

Peter Tounley walked close to him and scanned him imperturbably but with care. "What's up, Phidias?" The man made no articulate reply. He continued to grin and gesture. "Pain in oo tummy? Mother dead? Caught the cholera? Found out that you've swallowed a pair of hammered brass andirons in your beer? Say, who are you anyhow?" But he could not shake this invincible glee so he went away.

The dragoman's rapture reached its zenith when Coleman lent him to the professor and he was commissioned to bring a carriage for four people to the door at three o'clock. He himself was to sit on the box and tell the driver what was required of him. He dashed off, his hat in his hand, his hair flying, puffing, important beyond everything, and apparently babbling his mission to half the people he met on the street. In most countries he would have landed speedily in jail but among a people who exist on a basis of jibbering, his violent gabble aroused no suspicions as to his sanity. However, he stirred several livery-stables to their depths and set men running here and there wildly and for the most part futilely.

At fifteen minutes to three o'clock, a carriage with its horses on a gallop, tore around the corner and up to the front of the hotel where it halted with the pomp and excitement of a fire-engine. The dragoman jumped down from his seat beside the driver and scrambled hurriedly into the hotel in the gloom of which he met a serene stillness which was punctuated only by the leisurely tinkle of silver and glass in the dining-room. For a moment, the dragoman seemed really astounded out of speech. Then he plunged into the manager's room. Was it conceivable that Monsieur Coleman was still at luncheon? Yes; in fact, it was true. But the carriage was at the door! *The carriage was at the door!* The manager, undisturbed, asked for what hour Monsieur Coleman had been pleased to order a carriage. Three o'clock! Three o'clock? The manager pointed calmly at the clock. Very well. It was now only thirteen minutes of three o'clock. Monsieur Coleman doubtless would appear at three. Until that hour the manager would not disturb Monsieur Coleman. The dragoman clutched both his hands in his hair and cast a look of agony to the ceiling. Great God! Had he accomplished the herculean task of getting a carriage for four people to the door of the hotel in time for a drive at three o'clock, only to meet with this stoniness, this inhumanity? Ah, it was unendurable! He begged the manager; he implored him. But at every word, the manager seemed to grow more indifferent, more callous. He pointed with a wooden finger at the clock-face. In reality, it is thus that Greek meets Greek.

Professor Wainwright and Coleman strolled together out of the dining-room. The dragoman rushed ecstatically upon the correspondent. "Oh, Meester Coleman! The carge is ready!"

"Well, all right," said Coleman knocking ashes from his cigar. "Don't be in a hurry. I suppose we'll be ready presently." The man was in despair.

The departure of the Wainwrights and Coleman on this ordinary drive was of a somewhat dramatic and public nature. No one seemed to know how to prevent its being so. In the first place, the attendants thronged out en masse for a reason which was plain at the time only to Coleman's dragoman. And, rather in the background, lurked the interested students. The professor was surprised and nervous; Coleman was rigid and angry; Marjory was flushed and somewhat hurried; and Mrs. Wainwright was as proud as an old turkey-hen.

As the carriage rolled away, Peter Tounley turned to his companions and said: "Now that's *official*! That is the official announcement! Did you see Old Mother Wainwright? Oh, my eye, wasn't she puffed up! Say, what in hell do you suppose all these jay-hawking bell-boys poured out to the kerb for? Go back to your cages, my good people——"

As soon as the carriage wheeled into another street, its occupants exchanged easier smiles and they must have confessed in some subtle way of glances that now at last they were upon their own mission, a mission undefined but earnest to them all. Coleman had a glad feeling of being let into the family, of becoming one of them.

The professor looked sideways at him and smiled gently. "You know, I thought of driving you to some ruins but Marjory would not have it. She flatly objected to any more ruins. So I thought we would drive down to New Phalerum."

Coleman nodded and smiled as if he were immensely pleased but of course New Phalerum was to him no more nor less than Vladivostock or Khartum. Neither place nor distance had interest for him. They swept along a shaded avenue where the dust lay thick on the leaves; they passed cafes where crowds were angrily shouting over the news in the little papers; they passed a hospital before which wounded men, white with bandages, were taking the sun; they came soon to the arid valley flanked by gaunt naked mountains which would lead them to the sea. Sometimes to accentuate the dry nakedness of this valley, there would be a patch of grass upon which poppies burned crimson spots. The dust writhed out from under the wheels of the carriage; in the distance the sea appeared, a blue half-disc set between shoulders of barren land. It would be common to say that Coleman was oblivious to all about him but Marjory. On the contrary, the parched land, the isolated flame of poppies, the cool air from the sea, all were keenly known to him and they had developed an extraordinary power of blending sympathetically into his mood. Meanwhile the professor talked a great deal. And as a somewhat exhilarating detail, Coleman perceived that Mrs. Wainwright was beaming upon him.

At New Phalerum—a small collection of pale square villas—they left the carriage and strolled by the sea. The waves were snarling together like wolves amid the honey-comb rocks and from where the blue plane sprang level to the horizon, came a strong cold breeze, the kind of a breeze which moves an exulting man or a parson to take off his hat and let his locks flutter and tug back from his brow.

The professor and Mrs. Wainwright were left to themselves.

Marjory and Coleman did not speak for a time. It might have been that they did not quite know where to make a beginning. At last, Marjory asked: "What has become of your splendid horse?"

"Oh, I've told the dragoman to have him sold as soon as he arrives," said Coleman absently.

"Oh, I'm sorry . . . I liked that horse."

"Why?"

"Oh, because——"

"Well, he was a fine——" Then he too interrupted himself, for he saw plainly that they had not come to this place to talk about a horse. Thereat he made speech of matters which at least did not afford as many opportunities for coherency as would the horse. "Marjory, it can't be true. . . . Is it true, dearest? . . . I can hardly believe it. I—I——"

*   *   *   *   *

"Oh, I know I'm not nearly good enough for you."

"Good enough for *me*, dear?"

"They all told me so and they were right! Why even the American minister said it. Everybody thinks it."

"Why, aren't they wretches! To think of them saying such a thing! As if—as if *anybody* could be too——"

*   *   *   *   *

"Do you know——" She paused and looked at him with a certain timid challenge. "I don't know why I feel it but—sometimes I feel that I've been—I've been flung at your head."

He opened his mouth in astonishment. "Flung at my head!"

She held up her finger. "And if I thought you could ever believe it!"

"Is a girl flung at a man's head when her father carries her thousands of miles away and the man follows her all these miles and at last——"

Her eyes were shining. "And you really came to Greece—on purpose to—to——"

*　　　*　　　*　　　*　　　*

"Confess you knew it all the time! Confess!"

The answer was muffled. "Well, sometimes I thought you did and at other times I thought you—didn't."

*　　　*　　　*　　　*　　　*

In a secluded cove, in which the sea-maids once had played no doubt, Marjory and Coleman sat in silence. He was below her and if he looked at her he had to turn his glance obliquely upward. She was staring at the sea with woman's mystic gaze, a gaze which men at once reverence and fear since it seems to look into the deep simple heart of nature and men begin to feel that their petty wisdoms are futile to control these strange spirits, as wayward as nature and as pure as nature, wild as the play of waves, sometimes as unalterable as the mountain amid the winds; and to measure them, man must perforce use a mathematical formula.

*　　　*　　　*　　　*　　　*

He wished that she would lay her hand upon his hair. He would be happy then. If she would only, of her own will, touch his hair lightly with her fingers—— If she would do it with an unconscious air it would be even better. It would show him that she was thinking of him even when she did not know she was thinking of him.

Perhaps he dared lay his head softly against her knee. Did he dare?

*　　　*　　　*　　　*　　　*

As his head touched her knee, she did not move. She seemed to be still gazing at the sea. Presently idly caressing fingers played in his hair near the forehead. He looked up suddenly, lifting his arms. He breathed out a cry which was laden with a kind of diffident ferocity. "I haven't kissed you yet——"

THE TEXT: HISTORY AND ANALYSIS

THE TEXT: HISTORY AND ANALYSIS

THE THIRD VIOLET

No manuscript or typescript of *The Third Violet* has survived, and the only material that can be recognized as standing behind the novel is contained in two sketches in the late autumn of 1894. The first is the three-part "Stories Told by an Artist," published in the *New York Press* on October 28, 1894 (TALES, SKETCHES, AND REPORTS, *Works*, VIII [1973], 68–75). Chapters XIX and XX borrow extensively from these lighthearted anecdotes of impecunious young artists; in addition, the beginnings of Chapters XXI and XXV bear some relation to one of these parts, entitled "How Pennoyer Disposed of His Sunday Dinner," but the incidents are reversed and the characters changed. Finally, a passage near the start of Chapter XXVI (92.6–19) is much influenced by another sketch printed in the same issue of the *Press* on October 28, "In a Park Row Restaurant" (TALES, SKETCHES, AND REPORTS, pp. 328–331).[1]

The first direct reference comes in a letter that Crane wrote on or about December 27, 1895, to his editor Hitchcock at Appleton's:

Hartwood / Friday

Please acknowledge reciept.

Dear Mr. Hitchcock: Enclosed is "The Third Violet" in ms. There is only one. Typewriting is too new an art for the woods. If you think it well, have the thing type-writen—charged to my c/o—and send me the type written one to save the story. S.C.[2]

The Appleton typescript made from the manuscript became the printer's copy for the book. What was probably its carbon was

---

[1] In a special section of the apparatus following the Historical Collation appears a collation of the variants between Chapters XIX and XX and the novel in passages where the two texts are sufficiently parallel to make a record practicable. The texts in Chapters XXI and XXV are too divergent for meaningful collation. Immediately following is placed a section recording the variants between Chapter XXVI (Va. 92.6–19) and "In a Park Row Restaurant."

[2] *Stephen Crane: Letters*, ed. R. W. Stallman and L. Gilkes (New York University Press, 1960), p. 83.

the copy for the newspaper version syndicated by McClure, although the copyright notice in all newspapers is attributed to Crane.

A search of over forty newspapers has disclosed only the following six syndications:

N^1: *Philadelphia Inquirer,* October 25–November 13, 1896
N^2: *Pittsburg Leader,* October 25–November 15, 1896
N^3: *Portland Oregonian,* October 25–November 15, 1896
N^4: *Sunday Inter Ocean,* October 25–November 15, 1896
N^5: *New York World,* November 4–November 14, 1896
N^6: *San Francisco Chronicle,* October 5, 1896–January 24, 1897

How much, if at all, Crane revised the carbon of the Appleton typescript sent to the syndicate and distributed to subscribing newspapers in the form of proofs pulled from a common typesetting is not to be determined. What is clear, however, is that this newspaper text was in an earlier state than that in the ribbon typescript that was returned to him, revised, and at a later time given to the printer of the book for publication. According to the Library of Congress copyright record, the date was April 30, 1897.

Collation of the six known newspapers establishes beyond dispute the substantive readings of the underlying common proof from which each newspaper was set, and the readings of a number of the accidentals as well. However, although unanimity in an accidental form is ordinarily to be taken as faithfully reflecting the reading of the syndicate proof, evidence present in some anomalies suggests that a minority, or even a single newspaper, may on some very few occasions reflect more faithfully the proof than the styled majority. Some of Crane's eccentric or wrong spellings (repeated in the proof from the manuscript forms which had filtered through to the typescript) were corrected in most newspapers but occasionally reproduced in one or more. For instance, it is probable that the variant 'valueing' in N^5 at 4.34 represents such a case, and also 'harrie' in N^{1-3} (for *harry*) at 72.16 (cf. 27.22 where all prints [$-N^5$] read *harrie*). More certainly, one may adduce the reproduction in N^2 and in N^5 at 35.13 and in N^1 at 37.11 of Crane's almost invariable grammatical error of 'it's' for the possessive pronoun. Very likely the usual placement of quotation marks in N^5 before instead of after a dash in broken-off dialogue repeats Crane's manuscript custom copied in typescript and in proof, whereas the other newspapers correct it automatically save for a slip once in a while. The remains of a change of name from *Hollander* to *Hollanden* occasionally crop up in one or another newspaper although normalized by the rest. Significantly, 'Hollander' appears once in the book at 15.10. Insofar as can be judged from the evidence of the newspapers and one's estimate of the probable forms, the setting of the syndicate proof seems to have been relatively faithful to the typescript's accidentals. Moreover, although its substantives were subject to various small care-lessnesses, there seem to be few major errors. On the whole, then, to the extent that it can be reconstructed from the newspapers' evidence, the syndicate proof appears to be a relatively faithful witness to the carbon of the unrevised Appleton typescript that was its copy.

Hitchcock recognized that *The Third Violet* would come as a disappointment to its readers after *The Red Badge of Courage,* and he encouraged Crane to revise the book before publication. Crane's response has been misunderstood. On January 27, 1896, he wrote to Hitchcock:

I think it is as well to go ahead with The Third Violet. People may just as well discover now that the high dramatic key of The Red Badge cannot be sustained. You know what I mean. I dont think The Red Badge to be any great shakes but then the very theme of it gives it an intensity that a writer cant reach every day. The Third Violet is a quiet little story but then it is serious work and I should say let it go. If my health and my balance remains to me, I think I will be capable of doing work that will dwarf both books. [*Letters*, pp. 106–107]

Critics have been inclined to take this letter quite literally and—in the absence of collations of the two texts—to write as if Crane made no alterations in the book version from its syndicated newspaper form. The Historical Collation in the present edition shows very clearly that Crane thoroughly revised the typescript for the book while it was awaiting publication after the newspaper serialization had run its course. The interpretation of Crane's letter, then, must be modified. Possibly Crane changed his mind after writing it and so engaged himself to the revision that distinguishes the two texts. More likely, his meaning in the letter has been misconstrued. It may seem probable that Hitchcock was not at all concerned with urging a stylistic revision but instead that he hoped to secure from Crane a structural and narrative reworking, and perhaps one of tone, that would strengthen the novel. If Crane were referring to such a proposal, his letter is accurate in that he did nothing about the novel except to prune and vary its style. The only real difference in conception that can be detected was the minor but interesting change provided by his removal of much of the country dialect speech from Hawker's family, thus in part decreasing the social distance between the young lovers. This tinkering with the dialect was extended to a very slight formalization of a few colloquialisms in the speech of Hawker and of Hollanden.

The textual problem of *The Third Violet* has its complexities. It seems certain that neither the syndicate proof nor the book was set directly from holograph but instead that each radiates at equal distance from the Appleton typescript and its carbon made from Crane's manuscript at his request. As remarked, the substantive readings of the syndicate proof (although not all of its accidentals) can be recovered with complete accuracy. Insofar as these substantives, then, are at only one stage removed from the syndicate typescript, they are as authoritative in their transmission as the substantives of the book, set directly from the other copy of the typescript, albeit revised. Thus agreement between the syndicate proof and the book should automatically recover the exact readings of the typescript.[3] On the other hand, the typescript—the nearest document to the manuscript that can be reconstructed—was undoubtedly not the exact equivalent of the manuscript either in substantives or in accidentals; however, its recoverable features are the closest we shall ever come to ultimate authority, given the loss of the manuscript and its drafts.

When the recovered syndicate proof (N) and the book (A1) differ, three options exist: (1) N may be in error and A1 a correct transcript of the typescript; (2) A1 may be in error and N a correct transcript; or (3) N may be a correct reading from its typescript but the A1 variant may represent Crane's or an editor's revision made later in the Appleton copy of the typescript.[4] In his selection of readings from variation between the recovered syndicate proof and the book, the present editor has tried to take account of these possibilities and to choose the reading that seems best to fit the proper category as judged by the context and by Crane's usual style. In a small number of readings bibliographical conjecture as to the cause of the error may be applied, such as the hypothesis for memorial contamination in explaining the A1 error 'boat' for N 'moon' at 26.15. Occasionally a lack of unanimity among the newspapers will suggest independent sophistication of Crane's more ruggedly idiomatic phrases and lead to the view that A1 has joined one or more newspapers in its distrust of this edition's conjecturally established form of the typescript reading. For example, at 20.38–39 that the syndicate proof read 'Well, I shall tell it you' can be established with relative certainty because of the different means adopted by two newspapers to deal with this uncomfortable phrase as found in the other four: N^1 omits 'it' to read 'shall tell you' whereas N^4 adds 'to' to read 'shall tell it to you'. When A1, which in other places can be shown to normalize uncommon idiom, joins isolated N^4 in adding 'to', the problem resolves itself to the

---

[3] For the textual theory of authority and the process of its recovery in an eclectic text, see Bowers, "Multiple Authority: New Concepts of Copy-Text," *The Library*, 5th ser., XXVII (1972), 81–115; and "Remarks on Eclectic Texts," *Proof*, IV (1974), 13–58.

[4] The theoretical situation that N may be in error but A1 a revision of the original typescript reading from which N had departed is not worth considering as an active possibility since the case could never be demonstrated except in the case of a simple N misprint. Similarly, some of the A1 variants may have been created in proof; but, again, no means exist to distinguish authoritative proof changes from authoritative revision of the typescript—or unauthoritative proof-alterations from editorial marking of the typescript, or even from compositorial error or sophistication in the typesetting with or without error in N.

simple equation: Is it more likely that the N proof was in error and
A1 faithfully transmitted the typescript reading or that the N proof
was faithful and A1, whether editorially or compositorially, normalized the text? (This is to assume, of course, that in the revision of the
typescript for A1, Crane did not have second thoughts about an
idiom that he had employed in a natural manner.) Since 'tell it you'
appears to be an acceptable Crane colloquialism, the decision has
been made to retain it in the edited text as likely to represent the most
authoritative reading. A critical, or philological, basis is certainly significant in the reasoning, but the bibliographical evidence of the
N[1,4] variation was helpful in the final decision.

Other cruxes can be decided purely on critical grounds. For instance, the consistent A1 sophistication to 'bent' of the characteristic
'bended' (as at 44.26) found almost invariably in Crane's manuscripts and often present in one or more newspapers (whose compositors would scarcely invent it themselves) needs no particular
acumen to alter to the N reading as the authority. More speculative is
the adoption of N 'on' Second Avenue for the A1 Anglicism 'in'
Second Avenue (80.14, 81.4, 84.35), the latter an idiom that seems
to be alien to the United States but perhaps prompted by the birth or
training of a compositor who also produced in A1 wholly uncharacteristic spelling for Crane at this date ending in -our (see the Textual
Note to 80.14). On the other hand, the more neutral the variant, the
less evidence exists for making a critical judgment. Whether a character 'interrupted' (A1) or 'interposed' (N) (5.5), whether he 'observed' (A1) or 'blurted' (N) (13.17), or 'asked' (A1) or 'said' (N)
(14.29) is scarcely to be accounted as error and correction; instead,
such variants are to be credited to changes in the Appleton typescript,
whether by Crane or an editor, although some few may be compositorial "improvements." It would seem that most variants in this text
where positive grounds for suspicion of sophistication of N authority
do not exist must be included in the pervasive pattern of A1 alterations of original typescript readings on the whole reproduced faithfully by N. Since ordinarily these variants may be assigned to Crane's
latest intentions for his text,[5] they need to be respected by an editor
and incorporated in a critical eclectic edition.

The question of copy-text—it is generally agreed—is to be resolved
less on the authority of the substantives than on that of the accidentals. It is ordinarily simpler to insert revised substantive readings
from a later edition into the texture of an author's spelling, punctua-

[5] Of course, some editorial or compositorial variants that would separate a
reading in A1 from its N prototype are indistinguishable from Crane's authoritative revisions. A certain number of these, one expects, have not been detected on some ground or other and so have been accepted as Crane's own; but
for this situation there is no help, and the number of these cases should be
relatively smaller than the authoritative revisions in A1 variation as adopted in
the present text.

tion, capitalization, word-divisions, abbreviations, and emphasis in the earliest edition (typeset in closest relation to the holograph original) than it is to restore authoritative accidentals as replacement of compositorial styling in a reprint, whether or not substantively revised. In most cases of linear transmission this textual rule is generally advisable to follow. But revision within one arm of a radiating transmission from a lost common document, as is found in *The Third Violet*, introduces its own set of problems. In the case of a simple reprint it is scarcely arguable that the accidentals are less authoritative than those of the text on which it is based, one which is thus a step nearer to the forms of the holograph. Except for possible revision, the reprint accidentals have no access to fresh authority and merely restyle the edition that was their source. On the other hand, if there is no linear derivation but two texts which radiate independently from a common lost ancestor, it is clear that each has equal technical authority, even though an editor may come to believe that on the whole (but not necessarily in any specific case) one document offers a more faithful transcript than the other of the lost common authority. When one arm derives at a single remove from the lost source but the other at two or more removes, the extra stage or stages of the more distant document's transmission offer, in theory, more opportunity for accidental variation from authority than is present in the nearer document. Practice does not always agree with theory in this textual situation, however, for it may be that the document at only one remove was copied or typeset by an agent who altered the accidentals of the text more freely than occurred in the double transmission of the other arm through two more faithful workmen. Each case of radiation must be judged on its merits, therefore, although normally considerable weight in the choice of copytext is given to the document in closest relation to lost authority.

If *The Third Violet* had been represented on the one hand by only a single newspaper (at two removes from the unrevised typescript) and by the book (at one remove from a revised example of the same typescript) the issue of authority could be narrowly viewed. But instead of one newspaper there are six. This multiplicity of evidence in some respects is a blessing since it enables an editor to determine in many cases that the reading of any single newspaper (or sometimes of a minority) is generally unauthoritative. Also, when a sufficient—and often a complete—majority of newspapers agrees in a reading with the book form, something close to absolute authority can be established, so far as the documentary evidence permits.[6] On the other hand, although in a number of readings the evidence may be too conflicting to be trusted, the majority of the accidental forms

[6] One must reiterate that for *The Third Violet* "authority" must be defined only as the readings of the lost Appleton typescript, and not of the holograph behind it, which is unrecoverable on bibliographical evidence.

in the newspapers ordinarily do agree with one another as witnesses to the forms of the lost syndicate proof. As a consequence, insofar as this proof can be reconstructed in a trustworthy manner, it may be said to stand at the same remove from its typescript copy as the book from its copy, and thus to be of equal technical authority.

When these two authorities (only one fully complete, however) are matched, each exhibits accidental characteristics that resemble Crane's, as well as forms that are neutral and others that are uncharacteristic. To assess overall authority in such a situation is not easy, for quantitative agreement may, for editorial purposes, be less significant for the choice of a copy-text than a narrowly based qualitative agreement with Crane's more important and generally established system of accidentals. For *The Third Violet*, however, the fact that the reconstruction of the lost syndicate proof cannot be substantially complete, given the evidence of only six witnesses, disqualifies it for consideration as copy-text, and no other choice than the book can be contemplated. Nevertheless, the situation created by radiating authority is an unusual one, for it is evident to anyone closely acquainted with the most striking characteristics of Crane's system of accidentals as found in his manuscripts that the reconstructed proof, or occasionally the speculative evidence of even a half, or less, of the newspapers, is more like Crane than the corresponding readings of the book.[7] It follows that if, on the evidence of multiple authority, an editor chooses the critical approach for the accidentals as well as for the substantives, the theory of copy-text is more a formal than a practical working concept for this text. That is, the question of editorial convenience—instead of overall authority in respect to the accidentals of any single document (as in linear transmission)—may govern the choice of copy-text. Given the conventional system of recording variants that has been adopted throughout this edition of Crane's *Works*, the difficulties of listing rejected A1 readings from the mass of variants in six newspapers (as well as their own internal variation) would create a preposterous apparatus were an attempt made to adopt a hypothetically reconstructed syndicate proof as the copy-text. On practical as well as theoretical grounds, therefore, the book form (A1) has been selected as the copy-text. But the transmission of the newspapers through a radiating lost proof stage gives them a natural form of authority that may often be more faithful to Crane's characteristics than the accidentals of

---

[7] Sometimes this evidence is variable, apparently according to the characteristics of the different compositors who set different parts of the proof and the book. For example, in the first half or so of the novel the sparing use of exclamation marks in the newspapers as against the book's dialogue splattered with these exclamations is generally more characteristic of Crane's manuscripts. On the other hand, toward the end of the novel the situation reverses itself when the frequency increases in the newspapers and diminishes, in comparison, in the book.

the book, since the book's house styling seems to have been more thorough than that of the syndicate printer. Thus an editor seeking to reconcile accidental variants in multiple authorities in order to create from them an eclectic text that will be as close as the evidence permits to the typescript made from Crane's manuscript will draw freely on the newspaper accidental forms to emend those of the book when in his opinion the printer's setting of the book text has been less faithful to the details of the lost typescript, insofar as these can be determined as coinciding with Crane's usual system.

In the selection of substantives, a great deal more conservatism holds. Without question Crane revised the typescript that Appleton used—in some parts with particular thoroughness—but the well-grounded assumption is that this revision was unlikely to have extended to his accidentals in any significant respect except possibly in such matters as paragraphing and the addition and subtraction of dashes in the dialogue. Thus when a word in the book differs from the consensus of the newspapers, the odds favor it as an intentional revision in all cases when compositorial misunderstanding or sophistication of grammar and idiom is not in question, although of course editorial interference also needs to be considered. On the contrary, variation in the accidentals is to be taken as compositorial on one or the other side, each case to be judged on its merits. In a multiple-authority situation such as exists in *The Third Violet*, the normal respect given to the accidentals of the copy-text is not entirely applicable. When the accidentals of the lost syndicate proof can be recovered, these are as authoritative from a technical point of view as those of the book. Experience indicates, moreover, that in many respects this proof was set with greater fidelity than the carefully styled book to Crane's accidental characteristics as they could have been preserved in the Appleton typescript.

The List of Emendations, which necessarily records all alterations of the copy-text, with their sources, is a lengthy one since the present edited text is entirely eclectic. The first English edition (E1) being an unauthoritative reprint of A1, its readings do not appear in this List. The Historical Collation contains the variant substantive readings of E1 for the sake of the record, but any notice of its accidentals has been excluded because of their lack of authority. On the other hand, in theory any newspaper is as authoritative as any other, and a full record of their accidental variation from the edited text would be desirable from the point of view of completeness, even down to the record of a variant in one newspaper from the other five. Cases do arise in which it is clear that the syndicated proofs retained peculiarities from the typescript that derived directly from the manuscript, and it may be that only a single newspaper faithfully repeated these instead of normalizing them like the rest. Yet practical considerations must enter in this matter since such cases are certainly few and far between compared to the occurrence of casual and seemingly unauthoritative variations in one or two newspapers without significance and often with little chance that the real nature of their origin can be assessed.

Ultimately, whether the syndicate proof was right or wrong in any given reading (although the determination may be far from certain), the nature of its typesetting is of as much textual importance as the typesetting of the book. The identification of the exact reading of this proof is ordinarily established by the agreement of all six newspapers, usually by the agreement of five, and presumably the odds favor the agreement of four except in special circumstances. These degrees of certainty require a record when the proof variant has been editorially rejected in favor of the book. On the other hand, when three newspapers disagree with the common reading of the remaining three, the case for the reading of the proof is moot; yet the evidence for the reading is ordinarily contained in this evenly weighted variation and is worth consideration. The case for recording the rejected readings of one or of two newspapers is less arguable in the light of the confusion of evidence created in any list by such maverick variants as well as the general unlikelihood of their authority and the considerable expense of printing such a mass of material. With only a few special exceptions, therefore, variants have been ignored when only two newspapers, or one, have been concerned. When a newspaper reading has been accepted and appears in the List of Emendations, it is repeated in the Historical Collation only if it is substantive: the record of rejected accidentals consequent upon emendation of the copy-text is found in the List of Emendations and is not duplicated in the Historical Collation.

BIBLIOGRAPHICAL DESCRIPTIONS

The Library of Congress deposit copy of the first American edition of *The Third Violet* is datestamped April 30, 1897. The work was advertised as forthcoming in the March 13, 1897, issue of *Publishers' Weekly* and listed as published in the May 15, 1897, issue. The price was $1.

The description is as follows:

𝕿𝖍𝖊 𝕿𝖍𝖎𝖗𝖉 𝖁𝖎𝖔𝖑𝖊𝖙 | 𝕭𝖞 | 𝕾𝖙𝖊𝖕𝖍𝖊𝖓 𝕮𝖗𝖆𝖓𝖊 | 𝕬𝖚𝖙𝖍𝖔𝖗 𝖔𝖋 𝕿𝖍𝖊 𝕽𝖊𝖉 𝕭𝖆𝖉𝖌𝖊 𝖔𝖋 𝕮𝖔𝖚𝖗𝖆𝖌𝖊, | 𝕿𝖍𝖊 𝕷𝖎𝖙𝖙𝖑𝖊 𝕽𝖊𝖌𝖎𝖒𝖊𝖓𝖙, 𝖆𝖓𝖉 𝕸𝖆𝖌𝖌𝖎𝖊 | [publisher's device] | 𝕹𝖊𝖜 𝖄𝖔𝖗𝖐 | 𝕯. 𝕬𝖕𝖕𝖑𝖊𝖙𝖔𝖓 𝖆𝖓𝖉 𝕮𝖔𝖒𝖕𝖆𝖓𝖞 | 1897

Collation: [1]⁸ 2–13⁸; pp. [i–iv] 1–203 [204]; leaf measures 182 × 122 mm., top edge trimmed and stained yellow, other edges rough-cut; wove unwatermarked paper; endpapers and single initial and terminal flyleaves are text wove paper.

Contents: p. i: half-title, 'THE THIRD VIOLET'; p. ii: publisher's advt., '𝔒𝔱𝔥𝔢𝔯 𝔅𝔬𝔬𝔨𝔰 𝔟𝔶 𝔖𝔱𝔢𝔭𝔥𝔢𝔫 𝔚𝔯𝔞𝔫𝔢 . . . [lists *Red Badge, Little Regiment* and *Maggie*]'; p. iii: title; p. iv: 'COPYRIGHT, 1897, | BY D. APPLETON AND COMPANY. | Copyright, 1896, by Stephen Crane.'; pp. 1–203: text, headed 'THE THIRD VIOLET.'; p. 204: blank.

Binding: Light yellow brown (76. l.y Br) buckram. *Front*: '[red: floral orn.] | [first letter of each word in red, rest in black; red initial 'T' 2 lines deep in gilt panel with pattern of black lozenges] T²HE THIRD | VIOLET | [black] BY | [red and black] STEPHEN CRANE | [red: orn.]'. *Spine*: '[red: orn.] | [first letter of each word in red, rest in black] THE | THIRD | VIOLET | [red: orn.] | CRANE | [red: orn.] | APPLETONS'. *Back*: blank.

Dust Jacket: Tan (76. l.y Br) wove paper. *Front*: as the front cover except that the initial 'T' is in a pattern of black lozenges where gilt in binding. *Spine*: as binding. *Back*: blank. *Both flaps*: blank.

Copy Examined: University of Virginia–Barrett 551461.

Advance Copy: In the Barrett Collection is a copy (551462) internally identical to the first American edition, but lacking the publisher's advertisement on p. ii which, in this copy, is blank. The book is bound in tan paper wrappers, lacking endpapers and flyleaves. The front cover repeats exactly the title-page. Spine, back cover, and inner covers are blank. This appears to represent an advance copy especially made up by Appleton for copyright purposes in other countries.

The British Library deposit copy of the first English edition of *The Third Violet* was received on April 30, 1897. A listing appeared on May 6 and on May 8, 1897, in *Atheneum* and on May 15, 1897, in *Publishers' Circular and Booksellers' Record*. The price was six shillings.

The description is as follows:

THE THIRD VIOLET | BY | STEPHEN CRANE | AUTHOR OF | 'THE RED BADGE OF COURAGE,' ETC. | LONDON | WILLIAM HEINEMANN | 1897 | [*All rights reserved*]

Collation: π^2 1–13⁸ 14⁶; pp. [i–iv] [1] 2–220 (following the text are 16 unpaged leaves of publisher's advertisements stitched at the center fold and signed 'A'); leaf measures 189 × 126 mm., edges uncut; heavy laid unwatermarked paper, endpapers of cream wove paper, ads printed on light cream wove paper.

Contents: p. i: half-title, 'THE THIRD VIOLET'; p. ii: publisher's advt., '*By the same Author* . . . [lists *Red Badge, Little Regiment, Maggie, Black Riders*]'; p. iii: title; p. iv: blank; pp. 1–220: text, headed *'THE THIRD VIOLET'*; at the foot of p. 220 'BILLING AND SONS, PRINTERS, GUILDFORD'.

Binding: Tan (87. m. Y) linen cloth. *Front*: '[gilt-stamped] THE | THIRD | VIOLET | [gilt-stamped violet orn.] | STEPHEN CRANE'. *Spine*: '[gilt-stamped] THE | THIRD | VIOLET | STEPHEN | CRANE | HEINEMANN'. *Back*: publisher's cipher stamped in blind at lower right corner. A purple (219. deep P) ribbon, 14 mm. wide, is interlaced through cuts in the cloth of the cover and extends the width of front and back covers at center. The ribbon is buried beneath the midsection of the spine-strip, but may be presumed to be an unbroken length of material, secured inside the center edge of the front and back covers, under the paste-down endpapers.

Copies: British Library (datestamped April 30, 1897); Bodleian Library (Fic 2712.e.1380); University of Virginia–Barrett 551464.

Variant: A copy (551463) in the Barrett Collection of the University of Virginia Library, otherwise conforming in every particular with the first English edition, lacks the ribbon and cuts in the cover.

Six newspaper printings have been observed:

N¹: *Philadelphia Inquirer*, Sundays, October 25, 1896, p. 29; November 1, p. 29; November 8, p. 29; November 15, p. 29. On October 25, under a three-column title-cut '[superimposed on landscape with two women at left and a man at right] THE THIRD | VIOLET [to the left of 'Violet' in smaller face] BY | STEPHEN | CRANE.', Chapters I–VIII are in columns 1–8 with two illustrations: (1) ' "WHY DON'T YOU MARRY MISS FAIRHALL?" ' and (2) ' "DO YOU KNOW WHERE IS THE STAGE FOR HEMLOCK INN?" ' On November 1, under the same title-cut, Chapters IX–XVI are in columns 1–8 with three illustrations: (1) 'IN THE OX CART', (2) ' "Oh, Holly!" Cried the Girl, Impetuously "Do Tell Me How to Do That Slam-Bang Thing, You Know." ', (3) ' "YOU ARE MORE RIDICULOUS NOW THAN I HAVE YET SEEN YOU." ' On November 8, under a three-column title-cut '[superimposed on interior scene of two men seated by a table] THE | THIRD | VIOLET | BY | STEPHEN | CRANE', Chapters XVII–XXIII are in columns 1–8 with three illustrations: (1) 'The Dog Wagged His Tail and Sleepily Watched This Ceremony.', (2) 'FLORINDA LIGHTED A CIGARETTE AND PERCHING HERSELF ON A DIVAN SMOKED FIERCELY.', (3) 'TAKING AN ENVELOPE FROM HIS POCKET, HE EMPTIED TWO VIOLETS FROM IT TO THE PALM OF HIS HAND AND STARED LONG AT THEM.' On November 15, under the same title-cut as November 8, Chapters XXIV–end are in columns 1–8 with three illustrations: (1) 'HE PICKED IT UP.', (2) 'THEY STOOD GAZING AT THE PICTURE.', (3) 'Pontiac, Hawker and Hollie in the Cafe.' The N¹ artist who supplied the title-cuts redrew one of the syndicate cuts and added four more; these are: October 25, no. 1 (redrawn), no. 2; November 1, no. 3; November 8, no. 2; and November 15, no. 2.

N²: *Pittsburg Leader*, Sundays, October 25, 1896, p. 23; November 1, p. 23; November 8, p. 23; November 15, p. 23. On October 25, under a two-column headline 'THE THIRD VIOLET. || BY STEPHEN CRANE. || [Copyright, 1896, by Stephen Crane.]', Chapters I–VIII are in columns 1–7 with one illustration: ' "Here she comes now," said Hollie' (same subject as N¹, no. 1, but the syndicate cut). The title is the same for all four Sundays, but the copyright notice reads 'Copyrighted 1896 by Stephen Crane' for the last three issues. On November 1, Chapters IX–XVI are in columns 1–6 with two illustrations, nos. 1 and 2 of N¹ for the same date. On November 8, Chapters XVII–XXIII are in columns 1–6 with two illustrations, nos. 1 and 3 of N¹ for the same date. On November 15, Chapters XXIV–end are in columns 1–7 with two illustrations, nos. 1 and 3 of N¹ for the same date.

N³: *The Sunday Oregonian* (Portland), Sundays, October 25, 1896, p. 16; November 1, p. 16; November 8, p. 16; November 15, p. 16. Headline title across first column is the same each day 'The Third Violet. || By Stephen Crane. ||' The copyright notice appears at the head of the beginning chapter on each day and reads '(Copyright, 1896, by Stephen Crane.)'. N³ divides the text as N² does and contains the same illustrations for each day.

N⁴: *The Sunday Inter Ocean* (Chicago), Sundays, October 25, 1896, p. 37; November 1, p. 37; November 8, p. 37; November 15, p. 37. The division of text is as N¹⁻³; the illustrations are those of the syndicate, with an additional one supplied on October 25: 'HE HAD LEFT HER ON A BOWLDER, WHERE SHE WAS PROVISIONALLY HELPLESS.' The title-cut, signed 'C. Petford', for October 25 reads '[superimposed on a sketch of a train coming through a cutting] THE THIRD VIOLET [flower] | BY STEPHEN CRANE· | ·COPYRIGHT, 1896, BY STEPHEN CRANE·'. The November 1 title-cut and copyright notice are the same as those for October 25 except that the sketch is of two men, a woman, and an ox cart and is signed 'P'. The title-cut for November 8 and 15 is as follows: 'THE THIRD VIOLET [below to left artist's palette and three violet plants] | BY STEPHEN CRANE. || COPYRIGHT, 1896. BY THE AUTHOR.', signed 'Pet'.

N⁵: *The World* (New York), November 4, 1896, p. 7; November 5, p. 5; November 6, p. 7; November 7, p. 5; November 9, p. 7; November 10, p. 7; November 11, p. 7; November 12, p. 7; November 13, p. 7; November 14, p. 5. The two-column title-cut, signed 'TEP', is the same for each day and reads '[superimposed on a landscape with an inn at lower left, onto which is superimposed a portrait of Crane surrounded by violets] THE | THIRD | VIOLET [flower] | BY STEPHEN CRANE.' The notice '(Copyrighted, 1896, by Stephen Crane.)' heads the text on each day. On November 4, Chapters I–III are in columns 1–6 with four illustrations: (1) Decorative initial 'T' with train, (2) 'A WHIRL OF ASTONISHMENT WHIRLED THROUGH HIS HAIR.', (3) ' "SAY HAWKER," HE SAID SUDDENLY, "WHY DON'T YOU MARRY MISS FANHALL?" ', (4) ' "HERE SHE COMES NOW." ', all signed 'TEP'. On November 5, Chapters IV–VI are in columns 1–6 with four illustrations: (1) Decorative initial 'O' with women seated on a porch, (2) 'HE SUDDENLY CONFRONTED THE OTHER MAN.', (3) ' "AND RIVALS, TOO. GOOD LORD! THE WOODS MUST BE CROWDED WITH THEM." ', (4) ' "I WONDER WHY THEY DON'T COME DOWN." ' Nos. 1 and 2 are signed 'TEP'. On November 6, Chapters VI(continued)–IX are in columns 1–6 with three illustrations: (1) Decorative initial 'W' with Hawker lying back in the long grass, (2) 'HAWKER AND MISS FANHALL WERE LEFT ALONE STARING AT THE WHITE BUBBLES IN THE BLACK POOL.', (3) 'HAWKER WHEELED AND AN OATH SPUN THROUGH THE SMOKE.' Nos. 2 and 3 are signed 'TEP'. On November 7, Chapters X–XIII are in columns 1–6 with four unsigned illustrations: (1) Decorative initial 'W' with six people grouped around a tennis court, (2) ' "WHAT?" SAID THE OLD MAN. HE WAS TUGGING AT HIS RIGHT BOOT AND HIS TONE WAS VERY IRASCIBLE.', (3) ' "YOU SEE," SAID THE OTHERS, "IT IS AS I SAID, HE HAS COME BACK." ', (4) 'OGLETHORPE.' On November 9, Chapters XIV–XVI are in columns 1–6 with three illustrations: (1) Decorative initial 'A' with lake scene of fishermen and a dog, (2) ' "AREN'T THEY NICE OLD THINGS?" SHE SAID AS SHE STOOD LOOKING INTO THE FACES OF THE TEAM.', (3) ' "WHAT YOU GIGGLING AT?" SAID HOLLANDEN.' No. 3 is signed 'TEP'. On November 10, Chapters XVII–XIX are in columns 1–6 with five illustrations: (1) Decorative initial 'O' with Oglethorpe and Hollanden deep in conversation, (2) ' "THERE IS NO SENSE IN YOU FOLKS PESTERIN' TH' BOY." ', (3) 'SUDDENLY SHE DREW A VIOLET FROM A CLUSTER OF THEM UPON HER GOWN AND THRUST IT OUT TO HIM.', (4) 'THE OLD FOLKS.', (5) 'THEY HAD ALL TURNED TO SCAN THE GIRL'S FACE.' Nos. 2, 3, 4, and 5 are signed 'TEP'. On November 11, Chapters XX–XXII are in columns 1–6 with four illustrations: (1) Decorative initial 'H' with dog entering artists' studio, (2) ' "HOW'S THE WOLF, BOYS—AT THE DOOR YET?" ', (3) 'FLORINDA CURLED AGAIN ON THE DIVAN AND LIT A CIGARETTE.', (4) 'HAWKER CALLS ON MISS FANHALL.' The first three are signed 'TEP'. On November 12, Chapters XXIII–XXIV are in columns 1–6 with four illustrations: (1) Decorative initial 'T' with wine bottle and glasses superimposed on head of a man smoking, (2) '"HE CAN'T CARRY THE SALAD WITH THOSE GLOVES."', (3) 'INTO THIS TANGLED MIDNIGHT HAWKER CONDUCTED FLORINDA.', (4) '"WHY, I'M NOT MEAN TO YOU," HE SAID.' The first three are signed 'TEP'. On November 13, Chapters XXV–XXVIII are in columns 1–6 with five illustrations: (1) Decorative initial 'I' with two artists talking—one seated, one standing, (2) '"OH!" SAID HAWKER.', (3) '"MR. WILLIAM HAWKER, MR. PONTIAC."', (4) '"I WONDER WHAT THOSE TWO FOOLS ARE BELLOWING AT?" SAID HAWKER.', (5) '"DAMN IT!" SAID HAWKER TO HIS COFFEE CUP.' All are signed 'TEP'. On November 14, Chapters XXIX–end are in columns 1–6 with four illustrations: (1) Decorative initial 'W' with interior of drawing room showing large window, a chandelier and two people seated on a sofa, (2) '"SHUT UP!" SAID WRINKLES, SUDDENLY. LISTEN!"', (3) '"I CAN'T PAINT. I CAN'T PAINT FOR A DAM."', (4) '"OH DO GO! GO, PLEASE."' The second is signed 'TEP'.

N⁶: *San Francisco Chronicle*, Sundays, October 25, 1896, p. 14; November 1, p. 14; November 8, p. 14; November 15, p. 14; November 22, p. 12; November 29, p. 14; December 6, p. 14; December 13, p. 13; December 20, p. 18; December 27, p. 15; January 3, 1897, p. 40; January 10, p. 13; January 17, p. 13; January 24, p. 13. On October 25, November 1, 8, 15, 22, and 29 the two-column title-cut is 'The Third Violet. || By STEPHEN CRANE.' The copyright notice on October 25 and November 8 across the first column is '(Copyright, 1896, by Stephen Crane.)'; on November 1 and 15, to the left of the first column and the right of the second, it reads, spaced, 'Copyright, 1896.) (By Stephen Crane.'; on November 22 and 29 it reads, to the left of the first column, and the right of the second '(Copyright, 1896. By Stephen Crane.)'. The two-column title-cut for December 6, 13, and 27 within a decorated rectangle reads 'The Third Violet. || By STEPHEN CRANE. || [to the left] (Copyright, 1896 [to the right] By Stephen Crane.)'. The full seven-column title-cut for December 20 reads '[two cupids playing within circle, orn.] THE THIRD VIOLET. [orn., two cupids playing within circle] || By STEPHEN CRANE.'; at the head of the second column 'Copyright, 1896.'; at the head of the sixth column 'By Stephen Crane.' The seven-column title-cut for January 3 and 10 is '[orn.] "THE THIRD VIOLET," BY STEPHEN CRANE. [orn.]'. The copyright notice for January 3 across first column reads '(Copyright, 1896. All Rights Reserved.)'; for January 10, across first column it reads '(Copyright, 1896, by Stephen Crane.)'. The seven-column title-cut for the last two days, January 17 and 24, is '[orn.] "THE THIRD VIOLET." BY STEPHEN CRANE. [orn.]'. The copyright for January 17 across first column is 'Copyright, 1896, by Stephen Crane.'; there is no notice for January 24. On October 25, Chapters I–III are in columns 1–7 with one illustration: '"Why, Will. we're awful glad t' see yeh!"' On November 1, Chapters IV–VI are in columns 1–7 with one illustration: 'Hollanden Established Himself in an Oratorical Pose on a Great Weather-Beaten Stone.' On November 8, Chapters VII–VIII are in columns 1–7 with one illustration: 'She Gazed Off at the Water.' Illustrations for the first three days are signed 'LEON BOILLOT'. On November 15, Chapters IX–X are in columns 1–7 with one illustration: '"I don't believe it at all," she exclaimed.', signed 'LEWIS'. On November 22, Chapters XI–XII are in columns 1–7 with one illustration: '"There's another fellah come."', signed 'LEWIS'. On November 29, Chapters XIII–XIV are in columns 1–7 with one illustration: '"How d'yeh do?"', signed 'LEWIS'. On December 6, Chapters XV–XVI are in columns 1–7 with one illustration: 'He Comprehended Them Both in a Swift Bow.', signed 'LEWIS'. On December 13, Chapters XVII–XVIII are in columns 1–7 with one illustration: 'Suddenly She Drew a Violet and Thrust It Out to Him.', signed 'LEWIS'. On December 20, Chapters XIX–XX are in columns 1–7 with no illustration. On December 27, Chapters XXI–XXII are in columns 1–7 with an uncaptioned illustration showing Florinda entering the artists' studio, signed 'LEWIS'. On January 3, Chapters XXIII–XXIV are in columns 1–7 with one illustration: 'As they stood on the steps of the flat she slowly turned and looked up at him.' On January 10, Chapters XXV–XXVI are in columns 1–7 with one illustration: 'He Sat Braced Nervously Forward on a Little Stool Before His Easel.' On January 17, Chapters XXVII–XXIX are in columns 1–7 with one illustration: '"Poverty isn't anything to be ashamed of.', signed 'LEWIS'. On January 24, Chapters XXX–end are in columns 1–7 with one illustration: 'With Heroic Effort She Slowly Raised Her Eyes Until They Met His.', signed 'LEWIS'.

ACTIVE SERVICE

The main typescript for *Active Service*, here called TMs¹, is preserved in the Special Collections of the Columbia University Libraries. It is composed of 190 sheets of white wove foolscap, measuring 330 × 203 mm. and is unwatermarked. In addition, this document contains eleven leaves from a different typescript (TMs²), the first five providing the only typescript copy for Chapter V but the remaining six duplicating the four TMs¹ leaves for Chapter VI. The typescript TMs¹ is untitled, except for a notation 'Active Service: | by Stephen Crane' in a strange hand. Each chapter is headed 'CHAPTER -I- [-II-]' (Chapter XXV lacks the hyphens); each begins on a new leaf and is separately paged, starting with its second leaf, the numbers being typed in the upper right-hand corner. The chapter number appears on each leaf in the upper left-hand corner. This typescript served as the printer's copy for the Heinemann edition of 1899 in England and is marked with the names of the compositors.

The typing was done on the Crane typewriter, which had no right-hand margin release, and so a number of lines are missing the final letter(s), or final punctuation, not all of these having been supplied by hand. The typing is clearly an amateur job, with many x'd-out false starts, and a number of overlooked misspellings, errors, eye-skips, and the like. Exclamation marks are manufactured by a hand-drawn ink downstroke over a typed period. The wayward spelling not only reproduces various of Crane's own characteristic misspellings but adds many others that are similar to those in identifiable type-scripts made by Cora Crane. That Cora was the typist here admits of little doubt, and it is also evident that she was copying a manu-script by Crane, either in his own hand or perhaps in part dictated by him. But any dictation that may have occurred would appear to have been substantially less than his autograph inscription, on the evidence of a number of correct spellings that Cora would ordinarily have got wrong if left to her own devices in typing from her own inscription. Occasional typed-in interlineations of missing words ap-pear, or corrections of deletions, apparently made before the sheet was removed from the typewriter.

The typescript is a blue ribbon copy from fol. 1 to the end of Chapter xviii on fol. 122 (except for fols. 26–36 which are black ribbon and represent inserted leaves from another typescript), and thereafter a black carbon except for the blue ribbon page 163 which looks as though it may have been retyped especially for the printer as a substitute for a faulty carbon. It has a unique chapter designa-tion, since 'CHAPTER XXV' is typed to the left of center whereas all other pages of this typescript simply have the chapter number set off by hyphens; hence one may conjecture that the carbon of this page was found to be defective or was damaged at the printer. Owing to some accidents, perhaps at the printer, it is incomplete.[1] Folios 117–119, the first three pages of Chapter xviii, have their lower right corners torn off; fols. 120–121 (the candle . . . uproar [231.11–233.13]) are crumpled and torn; fol. 164 shows extra signs of wear and tear, possibly the reason for this is connected with the retyping of fol. 163; fols. 170 (the first leaf of Chapter xxvi) and 173 are crumpled and torn. After fol. 164, fols. 165–169 ending Chapter xxv (Everything . . . anyhow." [279.7–283.32]) are wanting, except for a minute fragment, possibly the foot of fol. 168; fol. 170 beginning

[1] That the typescript is preserved in the Columbia University Libraries' Crane Collection indicates that it came from Brede and had been preserved by the Cranes. The accidents do not seem to be of the kind that would happen while it was in their possession.

Chapter XXVI and fol. 172 are mutilated, and intervening fol. 171 (I don't know . . . man in [285.5–286.7]) and fols. 173–178 (man . . . presently the [287.7–293.5]) are wanting. It can hardly be fortuitous that these gaps occur at the ends of chapters and occasionally at their beginnings.

An anomaly is present in this typescript. Chapter V is replaced by a different typescript from the TMs[1] made by Cora. This TMs[2], foliated 42–46 on the typewriter, is a black ribbon professional typing job on American-made laid paper (267 × 203 mm.) with vertical chainlines and the watermark 'U.S. LINEN'. Chapter V is followed by Chapter VI of the same typing and paper, foliated 47–52, and then by duplicate Chapter VI of the original English typescript by Cora. The English printer, who numbered the leaves of the typescript from 6 to 212 (accepting TMs[1]'s typed 1–5), included this strange TMs[2] typescript Chapter V (which indeed was the only copy for this chapter) as his fols. 26–30, and then foliated Chapter VI of TMs[2] as 31–36, continuing with the TMs[1] duplicated Chapter VI as fol. 37, etc. A portion of the proof of the Heinemann first edition (E1) preserved at Columbia contains a correspondingly duplicated typesetting of Chapter VI, including the chapter number, despite the fact that this had been altered on the typescript to VII. From the printer's continuous foliation and from his renumbering of the TMs[1] chapters in the copy starting with VI as VII, it is clear that TMs[1] Chapter V was never in his hands and that he did not recognize that TMs[1] Chapter VI duplicated TMs[2] Chapter VI copy. The error in the printer's blue-pencil renumbering of the chapters to the end was probably discovered when proofs were pulled of the setting up to the first page of falsely numbered Chapter XI, as found in the Crane Collection, but the mistake was corrected in TMs[1] by the printer's deleting his blue-pencil renumbering of Chapter IX as X, and also his renumbering of X–XIII, XV–XX, XXII–XXVI, and XXVIII–XXXI one number ahead. Heading Chapter XXV on fol. 162 is another handwritten 'Active Service | Stephen Crane' like that on fol. 1 but in a different hand. One may conjecture that this marks the receipt of the last batch of copy, Chapters XXV–XXXI. The mixup in the English printer's copy, however, would seem to have no bearing on an independent error in the typesetting and printing of the Stokes edition in New York (A1) according to which Heinemann's Chapters IX and X are combined as A1 Chapter X so that the thirty-one chapters of TMs[1] and E1 become thirty in A1. Possibly this irregularity reflects an error made by the typist of TMs[2]—the printer's copy for A1—who may have failed to notice the chapter heading for X in the TMs[1] carbon sent to the United States.

The appearance of Chapters V and VI from TMs[2] in the Heinemann's printer's copy affected the text of both the English and the American editions. As shown by the preserved set of early proofs,

Heinemann's printer had set Chapter vi from TMs[2] immediately following the TMs[2] unique copy for Chapter v, and then in error continued with TMs[1] Chapter vi. When the mistake was discovered, it was natural that the printer would remove the second of the two Chapter vi versions and repage after the first. Thus the Heinemann edition was set from TMs[2] in Chapters v and vi, and the original typesetting of Chapter vi from TMs[1] was distributed and is preserved only in the proofs.

Correspondingly, the Stokes American edition in these chapters is the mirror image of the Heinemann, since its Chapters v and vi were set not from the preserved version of the text as found in TMs[2] —the American intruder in the English printer's copy—but instead from some lost typescript in another tradition that can only be TMs[1], the original Cora typescript. This is a strange set of circumstances, not entirely explicable but certainly related in some way to the textual history of publication in England and in the United States, including the newspaper serialization in the latter country.

Except for Chapters v and vi, which present a special problem, the facts about the textual transmission are these. Heinemann's English edition (E1) is clearly set from the preserved Cora typescript TMs[1], which contains the Heinemann printers' names, galley markings, and continuous paginal numbering, and which exhibits common errors with the book. The Stokes edition (A1) is set from some typescript other than a carbon of TMs[1]. The very considerable number of substantive variants are too many to have been compositorial, and the styling has distinctive features differing from TMs[1]. The first question is whether TMs[2], the presumed copy for A1, derived from Crane's manuscript directly or from TMs[1]. The evidence in such a case is difficult to come by, since common irregularities between TMs[1] and A1 need not result from a linear relationship but could occur in two radiating documents repeating some manuscript anomalies. For instance, that TMs[1] and A1 (joined by one of the newspapers, N[1]) agree in the spelling 'Mesalonghi' (163.29 *et seq.*) is not evidence, for this could have been the manuscript spelling and it is in fact the preferred spelling. Similarly, the error in usage 'illusions' in the same documents for 'allusions' (266.32) could have originated with Crane, and also the shared grammatical error 'or' for 'nor' (323.32) in TMs[1],A1. Properly, the evidence should bear on mistakes or peculiarities that may be presumed to have originated in the typing and not in the holograph. A certain number of such readings are present. Some are more doubtful than others, of course. That is, when A1 follows TMs[1] in the misspelling 'pantomined' at 167.23 but not in 'pantomine' at 260.30; or in 'stupified' at 216.16 but not elsewhere; or perhaps in 'callouse' for *callous* at 179.28, misspellings in the manuscript could still have been the origin. Somewhat better evidence may perhaps be found in the A1 agreement with TMs[1] at

129.21 and 130.12, the only two times that TMs[1] (and A1) does not use the capital in the title 'Sunday Editor'. Even more to the point, it is interesting to see A1 follow what seems to be, but is not demonstrably, Cora's peculiarity 'everytime' at 166.28 but not at 175.35. Physical evidence appears to be present, however. Several mistakes in hitting the keys of the typewriter in TMs[1] have affected the A1 readings. The first, unfortunately, is not evidence. At 124.15, TMs[1] 'wallx' becomes 'walls' in A1, but also in E1. The context is neutral for singular or for plural, but the fact that the two keys are adjacent, one above the other, on the keyboard suggests that both A1 and E1 were correct to interpret the mistake as the plural. Better evidence comes at 208.8 where TMs[1] read 'say' but the A1 guess 'sat' is better than E1's 'set' since 't' and 'y' are next to each other on the typewriter. Still better evidence appears at 269.14 where both TMs[1] and A1 share the common error of 'sunthing' for dialect 'sumthing', again because the wrong one of two side-by-side keys was hit. But the clincher is at 326.30 where TMs[1] 'theu' is set as 'then' in A1 and in E1, although the second newspaper, N[2], recognized correctly that the reading should be 'they'. Again two adjacent keys are involved in the error, but the more important point is that A1 'then' could have derived only from TMs[1] 'theu'.

Two other readings have an important bearing on the case if, as will be shown below, the evidence of the newspapers be admitted on the grounds that the copy from which their common proof was set was identical with that behind A1. At 320.31 TMs[1] 'tell-bearing' is repeated as 'tellbearing' in N[1], although in the other prints it has been corrected to the obvious 'tale-bearing'. It would seem that N[1] could have derived this reading from TMs[1] only if its copy, TMs[2], had literally transmitted the typescript error, one not clearly to be attributed to the manuscript. Similarly, the uncorrected TMs[1] reading 'person' at 327.11, found in both newspapers N[1] and N[2] and thus manifestly derived from their common proof, must derive from TMs[1] where it was typed as 'person' but corrected by hand to 'parson'. Evidently the copy for the newspaper proof had not had the mistake corrected but contained the original TMs[1] typing error; the A1 compositor or proofreader seems to have corrected the reading on its sense.

What is perhaps the strongest evidence for the derivation of TMs[2], and thus of A1, from TMs[1] is found in Crane's revisions (not corrections) introduced by hand in TMs[1] and faithfully reproduced in A1. Such alterations as 'her' for TMs[1] original 'his interlocutors' (247.2), or 'comic' for 'ludicrous' (252.3), or 'hurrying' for 'moving' (259.8) are true changes of mind by the author, scarcely to be attributed to the underlying manuscript. The case is of course considerably strengthened by the presence of Chapters v and vi in the printer's copy for E1 in the form of a professional script typed in the

United States and consecutively foliated by the typist. This typescript could not have derived from the manuscript unless we were to hypothesize the almost impossible situation by which the manuscript itself was sent to America instead of a copy of Cora's typescript, as is practically demonstrated by the internal evidence.

For Chapter VI a copy of TMs[1] was used by Stokes's printer, on the evidence of the shift in the forms of the accidentals as well as the A1 agreement with the substantives of TMs[1] that are variant from those in preserved TMs[2]. It is evident that the same textual situation held for Chapter V even though the case cannot be demonstrated because of the missing TMs[1] copy for this chapter. Hence no reason exists to posit the existence of more master typescripts than are represented by TMs[1] and TMs[2] as known by its two preserved chapters. The case for the remainder of TMs[2] as the printer's copy for A1 (and the syndicated newspaper proofs) is conjectural, of course, since no chapters of TMs[2] used by A1 are in existence. However, the hypothesis has general probability behind it, and it may be backed by the evidence that the substantive variants between TMs[1] and TMs[2] in Chapter VI and between A1 (set from TMs[1]) and TMs[2] in Chapter V are similar in nature to the numerous variants between TMs[1] and A1 (conjecturally set from TMs[2]) in the other chapters. Indeed, if these two chapters of a typescript made in the United States are not representative of the typescript copy behind A1, it is difficult to know what they could be. Certainly, A1—aside from Chapters V–VI, discussed above—could not have been set from a carbon or ribbon copy of TMs[1].

Except for Chapters V and VI, the agreement of the two known syndicated newspaper versions, the *Chicago Times-Herald* (N[1]) and the *Buffalo Courier* (N[2]), with the A1 readings variant from TMs[1] is so general as to divorce N[1-2] from the possibility of having any direct derivation from TMs[1]. The association of N with A1 could have come about in any one of four ways: (1) if A1 proof had been the printer's copy independently for each newspaper or for their common proof copy; (2) if the same typescript copy that had been (or was to be) used for setting A1 had been passed between the newspapers; (3) if a syndicate typesetting from a copy of TMs[2] had been made and the proofs pulled from this for subscribing newspapers had also been used as printer's copy for A1; or (4) if A1 were set from a copy of TMs[2] and the same example of the typescript had been used as copy for the syndicate typesetting that furnished common proof copies to the newspapers. Of these four possibilities only the last agrees with the textual evidence. The first is impossible, for the unique A1 variants would not have proved unique if they had existed in the only A1 typesetting that could have been passed on to the newspapers; moreover, these variants are not always of the nature of the A1 later proof-corrections for the perfection of copy, the N readings thus representing the early proof originals. Indeed, the co-incidence of N^{1-2} readings, occasionally, against A1 but agreeing with TMs¹ would not be explicable under these circumstances. The second runs aground on the same evidence of the occasional unique agreement of N^{1-2} against A1. If the same TMs² had been passed around, so that all three documents radiated independently from it, the unique A1, N^1, and N^2 readings would be readily explicable, but not the series of readings that link N^{1-2} together as a unit against A1, in such matters as the mistake 'genius' for 'journal' (129.7), 'drearying' for 'dreaming' (188.30), or certainly not the omission of words in N^{1-2} (where A1 agrees with TMs¹) such as 'its' (119.30), 'not' (194.6), 'lucky' (215.30), or 'going' (219.3). Such readings as TMs¹, E1, and A1 'on up' at 184.12 but N^1 'up in' and N^2 'up on' evidence some corruption of copy each newspaper had encountered and solved in a different manner. The third hypothesis, radiation of A1, N^1, and N^2 from a common set of proofs, fails because of the same difficulties encountered in the first and second cases. Only the fourth reconciles all evidence. The common readings of A1 and N^{1-2} against TMs¹ derive from the lost TMs² typescript, which was the printer's copy for A1 and also for the syndicate proof-setting. The unique A1 variants against TMs¹ and N^{1-2} represent A1 compositorial departures from copy or later variants from proofreading;[2] the unique N^{1-2} variants against TMs¹,A1 readings are the printer's errors in the syndicate proof. When N^1 or N^2 disagree with each other and with TMs¹ and A1, the variant must result from an individual newspaper type-setting error, but if the variant from the other newspaper and A1 (or N^{1-2} agreement against A1) concurs with the TMs¹ reading, the odds favor the hypothesis that the A1 reading represents an un-authoritative variant and that copy has been reproduced accurately in N.

To sum up the main outline of the textual transmission of *Active Service*, then, it would seem that Cora's TMs¹ was the Heinemann's printer's copy, and that a copy of TMs¹ was sent to the United States to Stokes, where it was considerably edited before being retyped to form TMs², the copy for A1 and presumably for the syndicated common proofs distributed by McClure to subscribing newspapers. A few details can be filled in by reference to correspondence about the book, although as many questions are raised as are answered by the in-complete record.

The correspondence between Crane and Stokes about *Active Service* has not been preserved, but there are some letters from Crane to to his New York agent Paul Reynolds which leave unclear the im-portant question of the relation of Reynolds to Stokes. On February 13, 1899, Crane wrote that he had nearly finished half of the big

_____

[2] No evidence suggests that these or the unique N^{1-2} variants derive from a TMs² in two different states of manuscript annotation.

novel and would send this half to Reynolds in about three weeks if Reynolds thought there would be a chance of an advance on the sample for serialization rights. The book rights, he stated, belonged to Stokes (Syracuse University transcript). This may be the first hard news that Reynolds had of *Active Service,* on the evidence of a letter conjecturally dated December, 1897, in which Crane informed Reynolds of a proposition he had made to McClure to advance £200 on the first of January for the book rights "to my new Greek novel— not yet begun" (*Letters,* p. 157). On March 2, 1899, Crane expected the 80,000-word novel to be completed by the end of the month. "Stokes and Co. dont wish me to sell the American serial rights but I think if you tackled all those news-papers for a big summer serial we could make fifteen hundred dollars out of it. Would a good half of the novel be of any service to you to begin preliminary work with? If so I can send it to you upon reciept of your reply to this letter" (Syracuse University transcript). On March 16 Crane reported completion of 47,000 words and progress at the rate of 10,000 words per week. "I dont suppose that the Stokes Co. will be pleased to have the story run as a serial in America" (Syracuse University transcript). On March 25 he wrote that under separate cover he was sending Reynolds eighteen chapters, about 46,000 words, the rest to come in batches of 10,000 words. Reynolds, he hoped, would make a very successful sale of the American serial rights. "As I told you, Stokes & Co. have the book rights" (Syracuse University transcript). The last dated letter, of March 30, 1899, enclosed 10,000 more words— Chapters XIX–XXII (Syracuse University transcript). Stallman and Gilkes print an undated letter that reads, in part: "As for 'Active Service,' Stokes and Company have, without my knowledge or permission, been attempting to sell it serially. I have told them that I wanted you to conduct that matter and in order to pervent confusion I send you word at the earliest possible moment" (*Letters,* p. 219). Probably this letter is later than that of March 30, but it must certainly precede by some time the copyright by McClure of the newspaper syndicated text on July 21, 1899.[3]

This correspondence suggests that Crane dealt directly with Stokes about the finances, and presumably the copy, and that he used Reynolds as an independent agent only for the American serial rights. The interest for the present discussion rests, therefore, on the narrow question of the relation of the copy that Crane sent to Reynolds to that he mailed to Stokes, and of these copies to the one provided McClure **for** syndication. The only evidence (other than the textual) concerns the shift in the Heinemann's printer's copy from a blue ribbon typescript to a black carbon beginning with Chapter XIX, a shift coinciding with the dispatch of the first eighteen chapters to Reyn-

[3]Thus Stallman's conjectural dates of May–November may be narrowed, very likely, to April–June, perhaps later in this span than earlier.

olds on March 25, 1899. It is a reasonable conjecture—but only a conjecture—that on February 13, 1899, the novel was still in manuscript and that Crane sent off the first eighteen chapters on March 25 as soon as they were typed.[4] We know that after this point Crane seems to have mailed the ribbon copy to the United States, reserving one of the carbons for Heinemann. But whether it was the ribbon copy that thereafter was sent to Reynolds is quite another matter, for one would expect this to be reserved for Stokes. All that we know is that from Crane's point of view it was more important for Reynolds to receive the chapters as they were written and typed than for Stokes, since Crane was particularly anxious to secure an advance on the serialization—by May 1 at the latest, as he urged Reynolds in his letter of March 25, unless the sale was to the newspapers, in which case it would seem that he expected delayed payment.[5] Indeed, this urgency to get Reynolds started and some money flowing in is implied in a letter of March 17, 1899, to his English agent James Pinker: "I have delayed sending you a copy of the first half of the book in order that I might get a copy off to Reynolds" (*Letters*, p. 218). The lack of mention of Stokes may be significant here.

We now enter an area where conjecture alone can rule in the absence of any proper evidence. If after completing 53,000 words by March 25 Crane had not relaxed (since enough had then been written to warrant the urgently needed advance from serialization), and if he continued at his proposed rate of 10,000 words per week, he may have finished *Active Service* by late April, with the typing concluded shortly afterward in early May. On April 25, 1899, Cora wrote to Pinker that she was sending him twenty-two chapters, the balance to follow at the end of the week.[6] Since Chapters xix–xxii had been

---

[4] Cora's typing speed is not known. If she had completed 46,000 words, or eighteen chapters, shortly before March 25, she would have typed the next 10,000 words (four chapters) by March 30. Thus if Crane had completed and revised the first eighteen chapters by about the third week of February, she could have completed the typing of the first mailing in four to five weeks, or close to March 25. From the statement that the book stands at 53,000 words on March 25, although only 46,000 words are being sent, it seems evident that Crane was anxious to mail copy before Cora had typed beyond Chapter xviii although (if revised) the manuscript would have been available for perhaps another two chapters. Five days later she had completed approximately another 10,000 words.

[5] His letters urge Reynolds to deal directly with the newspapers himself, in effect acting as his own syndicate; Crane had tried to form such a syndicate for his postwar Havana dispatches. Under such circumstances it would appear that the individual newspapers would pay only on publication, and sometimes later. Since *Active Service* was subsequently sold for syndication through McClure, an advance may have been paid, but no record is available nor are the circumstances of sale known for certain, whether it was through Stokes or through Reynolds. See below, pp. 354–358.

[6] *Letters*, p. 219. Pinker was to handle the English serial rights (which never materialized). He may also have handled the book sale, but this is not mentioned.

dispatched to Reynolds on March 30, several weeks earlier, the inference may be drawn that typing had not proceeded as planned in batches of 10,000 words for Reynolds. The printer's or publisher's handwritten retitling of the Heinemann typescript at the head of Chapter xxv indicates that this was the start of the second lot of copy received. It would seem, then, that after the typing and dispatch of Chapters xix–xxii, Chapters xxiii–xxiv were made up and presumably sent off; but that thereafter there could have been a delay, for Cora's promise to Pinker on April 25 that the rest would be available within a week might actually have been fulfilled only by Chapters xxiii–xxiv. If all copy after Chapter xxiv was held until completion of Chapter xxxi, Reynolds could easily not have received final copy until mid-May, and probably later.

What we do not know is whether Crane held off providing Stokes with the carbon of Chapters i–xviii and presumably the ribbon of xix–xxxi (or more likely of xxv–xxxi) until completion, or whether (probably through Dominick, Stokes's agent in London) Stokes received copy—perhaps in four sendings—like Reynolds,[7] or in two like Heinemann. Since the whole relation of Crane and Stokes is unknown, we cannot tell whether he was working to an advance already paid in, to an advance on the receipt of some copy, or to an arrangement in which payment would be held up until the entire copy had been received. All one can remark is that in the slight evidence preserved there is no hint of any urgency in providing Stokes with copy, but only Reynolds. It is possible, of course, that when on April 25 Cora mailed Chapters i–xxii to Pinker (presumably for Heinemann although also with some thought of English serial rights) she also mailed the same set of chapters to Stokes. Since the newspapers serialized the story uncomfortably close to its publication date of October 7, it may be that Stokes did not receive the final copy (and interested McClure in the syndication) until mid to late May at the earliest. However, all external evidence is wanting whether it was Reynolds or Stokes who concluded the arrangements with McClure in time for the type to be set and the newspaper form copyrighted on July 21. It is singularly unfortunate that the letter is undated in which Crane defends himself to Reynolds about Stokes's attempts to serialize (*Letters*, p. 219); but whatever the date, it would seem that the letter precedes the sale to McClure and certainly

---

[7] Ordinarily the point might have textual significance, since if there were a delay, opportunity would theoretically have been offered Crane to revise readings in the Stokes copy of the typescript in a manner denied to the Reynolds copy. However, the fate of the Reynolds copy is completely unknown and so no opportunity exists to compare it with the Stokes. All one can say is that a comparison of A1 with TMs1 in Chapters xix–xxxi known to have been revised by Crane in both the Heinemann and Stokes copies does not produce readings in A1 that can be identified as a further round of authorial revision.

the copyrighting, unless Crane is lying to Reynolds after the event. The odds would seem to favor the view that despite Crane's objections Stokes continued efforts to syndicate the novel and finally succeeded, presumably without reference to Reynolds. The hypothesis rests on the fact that whatever copy of Crane's typescript it was that was sent to Stokes,[8] it served, after thorough editing, as the basis for a new typescript, and this TMs[2] became the copy for the book and also for the McClure setting from which proofs were pulled to send to the newspapers. It is this typescript that appears as Chapters v and vi among the leaves of Cora's TMs[1] used as printer's copy in England by Heinemann.

The number of variant readings (some of them errors and misunderstandings) common to the book and the newspapers indicates that before this American TMs[2] was made up, Cora's copy was considerably edited. Although TMs[1] was set by Heinemann in its rough condition, with much normalization, it was evidently considered unsuitable for printer's copy in the United States because of its numerous misspellings, its nonexistent or erratic punctuation (by publisher's standards), and—quite clearly—because of the editor's view that the style and expression needed improvement. Moreover, one may guess—although here the evidence is confused—that a better copy than that received from Cora was necessary for a successful sale to newspapers.[9] That Stokes would have such an edited new typescript made up for publishing and for sale seems natural; that Reynolds would edit TMs[1] so severely before handing it over to a typist is unsupported by any parallel in his other dealings with Crane. Of the ribbon copy and the probable three carbons that Cora made up of TMs[1] (as for *The O'Ruddy*), then, one copy went to Heinemann, one to Pinker,[10] one to Stokes, and one to Reynolds. It would seem that the Pinker and Reynolds sets for serialization were never used and that the Stokes set was discarded after retyping, its derivative TMs[2] being known now only for Chapters v and vi inserted in the English printer's copy.

[8] This is to assume that Reynolds did not have the typescript copy of TMs[1] made himself and then turned TMs[2] over to Stokes, a most unlikely proceeding since Crane's letters about serialization show clearly that Reynolds had nothing to do with the sale of the book to Stokes and its publication. Moreover, Reynolds never edited other of Crane's works in this cavalier fashion.

[9] That the Stokes proof was not sold to McClure for its setting of the proof to mail to newspapers is indicated by the various unique A1 readings in which the newspapers agree with TMs[1]. These cannot all be proof-alterations in the book made for revises subsequent to the sale of the first set of proofs. Correspondingly, the various unique readings in which the newspapers join against A1 when it agrees with TMs[1] indicate that A1 could not have been set from the syndicate proof.

[10] If Pinker handled the dealings with Heinemann, as is likely, as well as attempting to sell the English serial rights, he may have had two copies of the typescript.

We come now to the vexed question of Chapters v and vi. Any explanation must take account of the curious appearance in the Heinemann's printer's copy of these chapters of the Stokes typescript, especially in its ribbon copy, although only Chapter v of Cora's typescript is missing. Moreover, the fact must be faced that along with this apparent repair of defective English copy, a disruption appears in the American edition, which for these two chapters is set from what must be the Stokes copy of Cora's typescript (carbon of TMs[1]) and not from TMs[2], which served as copy for the rest of the volume. Finally, the anomaly of this shift in the A1 printer's copy must be connected in some plausible way with the fact that Chapters v and vi were not printed in N[2], and the copy in N[1] for Chapter vi (and very likely for v as well) was not the syndicate typesetting from TMs[2] but instead the A1 Stokes proofs.

It is a reasonable hypothesis that the only cause for the appearance of the American typescript for Chapter v among the English papers lay in some accident whereby the chapter was missing from the Heinemann ribbon copy and could not be recovered by retyping the manuscript, which may have been discarded after Cora had copied TMs[1] from it. Thus, it would seem, Heinemann (or Crane) had to make direct application to Stokes in the United States.[11] Apparently there was some mixup in the request or in Stokes's response to it, so that Chapter vi was sent as well as Chapter v, although vi was not required. The placement of this superfluous Chapter vi in its TMs[2] form after TMs[2] Chapter v is readily explained by supposing that Heinemann's printer saw the Chapter v heading on the first leaf and assumed that all the copy was for this chapter; hence he inserted and foliated it without recognizing that he had duplicated Chapter vi.

However, the real problem comes in relating this repair of the English printer's copy to the use of TMs[1] as printer's copy for Chapters v and vi in the Stokes edition, compounded by the apparent difficulty found in providing any copy at all for McClure's syndication. The defect in the copy seems firmly established in England, not as

---

[11] Of Crane's novels only the manuscripts of the early *Red Badge of Courage* and the posthumous *O'Ruddy* have come down to us. Crane gave the *Red Badge* to a friend; and Cora does not seem to have been concerned in the preservation of *The O'Ruddy* manuscript since it was not kept among the papers at Brede that eventually went to Columbia University. Crane kept other manuscripts if they were drafts or unsold material not yet revised and rewritten, and Cora preserved anything, later, that she thought could be sold for publication; but there is no evidence that either one valued the manuscripts for their own sakes. Hence it is possible that the manuscript was indeed discarded when the typescript had been made. Why Pinker or Reynolds could not have supplied the chapters is not to be guessed at, unless Pinker had had only the Heinemann copy. On the evidence, Heinemann may have applied to Stokes directly as the most obvious choice once Crane could not furnish copy from manuscript.

originating in the United States;[12] all the results stem from this central point.

If it is true, as it seems, that Heinemann was wanting only Chapter v and that the Stokes's sending of Chapter vi was a mistake, the fact of a deficiency in England of only Chapter v but a disruption of the text in America in both Chapters v and vi can be reconciled. The working hypothesis that connects the two depends heavily upon the time factor. The need for such precision of accident in series is disturbing; nevertheless, of all evils the suggested hypothesis seems the least. Two mixups seem to have occurred from the emergency request made to Stokes for copy. First, Stokes took it that Chapter vi was required as well as v, or else vi was included inadvertently. Second, the Stokes ribbon copy of TMs[2] was mailed instead of the chapters of TMs[1] that had been its source, possibly through some secretarial misunderstanding of the instructions. This mistaken mailing of Chapters v and vi of TMs[2] must have occurred (a) shortly before the typesetting of A1 was to start and (b) before copy had been sent to McClure.

The difficult part of any hypothesis is, unfortunately, the oddity that, on the evidence, the mailing of the ribbon copy of TMs[2] Chapters v and vi to Heinemann seems to have prevented both Stokes's printers and McClure's from using the TMs[2] text for these chapters. There seems to be only one choice between the equally distasteful hypotheses either that perhaps only one copy, the ribbon, had been made of TMs[2] (despite Stokes's determination to serialize the novel instead of Reynolds) or the alternative that the error involved sending to London not only the ribbon but also a carbon copy of the two chapters, only one having been made. The evidence is inexorable that the Stokes compositors had to revert to the file copy of TMs[1] in the absence of any copy of TMs[2] for Chapters v and vi, and that these chapters were never set up in the McClure proof-typesetting: the later-published *Buffalo Courier* did not receive copy for this section, whereas the *Chicago Times-Herald* seems to have been alerted by the missing chapter numbers to make a successful effort to secure a text,

[12] Although it is tempting to reverse the events and to take this deficiency in the McClure copy as the operative cause of the whole disruption, any hypothesis would be too complex for belief that required one to conjecture that the copy of TMs[1] sent to the United States was deficient at least for Chapter v and presumably for Chapter vi, and that TMs[1] chapters had to be sent to the United States to repair the gap but did not arrive in time for the syndicate to use. This would not work, for the *Chicago Times-Herald* did find copy from Stokes proof. However, the chief obstacle is the difficulty of proposing that in returning copy to England, Stokes substituted TMs[2], whereas there would have been no reason to make up such a typescript for the chapters if they had already been set in proof from TMs[1]. Moreover, the chapters are numbered continuously in TMs[2], showing that Chapters v and vi should have been present from the start.

which turned out to be the Stokes proofs for A1. Fortunately, whether McClure set up proofs for the rest of the novel from the identical copy of TMs² used by the Stokes compositors or from a hypothetical carbon, which would be the same, is of no textual consequence. Indeed, we know nothing of the relation of the syndication to Stokes except that the publisher must have provided the copy. There are at least three oddities about this syndication: first, the extremely brief interval between newspaper appearance and book publication; second, the small number of newspapers (perhaps no more than the identified two) that subscribed; and third, the fact that the newspaper copyright was made in Crane's name, not in McClure's. There is at least an outside chance that McClure, in the end, acted only as Stokes's agent, not as an independent purchaser; if so, it might not be beyond belief that Stokes had both book and newspaper proofs set up in the same shop and from the same copy of TMs² (and TMs¹ for Chapters v and vi), as Harper set up both magazine and book texts in their separate formats for Crane's "A Little Pilgrim."

The evidence for Chapter vi as set in N¹ from the A1 proofs is stronger than for Chapter v, but the anomaly that Chapter v was set from a copy of TMs¹ and Chapter vi from proofs is not to be seriously contemplated, and the same sort of copy must have served for both chapters. In Chapter vi five substantive variants [13] pair TMs¹⁻² against A1,N¹; this is the bedrock evidence that the N¹ copy had to derive from A1 and not from TMs¹ or TMs². In two substantive readings [14] A1 and N¹ agree with TMs² against TMs¹, the first supplying a necessary word omitted by TMs¹. The second reading is perhaps the result of a handwritten revision in the copy of TMs¹ sent to the United States but not transferred to the ribbon copy of TMs¹ for Heinemann, or is an editorial substitution by the Stokes editor.[15] Moreover, there are four substantive or semi-substantive readings [16] in which A1 and N¹ agree with TMs¹ against TMs². Although eight further substantive readings appear in N¹, Chapter vi, which are unique to it,[17] in this chapter no unique A1 substantive occurs in which N¹ does not join

[13] These are TMs¹⁻² *fine* (143.9) for A1,N¹ *a fine*; TMs¹⁻² *singular* (143.12) omit A1,N¹; TMs¹⁻² *murmured* (144.30) for A1,N¹ *answered*; TMs¹⁻² *still I* (144.38) for A1,N¹ *I still*; TMs¹⁻² *instructions* (146.22) for A1,N¹ *instruction*.

[14] These are TMs²,A1,N¹ *men* (143.3) omit TMs¹,E1(p²); TMs²,A1,N¹ *cried* (143.17) for TMs¹,E1(p²) *said*.

[15] The possible status of other A1 variants in the first eighteen chapters is discussed later.

[16] These are TMs¹,A1,N¹ *"Now (no ¶)* (143.21) for TMs² ¶ *"Now*; TMs¹,A1,N¹ *isn't* (143.27,28[twice]) for TMs² *ain't*; TMs¹,A1,N¹ *that is* (145.8) for TMs² *this is*; TMs¹,A1,N¹ *toward* (146.5) for TMs² *towards*.

[17] These are TMs¹⁻²,A1 *we* (143.24) for N¹ *you*; TMs¹⁻²,A1 *staff* (143.25) for N¹ *staffs*; TMs¹⁻²,A1 *I've* (144.8) for N¹ *I have*; TMs¹⁻²,A1 *this* (144.35) for N¹ *the*; TMs¹⁻²,A1 *was in hell* (144.36) for N¹ *would suspend*; TMs¹⁻²,A1 *impetuous* (145.17) for N¹ *imperious*; TMs¹⁻²,A1 *in* (145.22) for N¹ *of*; TMs¹⁻²,A1 *Then . . . it."* (146.6–14) omit N¹.

either against TMs^1 or TMs^2. Except for the eight unique N^1 variants, then, the agreement of A1 and N^1 in substantives is complete.

In Chapter v the opportunity to make comparisons with TMs^1 is lost, but an analogy can be drawn for its evidence by seeing what would have been available in Chapter vi if TMs^1 had also been missing there. In Chapter v eleven substantive or semi-substantive variants [18] separate paired $A1,N^1$ from TMs^2, and seven unique N^1 substantives occur.[19] Significantly, in contrast to the lack of such evidence in Chapter vi, there are three unique A1 substantive variants in Chapter v versus TMs^2 and N^1 agreement.[20] Instead of treating these as sophistication in the N^1 typesetting that fortuitously agrees with TMs^2, it is better to regard them, on the whole, as evidence that proof-changes were made in A1 away from copy at a point later than the setting of N^1 from A1 proofs, or else as A1 compositorial departures from copy. As the case stands, otherwise, the variants in Chapter v between A1 and N^1 (A1 deriving from lost TMs^1) on the one hand and TMs^2 on the other appear to be a mixture in TMs^2 of typist's variants [21] and of editorial markings made in America in the pages of TMs^1 in preparation for its transcription in TMs^2. In Chapter vi the presence both of TMs^1 and of TMs^2 provides a sharper distinction. If the textual hypothesis is correct, the five noted paired variants separating $A1,N^1$ from TMs^{1-2} can represent only A1 compositorial departures from copy, this leaving the four readings in which A1 and N^1 agree with TMs^1 against TMs^2 as TMs^2 typist's errors. These figures offer a higher proportion of A1 compositorial changes (and possibly of TMs^2 typist departures from copy) and a lower proportion of editorial changes in the TMs^1 by Stokes (at least in Chapter vi) than seems usual, a matter that is discussed later. On the whole, however, the evidence about the A1 editor and the compositors that is revealed in both chapters by the testimony of N^1 is of

[18] These are $A1,N^1$ *circled* (139.8) for TMs^2 *circled about*; $A1,N^1$ *no* ¶ (139.9,13) for TMs^2 ¶; $A1,N^1$ *with sarcasm* (139.11) for TMs^2 *sarcastically*; $A1,N^1$ *comforts* (139.13) for TMs^2 *comfort*; $A1,N^1$ *clinking* (140.9) for TMs^2 *clicking*; $A1,N^1$ *people* (140.22,23) for TMs^2 *folks*; $A1,N^1$ *Afterward* (140.27) for TMs^2 *Afterwards*; $A1,N^1$ *Coleman?"* (141.27) for TMs^2 *Coleman," he said*; $A1,N^1$ *don't* (142.10) for TMs^2 *wouldn't*.

[19] These are $A1,TMs^2$ *had* (139.21) omit N^1; $A1,TMs^2$ *a window* (139.27) for N^1 *his window*; $A1,TMs^2$ *chips* (140.9) for N^1 *cups*; $A1,TMs^2$ *Washurst* (140.12) for N^1 *Washington*; $A1,TMs^2$ *hell of a* (140.34–35) for N^1 *fine*; $A1,TMs^2$ *damned* (141.1) omit N^1; $A1,TMs^2$ *This . . . in.* (141.19–20) omit N^1. The misprint at 139.6, N^1 *order* for $A1,TMs^2$ *odor*, has not been counted.

[20] These are TMs^2,N^1 *brakeman's* (139.18) for A1 *brakemen's*; TMs^2,N^1 *at* (139.21) for A1 *in*; TMs^2,N^1 *fellow* (140.15) for A1 *a fellow*.

[21] Possibly two of these can be identified in the paragraphing of TMs^2 at 139.9 and 139.13 where no $A1,N^1$ paragraph occurs, and the Anglicized 'Afterwards' at 140.27 for $A1,N^1$ 'Afterward', Crane's usual form. These correspond to the difference in paragraphing in Chapter vi between TMs^1 and TMs^2 at 143.21 and the TMs^2 form 'towards' for TMs^1 'toward' (146.5).

considerable textual interest, and the single piece of evidence that N^1 confirms of authorial or editorial revision in the copy of TMs^1 sent to Stokes but not transferred to the Heinemann copy is particularly valuable.

The working hypothesis that TMs^2 was a professional American typing job of an editorially altered example of Cora's typescript (TMs^1) sent to Stokes and that TMs^2 was the printer's copy for A1 and the newspapers settles enough problems so that it is possible to move on to consider the authority of the different preserved documents and the ultimate question of the reasons for the selection of copy-texts. The main copy-text must of course be TMs^1, the Cora Crane typescript that was used as printer's copy for the Heinemann edition, E1. This was typed directly from holograph, or just possibly in some small part from Crane's dictation, and therefore it stands in the nearest relation of any preserved document to the lost manuscript. Its value is considerable. Other Cora typescripts of Crane's manuscripts have shown that on the whole she was a relatively faithful transcriber of his words, and indeed in the present typescript the number of times she x'd out false starts of errors or of eyeskips, the substitution of one word for another (her greatest sin), impossible spellings, and the like, gives us some indication that she was attempting to exercise real care. However, for better or for worse, when the results were not revised subsequently by Crane, what she typed is all that we have of a text with any authority: the evidence holds that TMs^2—the copy for A1 and the newspaper proof N—derives from TMs^1 and, with only a few possible exceptions, can have no authority whatever.

The question must be raised whether any of the numerous TMs^2 variants from TMs^1 either in Chapter VI, the only preserved sample for comparison of both, or as identified elsewhere by agreement of N^{1-2} with A1,[22] can be regarded as authoritative. If one disregards the easy cases where TMs^2 seems to have corrected TMs^1 errors, for instance, TMs^2 'surpassed' for TMs^1 'surpasses' (119.25) or TMs^2 'placed' for TMs^1 'places' (128.5), either on its own responsibility (editor's or typist's) or on a hypothetical Cora correction in TMs^1

[22] Since the McClure proof, N, the common source of N^{1-2}, was set from a copy of TMs^2, the readings in which N^{1-2} agree may be taken to reproduce the proof typesetting. When these coincide with the A1 typesetting, we may assume that we have recovered the TMs^2 reading whether or not it agrees with TMs^1. In cases of N^{1-2} agreement against A1, when N^{1-2} agree with TMs^1 the variant is revealed as an A1 compositorial error or later proof change; correspondingly, when N^{1-2} agree against A1 but A1 agrees with TMs^1, the N reading must be an error in the McClure typesetting. N^1 or N^2 variants from each other may be unique, in which case the uniqueness is evidence of an error by the individual newspaper compositor; or if a single newspaper agrees with A1 or with TMs^1 the line of derivation and that of deviation will ordinarily be revealed except in cases of independent sophistication when the agreeing newspaper might in fact have been set from copy that read with the other N variant.

not present in the preserved example, the only authoritative variants possible would be those that reproduce autograph revisions or corrections that might have been present in the copy of TMs[1] sent to the United States but had not been transferred to the copy destined for Heinemann. The evidence is clear that not all TMs[2] substantive variants (or even a moiety) can represent such autograph alterations. Although many TMs[2] variants are relatively neutral and could as readily result from revision as from corruption—such as A1+ 'at the moment' for TMs[1] 'at that moment' (114.1), or 'me to flirt' for TMs[1] 'to see me flirt' (148.11)—some represent real errors of judgment in an attempt to 'improve' Crane's text or else simple misunderstanding and an ill-advised attempt at correction. Examples are A1+ 'plight of' for TMs[1] 'plight' in a cablegram (161.14) or 'at all' for 'all' in another cable (178.36); the typist(?) error 'actually' for 'acutely' (170.4); 'he' for '[1]they' (170.14); 'tail of the squadron' for 'tails of the squadrons' (172.32); 'newspapers' for 'newspaper' (179.1); 'American' for 'the American' (179.7); the omission of 'other' (188.9) and of 'himself' (189.8); the misunderstanding 'place' for 'plane' (191.22); the error 'natives' for 'native horses' (210.17) and of 'ride it' for 'ride' (210.10); the substitution of 'shape' for 'shade' (225.35), of 'by' for 'on' (260.25), or of 'fiercely' for 'fearfully' (263.10). These and many more would seem in some cases, though not in all, to go beyond a typist's usual departures from copy and to represent the actual application of an editor to the marking of the copy of TMs[1] that was to be transcribed as TMs[2]. Moreover, although the possibility always remains that here and there a plausible reading in the first eighteen chapters represents a lost Crane revision, the number of variants is far too great for A1 as a whole to be considered more authoritative in its substantives than TMs[1].

Considerations exist, however, that suggest that some of the A1+ variants could in theory be authoritative. It is curious that the blue ribbon TMs[1] copy of the first eighteen chapters given to Heinemann contains only one interlined verbal addition that might be rated as a possible revision instead of a simple correction (and this is not in Crane's hand), whereas eighty-nine of Crane's own revisions or corrections are found in the carbon TMs[1] pages that start with Chapter XIX. On the other hand, a form of mechanical correction of missing letters and punctuation at the ends of lines caused by the lack of a margin release, and also of some of the more egregious errors within the lines, are corrected by Cora in Chapters I–XVIII and equally in XIX–XXXI. Hence two layers of correction and revision are present. The first was made by Cora in pencil in Chapters I–XVIII of the ribbon typescript (less the inserted leaves from TMs[2]) and as carbon impressions from her similar correction on the lost ribbon copy in the carbon leaves of the typescript starting with Chapter XIX. These alterations represent Cora's attempt to correct the more obvious defects of her typescript and are without authority. The second layer was made in blue ink (except for four alterations in black ink on fols. 192–193) and are demonstrably in Crane's hand. Although some represent correction of mechanical errors, the majority are revisions.[23] These authorial alterations make their initial appearance in TMs[1] only with Chapter XIX, which marks the start of the second batch of typescript sent to Reynolds and also of the use of the carbon of TMs[1] as Heinemann's printer's copy. It is noteworthy that with a few exceptions, the holograph ink changes in the TMs[1] carbon of Chapters XIX–XXXI are also found in the text of A1+ derived from TMs[2]; hence they must have been transferred in some manner to the ribbon copy of TMs[1] sent to the United States.

Two important questions are raised by this evidence. First, was the Heinemann carbon of TMs[1] the primary document that Crane looked over starting with Chapter XIX, so that the ribbon copy assumed to have been sent to Stokes had these authoritative readings transferred to it from the preserved carbon; or second, was some other copy (presumably for Stokes) the primary one, so that the preserved Heinemann carbon contains alterations that Crane transferred to it from this other copy, in which case by accident he might have omitted some changes that he had originally made? According to the first possibility, all A1+ variants from the typed or altered text of the carbon in Chapters XIX–XXXI would almost automatically become unauthoritative; in the second, some A1+ variants—if they could be identified—might have a claim to authority in this area on the hypothesis that they represent original alterations accidently not transferred to the carbon. In this connection a distinction must be made between Crane's ink changes and Cora's carbon-impressed corrections which would have been identical in both copies.

The evidence suggests that the first option is the correct one and that the carbon of Chapters XIX–XXXI ultimately sent to Heinemann was the original authorially corrected copy from which the changes were transferred to the copy for Stokes. For example, three of Crane's ink changes were not, in fact, transferred to the copy for America. In Chapter XXI at 251.17 Crane altered TMs[1] typed 'pulling and pucking' in blue ink to 'puling and puking', which of course is the reading of E1 set from this copy. But in A1 and N[1-2] the reprinting of the original error demonstrates that this change in the carbon was never transferred to the typescript copy from which TMs[2] was made. Exactly the same situation holds in Chapter XXIX at 308.22 where the typed error 'past' was altered in black ink to 'pass', the reading of

---

[23] As samples, one may note 'comic' for TMs[1] 'ludicrous' (252.3), 'hurrying' for 'moving' (259.8); the supplying of missing 'thought of' (259.28), and 'even' (276.26); and the substitution of 'betrothal' for 'engagement' (324.7) and of 'played in' for 'touching' (328.33). The full roster is given in the List of Emendations.

E1 (and by compositorial correction of N^2), but 'past' appears in A1 and N^1. Finally, at 327.11 in Chapter XXXI Crane's interlined correction of 'parson' for typed 'person' was corrected on its merits by A1 but TMs^2, on the evidence of 'person' in N^{1-2}, read uncorrected 'person'. These readings show that any loss in transfer was made in the copy of the typescript sent to Stokes, and thus that the Heinemann carbon was the original marked by Crane. We cannot be sure whether Crane or Cora copied the original revisions from preserved TMs^1 into the typescript that stands in back of TMs^2. Knowing Crane's working habits, one may safely conjecture that it was Cora and thus at least one may conjecturally remove the slight possibility that if it had been Crane he could have inserted fresh revisions during the process even while inadvertently omitting others. It follows that if we respect the available evidence and take it that Crane reviewed the Heinemann carbon of TMs^1 and from this corrected and revised carbon Cora transferred the alterations (although not impeccably) to the ribbon copy for Stokes, an editor need expect no authoritative variants from preserved TMs^1 to have appeared for Chapters XIX–XXXI in the copy sent to the United States which was retyped as TMs^2 and served as printer's copy for A1 and N; thus any emendation of the TMs^1 text in this area accepted from the American prints can be only in the nature of necessary but unauthoritative correction.

For Chapters I–XVIII the case is by no means so simple because the bibliographical evidence present for Chapters XIX–XXXI is wanting that would support a firm decision. If the copy intended for Heinemann had always been that revised by Crane, the preserved ribbon copy for I–XVIII should have been altered, but in fact no signs of Crane's hand are present in the first eighteen chapters of TMs^1 nor do Cora's alterations (except for the doubtful 'that' at 165.21) offer any support for a hypothesis that she was transferring Crane's changes from another copy, since they are corrections only and not the revisions which distinguish most of Crane's alterations in Chapters XIX–XXXI. Because Crane read over and made a number of alterations in the second batch of typescript beginning with Chapter XIX it need not follow necessarily that he did so for the first eighteen chapters of the initial typing. However, the possibility must be considered that although authorial changes are not found in the ribbon section of the Heinemann TMs^1, they could have been present in the carbon of the first eighteen chapters sent to Stokes and thus they have been preserved among the A1+ variants from TMs^1.

In this important textual question what evidence may be adduced is obscure and even conflicting; nevertheless, some tentative relations between the bits and pieces may be perceived. The figure of 47,000 words Crane reported to Reynolds on March 16 agrees with a letter to Pinker the next day apologizing for the delay in sending him the first half of the book on the ground that he must get a copy off to Reynolds. The delay between March 16 and the mailing of about 46,000 words of Chapters I–XVIII to Reynolds on March 25 was probably due to the typing of the last four or five chapters, certainly not of the whole manuscript. By March 25 he had written 53,000 words and Cora seems to have typed these, and more, by March 30 when Chapters XIX–XXII were sent off. It may be that Crane wanted Reynolds to receive as many chapters as possible in the first installment so that there would be enough narrative to interest prospective purchasers in the serial rights, and he did not wish to interrupt the typing in order to prepare a copy for Pinker. (He seems never to have had much hope that Pinker could sell the serial rights in England.) His promise to Reynolds of 10,000 words a week was kept for Chapters XIX–XXII, most of which had been written when the promise was made, however. After that point the letters to Reynolds are not preserved (save for the undated one about Stokes trying for the serialization) and the evidence becomes obscure. For example, if Reynolds had been sent more copy in April, it is difficult to understand why as late as April 25 Cora dispatched to Pinker only Chapters I–XXII, which had been prepared for Reynolds as early as March 25. On the other hand, there is the fact that when Heinemann received Chapter I the note 'Active Service by Stephen Crane' was made on the typescript of the first page but no other note until the same formula appeared on the initial page of Chapter xxv, a clear sign—so far as one can tell—that Heinemann was sent Chapters I–XXIV as the first consignment and Chapters xxv–xxxI as the second. This suggests the possibility that at some unknown date Chapters XXIII–XXIV had been mailed to Reynolds but that a delay could have occurred thereafter. It cannot be determined whether the fact that Pinker received only the first twenty-two chapters on April 25 means that the following chapters had not been typed and sent to Reynolds until a later date, although it is a fair presumption. It may be an acceptable conjecture, however, that the consignment of copy to Heinemann and to Stokes was simultaneous, in which case Stokes, like Heinemann, would have received two batches of copy at different times, certainly after April 25 and perhaps considerably later. The mixup about Chapter v must have taken place after TMs^2 was prepared but before the McClure typesetting started. Since the McClure copyright on July 26 was almost necessarily entered on completion of the syndicate typesetting, it is likely that the actual sale, or lease arrangement, was negotiated perhaps as late as June, but whether on the basis of the first twenty-four chapters or of the whole novel cannot be known. Murky as this evidence is, it suggests that Crane relaxed after the mailing of Chapters XIX–XXII to Reynolds on March 25 and that he may not have set to work to complete the novel until a date later than April 25, Chapters XXIII and XXIV perhaps having been in draft but not typed and therefore in a state to be readily prepared when book copy was required. Given the time needed for Stokes to receive copy across the Atlantic, to edit TMs[1], and to have it typed into TMs[2] before the McClure typesetting could begin that was finished by July 26, Crane may not have completed the novel before the end of May. It would seem unlikely that either Heinemann or Stokes would have been sent copy before Pinker received his twenty-two chapters on April 25; and if the evidence of the notes that Heinemann applied to Chapters I and xxv is to hold, some interval after April 25 would have been necessary for the revision and typing of Chapters xxiii and xxiv, and then certainly for the composition of xxv–xxxi and their typing.

The interest that attaches to this conjectural reconstruction is more than academic, for there may be some bearing on the vexed question of the parts of the typescript that Crane revised and therefore on the authority of certain A1+ readings in the first eighteen chapters.[24] The blue ink revisions in the Heinemann carbon of TMs[1] begin in Chapter xix and extend into xxxi. Thus they bridge the gap between the copy in Chapters xix–xxii sent to Reynolds on March 25 and the rest, including the two parts of the Heinemann copy distinguished by the notation on Chapter xxv. This evidence suggests that Crane did not make these revisions as the result of a single review of Chapters xix–xxxi but that he looked over the Heinemann TMs[1] carbon at least twice, and perhaps even three times if he also had the changes made in the copy of Chapters xix–xxii sent to Reynolds. For several reasons it seems probable that he had. An attempt to reconstruct the writing-in of the blue ink revisions admits only two main hypotheses: (1) Crane did not revise copy for Chapters xix–xxxi until the respective typescripts for Heinemann and Stokes were complete and being prepared for book publication, or (2) his revision was a continuous process as Cora typed chapters, or at least as the respective batches were being prepared for mailing. The first has a tempting plausibility, and it would account for the fact that Stokes's edition printed the known revisions as well as Heinemann's. The vital question is raised, however, why if Crane delayed revision until the time to prepare book copy, the revisions are found in the Heinemann TMs[1] only in the carbon section beginning with Chapter xix and not in the ribbon copy of I–xviii, the very section representing the first lot of copy to be mailed to Reynolds on March 17. Since Crane was prepared to revise Chapters xix–xxiv at a different time

[24] A complication in assessing the authority of A1 variants when they cannot be identified, as in Chapters xix–xxxi, by Crane's autograph is that Cora's corrections of TMs[1] when they went beyond mechanical matters may not all have reflected Crane's wishes. For example, at 222.29 her pencil alteration of 'upon' to 'on' could be suspicious, for 'upon' is more characteristic of Crane and 'on' may reflect only her own notions of idiom. See also the Textual Note to 171.37.

from xxv–xxxi, no satisfactory reason offers itself why—if he were preparing the typescript for publication—he should have started at xix and not at i, for there is every evidence that i–xxiv were submitted to Heinemann as a unit. One seems forced into the second alternative, that his revision was a relatively continuous process, at least as copy was prepared for dispatch. If this is so, then Chapters xix–xxii were revised as a unit, probably xxiii–xxiv as another, and xxv–xxxi as a third, but never the whole at one time as a single preparation for the books.

The all-important question then arises whether in this same manner, or any other, Crane revised Chapters i–xviii before their dispatch to Reynolds and perhaps to Stokes. Again, two major alternatives suggest themselves: (1) Crane never did revise these early chapters in preparation for their mailing to Reynolds, or (2) revision was in fact made but, on the evidence, was not transferred to the Heinemann ribbon copy of TMs[1]. Unfortunately the choice between these options is not so clear-cut as between the earlier two. It might be possible to argue that if Crane had not worked over the typescript of the eighteen chapters until he received Reynolds' affirmative response to his March 2 letter, he would have had no time to go through and revise the typescript before it went off on March 25, the interval between the two dates suggesting that he had the copy bundled up with little or no delay immediately on hearing from Reynolds. Thereafter, one would need to argue, he had more leisure and could engage himself to revision. Such a view cannot be rebutted but it has its weaknesses. Since it seems reasonable to assume that he revised Chapters xix–xxii before mailing them to Reynolds, the lapse of five days between the two sendings does not suggest much spare time, although if he had read over every chapter as Cora typed it, the burden would not have been very great. On the other hand, it is difficult to reconcile his sudden zeal for assuring himself of the correctness of the copy starting with Chapter xix with a complete indifference to the state of the first eighteen chapters in the ribbon copy, a problem that is not confined to this first alternative, however. Moreover, although he may have delayed revision and then been caught short, as suggested as a possibility, it should be considered that after his first letter of March 2 he was expecting to send copy to New York immediately if Reynolds accepted the proposals for serialization, and he had had plenty of time between that date and March 25 to prepare the copy. (One may assume that Cora's independent correction of her typescript in all copies was made on a current basis, on the evidence that her corrections for Chapters xix–xxxi were made through carbon paper.) The anomaly might be reconciled if one were to speculate that before he began to mail copy and assumed the burden of a 10,000-word-per-week deadline (which, however, did not last very long), he had more leisure to revise the manuscript before typing, whereas after Chapter

XVIII he may have felt the need for a final look at the typescript since he had had less opportunity to rework the manuscript.[25] If this attitude held it might explain the lack of attention to the earlier chapters in the Heinemann ribbon copy (and hence in the Stokes carbon), although the evidence does not, in fact, support any hypothesis that he revised in the typescript what through haste he had neglected in the manuscript.[26]

The second alternative hypothesizes a correction and revision in the earlier Chapters I–XVIII, similar to that in XIX–XXXI, but one that for some reason was not transferred to the Heinemann ribbon copy. It may seem natural to conjecture that as the typescript of the earlier chapters was prepared and corrected by Cora, Crane would give it some attention to set right overlooked typing errors (unless he was so lazy as to trust Cora's own correction implicitly) and to take the opportunity to improve any readings that caught his attention on review. If he had done so, the related question arises why such alterations were not transferred to the Heinemann printer's copy and also whether, on the contrary, they had been inserted in the carbon of TMs[1] from which Stokes's TMs[2] printer's copy was derived. The only reason that may be advanced for a failure to mark up the Heinemann copy (already corrected by Cora) with Crane's own hypothetical revisions is that they were not transferred from the carbon he had used because when the time came to prepare copy of Chapters I–XXIV for Heinemann the revised carbon for I–XVIII was no longer available and Crane (then under pressure to complete the novel) did not trouble to engage himself to an independent rereading and revision.[27] If unavailability is the answer, the circumstances need reconstruction. Again, there would seem to be only one possibility—that the carbon containing the revisions had been inadvertently sent to the United States before the need to transfer its markings was recognized. In theory this unique marked copy could have been that mailed to Reynolds or to Stokes, but the conjectural reconstruction of events (and especially the assignment of Chapters I–XXIV as the first lot of

[25] The manuscript of *The O'Ruddy* shows not only revision made currently during the course of the writing but also alterations on rereading the pages after initial inscription.

[26] One may remark, however, that he should have seen that his confidence in the typing and in Cora's correction of it was misplaced, since in Chapters XIX–XXXI the alterations that he made were sometimes the correction of her mistakes (chiefly the addition of skipped words) as well as true revisions. Crane's wish to revise his copy must not be overemphasized. Revision seems to have been purely incidental to his going through the pages, and even with correction in mind he was so careless that he missed a number of serious errors.

[27] Although it is not proper evidence in the present case, one may remark that on other occasions Crane never attempted to insure that his short stories were in an equally revised state for publication both in the United States and in England by sending late alterations to one or other country for insertion after the dispatch of the original copy.

copy for both book publishers) almost requires the copy to have gone to Reynolds. That is, we know from Crane's March 17 letter to Pinker that he wanted to get copy to Reynolds before all else, the reason clearly being that Reynolds was to sell the serial rights with the utmost speed. Preparation of copy for Reynolds that delayed a sending to Pinker should have involved more than the packaging and ought to have included a review, with handwritten alterations, either by Cora or by both Crane and Cora. The interval between his receipt of Reynolds' affirmative response to his March 2 letter and the mailing of copy on March 25 could scarcely have been more than a day or two. It follows that if on March 17 he was already preparing copy for Reynolds before receipt of Reynolds' letter, and if his alterations had not been transferred to the other copies, and this fact had been forgotten, it would have been quite possible for Cora inadvertently to send off on March 25 the only copy that contained Crane's revisions.[28]

If these considerations are at all valid, it then follows that the hypothetical revisions in I–XVIII could not have been present in Stokes's copy of these chapters any more than in Heinemann's unless for some reason Reynolds had turned over to Stokes his own copy of marked TMs^1 in time for the typing of TMs^2. That such a transfer of copy from Reynolds to Stokes would occur is problematic in the extreme. Reynolds had no connection with Stokes's ownership of the book rights, and since Stokes could scarcely have relied on his copy from Reynolds instead of from Crane directly, no need existed for Stokes to want the Reynolds carbon or to be in a position to demand it. For all we know, until Stokes concluded arrangements with McClure, presumably after receipt of the first batch of copy, Reynolds was continuing his efforts to sell the serialization rights, and the typescript would have been in other hands for examination.[29] No connection can be traced between the Reynolds and the Stokes copies

[28] The alternative, that this single marked copy went to Stokes before its revisions could be transferred to the Heinemann typescript, is less attractive. No evidence exists that Stokes was rushed copy at the time of the mailing to Reynolds, and it is a natural assumption that the book copy for England and America would have been retained and consigned at the same time. If the evidence of the new heading marked on Chapter xxv of the Heinemann carbon is valid, Stokes would have received Chapters I–XXIV in one lot at the time Heinemann was given copy for the start of typesetting. If this is so, it would be considerably more difficult to explain the inadvertent dispatch of revised Chapters I–XVIII to Stokes but the transfer to Stokes's ribbon copy of XIX–XXIV of the autograph revisions in these chapters from the Heinemann carbon. The break between nonrevision and revision in the Heinemann typescript occurring after Chapter XVIII, the last chapter to be included in the initial sending to Reynolds, argues powerfully for the hypothesis that Reynolds was inadvertently mailed the only copy of the carbon that Crane had revised—providing, of course, that he had indeed revised I–XVIII as he was later to work over XIX–XXXI.

[29] That Stokes did not use the Reynolds TMs^1 to send to McClure is sufficiently demonstrated by the N readings without the evidence that Chapters V–VI were missing in the McClure copy.

of TMs[1]; hence if Reynolds were in fact sent the revised carbon, these alterations were lost and appeared neither in A1 nor in E1.

All logical possibilities, it would seem, end in the same conclusion. If Crane never did revise Chapters I–XVIII, then of course the variants in A1 have no authority in comparison with the TMs[1] readings. If he did revise the chapters, whether at one time for book publication or at intervals as Cora typed them, no apparent reason exists to suppose that the alterations were transferred to the Stokes carbon but not to the Heinemann ribbon copy. If they found their way, as seems plausible, to the Reynolds carbon, they were never turned over to Stokes and thus A1 has no readings with peculiar authority as against the overall authority of Heinemann's TMs[1].[30] This is the working hypothesis the transmissional evidence suggests. It is now incumbent to examine the evidence of the text itself in Chapters I–XVIII as against that of XIX–XXXI to see if the variant readings on the whole concur with the working hypothesis. If serious reservations develop that certain of the A1+ readings betray Crane's revising hand, an editor will need to consider whether he should emend the TMs[1] copy-text conservatively to admit such conjecturally authoritative readings even if he is in the uncomfortable position of having no hypothesis to account for their presence in A1. On the other hand, if the evidence is ambiguous, uncertain, and subject to the interpretation that the A1 readings are editorial,[31] one may be justified in retaining the working hypothesis of transmission that leads to the rejection of all A1 variants except those that are convenient to adopt as corrections of TMs[1] errors.

The analysis may well start with the substantive authoritative alterations in Chapters XIX–XXXI attested by Crane's hand in blue ink. These forty-eight changes occur in a space of seventy-six extant typescript pages of an original eighty-seven. The alterations are divided between twenty additions to the text, twenty-four substitutions of letters, words, or phrases, and four deletions. However, of the twenty additions, eleven insert words or a final plural 's' that were obviously omitted in error by Cora, or which were inserted in a space she had left when she could not read the text, and so must be classed as corrections,[32] leaving only nine that at the most may be called re-

---

[30] Except, of course, when TMs[1] is wanting, as in Chapter v and in the missing pages later in the typescript. In the first case TMs[2] shares equal authority with A1; in the second, E1 is one stage closer to TMs[1] authority than is A1.

[31] Any reading unique to A1 must be accounted unauthoritative and the result of the compositor's or proofreader's alterations. Only A1 variants confirmed by either N[1] or N[2], or preferably both, can be certain to derive from TMs[2] and thus from a hypothetically author-revised copy of TMs[1].

[32] These are SC(c) *things* (235.16) for TMs(u) *thing*; SC(c) *was* (248.7) omit TMs(u); SC(c) *Nora . . . odd* (249.1) omit TMs(u); SC(c) *sprung* (250.15) omit TMs(u); SC(c) *not* (260.27; 261.7) omit TMs(u); SC(c) *as* (276.7) omit TMs(u); SC(c) *so* (309.36) omit TMs(u); SC(c) *kept* (311.24)

visions,[33] and it seems probable that some of these were actually corrections of Cora's eyeskips. Of the twenty-four substitutions, fourteen repair typing errors and misreadings or Crane's own mistakes and are therefore simple corrections.[34] The remaining ten appear to be stylistic revisions.[35] Of the four deletions, one removes a word repeated in error in the typescript and three are most probably stylistic revisions.[36] Taking the substitutions as one form of alteration and the additions and deletions together as another, the substantive variants that result are almost equally balanced between corrections and revisions (with some slight tilt toward corrections), and in these chapters no more than twenty-two true revisions (very likely fewer) are present of readings that on the face of it would in their original form have aroused no critical concern. The revisory substitutions are mostly on a one-for-one basis, like *glazed* for *dazed* or *hurrying* for *moving*. Such a change as *betrothal* for *engagement* seems to be due to an attempt at precision of usage, almost in the nature of a correction, like the substitution of *Wainwrights* for *Wainwright party* (since in fact the look was *at*, not *from*, only the husband and wife), or the change of *repeated* to *responded* when the words in question had not been spoken previously. The change of *his interlocutors* to *her* removes a stilted expression, the substitution of *played in* for *touching* sharpens detail, but the reasons for altering *ludicrous* to *comic*, for example, remain obscure. The additions that are revisions may sharpen detail as in

---

omit TMs(u); SC(c) *trays* (316.34) for TMs(u) *tray*; SC(c) *mood* (321.20) omit TMs(u).

[33] These are SC(c) *grey* (238.14) omit TMs(u); SC(c) *even* (238.24) omit TMs(u); SC(c) *so* (238.29) omit TMs(u); SC(c) *a base suspicion,* (241.12–13) omit TMs(u); SC(c) *thought of* (259.28) omit TMs(u); SC(c) *he received . . . neck* (260.13–14) omit TMs(u); SC(c) *thus* (261.22) omit TMs(u); SC(c) *even* (276.26) omit TMs(u); SC(c) *to* (322.9) omit TMs(u).

[34] These are SC(c) *rascal. A* (237.8) for TMs(u) *rascale a*; SC(c) *doleful. She* (247.13) for TMs(u) *doleful she*; SC(c) *devotedly* (251.10) for TMs(u) *devoted*; SC(c) *talk. If* (251.25) for TMs(u) *talk if*; SC(c) *glowed* (251.27) for TMs(u) *glowered*; SC(c) *hum* (252.8) for TMs(u) *line*; SC(c) *resented* (253.12) for TMs(u) *resentful*; SC(c) *it. Even* (253.22) for TMs(u) *it even*; SC(c) *note* (256.8) for TMs(u) *not*; SC(c) *far to* (256.15) for TMs(u) *for*; SC(c) *the* (276.14) for TMs(u) *her*; SC(c) *has* (321.29) for TMs(u) *had*; SC(c) *parson* (327.11) for TMs(u) *person*.

[35] These are SC(c) *her* (247.2) for TMs(u) *his interlocutors*; SC(c) *comic* (252.3) for TMs(u) *ludicrous*; SC(c) *Wainwrights* (256.30) for TMs(u) *Wainwright party*; SC(c) *glazed* (257.10) for TMs(u) *dazed*; SC(c) *hurrying* (259.8) for TMs(u) *moving*; SC(c) *a* (260.33) for TMs(u) *the*; SC(c) *responded* (278.11) for TMs(u) *repeated*; SC(c) *cried* (282.7) for TMs(u) *said*; SC(c) *betrothal* (324.7) for TMs(u) *engagement*; SC(c) *played in* (328.33) for TMs(u) *touching*.

[36] These are SC(c) *others* (240.12) for TMs(u) *the others*; SC(c) *Coke* (250.16) for TMs(u) *Coke Coke*; SC(c) *indicating the Wainwrights* (259.11) for TMs(u) *indicating to the Wainwrights*; SC(c) *coffee* (294.6) for TMs(u) *coffees*.

the prefixing of *grey* to *rag* or slightly increase the force as in the two insertions of *even*. Some may be idiomatic, as the addition of *so* and possibly of *thought of*. Only two are at all extensive, and even so one merely inserts a simple rhetorical repetition for emphasis in *a base suspicion*, and the other a clause to include a detail that would justify the later description that Marjory wiped the blood from Coleman and bemoaned his bruises. Of the deletions, the excision of *the* removed the implication that all of the other students reproached Coleman; the deletion of *to* in *indicating to the Wainwrights* removed an ambiguity; and the removal of the final 's' of *coffees* probably corrected the typist's eyeskip to the series of plurals immediately following.

Crane did not, in fact, confine himself to substantive alterations, but concerned himself with an extensive correction of Cora's faults in the accidentals. He added ink strokes to fourteen periods and one comma to change them to exclamation points. Cora had faithfully copied his own characteristic inscription of *don't*, *won't*, and *can't* without the apostrophe; he added necessary apostrophes to the ten such words that he observed. He added quotation marks on four necessary occasions, inserted a comma thrice, a semicolon once, and an end-of-the-line hyphen for a broken word once. Twenty-four times he corrected Cora's mechanical errors in typing, a few misreadings, and various of her misspellings. To the total of forty-eight substantive alterations of various kinds, then, he added sixty-seven corrections of more or less mechanical or formal errors in the accidentals. In addition to these blue ink changes there are four black ink notations on fols. 192–193. Only one of these changes represents a complete word, and while the hand is not unlike Crane's, it could equally well be Cora's. However, if these alterations are Cora's, they are her only ink corrections in this second half of the typescript. Her medium in this carbon portion is pencil, or a carbon impression from the lost ribbon copy, and since she used pencil exclusively for the first eighteen (ribbon) chapters it is a fair assumption that she continued this practice for those chapters which survive only as carbon impressions in the latter portion of the typescript. Although the evidence is unsatisfactory, the editor leans toward the view that for these two folios black ink happened to be more readily available to Crane (there are no blue ink changes on fols. 192–193); nevertheless, as there is some possible doubt, these four notations have not been included in any of the preceding footnotes or counts. When assessing the possibility of authorial alterations in A1+ the evidence must be confined to the substantives, including paragraphing and syntactical adjustments such as the formation of two sentences from one or the running together of two separate sentences.

In these same chapters, in addition to about twenty necessary substantive corrections (mostly substitutions but a few additions),

A1+ contain ninety-one substantive variants which in the nature of
the case can have no claim to authority. The largest group consists
of thirty-seven omissions, usually of single words but several times of
sentences. This is followed by twenty-eight verbal substitutions, then
by thirteen additions, four transpositions, and finally by eleven outright errors or obvious misunderstandings, all of these substitutions.
We cannot assume that every variant represents an editorial marking
in the TMs[1] copy, for the typist of TMs[2] must be considered. Ordinarily there is no way of distinguishing the source, but the peculiarities of the textual transmission of Chapter VI in which both TMs[1]
and TMs[2] are preserved enables a clear discrimination. In this short
chapter five substantive variants occur in which A1 (and N[1]) agree
against TMs[1-2] (see footnote 13). These we may discard from consideration as A1 compositorial departures from its lost TMs[1] copy,
since TMs[2] (derived from the lost marked TMs[1] copy) agrees with the
preserved TMs[1]. On the contrary, four substantive variants occur in
which A1, TMs[1] (its copy here), and N[1] (from A1 proof) agree
against TMs[2] (see footnote 16). Since A1 was set from the same lost
edited example of TMs[1] that independently produced TMs[2], variation
between A1 (and N[1]) and TMs[2] must represent typist's changes in
making up TMs[2]. These four variants break down to one unique
difference in paragraphing (143.21), one semi-substantive use of
towards for *toward* (146.5), three substitutions of *ain't* for *isn't* in
dialogue (143.27,28 [*twice*]), and the substitution of *this* for *that*
in the clause *if you think that is the way that suits you* (145.8–9),
evidently an attempt to avoid the repetition of *that*. The sample is
too small to be extrapolated with any confidence, but the two clear-
cut cases of verbal substitution in six typescript pages if applied to
the seventy-nine pages preserved in Chapters XIX–XXXI would yield
an expectancy of about twenty-six typist substitutions in this area as
against a total of about forty-eight variants of this type, including
errors as well as corrections. Although no examples of typist's omissions or additions are found in this chapter, the appearance of two
substitutions—one the triple change of *isn't* to *ain't* going well
beyond the function of a typist—has some general significance. Yet
how untrustworthy statistics may be when based on such a small
sample can be illustrated by the fact that in Chapter VI only one
possible example can be detected of substantive annotation in the
lost Stokes TMs[1]. At 143.17 TMs[1] (and the E1 proof) reads *said* but
TMs[2], and A1 and N[1], print *cried*. Since for this reading the Stokes
example of TMs[1] was the printer's copy for A1, it is clear that the
only way *cried* could have got into TMs[2] and also have been reproduced by A1 was that it was marked as a substitute for *said* in the
Stokes carbon of TMs[1]. If in turn this one example were extrapolated
to cover the typescript pages of XIX–XXXI, it would produce no more
than twelve or thirteen expectable editorial annotations, a figure that

is nonsensical when the actual total of verbal substitutions is considered over and above the extrapolated statistics for the typist. All one can say is that in the regrettably small amount of text represented by Chapter VI, both typist and editorial substitutions for words in the TMs[1] copy may be perceived, each of a superficially revisory nature not to be assessed as simple corrections.

It is now useful to compare the unauthoritative variants identified in Chapters XIX–XXXI with the complete set of substantive differences for Chapters I–XVIII (less Chapter VI) that can be distinguished on the evidence of N from those unique variants of A1 that would have arisen either from compositorial departure from copy or from proofreader's alterations. These variants, 214 in all, consist of 101 verbal substitutions, 60 omissions, 46 additions, and 7 transpositions. When N in one or the other of its witnesses agrees with A1 in a variant from TMs[1], ordinarily the variant can be taken as a reading from TMs[2]. These TMs[2] variants will be a combination of typist's alterations and of markings in the TMs[1] copy used by the typist. Whether the markings give evidence of editorial or of authorial origin is the crucial question. At the start one may conjecturally discard the omissions found in A1+. In Chapters XIX–XXXI although only two autograph changes deleted any word as a revision, there were more than thirty-six such omissions, ranging from single words to phrases and even to sentences. Some of these may have resulted from typist errors,[37] but most, one may suppose, were editorial improvements. On this evidence, one would expect to find only two or three possible authorial omissions in the first eighteen chapters that might be assigned to Crane's revision.[38] Even more certainty can be assumed in rejecting all cases of transpositions, as at 114.15–16, 121.8, and 149.28.[39] Again, Crane himself in the later chapters made no transpositional adjustments although three are found among the unauthoritative variants.[40] In general, some of Crane's idiosyncratic distortions of word order were always fair game for alteration

[37] In Chapter VI the typist did not omit any reading, but she could not have been impeccable in this matter and one may notice that at 143.12 in this chapter the compositor skipped a word.

[38] As in the later chapters, Chapters I–XVIII show a constant pattern of omitted single words and phrases. The more important larger omissions corresponding to those, later, at 301.10 and 315.17–18, are 133.27–28, 178.4–5, 187.16–17, and 225.7–8.

[39] The only transposition to give one pause is at 190.14 in which TMs[1] is altered in A1+ to produce a typical Crane split infinitive, *but the dragoman was able to not understand it* where TMs[1] had *not to understand*. But since the A1 change is also found in E1 independently, it would seem that both agents "corrected" the order and it is unlikely that Crane marked the shift either in Stokes's TMs[1] or in the E1 proof.

[40] These occur at 235.5, 297.2, and 314.4. Whether they were editorial or typist errors cannot be determined, of course. In Chapter VI at 144.38 the compositor transposed two words.

throughout his career. This leaves over fifty additions and perhaps half again as many substitutions to consider as the only variation where Crane's hand has any chance of being detected.

If statistical extrapolation could give us a hint, among the substitutions one might expect perhaps as many as twenty-seven authoritative readings in the first eighteen chapters if Crane had actually worked over the copy. However, in the later chapters slightly over half of Crane's changes of this order were simple corrections of error, which in the initial chapters could scarcely be distinguished from similar editorial or typist correction; and thus, statistically, perhaps no more than thirteen to fourteen revisions might be expected. From the mass of evidence one can immediately discard the unassignable differences between singulars and plurals, many of which are manifest errors in A1, such as TMs[1] *illustrations* but A1+ *illustration* (130.13), *tails of the squadrons* but *tail of the squadron* (172.32), *newspaper* but *newspapers* (179.1), or *protests* but *protest* (197.35). A few are neutral and though acceptable in A1+ are probable errors, like TMs[1] *deck* but A1+ *decks* (147.11), *woods* but *wood* (195.31), or *shoulders* but *shoulder* (201.13). A pattern of pronominal changes in A1+ is not typical of Crane's revisions and often exhibits misunderstanding of the text or simple error, like TMs[1] *this* but A1+ *his* (114.35; 138.15), *his* but *this* (170.18), *he* but *we* (127.8), *its* but *his* (130.34), *they* but *he* (170.14); or alterations between demonstratives and articles like TMs[1] *at that* but A1+ *at the* (114.1), *the* but A1+ *this* (126.9; 198.6). Similarly, small differences in connectives are unassignable but probably show error in A1, such as TMs[1] *or* but A1+ *and* (127.25), or other minor changes like TMs[1] *upon* but A1+ *on* (113.6), *by* but *of* (119.5), *that* but *which* (167.29), *to* but *on to* (174.29), or *to* but *in* (206.29). Neutral changes of tense not properly corrective are nonevidential, such as TMs[1] *has* but A1+ *had* (132.11), *is* but *was* (166.23), or such variants as TMs[1] *began* but A1 *begun* (198.4) or *were* but *was* (201.12). The occasional introduction or reduction of contractions is quite unassignable, like TMs[1] *is not* but A1+ *isn't* (116.33; 117.14), *need not* but *needn't* (121.14), or the reverse with *You're* but *You are* (161.7).[41] Small grammatical distinctions like TMs[1] *unmistakably* but A1+ *unmistakable* (124.3), *courier* but *courier's* (167.9), *loudly* but *loud* (220.34), or syntactical distinctions like TMs[1] *race* but A1+ *racing* (147.5) are all not characteristic of Crane's concerns. More neutral, perhaps, are such attempts at variation as TMs[1] *called* but A1+ *cried* (130.12), *seemed* but *appeared* (165.21), or the identifiable marked-copy change in Chapter VI from *said* to *cried* (143.17). All such changes are paralleled among the unauthoritative variants from TMs[1] that A1+ exhibits in Chapters XIX–XXXI; hence no posi-

---

[41] One may recall the typist's triple change of *isn't* to *ain't* in Chapter VI, for example.

tive evidence for authorial intention can be adduced but instead only the constant attention of the Stokes editor and the occasional sophistication or inadvertent differences produced in the typing of TMs[2].

From what remains after obvious corrections have also been discarded, only a short list can be made up that might constitute authorial revision, and various of these items are probable mistakes in A1+. Thus TMs[1] *lad* but A1+ *lady* (126.18), *agonized* but *agonizing* (168.27), *appeared* but *happened* (218.20), and *shade* but *shape* (225.35) are certainly wrong in A1, and no confidence can be felt in such variants as TMs[1] *trampled* but A1+ *tramped* (115.1), or *slightest* but *lightest* (132.5), or *Somewhere in* but *Somehow on* (130.29). Even with the more striking TMs[1] *cold* but A1+ *cool* (113.1) it is difficult to think of Crane having written the first but then changing his mind to so similar a second. On the sense, such a reading as TMs[1] *plane* but A1+ *place* (191.22) shows clear-cut sophistication, and *black* but A1+ *blank* (191.17) is in the same category. When all is done, only a mere handful of substitutions could possibly be argued for if the touchstone of added precision be applied as found in such authorial revisions in XIX–XXXI as *the Wainwrights* for *the Wainwright party* (256.30), *responded* for *repeated* (278.11), or *betrothal* for *engagement* (324.7). Of these perhaps A1+ *wine bottle* for TMs[1] *bottle of wine* (151.24) is the most prominent, for it might be better to suppose that a drunken spectator would throw an empty rather than a full bottle of wine on the stage by mistake for a bouquet. It could be argued that A1+ *They expected me to flirt* is more precise than TMs[1] *They expected to see me flirt* (148.11), but the reasoning might seem to be finespun. At 201.38 Cora typed *dim* and then left a space when she could not decipher the rest of the word. The E1 compositor guessed very badly at *dim chances* in comparison to the A1+ reading *dimensions*, which has the ring of truth, but whether because of editorial ingenuity or because Crane filled in the gap is not determinable. In short, it would seem that no substitution was beyond the capacity of an editor who was prepared, in the later chapters, to replace TMs[1] *persistently* with *desperately* (246.31), *plan* with *idea* (277.36), *delighted* with *obliged* (278.15), *flaming* with *burning* (302.24), *visit* with *purposes* (303.20), *dolefully* with *mournfully* (304.11), or *acutely* with *actually* (299.15), a reading found with the same variant in the earlier section as well (170.4).

The case for the A1+ additions in the first eighteen chapters allows for a greater difference of opinion. In Chapters XIX–XXXI Crane's additions to the text were evenly divided between the correction of obvious error and either improvement or the correction of less apparent error, so that relatively few may be classed as true second thoughts. The longest at 260.13–14 adds a clause *he received a gun-butt emphatically on the side of the neck* when on review he saw the necessity to account for Coleman's blood, for no detail in the original episode would justify his wounds and bruises. Whether his rhetorical repetition *a base suspicion* (241.12–13) repaired an eye-skip or was a revision cannot be known. For the others, the addition of *grey* in *wet grey rag* (238.14) makes for a more visual description, but the rest of his ministrations are minor indeed. In these same chapters unauthoritative A1+ additions that are not necessary corrections are of about the same number and are mostly trivial, quite obviously an editor's attempt to make the expression more natural, such as *money enough* in A1+ for TMs¹ *money* (248.13), *any time* for *time* (265.9), *all in the carriage* for *all the carriage* (277.8), or *half of the men* for *half the men* (282.14). A few seek to improve the sense more than the style, such as *most serious* for *serious* (274.38), *then halted* for *halted* (299.9), *rest once upon* for *rest upon* (299.10), and *even seem* for *seem* (304.14) (N¹⁻²: *ever*). None represents more than a single word. The general run of the A1+ additions in Chapters I–XVIII are of the same neutral character; for example, A1+ *a faith* for TMs¹ *faith* (114.26), *own march* for *march* (121.27), *So Coleman* for *Coleman* (180.29), or *heard from behind* for *heard behind* (193.1).

At the most no more than eighteen merit serious consideration as possible authorial revisions, and in some of these the appearance is superficial since they arose through editorial misunderstanding or obvious sophistication, as in *as fresh as* for TMs¹ *as* (187.25), or *to cover the* for *to the* (198.20), or *ride it* for *ride* (210.10), or *enough fire* for *fire* (215.32). There remain a few simple additions that could as easily be editorial as authorial improvements. Whether the professor said that travel would be a *cure* or the A1+ *sure cure* (122.26) can scarcely be adjudicated, or whether the Chicago man answered *Oh, nothin', whatever* or *Oh, nothin'. Nothin', whatever* (150.12), or whether the party should make a *stout-hearted dash* for Arta or a *good, stout-hearted dash* (209.10). Even whether Crane would feel it necessary to specify that Nora bared her neck or bared it to Coleman (227.7) is doubtful [42] or that he would increase Coke's profanity by adding *damn* as in A1+ (with N¹ providing a two-em dash and N² omitting) before *peoples* in TMs¹ *what in hell are these two peoples fighting for anyhow* (209.32). Given an editor who substituted words freely in working over TMs¹, no reason exists why he should not elaborate at his fancy by addition. If he could specify that Nikopolos was only three miles *away* from Prevasa, when TMs¹ read *three miles from* (186.9), he might as easily specify that Coleman should order the party to go *up* about a hundred feet into the *wood* instead of TMs¹ *go about . . . into the woods* (195.20–21).

---

[42] Not to crush the wings of a butterfly, the A1 addition of *to him* after *baring* suggests wrongly in fact that under his gaze she made some adjustment of her gown, whereas it is clear in context that Crane meant only that she was dressed in a gown that showed her neck.

Several readings may give one pause, however. An unsolicited contribution to the newspaper might request return, if rejected, *in the enclosed envelope* (125.24), but the A1+ *enclosed stamped envelope* could represent Crane's precision or an editor's reproduction of the professional formula. That the Athenians observing Coleman's speed in buying horses and hiring a groom came out to *watch this surprising man* or *this surprising young man* (161.25) as in A1 again could be authorial or editorial detail; but the addition of Crane's frequently used word *wild* at 203.19 to the *gratitude* of the students gives one pause, as does the addition of *lowly* before *breathed* (196.4), more especially because of its awkwardness. These pretty well cover the ordinary evidence. More striking are three extended additions. One may have no significance since the omission was an obvious error that any reader, even a casual one, would detect. At 228.28–31 TMs[1] (and E1) reads:

"I am awfully tired," said Coleman thickly. "Wouldn't you like a little more of that champagne?"

That there has been an eyeskip in the typescript is evident, for it cannot be Coleman who continues his statement of fatigue with an invitation to Nora to drink champagne. The A1+ version neatly adjusts the difficulty.

"I am awfully tired," said Coleman thickly. "I think I will go home and turn in."
"You must be, poor boy," said Nora tenderly. "Wouldn't you like a little more of that champagne?"

If this is editorial patchwork, it is very good; it even recalls that when Coleman had first arrived, Nora *arose saying softly: "You look tired, almost ill, poor boy. I will give you some brandy"* (226.19–20). The second and third examples are not, apparently, cases of eyeskip —although they may be, of course—but of elaboration. In the first, when the Greek soldiers advance into Turkey they meet an old peasant who greets them ecstatically. TMs[1] then reads: *Behind the hedge of dry brambles there were more indications of life and the peasant stood up and made beseeching gestures. Soon a whole flock of miserable people in crude and comic smocks, prancing* (E1: *pranced*) *here and there uproariously embracing and kissing their deliverers* (184.3–7). Oddly, perhaps, A1+ add after *miserable people* the phrase *had come out to the Greeks, men, women, and children.* The detail that they comprised men, women, and children is by no means essential (and the specification may not altogether go with the dress of smocks for the women and children), but an editor (or an author) might like to make it clear that the people had indeed left the protection of the hedge and were prancing in front of it, not behind. The second expansion exhibits the same care for the connection of events. The retreat of the Greek forces has left Coleman exposed, and after the dragoman in a panic awakened him, the dragoman then *ran off to the little grey horse and frenziedly but skilfully began to bind the traps upon the pack-saddle. "Come. Come. Come. Queek! Queek!" They slid hurriedly down a bank to the road* . . . (190.32–35). However, in A1+ the urging "*Come* . . . *Queek!*" follows the addition *He appeared in a moment tugging at the halter. He could only say:*. The distinction is between the dragoman shouting *Come* while he was packing the horse but followed without transition by the action of their sliding down the bank, and the A1+ completion of the packing, the plea to *Come* delivered before Coleman, and then the hurried flight. The point is a small one, and again whether it would occur to a scrupulous editor concerned with apparent gaps in the action, or to an author, is scarcely demonstrable, for no parallels to these additions either by author or by editor appear in Chapters XIX–XXXI. (It is not really evidence that on the very next page the editor makes two almost wilful sophistications in substituting *blank* for *black* and *place* for *plane* at 191.17,22.)

The interpretation of this evidence can be no more than a matter of opinion. It is impossible to state categorically that the editor in these two relatively adjacent passages did not fill in what he regarded as gaps in Crane's continuity in the same spirit with which he frequently altered Crane's choice of words, as well as his characteristic idioms and syntax, in order—as he must have felt—to make a more presentable narrative for the reader. It is impossible, also, to state that in these latter two expansions Crane was not himself adding detail that he thought desirable. (The agent who patched the major eyeskip is not to be determined, but he should have been the same as the one who made the expansions.) Except for a very few single interpolations like *stamped, nothin', young, lowly,* and *wild,* the simple additions are either neutral or quite definitely on the side of the editor. Yet on the evidence of the mixed variants in Chapters XIX–XXXI, the large number of nonauthorial alterations does not preclude the appearance of a few authorial revisions as distinguished from unassignable corrections like *impertinence* for TMs[1] *importance* (120.22) or some—like *passing* for *passing into* (170.26) or *different* for *indifferent* (209.23)—so obvious that they were also corrected independently in E1.

Hazy as is the situation, an editor must make up his mind whether there is possible authority in some A1+ variants in the first eighteen chapters, or none. If there seems to be authority, he is bound to select for inclusion in his text those that appear to have the best claim to being Crane's. If none, then all A1+ variants must be rejected save for those necessary corrections that must be made in the TMs[1] copy-text regardless of source. Faced with this dilemma the present editor has come to believe that on the balance the evidence is stronger for nonauthority than for authority. Admittedly, the reconstruction is purely conjectural of the events that led to the lack of authorial revision in the ribbon part of the Heinemann typescript as against the presence of Crane's autograph alterations in the carbon. But if it comes anywhere near the truth, authorial revisions—if they ever existed—could not have found their way into the Stokes carbon of the first eighteen chapters except by the most extraordinary oversight that somehow differentiated Chapters I–XVIII from XIX–XXII and then from XXIII–XXIV, and XXV–XXXI, without regard for the Reynolds copy of the first eighteen chapters dispatched on March 25. The editor's failure to construct a reasonable explanation that would account for the presence of such revisions in the Stokes copy of I–XVIII weighs heavily in influencing his opinion. Also of some weight is the apparent lack of positive evidence in I–XVIII for authorial substitutions even though more plausible evidence may seem to exist in favor of authorial additions; however, some of the more attractive of these (apart from the two, or three, major expansions) are more than suspect of editorial sophistication and general improvement. To rest practically the whole case on a conjectured authorial origin for the added bridge passages at 184.3–7 and 190.34, against the weight of the other evidence, is too great a risk in the present editor's opinion. The editorial principle that has guided the formation of this text, then, is based on the hypothesis that none of the A1+ variants in Chapters I–XVIII is demonstrably authorial.

To sum up, finally, the choices of copy-text in this edition, for reasons that are clear, TMs^1 is the general copy-text. In later chapters when from time to time TMs^1 is wanting or defective, the Heinemann edition E1 becomes the copy-text since it is at only one remove from the missing typescript, its printer's copy. However, since compositorial (and editorial proofreading) changes both accidental—and to a slighter degree substantive—intervene between copy and the E1 print (as demonstrable when TMs^1 is present), the claims of A1+ as an emending agent in these areas need serious consideration. The A1+ readings, though at two removes from TMs^1, on some occasions demonstrably preserve TMs^1 more faithfully than E1 and must be utilized.

In Chapter V when TMs^1 is wanting throughout, both A1 and TMs^2 radiate from lost TMs^1 at the same distance. As a result, each has technically equal authority and copy-text in the usual sense of the word does not exist.[43] Nevertheless, for convenience some peg must support the apparatus, and TMs^2 has been chosen as copy-text for Chapter V on the grounds that it seems on the whole to reproduce what one may assume were the TMs^1 accidentals with slightly more faithfulness than is found after the housestyling of the A1 compositor who was utilizing the same document. In Chapters I–IV,

[43] See Bowers, "Multiple Authority: New Concepts of Copy-Text," *The Library*, 5th ser., XXVII (1972), 81–115; "Remarks on Eclectic Texts," *Proof*, IV (1974), 13–58.

VII–XVIII, readings from A1+ may be used as necessary corrections but not as revisory emendations of the copy-text owing to the editorial theory adopted for these chapters. In Chapters XIX–XXXI it is practically demonstrable that A1+ can have no authority independent of TMs¹; hence alterations in these chapters drawn from A1 are simple corrections.

Finally, the authority of the proofreading of E1 comes into question, for we know from the Columbia University Crane Collection that the Cranes had in their possession the proof for the first ten chapters at least.[44] That this copy is unmarked means nothing, for it is unlikely that Cora (or Crane) would have transferred to their file copy any revisions or corrections they had marked in the set that was presumably returned to Heinemann. Within the preserved pages of the proof, comparison of the text with E1 establishes the proof-alterations made in the copy by some agent, but elsewhere proof-correction cannot be distinguished in E1 from compositorial departure from copy. Crane was not noted as a careful proofreader and he generally shirked the task. Thus it is impossible to tell with any certainty whether some of the few identifiable E1 substantive proof-alterations are his or the publisher's. Most are concerned with correcting typescript accidentals too faithfully reproduced, as in 'portentious' changed to 'portentous' (116.2) or 'greight' to 'freight' (129.6), a few of these ill-advisedly as in the change at 137.4 of correct 'Editor' to 'editor', or else they correct errors in typesetting, such as 'wound' altered to 'would' (123.16), 'them' to 'then' (126.28), or 'abroad' to 'aboard' (150.28). The TMs¹ error 'importance' (which should have been 'impertinence' as in A1) was repeated in the original proof but altered in E1 on the general sense to 'blasphemy' by a corrector (120.22), without authority, one would think, although the case is not demonstrable. On the whole it is just to say that in the pages covered by the proofs no reading in E1 variant from the proof can with certainty be called an authorial revision.[45] The other

[44] Actually, the pages of this run of proof through the first page of Chapter XI are interrupted by a gap from page 59 in Chapter VII through page 82 near the end of Chapter IX (152.10–169.5).

[45] The best candidates are notably weak. For example, the proof followed what appears to be a TMs¹ error at 170.26 in copying the 'into' later omitted in E1 by correction; but since A1+ independently read with E1, no conclusions about authorial proof-correction can be drawn here unless one were simultaneously to conjecture that 'into' had also been deleted by Crane in the marked copy of TMs¹ used to set A1. This is possible, of course, but it would represent an almost unique case. E1 (and A1) 'in all' for TMs¹ and proof 'at all' (174.2) is in the same category. The addition of 'up' by E1 at 175.12, missing in TMs¹ and the proof, cannot be taken seriously as anything other than a proofreader's tinkering. It is interesting to observe that if the proofs had not been preserved to distinguish the actual alterations, it might have been tempting to speculate that such an omission in E1 as 'said the girl' at 116.15, the reading of TMs¹, could have represented Crane's own preference; but since we have the printer's

class of alteration, the corrections, might have stemmed from author or publisher; they are indifferent except when in a few cases they are wrong.

BIBLIOGRAPHICAL DESCRIPTIONS

The British Library deposit copy of the first English edition of *Active Service* was received on November 2, 1899. A listing for the work appeared in *Atheneum* on October 28, 1899, and in *Publishers' Circular and Booksellers' Record*, on November 11, 1899. The price was six shillings.

The description is as follows:

Active Service | By | Stephen Crane | Author of | "Pictures of War," "The Third Violet," etc. | London | William Heinemann | 1899

Collation: [A]² B–I⁸ K–U⁸ X⁶; pp. [i–iv] [1] 2–315 [316]; leaf measures 189 × 124 mm., edges rough-cut; heavy wove coated paper, unwatermarked; endpapers are text wove paper.

Contents: p. i: half-title, 'Active Service'; p. ii: Heinemann advt., 'New 6s. Novels . . . [10 titles]'; p. iii: title; p. iv: '[lower left] *This Edition enjoys Copyright in all | Countries signatory to the Berne | Treaty, and is not to be imported | into the United States of America. | All rights, including translation, reserved.*'; pp. 1–315: text, headed 'ACTIVE SERVICE'; p. 316: 'RICHARD CLAY & SONS, LIMITED, | LONDON & BUNGAY.'

Binding: Tan (76. l.y Br) rough linen cloth. *Front*: '[black] Active Service | [deep orange (51. deep O)] *By Stephen Crane* | [sword orn. in deep orange (51)]'. *Spine*: '[black] Active | Service | [deep orange (51)] *By Stephen | Crane* | [publisher's device in black outline with deep orange detail] | [black] Heinemann'. *Back*: sword orn. in deep orange (51).

Copies: British Library (datestamped November 2, 1899); Bodleian Library (Fic 271z.e.1826); University of Virginia–Barrett 551291.

Copyright for the first American edition of *Active Service* was applied for on October 7, 1899. One of the Library of Congress' deposit copies is in the Rare Book Division (PS1499.C85A7 1899) and has on the verso of its title-page the following notation: '58059 | Sep. 11–'99.' There are also two ink stamps: 'Library of Congress Office of Register of Copyrights Oct. 7–1899' and '2nd copy delivered to the Library of Congress Oct 9–1899.' The second deposit copy (PZ3.C852A) has all the elements described above on the verso of

---

copy here and both proof and book diverge from it in the omission, it is clearly identifiable as a compositorial error.

its title-page plus the number '43083' stamped above the copyright date and next to the October 7 stamp is a stamped 'second copy'. *Publishers' Weekly* noted the volume on September 16, 1899, advertised it on September 30, and listed it on October 14. The price was $1.25.

The description is as follows:

ACTIVE | SERVICE | 𝔄 𝔑𝔬𝔟𝔢𝔩 | BY | STEPHEN CRANE | AUTHOR OF "THE RED BADGE OF COURAGE," | "GEORGE'S MOTHER," ETC., ETC. | [orn.] | NEW YORK | FREDERICK A. STOKES COMPANY | PUBLISHERS

Collation: [1–22]⁸, pp. [i–vi] [1] 2–345 [346]; leaf measures 187 × 122 mm., all edges trimmed; laid paper, cream coated endpapers.

Contents: p. i: half-title, 'ACTIVE SERVICE.'; p. ii: blank; p. iii: title; p. iv: '*Copyright, 1899,* | *By Stephen Crane* | *Copyright, 1899,* | *By Frederick A. Stokes Company*'; p. v: dedication 'To E. A.'; p. vi: blank; pp. 1–345: text, headed 'ACTIVE SERVICE'; p. 346: blank.

Binding: Olive green (lighter than 110 gy. Ol) linen cloth. *Front*: '[dark olive green 128. d. gy. Ol G)] ACTIVE | SERVICE [following both title words, extending over the space of the two lines, is a leaf-branch orn. in very pale green (148. v. p. G)] | STEPHEN · CRANE | [beneath is a stylized fruit-tree design in very pale green (148. v. p. G); at center foot, the initials 'T B H']'. *Spine*: '[dark olive green (128)] ACTIVE | SERVICE | [leaf orn. in very pale green (148)] | [dark olive green (128)] STEPHEN | CRANE | [fruit-tree design in very pale green (148)] | [dark olive green (128)] STOKES'. *Back*: blank.

Copy: University of Virginia–Barrett 551294.

Variants: In the Barrett Collection of the University of Virginia Library is an advance copy (551292) internally identical to the first American edition, bound in cream paper wrappers with the title and design as on the front cover of the first American edition, but printed in dark yellow green (137. d. y G). The spine strip is chipped away and may have contained printed matter. The back cover is lacking as well. Inside the front cover is an advertisement for the Stokes publication, *Simon Dale* by Anthony Hope.

The Toronto edition, also published in 1899, is printed from the plates of the first American edition on laid paper. Collation by gatherings and pagination are the same. The title-page contains the variant imprint 'TORONTO: | WILLIAM BRIGGS. | 1899.' The title-page verso (p. iv), which contains the copyright notice in the first American edition, is blank in the Toronto edition. The book is bound in light gray paper wrappers, printed on the front cover as on the first American edition, but with lettering in bright red (36. deep r O) and foliated design in green (141. s. G). The spine is also as the first American edition, but with lettering in red (36), design in green (141), and the publisher's name 'BRIGGS' at the foot instead of 'STOKES'. The back and inner covers of the wrapper are blank.

Two newspaper printings have been observed:

N¹: *The Chicago Times–Herald*, Sundays, August 6, 1899, Part 5, pp. 1–2; August 13, Part 5, pp. 2–3; August 20, Part 5, p. 2; August 27, Part 5, pp. 6–7; September 3, Part 5, p. 6; September 10, Part 5, p. 6; September 17, Part 5, p. 6; September 24, Part 5, p. 6; October 1, Part 5, p. 6. August 6 and 13 have a full-page-spread title-cut 'ACTIVE | SERVICE | BY STEPHEN CRANE · [on a scroll with a soldier to the left and a figure holding a newspaper to right all superimposed on waves]'; signed 'Morgan'. The full-page title-cut for the remaining installments appears at the beginning on each day '[within ruled oblong, two ornaments] ACTIVE SERVICE [two ornaments] BY STEPHEN CRANE.' The notation '[COPYRIGHT, 1899, BY STEPHEN CRANE.]' appears at the head of the first column on August 6, 13, 20, 27, and September 3. On August 6, p. 1, Chapters I–III are in columns 1–7 with six illustrations: (1) '"GO AWAY!" CRIED HER FATHER IN A RAGE. "GO AWAY, GET OUT!"', (2) full-length portrait of Coleman with script legend 'RUFUS COLEMAN' on a scroll, (3) '"THINK OF THE CAMEL RIDES WE'LL HAVE!" CRIED COKE.', (4) 'THERE WERE NO BLOWS; IT WAS A BATTLE OF PRESSURE.', (5) inset on (4) with script legend 'PROFESSOR WAINWRIGHT STOOD | AT THE DOOR OF HIS RECITATION | ROOM.', (6) '"MY HEART IS BROKEN! MY HEART IS BROKEN!"' Nos. 1–4 and 6 are signed 'Morgan'; p. 2, continuation of Chapter III and Chapters IV–VI are in columns 1–7. On August 13, p. 2, Chapters VII–IX are in columns 1–7 with three illustrations: (1) '"WELL, OF ALL UNGALLANT MEN, RUFUS COLEMAN, YOU ARE THE STAR!"', (2) full-length portrait of man with, inset on a scroll, script legend 'LONDON | CORRESPONDENT | OF THE | ECLIPSE', (3) '"THE WAINWRIGHTS?" SAID THE MINISTER. "WHY, I MYSELF AM IMMENSELY CONCERNED ABOUT THEM."' No. 1 is signed 'Morgan'; p. 3, continuation of Chapter IX and Chapter X (run together with no heading for Chapter X) are in columns 1–7. On August 20, p. 2, Chapters XI–XIII are in columns 1–7 with two illustrations: (1) 'HE COULD ONLY SAY: "COME! COME! COME! QUEEK! QUEEK!"' and (2) '"HE THREW HIS GRIMY FEZ IN THE AIR AND CROAKED OUT CHEERS, WHILE TEARS WET HIS CHEEKS."', both signed 'Morgan'. On August 27, p. 6, Chapters XIV–XVI are in columns 1–7 with three illustrations: (1)

'THE PROFESSOR WAS AT LAST ABLE TO MAKE HIS FORMAL SPEECH.', (2) ' "NOW," HE SAID, "DO YOU KNOW THAT YOU ARE RAISING THE VERY DEVIL?" ', (3) 'UNCONSCIOUSLY HE STRETCHED HIS HANDS IN SUPPLICATION OVER HIS CHARGES, "DON'T MOVE! DON'T MOVE! AND KEEP CLOSE TO THE GROUND!" ' Nos. 2 and 3 are signed 'Morgan'; p. 7, the conclusion of Chapter XVI is in column 4. On September 3, p. 6, Chapters XVII–XIX are in columns 1–7 with two illustrations: (1) 'HIS FEET WERE SCARCELY OVER THE THRESHOLD BEFORE HE HAD CONCLUDED THAT THE TIGRESS WAS NOW GOING TO TRY SOME VELVET PURRING. NORA SAT FACING THE DOOR.' and (2) 'THEY WERE IN THE MIDST OF THESE FESTIVITIES WHEN THE DOOR OPENED AND DISCLOSED THE PROFESSOR.' Both are signed 'Morgan'. On September 10, p. 6, Chapters XX–XXII are in columns 1–7 with two illustrations: (1) ' "YOU LOOK AS IF SOME ONE HAD KICKED YOU DOWNSTAIRS." ' and (2) 'SHE LAID HER HAND ON HIS ARM AND WITH THE STRENGTH OF FOUR MEN HE TWISTED HIS HORSE TOWARD THE INN.' Both are signed 'Morgan'. On September 17, p. 6, Chapters XXIII–XXV are in columns 1–7 with two illustrations: (1) 'THE STUDENT CLATTERED INTO THE COMPARTMENT. "HELLO, COLEMAN! DIDN'T KNOW YOU WERE HERE." AT HIS HEELS CAME NORA BLACK, COKE AND MARJORY' and (2) 'HE HELD HER CLOSE TO HIM. "BUT YOU ARE MINE, REMEMBER," HE SAID, FIERCELY.' No. 1 is signed 'Morgan'. On September 24, p. 6, Chapters XXVI–XXVIII appear in columns 1–7 with one illustration: 'THE GIRL TURNED HER FACE TO THE PILLOW AND HELD OUT A HAND OF PROTEST. "DON'T, MOTHER! DON'T!" ', signed 'Morgan'. On October 1, p. 6, Chapters XXIX–XXXI are in columns 1–7 with one illustration: 'HE BREATHED OUT A CRY WHICH WAS LADEN WITH A KIND OF DIFFIDENT FEROCITY. "I HAVEN'T KISSED YOU YET——" ', signed 'Morgan'.

N²: *The Buffalo Courier*, Sundays, August 27, 1899, p. 4; September 3, pp. 4, 11; September 10, pp. 8, 11; September 17, pp. 8, 11; September 24, pp. 8, 11; October 1, pp. 8, 11; October 8, pp. 16–17; October 15, pp. 16–17; October 22, pp. 16–17; October 29, p. 16. On August 27, p. 4, under the full-page title-cut '[to the left, cupid playing with two pendant hearts] ACTIVE [orn.] SERVICE BY | STEPHEN | CRANE [to the right, framed landscape with soldiers]' signed 'O. E. Cesar '99', Chapters I–II are in columns 1–7. On September 3, p. 4, under a full-page title-cut '[to the left, sailing ship in oval] ACTIVE [two heart-shaped lockets] SERVICE [to the right, Greek soldier's head in circle] | BY STEPH[orn. obscures] CRANE' signed 'O. E. Cesar '99', Chapters II(continued)–III are in columns 1–7; p. 11, columns 4–5 contain the conclusion of Chapter III and Chapter

IV. On September 10, p. 8, under a five-column title-cut '[to the left, two pierced hearts] ACTIVE [vignette of steam ship] SERVICE [to the right, framed scene of soldier firing rifle] | BY | STEPHEN CRANE.', Chapters V–VII (*i.e.* VII, VIII, and IX) are in columns 1–6; p. 11, the continuation of N² Chapter VII is in column 4. On September 17, p. 8, under the same title-cut as August 27, but lacking the cupid to the left and the framed picture to the right, Chapters IX–X are in columns 1–5; p. 11, columns 4–5 contain Chapters X(continued)–XI. On September 24, p. 8, under the title-cut used on September 3, but lacking the Greek soldier's head to the right, Chapters XI(continued)–XIII are in columns 1–7; p. 11, columns 1–3 contain the conclusion of Chapter XIII. On October 1, p. 8, under the title-cut used for September 24, Chapters XIV–XV are in columns 1–7; p. 11, columns 5–6 contain the conclusion of Chapter XV. On October 8, p. 16, under the title-cut used for September 3, Chapters XVI–XVIII are in columns 1–7; p. 17, columns 1–5 contain the conclusion of Chapter XVIII–XX. On October 15, p. 16, under the title-cut used for September 3 and October 8, Chapters XX(continued)–XXIII are in columns 1–7; p. 17, columns 1–5 contain Chapters XXIII(continued)–XXV. On October 22, p. 16, under the same cut as the two previous weeks, Chapters XXV(continued)–XXVIII are in columns 1–7; p. 17, columns 1–7 contain Chapters XXVIII(continued)–XXIX. On October 29, p. 16, under a two-column title-cut '[within broken-ruled rectangle ACTIVE SERVICE]' Chapters XXIX(continued) to the end are in columns 1–7.

N² prints twenty-one of the illustrations found in N¹, plus one not found in N¹. The order of appearance and captions vary in N². Listed below is the order in which the N² illustrations appear together with their captions; where identification is not readily apparent, a cross reference is given to the corresponding issue and number of illustration in N¹:

August 27, p. 4: (1) 'THERE WERE NO BLOWS; IT WAS A BATTLE OF PRESSURE.' (2) inset script legend 'PROFESSOR WAINWRIGHT STOOD | AT THE DOOR OF HIS RECITATION | ROOM.' (3) 'HER FATHER LOOKED UP QUICKLY WITH A SCOWL. "GO AWAY," HE CRIED IN A RAGE. "GO AWAY."'

September 3, p. 4: (1) Coleman Portrait. (2) '"AND JUST THINK OF THE CAMEL RIDES WE'LL HAVE," SAID COKE.' (3) '"OH, MY HEART IS BROKEN! MY HEART IS BROKEN!"'

September 10, p. 8: (1) 'A TALL, FAIR WOMAN CAME UP TO COLEMAN.' (N¹: August 13, No. 1). (2) inset script legend 'LONDON | CORRESPONDENT | OF THE | ECLIPSE.' (3) '"THE WAINWRIGHTS!" EXCLAIMED THE MINISTER.'

September 17, p. 8: 'HE COULD ONLY SAY: "COME! COME! QUEEK! QUEEK!"'

September 24, p. 8: '"LIE DOWN," HE SAID.' (N¹: August 27, No. 3).

October 1, p. 8: (1) 'THE PROFESSOR MADE HIS SPEECH.' (2) ' "NORA," HE SAID, "DO YOU KNOW THAT YOU ARE RAISING THE VERY DEVIL?" '

October 8, p. 16: (1) 'THEY WERE IN THE MIDST OF THE FESTIVITIES WHEN THE DOOR OPENED.' (2) ' "YOU LOOK AS IF SOMEONE HAD KICKED YOU," SHE SAID CANDIDLY.' (3) 'THE HOWLING GREEK.' (N[1]: August 20, No. 2); *page 17* (4) 'SHE LAID HER HAND ON HIS ARM AND WITH THE STRENGTH OF FOUR MEN HE TWISTED HIS HORSE TOWARDS THE DOOR OF THE INN.'

October 15, p. 16: (1) 'THE CORRESPONDENT, LEANING FORWARD, WAS WATCHING HIM ALMOST BREATHLESSLY.' (not in N[1]; signed 'Morgan'). (2) 'NORA SAT FACING THE DOOR.' (N[1]: September 3, No. 1); *page 17* (3) 'THE GIRL TURNED HER FACE TO THE PILLOW AND HELD OUT A HAND IN PROTEST. "DON'T, MOTHER! DON'T!" '

October 22, p. 16: (1) 'HE LOOKED UP SUDDENLY, LIFTING HIS ARMS. HE BREATHED OUT A CRY WHICH WAS LADEN WITH A KIND OF DIFFICULT FEROCITY: "I HAVEN'T KISSED YOU YET." '; *page 17* (2) ' "OH!" THEY SAID, WHEN THEY SAW THE OCCUPANT OF THE CARRIAGE. "OH!" COLEMAN WAS FURIOUS.' (N[1]: September 17, No. 1).

The illustration dropped from N[2] was N[1]'s No. 2 of September 17.

APPENDIXES

THE THIRD VIOLET

TEXTUAL NOTES

3.25 employees] N[1,3-4,6] 'employes' certainly reflects the spelling of the N proof and very likely of the typescript and Crane manuscript. Crane would have had little idea that whereas 'employe' was an acceptable spelling of the singular, the plural was 'employees'. Properly, 'employés' as well as 'employées' is acceptable in British usage, but the newspapers had no acute accent and at this date Crane would scarcely have been aware of such a refinement.

4.21 leggins] This is the older-fashioned form and the one Crane is most likely to have used since it is improbable that it was the invention of the N proof compositor. The A1 (and N[5]) 'leggings' is a modernization.

5.23 Yes] The variant readings 'Yess' of N[2] and 'Yees' of N[5] indicate either a typo in the proof or a typist's mistake passed on but normalized by the other newspapers. That this was some dialect form in the typescript that got corrupted is not especially likely, since the standard dialect form is 'yep'. For other cases, see 'want' with the variants 'want'' in N[5] and 'wan't' in N[6] (8.1); N[1-3] 'padding' but N[4-6] 'paddling' (22.23).

10.5 then$_\wedge$] Ordinarily, the agreement of N[2,4-6] in a comma after 'then' (N[1,3] joining A1 in no comma) would indicate the reading of the proof. But on the evidence of 11.33 'Oh, then you saw her in the stage', in which only N[3] has a comma after 'then', the syntax is not necessarily parenthetical, and it may be that N[2,4-6] have here sophisticated the proof.

20.39 tell it you] That A1 'tell it to you' is a sophistication is strongly suggested by the difficulty two newspapers had in accepting the idiom of their proof. N[4] joined A1 in adding 'to', whereas N[1] simply omitted 'it' and read 'tell you'.

21.23 took seat] Ordinarily N[2] 'took seat', which alone preserves Crane's usual phrase, would furnish insufficient evidence for emendation against A1 and the other five newspapers' agreement in 'took a seat'. But at 57.1 occurs an example of how compositors would alter this phrase. Here 'took seat' filters through A1 and N[3-4], but N[1] reads 'took a seat', and N[2,5-6] 'took his seat'. This indication of the unwillingness of compositors to follow Crane in his usual locution shows that at 21.23 the copy almost certainly read 'took seat'.

26.15 moon] It seems probable that 'boat' from the line above in A1 contaminated the typescript 'moon' as is found in $N, and hence that the A1 compositor made a memorial error. The use of 'fall upon' indicates clearly that Crane's original intention was certainly to have the rays of the moon fall upon the girl's head from the sky. Why he deleted 'full' before 'upon' is obscure. If this change was part of an alteration of concept, and Crane intended 'flashing rays' to come from the reflection of the moon on the water, then one might be able to defend the change from 'moon' to 'boat' as meaning *as seen from the boat*, or, perhaps better, *as caused by the ripples the boat made moving through the water*. But the expression is very strained, even if one thinks of it as only a partially completed revision of concept. The odds would seem to favor a memorial corruption in A1 instead of conscious alteration of the typescript perhaps imperfectly reproduced. For similar cases of memorial contamination, see 60.22 and 85.7.

28.7 close] It may well be that $N 'closer' was what Crane originally wrote. Hawker had been standing and now for the first time he took a seat. Under ordinary circumstances to pull a chair closer would imply sitting in the chair before altering its position; but here Crane seems to have intended Hawker, before taking his seat, to pull a chair closer to the window than it had been placed in the room. The presence of what seems to be Crane's alteration of N 'irremediable' to 'long' in the preceding sentence, and then the insertion of 'out' after 'stared' in the next clause suggests that he altered 'closer' to 'close' at the time of making these other revisions. An easier and simpler reading results.

43.7 Billie] Although 'Billie' has been applied to Hawker previously at 23.14, this is the first indication that the typescript read 'Billee', as here in $N. The spelling 'Billee' is also found at 50.8 in $N($-N^6$) as well as in N^5 alone at 50.16 and 54.14 and in $N^{1,5}$ at 50.21. The variable normalization given what, in many places, must have been typescript spellings of 'Billee' makes it uncertain whether 'Billie', invariable in A1, is one of the usual unauthoritative normalizations with which this text is so free or else an authorial second thought, allied to the removal of colloquialisms from Hawker's speech. In the absence of any evidence, the A1 authority may hold although there is no certainty that Crane did not continue to intend the spelling 'Billee'. Yet it may be that he had no fixed ideas about its spelling: for example, 'Billee' appears as a variant for 'Billie' just once in *George's Mother* (173.30), and so was emended to the usual form in the edited text.

44.26 looking] The N^3 change to secure parallel structure of 'looked' with 'bended' suggests that the A1 'looked' is also a sophistication of a typical piece of structural looseness faithfully reproduced in the other newspapers. Earlier, N^1 'bending' is quite clearly not authoritative but an attempt to make the word parallel with 'looking' in the proof. For a similar construction, see 85.33–34, ' "Florinda," he cried, as if enlightened, and gulping suddenly at something in his throat.'

48.20 interrogations] The A1 singular is very likely an editorial or compositorial sophistication of Crane's typical idiosyncratic use of the plural.

For examples, see THE RED BADGE OF COURAGE, 14.4, 38.35, 47.13, 54.23, 62.9, 71.25, and 99.4.

50.8 where you] On the evidence of $N^{1,5-6}$, the typescript read colloquially 'where you'; on the evidence of N^{2-4}, three newspaper compositors were sufficiently disturbed so that they sophisticated it to 'where are you'. The A1 'where are you' appears to agree with N^{2-4} as an unauthoritative correction. For a similar example, see 50.13–14 'show it you' in $N^{1,3-5}$ versus 'show it to you' in $N^{2,6}$ and in A1, but more particularly 54.35 ' "What you giggling at?" ' in $N^{1,3,5}$, altered in $N^{2,4,6}$ to the more usual 'are you', the reading of A1 as well.

52.5 in] That A1 'into' is a manifest editorial or compositorial sophistication of $N 'in' is indicated by the repetition of the phrase at 52.22, where A1 retains 'in' but N^3 alters to 'into'. Another probable A1 normalization of N 'in' occurs at 68.34. Just possibly the single N^3 'in' at 13.31 where all other authorities read 'into' preserves the original reading and is not an isolated error. For a possible analogue, also, see the Textual Note to 86.15. 54.18 near to] $N 'near the ground' may well represent the authoritative reading and A1 'near to' a compositorial sophistication, but one may compare ACTIVE SERVICE 'Often he bent near to the embers of the fire' (187.16).

55.9 ingenuous] Crane had no clear idea of the distinction between the meanings of *ingenious* and *ingenuous* (indeed, the confusion is an ancient one) and was likely to use the first when he meant the second. The appearance of 'ingenious' in N^5, along with A1, indicates that the underlying typescript read 'ingenious' and that the other newspapers corrected it to 'ingenuous'.

60.22 home] The A1 insertion of 'come' before 'home' seems a relatively clear case of memorial contamination from 'can come' in the next line. One can scarcely envisage this as a revision.

62.19 bended] Given what seems to be an error 'you' in A1 for $N 'we' at 62.18, perhaps by contamination, it is a reasonable guess that Crane did not himself remove 'bended' here but the compositor, or editor, omitted it as an idiosyncratic form instead of changing it to 'bent' as at 21.15 and 44.26 in A1.

63.25 How are we] $N^{1,5}$ 'How we' may well reflect the copy reading (as at 63.33 in $N) sophisticated by the other authorities including A1. There is an outside chance, however, that independently both newspapers hit upon the same colloquial construction. On the other hand, it seems more probable to take it that if A1 'we've' is a revision at 63.33, then A1 'are we' is also a revision at 63.25. The two readings ought to stand or fall together. Although the colloquialism is sometimes employed in the city, it was a characteristic of Hawker's sisters, where no change occurred. Thus it is sufficiently possible that the A1 reading represents a removal of colloquial speech from city characters, one of the lines of Crane's revision. See also the readings at 70.5, 76.16, and 76.31.

63.31 "And . . . that."] On the evidence, the typescript was confused here. Since $N(-N^3)$ read 'settled', one must take it either that this is an error for A1,N[3] 'settles' or else that the quotation marks about 'And . . . that' are wrong in A1,N[2-3,6] and the sentence is not part of the quotation. It would seem that quotation marks stood in the typescript—particularly on the evidence of the styling of N[3] to 'isn't, . . . "and'—but that the error 'settled' led the compositors of N[1,4-5] to misunderstand the sense and omit the marks. The compositors of N[2,6] seem to have followed copy in reproducing the error 'settled' and the correct quotation marks, whereas only N[3] corrected the text, as in A1. The presence both of the preterite 'settled' and of the quotation marks shows that the intention of the copy was to treat the words as dialogue. The copy itself may have been in error, of course, for the typist may have added the marks mistakenly, particularly under the impression that 'And' could begin dialogue but not a narrative sentence.

72.16 opportunity] Given Crane's tendency to omit the article before a noun in similar constructions, the odds favor here the reading of \$N(−N[5]) and the probability that in inserting 'an' both A1 and N[5] have unauthoritatively altered the text.

76.30 deprecating] \$N 'deprecating' appears to be the right word. It is not entirely clear, however, whether A1 'depreciating' is a misunderstanding by the compositor or else an original confusion existing in the manuscript and typescript, with the compositor of the newspaper proofs making the right guess. Given Crane's uncertain handling of words like this, the latter is a probable enough hypothesis.

80.14 On] Here and at 81.4 \$N 'on' for A1 'in' is almost certainly the authoritative idiom. The A1 'in' is an Anglicism, very likely due to the compositor, who uses the -our British spellings. A case in point comes at 105.29 where A1 as well as \$N read 'on the street' but E1 alters to 'in the street'.

81.24–25 excepting] \$N 'excepting' becomes 'only' in A1, presumably to avoid the jingle with 'expect'. Whether or not the agent was Crane, the alteration was incomplete since it reverses the intended sense. If the change had been carried through on the basis of 'only', the 'not' in 81.22 and 81.24 should have been removed, although with some possible effect on the construction of 'and then you expect to see mittens'. On the whole, since the source of the alteration is not certain, it seems better to revert to the original reading, apparently as represented in \$N, than to leave the passage as the nonsense produced by A1 without the further change to straighten out the difficulty created by 'only', a change for which no documentary authority exists.

85.7 face] Given the repetition that follows in 'The street in front', it is more probable that \$N 'face' became A1 'front' by memorial contamination than that Crane or an editor deliberately altered the idiomatic phrase. The omission of 'in front' by N[2] is odd, however, as if it were an attempt to avoid the repetition; but since N[2] reads 'face' also, the omission should be fortuitous. For another example of such contamination, see 93.13.

86.15 to] For a use of 'to' by A1 where N[5] normalizes to 'into', see 71.18. What evidence there is elsewhere suggests A1 normalization without authority: such cases as A1 'into' but N 'in' as at 52.5 and 68.34 may be analogous.

90.23 remember] It is an open question whether $N 'remember' was contaminated by 'remember distinctly' in the repetition in 90.24 or whether the repetition was supposed to be exact and A1 sophisticated the first to the more natural idiom; the latter is the guess made by the present editor.

92.2 cash‸desk] The A1 variant 'cash-box' comes a few words above a serious A1 error 'practical' for 'practiced' and in an area in which for some unknown reason the A1 substantive variants appear to be largely untrustworthy. It is a reasonable conjecture that 'cash desk' was an unfamiliar term and was unauthoritatively altered to the conventional 'cash-box'. It is more difficult to envisage the reason for an authorial change or for N corruption.

92.3 practiced] $N 'practiced' seems to be the word required even though there is a very slight chance that A1 'practical' represents Crane's misuse of the word. *Practical* could be defended, however, if one took it that her amiability was not inherent but was fostered by the practical consideration that the restaurant was full and her customers were providing her with a profitable evening. Her amiability, thus, would have stemmed from practical motives. It may be thought, however, that this interpretation is more strained than necessary to avoid the natural emendation. The A1 substitutions for $N readings are not always immaculate and may represent compositorial blunders, like 98.1–2 or, earlier, 85.7 and then 93.13.

94.16 they] It is possible that A1 'you' is addressed by Hollanden to the two combatants; however, $N 'they' continues the previous form of address and appears to be correct. In A1 the shift to 'you' seems to have been made to avoid a superficially confusing reference in two contiguous sentences: the first to the people of the establishment and the second to the proprietor and the little man. This finicky alteration is more likely to be an editor's or compositor's than Crane's. It is worthy of note that shortly, at 94.24, A1 makes what may be an editorial change of 'to be' to 'being' in order to avoid repetition with 'to be detestable'; and, again shortly, the editor seems to have omitted the 'I' of $N at 94.28 through a misunderstanding that the one who had not changed was Hollanden (still talking like a granny) whereas the point is that it is Hawker who asserts that he himself has not changed. In this area the alterations are not demonstrably authorial.

98.1–2 windows, he] The $N plural is correct and the A1 singular an error, on the evidence of 'the two windows' at 89.2 and 'the room of the great windows' at 108.1. Probably by misspacing, the compositor created 'window she' from 'windows he'.

99.28 was] Crane persistently used a singular verb with what he regarded as a collective subject, and editors and compositors almost as persistently corrected what they regarded as his false grammar, as here. For another example, see THE RED BADGE OF COURAGE 51.6–7, 'With the courageous words of the artillery and the spiteful sentences of the musketry was mingled red cheers.'

102.2 ablaze] A1 'oblige' can be defended, of course, but the idiom is a less natural one and the word seems to have resulted from some form of misreading.

103.35 pinching] Either A1 'punching' or $N 'pinching' is an error, probably a misreading. In view of the statement that 'Florinda's fingers tore at Wrinkles' coat sleeve', it may be suggested that $N 'pinching' is the more appropriate in context, but the case is obviously uncertain.

110.9,11–12 freely-given] The A1 double mistake of a dash instead of a hyphen to separate these two words would seem to reflect a misunderstood hyphen in the typescript copy. If so, the unhyphenated form in N²⁻⁶ would reflect not the typescript but the practice (or correction) of the compositor of the N proof. The hyphens must have been oddly typed, perhaps with excessive spaces.

EDITORIAL EMENDATIONS IN THE COPY-TEXT

[NOTE: The copy-text is A1: *The Third Violet*, D. Appleton and Company, New York, 1897. The other texts collated are: N[1]: *Philadelphia Inquirer*, Sundays, Oct. 25, Nov. 1, 8, and 15, 1896; N[2]: *Pittsburg Leader*, Sundays, Oct. 25, Nov. 1, 8, and 15, 1896; N[3]: *The Sunday Oregonian* (Portland), Oct. 25, Nov. 1, 8, and 15, 1896; N[4]: *The Sunday Inter Ocean* (Chicago), Oct. 25, Nov. 1, 8, and 15, 1896; N[5]: *The World* (New York), Nov. 4–7, 9–14, 1896; and N[6]: *San Francisco Chronicle*, Sundays, Oct. 25, Nov. 1, 8, 15, 22, 29, Dec. 6, 13, 20, 27, 1896, Jan. 3, 10, 17, and 24, 1897. E1: *The Third Violet*, William Heinemann, London, 1897, is derived from A1 and is without authority. Every editorial change from A1 is recorded for the substantives, and every change in the accidentals as well save for such silent typographical alterations as are remarked in "The Text of the Virginia Edition," prefixed to Volume 1 of this edition. Asterisked readings are discussed in the Textual Notes. The note *et seq.* signifies that all following occurrences are identical in the text and thus that the same emendation has been made without further notice. An alteration assigned to V is made for the first time in the present edition if by *the first time* is understood *the first time in respect to the texts chosen for collation.* The wavy dash ($\sim$) represents the same word that appears before the bracket and is used exclusively in recording punctuation or other accidental variants. An inferior caret ($_\wedge$) indicates the absence of a punctuation mark. The dollar sign ($) is taken over from a convention of bibliographical description to signify *all* texts so identified. That is, if N represents newspaper versions in general, and N[1-6], the six collated newspapers, then $N would be a shorthand symbol for all these six texts; where a text subsumed under the $ notation is excluded from agreement, this is shown by the use of the minus sign. Thus such a notation as $N($-$N^2)$ would mean that all of the N texts agree with the noted reading to the left of the bracket except for N[2], which by its absence from the $N list of agreements must therefore agree with the reading to the right of the bracket unless otherwise specified. A lengthier way of expressing the same situation would be N[1,3-6]. A plus sign is used as a shorthand indication of the concurrence of all collated editions following the cited edition; for instance, if A1 and all the newspapers and E1 agree in a reading which has been emended by a V emendation, then the entry would read: '7.32 *Perkinson's*] V; Perkinson's A1+($-$N[2]); '$\sim$' N[2]', meaning that A1, N[1,3-6] and E1 all agree in the roman reading, but that N² encloses the word in single quotes. In this volume all chapter headings and section breaks have been ignored in computing the page and line references.]

3.3   steeps,] N$^{1-3}$; ~ $_\wedge$ A1,N$^{4-6}$

3.4   passengers,] N$^{1-2,5}$; ~ $_\wedge$ A1,N$^{3-4,6}$

3.11   paint box] N$^{2-3,5-6}$; ~ - | ~ A1; ~ - ~ N^1; paintbox N^4

3.16   interest$_\wedge$] N$^{1-2,5-6}$; ~ , A1, N$^{3-4}$

3.19   cried:] $N(−N^6); ~ , A1, N^6

3.19   down."] $N; ~!"A1

3.19; 4.12   nurse maid] N^5; nursemaid A1,N$^{3-4,6}$; ~ - ~ N$^{1-2}$

3.25   other] $N; the other A1

*3.25   employees] stet A1,N^{2,5}

3.27   say:] $N; ~ , A1

3.29   hair$_\wedge$] N$^{1-2,5-6}$; ~ , A1,N$^{3-4}$

3.30; 4.7   said:] $N; ~ , A1

3.31   Yes—certainly—] $N; ~ , ~ , A1

4.1   though.] N$^{1-2,4,6}$; ~ ! A1,N^{3,5}

4.2   murder.] N^{2,4,6}; ~ ! A1,N^{1,3,5}

4.2   eyes."] $N; ~ !" A1

4.6   Inn."] $N(−N^3) (N^2: inn.); ~ ?" A1,N^3

4.13   woman$_\wedge$] N$^{1,5-6}$; ~ , A1, N$^{3-4}$; N^2 illegible

4.16   vehicle,] $N(−N^6); ~ $_\wedge$ A1,N^6

4.21   long$_\wedge$] $N; ~ , A1

*4.21   leggins] $N(−N^5); leggings A1,N^5

4.24   seat$_\wedge$] N$^{1-2,5}$; ~ , A1,N$^{3-4,6}$

4.25   stage,] $N; ~ $_\wedge$ A1

4.28   a-slant] N^{1,6}; aslant A1, N$^{2-5}$

4.28   a-slant$_\wedge$] $N(−N^3); ~ , A1, N^3

4.30   road$_\wedge$] N$^{1-2,5-6}$; ~ , A1,N$^{3-4}$

4.37   fishing$_\wedge$ . . . hunting$_\wedge$] $N(−N^3); ~ , . . . ~ , A1; ~ $_\wedge$ . . . ~ — N^3

4.38; 5.1   shot] $N(−N^1); shoot A1,N^1

5.9   hills$_\wedge$] $N(−N^3); ~ , A1,N^3

5.15   seat$_\wedge$] N$^{1-2,5}$; ~ , A1,N$^{3-4,6}$

5.17   arm$_\wedge$] $N(−N^4); ~ , A1,N^4

5.20   inn$_\wedge$] N$^{1-2,5}$ (N^{1,5}: Inn); ~ , A1,N$^{3-4,6}$

5.22   said:] N$^{1,4-6}$; ~ , A1,N^3; ~ ; N^2

*5.23   Yes] stet A1

5.23   Hawker$_\wedge$] $N; ~ , A1

5.23   roared:] $N; ~ , A1

5.26   city,] N$^{1-2,4,6}$; ~ $_\wedge$ A1,N^{3,5}

5.33   man:] $N; ~ , A1

5.36   shadows,] N$^{2-5}$; ~ $_\wedge$ A1,N^{1,6}

5.36   assassin-like] $N(−N^4); assassinlike A1,N^4

6.4   man,"] $N; ~ !" A1

6.4   ardor] $N; ardour A1

6.5   dog$_\wedge$] N$^{1-2,5-6}$; ~ , A1,N$^{3-4}$

6.6   setter$_\wedge$] N$^{2,4-6}$; ~ , A1,N^{1,3}

6.13   kitchen$_\wedge$] N$^{1-2,4}$; ~ , A1, N$^{3,5-6}$

6.16   shouted:] $N; ~ , A1

6.16   is.] $N(−N^3); ~ ! A1,N^3

6.17   Will— . . . Will—"] N^6; ~ ! . . . ~ !" A1; ~ — . . . ~ ," N$^{1,3-4}$; ~ — . . . ~ " — N^{2,5}

6.18   you."] $N (N$^{1-3,5-6}$: yeh; N^4: yen); ~ !" A1

6.19   interrogation,] $N(−N^6); ~ $_\wedge$ A1,N^6

6.19   paint box] N$^{1,4-6}$; ~ - ~ A1, N$^{2-3}$

6.21   rocking chair] $N(−N^1); ~ - ~ A1,N^1

6.23   mother,"] $N(−N^3); ~ !" A1,N^3

6.25–26   Meanwhile,] $N(−N^1); ~ $_\wedge$ A1,N^1

6.31   clamored] $N; clamoured A1

7.3   buggy."] $N; ~ !" A1

7.7   Well! We'll] N$^{2,4-6}$; ~ , we'll A1,N^{1,3}

7.12   barn$_\wedge$] N$^{2,4-6}$; ~ , A1,N^{1,3}

7.17   supper,] $N; ~ $_\wedge$ A1

7.24   Yeh.] $N(−N^3) (N^{2,5}: Yep); Yeh? A1; Yes? N^3

7.28   Drowned$_\wedge$] $N; ~ , A1

7.28 feller."] $N(−N⁴); ~ !" A1,
N⁴

7.29 getting] V; gitting A1;
gittin' $N(−N³); gettin' N³

7.32 *Perkinson's*] V; Perkinson's
A1+(−N²); ' ~ ' N²

7.33 moment‚ₐ] N¹⁻²,⁵⁻⁶; ~ , A1,
N³⁻⁴

7.33 added‚ₐ] N²⁻³,⁵⁻⁶; ~ , A1,N¹,⁴

7.33 weakly:] N²⁻⁵; ~ , A1,N¹,⁶

7.37 scared‚ₐ] $N(−N⁴); ~ , A1,
N⁴

7.39 fall.] $N (N⁵: Fall.); ~ ;
A1

8.5 school teacher] N¹,⁴⁻⁶; ~ - ~
A1,N²; schoolteacher N³

8.7 ²it‚ₐ] N¹⁻²,⁵; ~ , A1,N³⁻⁴,⁶

8.11 odor] $N; odour A1

9.2 York,] N²⁻⁵; ~ ₐ A1,N¹,⁶

9.4 said.] $N(−N³); ~ ; A1; ~ :
N³

9.4 county] N¹⁻³,⁶; County A1,
N⁴⁻⁵

9.6 equipment‚ₐ] $N(−N³); ~ ,
A1,N³

9.7 maneuvering] $N(−N⁵);
manœuvring A1; manoeuvring
N⁵

9.9 o'clock‚ₐ] N¹⁻²,⁵; ~ , A1,N³⁻⁴,⁶

9.10 rumor] $N; rumour A1

9.13 shadows‚ₐ] N¹⁻²,⁶; ~ , A1,
N³⁻⁵ (N⁵ *uncertain*)

9.15–16 believed‚ₐ probably‚ₐ] $N;
~ , ~ , A1

9.18 Finally‚ₐ] $N; ~ , A1

9.19; 11.8,10,12,26 color] $N;
colour A1

9.19 scheme."] $N(−N⁴); ~ !"
A1,N⁴

9.20 At (*no* ¶)] N¹⁻³; ¶ A1,N⁴⁻⁶

9.22 boy.] N¹⁻²,⁵⁻⁶; ~ ! A1,N⁴; ~ ;
N³

9.23 canvas,] $N(−N⁴); ~ ₐ A1,
N⁴

9.27 out‚ₐ] $N; ~ , A1

9.28 said:] $N(−N²); ~ , A1,N²

10.3 Hawker. "A] $N(−N³); ~ ,
"a A1; ~ : "a N³

*10.5 then‚ₐ] *stet* A1

10.6 Hawker,] N²⁻⁵; ~ ₐ A1,N¹,⁶

10.9 Oh,"] $N(−N³); ~ !" A1,N³

10.15 now‚ₐ] $N; ~ , A1

10.21 else."] $N; ~ !" A1

10.26 'Quite dark,'] N²,⁴⁻⁶; ₐ ~
~ ‚ₐ A1,N¹; ₐ ~ ~ !ₐ N³

10.26 Hollanden‚ₐ] N¹,⁵⁻⁶; ~ , A1,
N²⁻⁴

10.31–32 morning.] $N; ~ ! A1

10.34 Hollanden,] N²⁻⁴,⁶; ~ ₐ A1,
N¹,⁵

11.4 laughed. "You] $N (cackled
shamelessly. "You); ~ ; "you
A1

11.8 ke-plunk] N¹,³⁻⁴,⁶; kerplunk
A1,N²,⁵

11.9 Hollanden,] $N; ~ ₐ A1

11.12 'What . . . eyes?'] N²,⁵;
ₐ ~ . . . ~ ? ₐ A1,N¹,³⁻⁴,⁶

11.16 yourself‚ₐ] $N(−N³); ~ ,
A1,N³

11.31 her‚ₐ] $N; ~ , A1

11.33 thief.] $N; ~ ! A1

11.34 here‚ₐ] N¹,⁴⁻⁶ (here and
howled‚ₐ); ~ , A1; here and
howled, N²⁻³

11.35 belabored] $N; belaboured
A1

11.36 that,"] $N; ~ !" A1

11.37 me.] $N; ~ ! A1

11.38 now."] $N; ~ !" A1

12.9 cried:] $N(−N⁴); ~ , A1,N⁴
(N⁴ *uncertain, possibly period*)

12.9 are.'] N¹⁻³,⁶; ~ !' A1,N⁴⁻⁵

12.10 endeavored] $N; endeav-
oured A1

12.15 her:] $N; ~, A1

12.17 saying:] N¹⁻⁴; ~ , A1,N⁵⁻⁶

12.17 charming.'] $N; ~ !' A1

12.21 me is:] $N(−N⁶) (N¹⁻⁴
omit is); ~ ~ , A1,N⁶

12.24 wives— . . . mothers—]
$N(−N³); ~ , . . . ~ , A1,N³

12.26 Cannot] $N(−N²); Can
not A1,N²

12.29 them."] $N; ~ !" A1

12.31 question.] $N(−N⁴); ~ :
A1,N⁴

12.31 recruited.] $N(−N³); ~ ?
A1,N³

13.2 Hollanden. "Almost] $N;
~ , "almost A1

13.3 question$_\wedge$] N$^{2,5-6}$; $\sim$, A1, N$^{1,3-4}$
13.5 Hawker. "And] $N; $\sim$, "and A1
13.6 them$_\wedge$] $N; $\sim$, A1
13.7 -houses] N$^{3-6}$; $_\wedge$ $\sim$ A1,N$^{1-2}$
13.7 houses$_\wedge$] N$^{2-5}$; $\sim$, A1,N^{1,6}
13.8 Hollanden. "Of] $N; $\sim$, "of A1
13.11 consideration. "Only] $N (−N^6); $\sim$, "only A1; $\sim$; only N^6
13.14 you—] N$^{1-2,5-6}$; $\sim$, A1,N$^{3-4}$
13.21 gloomed$_\wedge$] N$^{2,4-6}$; $\sim$, A1, N^{1,3}
13.21 said:] $N; $\sim$, A1
13.31 face$_\wedge$] N$^{2,5-6}$; $\sim$, A1,N$^{1,3-4}$
13.31 passionately:] $N; $\sim$, A1
13.32 business."] $N; $\sim$!" A1
13.34 eye$_\wedge$] N$^{2,4-6}$; $\sim$, A1,N^{1,3}
13.35 it. A] $N; $\sim$ — a A1
14.1 distance$_\wedge$] N$^{2,5-6}$; $\sim$, A1, N$^{1,3-4}$
14.3 to-morrow.] $N(N^4: tomorrow); $\sim$? A1
14.6 clever,"] $N; $\sim$!" A1
14.6 Hawker$_\wedge$] N$^{3-6}$; $\sim$, A1,N$^{1-2}$
14.8 too.] $N; $\sim$! A1
14.9 then,] $N; $\sim$ $_\wedge$ A1
14.9 money.] $N; $\sim$! A1
14.10 them,] $N(−N^1); $\sim$ $_\wedge$ A1, N^1
14.11 around.] $N; $\sim$! A1
14.12 cheerfully. "You've] $N; $\sim$; "you've A1
14.13,15 understand$_\wedge$] $N; $\sim$? A1
14.13 kindly$_\wedge$] N$^{1-2,5-6}$; $\sim$, A1, N$^{3-4}$
14.15 week$_\wedge$] N$^{2,5-6}$; $\sim$, A1,N$^{1,3-4}$
14.15 tolerantly,] $N(N$^{1-2,4-6}$: tolerably; N^3: tolorably); $\sim$ — A1
14.15 kindly$_\wedge$] $N(−N^4); $\sim$, A1, N^4
14.17 Hollie,"] $N(−N^5); $\sim$!" A1; $\sim$ $_\wedge$ N^5
14.18 Yes—yes—] N$^{1-2,4,6}$; $\sim$, $\sim$, A1,N^{3,5} (N^5: Yes, ys)
14.18 peacefully. "A] $N; $\sim$; "a A1

14.19 again$_\wedge$] $N(−N^3); $\sim$, A1, N^3
14.21 go."] $N; $\sim$!" A1
14.22 painter$_\wedge$] $N(−N^3); $\sim$, A1,N^3
14.24 There—there,] N$^{1-2,4,6}$; $\sim$! $\sim$! A1; $\sim$, $\sim$, N^{3,5}
14.24 fool.] $N; $\sim$! A1
14.30 idiot,"] $N(−N^6); $\sim$!" A1,N^6
14.32 replied:] $N; $\sim$, A1
15.8 gone,"] $N; $\sim$?" A1
15.9 gone."] $N(−N^5); $\sim$?" A1, N^5
15.10 Hollanden] $N; Hollander A1
15.12 gone."] $N; $\sim$?" A1
15.13 falls$_\wedge$] N$^{2,5-6}$; $\sim$, A1,N$^{1,3-4}$
15.15 exclaimed:] $N; $\sim$, A1
15.18 Providence$_\wedge$] $N; $\sim$, A1
15.19 Hollanden$_\wedge$] N$^{4-6}$; $\sim$, A1, N$^{1-3}$
15.20 brink. "Don't] $N(−N^4); $\sim$, "don't A1,N^4
15.23 men$_\wedge$] N$^{2-3,5-6}$; $\sim$, A1,N^{1,4}
15.25 history$_\wedge$] N$^{2-3,5-6}$; $\sim$, A1, N^{1,4}
15.30 cried:] $N; $\sim$, A1
16.4 prophet$_\wedge$] N$^{2,5-6}$; $\sim$, A1, N$^{1,3-4}$
16.6 carven] $N; carved A1
16.15 things$_\wedge$] N$^{2-3,5-6}$; $\sim$, A1, N^{1,4}
16.15 defense] $N; defence A1
16.17 mathematics$_\wedge$] $N(−N^3); $\sim$, A1,N^3
16.21 populace$_\wedge$] N$^{2-4,6}$; $\sim$, A1, N^{1,5}
16.26 paragraphs$_\wedge$] N$^{1-2,5-6}$; $\sim$, A1,N$^{3-4}$
16.29 Hollanden$_\wedge$] N$^{2,5-6}$; $\sim$, A1, N$^{1,3-4}$
16.31 sister. "You] N$^{1-3}$; $\sim$, "you A1,N$^{4-6}$
16.34 Hollanden,] $N; $\sim$ $_\wedge$ A1
16.39 others?"] $N(−N^3); $\sim$." A1; $\sim$!" N^3
17.1 Hollanden,] N$^{1,3-4}$; $\sim$ $_\wedge$ A1, N$^{2,5-6}$
17.3 purposely."] $N; $\sim$!" A1
17.5 Hollie."] $N; $\sim$!" A1

17.13 Hollie. You] $N(-N^4); \sim$, you A1; $\sim$; you N^4

17.18 away. Whereupon] $N; $\sim$; whereupon A1

17.19 chorus:] $N^{3-6}; \sim$, A1; $\sim$. N^{1-2}

17.20 back.] $N; $\sim$! A1

17.21 didn't."] $N; $\sim$!" A1

17.24 are.] $N; $\sim$! A1

18.2 and$_\wedge$] $N^{3,5-6}; \sim$, A1,$N^{1-2,4}$

18.3 warily$_\wedge$] $N^{3-6}; \sim$, A1,N^{1-2}

18.12 Yes. Of] $N^{1,5}; \sim$, of A1, $N^{2,4,6}; \sim$; of N^3

18.12 finer$_\wedge$ . . . rate$_\wedge$] $N^{1,4-6}; \sim$, . . . $\sim$, A1,N^{2-3}

18.17 it.] $N^{2,4-5}; \sim$? A1,$N^{1,3,6}$

18.23 You,"] $N^{1,4-5}; \sim$!" A1, $N^{2-3,6}$

18.25 life$_\wedge$] $N^{1,4,6}; \sim$, A1,$N^{2-3,5}$

18.29 answered$_\wedge$] $N^{1,4-5}; \sim$, A1, $N^{2-3,6}$

19.1 woman$_\wedge$ . . . for$_\wedge$] $N^{3,5}; \sim$, . . . $\sim$, A1,$N^{1-2,4,6}$

19.4 head. "No] $N; $\sim$, "no A1

19.10 He] N^{2-5}; he A1,$N^{1,6}$

19.12 said:] $N (said to Hawker:); $\sim$, A1

19.15 heaven] $N; Heaven A1

19.16 heiresses,] $N^{2,5-6}; \sim$ $_\wedge$ A1, $N^{1,3-4}$

19.17 this,] $N^{2-3,6}; \sim$ $_\wedge$ A1,$N^{1,4-5}$

19.33 Well—] $N; $\sim$, A1

20.2 that."] $N; $\sim$!" A1

20.7 her,] $N^{2,4-5}; \sim$ $_\wedge$ A1,$N^{1,3}$

20.8 water$_\wedge$] $N(-N^1); \sim$, A1, N^1

20.8 swirling$_\wedge$] $N; $\sim$, A1

20.12,17 moss$_\wedge$] $N(-N^1); \sim$, A1,N^1

20.23 beautiful.] $N(-N^6); \sim$! A1,N^6

20.25 motions$_\wedge$] $N^{2-3,5}; \sim$, A1, $N^{1,4,6}$

20.27 a-back] N^{1-3}; aback A1,N^{4-6}

20.27 a-back$_\wedge$] $N; $\sim$, A1

20.29 fool.] $N; $\sim$! A1

20.30 little] $N; the little A1

20.30 ants$_\wedge$] $N^{2-5}; \sim$, A1,$N^{1,6}$

20.31 important.$_\wedge$] $N; $\sim$.— A1

20.31 alone."] $N(-N^6); \sim$!" A1,N^6

20.32 investigations$_\wedge$] $N^{1-2,4}; \sim$, A1,$N^{3,5-6}$

20.35 Hawker,] $N(-N^2); \sim$ $_\wedge$ A1,N^2

20.37,38 pointing.] $N; $\sim$? A1

*20.39 it you] $N^{2-3,5-6}$; it to you A1,N^4; you N^1

21.1 time,] $N^{2-3,5}; \sim$ $_\wedge$ A1,$N^{1,4,6}$

21.13 severity:] $N; $\sim$, A1

21.14 folk-lore] $N^{3,5-6}$; folklore A1,$N^4; \sim$ - | $\sim$ N^{1-2}

21.15 bended] $N; bent A1

21.15 said. "They're] $N(-N^1); \sim$, "they're A1,N^1

21.17–18 and$_\wedge$ . . . -tops$_\wedge$] $N^{1-2,5}; \sim$, . . . $\sim$, A1,$N^{3-4,6}$

21.19 is."] $N; $\sim$!" A1

*21.23 took seat] N^2; took a seat A1,$N(-N^2)$

21.24 tree$_\wedge$] $N(-N^6); \sim$, A1,N^6

21.24 is. Whenever] $N; $\sim$, whenever A1

21.25 wits— . . . nature—] $N; $\sim$, . . . $\sim$, A1

21.26; 22.2 luck."] $N; $\sim$!" A1

21.28; 22.3 Hurry,] $N; $\sim$! A1

21.28; 22.3 said. "They're] $N (They are); $\sim$; "they're A1

22.7 listened$_\wedge$] $N(-N^4); \sim$, A1, N^4

22.18 said:] $N; $\sim$, A1

22.20 said:] $N(-N^5); \sim$, A1; $\sim$. N^5

22.20 good,] $N^{1,3,6}; \sim$ $_\wedge$ A1,$N^{2,4-5}$

22.22 hills$_\wedge$] $N^{1-2,5-6}; \sim$, A1,N^{3-4}

22.24 sing$_\wedge$] $N^{1-3,6}; \sim$, A1,N^{4-5}

22.25 quarreling] $N(-N^5); quarrelling A1,$N^5$

22.32 leaves$_\wedge$] $N^{1-2,5-6}; \sim$, A1, N^{3-4}

22.35 no.] $N(-N^4); \sim$ — A1,N^4

22.37 painter,] $N^{1,3-4,6}; \sim$ $_\wedge$ A1, $N^{2,5}$

23.3 scornfully. "Of] $N; $\sim$; "of A1

23.4 her$_\wedge$ . . . you$_\wedge$] $N(-N^4); \sim$, . . . $\sim$, A1,N^4

23.5 cried:] $N; $\sim$, A1

23.8–9 And$_\wedge$ of course$_\wedge$] $N; $\sim$, $\sim$ $\sim$, A1

23.9–10 now$_\wedge$ . . . circum-
stances$_\wedge$] \$N(−N³); ∼ , . . .
∼ , A1; ∼ , . . . ∼$_\wedge$N³

23.13 puffing. "Of] \$N; ∼ , "of
A1

23.19 grimly. "And] \$N(−N⁴);
∼ , "and A1,N⁴

23.20 chance."] \$N; ∼ ?" A1

23.21 chump,"] \$N; ∼ !" A1

23.21 Hollanden$_\wedge$] \$N; ∼ , A1

23.24–25 Stanley$_\wedge$ the setter$_\wedge$]
N²,⁴⁻⁶; ∼ , ∼ ∼ , A1,N¹,³

23.28 Hawker$_\wedge$] \$N(−N³); ∼ ,
A1,N³

23.29 work$_\wedge$] N¹⁻²,⁵⁻⁶; ∼ , A1,N³⁻⁴

23.29 ²to] \$N; omit A1

23.33 No.] N²,⁴⁻⁵; ∼ , A1,N¹,⁶;
∼ ; N³

23.35 said. "But] \$N; ∼ , "but A1

23.37 you.] N¹⁻²,⁵⁻⁶; ∼ ! A1,N³⁻⁴

23.38 moon,] N³⁻⁴,⁶; ∼$_\wedge$ A1,N¹⁻²,⁵

24.3 dog$_\wedge$] \$N; ∼ , A1

24.5 But,] N¹⁻²,⁵⁻⁶; ∼$_\wedge$ A1,N³⁻⁴

24.13 tomatoes$_\wedge$] \$N(−N⁶); ∼ ,
A1,N⁶

24.19 But,] \$N; ∼$_\wedge$ A1

24.26 while,] \$N(−N¹) (N⁴:
awhile); ∼$_\wedge$ A1,N¹

24.31 'One's own people,'] N²⁻³,⁵⁻⁶
(N⁵: people?'); $_\wedge$ ∼ ∼ ∼ !$_\wedge$
A1; $_\wedge$ ∼ ∼ ∼ ,$_\wedge$ N¹,⁴

25.1 said. "One's] \$N(−N⁵); ∼ ,
"one's A1,N⁵

25.3 appreciation,] N²,⁴,⁶; ∼ !
A1,N³; ∼ ? N¹,⁵

25.3 indeed."] \$N; ∼ !" A1

25.6 threshed] \$N(−N⁴);
thrashed A1,N⁴

25.11 said:] \$N; ∼ , A1

25.15 said. "Of] \$N; ∼ , "of A1

25.15 ¹it$_\wedge$] \$N(−N³); ∼ , A1,N³

25.17 Hollanden, perhaps,] \$N;
∼$_\wedge$ ∼$_\wedge$ A1

25.18 it. Of] \$N; ∼ , of A1

25.21 ²it$_\wedge$] \$N; ∼ , A1

25.23 exhibit$_\wedge$] N²,⁵⁻⁶; ∼ , A1,
N¹,³⁻⁴

25.24 remembered] \$N; remem-
ber A1

25.24 you$_\wedge$] N¹⁻³,⁶; ∼ , A1,N⁴⁻⁵

25.25 moment$_\wedge$] \$N; ∼ , A1

25.25 added:] \$N; ∼ , A1

25.26 good$_\wedge$] \$N(−N¹); ∼ , A1,
N¹

25.26 anyhow."] \$N(N⁶: any-
way); ∼ !" A1

25.30 persisted$_\wedge$] N¹⁻³; ∼ , A1,
N⁴⁻⁶

25.34 girls$_\wedge$] N¹⁻²,⁵⁻⁶; ∼ , A1,N³⁻⁴

25.36 girl,] \$N(−N⁵); ∼$_\wedge$ A1,N⁵

25.36 suddenly.] N¹⁻²,⁴; ∼ , A1,
N³,⁶; N⁵ illegible

25.36–37 to-morrow."] \$N; ∼ !"
A1

26.1 good$_\wedge$] N¹⁻³; ∼ , A1,N⁴⁻⁶

26.2 college$_\wedge$] N¹⁻²,⁶; ∼ , A1,N³⁻⁵

26.12 top$_\wedge$] N²⁻⁵; ∼ , A1,N¹,⁶

26.13 strange$_\wedge$] N¹⁻²,⁵⁻⁶; ∼ , A1,
N³⁻⁴

26.14 lake shore] \$N(−N²);
lakeshore A1; ∼ - | ∼ N²

*26.15 moon] \$N; boat A1

26.16 seat$_\wedge$] N¹⁻²,⁶; ∼ , N³⁻⁵

26.18 Hawker$_\wedge$] N¹⁻²,⁶; ∼ , A1,
N³⁻⁵

26.19 sub-consciously] \$N
(−N⁴); subconsciously
A1,N⁴

26.23; 27.9 said:] \$N; ∼ , A1

26.25 ¹will] \$N; shall A1

27.2 Fanhalls.] \$N(N⁵: Fan-
hall's); ∼ ! A1

27.2 him.] \$N; ∼ ! A1

27.3 too.] \$N; ∼ ! A1

27.6 fellow.] \$N; ∼ ! A1

27.7 rival.] \$N; ∼ ! A1

27.7 course.] \$N(−N⁶); ∼ ! A1,
N⁶

27.8 to-night."] \$N(N³⁻⁴:
tonight); ∼ !" A1

27.10 Yonder$_\wedge$] \$N; ∼ , A1

27.12–13 thrilling."] \$N; ∼ !" A1

27.16 said$_\wedge$] \$N(−N¹); ∼ , A1,
N¹

27.17 weariness:] N¹,³⁻⁵; ∼ , A1,
N²,⁶ (N² uncertain)

27.19 on,"] V; ∼ !" A1,E1,N³;
N¹,⁶ uncertain; ∼ ." N²,⁴⁻⁵

27.20 ceiling. "Don't] \$N; ∼ ,
"don't A1

27.20 yet.] \$N; ∼ ! A1

27.22 harry] N⁵; harrie A1,$N (—N⁵)

27.22 you.] $N; ~ ! A1

27.22 too."] $N; ~ !" A1

27.23 Hawker, suddenly∧] $N; ~ ∧ ~ , A1

27.24 duffer.] $N; ~ ! A1

27.25 man∧] $N; ~ , A1

27.26 ceiling."] $N; ~ ?" A1

27.28 up.] $N; ~ ! A1

27.29 business."] $N; ~ !" A1

27.30 Oglethorpe—] $N; ~ , A1

28.4 Oglethorpe.] $N; ~ ! A1

28.4 chumps.] $N; ~ ! A1

28.5 open∧] $N(—N⁵); ~ , A1,N⁵

*28.7 close] stet A1

28.8 calling:] N²⁻⁵; ~ , A1; ~ ∧ N¹·⁶

28.8,9 Good night] N²⁻³·⁵⁻⁶; ~ - ~ A1,N¹·⁴

28.10 said:] $N; ~ , A1

28.10 money."] N¹⁻⁴; ~ ?" A1, N⁵⁻⁶

28.11 has.] $N; ~ ! A1

28.12 situation."] $N(—N⁶); ~ !" A1,N⁶

28.13 brow∧] $N(—N⁶); ~ , A1, N⁶

28.14 here, sometimes] N²⁻³·⁵; ~ ! Sometimes A1,N¹·⁴; ~ ; ~ N⁶

28.16 fool,"] N⁴⁻⁶; ~ !" A1; ~." N¹⁻³(N¹ uncertain)

28.17 circumstances∧] $N(—N⁶); ~ , A1,N⁶

28.19 that.] $N(—N⁶); ~ ! A1; ~ , N⁶

28.22 was] N¹⁻³; were A1,N⁴⁻⁶

28.23 right.] $N; ~ ! A1

28.25 infant."] $N; ~ !" A1

28.30 And,] $N(—N⁶); ~ ∧ A1, N⁶

28.31 him."] N²·⁴⁻⁶; ~ !" A1,N¹·³

28.33 awhile] $N(—N⁶); a while A1,N⁶

28.35 would] $N; should A1

28.36 advice.] $N(—N¹); ~ ! A1, N¹

28.39 it.] N²⁻³·⁶; ~ ! A1,N⁴⁻⁵

29.1 fellow,] N²·⁴·⁶; ~ ∧ A1,N³·⁵

29.2 course∧] N¹⁻²·⁵; ~ , A1,N³⁻⁴·⁶

29.2 case,] N²⁻⁵; ~ ∧ A1,N¹·⁶

29.5 man?"] $N; ~ !" A1

29.19 lie."] $N(—N⁴); ~ !" A1, N⁴

29.21 ultimately. "And] $N; ~ ; "and A1

29.25 on.] $N(—N⁴); ~ ! A1,N⁴

29.29 silence,] $N(—N⁶); ~ ∧ A1,N⁶

29.29 said:] $N; ~ , A1

29.30 door,] N²⁻⁵; ~ ∧ A1,N¹·⁶

29.31 pilgrim."] N¹⁻²·⁴⁻⁵; ~ !" A1, N³·⁶

29.33 wheeled∧] $N; ~ , A1

30.3 tennis."] $N; ~ ?" A1

30.4 him,] $N(—N²); ~ ! A1,N²

30.11–12 supposed∧ of course∧] N²·⁵⁻⁶; ~ , ~ ~ , A1,N¹·³⁻⁴ (N³: suppose)

30.13 melee] $N; mêlée A1

30.15 walk."] $N(—N⁶); ~ ?" A1,N⁶

30.19 stubble∧] N¹·³·⁵⁻⁶; ~ , A1, N²·⁴

30.28 trees,] N¹⁻³·⁵; ~ ∧ A1,N⁴·⁶

30.29 began:] $N; ~ , A1

30.30 No. He] N¹·³⁻⁵; ~ , he A1, N²·⁶

30.30 said:] $N(—N³); ~ , A1; ~ . N³

31.6 Hollanden,] $N(—N⁴); ~ ∧ A1,N⁴

31.8 Hawker,] $N; ~ — A1

31.10 dog."] $N; ~ !" A1

31.12 not,"] $N; ~ !" A1

31.16 simple∧] N³·⁵⁻⁶; ~ , A1, N¹⁻²·⁴

31.20 Hollie] $N; Holly A1

31.21 Hawker∧] N¹·³·⁵; ~ , A1, N²·⁴·⁶

31.22 darkly. "You] $N; ~ ; "you A1

31.28 No. Not] $N(—N²); ~ , not A1,N²

31.33 There—there,"] $N(—N²); ~ ! ~ !" A1; ~ , ~ ," N²

31.34 oration."] N¹·⁴⁻⁶; ~ !" A1, N²⁻³

31.37 said,] N²⁻³·⁵⁻⁶; ~ ∧ A1,N¹·⁴

31.39 broadly——"] $N(—N⁵); ~ ——∧ A1; ~ "—— N⁵

32.2 rate$_\wedge$] N$^{1-2,4,6}$; $\sim$, A1,N^{3,5}

32.12 slowly:] \$N($-$N^5); $\sim$, A1; $\sim$. N^5

32.16 shoulder. "You] N$^{1-2,5}$; $\sim$, "you A1,N$^{3-4,6}$

32.18 again."] \$N; $\sim$!" A1

32.25 it! See it!"] \$N; $\sim$? $\sim$ $\sim$?" A1

32.29 decisively:] \$N; $\sim$, A1

32.35 excitedly$_\wedge$] \$N($-$N^6); $\sim$, A1,N^6

32.35 turn] \$N; turned A1

34.1 mother$_\wedge$] \$N; $\sim$, A1

34.4 boot$_\wedge$] N$^{1-3,5}$; $\sim$, A1,N^{4,6}

34.6 father$_\wedge$] N$^{1,3,5-6}$; $\sim$, A1,N^{2,4}

34.10 John. Folks] \$N($-$N^5); $\sim$ —folks A1; $\sim$, folks N^5

34.10 airs,] \$N($-$N^2); $\sim$; A1; $\sim$ $_\wedge$ N^2

34.13 man,] \$N($-$N^1); $\sim$ $_\wedge$ A1, N^1

34.17 'What girl!'] N$^{3-5}$ (N^5: girl?); $_\wedge$ $\sim$ $\sim$?$_\wedge$ A1,N$^{1-2,6}$ (N^6: girl!)

34.17 Why$_\wedge$] N$^{1-2,5-6}$; $\sim$, A1,N$^{3-4}$

34.20 mother,] N$^{2,4-5}$; $\sim$ $_\wedge$ A1, N^{1,3,6}

34.22 man$_\wedge$] N$^{2-3,6}$; $\sim$, A1,N$^{1,4-5}$

34.22 nor . . . nor] \$N($-$N^4); or . . . or A1,N^4

34.25 stairs$_\wedge$] N$^{2-3,5}$; $\sim$, A1, N^{1,4,6}

34.26; 35.4 said:] \$N; $\sim$, A1

34.26 -lookin'."] \$N; $\sim$!" A1

34.28 proud$_\wedge$] \$N($-$N^6); $\sim$, A1, N^6

34.31 he$_\wedge$] N$^{1,3,5-6}$; $\sim$, A1,N^{2,4}

35.3 sleep,"] \$N; $\sim$!" A1

35.3 father,] N$^{2-4,6}$; $\sim$ $_\wedge$ A1,N^{1,5}

35.4 time$_\wedge$] N$^{1-2,5}$; $\sim$, A1,N$^{3-4,6}$

35.4 John!"] \$N; $\sim$?" A1

35.8 demanded:] \$N; $\sim$, A1

35.9 you."] N$^{3,5-6}$(\$N: yeh); $\sim$?" A1,N$^{1-2,4}$

35.10 wide-eyed] \$N; wild-eyed A1

35.12 breakfast$_\wedge$] N$^{1-2,4}$; $\sim$, A1, N$^{3,5-6}$

35.16 parlor] V; parlour A1,E1

35.17 onto] \$N($-$N^6); on to A1,N^6

35.21 parlor] \$N; parlour A1

35.21 returned,] \$N($-$N^5); $\sim$ $_\wedge$ A1,N^5

35.23 said,] N$^{3-5}$; $\sim$ $_\wedge$ A1,N$^{1-2,6}$

35.32 rejoined$_\wedge$] N$^{1-3,6}$; $\sim$, A1, N$^{4-5}$

35.34 my,"] \$N($-$N^2); $\sim$!" A1, N^2

35.35 interested$_\wedge$] \$N($-$N^2); $\sim$, A1,N^2

36.2 wood,] N$^{1-4}$; $\sim$ $_\wedge$ A1,N$^{5-6}$

36.6 a] \$N; a | a A1

36.9 forest,] \$N($-$N^6); $\sim$ $_\wedge$ A1, N^6

36.14 sister—"] \$N($-$N^5); $\sim$," A1; Sister!" N^5

36.14 cried.] \$N; $\sim$, A1

36.21,24 Well!"] \$N; $\sim$," A1

36.22 Yep!] \$N; $\sim$. A1

36.28 Pa] N$^{1-2,4-5}$; pa A1,N^{3,6}

36.30 added:] N$^{1-3}$; $\sim$, A1,N$^{5-6}$; $\sim$ $_\wedge$ N^4

37.4 Hollanden$_\wedge$] \$N($-$N^4); $\sim$, A1,N^4

37.5 cried:] \$N($-$N^6); $\sim$, A1,N^6

37.6 coming."] \$N; $\sim$!" A1

37.9 dog$_\wedge$ . . . him$_\wedge$] N$^{1-3,6}$; $\sim$, . . . $\sim$, A1,N$^{4-5}$

37.11 court$_\wedge$] N$^{1-3,6}$; $\sim$, A1,N$^{4-5}$

37.13 sheep-trot] N$^{1-3}$; $\sim$ $_\wedge$ $\sim$ A1, N$^{4-6}$

37.14 said:] \$N; $\sim$, A1

37.15 Hawker?"] \$N($-$N^3); $\sim$." A1,N^3

37.21 summer$_\wedge$] N$^{1-3,5}$; $\sim$, A1, N^{4,6}

37.24 nod. "Just] \$N($-$N^3); $\sim$, "just A1; $\sim$; "just N^3

37.25 you."] \$N; $\sim$!" A1

37.28 inn$_\wedge$] N$^{1-3}$; $\sim$, A1,N$^{4-6}$

37.29 court,] N$^{1-4}$; $\sim$ $_\wedge$ A1,N$^{5-6}$

37.30 again$_\wedge$] N$^{1-3}$; $\sim$, A1,N$^{4-6}$

37.32 others. "It] N^1; $\sim$, "it A1, N$^{3-6}$; $\sim$, "It N^2

38.1 court$_\wedge$] \$N($-$N^4); $\sim$, A1, N^4

38.2 declare.] \$N; $\sim$! A1

38.2 ever."] \$N($-$N^6); $\sim$?" A1; $\sim$!" N^6

38.10 position."] \$N; $\sim$!" A1

38.11 dramatically:] $N(−N⁵); ~ , AI,N⁵

38.14 fellow."] $N(−N⁶); ~ !" AI,N⁶

38.19 owned∧] N¹⁻²,⁵; ~ , AI, N³⁻⁴,⁶

38.24 dear.] N¹⁻⁵; ~ ? AI

38.31 course. It's] N¹⁻⁴; ~ ∧ it's AI; ~ , it's N⁵⁻⁶

38.37 idea.] $N; ~ ! AI

38.39 child.] $N; ~ ! AI

39.1 ¹her.] $N; ~ ! AI

39.1 little∧ old∧] N³⁻⁵; ~ , ~ , AI,N¹⁻²,⁶

39.3 thing."] $N; ~ !" AI

39.6 hinge, you] N¹,³⁻⁵; ~ ∧ ~ AI,N⁶; ~ . You N²

39.8 said:] $N; ~ , AI

39.8 player,] $N; ~ ∧ AI

40.1 said∧] $N(−N³); ~ , AI,N³

40.1 greeting∧] $N; ~ , AI

40.1 Hawker:] $N; ~ , AI

40.5 Hawker,] $N; ~ ∧ AI

40.8 you.] $N; ~ ! AI

40.10 weren't∧] N¹,⁵⁻⁶; ~ , AI, N²⁻⁴

40.11 asked:] N¹⁻³,⁶; ~ , AI,N⁵; ~ . N⁴

40.17 said,] $N; ~ ; AI

40.19 Hawker,] N²⁻⁵; ~ ∧ AI,N¹,⁶

40.27 Stanley∧ the setter∧] N³,⁵; ~ , ~ ~ , AI,N¹⁻²,⁴,⁶

40.29 me—"] $N(−N⁵); ~ ," AI,N⁵

40.29–30 said. "Seems] N¹⁻²,⁴,⁶; ~ , "seems AI, N³,⁵

41.2 it∧ then∧] $N; ~ , ~ , AI

41.6 instantly. "Nothing] $N; ~ , "nothing AI

41.11 yellows∧] $N(−N⁴); ~ , AI,N⁴

41.17 quarreling] $N(−N⁵); quarrelling AI,N⁵

41.18 clamor] $N; clamour AI

41.18 Stanley∧ the setter∧] N⁵⁻⁶; ~ , ~ ~ , AI,N¹⁻⁴

41.20 there∧] $N; ~ , AI

41.21 fellow,"] N³⁻⁶; ~ ?" AI, N¹⁻²

41.26 said:] $N(−N⁶); ~ , AI, N⁶

41.30 again∧] N¹,⁴,⁶; ~ , AI, N²⁻³,⁵

41.33 well——"] N¹,³,⁵(N⁵: ~ " ——); ~ ," AI,N²,⁴,⁶

41.34 Oh,"] N¹⁻⁴; ~ !" AI,N⁵⁻⁶

41.38 know.] $N; ~ ? AI

41.39 Oh,"] $N(−N⁶); ~ !" AI, N⁶

41.39 added:] $N(−N⁴); ~ , AI; ~ ∧ N⁴

42.2 cried:] N¹⁻²,⁴; ~ ∧ AI,N⁵⁻⁶; ~ , N³

42.5 frowned∧] N¹⁻²,⁴,⁶; ~ , AI, N³,⁵

42.16 again:] $N; ~ , AI

43.1 lake∧] N¹,⁴⁻⁶; ~ , AI,N²⁻³

43.2,24 grey] V; gray AI,$N,EI

43.7 festivities,] N¹⁻⁴; ~ ∧ AI,N⁵⁻⁶

43.7,12; 44.9,15; 45.31; 46.10 said:] $N; ~ , AI

*43.7 Billie] stet AI

43.10 ¹it,] $N(−N¹); ~ ∧ AI,N¹

43.10 trouble∧] N¹⁻²,⁵; ~ , AI, N³⁻⁴,⁶

43.12 go."] $N; ~ !" AI

43.20 fool."] $N; ~ !" AI

43.21 Hawker∧] N¹⁻²,⁵⁻⁶; ~ , AI, N³⁻⁴

43.25 pines∧] $N(−N⁴); ~ , AI, N⁴

43.26 Hollanden∧] $N(−N³); ~ , AI,N³

43.27 Hollie,"] N¹,⁶; ~ !" AI; ~ ." N²⁻⁵

43.29 further] $N; farther AI

44.5 slowly,] N²⁻⁴; ~ ∧ AI,N¹,⁵⁻⁶

44.6 foliage.] $N(−N⁴); ~ : AI, N⁴

44.6 -ap! Blast] $N; ~ , blast AI

44.10 little."] N¹⁻²,⁶; ~ ?" AI, N³⁻⁵

44.12 Haw! Git-ap!] $N(N¹,³⁻⁴: Git-ap,); haw! git-ap! AI

44.13 Red. Git] $N; ~ , git AI

44.13 -ap!"] $N; ~ ! ∧ AI

44.17 there. Driving] $N(−N⁵); ~ , driving AI; ~ ; driving N⁵

44.19 skin] $N; shin AI

44.21 repeated:] $N; ~ , AI

44.23 Hawker,] $N; ~ ∧ AI

44.26 bended] $N(−N¹); bent
A1; bending N¹
44.26 yoke∧] $N^{1-2,6}$; ~ , A1,N^{3-5}
*44.26 looking] $N(−N³); looked
A1,N³
44.27 eyes∧] $N^{1-3,6}$; ~ , A1,N^{4-5}
44.28 them∧] $N^{1-2,4,6}$; ~ , A1,N^{3,5}
44.32 father,"] $N; ~ !" A1
44.33 Whoa—back—whoa!]
$N^{2,4-6}$; Whoa! Back! Whoa!
A1,N³; Whoa, back, whoa! N¹
44.37 do!"] $N; ~ ?" A1
45.1 girl, later,] $N(−N¹); ~ ∧
~ ∧ A1,N¹
45.2 things,"] $N^{1-2,4}$; ~ ?" A1,
$N^{3,5-6}$
45.2 said∧] $N^{1-3,6}$; ~ , A1,N^{4-5}
45.6 ox∧] $N^{2,5-6}$; ~ , A1,N^{1,3-4}
45.12 man,] $N; ~ ∧ A1
45.14 grinning. "Just] $N(Jest);
~ , "just A1
45.20 fellows.] $N^{1-2,4}$; ~ ? A1,
N^{5-6}; ~ ?? N³
45.25 said,] $N^{2,4-5}$; ~ ∧ A1,N^{1,3,6}
45.32 on∧] $N; ~ , A1
45.34 seat∧] $N^{1-2,4-5}$; ~ , A1,N^{3,6}
45.38 girl∧] $N^{1,5-6}$; ~ , A1,N^{2-4}
46.2 do? Would] $N(−N⁵); ~ ;
would A1; ~ , would N⁵
46.6 all.] $N; ~ ? A1
46.7 Yep. Always] $N; ~ ,
always A1
46.7 -foot,] $N^{1-3,6}$; ~ ∧ A1,N^{4-5}
46.9 Well!] $N(−N⁵); ~ , A1,N⁵
46.15–16 Stanley∧ the setter∧]
$N^{1,3}$; ~ , ~ ~ , A1,N^{2,4-6}
46.18 cheerfully:] $N; ~ , A1
46.22 awf'ly] $N; awfully A1
46.22 you."] $N; ~ !" A1
46.23 Why—"] N^{1-4}; ~ ," A1,
N^{5-6}
46.23 Hawker. "You] N^{1-4}; ~ ,
"you A1,N^{5-6}
46.33 attacks,] N^{1-4}; ~ ∧ A1,N^{5-6}
46.34 me!] $N; ~ . A1
47.1 Haw] $N^{3-4,6}$; Ha A1,N^{1-2,5}
47.3 alight∧] $N^{1-2,4}$; ~ , A1,N^{3,5-6}
47.6 time.] $N; ~ ! A1
47.7 us."] $N(−N⁶); ~ !" A1,N⁶
48.1 Fanhall."] $N; ~ !" A1

48.5 'Prank'?] V; '~ ?' N^{3-5}; ∧ ~
? ∧ A1,N^{1,6}; ∧ ~ ! ∧ N²
48.10 too,] $N(−N⁵); ~ ; A1,N⁵
48.10 ²can't.] $N; ~ ! A1
48.14 oration∧] $N(N⁴: ~ ∧
then,); ~ , A1
48.14; 49.1 said:] $N; ~ , A1
48.15 What's] $N; what's A1
48.17 them,] $N^{1-2,6}$; ~ ∧ A1,N^{3-5}
*48.20 interrogations] $N; inter-
rogation A1
48.20–21 nothing,"] $N; ~ !" A1
48.21 undertone:] $N; ~ , A1
48.24 nothing."] $N; ~ !" A1
48.26 morning,] $N^{1,3,6}$; ~ ∧ A1,
$N^{2,4-5}$
48.26 girl:] $N; ~ , A1
49.1 moment∧] $N; ~ , A1
49.1 "Well] $N; *battered type*
A1 ('Well)
49.2 said:] $N(−N⁶) ($N: replied); ~ , A1,N⁶
49.3 you—] $N; ~ , A1
49.6 Well—] $N; ~ , A1
49.12 you∧] N^{1-4}; ~ , A1,N^{5-6}
49.14 other∧] $N^{1-2,4-5}$; ~ , A1,N^{3,6}
49.14,28 said:] $N(−N⁶); ~ ,
A1,N⁶
49.17 bluntly:] $N(−N⁶); ~ ,
A1,N⁶
49.19 No!] $N(−N²); ~ . A1,N²
49.21–22 continued:] $N(−N⁶);
~ , A1,N⁶
49.24 stammered:] $N(−N⁶);
~ , A1,N⁶
49.31 indignantly:] N^{2-5}; ~ , A1,
N⁶; ~ . N¹
49.31 you."] $N; ~ !" A1
49.33 sneered. "Of] $N^{1-2,4-5}$; ~ ,
"of A1,N⁶; ~ ; "of N³
49.33,34(*twice*) not.] $N(49.33:
N⁵: ~ ∧); ~ ! A1
49.35 vouchsafed∧] $N^{1,3-4}$($N:
concluded); ~ , A1,N^{2,5-6}
49.35–36 eyeing] N^{1-3}; eying A1,
N^{4-6}
49.37 ²am,"] $N(N⁵: *possibly
period*); ~ !" A1
50.3 magnificently:] $N; ~ , A1
50.8 ahem.] $N(−N⁵); ~ ! A1,
N⁵

*50.8   you] N[1,5-6]; are you A1,N[2-4]
50.11   slam-thing] $N(−N[5]);
        ∼ ∧ ∼ A1,N[5]
50.12   racquet] $N(−N[6]); racket
        A1,N[6]
50.14   [1]you] N[1,3-5]; to you A1,N[2,6]
50.16   Billie."] $N(N[5]: Billee);
        ∼ !" A1
50.17   friend.] $N(−N[6]); ∼ , A1;
        ∼ ; N[6]
50.18   Good-by."] $N(N[1-2]: bye);
        Good-bye!" A1
50.32   time∧] $N(−N[3]); ∼ , A1,
        N[3]
50.32   observed:] $N; ∼ , A1
50.35   it. As] $N; ∼ —as A1
50.38   declare∧] $N(−N[6]); ∼ ,
        A1,N[6]
52.1   Hollanden∧] $N(−N[3]); ∼ ,
        A1,N[3]
*52.5   in] $N; into A1
52.6   expression∧] N[1-2,5-6]; ∼ , A1,
        N[3-4]
52.7   his] $N; its A1
52.10   answered∧] N[1-2,4,6]; ∼ ,
        A1,N[3,5]
52.11   me∧] N[1-2,4,6]; ∼ , A1,N[3,5]
52.13   Ah?"] N[1-2,4-5]; Ah!" A1,
        N[3,6]
52.14   Hollanden∧] N[1-2,4]; ∼ , A1,
        N[3,5-6]
52.16   swain∧] $N; ∼ , A1
52.21   Why∧] N[1-2,6]; ∼ , A1,N[3-5]
52.27   replied,] N[2-3,5-6]; ∼ ∧ A1,
        N[1,4]
52.27   ironically. "Not] $N(−N[3]);
        ∼ , "not A1,N[3]
52.30   feelings] $N; feeling A1
53.3   began:] $N; ∼ , A1
53.7   thing,] N[1-2,4-5]; ∼ ∧ A1,N[3,6]
53.8   any one's] N[3-6]; anyone's
        A1,N[1-2]
53.10,14,23   said:] $N; ∼ , A1
53.20   affairs∧] N[2,4-6]; ∼ , A1,N[1,3]
53.25   'Mean this time?'] N[2-3,6];
        ∧∼ ∼ ∼ ? ∧ A1,N[1,4-5]
53.27   said,] N[2-3,5-6]; ∼ ∧ A1,N[1,4]
53.28−29,31   event∧ . . . events∧]
        $N; ∼ , . . . ∼ , A1
53.29,32   ill-fortune] $N(−N[4]);
        ∼ ∧ ∼ A1,N[4]

53.30   yourself∧] N[1,4-5]; ∼ , A1,
        N[2-3,6]
53.33   clever,"] $N; ∼ !" A1
53.34   event∧] $N; ∼ , A1
53.34   events∧] N[1,4-6]; ∼ , A1,N[2-3]
53.39   said,] N[2-3,5]; ∼ ∧ A1,N[1,4,6]
54.2   answered,] N[3,5]; ∼ ∧ A1,
        N[1-2,4,6]
54.9   know∧ . . . know∧] N[2,5-6];
        ∼ , . . . ∼ , A1,N[1,3-4]
54.11   Hollanden,] N[2-3,5]; ∼ ∧ A1,
        N[1,4,6]
54.15   man.] $N; ∼ ! A1
54.16   dog."] $N; ∼ !" A1
54.18   trail∧] N[2-3,6]; ∼ , A1,N[1,4-5]
54.18   then∧] N[1-2,5-6]; ∼ , A1,N[3-4]
*54.18 near to] stet A1
54.18   ground∧] N[2,5-6]; ∼ , A1,
        N[1,3-4]
54.21   Indeed,] $N(−N[2]); ∼ ∧
        A1,N[2]
54.21   is,"] $N; ∼ !" A1
54.24   reason∧] N[1-2,6]; ∼ , A1,
        N[3-5]
54.26   slam.] $N; ∼ : A1
54.27   see—] N[1-4,6]; ∼ ! — A1;
        ∼ ? — N[5]
54.31   ground.] $N; ∼ ! A1
54.33   Afterward∧] N[2,5-6]; ∼ , A1,
        N[1,3-4]
54.35   you] N[1,3,5]; are you A1,
        N[2,4,6]
55.8   Hollanden.] N[2,5-6]; ∼ , A1,
        N[1,3-4]
*55.9   ingenuous] $N(−N[5]);
        ingenious A1,N[5]
55.17   last∧] N[1,4-6]; ∼ , A1,N[2-3]
55.20   parlors] $N; parlours A1
55.25   monotone∧] $N; ∼ , A1
55.25   [2]branch∧] N[1,3-4,6]; ∼ , A1,
        N[2,5]
56.1   Hollanden∧] $N(−N[4]); ∼ ,
        A1,N[4]
56.1   girls] N[2-3]; girl A1,N[1,4-6]
56.2   well∧being] N[1-2,4,6]; ∼ - ∼
        A1,N[3,5]
56.9   answered,] N[2,4-6]; ∼ ∧ A1,
        N[1,3]
56.9   stiffly∧] N[1-2,6]; ∼ , A1,N[3-5]
56.15   shall, of course,] N[1-2,5-6];
        ∼ ∧ ∼ ∼ ∧ A1,N[3-4]

56.18 dear—] N[1,3-4,6]; ~ ! A1,
N[5]; ~ , N[2]

56.33 good-night] N[3-5]; Good- |
~ A1,N[2]; ~ _∧ ~ N[1]; ~ - | ~ N[6]

56.34 attentions] $N; attention
A1

56.35 chaperone] N[1-2,6];
chaperon A1,N[3-5]

56.37 say:] $N(−N[2]); ~ , A1,N[2]

56.37 nervous."] $N; ~ !" A1

57.6 door,] $N(−N[1]); ~ _∧ A1,N[1]

57.10 girl:] $N; ~ , A1

57.19,22,23,26,27 Good-by]
N[2,4-6]; Good-bye A1,N[1,3]

57.23 feverishly_∧] $N(−N[4]); ~ ,
A1,N[4]

57.29 door mat] N[1-2,4]; ~ - ~ A1,
N[3,5]; doormat N[6]

57.30 thump-] N[1-2,4,6]; ~ , A1,
N[5]; ~ — N[3]

57.30 [2]thump_∧] $N; ~ , A1

57.31 enthusiasm_∧] N[1-3,6]; ~ ,
A1,N[4-5]

57.33 uncurled_∧] $N; ~ , A1

57.39 door mat] N[2,4]; ~ - ~ A1,
N[1,3,5]; doormat N[6]

58.2 door mat] N[2]; ~ - | ~ A1;
~ - ~ N[1,3,5]; doormat N[4,6]

58.2 steps_∧] N[2,5-6]; ~ , A1,N[1,3-4]

58.4 house,] N[1,3-5]; ~ _∧ A1,N[2,6]

59.9 Oh,"] $N; ~ !" A1

59.11 observed:] $N; ~ , A1

59.13 girl.] $N(−N[5]); ~ — A1,
N[5]

59.17 table_∧] $N(−N[1]); ~ , A1,
N[1]

59.17 and_∧ . . . hat_∧] $N
(−N[5]); ~ , . . . ~ , A1,N[5]

59.18 mother_∧] N[1-3,6]; ~ , A1,
N[4-5]

59.26 ain't. 'Cept] $N(N[1]: aint);
ain't—'cept A1

59.28 him,] $N('im); ~ _∧ A1

59.30 lightnin',"] $N(−N[5]); ~ !"
A1,N[5]

59.30 man,] N[1-2,4-5]; ~ _∧ A1,N[3,6]

60.8 face_∧] N[1-4]; ~ , A1,N[5-6]

60.15 more. But] $N(−N[6]); ~ ;
but A1; ~ , but N[6]

*60.22 home] $N; come home A1

60.23 best_∧] $N(−N[5]); ~ , A1,
N[5]

60.24 York,] $N(−N[5]); ~ _∧ A1,
N[5]

60.28 now.] $N; ~ ! A1

60.32 him:] $N; ~ , A1

60.36 blazes."] $N(−N[6]); ~ !"
A1,N[6]

61.3 does_∧]$N(−N[6]); ~ , A1,N[6]

61.6 a slate] $N(−N[3]); slate
A1,N[3]

61.6,10 color] $N; colour A1

61.6 Lord,] $N; ~ ! A1

61.10 up_∧] N[1-4]; ~ , A1,N[5-6]

61.15 stupid_∧] $N; ~ , A1

61.18 'Is . . . all!'] N[3-4,6](N[6]:
all?); _∧ ~ . . . ~ ? _∧ A1;
_∧ ~ . . . ~ ! _∧ N[1,5];
_∧ ~ . . . ~ ?" N[2]

61.23 mother:] $N; ~ , A1

61.27 declare.] $N; ~ ! A1

61.30 funny. John,] $N; ~ , ~ .
A1

62.1 dry goods] N[1-2,4]; ~ - ~ A1,
N[5-6]; drygoods N[3]

62.4 Heavens,"] N[1-2,4]; ~ !" A1,
N[3,5-6]

62.9 two_∧] $N; ~ , A1

62.10 it,"] N[1-2,4-5]; ~ !" A1,N[3,6]

62.11 Wrinkles,"] $N; ~ !" A1

62.14 There! That's right.] $N;
~ , that's ~ ! A1

62.14 Now,] $N(−N[6]); ~ _∧ A1,
N[6]

62.15 inquisition.] $N; ~ ! A1

62.16 peacefully.] $N; ~ ! A1

62.18 we] $N; you A1

62.19 Pennoyer_∧ . . . down_∧]
N[2-3]; ~ , . . . ~ , A1,N[1,4-6]

*62.19 bended] $N; omit A1

62.21 *Monthly Amazement*] E1;
Monthly Amazement A1,$N

*62.22 may] $N; will A1

62.23 to-morrow_∧] N[1,4-6]; ~ ,
A1,N[3]

62.30 Occasionally (*no* ¶)] $N;
¶ A1

63.1 slumbering_∧] $N; ~ , A1

63.2 that] $N; which A1

63.5 structure_∧] N[1-2,4]; ~ , A1,
N[3,5-6]

63.10 about$_\Lambda$] N$^{1-2,4-5}$; ~ , A1, N^{3,6}

63.11 labor] V; labour A1,E1; work $N

63.12 fully,] N$^{2-4}$; ~ $_\Lambda$ A1,N$^{1,5-6}$

63.17 stove$_\Lambda$] N^{1,5}; ~ , A1,N$^{2-4,6}$

63.18 -colored] $N; -coloured A1

63.19 places$_\Lambda$] N$^{1-2,5-6}$; ~ , A1, N$^{3-4}$

63.19 casts$_\Lambda$] $N(N^2: castes); ~ , A1

63.24 Eat!"] $N(−N^5); ~ ," A1; ~ ?" N^5

63.24 Wrinkles$_\Lambda$] $N(−N^5); ~ , A1,N^5

63.24 jeer.] $N; ~ ; A1

*63.25 are] stet A1,N$^{2-4,6}$

63.26 problem$_\Lambda$] N$^{1-2,5-6}$; ~ , A1, N$^{3-4}$

63.28 turf,"] N$^{1-2,4,6}$; ~ !" A1, N^{3,5}

*63.31 Wrinkles. "And . . . that."] N^{2,6}; ~ , "and . . . that." A1,N^3(N^3: Wrikles); ~ . $_\Lambda$And . . . that.$_\Lambda$ N$^{1,4-5}$

63.32 said:] $N; ~ , A1

63.37 bread$_\Lambda$] N$^{1,5-6}$; ~ , A1,N$^{2-4}$

63.38 yelled:] $N; ~ , A1

63.38 in."] N$^{1-4}$; ~ !" A1,N$^{5-6}$

64.1 opened$_\Lambda$] N$^{1-2,6}$; ~ , A1,N$^{3-5}$

64.3 Splutter,"] N$^{1-4}$; ~ !" A1, N$^{5-6}$

64.9–10 dinner—] $N(−N^3); ~ , A1,N^3

64.10 mention—] $N(−N^3); ~ , A1; ~ ; N^3

64.14 idiots.] $N; ~ ! A1

64.14 shame.] $N; ~ ! A1

64.18 Grief$_\Lambda$] $N; ~ , A1

64.20 jacket$_\Lambda$ . . . gloves$_\Lambda$] $N (−N^4); ~ , . . . ~ , A1,N^4

64.22 birds,"] $N; ~ !" A1

64.23 scrapes] $N; scrape A1

64.27 short$_\Lambda$] N$^{1-3,6}$; ~ , A1,N$^{4-5}$

64.28 trunk$_\Lambda$] $N(−N^5); ~ , A1, N^5

64.28 were] N^5; was A1,$N (−N^5)

64.29 chair$_\Lambda$] N$^{1-2,6}$; ~ , A1,N$^{3-5}$

64.34 table$_\Lambda$] $N(−N^6); ~ , A1, N^6

64.36–37 Here! That's . . . cof-fee."] $N; ~ , that's . . . ~ !" A1

65.3 table.] $N(−N^3); ~ ! A1; ~ ; N^3

65.6 Later$_\Lambda$] N$^{1-2,4-5}$; ~ , A1,N^{3,6}

65.6–7 satisfaction:] $N; ~ , A1

65.8 Florinda. "But] N$^{2,4-5}$; ~ , "but A1,N^{1,6}; ~ ; "but N^3

65.14 egg,"] $N; ~ !" A1

65.15 then. But] $N(−N^4); ~ ; but A1; ~ —but N^4

65.16 dudes. And] N$^{1,3,5-6}$; ~ — and A1,N^{2,4}

65.17 ^{2}lunch.] $N; ~ ! A1

65.19 sullenly:] $N; ~ , A1

65.20 gallery$_\Lambda$] N$^{1-2,5-6}$; ~ , A1, N$^{3-4}$

65.21 Yes,] N$^{1-3,6}$; ~ — A1,N$^{4-5}$

65.27 blowed.] $N; ~ ! A1

65.30 name,] N$^{2-4}$; ~ $_\Lambda$ A1,N$^{1,5-6}$

66.3 Florinda,] N$^{3-4,6}$; ~ $_\Lambda$ A1, N$^{1-2,5}$

66.6 course,] $N(−N^4); ~ $_\Lambda$ A1, N^4

66.12 me$_\Lambda$] N$^{1-2,5}$; ~ , A1,N$^{3-4,6}$

66.15 Florinda."] N$^{1-3,5}$; ~ !" A1; ~ ?" N^{4,6}

66.19 and$_\Lambda$] N$^{1-3,5}$; ~ , A1,N^{4,6}

66.20 divan$_\Lambda$] $N(−N^5); ~ , A1, N^5

66.23 kid,"] $N; ~ !" A1

66.23 Wrinkles] $N; Wrinkle A1

66.30 now$_\Lambda$] N$^{1,4-6}$; ~ , A1,N$^{2-3}$

66.30 hang$_\Lambda$] $N; ~ , A1

67.3 Wrinkles,] N$^{4-6}$; ~ $_\Lambda$ A1, N$^{1-3}$

67.5 Florinda. "It's] N$^{1-4}$; ~ , "it's A1,N$^{5-6}$

67.7 Grief. "Now] $N(−N^4); ~ , "now A1; ~ ; "now N^4

67.7 it.] $N; ~ ! A1

67.9 backwards] N$^{1-3,6}$; backward A1,N$^{4-5}$

67.12 indeed,] $N(−N^2); ~ $_\Lambda$ A1,N^2

67.13 then$_\Lambda$] $N(−N^5); ~ , A1, N^5

67.16 know.] $N; ~ ? A1

67.18 reflection$_\Lambda$] $N; ~ , A1

67.18; 68.25 said:] $N; ~ , A1

67.20 course,] $N; ~ ∧ A1
67.25 trade∧] N¹⁻²; ~ , A1,N³⁻⁶
67.30 street] $N; Street A1
67.31 Grief∧] $N(−N⁴); ~ , A1, N⁴
67.33 Splutter."] N¹⁻²,⁴⁻⁵; ~ !" A1,N³,⁶
67.33 coat∧] $N; ~ , A1
67.34 others:] N¹⁻⁴; ~ , A1,N⁶; ~ ∧ N⁵
67.38 soul,"] N¹⁻²,⁵; ~ !" A1, N³⁻⁴,⁶
68.1 Purple,"] $N(−N³); ~ !" A1,N³
68.7 Sanderson∧] $N(−N⁴); ~ , A1,N⁴
68.8 said:] $N(−N⁶); ~ , A1,N⁶
68.11 Or] $N; Oh A1
68.11 Pennoyer,] N³,⁵⁻⁶; ~ ∧ A1, N¹⁻²,⁴
68.11,14 *Amazement*] E1; Amazement A1,$N
68.12 would,] N²⁻⁴; ~ ∧ A1,N¹,⁵⁻⁶
68.12 money] $N; the money A1
68.17 *Eminent Magazine*] E1; Eminent Magazine A1,N¹,³⁻⁶ (N³: Emigrant); '~ ~' N²
68.20 got∧] $N(−N⁴); ~ , A1,N⁴
68.21 overdue∧] N¹⁻²,⁵⁻⁶(N¹: over | due); ~ , A1,N³⁻⁴
68.24 silence∧] $N; ~ , A1
68.30 Grief∧] N¹⁻⁴; ~ , A1,N⁵⁻⁶
68.32 You,"] N¹⁻²,⁴; ~ !" A1, N³,⁵⁻⁶
68.32 Sanderson,] N²,⁵⁻⁶; ~ ∧ A1, N¹,³⁻⁴
68.34 in] $N; into A1
68.36 Florinda.] N¹⁻³,⁵; ~ , A1, N⁴,⁶
68.38 it∧] N¹⁻²; ~ , A1,N³⁻⁶
69.1 Splutter,"] $N; ~ !" A1
69.2 Sanderson.] N¹⁻²,⁴,⁶; ~ : A1, N⁵(N⁵ uncertain: *possibly period*); ~ , N³
69.2 up."] $N; ~ !" A1
69.5 painters∧] N¹⁻³; ~ , A1,N⁴⁻⁶
69.5 Rotten] $N(−N³); rotten A1,N³
70.1 Pennoyer∧] $N(−N⁴); ~ , A1,N⁴

70.3 horse-car] N²⁻³; ~ ∧ ~ A1, N⁴,⁶; ~ - | ~ N¹,⁵
70.4 ¹Hello∧] N¹⁻²,⁴; ~ , N³,⁵⁻⁶
70.5 Penny,"] $N; ~ !" A1
70.5 What you] $N; What are you A1
70.15 b'ginger,"] N²⁻⁴,⁶; ~ !" A1, N⁵; ~ ." N¹
70.17 half way] $N; halfway A1
70.17 stairs∧] N¹⁻³,⁵; ~ , A1,N⁴,⁶
70.19 ¹Wolf∧] N³⁻⁴,⁶; ~ , A1, N¹⁻²,⁵
70.22 is.] $N; ~ ! A1
70.22 street] $N; Street A1
70.22 heaven∧] $N(N¹,³: Heaven); ~ , A1
70.23 breakfast∧—] $N; ~ ? — A1
70.25 himself∧] $N(−N⁴); ~ , A1,N⁴
70.27–28 breakfast∧] $N; ~ , A1
71.12 open∧] N¹⁻²,⁵⁻⁶; ~ , A1,N³⁻⁴
71.15 easel∧] N¹⁻²,⁶; ~ , A1,N³⁻⁵
71.16 friend,] $N; ~ ∧ A1
71.17 and∧] N¹,⁴,⁶; ~ , A1,N²⁻³,⁵
71.19 studio,] N¹⁻³; ~ ∧ A1,N⁴⁻⁶
71.20 labors] $N; labours A1
71.20 life∧ . . . frames∧] $N; ~ , . . . ~ , A1
71.22 Billie,] $N; ~ ! A1
71.26 Pennoyer.] $N(−N⁵); ~ , A1,N⁵
71.29 you,"] $N; ~ !" A1
71.31 place∧] $N(−N⁴); ~ , A1, N⁴
71.38 unpleasant∧] $N(−N⁴); ~ , A1,N⁴
72.4 den,] $N(−N⁴); ~ ∧ A1,N⁴
72.7 grimly. "You] N¹; ~ , "you A1,N²⁻⁴; ~ . "you N⁵; ~ , "You N⁶
72.12 Florinda∧] N¹⁻²,⁵⁻⁶; ~ , A1, N³⁻⁴
72.13 Great] $N(−N⁵); great A1,N⁵
72.13 Scott,"] $N(−N³); ~ !" A1,N³
72.16 part∧] N¹,³,⁵⁻⁶; ~ , A1,N²,⁴
*72.16 opportunity] $N(−N⁵); an opportunity A1,N⁵

72.19,22; 74.1,4,15   said:] $N;
~ , A1

72.20   so long] N[2-5]; ~ - ~ A1,
N[1,6]

72.21   Hawker.] N[1,3,5-6]; ~ , A1,
N[2]; ~ ∧ N[4]

72.25   know. But] $N; ~ ; but A1

72.25   him,] $N(−N[4]); ~ ∧ A1,
N[4]

72.31   well—] $N; ~ . A1

72.34   you,"] $N(−N[5]); ~ !" A1,
N[5]

72.35   him∧] $N; ~ , A1

72.36   said∧] $N(−N[3]); ~ , A1,
N[3]

72.37   say,"] $N; ~ !" A1

73.4   sake."] $N; ~ !" A1

73.9   Pl-e-a-se,] $N; ~ ∧ A1

73.13   Penny.] N[1,3-5]; ~ ? A1,N[2,6]

73.13   ²you∧] N[2,4-6]; ~ , A1,N[1,3]

73.20   Pl-e-a-se,] N[1-3,5]; ~ ∧ A1,
N[4,6]

74.2   drawing∧board] N[1-2,4]; ~ -
~ A1,N[3,6]; ~ - | ~ N[5]

74.6   say,"] $N(N[1]: say so); ~ !"
A1

74.7   hanged,"] $N; ~ !" A1

74.10   hanged,"] $N(−N[4]); ~ !"
A1,N[4]
thing

74.13   thing.] N[1,5-6]; ~ ? A1,N[2-4]

74.14   -durned."] $N(−N[4]); ~ !"
A1,N[4]

74.17   course,] $N; ~ ∧ A1

74.19   later,] N[1-3,6]; ~ ∧ A1,N[4-5]

74.20   demeanor] $N; demeanour
A1

74.22   other∧] $N; ~ , A1

74.31   -by."] $N(N[1-3]: bye);
-bye!" A1

75.1   door,] N[1,3,5]; ~ ∧ A1,N[2,4,6]

75.1–2   ¹Billie. . . . here.] $N
(N[2]: Bill); ~ ! . . . ~ ! A1

75.10   no.] $N; ~ ! A1

75.11   man?] N[2-4,6]; ~ ! A1; ~ .
N[1,5]

75.12   mean.] N[1-3,5]; ~ ! A1,N[4,6]

75.12   no.] $N(−N[4]); ~ ! A1,N[4]

75.14   Hawker∧ . . . face∧]
N[2-3,5]; ~ , . . . ~ , A1,N[1,4,6]

75.16   Hawker,] $N; ~ ! A1

75.16   ²true?] $N(−N[6]); ~ . A1,
N[6]

75.17   rascal.] N[1-3,5]; ~ ! A1, N[4];
~ , N[6]

75.17   picture."] $N(−N[4]) ($N:
picter); ~ !" A1,N[4]

75.20   noon∧] $N(−N[6]); ~ , A1,
N[6]

75.20   corridor∧] N[1,3-5]; ~ , A1,
N[2,6]

75.30   Wrinkles. "We] $N; ~ ,
"we A1

75.34   Wrinkles∧] $N; ~ , A1

75.39   time∧] $N(−N[6]); ~ , A1,
N[6]

76.1   said:] $N(N[4] *uncertain*);
~ , A1

76.4   quit,] $N; ~ ∧ A1

76.5   ha,] $N; ~ ! A1

76.6   Wrinkles. "But] $N; ~ ;
"but A1

76.13   Splutter,"] $N(−N[6]); ~ !"
A1,N[6]

76.14   girl∧] N[1-3]; ~ , A1,N[4-6]

76.15   dungeon-like] $N(−N[4]);
dungeonlike A1,N[4]

76.22   dull∧] $N; ~ , A1

76.22,27   grey] V; gray A1,$N,E1

76.23   cracky,"] $N(−N[5]); ~ !"
A1,N[5]

76.23   girl. "How] $N; ~ , "how
A1

76.23   Billie.] $N; ~ ! A1

76.27   us.] $N; ~ ! A1

*76.30   deprecating] $N; depreci-
ating A1

76.30   gloves. "Oh] $N; ~—"oh
A1

76.32   Hawker. "A] N[1,3,6]; ~ , "a
A1,N[2,4-5]

76.33   extraordinary. You] $N;
~ , you A1

76.35   us?"] $N(−N[3]); ~ ." A1,
N[3]

76.36   Why∧] $N(−N[2]); ~ , A1,
N[2]

76.37   on.] $N; ~ ! A1

77.1   stupid."] $N; ~ !" A1

77.7   steps,] $N(−N[5]); ~ ∧ A1,
N[5]

77.9   way,] N[1-3,5]; ~ ∧ A1,N[4,6]

77.11 strangely$_\wedge$] N$^{1-2,6}$; $\sim$, A1, N$^{3-5}$

78.11 up,"] $N; $\sim$!" A1

78.18 tumbler$_\wedge$] N$^{1-3,6}$; $\sim$; A1; $\sim$, N$^{4-5}$

78.21 pinched."] $N; $\sim$!" A1

78.22 duffer. You] $N(N^6: duffer!); $\sim$, you A1

78.22 chump,] $N; $\sim$ $_\wedge$ A1

78.23 sets.] $N(to.); $\sim$! A1

78.28 Florinda,] N$^{1,4-5}$; $\sim$ $_\wedge$ A1, N$^{2-3,6}$

78.30 Grief,] N^{2,5}; $\sim$ $_\wedge$ A1,N$^{1,3-4,6}$

78.31 But$_\wedge$] $N; $\sim$, A1

79.1 Florinda,] N$^{1-3,5-6}$; $\sim$ $_\wedge$ A1, N^4

79.10 *et seq.* spaghetti] $N; *spaghetti* A1

79.11 did once."] $N(N^1: once did); $\sim$ $\sim$?" A1

79.12 arms$_\wedge$] N$^{2,5-6}$; $\sim$, A1,N$^{1,3-4}$

79.15–16 politely:] N$^{1-4}$(N^1: positively); $\sim$, A1,N$^{5-6}$

79.16 No?"] N$^{5-6}$; $\sim$." A1,N$^{1-4}$

79.17 Florinda.] $N; $\sim$, A1

79.23 Pennoyer. "But] $N(−N^5); $\sim$, "but A1,N^5

79.34 Listen,"] $N(−N^2); $\sim$!" A1,N^2

79.36 clear$_\wedge$] $N; $\sim$, A1

79.36 muffled$_\wedge$] $N(−N^1); $\sim$, A1,N^1

80.2 gruffly:] N$^{1-4}$; $\sim$, A1,N$^{5-6}$

80.3 man,"] $N(−N^2); $\sim$!" A1, N^2

80.4 boy.] $N; $\sim$! A1

80.8 gloves,"] N$^{1,3-4,6}$; $\sim$!" A1, N^{2,5}

80.11 said:] N$^{1-4}$; $\sim$, A1,N$^{5-6}$

80.11 Billie."] $N(−N^2); $\sim$!" A1,N^2

*80.14 On] $N; In A1

80.14; 81.4 avenue] $N; Avenue A1

80.15 don't,"] N$^{1,4-6}$; $\sim$!" A1,N^2; $\sim$ $_{\wedge\wedge}$ N^3

80.17 Florinda.] N^{1,4,6}; $\sim$, A1, N$^{2-3,5}$

80.30 said:] $N(−N^6); $\sim$, A1, N^6

80.33 are. Ugly] $N; $\sim$—ugly A1

80.34 said:] $N; $\sim$, A1

80.36 dark$_\wedge$] N$^{3-6}$; $\sim$, A1,N$^{1-2}$

80.38 Oh,"] $N; $\sim$!" A1

80.38 Florinda$_\wedge$] N$^{1,3,5-6}$; $\sim$, A1, N^{2,4}

80.39 Hawker,] $N(−N^3); $\sim$ $_\wedge$ A1,N^3

81.4 on] $N; in A1

81.4 anxiously:] $N; $\sim$, A1

81.5 that."] $N; $\sim$!" A1

81.6 nonsense,"] $N(−N^2); $\sim$!" A1,N^2

81.7 not."] $N; $\sim$!" A1

81.8 Florinda. "It] $N(−N^3); $\sim$, "it A1,N^3

81.12 Billie,] $N; $\sim$; A1

81.12 then$_\wedge$] $N(−N^1); $\sim$, A1, N^1

81.17,19,20 grey] V; gray A1, $N,E1

81.20 grey.] $N(gray); $\sim$! A1

*81.24–25 excepting] $N; only A1

81.26 stairs$_\wedge$] $N(−N^2); $\sim$, A1, N^2

81.26 darkness$_\wedge$] N$^{3,5-6}$; $\sim$, A1, N$^{1-2,4}$

81.26 exclaimed:] $N; $\sim$, A1

81.26–27 Here! Look] $N; Here, look A1

81.27 fall."] $N(−N^3); $\sim$!" A1, N^3

81.28 girl.] $N; $\sim$! A1

81.29 Here! Give] $N(−N^2); $\sim$, give A1,N^2

81.30 There! Now,] $N; There—now$_\wedge$ A1

82.4 fool,"] $N; $\sim$!" A1

82.8 *et seq.* rabbits] $N; rarebits A1

82.9 tongues,"] N$^{2-4,6}$($N: tongue); $\sim$!" A1,N^5

82.12 Grief,] $N; $\sim$ $_\wedge$ A1

82.14 rabbits$_\wedge$] $N(−N^1); $\sim$, A1,N^1

82.15 Florinda. "Soon] $N (−N^3); $\sim$, "soon A1,N^3

82.16 $_\wedge$Pour] $N; —$\sim$A1

82.17 time$_\wedge$] $N(−N^3); $\sim$, A1, N^3

82.25　violets$_\wedge$] \$N; ～ , A1
82.25　you$_\wedge$] N$^{1-2,5-6}$; ～ , A1,N$^{3-4}$
83.9　guitar$_\wedge$] \$N; ～ , A1
83.9　serenade.] \$N; ～ , A1
83.11　up,"] \$N(−N^5); ～ !" A1,
　　N^5
83.12　again:] \$N; ～ , A1
83.16　business."] \$N(−N^5);
　　～ ?" A1,N^5
83.23　arose$_\wedge$] \$N(−N^3); ～ , A1,
　　N^3
83.25–26　demanded:] \$N; ～ ,
　　A1
83.29　on,] N$^{1-4}$; ～— A1; ～ ;
　　N$^{5-6}$
83.29,30,35　me.] \$N; ～ ! A1
83.29　$_\wedge$Grief] \$N; —Grief A1
83.31　shining.] \$N(N$^{2-4,6}$: ～ .");
　　～ ; A1
83.32　come$_\wedge$ my love$_\wedge$] N$^{2-3,6}$;
　　～ , ～ ～ , A1,N$^{4-5}$
83.32　me.] \$N(N$^{2-4,6}$: ～ ."); ～ !
　　A1
83.34　you.] \$N(−N^5); ～ ? A1;
　　～ ! N^5
83.34　$_\wedge$What] \$N; —What A1
83.37　curiosity.] \$N(N^5: ～ !); ～
　　——A1
83.39　Florinda,] N$^{1,3-4,6}$; ～ $_\wedge$ A1,
　　N^{2,5}
84.1　one$_\wedge$] \$N(−N^1); ～ , A1,N^1
84.2　announced:] \$N(−N^5); ～ ,
　　A1,N^5
84.4　any one] N$^{3-6}$; anyone A1,
　　N$^{1-2}$
84.5　Grief. "We'll] N$^{2-5}$; ～ ,
　　"we'll A1,N^{1,6}
84.6　honor] \$N; honour A1
84.12　dealing. "A] N^{2,5}; ～ , "a
　　A1,N^{1,6}; ～ ; "a N^3; ～ $_\wedge$ "A N^4
84.29　-by] N$^{3-6}$; -bye A1, N$^{1-2}$
84.30　Pennoyer,] N$^{2-4,6}$; ～ $_\wedge$ A1,
　　N^{1,5}
84.35　on] \$N; in A1
84.35　avenue."] \$N; Avenue!"
　　A1
84.39　What?] \$N(−N^5); ～ ! A1,
　　N^5
85.1　Me,] \$N(−N^4); ～ $_\wedge$ A1,N^4
85.2　Good-night] N^6; ～ $_\wedge$ ～ A1,
　　\$N(−N^6)

85.2　girl,"] \$N; ～ !" A1
85.3　onto] N$^{1-2,4-5}$; on to A1,N^{3,6}
　　(N^3: on | to)
85.4　up.] \$N; ～ , A1
85.4　stygian] \$N(−N^5); Stygian
　　A1,N^5
85.5　blackness:] N$^{1-2,4-5}$; ～ . A1;
　　～ , N^{3,6}
85.6　fire$_\wedge$escapes] N^{2,4,6}; ～ - ～
　　A1,N^{3,5}; ～ - | ～ N^1
*85.7　face] \$N; front A1
85.12　government$_\wedge$] N$^{2,4-6}$; ～ ,
　　A1,N^{1,3}
85.16–17　shopkeepers$_\wedge$ . . .
　　adjacent$_\wedge$] \$N(−N^1); ～ ,
　　. . . ～ , A1,N^1
85.21　on] \$N; omit A1
85.25　debris] \$N; débris A1
85.30　fire$_\wedge$escapes] N^{1,4}; ～ - ～
　　N$^{3,5-6}$; ～ - | ～ A1,N^2
85.30　escapes,] N$^{1,3-4,6}$; ～ $_\wedge$ A1,
　　N^{2,5}
85.31　pallor] \$N; pallour A1
85.31　darkness$_\wedge$] N$^{1,5-6}$; ～ , A1,
　　N$^{2-4}$
85.33　Florinda,"] \$N(−N^6); ～ !"
　　A1,N^6
86.1　Gamin] E1; Gamin A1,\$N
　　(−N^2); ' ～ ' N^2
86.5　table d'hote] \$N; table
　　d'hôte A1
86.6　Gamin] E1; Gamin A1,\$N
　　(−N^2); " ～ " N^2
86.8　payday] N$^{2-3}$; ～ - ～ A1;
　　～ - | ～ N^{1,5}; ～ $_\wedge$ ～ N^{4,6}
86.12　ten,"] \$N(10); ～ !" A1
86.15　Thunder,"] \$N(−N^2); ～ !"
　　A1,N^2
*86.15　to] \$N; into A1
86.17　Wrinkles$_\wedge$] N$^{1-2,4,6}$; ～ , A1,
　　N^{3,5}
86.20　fall$_\wedge$] N$^{2,4-5}$; ～ , A1,N^{3,6}
86.22　thing,"] \$N; ～ !" A1
86.27,28,29　cohn'fiel'] N^{4,6}; ～ - ～
　　A1,N$^{2-3,5}$
86.27　cohn'fiel',] \$N; ～ ' - ～ ; A1
86.29　'Way] N$^{1-2}$; $_\wedge$ ～ A1,N$^{3-6}$
86.30; 87.1　up,"] \$N; ～ !" A1
87.3　studio$_\wedge$] \$N; ～ , A1
87.5　him$_\wedge$] N$^{1-2,4}$; ～ , A1,N$^{3,5-6}$

87.10 powder smoke] N^{2,4}; ~ - ~
A1,N^5; powdersmoke N^1; ~ |
~ N^6

87.21 Oh,"] $N(−N^2); ~ !" A1,
N^2

87.25 Oh,"] $N; ~ !" A1

87.26 gone,] N$^{1-3}$; ~ $_\wedge$ A1,N$^{4-6}$

87.35 long$_\wedge$] N$^{1,3-4,6}$; ~ , A1,N^{2,5}

87.37 a-light] N$^{1-3}$; alight A1,
N$^{4-6}$

87.39 devil,"] $N(−N^5); ~ !"
A1; ~ ." N^5

87.39 shouted$_\wedge$] N$^{1-4}$; ~ , A1,
N$^{5-6}$

88.1 see!] $N(−N^3); ~ . A1;
~ ? N^3

88.6,9 tumbled,"] $N; ~ !" A1

88.6 delight. "We] $N; ~ , "we
A1

88.9 again,] $N(−N^3); ~ $_\wedge$ A1,
N^3

88.12 Yes. Go] $N; ~ , go A1

88.19 it?] $N; ~ ! A1

88.21 Hollanden,] N$^{1-2,5-6}$; ~ $_\wedge$
A1,N$^{3-4}$

88.25 Wrink,"] $N; ~ !" A1

88.27 coal$_\wedge$box] N^{4,6}; ~ - ~ A1,
N$^{2-3,5}$; ~ - | ~ N^1

89.2 windows$_\wedge$] N$^{2,4-6}$; ~ , A1,
N^{1,3,6}

89.3 brown stone] $N(−N^3)
(N^{2,5}: ~ | ~); brownstone A1,
N^3

89.9 swiftly$_\wedge$] N$^{1-2,4-5}$; ~ , A1,
N^{3,6}

89.10,12 said:] $N; ~ , A1

89.11 again."] $N(−N^2); ~ !"
A1,N^2

89.13 come."] $N; ~ !" A1

89.17 Finally$_\wedge$] $N; ~ , A1

89.17-18 "Hearts at War"] $N
(−N^2); $_\wedge$~ ~ ~ $_\wedge$ A1; $_\wedge$hearts
at war$_\wedge$ N^2

89.21 hastily. "The] $N; ~—
"the A1

89.23 is—] $N(−N^6); ~ , A1,N^6

89.28 Why—"] N$^{1-3}$; ~ ," A1,
N^{4,6}; ~ "— N^5

89.28 wider. "Nobody] N$^{1-3,5}$;
~ , "nobody A1,N^{4,6}

89.29 course!] $N; ~ , A1

89.30 'Nobody!'] $N(−N^2);
$_\wedge$nobody.$_\wedge$ A1; $_\wedge$Nobody!" N^2

90.1 Oh,"] $N(−N^4); ~ !" A1,
N^4

90.6 retorted$_\wedge$] N$^{1-3,6}$; ~ , A1,
N$^{4-5}$

90.8 discomfiture,] N$^{1-3,6}$; ~ $_\wedge$
A1,N$^{4-5}$

90.11 Oh,] $N; ~ ! A1

90.14 me$_\wedge$] N$^{1-2,6}$; ~ , A1,N$^{3-5}$

90.17 dog."] $N; ~ !" A1

90.18 asked:] $N; ~ , A1

90.22 moss$_\wedge$] $N(−N^4); ~ , A1,
N^4

*90.23 remember] $N; remember
it A1

90.25-26 before you$_\wedge$] N$^{2,5-6}$; ~
~ , A1,N$^{1,3-4}$

90.29 laughed$_\wedge$] $N(−N^4); ~ ,
A1,N^4

90.32 observed,] N$^{2-5}$; ~ $_\wedge$ A1,
N^{1,6}

91.1 course. As] $N; ~ , as A1

91.4 well——"] N$^{1,3-4}$; ~ ," A1,
N$^{2,5-6}$

91.4 Hawker.] $N(−N^6); ~ ,
A1,N^6

91.7 said:] $N(−N^6); ~ , A1,N^6

91.9 answered.] $N(N^1 *uncer-
tain*); ~ ; A1

92.1 door,] N$^{2-4,6}$; ~ $_\wedge$ A1,N^{1,5}

92.1 entrenched] N$^{1-4}$; in-
trenched A1,N$^{5-6}$

*92.2 cash$_\wedge$desk] $N(N^4:
cashdesk); cash-box A1

*92.3 practiced] $N(N^5: prac-
tised); practical A1

92.5 wide$_\wedge$] $N(−N^3)(N^6:
wild); ~ , A1,N^3

92.9 oaths,] $N(−N^1); ~ $_\wedge$ A1,
N^1(N^1 *uncertain*)

92.11 laborers] $N; labourers A1

92.13 Withal$_\wedge$] $N; ~ , A1

92.17 a fork] $N; fork A1

92.18 rapid$_\wedge$] N$^{1-2,6}$; ~ , A1,N$^{3-5}$

92.26 long$_\wedge$] $N(−N^4); ~ , A1,
N^4

92.27 hall,] N$^{2-4}$; ~ $_\wedge$ A1,N$^{1,5-6}$

92.29 person$_\wedge$] $N(−N^1); ~ ,
A1, N^1

92.31   and$_\wedge$] \$N($-$N^3); $\sim$, A1, N^3

93.2   tense$_\wedge$] N$^{1,4-6}$; $\sim$, A1,N$^{2-3}$

93.7   passionate$_\wedge$] N$^{1-2,6}$; $\sim$, A1, N$^{3-5}$

93.8   mad$_\wedge$] \$N; $\sim$, A1

93.10   creature,] \$N; $\sim$ $_\wedge$ A1

93.11   long$_\wedge$] N^{4,6}; $\sim$, A1,N$^{1-3,5}$

93.13   race] \$N; voices A1

93.14   brawlers$_\wedge$] N$^{1,4-6}$; $\sim$, A1, N$^{2-3}$

93.15   cafe] \$N; *café* A1

93.21   know,"] \$N; $\sim$!" A1

93.22   weary$_\wedge$] N$^{1-2,4,6}$; $\sim$, A1, N^{3,5}

93.22   din."] \$N($-$N^1); $\sim$!" A1; $\sim$?" N^1

93.24   Bohemian$_\wedge$] \$N(N^{4,6}: bohemian); $\sim$, A1

93.27   Ho,"] \$N($-$N^3)(N^1: No); $\sim$!" A1,N^3

93.27   Hollanden. "You're] \$N; $\sim$, "you're A1

93.29   him."] \$N($-$N^5); $\sim$!" A1, N^5

93.30   Hawker,] N$^{2-5}$; $\sim$ $_\wedge$ A1, N^{1,6}

93.32 ^{2}you.] \$N; $\sim$! A1

93.33   about?$_\wedge$] \$N; $\sim$?— A1

93.33   Hi,] \$N($-$N^2); $\sim$! A1,N^2

93.34   him—] \$N; $\sim$, A1

93.35   moment. Then] \$N; $\sim$; then A1

93.36   again.] \$N; $\sim$: A1

94.1–2 $_\wedge$I . . . out.$_\wedge$] \$N; —$\sim$ . . . $\sim$.— A1

94.2   course,] \$N; $\sim$ $_\wedge$ A1

94.3   last."] N$^{1-2,6}$; $\sim$!" A1,N$^{4-5}$

94.8   you,] \$N; $\sim$; A1

94.8   and$_\wedge$ moreover$_\wedge$] \$N($-$N^3); $\sim$, $\sim$, A1; $\sim$ $_\wedge$ $\sim$, N^3

94.10   consomme] \$N; *con-sommé* A1

94.12–13 $_\wedge$Oh . . . now.$_\wedge$] \$N; —$\sim$ . . . $\sim$.— A1

94.12   look—] \$N; $\sim$! A1

94.15   enough.$_\wedge$] \$N; $\sim$.— A1

*94.16   they] \$N; you A1

94.21 ^{1}dinner.] \$N; $\sim$! A1

94.21 ^{2}the dinner] \$N; dinner A1

94.22   eat—] \$N; $\sim$; A1

94.22–23 $_\wedge$Well . . . head.$_\wedge$] \$N; —$\sim$ . . . $\sim$.— A1

94.28   granny,"] \$N($-$N^6); $\sim$!" A1; $\sim$." N^6

94.29   right. Only] \$N; $\sim$, only A1

94.31   plain. You] \$N; $\sim$—you A1

95.2   man$_\wedge$] N$^{1,5-6}$; $\sim$, A1,N$^{2-4}$

95.7   gone!$_\wedge$] \$N; $\sim$.— A1

95.7 $_\wedge$Hi,] \$N(N^{2,5}: Hi!); "$\sim$! A1

95.7–8   Pontiac!$_\wedge$] \$N; $\sim$.— A1

95.8   here!"] \$N($-$N^3); $\sim$." A1, N^3

95.9   hair$_\wedge$] N^{1,4,6}; $\sim$, A1,N$^{2-3,5}$

95.12   them$_\wedge$] \$N($-$N^3); $\sim$, A1, N^3

95.13   Pontiac,"] \$N($-$N^2); $\sim$!" A1,N^2

95.14 ^{1}Hawker?$_\wedge$] \$N; $\sim$?— A1

95.21   firmly$_\wedge$ . . . silently$_\wedge$] \$N; $\sim$, . . . $\sim$, A1

95.25   stunning."] \$N($-$N^2); $\sim$!" A1,N^2

95.27   Yes. That's] N$^{1-2,6}$; $\sim$, that's A1; $\sim$; that's N$^{4-5}$

95.29   gossip,] N$^{1-2,6}$; $\sim$ $_\wedge$ A1, N$^{4-5}$

96.2   too. Honest] N$^{1-2,6}$; $\sim$ — honest A1,N^5; $\sim$; honest N^4

96.3   course,] N^{2,4,6}; $\sim$ $_\wedge$ A1,N^{1,5}

96.6   girl,] \$N($-$N^5); $\sim$ $_\wedge$ A1,N^5

96.13   Hawker.] \$N($-$N^5); $\sim$! A1,N^5

96.22   stunning.] \$N($-$N^2); $\sim$! A1,N^2

96.23   Scott,] N$^{1,3,5-6}$(N^6: Scot); $\sim$! N^{2,4}

96.24   said. 'There] \$N; $\sim$; 'there A1

96.25   model.' And] \$N; $\sim$,' and A1

96.27   beggar,"] N$^{1,3-4,6}$; $\sim$!" A1, N^{2,5}

96.32   soul.] \$N($-$N^5); $\sim$! A1, N^5

96.38   character. And] \$N; $\sim$ $_\wedge$ and A1

96.38–39 stunning."] $N^{1,3\text{-}4,6}$;
~ !" $A1,N^{2,5}$

97.1 it,"] $N^{1,4,6}$; ~ !" $A1,N^{2\text{-}3,5}$

97.3 model$_\wedge$] $N^{1,4,6}$; ~ , $A1,N^{2\text{-}3,5}$

97.8 late$_\wedge$] $N(-N^2)$; ~ , $A1,N^2$

*98.1–2 windows, he] $N(N^{5\text{-}6}$: windows$_\wedge$); window$_\wedge$ she $A1$

98.2 and$_\wedge$] $N^{1\text{-}2,4,6}$; ~ , $A1,N^{3,5}$

98.5 girl,] $N^{2\text{-}4,6}$; ~ $_\wedge$ $A1,N^{1,5}$

98.8 exactly—] $N(-N^5)$; ~ ; $A1,N^5$

98.10 heavens!] $N(-N^1)$; ~ —— $A1,N^1$

98.11 Yes. A] $N^{1\text{-}2,4,6}$; ~ , a $A1$, N^3; ~ ; a N^5

98.13 any one] $N(-N^1)$; anyone $A1,N^1$

98.17 Algiers$_\wedge$ . . . Turkey$_\wedge$] $N(-N^5)$; ~ , . . . ~ , $A1,N^5$

98.20 all. Excepting] $N(-N^5)$; ~ ; excepting $A1$; ~ — excepting N^5

98.21 color] N; colour $A1$

98.21 color$_\wedge$] $N^{1,3\text{-}4}$; ~ , $A1,N^{2,6}$; ~ . N^5

98.22–23 cigarettes$_\wedge$] N; ~ , $A1$

98.25 Oh,] N; ~ ! $A1$

98.28 drank] $N(-N^4)$; drunk $A1,N^4$

98.30 terrible$_\wedge$] $N^{1\text{-}2,4,6}$; ~ , $A1$, $N^{3,5}$

98.31 struggled$_\wedge$] $N(-N^5)$; ~ , $A1,N^5$

99.1 listen.] $N^{2,4\text{-}6}$; ~ : $A1$; ~ , N^1; ~ ; N^3

99.3–4 affairs,] N; ~ $_\wedge$ $A1$

99.4 too,] $N(-N^5)$; ~ ; $A1,N^5$

99.5 life$_\wedge$] $N^{1,3,5\text{-}6}$; ~ , $A1,N^2$; ~ . N^4

99.9 cannot] $N(N^4$: can- | not); can not $A1$

99.11 view$_\wedge$] $N^{1\text{-}3,6}$; ~ , $A1,N^{4\text{-}5}$

99.13 cigarettes$_\wedge$] $N(-N^4)$; ~ , $A1,N^4$

99.20 here,] N; ~ ! $A1$

99.23 studying$_\wedge$] $N^{1\text{-}2,6}$; ~ , $A1$, $N^{3\text{-}5}$

99.25 Paris$_\wedge$] $N^{1\text{-}2,6}$; ~ , $A1,N^{3\text{-}5}$

*99.28 was] N; were $A1$

99.28 shadow. This] $N(-N^5)$; ~ —this $A1,N^5$

99.29 time$_\wedge$] $N(-N^4)$; ~ , $A1$, N^4

99.36 heavens,] $N^{1\text{-}2,4,6}$; ~ ! $A1$, $N^{3,5}$

99.36 have] $N(-N^5)$; Have $A1$, N^5

99.37 remark.] $N^{1\text{-}3,6}$; ~ ? $A1$, $N^{4\text{-}5}$

99.39 course$_\wedge$] $N^{1\text{-}2,5\text{-}6}$; ~ , $A1$, $N^{3\text{-}4}$

100.8 Brave—] N; ~ ? $A1$

100.8 nonsense.] $N(-N^5)$; Non-sense! $A1$; nonsense! N^5

101.1 Grief,] $N(-N^1)$; ~ $_\wedge$ $A1$, N^1

101.2 Wrinkles,] $N(-N^2)$; ~ $_\wedge$ $A1,N^2$

101.4 Four!"] $N(-N^2)$; ~ ," $A1$, N^2

101.4 Pennoyer,] $N^{3\text{-}6}$; ~ $_\wedge$ $A1$, $N^{1\text{-}2}$

101.9 back$_\wedge$] $N(-N^6)$; ~ , $A1$, N^6

101.10 whispered:] $N(-N^2)$; ~ , $A1$; ~ . N^2

101.10 Three!"] N; ~ ." $A1$

101.11 Four!"] $N(-N^3)$; ~ ," $A1,N^3$

101.13 Now,] $N^{1\text{-}4}$; ~ $_\wedge$ $A1,N^{5\text{-}6}$

101.14–15 Jinks, don't] $N(-N^5)$; ~ ! Don't $A1,N^5$

101.15 reputation.] $N(-N^6)$; ~ ! $A1,N^6$

101.16 me$_\wedge$] $N^{2\text{-}4}$; ~ , $A1,N^{1,5\text{-}6}$

101.17 'em."] $N^{1\text{-}2,5}$; ~ !" $A1,N^4$; ~ ?" $N^{3,6}$

101.17 manner$_\wedge$] $N^{2\text{-}3,5}$; ~ , $A1$, $N^{1,4,6}$

101.20 woman$_\wedge$] $N(-N^4)$; ~ , $A1,N^4$

101.25 pipe$_\wedge$] $N^{1\text{-}4}$; ~ , $A1,N^{5\text{-}6}$

101.26 thanks.] $N(-N^5)$; ~ ! $A1,N^5$

101.28 canal] N; Canal $A1$

102.1 know,] $N^{1\text{-}2,6}$; ~ — $A1,N^5$; ~ ; N^4

*102.2 ablaze] $N(-N^3)$; oblige $A1$; blaze N^3

102.2 color] N; colour $A1$

102.3 here. And] N; ~ ; and $A1$

102.3 And$_\wedge$ besides$_\wedge$] N$^{1-3}$; $\sim$, $\sim$, A1,N$^{4-6}$

102.6 We] $N; we A1

102.6 aesthetic] N$^{1-2,5-6}$; æsthetic A1; esthetic N$^{3-4}$

102.8–9 aesthetic—yes] $N(N^4: esthetic); $\sim$. Yes A1 (æsthetic)

102.10 mine—] $N(−N^6); $\sim$; A1,N^6

102.11 up,"] $N(−N^5); $\sim$!" A1, N^5

102.12 Wrinkles,] N$^{4-6}$; $\sim$ $_\wedge$ A1, N$^{1-3}$

102.12 "Listen."] $N(−N^5); "$\sim$!" A1,N^5

102.16 wistfully:] $N; $\sim$, A1

102.20 arm$_\wedge$] N$^{1-2,4,6}$; $\sim$, A1,N^{3,5}

102.23 Four! And] $N; $\sim$; and A1

102.25 Oh] $N; O A1

102.25 lord] N$^{3-4,6}$; Lord A1,N$^{1-2,5}$

102.25 lord,"] $N(−N^5); $\sim$!" A1,N^5

102.25 others,] N$^{3-5}$; $\sim$ $_\wedge$ A1, N$^{1-2,6}$

102.26 know,"] N$^{1-2,4}$; $\sim$?" A1, N$^{3,5-6}$

102.29 grinning$_\wedge$] $N; $\sim$, A1

102.33 Hello,"] $N(−N^5); $\sim$!" A1,N^5

102.33 cried. "Who] $N; $\sim$, "who A1

102.34 place.] N$^{1,3-4}$; $\sim$? A1, N$^{2,5-6}$

102.35 Sh,"] N$^{1-3,6}$; $\sim$!" A1,N$^{4-5}$

102.37 fellows,"] N$^{1-2,4}$; $\sim$?" A1, N$^{3,5-6}$

102.37 Florinda,] N$^{1,3-5}$; $\sim$ $_\wedge$ A1, N^{2,6}

102.38 tone. Whereupon] $N; $\sim$; whereupon A1

102.39 S-s-sh."] N$^{1-2,6}$; $\sim$!" A1, N$^{3-5}$ (N^3: S-s-h)

103.3 bended] $N; bent A1

103.7 gruffly:] $N; $\sim$, A1

103.10 moment,] N$^{1-3,5}$; $\sim$ $_\wedge$ A1, N^{4,6}

103.12 "Oh,"] N$^{1-4}$; "$\sim$!" A1, N$^{5-6}$

103.13 coal box] N$^{1-2,4,6}$; $\sim$ - | $\sim$ A1; $\sim$ - $\sim$ N^{3,5}

103.15 stoutly:] N$^{1-2,5}$; $\sim$, A1, N$^{3-4}$; $\sim$ $_\wedge$ N^6

103.19,23 on,"] $N(−N^5); $\sim$!" A1,N^5

103.24 exclaiming$_\wedge$] $N; $\sim$, A1

103.27 you.] $N; $\sim$!— A1

103.27 $_\wedge$Be . . . tumble.$_\wedge$] $N; — $\sim$ . . . $\sim$.— A1

103.28 Wrink. Think] $N(N^5: Wrink!); $\sim$; think A1

103.30 O-o-oh,"] N$^{1-4}$(N^4: O-o-h); $\sim$!" A1,N$^{5-6}$

103.30 peach.] $N(−N^5); $\sim$! A1,N^5

103.32 Wrinkles'] N$^{1-3,6}$; Wrinkle's A1,N^4; Wrinkles's N^5

*103.35 pinching] $N; punching A1

103.35 me.] $N; $\sim$! A1

103.35 you.] $N(−N^5); $\sim$! A1, N^5

104.2 fire$_\wedge$escapes] N^{2,4,6}; $\sim$ - $\sim$ A1,N^{3,5}

104.4; 105.20 said:] $N; $\sim$, A1

104.10 most] $N; 'most A1

104.11 everything$_\wedge$] N$^{4-6}$; $\sim$, A1, N$^{2-3}$

104.11 listen$_\wedge$] $N; $\sim$, A1

104.12 fool$_\wedge$] $N; $\sim$, A1

104.13 helped$_\wedge$] N$^{2-3,5}$; $\sim$, A1, N^{4,6}

104.14 kid.] $N; $\sim$! A1

104.22 dejectedly.] $N(−N^5); $\sim$, A1,N^5

104.23 indifferently:] $N(remarked); $\sim$, A1

104.25 does. In] N$^{2-4,6}$; $\sim$ — in A1; $\sim$, in N^5

104.30 Yes$_\wedge$] N$^{2-3,6}$; $\sim$, A1,N$^{4-5}$

105.2 Florinda,] N$^{2-4}$; $\sim$ $_\wedge$ A1, N$^{5-6}$

105.8 be.$_\wedge$] $N; $\sim$.— A1

105.12 me."] $N; $\sim$!" A1

105.14 no. No. No.] N$^{3-6}$; no! no! no! A1; no. No! No! N^2

105.16 up$_\wedge$] N$^{2-3,5-6}$; $\sim$, A1,N^4

105.28–29 Splutter.] $N; $\sim$! A1

105.29 Don't$_\wedge$ . . . sake$_\wedge$] N$^{2-3,5}$; $\sim$, . . . $\sim$, A1,N^{4,6}

105.29   street.] $N; ~ ! A1
106.3   dark_] N[1-3,5]; ~ , N[4,6]
106.6   thoughtful_] N[1-2,5]; ~ , A1,
   N[3-4,6]
106.9   fro_] N[1-2,4-5]; ~ , A1,N[3,6]
106.10   eyeing] N[1-3,6]; eying A1,
   N[4-5]
106.11   easel_] $N; ~ , A1
106.13   wrong,] N[1,3-4,6]; ~ _ A1,
   N[2,5]
106.17   apart_] $N; ~ , A1
106.19   Aw,"] $N; ~ !" A1
106.19-20   good. . . . it.] $N;
   ~ ! . . . ~ ! A1
106.21   it. "That] N[2-5]; ~ — "that
   A1; ~ ; "that N[6]
106.22   vile. Aw,] $N; ~ ! ~ ! A1
106.24   now.] N[1,3,6]; ~ ? A1,
   N[2,4-5]
106.24-25   swear—] $N; ~ , A1
106.26   dismally.] $N; ~ : A1
106.26   ¹paint.] $N; ~ ! A1
106.27   damn.] N[1-3,5]; ~ ! A1;
   ——. N[6]
106.30   idiot.] $N; ~ ! A1
107.6   there.] $N; ~ ! A1
107.7   thing."] N[1-2,4,6]; ~ !" A1,
   N[3,5]
107.10   course,] $N(−N[4]); ~ _
   A1,N[4]
107.10-11   sneering. "Because]
   $N; ~ ; "because A1
107.12   fist,] N[1,4-5]; ~ _ A1, N[2-3,6]
107.13   demanded,] N[1,4-6]; ~ _
   A1,N[2-3]
107.14,29   heaven] $N; Heaven
   A1
107.15   Hollanden.] $N; ~ ; A1
107.15   But_] $N(−N[6]); ~ , A1,
   N[6]
107.20   once_] N[2,5-6]; ~ , A1,
   N[1,3-4]
107.23,30   blazes,"] N[1-2,5-6]; ~ !"
   A1,N[3-4]
107.25   me."] $N; ~ !" A1
107.27   Nature,] $N(nature);
   ~ ; A1
108.3   seated,] N[1,3,4-6]; ~ _ A1,N[2]

108.8   miserere] $N; *miserere* A1
108.9   began.] N[1-2,5-6]; ~ , A1,
   N[4]; ~ ; N[3]
108.11   away?"] $N; ~ !" A1
108.12   see_] N[1-2,4-5]; ~ , A1,N[3,6]
108.27   ²you_] N[2,5]; ~ , A1,
   N[1,3-4,6]
108.31   me.] $N; ~ ! A1
109.6   moment.] $N; ~ — A1
109.6   Here.] $N(−N[4]); ~ ! A1;
   ~ — N[4]
109.15   Moreover_] N[1,3-4]; ~ , A1,
   N[2,5-6]
109.22   stared] $N; started A1
109.24   heaven] $N; Heaven A1
109.25   us,] $N; ~ ! A1
109.29   him_] $N(−N[2]); ~ , A1,
   N[2]
109.29; 110.27   said:] $N; ~ ,
   A1
109.31   armor] $N; armour A1
109.31   armor,"] N[1,4,6]; ~ !" A1,
   N[2-3,5]
109.31   suppose_] N[1,4-6]; ~ , A1,
   N[2-3]
109.36   -by] $N(−N[1]); -bye A1,N[1]
110.2   violets,] N[1,3-4]; ~ _ A1,
   N[2,5-6]
110.5   others,] $N(−N[5]); ~ _ A1,
   N[5]
*110.9,11-12   freely-given] N[1];
   ~ — ~ A1; ~ _ ~ $N(−N[1])
110.11   murmured:] $N; ~ , A1
110.13   so."] $N; ~ !" A1
110.16   fool.] $N(−N[2]); ~ ? A1,
   N[2]
110.22   go.] $N(−N[6]); ~ ! A1,N[6]
110.22   Go.] N[1,3-5]; ~ ! A1,N[2,6]
110.22   Please.] N[3-6]; ~ ! A1,N[2];
   ~ , N[1]
110.23   go."] $N(N[2]: to); ~ !" A1
110.24   change,] N[1,3,5-6]; ~ _ A1,
   N[2,4]
110.25   forward_] $N(−N[4]); ~ ,
   A1,N[4]
110.28   effort,] N[1,4,6]; ~ _ A1,
   N[2-3,5]
110.28   a-light] V; alight A1+

WORD-DIVISION

1. *End-of-the-Line Hyphenation in the Virginia Edition*

[NOTE: No hyphenation of a possible compound at the end of a line in the Virginia text is present in the copy-text except for the following readings, which are hyphenated within the line in A1. Except for these readings, all end-of-the-line hyphenation in the Virginia text may be ignored except for hyphenated compounds in which both elements are capitalized.]

10.19	sister-|in-		71.4	ten-|thousand-
25.36	to-|morrow		83.15	two-|violet
67.29	Twenty-|third		84.12	show-|down

2. *End-of-the-Line Hyphenation in the Copy-Text*

[NOTE: The following compounds, or possible compounds, are hyphenated at the end of the line in A1. The form in which they have been transcribed in the Virginia text, listed below, represents the practice of the manuscript as ascertained by other appearances or parallels, or—failing that—by the known characteristics of Crane as seen in his manuscripts.]

6.18	whirlwind		57.22	Good-by
7.2	cross-roads		63.20	stove-pipe
8.2	five-acre		64.12	to-night
10.20	in-law		74.11	urchin-like
11.33	Ha-ha		74.14	gol-durned
16.2	weather-beaten		75.36	outlaws
20.25	war-like		80.26	pot-boiler
27.4	to-morrow		85.16	shopkeepers
43.19	afterthought		92.9	semi-distraction
44.40	overdoing		95.31	drill-sergeant
46.37	¹middle-aged		102.31	hallway
52.13	non-committal		106.21	thrust-way
56.33	good-night			

3. *Special Cases*

[NOTE: In the following list the compound is hyphenated at the end of the line in A1 and in the Virginia edition.]

5.33	Gol-|dern (i.e., Gol-dern)	70.18	Land-|lord (i.e., Landlord)

[NOTE: All substantive variants from the Virginia text are listed here. Since A1 and the syndicate proof radiate from the lost Appleton typescript, both have equal authority with respect to accidentals; therefore, the agreement of three or more newspapers in an accidental reading against the Virginia text is also listed here. A text not mentioned to the right of the bracket will either agree with the lemma before the bracket or will be lacking at that point. All cuts in the various texts are listed here.]

3.2　Grey] Gray N^{3-6}

3.9(*twice*); 3.22　stage$_\wedge$drivers] $\sim$-$\sim$ $N^{1,3,6}$

3.15　The (*no* ¶)] ¶ $N^{1,3,5}$

3.19　"Roger (*no* ¶)] ¶ $N^{1,3,5}$

3.19　A (*no* ¶)] ¶ $N^{1,3,5}$

3.20　by] with N^3

3.23　identities were] identity was N^3

3.25　other] the other A1

3.25　employees] employes $N^{1,3-4,6}$

3.27–28　Hawker (*no* ¶)] ¶ $N^{1,3,5}$

3.30　for] in $N

3.30　²that] *omit* $N

3.31　¹I] *omit* N^5

4.1　Wouldn't] Oh, lordie, wouldn't $N($N$^{3-4}$: Lordie)

4.2　her eyes] the eyes $N

4.22　anyhow] anyway N^4

4.23　set] were set N^4

4.27　front,] $\sim$ $_\wedge$ $N^{3-4,6}$

4.34　valuing] viewing N^1; valueing N^5

4.36　answered] said N^4

4.37　everything] everywhere N^5

4.38; 5.1　shot] shoot A1,N^1, E1

4.38; 5.1　bears] bear N^1

5.5　interrupted] interposed $N

5.6　every one] everyone $N^{1-2,6}$, E1

5.10　grip] a grip $N^{3.6}$

5.13　her] the $N

5.14　to her his] her to his N^4

5.18　conversation] conversational $N

5.19–20　"Train . . . interior.] *omit* $N

5.20　nine] 9 $N($−N^1)

5.21　travellin'] travelin' $N($−N^5)

5.22　waited] waiter N^2

5.23　Yes] Yess N^2; Yees N^5

5.23　face] face toward N^1

5.24　hain't] haint N^1; ain't N^4

5.28　Want] Wan N^6

5.30　fer] for E1

5.30　stay] stray $N

5.30　doorin'] dorin' N^2

5.32　On'y] O'ny $N^{1,4-6}$

5.32　²yeh] ye N^6

5.33,34　fifty] 50 N^{3-6}

5.33　' 'Tain't] 'Tain't $N^{1,5}$ (N^1: Taint); ' 'Taint N^4; 'Tain't N^6

5.34　-dern] $_\wedge$darn N^3; $_\wedge$dern N^4; -dearn N^5

5.34　On'y] O'ny $N($−N^3)

5.38　talk] conversation $N

6.1　gate,] $\sim$ $_\wedge$ $N^{1,4,6}$

6.6　gurgle] great gurgle $N

6.9　to each other] together N^3

6.11　dreat] drat N^2

6.14　had been] was N^6

6.16　and] *omit* N^3

6.18　to see you] t' see yeh $N ($N^4$: yen)

6.20 toward] towards N[2,5]

6.21 a] her $N

6.22 aside] *omit* N[2]

6.23 scanned] scranned N[2]

6.23 "Hello (*no* ¶)] ¶ N[1,3,5]

6.26 writhed] writhered N[2]

6.28 a] *omit* N[3]

6.30; 7.4,7,14,15,16,27,29; 8.6,7 you] yeh $N

6.30; 7.4,32 your] yer $N

7.1,25(*first*),36(*second*),38,39 (*twice*); 8.1 the] th' $N

7.1 you] yeh N[1-5]; yer N[6]

7.2 to the] t' th' $N(−N[3])

7.2(*second*),15; 8.2 to] t' $N

7.2 the stage] th' stage $N(−N[3])

7.3 you] yeh $N(−N[2]); yer N[2]

7.3,27; 8.5 And] An' $N

7.3,38; 8.5 we] we've E1

7.6 but——"] ~ "——— N[2,5-6]

7.8 They (*no* ¶)] ¶ N[3,5-6]

7.8 dove] dived N[5], E1

7.12 toward] towards N[1-2,5]

7.12 came] *omit* N[6]

7.13 grey] gray $N

7.14 you] yeh $N; you'd E1

7.15 hunt] hunt for E1

7.21 to] t' $N(−N[3])

7.21 'em] them N[3]

7.23 you] yeh $N(−N[2])

7.23 Lil'] Lill N[2]; Lil∧ N[3,6]

7.24 Yeh] Yep N[2,5]; Yes N[3]

7.28 pickerel] while pickerel N[3]

7.34 Pretty] Perty $N(N[1]: perty)

7.36 just] jest $N

7.36 about] 'bout $N

7.36 ¹the] th' N[1-4]

7.36 The] Th' $N(−N[6]); The' N[6]

7.38 because] b'cause $N

7.39 goin'] going N[1,6]

7.39 to] t' N[2-5]

8.1 want] want' N[5]; wan't N[6]

8.1 to] t' $N(−N[1])

8.1 And] An' N[3]

8.1-2 hoss∧team] ~ - ~ N[1-3] (N[1,3]: hoss-|team)

8.2 -acre] ∧acres N[3]; -acre lot N[4]

8.3 only] o'ny N[1,5]; on'y N[2-4]; on'ny N[6]

8.3 hand] han' $N

8.7,9 you'd] ye'd $N

8.7 and] an' $N(−N[3])

8.8 Monticello] Monticeller $N

8.14 dots] golden dots $N

9.1 Hollanden] Hollander N[4]

9.4 had] *omit* N[3]

9.8 *et seq.* toward] towards N[5]

9.9 nine] 9 $N

9.10 eleven] 11 $N; 11 o'clock N[4]

9.13 was] were E1

9.16 hill] hills N[2]

9.19 color-scheme] ~ ∧ ~ N[1,4-5]

9.21 Finally (*no* ¶)] ¶ $N(−N[4])

9.21 Finally∧] ~ , N[2,5-6]

9.27 quickly out] out quickly N[3]

10.2 a] her sister's $N

10.2 them] 'em $N

10.7 indignation] bitter indignation $N

10.13 simply] quite simply $N

10.14 I am] I'm N[1-2,4-5]

10.14 could] would N[3]

10.18 ¶ For] *no* ¶ $N(−N[5])

10.21 Hawker, "you] ~ . "You N[3-4,6]

10.23 expect, then,] ~ ∧ ~ ∧ N[2,4,6]

10.25 painter.] ~ ∧ feebly. N[1,3]; ~ , feebly. N[2,4-6]

10.26 voice] tone N[3]

10.36 is] are E1

11.1 there"—] ~ —" N[1-4]

11.4 Do,] ~ . N[2,5]

11.4 Hollanden laughed] he cackled shamelessly $N (N[2,5]: He)

11.12 color] color of N[2]

11.16 "Seems (*no* ¶)] ¶ N[3-5]

11.17 said.] said∧viciously. N[1,4-5]; ~ , viciously. N[2-3,6]

11.19 sorrow and gloom] Sorrow and Gloom N[4-5]

11.24 Hawker] Hawkie N[1]

11.33 thief.] thief, you old thief. $N

11.34 here] here and howled∧ $N(N[2-3]: howled,)

11.37 Hold] hold $N

12.1 Hollanden] Hollander N[1-2,5]; Hallonden N[3]

12.6 importantly] imporantly N[4]

12.12 but] *omit* N[3]

12.13 publicly∧] ~ . N[3]

12.21   is] omit N^{1-4}
12.27   Such] But N^4
12.28   away] *omit* N^2
12.31   all are] are all N^2
13.13   bad.] bad—that's bad. $N(N^6: \sim ; \sim \sim .)$
13.14   on to] onto N^5
13.16   eyes] eye N^6
13.16   deuced] dueced N^4
13.17   observed] blurted $N
13.18   Deuced] Dueced N^5
13.18   Hollanden] Hollander N^3
13.22   those] *omit* N^3
13.25   bad, too] too bad, too N^3
13.29   finally] frankly N^6
13.31   into] in N^3
13.34   this] the N^3
13.34   outburst] outbreak N^6
13.35   "You] "By cracky, you $N(N^6: \text{cranky})$
14.5   Eh?"] Eh? My stars." $N (N^3: \text{stars!})$
14.6   dev'lish] devilish N^6
14.8   too.] too. Good Lord! $N (N^4: \text{lord})$
14.11   around] round N^2
14.14   watch-tower] $\sim_\wedge\sim N^{1-2,5}$; $\sim$ - | $\sim N^6$
14.15   tolerantly] tolerably $N (N^3: \text{tolorably})$
14.22   What] What the blazes $N
14.24   Hollanden] Hollander N^1; Hollenden N^5
14.26   a] *omit* $N
14.29   asked] said $N
15.2   Hollanden,] $\sim_\wedge$ $N(-N^4)$
15.10   Hollanden] Hollander A_1
15.10   Hollanden,] $\sim_\wedge N^{3,6}(N^2$ *uncertain*)
15.18   he] He N^1,E_1
15.19   cried,] $\sim_\wedge N^{2-3,6}$
15.22   know] known N^3
15.24   I have] I've $N
15.31   scanning] canning N^2
15.31   ¹the] he N^2
16.6   carven] carved A_1,E_1
16.15   builded] built E_1
16.19   man$_\wedge$] $\sim$, $N^{2-3,6}$
16.20   concluded] considered $N

16.28   "I . . . Worcester.] Miss Worcester said: "I . . . true." $N
16.35   starts] start N^6
16.36   idea] brilliant idea $N
16.36   eyes] eye $N
17.6   Hollanden] Hollander N^5
17.14   younger] young N^2
17.24   don't] didn't N^4
18.2   looking] loking N^4
18.6   dreamily] dreamfully $N (-N^3)$
18.11   mean art] mean—I suppose you mean—art $N(-N^3)$ $(N^5: \text{Art})$; $\sim$ —I . . . mean art N^3
18.15   here."] here and take in God's exhibit." $N
18.21   should] *omit* N^4
18.21   more] *omit* N^2
18.23   cried—] cried, wrathfully, $N(N^{2,6}: \sim , \sim ; ; N^4: \sim_\wedge \sim ,; N^5: \sim_\wedge \sim —)$
18.23   'just . . . people.'] $_\wedge \sim$ . . . $\sim ._\wedge$ $N
18.25   I can't] can't N^5
18.26   her.] her, resentfully. $N (N^{4-5}: \text{her}_\wedge)$
18.27   be] be be N^3
19.6   "Well] He said: "Well $N (N^2: \sim \sim : ¶ " \sim)$
19.10   Well!] $\sim$, $N^{1,6}$; $\sim$? N^5
19.10   are] have N^5
19.10   you] are N^6
19.12   said:] said to Hawker: $N
19.18   The (*no* ¶)] ¶ $N
19.29   into] in $N
19.31   continued] said $N
19.34   do.] $\sim$! $N(-N^3)$
19.35   don't.] $\sim$! $N^{1-2,5-6}$
19.36   say] said $N
19.38   ¹did] *omit* N^{2-3}; do N^6
19.38   say,] $\sim_\wedge N^{1,3,6}$
19.40   for] for—for $N
19.40   heiresses] actresses N^5
20.1   said.] said$_\wedge$ bristling. $N (N^{1,3}: \text{said,})$
20.7-9   Far . . . nod.] *omit* N^6
20.8   drooped] dropped N^5
20.15   be so] to be N^3

20.17–18 Stanley . . . circum-
    stances.] *omit* N⁶
20.23 bird] birds N⁶
20.25 had_∧ perhaps_∧] ~ , ~ , N¹,⁴,⁶
20.30 little] the little A1,E1
20.31 old] *omit* $N
20.37 I am] I'm $N
20.39 it you] it to you A1,N⁴,E1;
    you N¹
21.9 in such case] *omit* E1
21.9,10,10–11,11 (*twice*) , of
    course,] ∧ ~ ~ ∧ N¹⁻²,⁵
21.12 After (*no* ¶)] ¶ $N
21.12 time,] ~ ∧ N¹⁻²,⁵
21.15 bended] bent A1,E1
21.20 very] *omit* $N
21.23 Suddenly (*no* ¶)] ¶ $N
    (−N⁴)
21.23 seat] a seat A1,$N(−N²),E1
21.27 boulder] bowlder N⁴,⁶
21.28–22.3 helpless . . . [¶] "Hur-
    ry] helpless. [¶] Hawker leaned
    his head on his hand and pon-
    dered, dejectedly: "It's the
    worst luck." [¶] "Hurry," she
    said. "They are waiting for
    us." [¶] Stanley . . . cleared.
    [¶] "Hurry N⁴
21.28; 22.3 They're] They are $N
21.29 sliding] sidling N³
22.7 very] *omit* N¹
22.11 of] off N⁵
22.18 "Well (*no* ¶)] ¶ N⁴⁻⁶
22.19 toward] towards N⁵,E1
22.22 home] homeward $N
22.22 sombre] somber N²⁻⁴,⁶
22.23 padding] paddling N⁴⁻⁶
22.24 Hollanden] Hollenden N³
22.25 lights] light N³
22.28 home] *omit* $N
22.29 writer] waiter N³
22.32 from] *omit* N⁴
22.35 hand] arm N⁴
22.36 asked] said $N
22.37 I] I'll N³
23.3 Hawker,] ~ ∧ N¹⁻²,⁵⁻⁶ (N⁶:
    Hanker)
23.12 were] are N³,⁶
23.15 a] such a $N
23.16 there] here N²

23.17–18 You . . . think.] *omit*
    E1
23.23 strode] strode on N⁴
23.29 ²to] *omit* A1
24.1 night] light N⁵
24.3 who_∧] that, N¹
24.6 "There] ∧ ~ N¹,⁴
24.7 times_∧] ~ , N²⁻⁴
24.8 credit] much credit $N
24.9 these] those N³,E1
24.14 first I] I first N⁶
24.15 ²paint.] paint. My tomato-
    can designs met, however,
    with instant favor. $N(N¹⁻²:
    tomato_∧can)
24.15 Later,] ~ ∧ N¹,⁴⁻⁵
24.16 green] the green N⁴
24.16 asparagus——] asparagus,
    and—— N⁶
24.22 We] Hence we $N
24.24 no] no—no $N
24.26 a while] awhile N⁴
25.3 "Yes (*no* ¶)] ¶ $N
25.6 threshed] thrashed A1,N⁴,E1
25.9 was] *omit* N³
25.14 haystack] ~ - | ~ N¹; ~ ∧ ~
    N²,⁶; ~ - ~ N³
25.16 remembered] remember N³
25.16 cried,] cried with a sudden
    scowl, $N(N⁴: cried,)
25.22 about] 'bout $N
25.23 about] of $N
25.24 remembered] remember A1,
    E1
25.25 said] said dejectedly $N
    (N³⁻⁴: said,)
25.25 After (*no* ¶)] ¶ $N
25.26 anyhow] anyway N⁶
25.27 so] *omit* N³
25.33 splashing] splashing about
    $N
25.33 squealing] a squealing
    N²⁻³,⁵
25.36,38; 26.21 Oglethorpe]
    Oglethrope N²
26.3 violets.] violets, although he
    remonstrates with me for not
    preferring a more fashionable
    flower or—or, maybe, a more
    expensive one. $N±(N⁴: flower
    —or, maybe,)

26.8 eleven] 11 $N
26.15 dock,] ~ $_\wedge$ N$^{1,4-5}$
26.15 flashing] bright E1
26.15 moon] boat A1
26.15 upon] full upon $N
26.21 I knew] *omit* N^3
26.25 and] *omit* N^4
26.25 ^{1}will] shall A1
27.2 the Fanhalls] Fanhall's N^5
27.6 so——] so partic—— $N
27.6 Say] say $N(−N^3)
27.11 he's] he is $N
27.12,21 Say] say $N
27.13 a] his N^6
27.14 the chair] a rocking chair $N(N^3: ~ - ~)
27.16 his] has N^4
27.16 shadow] the shadow N^6
27.22 too.] too. My sakes. $N(N^6: sakes!)
27.27 piper] paper N^2
28.1 ^{1}were] weer N^3
28.6 long] irremediable $N
28.7 close] closer $N
28.7 out] *omit* $N
28.10 train loads] trainloads N$^{3,5-6}$,E1; ~ - ~ N^4
28.11 streets] the streets N^4
28.18 sake$_\wedge$] ~ , N$^{1,4-5}$
28.21 to] *omit* $N
28.22 was] were A1,N$^{4-6}$,E1
28.23 like] just like N^6
28.23 balloon$_\wedge$] ~ , N^{1,4,6}
28.32 he] *omit* N^2
28.32 along] along just $N
28.35 would] should A1,E1
28.36 advice.] advice. The last thing I want from you is advice. $N (N^1: ^{1}advice!)
28.38–29.1 before, . . . he has] before. He has N^1
28.39 ^{1}it] *omit* N^6
29.1 He is] He's N^3
29.3–6 Miss . . . popular.] *omit* N^1
29.9 That's] That is N^2; That's a N^6
29.13 this] the $N
29.15–16 "You're . . . said.] *omit* N^5
29.21 a woman] women N^3

29.30 ¶ As] *no* ¶ N$^{1-4}$
29.33 ¶ Hawker] *no* ¶ $N(−N^5)
30.6 in] *omit* E1
30.8 began also] also began N^2
30.11–12 supposed] suppose N^3
30.16 she said] said she N$^{2-3}$
30.19 that] the N^6
30.22 until] till N^3
30.25 won't] don't N^5
31.1 suppose] don't suppose $N
31.1 nothing] *omit* $N
31.4 much] much space $N
31.6 eh] hey $N
31.11 he] *omit* N^3
31.16 the] that N^6
31.19 stern] as stern $N
31.20 You are] You're N^2
31.20 awf'ly] awfully N$^{2-3}$
31.21 I am] I'm N^2
31.27 Whose?"] Whose? The dog's?" $N(N^5: Whose, the)
32.2 scoffing] terrible scoffing $N
32.11 He . . . trees.] *omit* N^2
32.14 desire] vast desire $N
32.14 coat collar] ~ - ~ N^{1,5}; coatcollar N^4
32.16 the] a N^4
32.22 And—and] And $N(N^6: and)
32.24 soul! And] soul, and $N (N^6: soul;)
32.25 stage.] ~ ! $N
32.35 turn] turned A1
32.39 Now,] ~ $_\wedge$ N$^{2,4-5}$
33.9 at] with N^6
34.2 quilts] the quilts $N
34.10 and] an' $N
34.10 for] fer N$^{2-4,6}$
34.11 home] hum $N(−N^5)
34.16 said he] *omit* N^5
34.17,19; 35.6,9,18,23,37; 36.28 you] yeh $N(N^3: you *at* 35.18)
34.20–21 mournfully] mouthfully N^4
34.22 nor . . . nor] or . . . or A1,N^4,E1
34.25 step] first step $N
34.28 ^{1}and] an' $N(−N^5)

34.28(*second*),30; 35.26; 36.22
  (*twice*),23,25 and] an' $N
  (N¹: 'an *at* 34.28)
34.28 everything] ever'thing
  N²⁻⁴˒⁶
34.29 do you] d' yeh N¹⁻⁴; do yeh
  N⁵; d' ye N⁶
34.30 just] jest $N
34.30 leading him] a-leadin' 'im
  $N(N⁵: -leading 'in)
34.31; 36.20,23,28,29 him] 'im $N
35.2,3,6,9,30 to] t' $N
35.2 careₐ] ~ — $N
35.2 about] 'bout $N(−N¹)
35.6 I] I'd Eɪ
35.9 of your] 'a yer $N
35.10 wide-] wild- Aɪ,Eɪ
35.13 blue] cold blue $N(N²˒⁴:
  cold,)
35.13 its] it's N²˒⁵
35.15–17 At . . . stove.] *omit*
  $N
35.17 She slid] , and then slid N⁵;
  When he did appear she slid
  N⁶
35.17 the various] various N⁵
35.22 he sat] she was N⁵
35.28 Afterward] Afterwards N⁵
35.30 Going] Goin' $N
35.30; 36.18,19,23 the] th' $N
35.30 morning] mornin'
  $N(−N⁶); morning' N⁶
35.36 I'm] I am N⁶
36.1 going] again $N
36.3 lustre] luster N²˒⁴˒⁶
36.6 a] a | a Aɪ
36.7 heₐ tooₐ] ~ , ~ , N³⁻⁵
36.10 Hemlock] Hemblock N³
36.12 younger] youngest N⁵
36.14 to] t' $N(−N⁴)
36.14 the] th' $N(−N⁴)
36.15 to-day] t'-day $N(N³:
  t'day)
36.15(*twice*),18,19,22 fellow]
  fellah $N
36.16 What do] Whaddy $N
36.16 you] yeh $N(−N⁵); *omit* N⁵
36.20 driving] drivin' $N
36.22 looking] lookin' $N
36.23 oh] ah N²
36.24 ²her] *omit* N²˒⁵

36.26 your] yer $N
36.26 gabbling] gabblin' $N
  (−N³); grabbin' N³
36.28,29 a-hurting] a-hurtin' $N
37.1 the tennis] his tennis N²
37.7 which] that N⁵
37.9 of] of of N⁵
37.11 its] it's N¹
37.12 hit] bit N²˒⁴˒⁶
37.14–15 You didn't] Why didn't
  you N⁵
37.16 Hollanden] Hollander N²
37.27 with] in $N
38.3 at] in Eɪ
38.3 keysₐ] ~ , N³⁻⁵
38.4 a] *omit* N³
38.5 ecstasy] ecstacy N²˒³
38.6 would] *omit* N⁴
38.7–8 who was] *omit* Eɪ
38.13 he did] did he N⁶
38.14 Stayed] Staid N²⁻³˒⁵⁻⁶
38.18–19 Chambers Street Bank]
  ~ street bank N²; ~ - street
  bank N³; ~ - street Bank N⁶
38.19 stock] *omit* N³
38.22 it is] it's N³
38.24–26 The . . . her.] "Why,
  you foolish child, he's immensely rich." N⁶
38.28 courseₐ] ~ , N¹˒³˒⁵
39.4 to] of N⁴
39.4 yard, it] ~ ₐ ~ N¹; ~ ; ~ N⁵;
  ~ . It N⁶
39.4–5 hinge, you know. Of] ~ .
  You know, of N²
39.5 awful] awfully $N
39.7 ¹at] upon $N(−N⁵)
39.8 corps] group N⁵
39.10 others] other N⁶
39.10 my] *omit* N³
40.3 asked] said $N
40.6 interest was] interests were
  N³
40.11 silenceₐ] ~ , N²⁻⁴
40.31 about] of N³
41.1 ₐHer] " ~ N²⁻⁴˒⁶
41.5 swept] swept over N²
41.5 said,] ~ ₐ N¹˒³⁻⁴˒⁶
41.18 soused] soused N⁵,Eɪ
41.20 door mat] doormat N²˒⁴˒⁶
41.22 painter] pointer N³

41.31　wide] whole N⁴
41.34　said] cried $N
41.36　to] would N¹
41.37　don't] *omit* N³
41.38　so] *omit* N¹
41.38　sure] sure that N³
41.40　a man] man $N(—N³)
41.40　at all] *omit* N⁶
42.4　and] *omit* N³
42.9　"And (*no* ¶)] ¶ N²⁻³,⁵⁻⁶ (N³: ——And)
42.14　uninformed] uniformed N⁵
42.14　disreputable] disreptuable N⁶
43.2　gaunt] guant N⁵
43.2,24　grey] gray A1,$N,E1
43.4　in such cases] on such occasions N³
43.6　the song] this song N²
43.7　Billie] Billee $N
43.15　she] she has N³
43.24　high] *omit* N³
43.24　ferns] terns N⁵
43.27　cried] called $N(—N³); call N³
43.29　further] farther A1,E1
43.30　old] *omit* N³
43.31　¹to] at E1
43.31　innₐ] ~ , N²⁻⁴
44.1　vivid] a vivid N¹
44.7(*first*),19(*twice*),33,37; 45.9, 32; 46.7(*second*),18　you] yeh $N
44.7　your hides] yer ol' hides $N (N⁶: old)
44.7　²you] yeh $N(—N⁶); yer N⁶
44.7　haw?] haw, drat yeh! $N
44.19; 46.8　the] th' $N(—N³)
44.19　skin] shin A1,E1
44.19　minute.] minnet! $N
44.20　²Haw!] *omit* N⁶
44.26　bended] bent A1,E1; bending N¹
44.26　looking] looked A1,N³,E1
44.30　Hawₐ] ~ , N²⁻⁴,⁶
44.33　what] whaddy $N; what are E1
44.33　doing] doin' $N
44.35　Fanhall] Fanhill N⁵
45.7　at the] at that $N
45.8　herself] her $N

45.11　bite] bit N²
45.14　Just] Jest $N
45.16　them circuitously] then cautiously N²
45.22　kind of] kinda $N(N³: kind a)
45.22　aggravating] aggravatin' $N
45.23　can] kin $N
45.32　and] an' $N
45.32　He (*no* ¶)] ¶ N³,⁵⁻⁶
45.38　asked] said $N
45.39　Git-ap] Git-up E1
46.4　just] jes' $N
46.10　while] time $N
46.13　onₐ] ~ , N¹⁻²,⁴
46.18　cheerfully: (*no* ¶)] cheerfully: [¶] At last the old man said cheerfully: N⁶
46.21　interrupt] interpose $N
46.21　cried] said $N
46.22　awf'ly] awfully A1,E1
46.24,29–30; 48.30; 49.4,8,10　ox wagon] ~ - ~ N¹⁻³
46.25　courseₐ] ~ , N¹⁻⁴
46.25　retorted,] retorted, hotly, N⁶
46.29　everybody] ever'body $N
46.29　th'] the N⁵
46.30　to] t' $N
46.33　two] *omit* N³
46.34　blast] yeh blast $N
46.37　along] among $N
46.38　Fanhall] Fanall N³
46.39; 48.6　ox cart] ~ - ~ N¹⁻³
47.1　Haw] Ha A1,N¹⁻²,⁵, E1
47.2　Whoa there] Whoa, now. Whoa there $N(N²: , there; N⁵⁻⁶: now!)
47.2　Whoa, now!] *omit* $N
47.6　¶ "Oh] *no* ¶ $N(—N⁵)
48.3　yours] your N⁵
48.7　Mr. What's] Mr.—what's N⁵
48.12　Out . . . friends.] Hollanden was haranguing his friends out on the porch. E1
48.12　haranguing] harranguing N²; haranging N⁵
48.14　oration] oration then $N
48.20　Worcester girls] Worcesters $N

48.20 interrogations] interrogation A1,E1

48.29 meekness. "It] ~ , "it $N (N⁴: meekness;)

49.2 said] replied $N

49.10 I am] I'm N²,⁵

49.12 of] for E1

49.23 quite] omit N⁴

49.25 forever] for|ever E1

49.35 vouchsafed] concluded $N

49.37 heavens] heaven N¹

50.8 Billie] Billee $N(−N⁶)

50.8 you] are you A1,N²⁻⁴,E1

50.14 ¹you] to you A1,N²,⁶,E1

50.16 Billie] Billee N⁵

50.19 stalked] walked N²

50.20 to the girl] toward the girls N⁶

50.21 Billie] Billee N¹,⁵

50.23–26 "Why . . . him?"] omit N¹

50.23 nothing—] ~ , $N(−N⁴); ~ ; N⁴

50.24–25 stone crusher] ~ - ~ N²⁻³,⁵; stonecrusher N⁴

50.31 absurd.] ~ ! N¹,⁴⁻⁵

50.35 "And] "—and N¹,⁴,⁶

51.4 Hollanden] Hollanded N³

51.4 in] omit E1

52.5 to be] omit N³

52.5 in] into A1,E1

52.7 his] its A1

52.11–12 resemble] resembled N²

52.16 don't] didn't N³; doesn't N⁴⁻⁵

52.22 plunged] again plunged $N

52.22 in] into N³

52.22 again] omit $N

52.29 an] omit N⁴

52.30 feelings] feeling A1,E1

53.1 sorrows? Or] ~ . Or N²,⁴; ~ , or N⁶

53.10 Hollanden] Holland N⁵

53.11 Now,] ~ ∧ N¹⁻²,⁶

53.12 was] omit $N

53.16 suppose] suppose that N⁴

53.23 Afterward] Afterwards N¹⁻³,⁵

53.25–26 supposed] suppose $N

53.28 were∧ . . . course∧] ~ , . . . ~ , N³,⁵⁻⁶

53.33 awf'ly] awf-fly N³⁻⁴; awf'fly N⁵⁻⁶

53.35 air∧] ~ , N¹,⁴⁻⁵

53.39–40 wrathfully] mirthfully N⁴

54.8 concerning] about N²

54.8 a] omit N⁴

54.14 Billie] Billee N⁵

54.18 to] omit $N

54.21 fervently] fervidly $N(N³: fervedly)

54.23 we're] we are $N

54.25 it] omit $N

54.27 ²a] omit N⁵

54.27 underhanded] underhand N⁴⁻⁵

54.27 underhanded∧] ~ , N¹,³⁻⁴ (N⁴: underhand)

54.28 this] the N⁵

54.29 Look∧] ~ — N³⁻⁴

54.29 way∧] ~ , N²⁻⁴

54.30 to] omit N³

54.33 inn,] ~ ∧ N²,⁵⁻⁶

54.35 you] are you A1,N²,⁴,⁶,E1

54.36 thinking] just thinking N⁶

54.37 rejoined] replied N⁶

54.38 asked] said $N

55.6 "That (no ¶)] ¶ N²⁻³,⁵

55.8 people. But] people. I am of the people. But $N

55.9 ingenuous] ingenious A1, N⁵,E1

55.18 yes—] ~ , N²⁻⁴; ~ ; N⁵

56.1 girls] girl A1,N¹,⁴⁻⁶

56.13 in] omit N⁴

56.14 Sha'n't] Shan't N¹⁻²,⁴⁻⁶

56.28 Oh!] Er—oh, $N(N²,⁶; oh!)

56.29 old,] ~ ∧ N⁴⁻⁶

56.30 joined] joined in N⁴

56.34 attentions] attention A1,E1

56.34 and] omit N⁴

57.1,5,7 Oglethorpe] Oglethrope N⁶

57.1 seat] a seat N¹; his seat N²,⁵⁻⁶

57.4 ¶ "Why] no ¶ N¹,³⁻⁴,⁶

57.8 rate——] ~ , $N

57.8 picked] picked up E1

57.11 said∧] ~ , N²⁻³,⁶

57.16 Oglethorpe] Mr. Oglethorpe N²

57.17,18 Good-night] ~ ∧ ~ N¹·⁵⁻⁶
57.18 I'm] I am N²
57.19 Good-by.] ~ ! N¹·³⁻⁴(N¹·³:
   -bye)
57.29 sudden∧] ~ , N¹·³⁻⁴
57.30 as] omit N³
57.31 state] stage $N
57.32 curiously loud] curiosity N²
57.35 clear] omit N³
59.2,23(twice) the] th' $N
59.2,3(twice),6,24,26; 60.16,21
   (twice),22(twice),23(thrice),
   24,25; 61.27 you] yeh $N
59.3 slep'] slep∧ N¹⁻³; slept N⁴
59.6 kind of] kinda $N
59.9 his] the N⁴
59.9–10 the other] other N⁴
59.11,27; 61.23,27,30 going] goin'
   $N
59.11 to-day] t'day N¹·³⁻⁴; t'-day
   N²·⁵⁻⁶
59.13 the] his $N
59.16; 60.29; 61.28 for] fer $N
59.18 ¶ "Mary] no ¶ N¹·³⁻⁴
59.18 Mary!] ~ , N¹⁻³·⁶
59.18 belated] the belated N¹
59.21,24,25,28,29; 60.30 him] 'im
   $N
59.22 you] yeh $N(−N²)
59.22 ought to] oughta $N
59.23 wimen] wimmen N¹; wimin
   N³
59.23 pestering] pesterin' $N
59.25 leaving] a-leavin' $N
59.25 alone?] ~ . N¹⁻⁴
59.26 the] th' $N(−N⁶)
59.27; 60.22,24,29 and] an' $N
59.27; 60.18,22; 61.25 to] t' $N
60.2 breakfast] breakfasting $N
60.6 powder smoke] ~ - ~ N²⁻³;
   ~ - | ~ N⁵
60.7 He] And he $N
60.8 like . . . killing] omit E1
60.9 boughs] bough N³
60.10 "Oh (no ¶)] ¶ N³·⁵⁻⁶
60.10 I] omit N⁴
60.12 father∧] father, puffing $N
60.17 asked] said $N
60.19 Oh] oh $N(−N³)
60.22 the] th' N³⁻⁶
60.22 home] come home A1,E1

60.23,29,31; 61.30 can] kin $N
60.24 ought to] oughter $N
60.24 ²to] t' $N(−N⁴)
60.24 why—] omit N⁶
60.27 speech] speeches N³
60.28,30 just] jest $N
60.28 he] omit N²
60.29 out of] outa $N(N²: out a)
60.30 could have] coulda $N(N⁵:
   could a)
60.34 Yesterday!] ~ . N¹; ~ ? N²;
   ' ~ !' N³; ' ~ ?' N⁶
60.35 for two] for more than two
   N⁶
60.35 during the day] omit N⁶
60.37 the other day] yesterday $N
61.1 wrote——] ~ , —— N²;
   ——, N¹·³·⁶
61.1 Say] say $N(−N⁵)
61.2 pure] omit N⁶
61.6 a slate] slate A1,N³,E1
61.7 blazing] a blazing N⁶
61.8 ²and] omit N¹
61.19 recalled] remembered E1
61.21 you were] were you $N
   (−N⁶)
61.22 is] are N⁵
61.23 ²to] t' $N(−N²)
61.25 nothing] nothin' $N
61.27 before] b'fore $N
61.29 do] d' $N(N²: 'd)
61.30 funny. John,] ~ , ~ . A1
62.3 half] half of $N(−N³); a
   half of N³
62.18 we] you A1
62.19 bended] omit A1
62.20 at] omit $N
62.22 may] will A1
62.22–23 to-morrow. They . . .
   there] omit N²
62.30 Occasionally (no ¶)] ¶ A1
63.2 that] which A1
63.3 had] omit N⁵
63.3 afar] far N⁶
63.4 overturn] overrun N⁴
63.11 labor] work $N
63.11 was] is E1
63.19 casts] castes N²
63.20 stove-pipe] stovepipe N¹·³⁻⁴·⁶
63.20–21 wrong . . . hole in the]
   omit N²

63.21 then] *omit* N³
63.21 wall] hall E1
63.24 was] were E1
63.25 are] *omit* N¹·⁵
63.26–27 hour for dinner] dinner hour N³
63.31 "And . . . that."] ∧ ~ . . . ~ · ∧ N¹·⁴⁻⁵
63.31 settles] settled $N(–N³)
63.33 eat] *omit* N⁴
63.33 we've] we $N
63.33 got."] ~ · ∧ N²·⁴·⁶
63.36 arranging] arranged N⁴
64.3 cried] roared $N
64.5 like] *omit* N¹
64.6 have?] ~ , $N(–N⁵)
64.7 What's] What's—what's $N
64.8 Grief, "you've] ~ . "You've N²⁻³; ~ ; "you've N⁴
64.9 at] *omit* $N
64.12 You'd] You $N(–N³)
64.14 you.] ~ ? N²·⁴⁻⁶
64.23 scrapes] scrape A1
64.28 were] was A1,$N(–N⁵)
64.31 piece] slice $N
64.31 There!] ~ ; N¹; ~ , N³⁻⁴(N⁴ *possibly period*)
64.34 was] were N⁴
64.35 its] it's N⁶
64.38 ain't?"] ain't?" said Grief. $N
65.1 making] makin' N⁴
65.4 music box] ~ - | ~ N²⁻³·⁶
65.14 an—] ~ ∧ $N
65.14 they said] said they $N
65.19 to be] *omit* E1
65.19 oppressed] much oppressed N⁵
65.19 sullenly] suddenly N⁴
65.20 over] *omit* N³
65.20 they're] they are N⁵
65.24 Willie] willie N²·⁴
65.27 alongside] along side N⁵⁻⁶
65.29 Hawker's] Harker's N⁶
65.31 her] the girl's $N
66.5 still] *omit* N⁵
66.7 defiance] sudden defiance E1
66.12 give] care E1
66.12 about] for N⁶
66.19 lit] lighted N⁵
66.23 poor∧ little∧] ~ , ~ , N³·⁵⁻⁶

66.23 Wrinkles] Wrinkle A1,E1
66.26 that] *omit* N⁴
66.28 replied] said N¹
67.2 Still,] Still—still∧ $N(N⁵⁻⁶: still,)
67.7 said] exclaimed $N
67.8 where∧ . . . again∧] ~ , . . . ~ , N³·⁵⁻⁶
67.9 backwards] backward A1, N⁴⁻⁵,E1
67.10 course∧] ~ , N⁴⁻⁶
67.13 "But] "——but N¹⁻⁴
67.16 jay] gay $N
67.17 know] see $N
67.25 gas-fitter's] ~ ∧ ~ N¹·⁴; gasfitter's N³; ~ - | ~ N⁶
67.35 asked] said $N
68.11 Or] Oh A1,E1
68.12 money] the money A1,E1
68.15 You . . . me.] *omit* N⁴
68.17 *Eminent*] Emigrant N³
68.20 his] the $N
68.28 the] her $N
68.33 you,] ~ ∧ N¹·⁵⁻⁶
68.34 in] into A1,E1
68.37 I am] I'm N⁶,E1
70.2 den] end N³
70.3 bounce] bound N⁵
70.5 you] are you A1,E1
70.6 nine] 9 $N
70.11 No. Not] ~ ; not N³; ~ , not N⁵⁻⁶
70.11 so] *omit* N⁴·⁶
70.14 loosen] loose N¹
70.17 "'At . . . yet?'] " ∧ ~ . . . ~ ? ∧ N³·⁵⁻⁶
70.18 to-morrow] tomorrow N³⁻⁴; to- | morrow N⁵
70.19–20 Wolf—] ~ , N¹·⁴⁻⁶
70.22 heaven] Heaven N¹·³
70.23 cake] cakes N⁶
70.23 mean.] ~ ? N³·⁵⁻⁶
71.6 No.] ~ ! N¹⁻²·⁴
71.6 frame-maker] framemaker N³⁻⁴·⁶
71.8 Afterward] Afterwards N⁵
71.11 some one] someone N²,E1
71.13 effects] effect N⁵
71.16 Hawker] Rawker N⁵
71.18 to] into N⁵
71.23 What's] what's $N(–N⁵)

71.28   hand.] ~ ? $N^{1-2,4,6}$

71.37   Oh] oh $N

72.2   That's] that's $N

72.6 $last_{\wedge}$] ~ , $N^{1-2,6}$ (N^1 uncertain)

72.8   a fellow] me, fellow $N^{1-2,5-6}$ ($N^{2,5}$: $me_{\wedge}$)

72.9   heavens, did] heavens, give a man a chance. What did you expect, Splutter? Did $N

72.16   opportunity] an opportunity A_1,N^5,E_1

72.16   harry] harrie N^{1-3}

72.28   asked] said $N

72.31   couldn't] could not N^1

72.34   Nothing,] ~ — $N^{2-3,5}$

72.38   hit] have E_1

73.9   Pl-e-a-se] P-l-e-a-s-e $N

73.14   about] bout N^2; about it N^3

73.20   Pl-e-a-se] P-l-e-a-s-e $N(N^3$: P-l-e-a-se)

74.1   had] has N^{2-3}

74.1   was] is E_1

74.6   say] say so N^1

74.13   a] omit $N

74.14   gol-durned] durned E_1

74.16   a] the $N

74.21   What's] what's $N

74.21   asked] said $N

74.26   feeling] omit N^4

74.29   died] die N^1

75.1 ^{2}Billie] Bill N^2

75.6   She.] ~ ! $N^{2-3,5-6}$

75.7   She.] ~ ! $N(-N^4)$

75.16   is it] it is N^2

75.17   picture] picter $N

75.25   a] omit N^5

75.26   asked] said $N

75.27   a kind] kind $N(-N^1)$

75.35   worse] more $N

75.35   than] that N^3

75.38   I] II N^5

76.5   jumping] jumpin' N^3

76.6   know] know that $N

76.7   Wrinkles (no ¶)] ¶ $N^{2-3,5-6}$

76.8   snickered] sniggered $N

76.10–11   which, upon . . . charged] which was on . . . charging N^3

76.10 ^{2}upon] on $N

76.14   hallways] hall ways E_1

76.16   are] omit N^4

76.30   deprecating] depreciating A_1,E_1

76.31   you] are you N^5

77.3   tell——"] tell you——" $N(-N^5)$; ~ ~ "—— N^5

77.5   austere] tall and austere $N

77.10   has] had $N^{3,5}$

77.10   grievously] greviously $N^{1,5}$

78.9   window ledge] windowledge N^1; window-|ledge N^5; window-ledge N^6

78.18   the little] a little N^4

78.20   -dyed] -died N^3

78.23   sets.] sets, much as it would like to. $N

79.4   move] have N^6

79.10   spaghetti.] spaghetti. $N^{1-3,6}$

79.11   did once] once did N^1

79.14   inspiration] thought N^3

79.15–16   politely] positively N^1

79.19   trample] tramp E_1

79.26   Well] Er—well $N

79.26   know,] ~ — $N

79.28   know,] ~ $_{\wedge}$ $N^{3-4,6}$

79.30   so] omit N^3

80.7   displeasure] fine displeasure $N

80.8   cried] said N^2

80.12   replied] said N^2

80.14   On] In A_1,E_1

80.19   won't] don't $N^{1,3-4,6}$

80.22   voice] tone N^5

80.23   on] ahead $N

80.24   departed,] ~ $_{\wedge}$ $N^{3-4,6}$

80.28   Pennoyer. "It's] ~ , "it's N (N^2: Pennoyer; [N^5 uncertain])

80.30   What—what] What N^2

80.32   I am] I'm N^3

80.34   eyes] eye N^4

81.1   cigarettes] good cigarettes $N^{1-2,5-6}$

81.4   on] in A_1,E_1

81.8   Well,] ~ — $N^{3-4,6}$

81.10   heaven's] Heaven's N^5

81.11   cholly boys] ~ - ~ $N^{1-2,5}$; Cholly ~ N^6

81.13   Willie] willie N^{2-5}

81.14   business!] ~ ? $N^{1,4,6}$; ~ . $N^{2-3,5}$

81.16   you've] you have N^1

81.24 "You] "——you $N(N²:
  "——! You)
81.24–25 excepting] only A1,E1
81.29 the] that N²
82.7 Welsh] welsh N¹⁻³; Wesh N⁶
82.8 et seq. rabbits] rarebits A1,
  E1
82.8–15 rabbits . . . triumphant.] rabbits and finally
  they came very triumphant.
  N¹
82.9 tongues] tongue $N
82.9 Barbarians!] ∼ . N²,⁴,⁶
82.10 Pennoyer,] ∼ , disregarding
  the injunction, E1
82.14 Welsh] welsh N²⁻³
82.15 finished‸] ∼ , N²⁻³,⁶
82.16 eleven] 11 $N
82.16 the] omit N⁶
82.25 then. Weren't] ∼ ; weren't
  N²; ∼ ? ∼ N³,⁶
82.27 said he] he asked N³
82.28–83.2 "No . . . anything."]
  omit N¹
83.2 it's] it is $N
83.5 said] sad N²
83.14 rabbit] rarebit A1,E1;
  welsh-rabbit N¹⁻²; welsh-|rabbit
  N³; Welsh rabbit N⁴⁻⁶
83.15 said] asked N³
83.15–16 two-violet] ∼ ‸ ∼ N¹⁻²,⁴
  (N²: violent); 'two-violet' N⁵
83.20 There!] ∼ , $N
83.24 pend] end N¹; hang E1
83.25 him‸] ∼ , N²⁻⁴
83.26 "What (no ¶)] ¶ N³⁻⁵
83.31–35 "The . . . me."] omit
  N¹
83.31 shining.‸] ∼ ." N²⁻⁴,⁶
83.32 ‸Oh . . . me.‸] "∼ . . .
  ∼ ." N²⁻⁴,⁶
83.33 ‸My] " ∼ N²⁻⁴,⁶
84.1 the] omit $N
84.1 cigarettes,] ∼ ‸ N¹,⁴,⁶
84.3 Splutter?"] ∼ ?" asked
  Wrinkles $N
84.8 to] at $N
84.8 end] omit $N
84.9 table] tables $N
84.16–17 two . . . queens] two
  aces and two queens $N

84.23 When (no ¶)] ¶ $N
84.28 Wrinkles] Grief $N(−N¹)
84.31 "Beat 'em?"] omit N¹⁻²,⁴
84.32 said] replied $N
84.34,38; 85.3,23 Billie] Billy N⁶
84.35 on] in A1,E1
85.1 sometime] ∼ ‸ ∼ N¹,⁴,⁶
85.1 "Me (no ¶)] ¶ N³⁻⁵
85.2 They (no ¶)] ¶ N³⁻⁵
85.5+ (space)] no space $N
  (−N⁶)
85.7 face] front A1,E1
85.7 in front] omit N²
85.8 of] in N⁴
85.13 alderman] Alderman N¹,⁵⁻⁶
85.16 shopkeepers] the shop-
  keepers N³
85.21 on] omit A1,E1
85.25 debris] débris E1
85.28 I?"] I?" he said. $N
85.30 innumerable] the innumerable N³
85.33 enlightened,] ∼ ‸ N¹⁻³,⁵
85.36 schoolhouses] ∼ ‸ ∼ N¹⁻²;
  ∼ - ∼ N⁵
86.1,12; 87.23 check] cheque E1
86.9,12,17 ten] 10 $N
86.11 den‸] ∼ , N¹,³⁻⁴
86.17 morning,] ∼ ‸ N¹,⁶; ∼ — N²
86.15 to] into A1,E1
86.19–87.2 While . . . ballad.]
  omit N¹
86.26–29 ‸Oh . . . fiel'.‸] " ∼
  . . . ∼ ." N²,⁵; " ' ∼ . . .
  field'." N³
86.26 dat] that N⁴
86.26 niggah] nigger N⁴; niggeh
  N⁵⁻⁶
86.26 won'] won't N⁶
86.27 'Way] ‸ ∼ N³⁻⁶
86.27,29 d'] de N²
87.6,20 canvas] canvass N²
87.7–17 He . . . sword.] omit N³
87.7–8 dishevelled] disheveled
  N²,⁴,⁶
87.21 said,] ∼ ‸ N¹,³⁻⁴
87.26 had] was N⁴
87.29–30 The . . . east.] omit N¹
87.31 Once] One N³
87.33 the] a N⁴
87.35 period‸] ∼ , N¹,³⁻⁴

88.1   Hi,] $\sim_\wedge$ N[1,5-6]
88.1   fellow] feller $N
88.2   hit] take E1
88.7   There!] $\sim$, N[3-4,6]
88.9   ecstasy] ecstacy N[2,5]
89.6-7   headdress] $\sim$ - | $\sim$ N[1];
        $\sim$ - $\sim$ N[2-3]
89.16   receipts] recipes N[3]
89.23   rather] has rather $N
90.3   you are] you're N[1]
90.7   was apparently] apparently
        was $N
90.11   and] omit N[1]
90.16   age] ague N[5]
90.17   story-tellers] story-writers
        $N(N[4,6]: $\sim_\wedge\sim$)
90.18   reproachfully] with re-
        proach $N
90.23   remember] remember it A1,
        E1
90.28   fact,] $\sim_\wedge$ N[1,3,5]
91.1   He] omit $N
91.1   into] in to $N($-$N[2])
91.2   games——"] $\sim$ "—— N[2,5];
        $\sim$ · $_\wedge$ N[4]
91.6   have] omit N[3]
91.9   had] have N[4]
92.2   cash desk] cash-box A1,E1
92.3   practiced] practical A1,E1
92.5   wide] wild N[6]
92.11   breaths] breath N[5]
92.17   a fork] fork A1,E1
92.21   mad] omit N[1]
92.23   deviltry] devilry E1
92.24   movement] movements E1
92.25   air] the air N[5]
92.25   the smoke] smoke N[4]
92.26   bottles] bottle N[4]
92.27   maudlin] mandolin N[1,4]
93.3   them] omit N[1]
93.6   still] were N[4]
93.6   2their] the N[1]
93.6-7   instruments] in- |
        instruments N[6]
93.8-9   agitation] agitated N[2]
93.10   harried] harrowed N[2]
93.13   race] voices A1,E1
93.15   cafe] café E1
93.17   cognac] some cognac N[4]
93.18   flames] flame E1
93.24   Bohemian] bohemian N[4,6]

93.27   Ho] No N[1]
93.27   that's it] that it's N[5]
93.28   Look] look $N
93.31   Hollie] Tollie N[5]
93.32   heavens] Heavens N[5]
93.35-94.3   He . . . last."] omit
        N[3]
94.1   those] these N[6]
94.2   There] there $N
94.3   swiped at] swiped N[4]
94.6   a] omit N[1]
94.15   heaven's] Heaven's N[5]
94.16   out?] $\sim$! N[1-2,4]
94.16   they] you A1,E1
94.21   the dinner?] dinner? A1,E1
94.24   it is] it's $N
94.24   being] to be $N
94.28   Haven't] I haven't $N
95.6   graves] the grave N[2]
95.7   Lucian] Lucien $N
95.8   Hi,] omit N[2]
95.8   Hi,] $\sim$! N[3-4,6]
95.11   came] came forward N[1]
95.18   a great] an N[6]
95.20   understanding] misunder-
        standing N[1,3,5-6]
95.25   Stunning . . . stunning.]
        Stunning figure. N[3]; omit N[6]
95.26-96.5   "You . . . curious.]
        omit N[3]
95.27   the] her N[6]
95.28   2time$_\wedge$] $\sim$, N[2,4-5]
95.31   me you] me that you N[2]
96.4   you know] in fact $N
96.8   proprietory] proprietary
        N[3,5-6],E1
96.12   on] omit N[3]
96.16   any] that N[4]
96.18   anyway] any way E1
96.22   Charley] Charlie N[2]
96.23   Scott] Scot N[6],E1
96.24   'way] omit N[2]
96.25-26   2I . . . yours.] omit N[6]
97.1   Damn] D—— N[2],E1; Hang
        N[4]
97.1   coffee cup] $\sim$ - | $\sim$ N[3]; $\sim$ - $\sim$
        N[4-5]
97.1-2   accidentally] omit N[6]
98.1-2   windows, he] window she
        A1
98.4   and familiar] omit N[5]

98.13 ¹is] *omit* N⁵
98.16 he] we $N
98.16 servants, and] ∼ ∧ ∼ N¹,⁴;
∼ ! And N⁵
98.18 What's] what's N¹,³⁻⁴,⁶
98.22 monogrammed] mono-
gramed N¹,³
98.27 about] of $N
98.28 drank] drunk A1,N⁴,E1
99.5 makes] sort of makes $N
99.6 better∧ they] ∼ , ∼ N¹,³⁻⁴
99.7 an] *omit* N¹
99.11 proceed] proceed then $N
(N⁵: , then,)
99.11 sha'n't] shan't $N
99.13 monogrammed] mono-
gramed N¹⁻³
99.15 it.] it. You've hit it. $N
99.22 as] was N⁴⁻⁶
99.28 was] were A1,E1
99.36 Great] Good $N
100.1 one . . . never] none . . .
ever $N
100.9 created] is created N⁴
100.10 have] have not N⁶
101.2 you!] ∼ , N²,⁴,⁶
101.8 kept] *omit* $N
101.11 Pennoyer and Wrinkles]
Wrinkles and Pennoyer N⁴
101.13 out,] ∼ . N¹⁻²,⁴⁻⁵; *omit* N³
101.18 spaces] blank spaces $N
101.18 of] on N⁶
101.19 spot] part $N
102.1 you . . . find.] *omit* N³
102.2 ablaze] oblige A1,E1; blaze
N³
102.9 Now] now $N
102.12 paused] paused in E1
102.14 dulled∧] ∼ , N²,⁵⁻⁶(N⁵:
dull)
102.14 came] same N⁶
102.31 There] Then N¹
102.32 was] could be $N(N⁵:
could not)
102.35 at] to N³
102.37 asked] said $N
102.39 S-s-sh] S-s-h N³
103.3 bended] bent A1,E1
103.11 is!] ∼ . N¹,³,⁵; ∼ ? N²,⁶
103.11 suppose] s'pose $N
103.12 a] *omit* N⁵

103.12 divan,] ∼ ∧ N¹⁻³
103.14 ²she—] ∼ ∧ N²,⁴⁻⁶
103.18 'em] 'm N²⁻⁴
103.28 barn door] ∼ - | ∼ N⁴;
∼ - ∼ N⁵
103.28 door?] door? Look out! $N
(N⁶: out.)
103.28 come] are N³
103.28 come.] ∼ ! N¹⁻⁵(N³: are)
103.29 back.] ∼ ! $N
103.29 you.] ∼ ! $N(−N³)
103.30 O-o-oh] O-o-h N⁴
103.32–33 Wrink, Wrink, is] ∼ !
∼ ! Is $N
103.33 her,] ∼ ? N¹,³⁻⁵
103.34 Wrink?] ∼ ! N¹,³⁻⁴
103.35 pinching] punching A1,E1
104.0–105.34 CHAPTER XXXI |
In . . . idiot!"] *omit* N¹
104.10 No. There] No—there
N²⁻³,⁵⁻⁶; ∼ ; there N⁴
104.12 that it] *omit* E1
104.16 it.∧] ∼ ." N²⁻³,⁶
104.23 and∧] ∼ , N²⁻³,⁶
104.23 remarked indifferently] indifferently remarked $N
104.25 that] *omit* N⁴
104.27 way'?] ∼ ?' $N
105.8,10 do] *omit* N⁵
105.10 do you] you do $N(N⁵:
omit do)
105.14 No."] no, I don't!" E1
105.21 asked] said $N
105.27 Penny.] ∼ ! $N(−N⁶)
105.28 There!] ∼ . N²⁻³,⁵; ∼ ; N⁶
105.29 on] in E1
105.30 didn't] don't N⁴
105.33 not;] you are not, $N
(N³,⁶: not;)
106.0 XXXII] XXXI N¹
106.2 feet,] ∼ ∧ N¹⁻³
106.4 the hemlocks] hemlocks N⁶
106.4 boulders] bowlders N⁴,⁶
106.5 studio∧] ∼ , N¹⁻²,⁴
106.12 Hollanden . . . and]
When Hollanden . . . he $N
106.14 thing.] ∼ ! $N
106.15 tired.] ∼ ! $N
106.16–22 "What . . . weary.]
omit N¹
106.18 thing.] ∼ ! N⁴⁻⁶

106.20–21 ²I didn't . . . wanted.]
    omit N²
106.21 shouted] *omit* N²
106.21 thrust-way] thrustways E1
106.26–27 for a damn] *omit* N⁴;
    for a —— N⁶; for a dime E1
107.6 Damn] damn $N(−N⁴);
    burn N⁴
107.8 Why,] ∼ ∧ N²⁻³,⁵
107.8–9 perplexed] *omit* N⁶
107.12 he] He N¹⁻²,⁵
107.12 vaguely—"that] vaguely.
    "—that N¹⁻²,⁵; vaguely; "that
    N³; vaguely, "that N⁴,⁶
107.13–14 a curious] *omit* E1
107.17 which] that N²
107.18 a woman's] woman's N²
107.21 woman's] a woman's N¹
107.27 Nature] nature $N
107.30 again] gain N⁵
108.0 XXXIII] XXXII N¹
108.1 again entered] entered
    again $N
108.5 shovelling] shoveling N²⁻⁴,⁶
108.7–8 was . . . him] perhaps
    was to him $N(−N²); perhaps
    to him was N²(N¹: , perhaps,)
108.9 you,] ∼ — N¹,³,⁶
108.13 somewhere] *omit* N³
108.14 States] states N²⁻⁴
108.15 where] just where $N
108.19 you will] you'll N³

108.19 but] and N³
108.22 away] *omit* $N
108.22 time.] ∼ ! $N(−N⁶)
108.28 'way] away N²
108.28 ³where——] *omit* N⁶
108.28 See] see $N(−N⁶)
108.30 How] how $N(−N⁶)
109.1 ²can] will $N
109.3 court,] ∼ , N¹⁻²,⁴
109.7 ¹a] the N³
109.7 toward] towards N⁵,E1
109.10–11 I know . . . tenor]
    omit N¹
109.15 don't,] ∼ ." N³⁻⁴,⁶
109.22 ¶ Together] *no* ¶ $N(−N⁵)
109.22 stared] started A1,E1
109.27 then] yet $N
109.29 then] *omit* N⁶
109.30 serene] *omit* N⁶
109.34 But] *omit* N⁵
109.36 me."] ∼ .,∧ N¹⁻²,⁴
109.40 And you are] Are you N⁵
110.5 Dare] I dare E1
110.9,11–12 freely-given] ∼ — ∼
    A1; ∼ ∧ ∼ $N(−N¹)
110.17 Now] No N²
110.22 tearfulness:] ∼ . N¹⁻²; ∼ ,
    N⁶
110.23 go] *omit* N²
110.24 ¶ Under] *no* ¶ $N(−N⁵)
110.30 Later,] ∼ ∧ N²⁻³,⁵

Collation of Chapters XIX *and* XX *against "Stories Told by an Artist,"*
New York Press, *October 28, 1894*

[NOTE: The present text appears before the bracket; "Stories Told by an
Artist" is given the designation NYP and its readings appear to the right
of the bracket; the newspaper readings of *The Third Violet* are presumed
to agree with the sigla before the bracket unless specifically listed.]

62.2 are] is NYP
62.3 half a] a half of a NYP,N³;
    half of a N¹⁻²
62.5 in a] in his usual NYP
62.5–6 This . . . him] By it he
    had earned NYP
62.7–10 From . . . exclaimed.]

Wrinkles was a thrifty soul. A
sight of an almost bare cupboard maddened him. Even
when he was not hungry, the
ghosts of his careful ancestors
caused him to rebel against it.
He sat down with a virtuous

air. "Well, what are we going to do?" he demanded of the others. It is good to be the thrifty man in a crowd of unsuccessful artists, for then you can keep the others from starving peacefully. "What are we going to do?" NYP

62.11 bed.] bed. "You make me think." NYP

62.11–18 Wrinkles . . . Wrinkles.] *omit* NYP (*see* 62.7–10)

62.19 Pennoyer] Little Pennoyer NYP, $N

62.19 bended] NYP, $N; *omit* A1

62.20 scratching at a] scratching away at a NYP; scratching a $N

62.21 a] his NYP

62.21 "The (*no* ¶)] ¶ NYP, N⁵

62.22 may] NYP, $N; will A1

62.25 with . . . tolerance.] to him tolerantly, NYP

62.25–26 "Oh, . . . pityingly.] but at last Wrinkles could not omit a scornful giggle. He was such an old man, almost 28, and he had seen so many little boys be brave. "Oh, no doubt, Penny, old man." NYP

62.29 to this room] *omit* NYP

62.30 Occasionally (*no* ¶)] NYP, $N; ¶ A1

63.1 the] this NYP

63.1 which] that NYP

63.2 old] aged NYP

63.2 that] NYP, $N; which A1

63.3–8 The . . . room.] The light snow beat pattering into the window corners and made vague and gray the vista of chimneys and roofs. Often, the wind scurried swiftly and raised a long cry. [¶] Great Grief leaned upon his elbow. "See to the fire, will you, Wrinkles?" [¶] Wrinkles pulled the coal box out from under the bed and threw open the stove door preparatory to shoveling some fuel. A red glare

plunged at the first faint shadows of dusk. NYP

63.8 Pennoyer] Little Pennoyer NYP

63.10 a] his NYP

63.12 fully, . . . sad.] it saddened these youths. NYP

63.13 the gloom] darkness NYP

63.13 seemed to make them] always caused them to NYP

63.14 fretfully] *omit* NYP

63.16 masses] mass NYP

63.17 a] the NYP

63.17 dead] fierce NYP

63.18 were] were some NYP

63.19 were plaster casts] was a plaster cast NYP

63.19 with] dark with NYP

63.21 turned] twined NYP

63.22 elaborate] extensive NYP

63.24–34 "Eat . . . minds.] *omit* NYP

63.35–36 quick . . . upon] sad knock at NYP

63.36 ⁿthe] a NYP

63.37 gas] *omit* NYP

63.37 Pennoyer] little Pennoyer NYP

63.37 engaged in] busy at NYP

64.1–65.31 Miss . . . face.] Corinson entered . . . anyhow." (*see* Vol. VIII, 70.1–71.21) NYP

66.1–67.22 "He . . . Florinda.] Little Pennoyer's . . . world. (*see* Vol. VIII, 71.23–72.9) NYP

67.23 in this room] there, too NYP

67.23 he usually dined out] then he really ate NYP

67.24–25 At . . . trade] He had learned parts of the gasfitter's trade before he came to be such a great artist, NYP

67.25–26 were not identical] disagreed NYP

67.26 the opinions] that NYP

67.26–27 ²the . . . publications] every art manager in New York NYP

67.27–29 friend . . . to] plumber, a friend of his, for whose opinion he had a great deal of NYP

67.29 He] In consequence he NYP

67.30 street. . . . that] street and sometimes NYP

67.30–31 Wrinkles . . . him.] he openly scorned his companions. NYP

67.32–33 As . . . As] Purple was a good fellow, Grief said, but one of his singularly bad traits was that he always remembered everything. One night, not long after little Pennoyer's great discovery Purple came in and as NYP

67.33 ²he] *omit* NYP

67.33–34 to the others] *omit* NYP

67.35 asked Pennoyer] demanded Penny NYP; said Pennoyer $N

67.35 astounded.] astounded. Penny was always astounded when the rent came due. It seemed to him the most extraordinary occurrence. NYP

67.36 responded] said NYP

67.36 air] irritated air NYP

68.1–11 "Oh, . . . hastily, "if] Great Grief lay on the bed smoking a pipe and waiting for fame. "Oh, go home, Purple. You resent something. It wasn't me—it was the calendar." [¶] "Try and be serious a moment, Grief." [¶] "You're a fool, Purple." [¶] Penny spoke from where he was at work. "Well, if NYP

68.12 money.] money then. NYP; the money. A1

68.13 will,] will, dear, NYP

68.13 Grief.] Grief, satirically. NYP

68.13 You will] You'll NYP

68.15 You are] You're NYP

68.17 Pennoyer] little Pennoyer NYP

68.17 *Eminent Magazine*] Established Magazine NYP; Emigrant N³

68.19 would] will NYP

68.19 stack of blues] big blue chip NYP

68.20 his] the NYP

68.20 three] two NYP

68.24–69.5 After . . . Rotten."] It was . . . mummies. (*see* Vol. viii, 73.10–29) NYP

Collation of Beginning of Chapter xxvii *against "In a Park Row Restaurant,"* New York Press, *October 28, 1894*

[NOTE: The present text appears before the bracket; "In a Park Row Restaurant" is given the designation NYP, and its readings appear to the right of the bracket. See also Volume viii, 329.10–24.]

92.6 little handful of] *omit* NYP

92.6–13 ran . . . injury.] dashed about the room as if a monster pursued them, and they sought escape wildly through the walls. It was like the scattering and scampering of a lot of water bugs, when one splashes the surface of the brook with a pebble. NYP

92.14 ways] swift ways NYP

92.14 skill.] rare skill. Perspiration stood upon their foreheads, and their breaths came strainedly. NYP

92.15 people] customers NYP

92.16 assault. They] assault. The crumbs from the previous diner were swept off with one

fierce motion of a napkin. A
waiter NYP

92.16   two] too NYP

92.17   ¹a] the NYP

92.17   a fork] NYP; fork A1

92.17   Then] And then NYP

92.17–18   volley . . . was] volley, thumped down in haste, causing men to look sharp to see if their trousers were safe. [¶] There was in the air an endless clatter of dishes, NYP

ACTIVE SERVICE

TEXTUAL NOTES

114.27–28 machine, this] These words were seemingly omitted in TMs[1] by a typing error. Cora first typed 'this | machine, this clock, suddenly crumble' but then recognized an eyeskip and x'd out 'machine . . . crumble' before continuing with 'self-sustaining, self-operative'. By an error, evidently, 'machine, this' at the beginning of the line was deleted whereas the deletion should have begun with 'clock'. Whether the restoration of 'machine, this' in the copy for A1+ was made by Cora but not in Heinemann's ribbon copy, or whether the editor who went over TMs[1] before TMs[2] was typed recognized the error under the deleting x's and restored it, is not demonstrable.

114.33–34 Coleman!] The TMs[1] period is not necessarily an error, but it is slightly unusual after an obvious exclamation and may have derived from a failure to turn the period into an exclamation by hand, as was necessary for all exclamation marks in TMs[1]. If emendation is to be made, the E1 reading, under the circumstances, is superior to the A1 question mark although neither can be authoritative. For a clearer instance of an oversight in adding the exclamation by hand, see TMs[1] at 115.1 and 141.4.

124.15 walls] Both E1 and A1 read 'walls' for the TMs[1] mistake 'wallx'. That the plural is the right reading is strongly suggested by the closeness of the two letters on the keyboard so that 'x' is an easy typing error for 's'.

131.20 Edidor] The second 'd' is not absolutely clear in TMs[1] but that it is 'd' cannot be in doubt. The lack of clarity in the letter gave rise, however, to similar error in E1 and A1+, for the dialect 'Edidor' of TMs[1] is presumably justified by the insistence on the German origin of the speaker. The inventor is otherwise speechless and so comparisons are not available.

135.33 me] Crane's grammar was often so uncertain that TMs[1] 'I' is certainly what he wrote in all innocence. But since this incorrect usage is not supposed to be a socially characterizing device for Marjory, the conventional alteration of the printed editions is adopted.

137.39 feckless] Crane seems regularly to have confused 'feckless' with his version 'fetless'. For other examples, see the Textual Notes to "The Second Generation" and "Memoirs of a Private," pages 268.21 and 195.26 respectively in TALES OF WAR, *Works*, VI, and REPORTS OF WAR, *Works*, IX. Emendation of the nonce word seems justified, although *fetless* might well be recorded in dictionaries on historical principles.

141.4 Steady! Come off!] Since the exclamation point was a key on TMs[2] but had to be entered by hand above a period in TMs[1], it seems probable that the underlying manuscript had exclamation points here but that the marks were not added by hand in the Stokes copy of TMs[1] and therefore are not reflected in A[1] and N[1] set at this point from TMs[1]. See Textual Note to 114.33–34.

149.16 differently] The TMs[1] reading is somewhat obscure in its sense, but the A[1]+ reading 'indifferently' seems to be even less acceptable and probably represents a sophistication. It may be that what Crane had in mind was the sneer that all plays are likely to be bad but Whipple's was bad with a difference, the differences (that it did not conform to the popular formula, as indicated in the context) having deceived Nora into thinking that it was good.

150.36 look and whisper] This reading of TMs[1] (and E[1]) was altered in A[1]+ to the more natural 'look up', doubtless by editorial intervention. For the possibility that 'look and whisper' is what Crane actually wrote, see the Textual Note to 175.30.

165.31 had become] The past perfect fits the context best; under these circumstances it is as reasonable to conjecture that the manuscript—or TMs[1] by eyeskip—omitted the 'had', and its 'become' was corrected to 'became' in TMs[2], as that we are faced by a grammatical error or a TMs[1] misreading of the manuscript.

170.10 flickered] This word appears as 'flicked' in A[1]+ as well as in TMs[1]. Very likely it was Crane's mistaken usage for 'flickered' although a Cora misreading is not impossible. The E[1] reading 'flecked' is clearly a sophistication.

170.26 passing] TMs[1] 'passing into' appears to be a slip. From the subsequent narrative it is clear that the cavalry on their scouting expedition were not accompanied by the slower infantry which would have impeded their mobility. The infantry were covering only the makeshift bridge on the near or Greek side of the river (see 'Then the column curved along . . . to the shallows of the river' [172.39–173.1]). It is possible that TMs[1] 'into' is a memorial contamination anticipating 'proceed into Turkey'. However, despite the concurrence of the prints in the right reading, the source of correction is uncertain. E[1] here is not likely to be any more authoritative than A[1], especially since it is an alteration from the preserved proof.

171.37 world] In working over TMs[1] Cora (apparently in an operation independent from Crane's own later revision) deleted the 'l' of typed 'world' by a slash, an alteration followed by E[1]. The A[1]+ reading 'world' may have derived in TMs[2] either from an example of TMs[1] not so altered or else by the editor, on the sense, ignoring the change. 'Word' could be defended as the coronation provided by the written word of the press, but 'this word' lacks a referent in such a sense, and the context centers on the glorification of fighting men at having a spectator to their deeds who was disinterested since he was neither Greek nor Turkish, with no necessary implication that this spectator must be a reporter. The continuation of the passage with its amplification, 'this desire of men to have some disinterested fellows perceive their deeds', does not support the narrow suggestion that the deeds must necessarily be written about. Such a feeling among the soldiers would be useful for a war correspondent; but the soldiers' reaction was not necessarily triggered by the presence of a correspondent any more than by another foreign spectator. Since Cora's changes in TMs¹ are seemingly unauthoritative, the sense suggests the advisability of retaining the word as originally typed.

172.16 uniforms . . . were] The agreement of N² (set from TMs²) with TMs¹ indicates that the common error 'uniform . . . were' was present in TMs² copying TMs¹. Whether the error lay in the singular 'uniform' or the plural 'were' is scarcely to be demonstrated. Although 'were' could have been a contamination from the plural 'troopers', the simplest explanation is that 'uniform' is a typist error.

175.30 looked] The omission of 'at him' in TMs¹, followed by E1 but altered in A1+ to 'looked at him', presents a troublesome problem. The addition in A1+ has little or no chance of being authoritative, but it could of course be a correction of one of Cora's common eyeskips and therefore desirable to adopt. It is true that there can be no ambiguity here, for the fact that Coleman smiled in response indicates clearly enough that the major was not looking into the distance to see the source of the bullets. Nevertheless, the more natural phrase occurs at 182.11–12, 'he saw the captain of the battery looking at him'. Some possibility exists that Crane liked the idiom 'looked' without the usual following adverb. A reading at 215.37–38 'He heard a horse cantering up on his left side and looking he saw Nora' may offer a distant parallel. Much closer is the curious reading in TMs¹ (also followed by E1) at 150.35–36, 'Everybody saw Coleman read this card and then look and whisper to the deck-steward.' Here the A1+ alteration 'look up and whisper' may repair a Cora eyeskip but is probably a TMs² editorial or typist sophistication, for it is possible that Crane felt the use of 'to' after 'whisper' applied to both 'look' and 'whisper', and TMs¹ may reproduce faithfully what for better or for worse he wrote. On the whole, it may seem the better to let the TMs¹ readings stand in both places.

190.21 there] TMs¹ 'that there' is almost certainly authorial but in need of the correction applied by E1 and TMs². Crane was continuing the indirect discourse of 190.18–19, 'whispered to him swiftly that the game was to flee, flee, flee.' But parallel structure with the start of the new sentence 'The wing of the army . . .' requires the removal of 'that' beginning the second main clause of this compound sentence.

198.36 and the sex] That there was an eyeskip in TMs¹ is obvious, and equally obvious are the means both E1 and A1 used to correct the error. It may well be that both versions are unauthoritative, depending upon the agent who made the change in E1. The choice of E1 over the A1 reading, then, is made in part on its superiority in context and in part to allow for the remote possibility that Crane corrected the proof.

202.38 enlightened‸ immediately‸] The evidence suggests that TMs¹ reflects what was probably the manuscript lack of punctuation and that A1+ 'enlightened‸ immediately,' is the TMs² misinterpretation of the resulting ambiguity. In fact, E1 'enlightened, immediately‸' appears to represent the intended construction, in which 'immediately' should be associated with 'spun'. See 'The latter immediately went and bowed' (203.3).

203.12 at the strong finish] This difficult reading comes in Chapter XIV, which is still textually a gray area although with a strong supposition that no variant in A1+ stemming from TMs² can be authoritative. Thus the question is almost wholly one of whether the A1+ reading 'strong at the finish' is a necessary correction of a TMs¹ error 'at the strong finish'. The phrase 'at the strong finish' is not itself suspect, since only a few pages later we find 'I would rather look at a good strong finish at a horse-race' (205.33–34); instead it is the association of the phrase with the verb 'came in', which is invariably found as in the TMs² idiom, 'he came in strong at the finish'. In favor of the TMs¹ (and E1) reading is the evidence that elsewhere in this typescript Cora has not transposed words in such a manner; moreover, since 'strong' is essential to the idiom, its position in TMs¹ can scarcely be put down to her misinterpretation of the placement of a manuscript interlineation. If Crane did indeed write 'he came at the strong finish', the usual idiom was certainly in his mind but he was adapting it, albeit in a strained and individual manner, to the somewhat different meaning of a strong finish as found in Coleman's reference to his pleasure at a horse race. The emphasis shifts from the runner (or rider) holding enough energy in reserve so that he wins the race by a final spurt, although he has trailed the field up to the finish, to the other concept of a competitive, exciting struggle among equal contestants to cross the finish line the winner. The weight comes on the finish itself, its excitement (and danger), and not on the specific method of winning. If the ordinary idiom were to be altered to this different meaning, then Crane's unusual form does indeed express the actual situation better than the conventional one, which would imply that Coleman had held back, apparently not the winner, until the finish line. In context the students seem to be referring specifically to Coleman's firm leadership during the scare that they were blocked by the Turks on the road to Arta, and to the now triumphant conclusion of their adventure, and less to his original discovery and conduct of the party. The Turks turned out to be the friendly Greeks, which was the strong finish, but no criticism that Coleman had not also been a strong leader earlier could possibly be contained in the students' ecstatic outcries. Whether in the TMs¹ strained phrase or in the conventional A1+, the verb 'came in' causes difficulty; perhaps less literal difficulty is encountered in the TMs¹ phrase if it is conjectured to represent Crane's attempt to alter the sense of a conventional idiom to the precise circumstances he had in mind. The sense clearly is intended to be: Coleman fought through a serious emergency that occurred at the finish and he won.

208.8 sat] That A1+ made the right guess from TMs² about the TMs¹ error 'say' instead of E1's 'set' may be shown by the fact that t and y are next to each other on the keyboard, so that Cora merely struck the wrong letter as she often did.

215.14 broke] That both E1 and A1+ agree in 'broke' for TMs¹ 'looked' means only that both independently found the copy reading unsatisfactory.

Because of the somewhat odd use of 'look' at 150.36 and 175.30 (although in a quite different sense) the outside chance exists that Crane in the phrase 'looked . . . into' meant something like 'dropped in on' as in the common phrase for *come to visit*. But 'into' does not substitute for *in on* with 'looked' and it would seem that TMs[1] is in error through misreading or through copying some fault in the manuscript.

215.17 horses] The A1+ reading 'horse' was a superficially acute but not necessarily therefore authoritative change, although the editor would have had to recall that the little gray horse had been used as a packhorse. Crane may have forgotten, or else taken it for granted that some of the load would be distributed. The 'traps' at 215.16 would include more than the 'luggage' which at 210.22–24 was specified as carried by the gray horse. The editor of TMs[2], therefore, was very likely mistaken in his too narrow reading of the sense.

215.24 circumstance] That TMs[1] is correct in the singular and its derivatives in error in printing the plural 'circumstances' is indicated by 240.19 'There seemed to be a conspiracy of circumstance', which E1 sophisticates to 'circumstances'. See also 'arrangement of circumstance' at 253.3 which N[2] prints as 'circumstances'.

215.31–32 substance . . . only fire] The A1+ version 'substances . . . only enough fire' is an amusing case of literal-minded "improvement" by the editor behind TMs[2]. As indicated by his 'so to speak', Crane meant that the fire carried by Nora Black was figurative.

228.28–30 "I think . . . tenderly.] That there is a more serious error in TMs[1] (repeated in E1) than Cora's failure to indent a line of dialogue when the speech shifts to Nora seems evident, and it is certain that something following Coleman's statement of fatigue was skipped in error. TMs[2] addition has small chance of being authoritative but its insertion in the text is necessary. The editor was not beyond going back to 226.20 for 'poor boy' and creating a plausible and even characteristic exchange between the two. That Crane did not correct this obvious error in proof shows how careless, and even perhaps nonexistent, his reading must have been and how little E1 variants may be ascribed to authorial proof-correction.

269.14 sumthing] It is not likely that Crane would write TMs,A1+ 'sunthing' as broken English for *something*. The keys for *m* and *n* are next to each other on the typewriter, and Cora made a similar error at 270.29 where 'natter' was typed for 'matter'.

288.32 opinions] In the absence of TMs[1] the A1 reading 'opinions' may be taken to represent the typescript and the E1 'opinion' to be a sophistication influenced by the following 'keep your opinion'. For a parallel, see 'Mrs. Wainwright . . . had set about re-adjusting her opinions' (320.22–23).

289.16 could see] It is something of a toss-up whether E1 'could see' but A1+ 'could only see' is one of E1's numerous omissions or of TMs[2]'s numerous smoothings of phrase by addition. On the whole, the 'only' seems unnecessary although superficially attractive, and the E1 copy-text has been retained. Actually, it is of no importance in context whether the professor could see anything else in the room.

300.29 tragic muse] Since A1 and N derive through TMs[2] from the ribbon of TMs[1], which reads 'tragic muse' in its Heinemann carbon, the E1 'Tragic Muse' would appear to be without authority. However, in the preserved carbon typescript both the *t* and the *m* have had a horizontal stroke placed below them (transferring through the carbon paper from the ribbon copy) as if to distinguish the letters in some manner, perhaps representing some query by Cora. But Crane would not ordinarily have capitalized the phrase.

323.33 triumphant] The TMs reading 'triumph ant' leaves the question open whether E1 'triumph and' or A1+ 'triumphant' is the intended reading of the manuscript. Three small considerations join to favor the A1 reading. (1) It is true that Cora on a few occasions struck *t* for *d* (as for example at 326.1 'attentants') although the keys are not immediately above each other on the keyboard. But this is not a common error—*f* is her usual misstrike for *d*—and so the examples of *t* for *d* may instead represent her misspellings. (2) Some difficulty occurred in the typing that needed mending. By transfer, the carbon shows that on the ribbon copy she wrote a strong *h* in 'triumph' over a typed 'g'; thus it is possible that she skipped a space which she neglected to close when mending her typo by hand. (3) The sense requires 'triumphant': Marjory could scarcely be glowing with *triumph* over her parents or Coleman and the continuation of the sentence depends upon 'triumphant' for the effect on others of her beauty.

326.30 they] That Cora's error 'theu' in TMs[1] is a mechanical mistake for 'they' is indicated by the fact that the two keys are immediately adjacent. For a similar mistake, see 'deeplu' for *deeply* (118.4) and 'veru' for *very* (210.26). Thus the reading 'then' of all the prints save N[2] is a sophistication, and N[2] made the right guess.

327.9 plane] This is a quite probable reading in which all the prints follow TMs; moreover, an excellent parallel exists at 191.22–23 'All they saw of the universe was, in front of them, a plane faintly luminous near their feet but fading in six yards to the darkness of a dungeon.' Cora spelled 'plain' correctly at 113.17, 122.5–6, 206.30, and elsewhere, though she transposed it as 'palin' at 174.6 and 239.24.

EDITORIAL EMENDATIONS IN THE COPY-TEXT

[NOTE: Every editorial change from the typescript copy-text is recorded here except for the silent correction of the position of punctuation marks which, in the copy-text, frequently fell outside the closing quotes, and the correction of typographical errors, these being listed in a separate section following the emendations. TMs[1] is the copy-text for the first four chapters; TMs[2] (present for Chapters v and vi) is the copy-text for Chapter v; TMs[1] resumes as copy-text for Chapters vi–xxxi; where TMs[1] is lacking or mutilated, E1 (set from TMs[1]) becomes the copy-text. An emendation assigned to the Virginia edition (V) is made for the first time in the present edition if by *the first time* is understood *the first time in respect to the texts chosen for collation*, which for the present text comprise: TMs[1]: Cora Crane's typescript prepared on the Crane typewriter at Brede and now in the Special Collections of Columbia University Libraries; TMs[2]: American professional typescript for Chapters v and vi only, in the Special Collections of Columbia University Libraries; E1: *Active Service*, William Heinemann, 1899; E1(p): proof for E1 (present at 113.1–152.10 *Marjory . . . for it*; 169.6–177.21 *And . . . about the*) including a duplicated Chapter vi, one set from TMs[1] and the other from TMs[2], in the Special Collections of Columbia University Libraries—the symbol E1 occurring where E1 and E1(p) are both present indicates an agreement of the two, and only when they differ will the symbol E1(p) appear (a full collation of E1 vs. E1(p) starts on page 484); A1: *Active Service*, Stokes, New York, 1899; N[1]: *The Chicago Times-Herald*, Sundays, Aug. 6–Oct. 1, 1899; N[2]: *The Buffalo Courier*, Sundays, Aug. 27–Oct. 15 (lacking Chapters v and vi). Asterisked readings are discussed in the Textual Notes. The notation *et seq.* signifies that all following occurrences are to be taken as identical unless specifically listed to the contrary. The wavy dash (~) represents the same word that appears to the left of the bracket and is used exclusively in recording punctuation and other accidental variants. An inferior caret (ᴧ) indicates the absence of a punctuation mark. The plus sign (+) following a text symbol indicates that all texts (in the order listed in this headnote) following the text symbol agree with that text, i.e. '115.22–23 keen-eyed] E1+; ~ ᴧ | ~ TMs' simply means that E1(p),A1,N[1-2] all agree with E1 in hyphenating the compound as opposed to TMs, which did not hyphenate at the end of its line. The minus sign (−) similarly excludes a particular text from agreement with the preceding texts, i.e.

'128.24 bony-] E1+($-$N¹); boney- TMs,N¹.' The symbol SC(c) indicates Crane's holograph correction, TMs(u) symbolizes the uncorrected typescript, and TMs(c) indicates either Cora's correction or a typed correction; these are listed separately following the Historical Collation.]

113.19 endless,] E1+; $\sim_\wedge$ TMs

113.20 prepositions,] E1+; $\sim_\wedge$ TMs

113.29 petulant] E1+; petulent TMs

114.1 campus,] E1+; compus$_\wedge$ TMs

114.5 "Something] E1+; $_\wedge\sim$ TMs

*114.27–28 machine, this] TMs (u),A1+; omit TMs(c),E1

114.30–31 Coleman,] E1+; $\sim$. TMs

*114.33–34 Coleman!] E1; $\sim$. TMs; $\sim$? A1+

115.1 Marjory! Marjory!] E1; $\sim$! $\sim$. TMs; $\sim$, $\sim$, A1+

115.8 New York Eclipse] E1,A1; roman in TMs,N¹⁻²

115.16 Marjory,] E1+; $\sim_\wedge$ TMs

115.22–23 keen-eyed] E1+; $\sim_\wedge$ | $\sim$ TMs

115.24 outburst] E1+; out-burst TMs

115.38 dishevelment] E1+; dishevellment TMs

116.2 portentous] E1+; portentious TMs,E1(p)

116.6 three . . . -two] E1; 372 TMs,A1+

117.7 you,] E1; $\sim$— TMs,A1+

117.37 et seq. (except at 139.28, 29; 163.12; 164.21; 165.7; 179.11; 237.28,29; 247.40 [twice]; 251.28; 268.8; 274.38) its] E1+; it's TMs

118.21 theater] N¹⁻²; thestre TMs; theatre E1,A1

118.22 et seq. (all forms) Sophomores] A1+; Sophemores TMs,E1

119.5 pressure] E1+; presure TMs

119.21 infuriated] E1+; enfuriated TMs,E1(p)

119.25 surpassed] E1+; surpasses TMs,E1(p)

119.30 separate] E1+; seperate TMs

119.30 antagonists] E1+; antogonists TMs

120.6–7 privilege] E1+; previlege TMs

120.8 besieged] E1+; beseiged TMs

120.22 impertinence] A1+; importance TMs,E1(p); blasphemy E1

121.12 signaled] A1+; signalled TMs,E1

122.26 Separation] E1+; Seperation TMs

123.7–9 et seq. to 128.16 Michaelstown Tribune . . . New York Eclipse] E1,A1; roman in TMs,N¹⁻²

123.13 Afterward] N²; Afterwards TMs,E1+($-$N²)

123.15 foreigner's] E1+; foriegner's TMs

*124.15 walls] E1+; wallx TMs

124.16 appalling] E1+; apalling TMs

124.26 sunlight] E1,A1,N²; sun-light TMs; sun-|light N¹

124.28 office,] E1; $\sim_\wedge$ TMs,A1+

125.13,20 Little Rock Sentinel] E1,A1; roman in TMs,N¹⁻²

125.25 trolley] E1+; trolle TMs, E1(p)

125.25 Adventuring] E1+; Adventure TMs,E1(p)

125.36 Westerner] E1,N²; westerner TMs,A1,N¹

125.37 harangue] E1+; harrangue TMs

126.2 Western] N²; western TMs+($-$N²)

126.7 good nature] V; $\sim$ - $\sim$ TMs,A1,N²; $\sim$ - | $\sim$ E1,N¹

126.33   judicial] E1+; judic-|ical
TMs

126.38   Editor,] E1+(editor);
~ ∧ TMs

127.5   office-boy] E1; ~ ∧ ~
TMs,E1(p),A1+

127.15   East-side] N¹ (East∧
Side); east-side TMs,E1(p);
east∧side E1,A1,N²

127.38   curly-headed] E1+
(−N¹); ~ ∧ ~ TMs,N¹

128.5   placed] E1+; places TMs

128.8   æsthetic] E1,A1; aesthetic
TMs,N¹⁻²

128.11   stony] E1+; stoney TMs

128.24   bony-] E1+(−N¹);
boney- TMs,N¹

128.27   work 'em] E1+; work'em
TMs

129.4   conceited] E1+; conceeted
TMs(u); concieted TMs(c)

129.6   freight] E1+; grieght
TMs,E1(p)

129.21;130.12   Editor] V; editor
TMs+

130.5   circuitously] TMs(u),
E1+; circiutously TMs(c)

130.9   "They . . . outside,"]
E1+; ∧ ~ . . . ~ ,∧ TMs

130.23   -paper.] E1+; - ~ ∧ | TMs

131.1   contemptuous] E1+; con-
tempuous TMs

131.12   -sandwich] E1+; -sand-
which TMs

*131.20   Edidor] stet TMs

131.26   manœuvre] E1,A1;
manoevre TMs; maneuver
N¹⁻²

133.4   Well?"] E1; ~ "? TMs;
~ ," A1+

133.8   satanically] E1+; satani-
caly TMs(u); satanicly
TMs(c)

134.17   and—— No] E1+; ~
——*** ~ TMs

135.13   cried,] E1+(−N²); ~ ∧
TMs; ~ . N²

135.17   tranquillity] E1+; tranquility TMs

*135.33   me] E1+; I TMs,E1(p)

136.16   enquired] A1; nequired
TMs; inquired E1+(−A1)

136.39   cordiality] E1+; cordialty
TMs,E1(p)

137.2   triangle] E1+; tri-angle
TMs

137.5   the top] E1+; to top TMs

137.12   Coke!"] E1+; ~ !' TMs

137.19   shan't] E1+; shant TMs

137.22   Marjory!∧] E1+(~ .);
~ !" TMs

137.22   now,] E1; ~∧ TMs

137.34   room,] A1+; ~ ∧ TMs,E1

*137.39   feckless] V; fetless TMs+
(−N²); footless N²

138.13   Women∧—] E1+; ~ ,—
TMs

138.13   matter."] E1+; ~ .∧ |
TMs

138.19   women,] E1; ~ ∧ TMs;
~— A1,N¹

[TMs¹ is lacking for Chapter v;
copy-text is TMs². E1 derives from
TMs², A1 from lost TMs¹. All variants are listed.]

139.3   region∧] A1; ~ , TMs²,E1,
N¹

139.8   circled] A1,N¹; circled
about TMs², E1

139.9   "Well (no ¶)] A1,N¹; ¶
TMs²,E1

139.11   conductor] E1+; Conductor TMs²

139.11   with sarcasm] A1,N¹;
sarcastically TMs²,E1

139.11   sarcasm:]V; ~ ; TMs²
(sarcastically); ~— E1(sarcastically); ~ , A1; ~ . N¹,
E1(p) (E1[p]: sarcastically)

139.11   Maybe] E1+; May be
TMs²

139.12   road.] A1+; ~∧ TMs²;
~ ; E1

139.13   Amid (no ¶)] A1,N¹;
¶ TMs²,E1

139.13   comforts] A1,N¹; comfort
TMs²,E1

139.29   cars∧] E1+; ~ , TMs²

139.29   and glittering] E1+;
andglittering TMs²

140.3–4 upstairs] N¹; up stairs
TMs²,A₁; up-stairs E₁

140.9 clinking] A₁,N¹; clicking
TMs²,E₁

140.15 know. Why] E₁+; ∼ ∧
why TMs²,E₁(p)

140.20 lad.] E₁+; ∼ ∧ TMs²; ∼ ,
E₁(p)

140.22,23 people] A₁,N¹; folks
TMs²,E₁

140.22 were."] E₁+; ∼ ?" TMs²,
E₁(p)

140.27 Afterward] A₁,N¹; Afterwards TMs²,E₁

140.35 drinks."] E₁+; ∼ ·∧ TMs²

140.39 ²bet,] A₁,N¹; ∼ ∧ TMs²,
E₁

*141.4 Steady! Come off!] stet
TMs²,E₁

141.8 'Drunk'?] A₁,N¹('∼ ?');
∧ ∼ ∧? TMs²,E₁

141.18 pair!] A₁,N¹; ∼ . TMs²,
E₁

141.23 grill-room] A₁,E₁; ∼ ∧ ∼
TMs²; grillroom N¹

141.26 him,] A₁,N¹; ∼ ∧ TMs²,
E₁

141.27 Coleman?"] A₁,N¹; Coleman," he said. TMs²,E₁

141.29 The (no ¶)] A₁,N¹; ¶
TMs²,E₁

141.30 "The (no ¶)] A₁,N¹; ¶
TMs²,E₁

141.34–35 point-of-view] V; ∼ ∧
∼ ∧ ∼ TMs²+

142.2 thoughtfully. "It] A₁,N¹;
∼ , "it TMs²,E₁

142.7 sure,] E₁+; ∼ ∧ TMs²

142.9 Yes;] A₁,N¹; ∼ , TMs²,E₁

142.10 medieval] E₁+; mediae-
val TMs²; mediæval E₁(p)

142.10 don't] A₁,N¹; wouldn't
TMs²,E₁

142.12 rate,] E₁+; ∼ ∧ TMs²

142.14 Coleman.] E₁+; ∼ ,
TMs², E₁(p)

142.14 Easy?] A₁; ∼ ! TMs²,
E₁; ∼ . N¹

[TMs¹ is the copy-text for Chapter
vi but TMs² is present. The order of

textual authority is as follows:
TMs¹; E₁(p²) set from TMs¹; E₁
(p¹) set from TMS², A₁, and N¹
(set from A₁ proofs) of equal authority; and last, E₁, printed with
some corrections from its proof.
E₁(p¹) and E₁(p²) are so numbered because the Heinemann
proof placed E₁(p¹) first in order,
retaining this first version for
printed E₁, while E₁(p²), second
in order but set from TMs¹, was
discarded by Heinemann. An appearance of the form E₁(p²)+ will
signify the agreement of all texts
save TMS¹.]

143.2,22,23; 144.36,37 Eclipse]
E₁,A₁; roman in TMs¹⁻²,N¹

143.3 men] TMs²+; omit TMs¹,
E₁(p²)

143.20 trousers] TMs²+(E₁:
∼ -); trouser's TMs¹; trousers'
E₁(p²)

143.25 ammunition] E₁(p²)+;
ammunation TMs¹

143.28 ²great,] E₁(p²)+; ∼ ∧
TMs¹

143.29 free——"] E₁+; ∼ "——
TMs¹⁻²

144.6 vacation."] E₁(p²)+; ∼ ·∧
TMs¹

144.7 Vacation!] TMs²+; ∼ .
TMs¹; ∼ , E₁(p²)

144.7 et seq. Chapters vi–xiii
don't] E₁(p²)+; dont TMs¹

144.11 hasn't] E₁(p²)+; hasnt
TMs¹

144.17 Mind!] TMs²+; ∼ . TMs¹;
∼ , E₁(p²)

144.30 Sturgeon,] TMs²,E₁,N¹;
∼ ∧ TMs¹,A₁

145.11 cheque-book] E₁; ∼ ∧ ∼
TMs¹⁻²,A₁,N¹(A₁,N¹: check)

145.18 "'Tomorrow','"] V;
"'∼ ''", TMs¹; "∧To-|morrow∧,"
TMs²; "∧To-morrow∧," E₁+

145.24 fingers] E₁(p²)+; fin-
gures TMs¹

145.26 " 'Tomorrow',"] V;
"' ~ '", TMs¹; "ₐTo-morrowₐ,"
E1(p²)+

145.27 jiminy] TMs²+(E1:
Jiminy); jiming TMs¹, E1(p²)

145.28 mood.] TMs²; ~ , TMs¹,
E1+

145.33 et seq. (except in Chapters
XV–XVIII, XXVIII–XXIX) can't]
E1(p²)+; cant TMs¹

146.6–7 I must] E1(p²)+; I
must | I must TMs¹

146.18 is—"] TMs²,A1; ~ "—
TMs¹; ~ ," E1

146.21 it.] E1(p²)+; ~ : TMs¹

146.24 reasons!] TMs²,E1; ~ .
TMs¹,A1,N¹

146.30 pantomime] TMs²,E1,N¹;
pantomine TMs¹,A1

[TMs¹ is copy-text; TMs² is no
longer present.]

147.4 rhythmical] E1+; rythmi-
cal TMs

147.14 smoking room] E1,N¹;
~ ₐ ~ TMs,A1,N²

147.17; 149.39–150.1 wine-mer-
chant] E1; ~ ₐ ~ TMs,E1(p),
A1+

147.26 star!] V; ~ . TMs; ~ ,
E1+

147.30 word?] E1+; ~ ₐ TMs;
~ . E1(p)

148.6 the] E1+; | he TMs

148.9; 149.29,31 Fly by Night]
E1; roman in TMs, A1; 'Fly
by Night' N¹⁻²

148.15 north] E1+; North TMs

148.21 " 'Worked hard'!"] V;
"ₐ ~ ~ ' ₐ". TMs(u); "' ~
~ ' ₐ". TMs(c); "ₐ ~ ~ ₐ,"
E1+

148.25 that!] V; ~ . TMs; ~ ?
E1+

148.28 Gazette] E1,A1; Gazette
TMs,N¹⁻²

149.7 cost] E1+; coust TMs

*149.16 differently] stet TMs

149.32 on] E1+; in TMs

149.35 There!] E1; ~ . TMs; ~ ,
A1+

150.8 "He's] E1+; ₐ ~ TMs

150.9 elaborate] E1+; elabor-
tate TMs

150.12 airily] E1+; airely TMs

150.22 smoking-room] E1,N¹;
~ ₐ ~ TMs,A1,N²

150.25 et seq. (except in Chapters
XVI, XVIII, XXVIII–XXX)
won't] E1+; wont TMs

*150.36 look] stet TMs,E1

150.37 discreetly] E1+; dis-
cretely TMs

151.6 smoking-room] E1; ~ ₐ ~
A1+; somkingroom TMs

151.19 you.] E1+; ~ ? TMs,
E1(p)

152.16 isn't] E1+; 'tisn't TMs

152.30 "Confound] E1+; ₐ ~
TMs

152.38 discomfiture] E1+; dis-
comforture TMs

153.1 honor] A1+; honour TMs,
E1

153.24–25 receive] E1+; recieve
TMs

153.25 first-class] E1+; ~ ₐ ~
TMs

153.30 ¶ There] E1,N¹; no ¶
TMs,A1,N²

154.18 said:] A1+; ~ ₐ| TMs;
~ , E1

155.6 et seq. Eclipse] E1,A1; roman in TMs,N¹⁻²

157.10 recent] E1+; resent TMs

157.20 lightning] A1+; lighten-
ing TMs,E1

157.30 Walkley's] E1,N²; Walk-
leys TMs; Walkely's A1,N¹

158.7 humor] N¹⁻²; humour TMs,
E1,A1

158.15–16 seasick] A1+; ~ ₐ ~
TMs; ~ - ~ E1

158.30 Greek] E1+; Greeks TMs

159.11 salaams] E1+; salamms
TMs

159.11 salaamsₐ] A1+; ~ , TMs,
E1

159.17 arrival's] E1+; arrivals
TMs

159.23 staircase] E1; stair-case
TMs,A1+

159.25 foreign] E1+; foriegn TMs

160.12 er—] E1+; er$_\wedge$ (*space*) TMs

160.16 " 'Daughter',"] V; " ' $\sim$ ' ". TMs; " '$\sim$,' " E1,N²; "$_\wedge \sim _\wedge$," A1,N¹

160.18 villainous] E1+; villianous TMs

160.28 Christians] E1+; christians TMs

160.29 blanched] E1+; blanced TMs

160.31 Nikopolis?] E1+; $\sim$, TMs

161.24 dealer's] E1+; dealers TMs

161.32 medicines] E1,N¹⁻²; medecines TMs; medicine A1

163.18 snail's] E1+; snails TMs

163.29 too] E1+; to TMs

164.11–12 appalled] E1+; apalled TMs

164.35 Parisian] E1+; parisian TMs

165.4 field-glasses,] E1; $\sim _\wedge \sim _\wedge$ TMs,A1,N¹; $\sim _\wedge$ | $\sim _\wedge$N²

165.9 from] E1+; *omit* TMs

165.21 that] TMs(c)+; *omit* TMs(u)

165.22 accommodations] E1+; accomodations TMs¹

*165.31 had become] V; become TMs,E1; became A1+

166.7 tremulously] E1+; tremelously TMs

166.28 every time] E1,N¹⁻²; everytime TMs,A1

167.5 inefficient] E1+; ineffecent TMs

167.23 pantomimed] E1,N¹⁻²; pantomined TMs,A1

167.25 led] E1+; lead TMs

168.4 armor] N²; armour TMs+(−N²)

168.12 knolls] E1+; knowlls TMs

168.33,34 occurrence] E1+; occurance TMs

169.1 background] E1+; back-ground TMs

169.9 clearly,] E1+; clearlya TMs; clearly; E1(p) (*uncertain*)

*170.10 flickered] V; flicked TMs, E1(p),A1+; flecked E1

170.20 appeared,] E1+; $\sim _\wedge$ TMs

*170.26 passing] E1+; passing into TMs,E1(p)

171.4 philanthropic guardian] E1+; philantropic gaurdian TMs

171.20 rind] E1+; rhind TMs, E1(p)

171.29 existent] E1+(−N¹); existant TMs,N¹

*171.37 world] TMs(u),A1+; word TMs(c),E1

172.4 young,] E1+; $\sim _\wedge$ TMs

172.5 enough,] E1+; $\sim _\wedge$ TMs

*172.16 uniforms] E1,N²; uniform TMs,A1,N¹

172.17 equipped] E1+; equiped TMs

172.24–25 moustache,] E1+; $\sim _\wedge$ TMs

172.26 called$_\wedge$] E1+; $\sim$, TMs

173.15 an] E1+; and TMs

173.32 thick] E1+; think TMs

174.2 in all] E1+; at all TMs, E1(p)

174.10–11 trepidation] E1+; trepidition TMs

174.17 friend,] E1+; $\sim _\wedge$ TMs

175.16 occurs] E1+; occurrs TMs

175.18 hobbled,] E1+; $\sim _\wedge$ TMs

*175.30 looked] *stet* TMs,E1

175.35 every time] E1+; everytime TMs

176.3 pretension] E1+; pretention TMs,E1(p)

177.2 troop horses] V; $\sim$ - $\sim$ TMs+

177.13 Point] E1+; point TMs

177.29 whining] E1+; whineing TMs

178.23 battlefield] A1+; battle-| field TMs; battle-field E1

178.26 they] E1+; Thhey TMs (*possibly 't' struck over first 'h'*)

178.36 hazards$_\wedge$ . . . here$_\wedge$]
TMs(u); ~ — . . . ~ —
TMs(c),E1; ~ ; . . . ~ ; A1+
178.39 Turk,] E1+; ~ $_\wedge$ TMs
179.12 arousing] E1+; a rousing
TMs
179.28 callous] N²; callouse
TMs,A1; callus E1; callosity N¹
179.39 Plevna] E1+; plevna TMs
180.2 kilometers] A1+; Kilometres TMs; kilometres E1
180.4 river] E1,A1; River TMs,
N¹⁻²
180.18 the cavalry] A1+; cavalry
TMs,E1
180.30 day-light] V; daylight
TMs+
180.36 foreigner] E1+; foriegner
TMs
180.36 Athens,] E1,N¹⁻²; ~ $_\wedge$
TMs,A1
181.11 game." . . .] V; ~ "
x x x TMs; ~ " . . . E1; ~ ."
A1+
182.3 is] E1+; in TMs
182.17 an] E1+; a TMs
182.27 acknowledgment] E1+;
acknowledgement TMs
183.9 Further] E1+; Futher TMs
183.20 fez] E1+; fiz TMs
183.31 identical] E1+; indentical
TMs
183.33; 223.31 grimy] E1+;
grimey TMs
184.6 pranced] E1; prancing
TMs,A1+
184.35 horsemen] E1+(N¹:
horse-|men); horse-men TMs
185.11 leviathan] E1+; laviathan
TMs
185.12 downfall] E1+; down-fall
TMs
185.21 people,] E1+; ~ $_\wedge$ TMs
185.30 yielded] E1+; yeilded
TMs
187.2 lee] E1+; lea TMs
187.5 assiduously] E1+; assidi-
ously TMs
187.6 tin] E1+; tine TMs
187.23 shackles] E1+; schakles
TMs

187.31 heart,] E1+; ~ $_\wedge$ TMs
188.7 henchman] E1; henchmen
TMs,A1+
188.20 abutments] E1+; abutt-
ments TMs
188.33 to] E1+; thet TMs
189.1 stragglers] E1+; strang-
glers TMs
189.2 waning] E1+; waneing
TMs
190.3 his] E1+; omit TMs
190.19 north-ward] V;
northward TMs+
190.21 river] E1,A1; River TMs,
N¹⁻²
*190.21 there] E1+; that there
TMs
190.34 ²Queek!] A1+; ~ . TMs,
E1
190.39 ²rear-guard] E1,N¹; ~ $_\wedge$ ~
TMs,A1,N²
191.8 upon] A1+; with TMs; on
E1
191.19 dragoman:] V; ~ .
TMs+; ~ — E1
191.31; 196.14 precisely] E1+;
percisely TMs
191.33 regretted] E1+; regreted
TMs
192.32 other's] E1+; others TMs
192.38 barred;] A1,N²; barreda$_\wedge$
TMs; ~ , E1,N¹
193.2 footsteps] E1+; foot-steps
TMs
194.10 danger.] A1+; ~ $_\wedge$ TMs;
~ ; E1
195.25 authoritatively] E1+;
authoritively TMs
195.32 a] E1+; an TMs
196.25 counsel] E1+; council
TMs
196.26 because$_\wedge$] E1; ~ , TMs
196.27 counsel] E1; council TMs
196.37 away and . . .] V; ~ ~
x x TMs; away . . . E1; ~
~ — N¹; ~ ~ * * A1,N²
196.37–38 us and . . .] E1; ~ ~
x x TMs; ~ ~ — N¹; ~ * * A1,
N²
197.8 privileged] E1+; previ-
leged TMs

197.15 saviour,] E1+; ~ ∧ TMs
197.25 thither, speculating]
A1+; ~ . Speculating TMs;
~ : ~ E1
197.38 pre-empted] E1+;
preempted TMs
197.39 blankets] A1+; blanket
TMs,E1
198.2 temperament] E1+; tem-
perment TMs
198.13 words:] N¹; ~ . TMs,A1,
N²; ~ — E1
198.28 condescension] E1+;
condecension TMs
198.30 grandfather's] E1+;
grandfathers TMs
198.34 certainly,] E1+; ~ ∧ TMs
*198.36 and the sex] E1; omit
TMs; and so the sex A1+
198.36 embodied] E1+; enbodied
TMs
200.1 pallid] E1+; palid TMs
200.23 laggardly] E1+; lagardly
TMs
200.24 prodigiously] E1+; pro-
digously TMs
200.25; 205.3 discernible] E1+;
discernable TMs
200.25; 273.21 consummated]
E1+; consumated TMs
201.14 corps] E1+; corp TMs
201.38 no wise] A1+; nowise
TMs,E1
201.38 dimensions] A1+; dim
(space) TMs; dim chances E1
202.8–9 bridle-rein taut] E1+
(A1:-reins); bridlerein tawt
TMs
202.17 what] A1+; What TMs,
E1
202.20 do] A1+; Do TMs,E1
*202.38 enlightened∧ immedi-
ately∧] stet TMs
*203.12 at the strong] stet TMs, E1
203.25 appropriate] E1+; ap-
propreate TMs
204.11 pretentious] E1+; pre-
tentous TMs
204.18 you] E1+; You TMs
204.20 by] A1+; from E1; omit
TMs

204.29 "Did] E1+; ∧ ~ TMs
204.39 concerned,] E1+; ~ ∧
TMs
206.1 Coleman] E1+; mutilated
TMs
206.1 Were] E1+; Where TMs
206.25 river] E1,A1; River TMs,
N¹⁻²
206.28 stifled] E1+; stiffled TMs
207.11 thinks] E1+; think TMs
207.22 annihilated] E1+; annili-
lated TMs
*208.8 sat] A1+; say TMs; set E1
208.26 pow-wow] E1+; pow-pow
TMs
209.2 horses—] E1+; ~ ∧ TMs
209.3 mountain-side] E1+;
~ — ~ TMs
209.4 he] E1+; He TMs
209.4 wisely—] E1,A1,N²; ~ . —
TMs; ~ , N¹
209.5 to] E1+; of TMs
209.15 monarch,] E1+; ~ ∧ TMs
209.19 veritably] E1+; veritible
TMs
209.21 ingenuity] E1+; engenu-
ity TMs
209.31 hell] E1,A1; heel TMs;
—— N¹; the deuce N²
210.31 unwieldy] E1+; unweildy
TMs
210.32–33 contemptuous] TMs
(u),E1+; contemptous TMs(c)
211.1 bitterness,] E1+; ~ ∧ TMs
211.13 Looking] E1+; looking
TMs
211.18 querulously] E1+; quere-
lously TMs
211.28–29 floundered] E1+;
flounded TMs
211.32 were] E1+; where TMs
211.38 tin-plates] V; tin-|plates
E1; tin plates TMs+
212.30 d'] E1+; -'d TMs
213.7 a spirit] E1+; spirit TMs
213.14 forever] A1,N¹; for ever
TMs,E1; for-|ever N²
213.19 et seq. New York Day-
light] E1,A1; roman in TMs,
N¹⁻²

214.7 *Daylight*ₐ] TMs(u),A1;
~ , TMs(c),E1,N¹⁻²
214.11 Why,] E1+; ~ ₐ TMs
214.12 rustled] E1+(−N¹);
russled TMs; rushed N¹
214.15 'way] E1; ₐ~ TMs,A1+
214.29 mind,] E1+; ~ ₐ TMs
215.11 clamor] V; clamour E1+;
clammor TMs
*215.14 broke] E1+; looked TMs
*215.17 horses] *stet* TMs,E1
215.21 horses'] E1,N¹; horsesₐ
TMs,A1,N²
*215.24 circumstance] *stet* TMs
215.31 inflammable] E1+; in-
flamable TMs
*215.32 fire] *stet* TMs,E1
216.13 outright:] V; ~ . TMs+
(−E1); ~ — E1
216.16 stupefied] E1,N¹⁻²; stupified TMs,A1
216.24 seen] E1+; see TMs
216.26 it] E1+; *omit* TMs
216.26 advisable] E1+; advice-
able TMs
216.36 animatedly] E1+; animately TMs
217.3 President] E1+; president
TMs
217.7 *et seq. Daylight*] E1,A1;
Daylight TMs,N¹⁻²
217.20 point-of-view] V; ~ ₐ ~ ₐ
~ TMs+
218.9 *Fly by Night*] E1,A1(A1:
roman); Fly-by-night TMs;
'Fly by Night' N¹⁻²
218.24 tranquillity] E1+; tranquility TMs
219.4 pessimistically] TMs(u),
E1+; pessimisticly TMs(c)
220.18 Tounley,] E1+; ~ . TMs
220.25 re-assure] V; reassure
TMs+
222.1 God] E1+; god TMs
222.3 Aunt] E1+; aunt TMs (*unclear*)
222.9 Only . . .] E1; ~ * * *
TMs; ~ * * A1,N²; ~ ₐ N¹
222.21 Her] A1+; He TMs; His
E1

222.29 upon] TMs(u),A1+; on
TMs(c), E1
223.5 river] E1,A1; River TMs,
N¹⁻²
223.18 chaotic] A1+; choatic
TMs,E1
224.26 you. . . .] E1(3 *periods*);
~ . * * * TMs,A1+
224.26 much. . . .] E1 (3 *periods*); ~ ₐ * * TMs; ~ .
* * * A1+
224.34 apartment] E1+; appart-
ment TMs
225.12 toward] A1+; towards
TMs,E1
225.36 amber-like] E1+(−N¹);
~ ₐ ~ TMs; amberlike N¹
226.3 famous] E1+; famious
TMs
226.3 azure] E1+; asure TMs
226.8 street:] V; ~ . TMs,A1,N¹;
~ — E1; ~ , N²
226.23 opulence] E1+; oppu-
lence TMs
226.39 affect] A1+; effect TMs,
E1
227.5 hers] E1+; her's TMs
227.7 baring] E1+; bareing TMs
227.13 covetous] E1+; covetuous
TMs
*228.28–30 "I think . . . ten-
derly.] A1+; *omit* TMs,E1

[TMs *copy-text is present but mutilated.*]

229.2 pounded to the] E1+; TMs
mutilated
229.3 ²devil—to go to] E1+; TMs
mutilated
229.4 ²not . . . not] E1+; TMs
mutilated
229.5–6 of champagne. Then he]
E1+; TMs *mutilated*
229.6 mumbled:] A1+; ~ ; TMs;
~ — E1
229.6–7 cape . . . won't] E1+;
TMs *mutilated*
229.7 know.] E1+; ~ ₐ TMs
229.9 thanks . . .] E1; ~
* * * TMs,A1,N¹; ~ * * * *
N²

229.9   . . . there,] E1; * * *
~ ∧ TMs; * * * There∧ A1;
* * * There, N1-2

229.11   caress] E1+; carress TMs

229.14–15   Sweetheart . . .] E1;
~ * * * TMs,A1+

229.23   precedence] E1+; presi-
dence TMs

229.27   nor] E1,N2; or TMs,A1,N1

229.38   bodily."] E1+; TMs mutilated

229.39   see . . . Coke,] E1+;
TMs mutilated

230.1–2   as . . . were] E1+;
TMs mutilated

230.2–3   three . . . years] E1+;
TMs mutilated

230.3   years∧] N1-2; ~ , E1,A1

230.3   appear . . .] E1; ~ * * *
TMs,A1,N1; ~ * * * * N2

230.3–4   much . . . now."] E1+;
TMs mutilated

230.5   Coleman's . . . of] E1+;
TMs mutilated

230.6–7   tightly . . . either]
E1+; TMs mutilated

230.8,10   throw-down] A1+;
~ ∧ ~ TMs,E1

230.11   Sophomore] V; Sophe-
more TMs,E1; sophomore A1+

230.16   people's] E1+; peoples
TMs

230.18   calcium] E1+; calseum
TMs

230.22   noises,] E1+; ~ ∧ TMs

230.24   notorious] E1+; TMs
mutilated

230.28   -combatants] E1+;
-combantants TMs

230.30   knee,] E1+; ~ ∧ TMs

230.32   clamoring] N1-2; clam-
moring TMs; clamouring
E1,A1

230.33   say,] E1+; ~ ∧ TMs

230.34   it,] E1+; ~ ∧ TMs

230.35   jackass,] E1+; ~ ∧ TMs

230.39   speech, however,] E1+;
~ ∧ ~ ∧ TMs

231.3   Nothing,] E1+; TMs
mutilated

231.4   insulted] E1+; TMs mutilated

231.5   , and . . . beg] E1+; TMs
mutilated

231.7   "Mr.] E1+; ∧ ~ TMs

231.7   "what] E1+; "What TMs

231.7   have you to] E1+; TMs
mutilated

231.8–9   and . . . peered] E1+;
TMs mutilated

231.10   was expostulating] E1+;
TMs mutilated

231.11   excited . . . in] E1+;
TMs mutilated

231.13   light,] E1+; ~ ∧ TMs

231.16   Tounley,] E1+; ~ ! TMs

231.17   paid] E1+; TMs mutilated

231.18–19   jack-rabbit] E1,A1,N1;
~ ∧ | ~ TMs (unclear);
~ - | ~ N2

231.20   Well . . .] E1; ~ * * *
TMs,A1+

231.23   suffocating] E1+; suffi-
cating TMs

231.24   clear,] E1+; ~ ∧ TMs

231.25   Yes . . .] E1; ~ * *
TMs; ~ * * * A1+

231.25   you . . .] E1; ~ * *
TMs; ~ * * * A1+

231.26   correct . . .] E1; ~ * *
TMs; ~ * * * A1+

231.26   attributes] A1+; attribute
TMs (mutilated), E1

231.26   attributes . . . yes
. . .] E1; ~ * * ~ * * TMs,
A1+

231.28   "Oh (no ¶)] A1+; ¶ TMs,
E1

231.29   that,] E1+; ~ ∧| TMs

231.35   moment's] E1+; moments TMs

231.36   spoke,] E1+; TMs mutilated

231.37   Coke,] E1+; ~ ∧ TMs

232.1   defiance,] E1+; ~ ∧| TMs

232.4   1your . . .] E1; ~ —
TMs,A1+

232.4   2your . . .] E1; ~ ——
TMs; ~ — A1+

232.4   retire . . .] E1; ~ — TMs,
   A1+
232.4   and] E1+; < >nd TMs
232.6   moment,] E1+; ~ ∧ TMs
232.6   shrieked] E1+; TMs *mutilated*
232.9   Professor, I] E1+; TMs
   mutilated
232.10–11   riot as this∧] N²; TMs
   mutilated; ~ ~ ~ , E1+(−N²)
232.12   other's society∧] A1+;
   TMs *mutilated;* ~ ~ , E1
232.13   the] E1+; TMs *mutilated*
232.14–15   unwarranted] E1+;
   unwarrented TMs
232.15   but . . .] E1; ~ * *
   TMs; ~ * * * A1+
232.15   say . . .] E1; ~ * *
   TMs; ~ * * * A1+
232.16   breach . . .] E1; ~ * *
   TMs; ~ * * * A1+
232.16   to . . .] E1; ~ * * TMs;
   ~ * * * A1+
232.17   manner."] E1+; TMs
   muttilated
232.24–25   course . . .] E1; ~
   * * TMs; ~ * * * A1+
232.25   really] E1+; TMs *mutilated*
232.25   place . . .] E1; ~ * *
   TMs; ~ * * * A1+
232.26   be better . . . Coke]
   E1+; TMs *mutilated*
232.27   chosen an] E1+; TMs
   mutilated
232.31   (*twice*) Good-night] E1,
   A1; ~ ∧ ~ TMs,N¹⁻²
232.31   ²Good] E1+; TMs *mutilated*
232.33–34   retreated] E1+; TMs
   mutilated
232.35   yellow] E1+; TMs *mutilated*
232.38   removed] E1+; TMs *mutilated*
233.1   subdued,] E1+; ~ ∧ TMs
233.1   their places] E1+; TMs
   mutilated
233.2   extremely] E1+; TMs *mutilated*
233.3   floor] E1+; TMs *mutilated*

233.4   also referring] E1+;
   < >fering TMs *partially
   mutilated*
233.4–5   selfishness . . . part]
   E1+; TMs *mutilated*
233.5–6   there . . . of] E1+;
   TMs *mutilated*
233.10   it?"] E1+; TMs *mutilated*
233.12   a regular ruffian] E1+;
   TMs *mutilated*
233.12–13   tremendous uproar]
   E1+; TMs *mutilated*

[TMs *copy-text is present, not mutilated.*]

233.18   as] A1+; *omit* TMs,E1
233.18–19   partial] E1+; parial
   TMs
233.20   insane . . .] E1; ~ * *
   TMs; ~ * * * A1+
233.21   him . . .] E1; ~ * *
   TMs; ~ * * * A1+
233.21   ice . . .] E1; ~ * *
   TMs; ~ * * * A1+
233.22–23   it . . .] E1; ~ * *
   TMs; ~ ∧ A1+
233.23   all . . .] E1; ~ * *
   TMs; ~ . A1+
233.25   business . . .] E1;
   ~ * * TMs; ~ . A1+
233.25–26   dissenting] E1+; de-
   senting TMs
233.29   but . . .] E1; ~ * *
   TMs; ~ ∧ A1+
233.39   putting] E1+; puting TMs
235.10   beds . . .] E1; ~ x x x
   TMs; ~ * * * A1,N²; ~ .
   * * * N¹
235.10   true . . .] E1; ~ x x
   TMs; ~ , * * * A1,N¹; ~
   * * * N²
235.12   it. . . .] E1; ~ , x x
   TMs; ~ ∧ * * * A1,N²; ~ .
   * * * N¹
235.13–14   excellent . . .] E1;
   ~ x x TMs; ~ * * * A1,N²;
   ~ , * * * N¹
235.14   teacher . . .] E1; ~ x x
   TMs; ~ * * * A1,N²; ~ ,
   * * * N¹

235.16 things. . . .] E1; ~ ∧
x x TMs; ~ . * * * A1+
235.17 world. . . .] E1; ~ ∧ x x
TMs; ~ . * * * A1+
235.19 again. . . .] E1; ~ ∧
x x TMs; ~ . * * * A1+
235.20 " 'Induced',"] V; " ' ~ ' ".
TMs; " ' ~ ,' " E1; " ' ~ !' " A1,
N1-2
235.27 *et seq.* Chapters xix–xxiv
and xxv *to* 278.9 don't] E1+;
dont TMs
236.4 No,] E1+; ~ ∧ TMs
236.8 that . . .] E1; ~ x x
TMs; ~ — A1+
236.9 than . . .] E1; ~ x x
TMs; ~ — A1+
236.18–19 your . . . your . . .]
V; ~ x ~ x TMs; your∧ E1;
~ — ~ — A1,N1; ~ — ~ ∧ N2
236.22 but . . .] E1; ~ x x
TMs; ~ — A1+
236.25 suppose. . . .] E1; ~ x x
TMs; ~ * * * A1+
236.34 Coleman,] E1+; ~ . TMs
236.39 committed] E1+; com-
mited TMs
237.3 father,] E1+; ~ ∧ TMs
237.8 a——] E1+; ~ ∧ TMs
237.9 coolly] E1+; cooly TMs
237.10 you,] E1+; ~ ∧ TMs
237.16 Marjory!" screamed]
E1+; ~ ". Screamed TMs
237.23 preceding] E1+;
proceeding TMs
237.32 referred] E1+; refered
TMs
237.37–38 putrefaction] E1+;
putrifaction TMs
238.5 beginning] E1+; begining
TMs
238.14 grey] SC(c)+; *omit*
TMs(u)
238.24 even] SC(c)+; *omit*
TMs(u)
238.25 retriever] E1+; retreiver
TMs
238.26 spaniel] E1+; spanial
TMs
238.29 so] SC(c)+; *omit*
TMs(u)

238.30 balloons] E1+; baloons
TMs
239.8 course . . .] E1; ~ x x
TMs; ~ — A1+
239.9 know . . .] E1; ~ x x
TMs; ~ — A1+
239.12 Old] V; old TMs+
239.18 it . . .] V; ~ x TMs; ~ ∧
E1; ~ — A1,N2; ~ , N1
240.5 man. . . .] V; ~ . x x
TMs; ~ . A1+
240.6 you . . . we . . .] E1;
~ x x ~ x TMs; ~ — ~ —
A1+
240.6 like . . .] E1; ~ x TMs;
~ — A1+
240.8 equivalent] E1+;
equivelant TMs
240.16,17,18 preferred] E1+;
prefered TMs
240.29 benefaction] E1+;
benifaction TMs
240.31 deuce] E1+; duece TMs
240.37 apologetically] E1+;
opologetically TMs
241.3 2mind,] E1+; ~ ∧ TMs
241.6–7 morning. . . .] V; ~ .
x x TMs; ~ . . . E1; ~ . ∧
A1+
241.12–13 a base suspicion,]
SC(c)+; *omit* TMs(u)
241.26 desirous] E1+; desirious
TMs
241.31 vivacious] TMs(u),E1+;
vivacous TMs(c)
243.38 you] E1+; You TMs
244.8 "They'?"] E1; " ' ~ ' "?
TMs; " ' ~ ?' " A1,N2;
" ∧ ~ ∧ ?" N1
244.10 said. ". . . Well] V; ~ ,
"x x ~ TMs; ~ . . . "Well
E1; ~ , "* * ~ A1+
244.32 kid,"] E1+; ~ ". TMs
245.8 challenging] E1+;
challengeing TMs
245.22 No . . . no . . .] V;
~ x ~ x TMs; ~ — ~ — E1+
245.27 No,] A1+; ~ ∧ TMs; ~ —
E1

245.27 no . . .] V; ～x x TMs;
  ～ . . . E1; ～ * * A1;
  ～ * * * N¹⁻²
245.27–28 truly . . .] E1; ～x
  TMs; ～ * * A1+
245.28 word. . . .] V; ～x x
  TMs; ～ . . . E1; ～ * * A1+
245.36 it's] E1+; its TMs
246.2 truth . . .] E1; ～x x
  TMs; ～ * * A1,N²; ～ * * *
  N¹
246.2 him . . .] E1; ～x x TMs;
  ～ * * A1,N²; ～ * * * N¹
246.3 anything. . . .] E1; ～.
  x x TMs; ～. * * A1,N²; ～ ∧
  * * * N¹
246.9 Oh! Oh! Oh!] A1+; ～. ～.
  oh. TMs; ～, oh, oh. E1
246.13 Coke] E1+(−N²); Coleman TMs; Cole N²
246.15 No . . .] E1; ～x x TMs;
  ～— A1+
246.15 good . . .] E1; ～x x
  TMs; ～— A1+
246.16 him . . .] E1; ～x x
  TMs; ～— A1+
247.2 her] SC(c)+; his
  interlocutors TMs(u)
247.3 doggedly:] A1+; ～. TMs;
  ～, E1
247.4 Ahem,] E1+; ～. TMs
247.4 Why,] E1+; ～∧ TMs
247.5 It's] E1+; Its TMs
247.13 serious,] E1+; ～∧ TMs
247.19 villains] E1+; villians
  TMs
247.23 neither] E1+; niether
  TMs
247.23 could] E1+; come TMs
247.24 perhaps] E1+; Perhaps
  TMs
247.26 Their] E1+; There TMs
247.29; 249.13 Coke's] E1+;
  Cokes TMs
247.33 conceitedly] E1+;
  concietedly TMs
248.7 was] SC(c)+; *omit*
  TMs(u)
248.12; 260.35 beginning] E1+;
  begining TMs
248.23 when∧] E1+; ～, TMs

249.1 Nora and Coke were an
  odd] SC(c)+; (*space*) TMs(u)
249.10 Coke:] V; ～. TMs,A1,
  N¹⁻²; ～— E1
249.22 separate] E1+; seperate
  TMs
249.23 disapproval] E1+;
  disaproval TMs
249.25 but] E1+; by TMs
249.25 I would] E1+; would
  TMs
250.15 sprung] SC(c)+; (*space*)
  TMs(u)
250.16 Coke] SC(c)+; Coke
  Coke TMs(u)
250.32 outcries] E1+; out-cries
  TMs
251.10 devotedly] SC(c)+;
  devoted TMs(u)
251.17 puling and puking]
  SC(c),E1; pulling and pucking
  TMs(u),A1+
251.27 glowed] SC(c)+;
  glowered TMs(u)
251.30 down-right] V;
  downwright TMs; downright
  E1+
251.30 destruction] E1+;
  distruction TMs
251.36 aggregation] E1+;
  agregation TMs
252.3 comic] SC(c)+; ludicrous
  TMs(u)
252.8 hum] SC(c)+; line
  TMs(u)
252.16,17 outrage!] E1+; ～.
  TMs
252.17 consensus] N¹⁻²;
  concensus TMs,E1,A1
252.19 deep-drawn] E1,N¹;
  ～∧～ TMs,A1,N²
252.23 with a sort] E1,N²; with
  sort, TMs,A1; a sort N¹
252.33 artificial stimulant] E1+;
  artifical stimulent TMs
253.3 arrangement] E1+;
  arrange-ment TMs
253.12 resented] SC(c);
  resentful TMs(u)
253.28; 254.14 They] E1+; Thay
  TMs

253.29 ₍ₐ₎ribbons] E1+; - ~ TMs
253.31 easily] E1+; easy|ly TMs
253.37 professor,] E1+; professo|
TMs
254.3–4 yelled. [¶] The road]
SC(c)+; *type superimposed*
TMs(u)
254.9 circuit] E1+; circiut TMs
254.14 prisoner] E1+; prisner
TMs
254.27 nation's] E1+; nations
TMs
254.34 whining] E1+; whineing
TMs
254.38 mad-men] V; ~ ₍ₐ₎ ~ TMs,
A1,N¹; madmen E1,N²
256.8 note] SC(c),E1; not
TMs(u),A1+
256.15 far to] SC(c)+; for
TMs(u)
256.24 unarmed,] E1+; ~ ₍ₐ₎ TMs
256.29 privilege] E1+; previlege
TMs
256.30 at] SC(c)+; from
TMs(u)
256.30 Wainwrights] SC(c)+;
Wainwright party TMs(u)
257.4 imagined.] E1+; ~ ₍ₐ₎ | TMs
257.10 glazed] SC(c)+; dazed
TMs(u)
257.16 street.] E1+; ~ ₍ₐ₎ | TMs
257.24 why . . .] V; ~ x x TMs;
~ — E1; ~ * * A1,N²;
~ * * * N¹
257.24 am . . .] V; ~ x TMs;
~ — E1; ~ * A1,N²; ~ ₍ₐ₎ N¹
257.24 ready . . .] V; ~ x TMs;
~ — E1; ~ * A1,N²; ~ * * *
N¹
257.29 ear:] V; ~ . TMs; ~ —
E1; ~ , A1+
258.9 good . . .] E1; ~ x x
TMs; ~ * * A1,N²; ~ * * *
N¹
258.9–10 like . . .] E1; ~ x x
TMs; ~ * * A1,N²; ~ * * *
N¹
258.10 it . . .] E1; ~ x x TMs;
~ * * A1,N²; ~ * * * N¹
258.37 simultaneous] E1+;
simaltaneous TMs

258.38 throughout,] E1; ~ ₍ₐ₎
TMs,A1+
259.1 of the] E1+; of the | of the
TMs
259.8 hurrying] SC(c)+; moving
TMs(u)
259.28 thought of] SC(c)+; *omit*
TMs(u)
260.2 cartridges] E1+; cartriges
TMs
260.2; 272.38; 286.30 appalled]
E1+; apalled TMs
260.10 jolted] N²; jilted TMs+
(−N²)
260.13–14 he received . . .
neck;] SC(c)+; *omit* TMs(u)
260.13 received] E1+; recieved
TMs
260.19 others.] E1+; other₍ₐ₎| TMs
260.24 strong₍ₐ₎wood] E1+; ~ - ~
TMs
260.27; 261.7 not] SC(c)+; *omit*
TMs(u)
260.28 at] E1+; *omit* TMs
260.30 pantomime] E1+;
pantomine TMs
260.33 a] SC(c)+; the TMs(u)
260.35 beginning] E1+;
begining TMs
261.10 Oh . . .] E1; ~ x x TMs;
~ — A1+
261.10 bleeding . . .] E1; ~ x x
TMs; ~ — A1+
261.12,14–15,20; 262.8 handker-
chief] E1+; hankerchief TMs
261.22 thus] SC(c)+; *omit*
TMs(u)
261.36 dilapidated] E1+;
delipidated TMs
262.1 Peter,] E1,A1,N²(N¹:
unclear); ~ . TMs
262.4 ambitions,] E1+; ~ ₍ₐ₎ TMs
263.2 clamor] N¹⁻²; clammor
TMs; clamour E1,A1
263.7 go, go] E1+; ~ ₍ₐ₎ ~ TMs
263.15–16 motley] E1+; motely
TMs
263.20 piercing] E1+; peircing
TMs
263.22 stabbed] E1+; stabed
TMs

263.22 nor] E1,N¹; or TMs,A1, N²

263.30 pierced] peirced TMs

263.31–264.1 inn-keeper] V; innkeeper TMs+

264.1 siege] E1+; seige TMs

264.6 endeavor] N¹⁻²; endeavour TMs,E1,A1

264.27 us."] E1+; ∼ .ₐ TMs

266.31 inscrutable] E1+; incrutable TMs

266.32 allusions] E1,N²; illusions TMs,A1,N¹

267.9 out:] A1+; ∼ . TMs; ∼ , E1

267.14 baring] E1+; bareing TMs

267.25 Cupid's] E1+; cupids TMs

267.40 ye'] V; yeₐ TMs,E1; you A1+

268.6 intimacy] E1+; intimicy TMs

268.6 correspondent] E1+; Correspondent TMs

268.12 beaten] E1+; beatten TMs

*269.14 sumthing] E1; sunthing TMs+(−E1)

269.15 head.] E1+; ∼ ₐ | TMs

269.20 It] E1+; He TMs

270.18 despaired] E1+; dispaired TMs

270.22 interrupted] E1+; interupted TMs

270.22 Marjory:] V; ∼ . TMs+; ∼ — E1

270.22 professor] E1+; proffessor TMs

270.29 sufficient] E1+; sufficent TMs

271.8 horses.] E1+; ∼ ₐ | TMs

271.16 Nora's] E1+; Noras TMs

272.13 daybreak] E1+; day-break TMs

272.30 outlook] E1+; out-look TMs

272.31 future.] A1+; ∼ ₐ TMs; fortune. E1

273.19 stupefied] E1+; stupified TMs

273.21 consummated] E1+; consumated TMs

273.23 wondrous] E1+; wonderous TMs

274.10 was,] A1+; ∼ ₐ TMs,E1

274.20 espousal] E1+; esposal TMs

274.22 apostle] E1+; opostle TMs

274.28 aroused] E1+; arroused TMs

274.28 out:] A1+; ∼ , TMs(unclear),E1

274.29 here."] E1+; ∼ .ₐ TMs

274.32 Where's] A1+; where's TMs,E1

274.38 heaven] A1+; Heaven TMs,E1

275.1 first-class] E1+; ∼ ₐ ∼ TMs

275.2 closed] E1+; clossed TMs

275.7 distance:] A1+; ∼ . TMs; ∼ , E1

275.8 Didn't] E1+; Did'nt TMs

276.4 poignancy] E1+; poingancy TMs

276.7 as] SC(c)+; omit TMs(u)

276.14 the] SC(c)+; her TMs(u)

276.16 grocer's] E1+; grocers TMs

276.24 morning,] E1+; ∼ ₐ TMs

276.26 even] SC(c)+; omit TMs(u)

277.1 smiled] E1+; smilled TMs

277.1 relieved] E1+; relived TMs

277.3 naught] A1+; nought TMs, E1

277.15 isn't] E1+; is'nt TMs

277.15 Aren't] E1+; Are'nt TMs

277.17 over-coats] V; overcoats TMs+

277.18 them."] E1+; ∼ .ₐ TMs

277.20 interest] E1+; intrest TMs

277.22 meanwhile,] A1+; ∼ ₐ TMs,E1

277.25–26 advisability] E1+; advisibility TMs

277.34 Oh,] E1+; ∼ . TMs

277.37 exercise] EI+; exersize TMs

277.39 well-known] V; ~ ∧ ~ TMs+

278.3 did not] SC(c)+; didn't TMs(u)

278.11 responded] SC(c)+; repeated TMs(u)

[TMs *is wanting; EI is copy-text except for minute fragment, possibly the foot of fol. 168.*]

279.11 Patras∧] AI+; ~ , EI

279.13 pier∧] AI+; ~ , EI

279.16 fashion∧] AI+; ~ , EI

279.16 misery∧] AI+; ~ , EI

279.31 deck-house∧] AI; ~ - ~, EI; deckhouse∧ N¹; ~ ∧ ~ ∧ N²

280.5 eye-brows] V; eyebrows EI,N¹⁻²; ~ - | ~ AI

280.8 you∧] AI+; ~ , EI

280.9(*twice*) fiend] AI+; friend EI

280.15 him∧] AI+; ~ , EI

280.16 glad∧] AI+; ~ , EI

280.39 Wainwright. "We] AI+; ~ , "we EI

281.3 Good- (*no ¶*)] AI+; ¶ EI

281.6 acquaintance∧] AI+; ~ , EI

281.8 When (*no ¶*)] AI+; ¶ EI

281.15 French∧] AI+; ~ , EI

282.7 cried] SC(c)+; said TMs(u)

282.18 brightly∧] AI+; ~ , EI

282.30 'Glamour', 'Fascination',] V; ∧ ~ ∧! ∧ ~ ∧! EI; ' ~ ,' ' ~ ,' AI,N¹; ' ~ !' ' ~ !' N²

282.32 her, then,] AI+; ~ ∧ ~ ∧ EI

283.7 "If (*no ¶*)] AI+; ¶ EI

283.7 case— . . . musingly,] AI+; ~ , . . . ~ — EI

283.13 armor] N¹⁻²; armour EI, AI

283.14 someone] V; some one EI+

283.15 alone!] AI+; ~ , EI

[TMs *is copy-text, present but mutilated.*]

284.2 striving] EI+; TMs *mutilated*

284.3 words were] EI+; TMs *mutilated*

284.4 the] EI+; TMs *mutilated*

284.5 mountains that] EI+; TMs *mutilated*

284.7 The] EI+; TMs *multilated*

284.8 to] EI+; TMs *multilated*

284.26 Coleman'."] V; ~ '". TMs; ~ .'" EI+

284.29 Oh,] EI+; ~ . TMs(*unclear*)

285.5 know . . .] EI; ~ * * TMs,AI+

[TMs *is wanting; EI is copy-text.*]

285.7 to——] AI+; ~ . . . EI

285.11 ²Nonsense] AI+; nonsense EI

285.29 confusing∧] N¹⁻²; ~ , EI, AI

[TMs *is copy-text, present but mutilated.*]

286.19 part,] EI+; TMs *mutilated*

286.21 could,] EI+; TMs *mutilated*

286.30 Don't] EI+; Dont TMs

287.6 ¹the] EI+; TMs *mutilated*

[TMs *is wanting; EI is copy-text.*]

287.16 shield∧] AI,N¹; ~ , EI,N²

287.17 hands'] AI+; hand's EI

287.21 error∧] AI+; ~ , EI

287.24 judgement] V; judgment EI+

287.27 only] AI+; *omit* EI

287.37 thing.] AI+; ~ ! EI

287.39 probably∧] AI+; ~ , EI

288.11 church] AI+; Church EI

288.14 Finally∧] AI+; ~ , EI

288.19 "Well (*no ¶*)] AI+; ¶ EI

288.25 danger signal] AI+; ~ - ~ EI

288.27 asked. Her] AI+; ~ , her EI

288.31 weather-cock] AI+; weathercock EI

*288.32 opinions] AI+; opinion EI

289.6   as] A1+; that E1
*289.16   could see] *stet* E1
290.4   -room$_\wedge$] A1,N²; - ~ , E1,N¹
290.4   entrance hall] A1+; ~ - ~ E1
290.5   room,] A1+; ~ ; E1
290.6,24–25   gold$_\wedge$fish] A1+; ~ - ~ E1
290.6   license] A1+; licence E1
290.7   polished$_\wedge$] A1+; ~ , E1
290.12   them$_\wedge$] A1+; ~ , E1
290.12   said:] A1+; ~ , E1
290.12   Whiskers.] A1+; ~ ! E1
290.23   minions$_\wedge$] A1+; ~ , E1
290.26–27   room$_\wedge$ . . . mirrors$_\wedge$] A1+; ~ , . . . ~ , E1
291.6   skirts$_\wedge$] N¹⁻²; ~ , E1,A1
291.14   companions. "You] A1+; ~ , "you E1
291.15   schoolboys] A1+; school-boys E1
291.19   dripping$_\wedge$] A1+; ~ , E1
291.26,30   States] A1+; States' E1
291.26   minister] A1,N¹; Minister E1,N²
291.30   *et seq.*   minister] A1+; Minister E1
291.31   correctly attired] A1+; ~ - ~ E1
291.31   men$_\wedge$] A1+; ~ , E1
291.34   laughing$_\wedge$] A1+; ~ , E1
291.37   forever] A1+; for ever E1
292.24   thing$_\wedge$] A1+; ~ , E1
293.1   said:] A1+; ~ — E1
293.2   tonight] N²; to-night E1+ (−N²)
293.5   dinner$_\wedge$] A1+; ~ , E1
293.6   professor] E1+; proffessor TMs

[TMs *copy-text is present; normal collation resumes.*]

294.12   State Department] E1+; state department TMs
294.17   consist] E1+; insist TMs
294.37   ingenuous] E1+; engenuous TMs
295.19   No.] E1+; ~ ". TMs
296.13   'Going?'] E1; '~'? TMs; $_\wedge$~ ?$_\wedge$ A1+

296.14   Going!] E1; ~ ? TMs, A1+
296.21   to] E1+; *omit* TMs
296.30   it,] E1+; ~ . TMs
296.35   Oh . . .] E1; ~ * * TMs, A1,N²; ~ * * * N¹
297.4   " "It . . . go',"] V; " ' ~ . . . ~ ' ", TMs; " $_\wedge$ ~ . . . ~ $_\wedge$," E1,N¹⁻²; " ' ~ . . . ~ ,' " A1
297.4   humbly, "if] E1; ~ . "If TMs,A1+
297.19   there!"] E1+; ~ !$_\wedge$ TMs
297.20   Well,] A1; ~ $_\wedge$ TMs,E1, N¹⁻²
298.4   affect] E1+; effect TMs
298.5   student's] E1; students TMs; student A1+
299.19   tonight] N²; to-night TMs+(−N²)
299.22   that$_\wedge$] E1+; ~ , TMs
299.22; 300.4   the] E1+; *omit* TMs
299.31   pages] E1+; pagers TMs
299.36   likely] E1,N²; like TMs, A1,N¹
*300.29   tragic muse] *stet* TMs, A1+
301.11   cigar. . . .] V; ~ . * * TMs,A1,N²; ~ ? . . . E1; ~ . * * * N¹
301.12   fool. . . .] E1(3 *periods*); ~ . * * TMs,A1,N²; ~ * * * N¹
301.29   identify] E1+; indentify TMs
302.15   Why,] E1+; ~ $_\wedge$ TMs
302.20   lightnin'] E1,N²; lightenin' TMs,A1,N¹
302.21   goodness'] E1+; ~ $_\wedge$ TMs
302.29   professor,] E1+; ~ . TMs
303.24   sufficiently] E1+; suffuiciently TMs
303.28   errand] E1+; errant TMs
303.32   eliminating] E1+; eluminating TMs
303.39   ¹to] E1+; of TMs
304.8   eliminated] E1+; eluminated TMs
304.24   then, . . . Coleman,] E1+; ~ $_\wedge$ . . . ~ $_\wedge$ TMs

305.1 Spectator] E1,A1;
Spectator TMs,N$^{1-2}$

305.25–26 block-head] V;
blockhead TMs+

306.14 Well . . .] E1; ~ * *
TMs; ~ * * * A1+

307.19 reading-room] E1,N^1;
~ $_\wedge$ ~ TMs,A1,N^2

308.1 perceived] E1+; parceived
TMs

308.3 enough,] E1,N^1; ~ $_\wedge$ TMs,
A1,N^2

308.22 pass] SC(c),E1,N^2; past
TMs(u),A1,N^1

308.27 other. . . .] E1; ~ . * *
TMs,A1; ~ . * * * N$^{1-2}$

308.27 resistance] E1+;
resistence TMs

308.29 him. . . .] E1; ~ . * *
TMs,A1,N^2; ~ . * * * N^1

309.4 Honest!"] E1+; ~ ! $_\wedge$ TMs

309.36 so] SC(c)+; omit
TMs(u)

311.24 kept] SC(c)+; omit
TMs(u)

314.15 other's] E1+; others TMs

314.18 separation] E1+;
seperation TMs

314.21 long.] E1+; ~ , TMs

314.29 pantomime,] E1,N^1; ~ $_\wedge$ |
TMs; ~ $_\wedge$ A1,N^2

315.24 planned] E1+; planed
TMs

315.30 plumb] V; plum TMs+

316.4 Yours,] E1+; ~ $_\wedge$ TMs

316.7 kid] E1+; Kid TMs

316.11 loose] E1+; lose TMs

316.11 sometimes] E1; some
times TMs; some times A1,N^2;
sometimes N^1

316.12 separated] E1+;
seperated TMs

316.36 naturally,] E1,A1,N^2; ~
TMs,N^1

319.8 reading."] E1+; ~ . $_\wedge$ TMs

319.28 "'Marco',"] V; "'~'",
TMs; "'~,'" E1+

319.31 "'Marco'!"] V; "'~'"!
TMs; "'~,'" E1,N^2; "'~!'"
A1,N^1

319.32 'Marco'," . . . "'Marco'.]

V; '~'", . . . "'~'". TMs;
'~,'" . . . "'~.' E1+

320.18 Maude;] A1; ~ : TMs;
~ , E1,N^1; ~ ! N^2

320.31 tale-bearing] E1+(—N^1);
tell-bearing TMs; tellbearing
N^1

321.4 sigh] A1+; sign TMs,E1

321.5 headstrong] E1+;
head-strong TMs

321.7 mothers'] E1+; mother's
TMs

321.20 mood] SC(c)+; omit
TMs(u)

321.20 say . . .] E1; ~ * *
TMs,A1; ~ * * * N^1

321.22 income. . . .] E1; ~ .
* * TMs,A1; ~ . * * * N^1

321.22 know. . . .] E1; ~ . * *
TMs,A1; ~ . * * * N^1

321.26 precarious] E1+;
percarious TMs

321.29 has] SC(c)+; had
TMs(u)

321.30–31 Still . . . still . . .]
E1; ~ * * ~ * * TMs,A1;
~ — ~ — N^1

321.31–32 income . . .] E1; ~ *
TMs; ~ * * A1; ~ — N^1

321.32 That] E1+; that TMs

321.34 Still] E1+; still TMs

321.34 Still . . .] E1; ~ * *
TMs,A1; ~ — N^1

321.36–37 were. . . .] E1; ~ .
* * TMs,A1; ~ . * * * N^1

321.39 amiable. . . .] E1; ~ .
* * TMs,A1; ~ . * * * N^1

322.9 simply] SC(c)+; omit
TMs(u)

322.13–14 vicious] TMs(u),
E1+; vicius TMs(c) (doubtful)

322.21 But . . .] E1; ~ * *
TMs,A1+

322.25 upstairs] A1+; up-|stairs
TMs; up-stairs E1

322.32 Well . . . anyhow . . .]
E1; ~ * ~ * TMs,A1,N^2; ~ ,
~ , N^1

323.16–17 tranquillity] E1,N$^{1-2}$;
tranquility TMs,A1

323.23   ²man,] E1+; ~ ∧ TMs
323.26   politics] E1+; polotics TMs
323.32   nor] E1,N¹⁻²; or TMs,A1
*323.33   triumphant] A1+; triumph ant TMs(c); triumph and E1
323.39   tremulously] E1+; tremelously TMs
324.7   betrothal] SC(c)+; engagement TMs(u)
324.12   ear,] E1+; ~ ∧ TMs
324.18   care.] E1+; ~ , TMs
324.18   up,] E1+; ~ ∧ TMs
325.23   ceiling] E1+; cieling TMs
325.23   God] E1+; god TMs
325.26   unendurable!] E1,N¹⁻²; ~ ? TMs,A1
325.28   callous] E1+; callouse TMs
326.1   attendants] E1+; attentants TMs

326.25   Vladivostock] E1,N¹; Vladurstock TMs; Vladisvostok A1; Vladivurstock N²
*326.30   they] N²; theu TMs; then E1+(−N²)
*327.9   plane] stet TMs+
327.11   parson] SC(c),E1,A1; person TMs(u),N¹⁻²
327.19   sorry . . .] E1; ~ * * TMs,A1; ~ . * * * N¹⁻²
327.26   true. . . .] E1(3 periods); ~ ∧ * * TMs,A1; ~ . * * * N¹⁻²
327.26   dearest? . . .] E1; ~ ? * * TMs,A1; ~ ? * * * N¹⁻²
327.27   I——"] E1+; ~ —— ∧ TMs
328.10   sometimes] E1+; some times TMs
328.21   winds;] E1+(−N¹); ~ : TMs; ~ , N¹
328.33   played in] SC(c)+; touching TMs(u)

MECHANICAL ERRORS IN THE TYPESCRIPT

[NOTE: A number of faults in TMs[1] can be attributed not to copy or to the typist's own misspellings but to purely mechanical errors such as the transposition of letters and the striking of an adjacent key for the correct one. Errors of this conjectured nature have been removed from the List of Emendations and are reproduced here without the sigla in order to conserve space. All were automatically corrected in E1+.]

113.29	writint
114.11	Waht
114.35	fell
115.7	coice
115.26	personallly
118.4	deeplu
118.27	lived
120.4	hub-hub
120.32	Junioe
121.24	mat
123.29	mani-
126.19	Napopeon
126.32; 129.30	deak
127.8	enployed
127.10	bumgled
128.22	arist
128.24	compang
130.11	monley
130.28	interviwe
132.14	im pelled
133.7	improtant
133.24	go ing
136.3	Put
136.5	cise
137.2	fromed
145.5	[1]atke
145.21–22	monentary
146.12	batter
147.11	stwards
147.18	Chicgo
148.14	crashinf
148.17; 153.24; 156.10; 180.16; 198.28; 205.4; 241.3([1]of)	od

148.34	eys
148.39	hhe
150.22	afeter
151.33	oof
152.15	wwhat
152.28	satiafied
155.7	fron
158.2	actuallly
159.13	aprty
159.36; 248.17; 253.24; 256.4	thay
160.13	wnated
161.21	captial
161.23	at little
161.29; 163.13	fielf
161.38–162.1	epople
163.30	hia
165.15	demonstartions
165.28	rodinary
165.31	slve
168.12	mraking
171.11	suely
171.34	heraing
172.21	-perhaps
172.30	fron
173.6	forst
174.6; 239.24	palin
174.11; 238.5; 258.31	dragoamn
174.28	quests
175.5	compsed
175.31	repsonse
177.4	derpairing
180.2	OH

181.25	waht	212.1	thet
182.17	hrad	212.20	say
182.37	ras	213.6	queation
183.11	landscpac	214.29	chancing
184.23	isde	214.31–215.1	husbad
185.5	isdes	217.3	specicl
185.18	ans	218.3	ola
188.17	ebing	220.15	herslef
189.5	sdeadiness	224.39	whisket
189.18	fielfs	225.26	noight
190.22	parctically	225.28	drak
190.23	nemy	227.1	Fnacy
190.27	tsuttered	230.25	owrld
190.30	drowiness	234.2	herslf
190.32	offt	235.10	ture
191.11	opend	235.23	onlyone
192.1	rpoper	237.1	inctinct
192.10	ti	238.26	Perter
192.22	smae	239.12–13	Wwinwright
193.13	epxected	240.4; 328.14	flance
193.19	drakness	240.27	exprss
194.6	gangers	241.28	restectfully
194.7	²sopke	242.31	aquatted
194.15; 236.16	victroy	243.9	askek
195.30	Afyer	244.23	fao t
196.6	hanfcuff	245.30	ltitle
196.23	speak ing	246.22	must
197.17	psoition	247.18	palinly
197.33	liger	247.23	²ot
198.31	kinght	250.10	dount
200.6	rofles	251.13	ti
202.15	himjubilantly	251.23	judhement
203.11	¹Goodboy	252.13	woeld
203.16	enfuring	252.37	hehind
204.22	kew	253.39	anf
205.2	fell	254.14	prisnor
205.23	slihjtly	256.28	dlood
205.27	metion	258.22	bron
206.2	amswered	258.27	cartriages
206.25	bridgge	258.31	dragaamn
207.22	nothin	259.24	earht
207.22–23	Waniwright	259.25	sais
208.6	owrrying	260.1	crashedto
208.23–24	fociferously	260.24	barredhis
209.12	profeesor	261.31	openeda
209.13	siad	265.9	ime
210.26	veru	266.38	tlak
211.1–2	opportunitiers	267.24	o nly
211.15	hid	267.35	despiar
211.16	certred	267.36	improce
211.38	thee entire	268.1	NOW

268.26   batter
268.28–29   nervertheless
270.5   f
270.10   thesewords
270.29   natter
271.19   tounched
273.2   Colsely
273.36–37   notevil
274.9   ofher
274.11   approximacely
274.17   [1]he
274.20   thatthe
274.23   diseas
274.30   ceught
275.9   hisheels
277.16   Spartous
277.17   ape
278.4   antagnoize
286.18   uncheched

286.18   Mrajory's
294.7   apoletically
294.20   rescure
295.13   That'a
295.26–27   therealways
296.36   Mrs,
300.16   strudent
301.32   strating
303.32   WEll
304.5   professor-s
305.18   stirredup
315.38–39   Coleman-s
317.36,39   offiver
321.26   owrld
321.32   that
322.32   evrything
326.14   exchanhed
327.25   mant

WORD-DIVISION

1. *End-of-the-Line Hyphenation in the Virginia Edition*

[NOTE: No hyphenation of a possible compound at the end of a line in the Virginia text is present in the copy-texts except for the following readings which are hyphenated within the line in the typescript. Except for these readings, all end-of-the-line hyphenation in the Virginia text may be ignored except for hyphenated compounds in which both elements are capitalized.]

114.2	snow-|balls		189.17	Camp-|fires
114.21	pig-|market		197.23	half-|thoughts
116.35	fine-|minded		205.33	horse-|race
117.22	stand-|point		211.37	tin-|cups
121.9	class-|room		228.18	common-|places
123.3	fin-|like		245.31	block-|head
124.23	pearl-|misted		251.26	class-|rooms
125.26	re-|light		257.32	drawing-|room
127.26	under-|done		258.30	inn-|keeper
130.22	note-|paper		263.16,19	inn-|keeper
138.5	wide-|open		264.5	inn-|keeper
150.36	deck-|steward		266.15	hot-|headed
151.9	rain-|stricken		288.11	death-|bed
159.22	red-|carpeted		290.4	dining-|room
165.11,34	distinguished-|looking		291.6	smoking-|room
171.29	war-|correspondents		298.16	paper-|littered
173.39	good-|bye		301.22	Good-|night
179.5	bar-|keepers		301.29	self-|satisfaction
183.14	garden-|patch		307.10	self-|satisfied
184.34	corn-|color		314.24	top-|coat

2. *End-of-the-Line Hyphenation in the Copy-text*

[NOTE: The following compounds, or possible compounds, are hyphenated at the end of the line in the copy-text. The form in which they have been transcribed in the Virginia text, listed below, represents the practice of the manuscript as ascertained by other appearances or parallels, or—failing that—by the known characteristics of Crane as seen in his other manuscripts.]

113.12	dead-eyed		130.25	tempest-tossed
127.38	corn-cob		137.35	semi-circle

139.3	side-track	227.2	orris-root
148.18	deck-chair	239.35	housemaid
152.25	card-players	241.25	dark-browed
152.26	wine-merchant	256.3	broken-voiced
158.6	first-class	260.24	inn-keeper
183.30	ill-birth	261.19	half-coherent
184.26	pack-horses	265.1	re-assurance
191.25	daytime	274.35	common-place
208.28	open-mouthed	276.8	wooden-headed
211.35	saddle-bags	280.6	headlong

3. *Special Cases*

[NOTE: In the following list the compound is hyphenated at the end of the line in the copy-text and in the Virginia edition.]

128.1 office-|boy (i.e., office-boy) 264.28 inn-|keeper (i.e.,
226.27 camp-|table (i.e.,   inn-keeper)
   camp-table)

HISTORICAL COLLATION

[NOTE: All substantive variants from the Virginia text are listed here. Variants in accidentals are only recorded where TMs is not present, or in the case of Chapter VI where there is a second typescript designated TMs². A text not mentioned to the right of the bracket will either agree with the lemma before the bracket or will be lacking at that point. All cuts in the various texts are listed here.]

113.1   cold] cool A1+
113.6   upon] on A1+
113.17   arising] rising E1
113.18   his] the N²
114.1   at that] at the A1+
114.15–16 thoughtful and thoughtless] thoughtless and thoughtful A1+
114.18   he] be N²
114.26   faith] a faith A1+
114.27–28 machine, this] *omit* TMs(c),E1
114.35   this] his A1+
115.1   trampled] tramped A1+
115.10   arose] rose E1
115.14   witless] witness A1
115.22   in] with N¹
115.35   quite] *omit* A1
116.15   said the girl] *omit* E1
116.16   do not] don't A1+
116.20   to it] in it E1
116.25   often] *omit* A1
116.29   night] the night A1,N²
116.33; 117.14 is not] isn't A1+
117.33   wind] winds A1+
118.2   amid] amidst E1
118.9   a] the N¹
118.13   a block] block A1+
118.16   meeting] meet A1+
118.21   melee] *mêlée* E1; mêlée E1(p)
119.5   by] of A1+
119.12   hurled] hurried N²

119.13   in] with E1
119.19   Sophomore] Sophomores'. A1+(N¹⁻²: sophomores')
119.25   surpassed] surpasses TMs, E1(p)
119.30   clump] lump E1
119.30   its] *omit* N¹⁻²
119.33   register] resist E1
119.39   by] from E1
120.2   recitation] recreation- N²
120.11   of] the N²
120.15   circumstance] circumstances TMs(u),N¹
120.21   campaign] campaigns N¹
120.22   impertinence] importance TMs,E1(p); blasphemy E1
120.32   most] *omit* A1+
120.38   the] a N²
121.4   Austro-] Austria- N¹
121.5 *et seq.* forever] for ever E1
121.8   a quite] quite a A1+
121.14   still] *omit* E1
121.14   need not] needn't A1+
121.21–22 desperate, delivered himself] disheveled, stepped forward N¹
121.27   march] own march A1+
121.29   the] *omit* N¹
121.31   this all] all this E1
121.32   that] *omit* A1+
121.35   which] which apparently A1+
122.5   as] so E1; as E1(p)

122.5   plain!"] plain——" A1+
122.12   didn't] did not TMs(u), E1
122.13   known] known it A1+
122.20   yawed] yawned N2
122.25   scallywag] scalawag A1+ (N1-2: scallawag)
122.26   cure] sure cure A1+
123.4   bones] bone A1+
123.7   had] omit A1+
123.13   Afterward] Afterwards TMs+(−N1)
123.16   would] wound E1(p)
123.24   an] the A1+
123.29   huge and] huge N2
123.31   walks] walls E1
124.2   fish] a fish A1+
124.3   unmistakably] unmistakable A1+
124.7   shout] shouting N2
124.16   and] omit A1+
124.17   tops] the tops A1+
124.21   one's] one N1
124.25   slight] light N2
124.30   the elements . . . of] omit N2
125.18   other] the other A1+
125.24   enclosed] enclosed stamped A1+
125.25   Adventuring] Adventure TMs,E1(p)
125.34   of the] in the N1
125.39–126.1   inability] ability N1
126.1   habit] habits N2
126.5; 129.30; 130.3   Afterward] Afterwards N2
126.9   the banter] this banter A1+
126.12   apartment] department E1
126.12   there] omit A1+
126.15   of the] the A1+
126.18   lad] lady A1+
126.18   challenging] charging N1
126.28   then] them E1(p)
126.35   better] had better E1
127.5   then] omit E1
127.8   he] we A1+
127.16   grand] omit E1
127.22   had] omit A1
127.25   or] and A1+
127.28   assurance] assurances N1
127.29   stern] strange N2

127.30   he] omit N2
128.5   placed] places TMs
128.5   came] came in A1+
128.19   Schooner] Schoner E1
128.24   grisly] grizzly A1+
128.26   But] omit N1
128.27   around] round E1
129.2   page] paper N1
129.7   journal] genius N1-2
129.22   his] omit A1+
129.24   balls] omit E1
129.27   the] a N1
130.12   called] cried A1+
130.13   illustrations] illustration A1+
130.22   lapsed] relapsed N1
130.28   to] for N1
130.29   Somewhere in] Somehow on A1+
130.34   its] his A1+
131.20   Edidor] Editor E1+
131.22   toward] towards E1
131.37   sank] sang N2
132.1   lights] fights N2
132.1   the] omit N2
132.3   heavenwards] heavenward A1+
132.5   slightest] lightest A1+
132.11   has] had A1+
132.14   impelled] compelled N1
132.21   his] the N1
133.10   has] omit A1+
133.11   said] cried N1
133.16   that] omit A1+
133.21   I have] I've A1+
133.21; 134.16,16–17   do not] don't A1+
133.25   that] omit N1
133.27   not] not going TMs(going x'd-out); not going E1
133.27–28   You . . . point.] omit A1+
134.18   can not] cannot E1; can't A1+
134.18   Marjory] Majory A1
134.35   and] omit A1+
134.39   make] take A1,N1
135.24–25   "What . . . happened?'] "∧ ~ . . . ~ ? ∧ A1
135.27   in the] in a A1,N1; of a N2
135.33   me] I TMs,E1(p)

136.10 debris] *débris* E1
136.21 of a] of E1
136.23 'Explain'] ˄ ~ ˄ A1
136.26 glared] glanced A1
136.35 -tamed] -tame N²
137.4 Editor] editor E1+; Editor
　　　E1(p)
137.5 the top] to top TMs
137.6 clear] *omit* N¹
137.6 rang] ran A1; rank N²
137.9 idle and] *omit* A1+
137.12 " 'Camel rides',"]
　　　" ˄ ~ ~ ˄ ," A1
137.15 you] you'll E1; you will A1
137.18 friendly] a friendly A1+
137.28 even] *omit* A1+
137.39 feckless] fetless TMs+
　　　(−N²); footless N²
138.12 can] can't A1
138.13 they] the A1+
138.14–20 ¹"Marjory . . . al-
　　　ways——"] *omit* N²
138.15 this] his A1,N¹

*[Chapter v copy-text is TMs²; all
A1,N¹ accidentals as well as substantives are recorded that are not
listed in the Emendations. Unique
E1 accidental variants are not
listed; N² is missing for Chapter v.]*

139.1–142.15 By . . . bottle."]
　　　omit N²
139.3 region˄] ~ , TMs²
139.6 odor] order N¹
139.8 aisles˄] ~ , E1+
139.8 circled] circled about TMs²,
　　　E1
139.11 conductor] Conductor
　　　TMs²
139.11 with sarcasm] sarcastically
　　　TMs²,E1
139.11 Maybe] May be TMs²
139.12 road.] ~ ˄ TMs²; ~ ; E1
139.13 comforts] comfort TMs²,
　　　E1
139.14 cars˄] ~ , A1
139.16 heart˄] ~ , A1,N¹
139.16 dusky˄] ~ , A1,N¹
139.18 brakeman's] brakesman's
　　　E1(p); brakemen's A1
139.19 jolt,] ~ ˄ E1,N¹

139.21 had] *omit* N¹
139.21 at] in A1
139.21 York,] ~ ˄ N¹
139.24 sombre] somber N¹
139.25 prison house] ~ - ~ E1,N¹
139.27 a window] his window N¹
139.28 night˄] ~ , E1+
139.29 cars˄] ~ , TMs
139.29 glittering˄] ~ , A1,N¹
140.1 hall˄] ~ , A1,N¹
140.4 rooms˄] ~ , E1+
140.4 preliminary˄] ~ , E1,A1
140.6–7 men˄ . . . game˄] ~ ,
　　　. . . ~ , E1+
140.9 clinking] clicking TMs²,E1
140.9 chips] cups N¹
140.9 elected] electric E1(p)
140.12 Washurst] Washington N¹
140.15 fellow] a fellow A1
140.22,23 people] folks TMs²,E1
140.27 Afterward] Afterwards
　　　TMs²,E1
140.34–35 hell of a] fine N¹
141.1 damned] *omit* N¹
141.4 Steady! Come off!]
　　　~ .~ ~ . A1,N¹
141.11 grey˄] ~ , A1,N¹(N¹:
　　　gray)
141.15 murmured˄] ~ , A1
141.16 man˄] ~ , A1
141.19–20 This . . . in.] *omit*
　　　N¹
141.21 morning,] ~ ˄ N¹
141.27 Coleman?"] Coleman," he
　　　said. TMs²,E1
141.31 Now˄] ~ , A1,N¹
141.32 when˄] ~ , E1,A1
141.32 yesterday,] ~ ˄ N¹
141.33 heart,] ~ ˄ N¹
141.37 not˄ . . . times˄] ~ ,
　　　. . . ~ , A1
142.2 Coleman˄] ~ , A1,N¹
142.6 make,] ~ ˄ A1,N¹
142.10 don't] wouldn't TMs²,E1
142.14 "˄Easy?˄] "' ~ .' N¹

*[Chapter vi copy-text is TMs¹; TMs²
is present and all variants between
the two are given unless listed in
the Emendations; N² is missing for
Chapter vi. The order of textual au-*

thority is as follows: TMs¹; E1(p²), *set from* TMs¹; E1(p¹) *set from* TMs², A1, *and* N¹ (*set from* A1 *proofs*) *of equal authority; and last,* E1, *printed with some corrections from its proof.* E1(p¹) *and* E1(p²) *are so numbered because the Heinemann proof placed* E1(p¹) *first in order, retaining this first version for printed* E1, *while* E1(p²), *second in order but set from* TMs¹, *was discarded by Heinemann. An appearance of the form* E1(p²)+ *will signify the agreement of all texts save* TMs¹. E1(p²) *is understood to agree with the lemma to the left of the bracket unless otherwise noted.*]

143.1–146.30   Six . . . "Non-
      sense——"] *omit* N²
143.3   men] *omit* TMs¹,E1(p²)
143.4   times,] ∼ ∧ TMs²,E1,N¹
143.5   suspicion∧] ∼ , TMs²,E1
143.9   fine] a fine A1,N¹
143.11   recuperation∧] ∼ , TMs²+
143.12   singular] *omit* A1,N¹
143.15   office,] ∼ ∧ TMs²+
143.15   table∧] ∼ , TMs²,E1
143.17   "Rufus (*no* ¶)] ¶ E1
143.17   said] cried TMs²+
143.20   trousers] trouser's TMs¹;
      trousers' E1(p²)
143.21   "Now (*no* ¶)] ¶ TMs²,E1
143.24   we] you N¹
143.25   drill 'em—] ∼ '∼ ∧ | TMs²;
      ∼ '∼ ∧ E1(p¹)
143.25   staff] staffs N¹
143.27,28 (*twice*)   isn't] ain't
      TMs²,E1
143.31   fool-matters] ∼ ∧ ∼
      TMs²+
143.31   connected] concerned E1
144.2   scheme] scheme is TMs²+
144.3   Why∧] ∼ , TMs²+
144.5   answered.] ∼ , TMs²,E1
144.7   Sturgeon. "Why] ∼ , "why
      TMs²,E1
144.8   ¹I've] I have N¹
144.9   now∧] ∼ , E1(p²)+
144.13   you∧] ∼ , E1(p²)+

144.14   go∧] ∼ , TMs²,E1
144.14   success∧] ∼ ; E1(p²); ∼ ,
      TMs²+
144.15   right∧] TMs²,E1
144.15   time∧] ∼ , TMs²,E1
144.17   and] *omit* E1
144.18   cheque-book] ∼ ∧ ∼ TMs²,
      A1,N¹(A1,N¹: check)
144.20   much. And] ∼ , and TMs,
      E1
144.21   awhile] a while E1(p²)+
144.23   air∧] ∼ , TMs²,E1
144.24   Why∧] ∼ , TMs²,E1
144.27   Coleman.] ∼ , TMs²; ∼ ;
      E1
144.30   murmured] answered A1,
      N¹
144.32   War-correspondence]
      ∼ ∧ ∼ E1(p²)+
144.34   funny∧ but, really,] ∼ ,
      ∼ , ∼ , E1(p²); ∼ , ∼ ∧ ∼ ∧
      TMs²,E1
144.35   this] the N¹
144.36   it∧] ∼ , TMs²,E1
144.36   was in hell] would sus-
      pend N¹
144.37   *Eclipse.*] ∼ , TMs²; ∼ ; E1
      (*punctuation italic in* E1,
      roman in E1[p¹])
144.38   still I] I still A1,N¹
145.6   vacation∧] ∼ , TMs²,E1
145.6   way∧] ∼ , E1(p²)+
145.7   different?] ∼ . TMs²,E1
145.8   it∧] ∼ , E1(p²)+
145.8   that is] this is TMs²,E1
145.9   why,] ∼— TMs²,E1
145.11   book∧] ∼ , TMs²,E1
145.12   "Here's (*no* ¶)] ¶ E1
145.16,18,26,36–37; 146.26
      Tomorrow] To-morrow
      E1(p²)+
145.17   Oho] Oh E1(p²)
145.17   Sturgeon. "You're] ∼ ,
      "you're TMs²,E1
145.17   impetuous] imperious N¹
145.18,26   'Tomorrow'] ∧ ∼ ∧
      E1(p²)+
145.19   repeated∧] ∼ , TMs²,E1,N¹
145.21–22   momentary] monen-
      tary TMs¹; monetary E1(p²)

145.22 vaguely-defined] ～ ∧ ～ TMs²,E1,N¹
145.22 in] of N¹
147.27 jiminy] jiming TMs², E1(p²); Jiminy E1
145.29 years∧] ～ , TMs²,E1,N¹
145.31 lines∧] ～ , E1(p²)+
145.33 now∧] ～ , TMs²,E1
145.35 vacation.] ～ ; TMs²,E1
145.36 take. And∧] ～ , and, TMs², E1(p¹); ～ , and∧ E1
145.36–37 'tomorrow',] ∧ ～ ∧∧ TMs²
145.38 Coleman∧] ～ , TMs²+
145.39 cheque. Clear] ～ ; clear TMs²,E1
146.1 ¹you] you here E1
146.2 rested∧] ～ , E1(p²+)
146.2 it] omit TMs²
146.4–5 a thousand dollars] $1,000 N¹
146.5 toward] towards TMs²,E1
146.6–14 Then . . . it."] omit N¹
146.6 minute.] ～ , TMs²,E1
146.13 positively.] ～ , TMs²; ～ ; E1
146.18 reasons—] ～ , TMs²,E1
146.19 reasons.] ～ ! E1(p²); ～ , TMs²
146.22 instructions] instruction A1,N¹
146.23 there∧] ～ , TMs²,E1
146.25 dinner] dine E1
146.26 Coleman. "If] ～ , "if TMs²
146.27 pack——] ～ . TMs²,E1
146.30 Sturgeon.] ～ , TMs²
146.30 Nonsense——] ～ ! TMs², E1

[Chapter VII et seq.: TMs² is no longer present; only substantives are recorded.]

147.0 VII] v N²
147.2 -houses] -house N²
147.5 race] racing A1+
147.11 deck] decks A1+
147.14 settling] settled N²
147.15 diffident] a diffident A1+
147.20 salon] saloon N²
148.4 that] omit A1+
148.7–8 But . . . later.] omit N²

148.11 to see me] me to A1+
148.21 'Worked hard'] ∧ ～ ～ ∧ E1+
148.24 queen] Queen E1,N²
148.28 that] the A1+
148.31 any] an A1+
149.5 Whipple] Wipple E1
149.8 eight . . . dollars] $8,000 N¹
149.12 a . . . dollars] $1,000 N¹
149.16 differently] indifferently A1+
149.22 say] say that A1+
149.28 were always] always were A1+
149.32 on] in TMs
150.4 snapped] slapped N¹
150.6 conquest?] ～ . A1,N¹
150.10 Known] Know A1+
150.11 you] you there, A1,N²
150.12 nothin',] nothin'. Nothin', A1,N²; nothin'; nothin'∧ N¹
150.16 narrowed] narrow A1+
150.20 and profound] omit E1
150.23 much] omit A1+
150.28 aboard] abroad E1(p)
150.31 Tomorrow] To-morrow E1+(N²: ～ - | ～)
150.36 look] look up A1+
151.18 bad] a bad A1+
151.24 bottle of wine] wine bottle A1+
151.27 seem] seem to be A1
151.29 such a] a great A1,N²; a N¹
152.16 isn't] 'tisn't TMs
152.17 let's] let us N²
153.10 marked] omit N¹
153.14 et seq. toward] towards E1
153.15 accident] an accident N²
153.29 "Rufus."] omit N¹
154.15 Afterward] Afterwards E1
155.0 VIII] vi N²
155.4 only] omit N²
155.12 are] omit N²
155.14 immense . . . enormous] roman in A1+
155.20 me] omit A1+
156.2 came . . . directly] came in and seated themselves N²
156.17 a] omit A1,N²

156.20 sleeve] sleeves N²
156.23 siren . . . succubus] note of a siren N¹
156.27 my] me A1,N¹
156.36 his] *omit* N²
156.37 description] descriptions N¹
157.21 horses] horse A1,N²
157.26 debutante] *débutante* E1
157.26 too] *omit* N¹
157.27,30 Walkley] Walkely A1, N¹
157.34 a sort of an] *omit* A1; a N¹⁻²
157.36 When] CHAPTER VII | When N²
158.13 at] in N²
158.27 in his carriage] by his carriages N²
158.30 Greek] Greeks TMs
158.32–33 up on] upon A1+
158.33 *et seq.* cafes] *cafés* E1
158.38 that] *omit* E1
159.7 brown] *omit* A1+
159.9–10 and use . . . him] *omit* N²
159.16 off] of N²
159.17 thought] though N²
159.18 some] some of his A1+
159.22 files] fifty files N²
159.23 Coleman] Coleman's A1+
159.26 They] Then they N¹
159.30 didn't] did not N²
159.39 the Hon.] Hon. N¹
160.5 Directly] Director N²
160.8 am] an E1
160.14 begged] he begged N²
160.14 not] not to N¹⁻²
160.16 'Daughter',] ‸ ~ ‸ , A1+
160.25 gently] slowly E1
160.28 a] *omit* E1
160.33 *could . . . can't*] roman *in* A1+
161.2 about] *omit* E1
161.3 Pekin] Peking N¹
161.5 Well,] *omit* E1
161.7 You're] You are A1+
161.14 plight] plight of A1+
161.20 for] of E1
161.25 man] young man A1+
161.25 to] toward A1+

161.26 oriental] Oriental E1,A1, N²
161.32 medicines] medicine A1
161.33–162.6 He . . . important.] *omit* N²
161.35 last] least E1
163.29; 164.37 Mesalonghi] Missolonghi E1,N²
163.29 too] to TMs
164.1–2 howling . . . attacked] *omit* A1+
164.3 by] of N¹
164.19 eloquently] *omit* N²
164.19 he . . . plight] told him N²
164.20 of his] *omit* A1+
164.38 *et seq.* Agrinion] Agrinium E1
165.7–8 cross . . . crescent] Cross . . . Crescent E1
165.9 from] *omit* TMs
165.16 soldiers] the soldiers A1
165.20 ill-faith] ill-fate A1
165.21 seemed] appeared A1+
165.21 that] *omit* TMs(u)
165.31 had become] become TMs, E1; became A1+
165.32 establishment] establishing N¹
165.34 gentleman] gentlemen E1
166.11 his little] the little E1
166.11 almost] pretty near N²
166.22 was] had been A1
166.23 is] was A1+
166.23 last] latest A1
166.23 final] conclusive A1
166.31 or] or | or N²
166.36 back] the back A1+
167.9 courier] courier's A1+
167.10 his] the E1
167.20 inelegant] elegant A1
167.29 that] which A1+
168.1 momentous] a momentous N²
168.8 direction] directions N¹⁻²
168.9+ (*no space*)] CHAPTER X N²
168.27 agonized] agonising A1; agonizing N¹⁻²
168.34 detail] details N¹
168.38 little] *omit* A1+

169.1 green] *omit* A1+
169.8–9 it clearly,] *omit* N[1]
170.0 CHAPTER X] *omit* A1
170.1 long] a long A1+
170.3–4 reverberations] reverberation N[2]
170.4 acutely] actually A1+
170.10 flickered] flicked TMs, E1(p),A1+; flecked E1
170.14 [1]they] he A1+
170.18 his] this A1+
170.21 Turks] the Turks A1+
170.26 passing] passing into TMs,E1(p)
170.26–27 covering] men covering N[2]
171.2 had] *omit* N[2]
171.8 near] to N[2]
171.9 upon] on N[2]
171.9 a] *omit* A1+
171.21 his] the N[2]
171.25 this] his A1
171.32 proven] proved N[1]
171.35 they] *omit* N[2]
171.37 world] word TMs(c),E1
171.38 to have] who have N[2]
172.9 cheap] a cheap A1+
172.16 uniforms] uniform TMs, A1,N[1]
172.16 were] was A1,N[1]
172.16 [2]of] *omit* N[2]
172.20 noted] noticed N[2]
172.32 tails] tail A1+
172.32 squadrons] squadron A1+
172.33 who] which A1+
173.8 landscape] landscapes N[2]
173.9–10 on . . . stream] *omit* N[1]
173.18 sunrays] sun's rays N[1]
173.27 heaving] *omit* A1+
173.32 They] The E1(p)
173.33 troopers] troops E1
174.1 actual] active N[2]
174.2 in all] at all TMs,E1(p)
174.15 rattled] ruffled E1
174.27 gentleman] gentlemen N[2]
174.29 to] on to A1+
175.3 and] and | and N[2]
175.3 scrub] scrubs A1+
175.12 [2]to] up to E1; to E1(p)
175.13 white] *omit* A1+

175.17 sheep] sheeps E1(p)
175.20 with] to E1
175.30 looked] looked at him A1+
175.37 the] his N[2]
176.2 little] *omit* A1+
176.9 he] *omit* A1+
176.13 horses] heroes N[2]
177.0 XI] X A1
177.17 had not heard] did not hear A1+
177.18 if] whether N[2]
177.23 the salt] salt the N[1]
178.2 [1]in] of N[2]
178.2 Sudan] Soudan E1,N[2]
178.4–5 Some . . . salaries;] *omit* A1+
178.6 nor] or N[2]
178.13 took seat] took a seat N[1-2]
178.34 futile] *omit* A1+
178.36 all] at all A1+
178.39 was] were N[2]
179.1 newspaper] newspapers A1+
179.7 the American] American A1+
179.12 arousing] a rousing TMs
179.34 all] *omit* A1+
180.2 other] others A1
180.18 the cavalry] cavalry TMs, E1
180.20 it . . . consistent] *omit* N[1]
180.29 Coleman] So Coleman A1+
180.34 francs] franc N[1]
180.35 on] upon A1+
180.38 think] thing N[1]
180.39; 181.2; 182.5 *Much*] Much A1+
181.8 were] are N[1]
181.10 a] *omit* A1+
181.13 dumbfounded] dumfounded E1,N[1]
181.32 that that] that the N[1]
182.1 very] very very TMs(u) (TMs[c] *first* very *x'd-out*); very very A1+
182.3 is] in TMs
182.3 tell] tells N[1]
182.13 had been] was N[2]
182.17 an] a TMs

182.25   some] an A1+
182.31   green] great N1
182.32   so] *omit* N1
184.5   people] people had come out to the Greeks, men, women and children A1+
184.6   pranced] prancing TMs, A1+
184.10   that] the A1+
184.12   this] the A1+
184.12   on up] up in N1; up on N2
184.12   up] up to E1
184.21   and dancing about him] *omit* N2
184.30   in] even in A1+
184.30   life-time] life N2
185.15   1his] the N1
185.22   reason] season N1
185.24   a bad] bad A1+
185.25   feeling] feelings A1+
186.4   it, else] it. Else A1+
186.9   miles] miles away A1+
187.0   XII] XI A1
187.6   tin] tine TMs; tin mug A1+
187.10   the night] a night A1+
187.16–17   Often . . . watch.] *omit* A1+
187.21   it] *omit* A1,N2
187.25   as] as fresh as A1+
187.27   ghostly] ghastly N2
187.28   in] from N2
188.7   henchman] henchmen TMs, A1+
188.9   other] *omit* A1+
188.12   That] This E1
188.14   ¶ Coleman] *no* ¶ A1+
188.19   a] the A1+
188.20   and] *omit* A1+
188.23   even] *omit* E1
188.30   dreaming] drearying N1-2
188.33   absolute] absolutely N1
189.8   himself] *omit* A1+
189.10   with] *omit* N2
189.26   handily] happily E1
190.3   his] *omit* TMs
190.12   that] *omit* A1+
190.14   able . . . remained] *omit* N2
190.14   not to] to not E1+
190.21   Louros] Loures N1
190.21   there] that there TMs

190.34   pack-saddle.] pack-saddle. He appeared in a moment tugging at the halter. He could only say: A1+
190.38   already] *omit* E1
191.8   upon] with TMs; on E1
191.14   more] mere N1
191.17   black] blank A1+
191.22   plane] place A1+
191.33   regretted merely] merely regretted E1
191.36   circumstance] circumstances A1+
192.3   damned] d—d N1
192.10   jab] job E1
192.21   effect] effects A1+
192.22   terrors] torrents N1-2
192.27   knew] know A1
193.1   heard] heard from A1+
193.22   2up] *omit* A1+
193.22   This] The E1
193.24   Washurst] Washurt N2
194.0   XIII] XII A1
194.4   a] *omit* A1+
194.5   had] *omit* A1+
194.6   not] *omit* N1-2
194.7   but] *omit* A1+
194.18   the] a A1,N1
194.20   were] *omit* N2
194.22   to] *omit* E1
194.27   steady] as steady A1+
195.14   such a] such A1+
195.20   go] go up A1+
195.27   fingers] figure N1
195.28   them] it N1
195.31   woods] wood A1+
195.32   a] an TMs
195.36   his] the N1
196.3   at once] *omit* N2
196.4   they] they lowly A1+
196.6   a sort of] sort of a A1+
196.12   2the] *omit* A1+
196.25,27   counsel] council TMs
196.25–27   He . . . counsel.] *omit* A1+
196.37   away and] away E1
196.37   we] and then we A1+
197.1   1his] the N2
197.3   an] the A1+
197.6–7   circumstance] circumstances N2

197.11   set] *omit* E1; set out N¹
197.33   hopes] hope N¹
197.34   ²as] *omit* N²
197.35   protests] protest A1+
197.37   Washurst] Washrust N¹
197.39   blankets] blanket TMs,E1
198.4   began] begun A1,N²
198.6   the] this A1+
198.19   smoking] *omit* A1+
198.20   to] to cover A1+
198.29   him] his N¹
198.36   and the sex] *omit* TMs; and so the sex A1+
198.37   safety came] should safety come N²
200.0   XIV] XIII A1
200.15; 212.15   toward] towards N²
200.15   was] *omit* A1+
201.4   a] *omit* N¹
201.5   now] *omit* N¹
201.7   turned] returned E1
201.12   were] was A1
201.13   shoulders] shoulder A1+
201.14   corps] corp TMs
201.35   the] his N²
201.38   dimensions] dim chances E1; dim (*space*) TMs
202.1   weighted] weighed E1
202.8   slanted on] lanted to N²
202.8   -rein] -reins A1
202.23   this] his N²
202.38   enlightened‿ immediately‿] ~ , ~ ‿ E1; ~ ‿ ~ , A1+
203.1   ²of the] of that A1+
203.12   at the strong] strong at the A1+
203.19   gratitude] wild gratitude A1+
204.1   little] *omit* A1+
204.15   go to] go to to N²
204.20   by] *omit* TMs; from E1
204.26   up] out A1+
204.32   proven] proved N¹
204.33   practical] practically N²
205.10   for] to N²
205.20   sets] sits E1
205.31   think] think that A1+
205.33   ²at] in N¹
206.7   what] that E1,N²

206.18   dragomen] dragomans N¹
206.29   to] in A1+
206.34   eye] eyes N²
206.37   also] *omit* N¹
207.8   imaginations] imagination A1+
207.11   thinks] think TMs
207.20   is] *omit* N²
207.27   hill] hills N¹
208.0   xv] xiv A1
208.8   sat] say TMs; set E1
208.23   melee] *mêlée* E1; mêlée A1
208.30   role] *rôle* E1
208.30   horse] horses A1+
209.5   to] of TMs
209.10   stout] good, stout A1+
209.14   somehow] somewhat N²
209.19   veritably] veritible TMs
209.23   different] indifferent A1+
209.30   beers] beer N¹
209.31   hell] heel TMs; —— N¹; the deuce N²
209.32   two] two damn A1; two —— N¹
210.1   as] *omit* N¹
210.10   ride] ride it A1+
210.17   native horses] natives A1+
210.23   student] of the students N¹
210.31   as] was N²
210.31–32   not . . . even] not even capable of A1+
210.37   had had] had N¹
211.2   one] *omit* N¹
211.7   in . . . those] to any of those E1
211.13   in] on N²
211.22   a] the N²
211.33   troop] troops N²
212.10   polite] a polite A1+
212.23   all] *omit* A1+
212.28   had] *omit* A1+
213.1   his] her E1
213.3   extremely] *omit* N¹
213.7   a] *omit* TMs
213.7   some] *omit* A1+
213.9   Here they are.] *omit* A1+
213.11   of] *omit* N¹

213.19 *et seq. New York Day-light*] roman *in* N¹⁻²
214.0 XVI] xv A1
214.15 'way] way TMs, A1+
214.16 on further] any farther N²
214.16 *such*] such A1+
215.5 have] has N¹
215.6 even . . . and] either . . . or a E1
215.14 broke] looked TMs
215.17 horses] horse A1+
215.24 circumstance] circumstances E1+
215.30 extraordinary] extraordinarily A1
215.30 lucky] *omit* N¹⁻²
215.31–32 substance] substances A1+
215.32 fire] enough fire A1+
215.38 Nora] Nora Black A1+
216.8 raised] lifted A1
216.20–21 toward] towards A1
216.24 seen] see TMs
216.24 anyone] any one E1,A1
216.26 it] *omit* TMs
216.31 the white] white E1
216.35 place] places A1+
216.36 animatedly] animately TMs
217.5 ideas] *omit* E1
217.6 wont] won't A1,N²
217.9 protection] protector N¹
217.16 tourist's] tourists' N¹
217.19 actual] *omit* E1
217.36 great] *omit* N²
218.1 illumined] illuminated N²
218.2 on] upon A1+
218.4 meet] see N²
218.4,31 seems] seemed A1+
218.5 was] was being A1+
218.18 how] so N¹⁻²
218.20 appeared] happened A1+
218.31 seems] seemed A1+
218.35 this] the N¹
218.38 lose] loose E1
219.3 damned] —— N¹
219.3 going] *omit* N¹⁻²
219.3 tow] two N¹
219.3 further] farther N¹
219.10 Pete] Peter E1
219.12 it] *omit* A1+

219.16 onto] on to E1
219.20 think] thing N²
219.21 'round] ∧ ~ E1
219.33 damned] damn A1,N²; —— N¹
220.23 her] *omit* N²
220.31 me] my E1
220.34 loudly] loud A1+
221.1–2 Dear . . . ¹me.] *omit* N¹
221.12 then] *omit* A1+
222.0 XVII] xvi A1
222.1 God] god TMs
222.5–6 are not] are are not N²
222.7 me] my N²
222.12 to] at A1+
222.17 this] his N²
222.21 Her] He TMs; His E1
222.24 let] to let N²
222.29 upon] on TMs(c),E1
222.30 means] method N²
223.4 formulation] formation N¹⁻²
223.9 aplomb] *aplomb* E1
223.15 bad] *omit* A1+
223.32 ²all] *omit* A1+
224.7–8 It . . . waiting.] *omit* N²
224.31 a] the N²
224.39 glistening] glittering N²
225.1 laid] lay N²
225.4 ²that] *omit* A1+
225.7 hours] hour A1+
225.7–8 a new . . . succeeded in] *omit* A1+
225.12 toward] towards TMs,E1
225.35 shade] shape A1+
226.21 have] have got E1
226.23 her] the A1+
226.28 an] *omit* N²
226.30 rack] row E1; rank A1+
226.35 little] the N²
226.39 affect] effect TMs,E1
227.7 baring] baring to him A1+
227.8 with] in N²
227.11 monosyllable] monosyllables N¹
227.16 was] is A1
228.0 XVIII] xvii A1
228.3 ²all] *omit* A1+
228.20 and] *omit* N²

228.28–30 "I think . . . tenderly.] *omit* TMs,E1

[TMs *copy-text is present but mutilated.*]

229.9 not] *omit* N²
229.9 that's] that is N²
229.12 role] *rôle* E1
229.20 relapsed] lapsed A1+
229.27 nor] or TMs,A1,N¹
230.6 mouth] mouths A1+
230.29 toward] towards E1
230.35 damned] d—d N¹
231.5 irresponsibility] responsibility N²
231.12 Titanic] *omit* A1
231.15 proven] proved N¹
231.23 this] his A1+
231.26 attributes] attribute TMs, E1
231.36 out] *omit* A1+
232.27 with] with a A1+
232.33 bade] bidden N²
233.5 one] *omit* N²
233.7 may be] he A1 |

[TMs *copy-text is present; normal collation resumes.*]

233.18 as] *omit* E1
233.20 could not] couldn't A1+
233.22 quite] quiet A1
233.22–23 it . . . all . . . if] it all. If A1+
233.25 business . . . he] ~ . He A1+
233.29 repeated] responded A1+
233.33 was] were N²
233.38 collar] color N¹
234.1 in] into E1
235.0 XIX] XVIII A1
235.5 here see] see here A1+
235.11 ²one] *omit* E1
235.14 is] it N¹
235.16 *did*] did A1+
235.18 ¹ever] even N²
235.20–22 "Induced . . . arose.] *repeated in* N²
235.28 I] me N²
236.1 *is*] is A1+
236.9 mislead] misled A1+

236.18–19 your . . . your . . .] your_ E1
236.21 'Hospitality'?] _ ~ _ ? A1+
236.37 and abashed looked] an abashed look A1
237.4 humiliate] distress A1
237.5 meet] get A1+
237.23 preceding] proceeding TMs
237.24 an] the N¹
238.21 snark] snarl N¹
238.24 damned] d—d N¹
239.1–2 Another . . . it."] *omit* A1+
239.6 know] knows N¹
239.13 it] *omit* A1+
239.13 further] farther N²
239.37 even] even been A1,N²; ever been N¹
240.4 abased] abashed A1
240.15–17 He . . . breakfast.] *omit* N¹
240.19 circumstance] circumstances E1
240.33 *what*] what A1+
240.38–39 He . . . boudoir.] *omit* A1+
241.5 judge] judges N²
241.7 *may*] may A1+
241.12 guile] guilt N²
241.31 this] his N²
242.0 xx] XIX A1
242.11 rage] a rage N²
242.13 something] *omit* A1+
242.20 had] *omit* A1+
242.20 go] are N²
242.20 *can't*] can't A1+
242.31–243.1 The . . . floor.] *omit* N²
243.14 about] *omit* A1+
243.35 him. Beyond] ~ , beyond E1
244.7 *they*] they A1+
244.14; 253.38; 257.35 toward] towards E1
245.24 *was*] was A1+
245.26 if] though A1
245.27 a] an N²
246.2 *is*] is A1+
246.4 to] in E1
246.6 know] knew N¹

246.13　Coke] Coleman TMs; Cole
　N²
246.16　²too] to N²
246.23　(twice)　Will] Will A1+
246.24　clenched] clinched N¹
246.25　no] not N²
246.29　is] is A1+
246.31　persistently] desperately
　A1+
247.11　known] know N²
247.23　could] come TMs
248.1　unhappiness] happiness
　N¹⁻²
248.7　divided] known N¹⁻²
248.13　money] money enough
　A1+
248.20　the] omit N²
248.26　set] sent E1
248.28　two] omit E1
249.0　xxi] xx A1
249.2　to] on N²
249.14　¹are . . . not] you are A1
249.24　your safe] you safe A1
249.25　but] by TMs
249.25　I would] would TMs
249.28　silent_∧ in reality_∧] ~ _∧ ~
　~ , E1; ~ , ~ ~ _∧ A1
249.30　like] omit A1+
250.5　require] requires N²
250.28–29　moment] movement
　N¹
250.29　role] rôle E1
250.30　one] omit A1+
250.37　et seq.　Agrinion]
　Agrinium E1
250.39　at] to N²
251.9　²this] that N²
251.17　puling and puking] pulling
　and pucking TMs(u),A1+
251.28　here] omit A1+
251.32　that] omit N²
251.34　consciences] conscience N²
252.6　monkey] donkey N²
252.15　high] omit A1+
252.16　What] What A1+
252.19　damned] d—d N¹
252.20　completely] complete A1+
252.23　with a] with TMs,A1; a N¹
253.2　mid] amid N²
253.3　circumstance] circum-
　stances N²

253.12　resented] resentful N¹⁻²
253.13　came] come E1
253.18　yawp] yawn E1
253.18　their] his A1
253.21　someone] some one E1,A1,
　N¹
253.34　such] such a N²
254.12–13　All . . . hoofs.]
　omit N²
254.17　had] omit A1+
254.19　²any] and E1
254.22　noted] noticed A1+
254.23　his] their N²
254.34　-browed] -browned E1
254.37　launched] launching E1
255.4　on to] onto N¹
255.8　up] omit A1+
256.0　xxii] xxi A1
256.1　the throng] omit A1+
256.4　ongry] angry A1+
256.7　must] must A1+
256.8　note] not TMs(u),A1+
256.10　on] no N²
256.11　Make] Make A1+
256.12　note] note A1+
256.29　amok] amuck A1+
257.3　²do something] omit E1
257.4　have even] even have E1
257.23　is] is A1+
257.24　It] I N¹
257.25　admitted] admitting N¹
257.36–37　his Marjory] omit N²
257.38　his left] one N²
258.7　a disdain] omit N¹
258.9　faces] facts N²
259.10　somewheres] somewhere
　A1+
259.20　laid] lain N¹
259.35　had] omit A1+
259.35　begun] began N²
259.39　wide] omit A1+
260.1　clang] clank N¹
260.10　jolted] jilted TMs+(−N²)
260.19　others] other| TMs
260.20　Billie] Billy A1
260.24　had] omit N²
260.25　on] by A1+
260.28　at] omit TMs
261.2　darker] omit N²
261.2　stepped] steered N¹
261.4　was] is N²

261.5   did] did A1+
261.5   Isn't] Is A1+
261.13–14   tearful] tearfully A1+
261.33   those] thosc A1+
263.0   XXIII] XXII A1
263.2   door] doors TMs(u),E1
263.10   fearfully] fiercely A1+
263.19   pow-wow] pow-bow A1
263.22   neither . . . nor] neither
        . . . or TMs; either . . . or
        A1,N²
263.25   go] go up N²
264.6–7   in the devil] omit N¹
264.8   by] with N²
264.12   convinced] now convinced
        N²
264.12   his] this A1
264.19   went] was A1+
264.22   feminine] omit A1+
264.23   ²in] omit N¹
264.30   was] omit A1+
264.32   carriages] carriage A1+
264.34   O-o-oh] O-o-h E1
264.35   Rufus] Refus N²
264.36   huve] have A1+
265.5   do] do A1+
265.9   time] any time A1+
265.11   their] the A1+
265.15   like] omit A1+
265.26   need] need A1+
265.29   in any way] omit A1+
266.1   foreseen] seen N¹
266.8   so] so A1+
266.10   to convey] omit A1+
266.19   do] do A1,N²; omit N¹
266.32   allusions] illusions TMs,
        A1,N¹
267.2   Marjory] Marjorie N¹
267.14   denouement] dénouement
        E1
267.15   fleur de lys] fleur de lys
        E1; fleur-de-lis A1+
267.18   thousand] thousands N²
267.22   ²of] omit A1+
267.35   of] for E1
267.40   ye'] you A1+
268.4   repartee] repartee E1
268.20   not] omit N²
268.22   away] omit N¹
268.27   at] with A1+
269.12   Coleman's] Colemans N²

269.14   want] wants A1
269.14   sumthing] sunthing
        TMs,A1+
269.20   It] He TMs
270.0   XXIV] XXIII A1
271.4   afterward] forward E1
271.19   the spur . . . horse] his
        horse with the spur, E1
271.21   turn] return A1
271.30   all] it all A1+
272.8   of himself] himself A1+
272.24   specially] special E1
272.31   future] fortune E1
273.10   was] were N²
273.12   unimportant] important N²
273.24   surpassing] surprising N²
273.28   an affectionate] omit A1+
273.33   of] to A1
274.7   this] his this N²
274.29   here] here A1+
274.38   serious] most serious A1+
274.38   carriages] diligencia A1+
274.39   had] had had A1+
276.0   XXV] XXIV A1
276.17   conditions] traditions A1+
276.24   actual] omit E1
277.3   naught] nought TMs,E1
277.4   directly] omit E1
277.6   a] omit A1+
277.8   all] all in A1+
277.36   had had no plan] had no
        idea A1+
278.15   delighted] obliged A1+
278.27   unconventionally] uncon-
        ventional A1+
278.30   for] of N²
278.36   Mesalonghi] Missolonghi
        E1

[TMs is wanting; E1 is copy-text;
all accidental variants are recorded.]

279.7   terrors] errors N²
279.8   easily,] ~∧ N¹
279.8   over-estimate] overestimate
        A1+(N²: ~-|~)
279.14   gulls] the gulls N²
279.15   placid∧] ~ , N²
279.15   oriental] Oriental A1,N²
279.17   travellers] travelers N¹⁻²
279.20   Corinth,] ~∧ N¹

279.27 course. It] ~ ∧ it N²
279.29; 280.6,12,21 Coleman∧]
~ , A1
279.31 deck-house] deckhouse N¹;
deck house N²
279.35 seemed, more,] ~ ∧ ~ ∧ N²
279.38 pause,] ~ ∧ N¹
280.1 plains] Plains A1,N²
280.9 (twice) fiend] friend E1
280.13,19 Marjory∧] ~ , A1
280.19 wearily,] ~ . N¹⁻²
280.25 manner,] ~ ∧ N²
280.29 ²not] would not A1+
280.31 would not] not to A1+
280.35 daughter,] ~ ∧ N²
280.36 ²in] is N¹
281.3 Good-bye] Good-by N¹
281.3 to Coleman] omit A1
281.5–6 from . . . Athens] omit
N¹
281.5 Patras] there N²
281.6 a dismissal] the dismissal
N¹
281.9 again,] ~ ∧ N¹
281.9 man] men N¹
281.11 train∧] ~ , A1,N²
281.18 to be] omit A1+
281.21 inn∧] ~ , A1+
281.21 budge] budge A1+
281.30 would] should A1+
281.34 singular] singularly A1
281.37 Nora∧] ~ , A1+
281.38 silent] omit A1+
282.5 She . . . him] roman in
A1+
282.6,7 her] her A1+
282.7 old] omit A1+
282.7 he] he A1+
282.14 half] half of A1+
282.19 does] does A1+
282.34 the gloom] a gloom A1+
282.36 be not] not be A1+
282.36 value] great value A1+
282.37–38 It . . . them.] omit
A1+
283.4 said∧] ~ , A1
283.4 were] are N¹
283.11 The] That N²
283.15 Nora∧] ~ , A1
283.18 say!] ~ . A1,N²
283.22 Afterward,] ~ ∧ N¹

283.25 lady∧] ~ , A1+
283.29 does] does A1+
283.30 Nora∧] ~ , A1,N²
283.32 for∧] ~ , A1+
283.32 anyhow] any how N¹; anyway N²

[TMs copy-text is present but mutilated.]

284.0 xxvi] xxv A1
284.28 It] I N¹
284.29–30 our . . . his] roman in
A1+
284.30 I am] I'm A1
285.2 meant] mean N¹⁻²
285.4 our] our A1+

[TMs is wanting; E1 is copy-text;
all accidental variants are recorded.]

285.13–14 like . . . parrot]
omit N¹⁻²
285.15 Wainwright,] ~ ∧ N²
285.17 me] be N²
285.28 Athens∧] ~ , A1
285.33–34 but, . . . minutes,]
~ ∧ . . . ~ ∧ N¹
285.37 feeling∧] ~ , N²
285.37 dinner∧] ~ , A1
286.1 light;] ~ : A1
286.2 mother∧] ~ , A1
286.7 man∧] ~ , N²

[TMs copy-text is present but mutilated.]

286.8 from] omit A1+
286.10 ²like] omit A1
286.13 here] omit A1+
286.14 this] the E1
286.30 appalled] appalled to N²
287.1 She] See E1

[TMs is wanting; E1 is copy-text;
all accidental variants are recorded.]

287.7 knelt∧] ~ , A1+
287.9 lost . . . everything . . .]
~ — ~ — A1+
287.12 by] from A1+
287.13 grey] gray N¹⁻²

287.17 hands'] hand's E1
287.20 there] *omit* A1+
287.27 only] *omit* E1
287.30 was a] was such a A1
288.4 it. . . .] ~ . * * * A1,N¹;
~ . * * * * N²
288.6 daddy. . . .] ~ . * * *
A1,N¹; ~ . * * N²
288.7 The (*no* ¶)] ¶ A1+
288.11–12 death-bed] deathbed N¹
288.12 low∧] ~ , N²
288.17 emotion,] ~ ∧ N¹
288.19 demanded∧] ~ , A1
288.26 ¶ "Please] *no* ¶ N¹
288.30; 289.10 said∧] ~ , A1+
288.32 opinions] opinion E1
288.32 *could*] could A1+
288.36 now∧] ~ , A1+
288.36 you.] ~ ! A1+
288.37 professor∧] ~ , A1
289.2 snarled∧] ~ , A1,N²
289.3 it] It N¹
289.6 as] that E1
289.8 us∧] ~ , A1+
289.11 Wainwright∧] ~ , A1+
289.15 went∧] ~ , A1,N²
289.15 tip-toed] tiptoed A1+(N²:
~ - | ~)
289.16 see] only see A1+
289.16 pillow∧] ~ , A1,N²
290.0 XXVII] XXVI A1
290.2 hotel,] ~ ∧ N¹
290.4; 291.6–7 smoking-room]
~ ∧ ~ A1,N²
290.4–5,29 dining-room] ~ ∧ ~
A1,N²
290.5 of the] of this A1+
290.6 fish,] ~ ∧ N¹
290.13 the] their A1+
290.14 authority,] ~ ∧ N²
290.14 and,] ~ ∧ N¹
290.15 hotel-keeper] hotelkeeper
N²
290.17 impudence,] ~ ∧ N¹
290.17 attitude,] ~ ∧ N²
290.18 long] *omit* A1+
290.18 speeches,] ~ — N²
290.26 it∧] ~ , N²
290.31 them,] ~ ∧ N²
291.1 fountain,] ~ ∧ N²
291.5 was] were N²

291.14 Coke∧] ~ , N¹
291.22 naggled] haggled A1+
291.23 him] him like an outright
parrot N¹
291.26 departure,] ~ ∧ N¹
291.28–29 There . . . them.]
omit N²
291.33 hotel-keeper] hotelkeeper
A1,N²
291.34 minister,] ~ ∧ N²
291.36 trusted, . . . are;]
trusted, and, . . . are, A1+
(N²: trusted∧)
292.7,9,23 minister∧] ~ , A1
292.14 at] in A1+
292.28 *man*] man A1+
292.29 Billie] Pillie N¹
292.31 minister,] ~ ∧ N²
293.1 end,] ~ ∧ N¹⁻²
293.1 is] are A1+
293.4 a] the N²

[TMs *copy-text is present; normal
collation resumes.*]

293.18 *might*] might A1+
293.25 calmly] calmy A1
293.27 ¹Oh] *omit* A1+
294.4 the] *omit* E1
294.9 sang] rang N¹
294.9 their] the A1+
294.12 whereabouts] whereabout
N²
294.17 consist] insist TMs
295.11 you] your E1
295.15 Wainwright∧] ~ — A1+
295.17 Everyone] Every one E1
295.25 *debut*] *début* E1; debut
A1+
295.26 there] they N²
295.31 when] when it E1
296.10 sleep, he] ~ . He N¹⁻²
296.11 *are*] are A1+
296.21 to] *omit* TMs
297.1 if] *omit* N²
297.2 a choking] choking a A1+
297.4 go] do N²
297.4 humbly, "if] ~ . "If TMs,
A1+
297.9 as] *omit* A1+
297.12 heard of] head of N¹;
omit N²

297.23   then] *omit* E1
297.25   *worst*] worst A1+
298.0   XXVIII] XXVII A1
298.3   a] *omit* N[1-2]
298.4   affect] effect TMs
298.4   express] impress N[2]
298.5   student's] student A1+
298.9   supplicant] suppliant N[2]
298.12   on] at N[2]
298.21   represented] presented N[1-2]
298.24   first] *omit* N[1-2]
299.9   halted] then halted A1+
299.10   rest] rest once A1+
299.15   acutely] actually A1+
299.22; 300.4   the] *omit* TMs
299.36   likely] like TMs,A1,N[1]
300.12   *care*] care A1+
300.15   ways] way E1,N[2]
300.28   man] men E1
300.29   tragic muse] Tragic Muse E1
300.36   blank] black E1
301.3   toward] towards A1
301.10   , sir, . . . anything] *omit* A1+
301.10-11   you sit . . . Will] *omit* E1
301.24   how] now A1,N[1]
301.30   was] were N[2]
301.37   a while] awhile A1+
302.8   seemed] here seemed A1+
302.11-18   *Arranged . . . Coleman?*] roman in A1+
302.14   professor. Then] ~ , when E1
302.24   flaming] burning A1+
302.28   Grrr] G-r-r-r E1
302.37   *dare*] dare A1+
303.2   found] had found N[2]
303.17   any] a A1+
303.20   visit] purpose A1+
303.32-304.12   Well . . . proceed.] *omit* N[1]
303.32   main] *omit* A1,N[2]
303.39   retort] reply E1
303.39   [1]to] of TMs
304.11   dolefully] mournfully A1+
304.14   seem] even seem A1; ever seem N[1-2]
304.29   was] were N[2]
304.32   any one] anyone N[1]

304.35   somebody] a man A1+
305.16   active] very active N[1]
306.5   they] *omit* E1
307.0   XXIX] XXVIII A1
307.1   of a] of E1
307.5   [1]his] the A1+
307.26   a] an E1
308.4   [2]was] were N[2]
308.8-9 Wainwright] Weinwright N[2]
308.11   of] *omit* E1
308.18,20   *my*] my A1+
308.19,20   *you*] you A1+
308.22   pass] past TMs(u),A1,N[1]
308.39   tell] fell N[2]
309.8   the journey] his journey A1+
309.11-12   descriptions] description E1
309.21   conclusion] conclusions N[2]
310.16   arose] rose E1
310.18   thing!] ~ ? E1
310.19   these] those N[2]
310.39   was not yet] had not yet been A1+
311.3   please] *omit* A1+
311.5   happy——] ~ . E1
311.11   cheerful?] ~ . E1
311.17   or] of A1+
311.22   trousers] trousers' A1
311.33   arising] rising E1
312.14   king's] King's E1,N[2]
312.18   Hear] Heard E1
312.32   nor] or A1+
313.20   everlastingly] everlasting A1,N[2]
313.29   hell] —— N[1]
313.29,32   *you*] you A1+
313.30   damned] d—— N[1]
313.33   what] that N[2]
313.35   go] go and E1
313.37   You] You'd E1
313.38   me] my N[2]
314.4   not at present] at present not A1+
314.5   hear] heard E1
314.21   to] in E1
314.34   *Is it true?*] roman in A1+
315.6   done] *omit* E1
315.13   damn] d—— N[1]

315.13 *let*] let A1+
315.17–18 nursing . . . latter]
    omit A1+
315.19 happening] happened N[2]
315.30 plumb] plum TMs+
316.8 Blues] blues E1,N[1]
316.12–30 When . . . aim-
    lessly.] *omit* N[2]
316.17 [1]in] *omit* A1,N[1]
316.26 *horrible*] horrible A1+
317.13 suddenly] *omit* E1
317.13 you] *omit* N[2]
317.17 more] *omit* A1+
317.24 *he*] he A1+
317.31 *rich*] rich A1+
317.32 can] rich can N[1]
317.35 *prince*] prince A1+
318.3 *awful*] awful A1+
318.3 *does*] does A1+
319.0 xxx] xxix A1
319.31 again] *omit* N[2]
319.32 cried . . . Marco'.] *omit*
    N[1]
320.11 *serious . . . means*] ro-
    man *in* A1+
320.23–24 unconscious] conscious
    N[2]
320.27 if] of N[1]
320.31 tale-bearing] tell-bearing
    TMs; tellbearing N[1]
320.35 [2]of] with A1+
321.4 sigh] sign TMs,E1
321.7 *We*] We A1+
321.7 mothers'] mother's TMs
321.17–322.2 "Well . . . him."]
    omit N[2]
321.25 doesn't] don't E1,N[1]
321.28 they] he A1,N[1]
321.28–29 *income . . . ability*]
    roman *in* A1+
322.8 *me*] me A1+
322.15 *some*] some A1+
322.25 walking] talking A1+
322.26 if he] he if A1
322.33 great] good N[1]
323.3 a] the A1
323.8 was] were E1

323.15 *wouldn't*] wouldn't A1+
323.17–18 *did . . . exactly*] ro-
    man *in* A1+
323.32 nor] or TMs,A1
323.33 triumphant] triumph ant
    TMs; triumph and E1
324.0 xxxi] xxx A1
324.1 the one] one N[1]
324.6 employees] employe's E1;
    employes A1,N[1]
324.9 least] last N[1]
324.30 street] streets E1
324.31 jail] gaol E1
325.1 jibbering] gibbering E1
325.6 a gallop] the gallop E1
325.6 around] round E1
325.13–14,16,19,21 Monsieur] M.
    N[1]
325.15 *The . . . door!*] roman *in*
    A1+
325.22 in his hair] *omit* N[2]
325.23 God] god TMs
325.25 this] *omit* N[1-2]
325.34 ashes] the ashes N[2]
326.1 en masse] *en masse* E1
326.8 *official*] official A1+
326.10 hell] —— N[1]
326.17 [2]of] or A1+
326.25 Vladivostock] Vladurstock
    TMs; Vladisvostok A1; Vladi-
    vurstock N[2]
326.25 Khartum] Kartoum A1,N[2]
326.30 they] theu TMs; then E1+
    (−N[2])
326.35 half-disc] disc N[2]
327.11 parson] person TMs(u),
    N[1-2]
327.27 I—I——] —I—— A1;
    ∧I—— N[1-2]
327.29 *me*] me A1+
327.33 *anybody*] anybody A1+
327.36 [2]I've been] *omit* N[1]
328.1 astonishment] amazement
    E1
328.19 and . . . nature] *omit* N[2]
328.32 sea] seas N[2]

COLLATION OF E1 VERSUS E1(p)

[NOTE: The lemma reading is that of the Virginia edition, with the variant reading to the right of the bracket. E1: *Active Service*, Heinemann, 1899; E1(p): proof for E1 (present at 113.1–152.10 *Marjory . . . for it*; 169.6–177.21 *And . . . about the*) including a duplicated Chapter VI. E1(p) is preserved in the Special Collections of the Columbia University Libraries.]

113.12   mantle] mantel E1
115.31   well-known] ~ ∧ ~ E1
116.2   portentous] portentious E1(p)
116.14   " 'Rufus' ! "] " ' ~ ! ' " E1
118.18   foes.] ~ ∧ E1(p)
118.21   melee] mêlée E1(p); mêlée E1
119.21   infuriated] enfuriated E1(p)
119.25   surpassed] surpasses E1(p)
119.35; 120.34–35   classmen] class-men E1
120.22   impertinence] importance E1(p); blasphemy E1
122.5   as] so E1
123.16   would] wound E1(p)
125.3   display] displav E1(p) (*doubtful*)
125.25   trolley∧] trolle- E1(p); trolley- E1
125.25   Adventuring] Adventure E1(p)
126.28   then] them E1(p)
127.5   office-boy] ~ ∧ ~ E1(p)
127.15   -side] ∧ ~ E1
129.6   freight] grieght E1(p)
130.31   projects,] ~ ∧ | E1(p) (*comma dropped out*)
131.20   gasped:] ~ — E1(p); ~ , E1
134.32   sense∧] ~ , E1
135.11   Good∧afternoon] ~ - ~ E1
135.25   absurd.] ~ ! E1

135.33   me] I E1(p)
136.5   vise-] cise- E1(p); vice- E1
136.39   cordiality] cordialty E1(p)
137.4   Editor] editor E1
139.9   for?"] ~ ? ∧ E1(p)
139.11   with sarcasm:] sarcastically. E1(p); sarcastically— E1
139.18   brakeman's] brakesman's E1(p)
139.29   cable∧cars] ~ - ~ E1(p)
139.29   glittering∧like] ~ - ~ E1(p)
140.9   elected] electric E1(p)
140.15   know. Why?"] ~ ∧ why?" E1(p)
140.20–21   lad. I] ~ , ~ E1(p)
140.22   were.] ~ ? E1(p)
141.30   arm.] ~ ∧ E1(p)
142.10; 171.13   medieval] mediæval E1(p)
142.14   Coleman.] ~ , E1(p)
142.14   Man] man E1(p)
142.15   bottle."] ~ . ∧ E1(p)

[NOTE: E1(p) *contains two versions of Chapter* VI. *The first version had the same pagination as* E1 *and was the final printed version, although it was set from TMs²; because of its position in the proof it shall be shown here as* E1, *if in agreement with* E1, *and as* E1(p¹) *when variant. The second version of Chapter* VI *was set from TMs¹;*

this version shall be shown as E1(p²), for the pagination was continued in E1(p) as if this were a subsequent chapter rather than a repetition.]

143.3　men] *omit* E1(p²)
143.8　office∧] ～ , E1
143.15　office,] ～ ∧ E1
143.15　table∧] ～ , E1
143.16　surveying] surverying E1(p²)
143.17　"Rufus (*no* ¶)] ¶ E1
143.17　said] cried E1
143.18　scheme. A] ～—a E1(p²)
143.20　trousers∧pockets] trousers'∧ | ～ E1(p²); ～-～ E1
143.21　"Now (*no* ¶)] ¶ E1
143.25　'em—] '～ ∧ E1(p¹); '～ — E1
143.27,28(*twice*)　isn't] ain't E1
143.28　¹that∧] ～ , E1
143.31　fool-matters] ～ ∧ ～ E1
143.31　connected] concerned E1
144.2　scheme] scheme is E1
144.3　Why∧] ～ , E1
144.5　answered.] ～ , E1
144.7　Vacation!] ～ , E1(p²)
144.7　Sturgeon. "Why] ～ , "why E1
144.14　success∧] ～ ; E1(p²); ～ , E1
144.15　right∧] ～ , E1
144.15　time∧] ～ , E1
144.17　Mind!] ～ , E1(p²)
144.17　Sturgeon∧] ～ , E1(p²), E1; ～ ∧ E1(p¹)
144.17　chair∧and] chair, ∧ E1
144.20　much. And] ～ , and E1
144.23　air∧] ～ , E1
144.24　Why∧] ～ , E1
144.27　Coleman.] ～ ; E1
144.34　funny∧but, really,] ～ , ～ , ～ , E1(p²); ～ , ～ ∧ ～ ∧ E1
144.37　*Eclipse.* "But] ～ ; "but E1 (*semicolon roman in* E1[p¹])
145.2　course∧] ～ , E1
145.6　vacation∧] ～ , E1
145.7　different?] ～ . E1
145.8　No,] ～ ; E1

145.8　that] this E1
145.9　why,] ～ — E1
145.12　"Here's (*no* ¶)] ¶ E1
145.17　Oho] Oh E1(p²)
145.17　Sturgeon. "You're] ～ , "you're E1
145.21–22　momentary] monetary E1(p²)
145.22　vaguely-defined] ～ ∧ | ～ E1
145.23　grinned∧] ～ , E1(p²)
145.25　indifference∧] ～ , E1(p²)
145.27　jiminy] jiming E1(p²); Jiminy E1
145.35　vacation.] ～ ; E1
145.36　take. And∧] ～ , and, E1(p¹); ～ , and∧ E1
145.36–37　'tomorrow',] 'to-morrow,' E1(p²); ∧to-morrow∧, E1
145.38　Coleman∧] ～ , E1
145.39　cheque. Clear] ～ ; clear E1
146.1　you] you here E1
146.5　toward] towards E1
146.6　minute.] ～ , E1
146.11　course∧] ～ , E1
146.12　say∧] ～ , E1
146.13　positively.] ～ ; E1
146.18　suddenly.] ～ , E1(p²); ～ ; E1
146.18　reasons—] ～ , E1
146.19　reasons."] ～ !" E1(p²)
146.25　dinner] dine E1
146.26　Coleman. "If] ～ , "if E1
146.27　pack——] ～ ." E1
146.29　sentiment,] ～ . E1(p¹); ～ , E1
146.30　Nonsense——] ～ !" E1

[*Chapter* VI *ends.*]

147.17　wine-merchant] ～ ∧ ～ E1(p)
147.26　cried∧] ～ , E1
147.30　word?] ～ ." E1
149.39–150.1; 150.5,9　wine-merchant] ～ ∧ ～ E1(p)
150.7　brandy∧and∧soda] ～ - | ～ ∧ ～ E1(p); ～ - | ～ -～ E1
150.12　nothin',] ～'∧ | E1
150.26–27　"Why . . . ∧you] | '～ . . . | '～ E1(p)

150.28 aboard] abroad E1(p)

151.19 you."] ~ ?" E1(p)

152.10–169.5 either . . . devil-dog?] E1(p) *lacking*

169.9 clearly,] ~ ; E1(p) (*uncertain*)

170.10 flickered] flicked E1(p); flecked E1

170.26 passing] passing into E1(p)

171.15 game,] ~ ∧ E1

171.19 stood] stdod E1(p)

171.20 rind] rhind E1(p)

171.24; 172.14–15 troop∧horses] ~ - ~ E1

171.29–30 war-correspondents] ~ ∧ ~ E1

171.30 war-offices] ~ ∧ ~ E1

172.4 proud∧] ~ , E1

172.9 war-correspondent] ~ ∧ ~ E1

172.9 arises,] ~ ∧ E1

172.21 by∧perhaps∧] ~ — ~ ∧ E1(p); ~ , ~ , E1

172.38 intrenchments] entrenchments E1

173.18 sunrays] sun-rays E1

173.29 line.] ~ , E1(p)

173.32 They] The E1(p)

173.34 proudly∧] ~ , E1

174.2 ¹in] at E1(p)

174.27 courteously,] ~ . E1(p)

174.30 could] |ould E1(p) (*unidentified hand added 'c' in margin*)

174.30 it∧] ~ , E1

175.2 grass;] ~ — E1

175.12 almost] almost up E1

175.17 sheep] sheeps E1(p)

176.3 pretension] pretention E1(p)

177.20 fellow∧correspondents] ~ - ~ E1

ALTERATIONS IN THE TYPESCRIPT

Crane's Holograph Alterations in the Typescript

[NOTE: All changes made by Crane are listed; the medium is blue ink unless otherwise noted.]

235.16 things] 's' *added at end of line*

236.39 atrocity] 'a' *over* 'o'

237.8 rascal. A] *a final* 'e' *deleted from* 'rascal'; 'A' *over* 'a'; *period inserted*

237.21–22 catastrophe] 'e' *over* 'y'

238.14 grey] *interlined with a caret*

238.24 even] *interlined with a caret*

238.29 so] *interlined with a caret*

240.4 abased] *second* 'a' *inserted with a caret*

240.8 guilt] 'g' *over* 'q'

240.11–12 lettuce] *first* 't' *inserted with a caret*

240.12 others] *preceded by deleted* 'the'

240.21 benefaction] *second* 'e' *over* 'i'

241.12–13 a base suspicion,] *interlined*

242.9 pulverize] 'r' *inserted with a caret*

247.2 her] *interlined above deleted* 'his interlocutors'

247.6 that,] *comma inserted*

247.8 "It] *quotes inserted*

247.13 doleful. She] *period inserted;* 'S' *over* 's'

247.21 aspirations] *first* 'i' *over* 'e'

248.6 Apparently] TMs 'apparent|ly' *with stroke to make uppercase* 'A'; *hyphen inserted at end of line*

248.7 was] *inserted at end of line*

248.9 campaigns] 'e' *deleted before* 's'

248.15 "I've] *quotes inserted*

249.1 Nora . . . odd] *inserted in a space left by the typist*

250.15 sprung] *inserted in a space left by the typist*

250.16 Coke] *followed by deleted* 'Coke'

250.27 in] TMs 'In' *reduced with a slash*

250.33 deference] 'f' *preceding* 'f' *deleted*

251.10 devotedly] 'ly' *interlined with a caret*

251.17 puling and puking] 'l' *following* 'l' *and* 'c' *before* 'k' *deleted*

251.23 gentlemen!] *exclamation altered from period*

251.25 beginning] *second* 'n' *interlined*

251.25 talk. If] *period inserted;* 'I' *over* 'i'

251.27 glowed] *altered from* 'glowered'

252.3 comic] *interlined above deleted* 'ludicrous'

252.8 hum] *interlined above deleted* 'line'

252.27 gutturally] *second* 'u' *over* 'e';* 'al' *interlined with a caret*

252.37 trivialities] 'a' *interlined with a caret*

252.39 triviality] 'a' *interlined with a caret*

253.12 resented] 'ed' *over* 'ful'

253.22 it. Even] *period inserted;* 'E' *over* 'e'

254.3–4 yelled. [¶] The road] *interlined, with paragraph sign preceding* 'The', *above deleted typed* 'yelled. The road' *of which* 'The road' *superimposed at paragraph point onto typed* 'yelled.'

254.11 waist] *interlined above deleted* 'waste'

256.8 note] 'e' *added*

256.12 note,"] *comma and quotes inserted*

256.15 far to] *interlined above deleted* 'for'

256.30 at the Wainwrights] 'at' *interlined above deleted* 'from'; 's' *inserted before deleted* 'party'

257.10 glazed] *interlined above deleted* 'dazed'

259.8 hurrying] *interlined above deleted* 'moving'

259.11 the] *preceded by deleted* 'to'

259.19 offensive,] *comma inserted*

259.28 thought of] *interlined with a caret*

260.13–14 he received . . . neck;] *interlined with a caret* (TMs: 'recieved')

260.27; 261.7 not] *interlined*

260.33 a] *interlined above deleted* 'the'

261.12,14–15 handkerchief] 'd' *interlined with a caret*

261.22 thus] *interlined*

276.7 as] *interlined with a caret*

276.9 nature of a preservative] *slash inserted to separate* 'natureof'; 'a' *of* 'preservative' *over* 'e'

276.14 the] *interlined above deleted* 'her'

276.26 even] *interlined with a caret*

278.3 did not] *interlined with a*

caret above deleted Cora *alteration*

278.11 responded] *interlined with a caret above deleted* 'repeated'

278.20 billings-] 'b' *over illegible letter*

282.7 cried] *interlined with a caret above deleted* 'said'

282.8 don't] *apostrophe inserted*

284.15 ¹odd] 'o' *mended*

284.16(*twice*),18,19,25; 286.12,23,26(*twice*),29 (*twice*),34 [*exclamation point*]] *altered from a period*

284.25; 286.15,25(*twice*), 27(*twice*) don't] *apostrophe inserted*

286.25 mother! Don't!] *first exclamation altered from a comma, second from a period*

286.29 "Oh] *quotes inserted*

286.32 won't . . . ²can't] *apostrophes inserted*

294.6 coffee] *a final* 's' *deleted*

307.14 her] *written over illegible letters* (*black ink*)

308.2 immortal] TMs 'im-|-mortal' *with second hyphen inserted* (*black ink*)

308.16 ¶ "Yesterday] *paragraph sign inserted* (*black ink*)

308.22 pass] *final* 's' *over* 't' (*black ink*)

309.36 so] *interlined with a caret*

311.24 kept] *inserted at end of line*

312.32 often] 'o' *over* 'a'

316.16 perching] 'h' *over illegible letter*

316.34 trays] 's' *added*

321.20 mood.] *interlined with a caret which deleted a period following* 'thoughtful'

321.29 has] 's' *over* 'd'

322.9 simply] *interlined with a* **caret**

324.7 betrothal] *interlined above deleted* 'engagement'

326.4 nervous;] *semicolon inserted after deleted question mark*

327.11   parson] *interlined above deleted* 'person'

328.33   played in] *interlined above deleted* 'touching'

Cora Crane's Holograph Alterations in the Typescript

[NOTE: This listing excludes all additions to words at the ends of lines and simple corrections of spelling errors. Cora's medium was pencil on ribbon and carbon, except where corrections were made by hand on the ribbon copy and survive only as carbon impressions; at these points the notation 'carbon' is used.]

[TMs *ribbon copy*]

117.33   wintry] *an 'e' before 'r' deleted*

120.15   circumstance] *a final 's' deleted*

122.12   didn't] *altered from* 'did not'

131.2   called] *preceded by deleted* 'come'

132.16   distinguish] *final 'ed' deleted*

133.8   satanically] *third 'a' deleted* (*see* Emends)

161.23   ¹a] *a final 't' deleted*

161.31   food] *a final 's' deleted*

164.20   Nikopolis] *followed by a deleted period*

165.21   that] *interlined with a caret*

171.37   world] 'l' *deleted* (*see* Emends)

178.36   party₍ₐ₎] *an inserted dash deleted*

178.36   hazards . . . here] *dashes inserted after both words* (*see* Emends)

184.20   group] *a final 's' deleted*

191.38   crawl] *altered from* 'scrawl'

206.10   deliberately] *altered from* 'deliberatedly'

206.14   had] *preceded by deleted* 'he'

206.18   dragomen] 'e' *interlined with a caret above deleted* 'a'

213.14   forever] *an attempt made to separate with vertical strokes before and after first* 'e'

213.19; 214.7   *New York Daylight*] *italicization added*

214.5   if] 'f' *over* 't'

214.7   Daylight] *a following comma inserted* (*see* Emends)

217.3   President] *followed by a deleted period* (*see* Emends)

222.29   upon] 'up' *deleted by slash* (*see* Emends)

227.4   half-closed] *hyphen inserted*

232.5   Retire!" Whereupon] TMs '¶ Whereupon' *with line drawn from* 'Retire!"' *to indicate run-on*

232.34   room] *followed by a deleted period*

233.27   Well,] *comma inserted*

233.33   Arta] *followed by a deleted period*

234.4   other] *a final 's' deleted*

[TMs *black carbon copy*]

235.20   word] 'l' *after* 'r' *deleted*

241.31   vivacious] *second* 'i' *deleted* (*carbon; see* Emends)

247.31   -boy] *followed by deleted period* (*carbon*)

254.13   click] *a final 's' deleted* (*carbon*)

269.2   too] *the final 'o' interlined with a caret* (*carbon*)

270.8   from] *interlined with a caret above deleted* 'with' (*carbon*)

276.15   acutely,] *comma inserted* (*carbon*)

277.21   not] *interlined with a caret*

278.3   did not] *altered from* 'didn't' (*see* Crane *alterations*)

284.28   behavior.] *following closing quotes deleted* (*carbon*)

297.13 going to] *followed by deleted* 'do'

300.29 tragic muse] *strokes appear under the* 't' *and* 'm' (*carbon; see* Emends)

301.2 lain] *followed by deleted* 'in' (*carbon*)

307.29 wait."] *quotes inserted* (*carbon*)

Typed Alterations in the Typescript

[NOTE: All corrections of misspellings, additions to words at the end of lines, false starts, and deletions caused by the realization of eyeskips have been ignored in this listing.]

113.14 swarmed] *preceded by x'd-out* 'swayed'

113.26 mind] *preceded by x'd-out* 'head'

114.7 them] *preceded by x'd-out* 'him'

114.26 faith] *preceded by x'd-out* 'delight'

114.28 ¹self-] *preceded by x'd-out* 'machine, this clock, suddenly crumble'

114.37 simply] *preceded by x'd-out* 'blushed'

119.36 ²Get back,] *interlined with a caret*

121.1 changes] *preceded by x'd-out* 'replacements'

121.17 on] 'o' *over* 'i'

121.25 to] *interlined with a caret above x'd-out* 'of'

121.30 cried] *preceded by x'd-out* 'said'

124.39 a comrade's] *preceded by x'd-out* 'insolence'

126.36 dismal] *preceded by x'd-out* 'littl'

129.20 a] *interlined with a caret*

130.1 it] *preceded by x'd-out* 'his ha'

130.2 of] *preceded by x'd-out* 'like'

130.17 faces] *preceded by x'd-out* 'names'

130.29 in] 'i' *over* 'o'

130.33 on] 'o' *over* 'i'

131.18 the] *interlined with a caret*

132.14 behind] *preceded by x'd-out* 'back'

133.27 not] *followed by x'd-out* 'going'

135.14 a] *interlined with a caret above x'd-out* 'the'

136.27 to Greece] *preceded by x'd-out* 'away'

144.24 may] *interlined with a caret above x'd-out* 'might'

145.17 Oho] 'o' *over a comma*

148.16 declaiming] *preceded by x'd-out* 'declaring'

148.39 forget] *preceded by x'd-out* 'change'

149.16 bad,] *followed by x'd-out* 'bad'

155.2 in] 'i' *over* 'o'

157.16 his mind] *preceded by x'd-out* 'himself cynically in'

164.5 armies] *interlined with a caret*

165.17 ¹to] *interlined with a caret above x'd-out* 'at'

165.17 diligence] *followed by x'd-out* 'proceeded,'

166.7 that] *interlined with a caret*

171.27 judged] *preceded by x'd-out* 'had'

171.30 governments] *preceded by x'd-out* 'the'

173.16 fumed] *interlined with a caret above x'd-out* 'fuming'

173.23 bridge] *preceded by x'd-out* 'river'

175.5 of] *interlined with a caret*

175.14 advance] *a final* 'd' *x'd-out*

178.38 to] *interlined with a caret above x'd-out* 'of'

179.11 to] *interlined with a caret*

182.1 very] *preceded by x'd-out* 'very'

184.25 a] *interlined with a caret*

190.2 with] *interlined with a caret above x'd-out* 'which'

190.30 luxurious] '-ous' *added after x'd-out* 'ant'

191.1 his] *preceded by x'd-out* 'to'

192.12 induce] *interlined with a caret above x'd-out* 'make'

192.37 it] *preceded by x'd-out* 'of'

194.29 lips] *preceded by x'd-out* 'teeth'

195.20 go] *preceded by x'd-out* 'go get'

198.27 in] 'i' *over* 'o'

201.38 dimensions] 'dim' *followed by a space in which appears a black ink question mark within parentheses; probably the printer's notation*

203.22 ¹had] 'd' *over* 's'

210.6 Coleman] *followed by x'd-out* 'said'

211.16 could] *interlined with a caret*

211.28 Often] *typed over* 'After'

212.20 bulge] *preceded by deleted* 'kin'

216.26 to] *interlined with a caret*

224.24 yet] *interlined with a caret*

224.37 In] *interlined with a caret above x'd-out* 'the'

224.38 possibility] 'y' *over* 'i'; 'es' *deleted by hand*

229.24 had] *preceded by x'd-out* 'are'

231.24 expressions] *final* 's' *interlined with a caret*

233.20 control] *preceded by x'd-out* 'seperate'

235.22 American] *interlined with a caret above x'd-out* 'hundred'

242.18 sinister] *interlined with a caret above x'd-out* 'singular'

244.9 them] *preceded by x'd-out* 'him'

245.14 way] *preceded by x'd-out* 'street'

250.5 introduction] *preceded by x'd-out* 'duty'

250.6 owe] *followed by x'd-out* 'you'

250.18 Coleman] *followed by x'd-out* 'with his'

251.17 that] *interlined with a caret*

252.1 intensified] 's' *followed by x'd-out* 'ely'

253.16 this] 'i' *over* 'e'

255.5 driver] *preceded by x'd-out* 'danger'

257.28 and] *interlined*

259.1 far] *interlined*

259.19 which] *preceded by x'd-out* 'was'

259.23 a] *interlined with a caret above x'd-out* 'the'

260.15 always] *interlined above x'd-out* 'almost'

265.27 must] *followed by x'd-out* 'be'

267.21 between] *preceded by x'd-out* 'of'

268.27 exactly] *preceded by x'd-out* 'see'

271.11 accepted] *interlined with a caret above x'd-out* 'expected'

271.32 serious] *interlined with a caret*

272.29 a] *interlined with a caret*

273.20 unashamed] *first* 'a' *interlined*

276.17 deplore] *followed by x'd-out* 'in'

277.6 conventional] *preceded by x'd-out* 'conversation'

277.35 protest] *followed by partially x'd-out* 'if'

297.6 ¹no] *interlined with a caret*

297.27 stared] *preceded by x'd-out* 'started'

304.8 after] *followed by x'd-out* 'all'

304.23 have] *interlined with a caret*

305.13 and innocent] *interlined with a caret*

308.3 common] *interlined with a caret above x'd-out* 'coming'

308.11 of] *interlined with a caret*

309.34   man] *followed by x'd-out*
'seemed'

314.18   badly] *preceded by x'd-out*
'boldly'

315.1   Is] *preceded by x'd-out*
'What'

320.3   are] *preceded by x'd-out*
'were'

324.4   is] *interlined with a caret*
above x'd-out 'was'

326.4   angry;] *semicolon over*
question mark

326.5   was] *followed by x'd-out*
'somewhat'

327.9   where] *interlined with a*
caret

328.20   unalterable] '-able' *inter-*
lined with a caret above x'd-
out 'ed'